JAMES THURBER

JAMES THURBER

WRITINGS AND DRAWINGS

THE LIBRARY OF AMERICA

For copyright holders and publication rights,
see Acknowledgments, pages 993–94.

The paper used in this publication meets the
minimum requirements of the American National Standard for
Information Sciences—Permanence of Paper for Printed
Library Materials, ANSI z39.48—1984.

Distributed to the trade in the United States
by Penguin Books USA Inc
and in Canada by Penguin Books Canada Ltd.

Library of Congress Catalog Number: 96–5853
For cataloging information, see end of Notes.
ISBN 1–883011–22–1

First Printing
The Library of America—90

Manufactured in the United States of America

GARRISON KEILLOR
SELECTED THE CONTENTS FOR THIS VOLUME

Contents

from *Let Your Mind Alone!* (1937)
   Let Your Mind Alone!

from *Fables for Our Time & Famous Poems Illustrated* (1940)

Uncollected Pieces

FROM

IS SEX NECESSARY?

OR

WHY YOU FEEL THE WAY YOU DO

The Nature of the American Male:
A Study of Pedestalism

IN NO other civilized nation are the biological aspects of love so distorted and transcended by emphasis upon its sacredness as they are in the United States of America. In China it's all biology. In France it's a mixture of biology and humor. In America it's half, or two-thirds, *psyche*. The Frenchman's idea, by and large, is to get the woman interested in him as a male. The American idea is to point out, first of all, the great and beautiful part which the stars, and the infinite generally, play in Man's relationship to women. The French, Dutch, Brazilians, Danes, etc., can proceed in their amours on a basis entirely divorced from the *psyche*. The Chinese give it no thought at all, and never have given it any thought. The American would be lost without the *psyche*, lost and a little scared.

As a result of all this there is more confusion about love in America than in all the other countries put together. As soon as one gets the psychical mixed up with the physical—a thing which is likely to happen quite easily in a composing-room, but which should not happen anywhere else at all—one is almost certain to get appetite mixed up with worship. This is a whole lot like trying to play golf with a basketball, and is bound to lead to maladjustments.

The phenomenon of the American male's worship of the female, which is not so pronounced now as it was, but is still pretty pronounced, is of fairly recent origin. It developed, in fact, or reached its apex, anyway, in the early years of the present century. There was nothing like it in the preceding century. Throughout the nineteenth century the American man's amatory instincts had been essentially economic. Marriage was basically a patriotic concern, the idea being to have children for the sake of the commonwealth. This was bad enough, but nevertheless it is far less dangerous to get the commonwealth mixed up with love than to get the infinite mixed up with love.

There was not a single case of nervous breakdown, or neurosis, arising from amatory troubles, in the whole cycle from

1800 to 1900, barring a slight flare-up just before the Mexican and Civil wars. This was because love and marriage and children stood for progress, and progress is—or was—a calm, routine business. "Mrs. Hopkins," a man would say to the lady of his choice (she was a widow in this case)—"Mrs. Hopkins, I am thinking, now that George* has been dead a year, you and I should get married and have offspring. They are about to build the Union Pacific, you know, and they will need men." Because parents can't always have men-children when they want them, this led to almost as many women as men working on the Union Pacific, which in turn led to the greater stature of women in the present Northwest than in any other part of the nation. But that is somewhat beside the point. The point is that men and women, husbands and wives, suitors and sweethearts, in the last century lived without much sentiment and without any psycho-physical confusion at all. They missed a certain amount of fun, but they avoided an even greater amount of pother (see Glossary). They did not worry each other with emotional didoes. There was no hint of Pleasure-Principle. Everything was empiric, almost somatic.†

This direct evasion of the Love Urge on the part of Americans of the last century was the nuclear complex of the psycho-neurosis as we know it today, and the basis for that remarkable reaction against patriotic sex which was to follow so soon after the Spanish-American war.

At the turn of the century, the nation was on a sound economic basis and men had the opportunity to direct their attention away from the mechanics of life to the pleasures of living. No race can leap lightly, however, from an economic value to an emotional value. There must be a long period of

*The late George Hopkins.

†The word "somatic" has been left out of the glossary because of the confusion which the dictionary itself seems to be in over the meaning of the term. "Pertaining to the wall of the body" is as close as the New International comes to what we have in mind here, but it goes right on to use "parietal" as a synonym and parietal means "pertaining to order within the buildings of a college." Then again the word goes back to the old Indian, or East Indian, root *Soma* which means a god, a liquor, and an asclepiadaceous climbing shrub (*Sarcostemma acidum*). Furthermore, if your eyes stray even a fraction of an inch, in looking up "somatic," you are in "sölvsbergite" which includes the feldspars, ægirite, grorudite, and tinguaite.

Übertragung, long and tedious. Men were not aware of this, thirty years ago, because the science of psychology was not far advanced, but nature came to their aid by supplying a tem-

Fig. 1. Sex Substitutes (Übertragung Period): Baseball.

porary substitute for an emotional sex life, to tide them over during the period of *Übertragung*. This substitute took the form of games. Baseball assumed a new and enormous importance, prize-fighting reached its heyday; horse-racing became an absorption, bicycling a craze.

Now women, naturally intraverts, could not easily identify themselves with baseball or prize-fighting (they admired Christy Mathewson and Terry McGovern, but that was about all); they took but slowly to horse-racing; and they giggled and acted the fool when they first tried to balance themselves on a bicycle. They drew away from men and from men's concerns, therefore—there was no more of the old Union Pacific camaraderie—and began to surround the mere fact of their biological destiny with a nimbus of ineffability. It got so that in speaking of birth and other natural phenomena, women seemed often to be discussing something else, such as the Sistine Madonna or the aurora borealis. They became mysterious to themselves and to men; they became suddenly, in their own eyes, as capable of miracle and as worthy of worship as Juno and her sisters. This could not go on. The conflict was ineluctable.

Fig. 2. Sex Substitutes (Übertragung Period): Bowling.

When men, wearied of games, turned to women with that urgency so notable in the American male for its simplicity and directness, they found them unprepared for acceptance and surrender. The process of adjustment in courtship and in marriage became more involved than it had ever been before in the history of the country, if not in the history of the world. The new outdoors type of American man, with all his strength and impetuosity, was not easily to be put off. But the female, equipped with a Defense far superior in polymorphous ingenuities to the rather simple Attack of the male, was prepared. She developed and perfected the Diversion Subterfuge. Its purpose was to put Man in his place. Its first manifestation was fudge-making.

The effectiveness of fudge-making in fending off the male and impressing him with the female's divine unapproachability can not be over-estimated. Neither can its potentiality as a nuclear complex. The flitting from table to stove, the constant necessity of stirring the boiling confection, the running out-

FUDGE-MAKING

"The female, equipped with a Defense far superior in polymorphous ingenuities to the rather simple Attack of the male, developed, and perfected, the Diversion Subterfuge. The first manifestation of this remarkable phenomenon was fudge-making."

of-doors to see if the candy had cooled and hardened, served to abort any objective demonstrations at all on the part of the male. He met this situation with a strong Masculine Protest. He began to bring a box of candy with him when he called, so that there would not be any more fudge-making. These years constituted the great Lowney's era in this country. Brought back to where she had started, face to face with the male's simple desire to sit down and hold her, the female, still intent upon avoidance of the tactual, retaliated by suggesting Indoor Pastimes—one of the greatest of all Delay Mechanisms. All manner of parlor games came into being at this period, notably charades,* which called for the presence of

*See Glossary, definition No. (1).

other persons in the room (Numerical Protection). The American male's repugnance to charades, which is equaled, perhaps, by his repugnance to nothing else at all, goes back to those years. The Masculine Protest, in this case, was a counter-suggestion of some games of his own, in which there was a greater possibility of personal contact. His first suggestions were quite primitive, such as that it would be fun to count up to a hundred by kissing. The female's response was the famous one of Osculatory Justification. There must be, she decreed, more elaborate reasons for kissing than a mere exhibition of purposeless arithmetical virtuosity. Thus Post Office and Pillow were finally devised, as a sort of compromise. Neither was satisfactory to either sex. The situation became considerably strained and relationships finally trailed off into the even less satisfactory expedient of going for long rides on a tandem bicycle, which has had its serious effects upon the nature of the American man. He liked, for one thing, to do tricks on a bicycle. The contraption was new to him, and he wanted to do tricks on it. One trick that he liked especially was riding backwards. But there wasn't one woman in ten thousand, riding frontwards on the rear seat of a tandem wheel, who would permit her consort to ride backwards on the front seat. The result of all this was not adjustment, but irritability. Man became frustrated.

Frustration wrought its inevitable results. Men began to act jumpy and strange. They were getting nowhere at all with women. The female gradually assumed, in men's eyes, as she had in her own, the proportions of an unattainable deity, something too precious to be touched. The seed of Pedestal-ism was sown. The male, in a sort of divine discontent, began to draw apart by himself. This produced that separation of the physical and the psychic which causes the adult to remain in a state of suspended love, as if he were holding a bowl of goldfish and had nowhere to put it. This condition nowadays would lead directly to a neurosis, but in those days men were unable to develop a neurosis because they didn't know how. Men withdrew, therefore, quietly and morosely, to their "dens." It was the epoch of the den in America. Some marvelous ones sprang into being. Their contents were curiously significant. Deprived of possessing the female, the male worked off his Possessive Complex by collecting all manner of bibelots and bric-à-brac. The average den contained a paper-weight from Lookout Mountain, a jagged shell from Chickamaugua, a piece of wood from the *Maine*, pictures of baseball players with beards, pictures of bicycle champions, a yellowing full-page photograph of Admiral Schley, a letter-

"There wasn't one woman in ten thousand, riding frontwards on the rear seat of a tandem wheel, who would permit her consort to ride backwards on the front seat. The result of all this was not adjustment, but irritability. Man became frustrated."

opener from Niagara Falls, a lithograph of Bob Fitzsimmons, a musket-badge from the G. A. R. parade, a red tumbler from the state fair, a photograph of Julia Marlowe, a monk's head match-holder, a Malay kriss, five pipe racks, a shark's tooth, a starfish, a snapshot of the owner's father's bowling team, colored pictures of Natural Bridge and Balanced Rock, a leather table runner with an Indian chief on it, and the spangled jacket of a masquerade costume, softly shedding its sequins.

Fig. 3. Sex Substitutes (Übertragung Period): Craps.

The den was the beginning of male sublimation in this country, but the fruits of that sublimation were slow in ripening. At the start, in fact, they were in a state of absolute suspension. Man began to preoccupy himself with anything, no matter how trivial, which might help him to "forget," as the lay expression has it. He thought up childish diversions, at which one person can amuse himself, and to justify his absorption in these futile pastimes he exaggerated their importance, as we shall see. These diversions included the diabolo, the jig-saw puzzle, linked nails and linked keys, which men took apart and put back together again, and most important of all, pigs-in-clover.

During this period almost no achievements of value, in art, science, or engineering, were forthcoming in the nation. Art, indeed, consisted chiefly of putting strange devices on boxes with the aid of a wood-burning set. The commonest device was the swastika, whose curiously distorted conformation

Fig. 4. Sex Substitutes (Übertragung Period): Six-day Bicycle Racing.

bears no discernible relationship to any known phallic symbolism. Those years were blank, idle, lost years. Outside affairs of all kinds were neglected. Men retired to their dens and were not seen for days. The panic of 1907 was a direct result. It might be interesting to examine into a typical case history of the period.

CASE HISTORY

George Smith, aged 32, real estate operator. Unmarried, lived with mother. No precocious mother fixation. Had freed his libido without difficulty from familial objects, and was eager to marry. Had formed an attachment in 1899, at the age of 29, with a young virgin. Her Protective Reactions had been immediate and lasted over a period of three years, during which he had never even held her hand. Defense Devices: usually euchre (four-handed), or pedro. Definite and frequent fudge-making subterfuge. Post Office and Pillow, both with low degree of success.

Smith's separation between the physical and the psychic occurred in 1902, the direct stimuli presenting themselves on June 6th of that year, examination (by Dr. Matthiessen) showed. On that day Smith ran, frightened, from a barbershop in Indianapolis, where he lived. Inside the shop, on the floor, a middle-aged man named Herschel Queeper had thrown a fit. Queeper had been trying for two days to get three little balls, under a glass in a tiny round box, to roll into an opening made for them (common pigs-in-clover puzzle). But no sooner would he get the third one in than one, or perhaps both, of the others would roll out. Mrs. Queeper was beginning to wonder where he was.

Smith withdrew to his den and pondered and fiddled around and made Unconscious Drawings (Cf. Plates I, II, III and IV). He turned his attention from the object of his amorous affections to a consideration of the problems of pigs-in-clover. The usual Justification of Occupation occurred. It took the form of exaggerating the importance of finding out whether the puzzle could possibly be solved, and of working out a methodology of solving it more readily, if it could be solved at all. The case procured one of the little boxes and began to roll the balls toward the opening. At first he set about it quite calmly. There were no immediate signs of mental deterioration, either malignant or benign. But although the case got all the balls into the opening, thus proving that it could be done, he never got them all in at the same time. In the second month he threw a brief fit. This, today, would ordinarily prove the first step toward a complete physico-psychic breakdown, but in those days neuroses were staved off longer, owing to the general ignorance of psychology, and Smith not only calmly examined the effect of the fit upon himself, without calling in any scientists, but determined to go on and examine the effect of fits upon others. He decided, however, that it would be difficult to examine the effects of puzzle-fits upon men, because men brooked no examination when they were intent upon puzzles, and so he hit on the idea of having his dog, an animal named Dewey, play with the little round box until it threw a fit. But when he called in his dog

UNCONSCIOUS DRAWING: PLATE I.
Unconscious drawings, as they are called in psychoanalytical terminol-
ogy, are made by people when their minds are a blank. This drawing
was made by Floyd Neumann, of South Norwalk. It represents the Male
Ego being importuned by, but refusing to yield to, Connecticut
Beautiful.

he found, after several experiments, that the dog could not hold the box in either its right or left paw.* Furthermore, the animal was profoundly incurious about the puzzle.†

"Furthermore, the animal was profoundly incurious about the puzzle."

Undismayed, Smith decided that somewhere in Indianapolis there must be a dog adroit enough to handle the box and sagacious enough to grasp the idea behind it, and with a view to finding such an animal, he determined to get all the dogs in town, and all the pigs-in-clover puzzles in town, into one room and see what would happen. (Apotheosis Complex, with Plurality Fallacy.)

Smith was able, however, to round up only about 85 per cent of the dogs of the city, because there were many who were too busy to get away at the time. Even so, 85 per cent of the dogs in Indianapolis was more than had ever been got together in one room before. The case attempted to explain the problem to the dogs in short, one-syllable talks, but the bedlam was too loud and too prolonged for him to make himself heard. Fifty or more St. Bernards and a few dozen Chesapeake spaniels listened, half-heartedly, but the others made holiday. Furthermore, eighty-four bulldogs would not permit themselves to be muzzled, and this added to Smith's difficulties. Thus, on the fifth day of the singular experiment,

*This presented a difficulty that has not been overcome to this day.
†This disinterest held good up until the day of the dog's death.

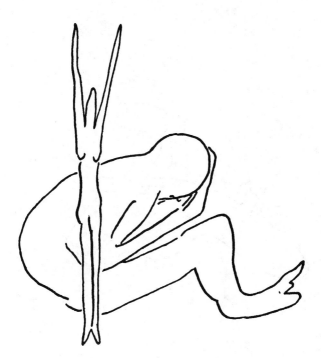

UNCONSCIOUS DRAWING: PLATE II.
This was drawn by Peter Zinsner, 564 DeKalb Avenue, Brooklyn, with-
out knowing it. We here see Sublimation in conflict with the Libido.
Peter has reached a point in life where women seem so divine he doesn't
dare call them up on the phone. Yet they still call him.

UNCONSCIOUS DRAWING: PLATE III.
This is the work of Grace McFadden, aged 11, of Bucyrus, Ohio (R.F.D. #3,
Bucyrus 6021, Ring 3), and was drawn on the day that Principal K. L.
Mooney, of the Paulding County Concentration Grade Schools, was
married. Here the Pleasure-Principle and the Wish Motive are both
overshadowed by the Bridegroom Fallacy.

Smith, hearing a remarkable hullaballoo belowstairs (he worked in the attic), descended to the parlor, where he discovered the bulldogs engaged in a sort of tug-of-war, using a body Brussels carpet as a rope. (The case's mother had several days before retreated to French Lick, in a rundown condition.)

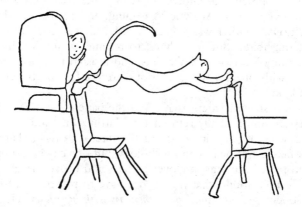

This drawing was made from an old 1901 lantern slide often used by Dr. Karl Zaner in his illustrated lecture, "What Can We Learn from Animals?" Dr. Zaner has always contended that we can learn nothing of importance from animals beyond a few pointers on the art of relaxation. "Their general activities are, as a rule, not only meaningless to man, but frequently to themselves as well. This particular cat, for example, probably had nothing special in mind at all."

Smith grasped the carpet firmly, with some idea of wresting it away from the dogs, whereupon all of them save three began to pull against him.* The Exaggeration Complex under which the case was laboring gave him strength enough to meet with some small success in his first efforts to take the carpet away from the dogs. He pulled them as far as the bay window in the parlor, largely because they had not settled down seriously to winning. When they did, however, the total of three hundred and twenty-four solidly implanted feet and the virtually

---

*These three had closed their eyes, to hang on, and did not see Smith.

immeasurable tugging potentiality were too much for Smith. He was slowly pulled out into the hall, through the front door, and into the street. He stubbornly contested every inch of the way until a drug store, three blocks away, was reached. Here some one had the presence of mind to call out the fire department.

Dr. Matthiessen, who took the case at about this period in its development, attempted to reduce the Magnification of Objective, first by Analytic Reasoning, and then by cold applications. Neither was successful. Matthiessen could not divert the libido. Smith declined to resume his interest in the feminine object of his affections, and insisted that his experiment with puzzles was a glorious project for the benefit of mankind.

It was sheer accident that saved the patient—not Dr. Matthiessen. Smith finally refused Dr. Matthiessen admittance to his house, nor would he go to the doctor's office, claiming that he did not believe in psychology, but one day he dropped one of the little pigs-in-clover puzzles and broke the glass in it. He then found that he did not have to roll the balls into the openings, *but could push them in with his finger*. He got a hammer and broke the glass in all the thousands of puzzles he had brought to his home for the dogs, and solved every one of the puzzles by pushing, not rolling. This instantly released him from his complex by the Gordian Knot principle of complex release. He thus gained the necessary confidence and sense of power to feel worthy of the woman with whom he was in love, and he finally married her. The marriage was of average success.

Marriages, however, were frequently delayed much longer than in the case of George Smith, and it was not, indeed, until 1909 that the usual norm was restored. Meanwhile, in between the time of the first general separation of the physical and the psychic in this country, and the final culmination in marriages, a period of sublimation set in. This followed directly on the heels of the remarkable and lamentable era of preoccupation with trivial diversions and was characterized by an extravert interest in truly important projects and activities. The airplane was brought to a high stage of development, the telephone transmitter was perfected, tungsten replaced carbon as

UNCONSCIOUS DRAWING: PLATE IV.

The mood captured in this drawing is a rare one indeed, and Dr. Karl Zaner considers the sketch the finest in his collection. Here the masculine sense of Ironic Detachment rises superior to the Love Urge and can take it or let it alone. The drawing was sent to Dr. Zaner by Mrs. Walter L. Mouse (née Kathleen Schaaf), recently divorced wife of the author of the drawing, Walter L. Mouse, of Columbus, Ohio.

a filament for incandescent lamps, better books were written, art progressed, there was a cultural advance generally and the birth of a new Æsthetic, and people began to get at the real facts in the Thaw case. Nevertheless, Pedestalism has left its serious effects. It is doubtful if they will fully wear off for another fifty or seventy-five years.

The Lilies-and-Bluebird Delusion

T HE YOUNG BRIDEGROOM who unexpectedly discovers that his wife has been brought up in extreme unawareness of the true facts of life and believes in some variant of the Birds and Flowers Delusion (that is, that birds and flowers have something to do with the emotional life of persons), is faced with a situation calling for the greatest tact and tenderness. It won't do any good for him to get mad, or to indulge in self-pity, crying, "Oh, how sorry I am for me!" and only a coward would go directly into a psycho-neurosis without first trying to win his wife over to acceptance of things as they are.

I have in mind the case of a young lady whose silly mother had taught her to believe that she would have a little son, three years old, named Ronald, as soon as her husband brought a pair of bluebirds into a room filled with lilies-of-the-valley. The young woman (to say nothing of the young man) was thus made the victim of one of the extremest cases of Birds and Flowers Fixation which has ever come to my attention. I shall transcribe, from Dr. Tithridge's notes, the first dialogue on the subject that took place between the young couple. This dialogue was carefully reconstructed by Tithridge from the account of the incident as given by the young husband, who sought his advice and counsel.

On the evening of the 25th of June, when the couple were married, the young husband entered their hotel suite to find it literally a garden of lilies-of-the-valley. He was profoundly touched, but baffled, and asked his wife who was dead.

"Where are the bluebirds?" she replied, coyly.

"What bluebirds?" he demanded.

"*The* bluebirds," she said, blushing.

Unfortunately, but not unnaturally, the bridegroom did not know what the bride was talking about. What was of the extremest importance to her, was to her husband merely an idle whim, a shadowy fancy. Obviously, the young couple should have talked such matters over long before, but they hadn't, and there they were. He strove to change the subject, whistled, lighted cigarettes, for he was nervous enough the way it was, but she kept recurring to the bluebirds. His bewilderment became tinged with some alarm, for during their courtship he had put forth no great effort to examine into her

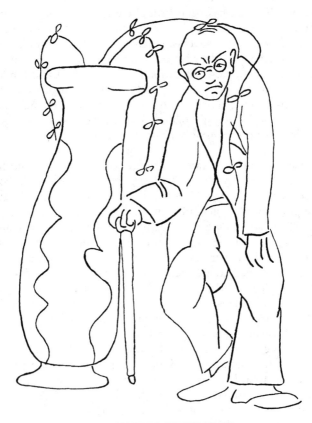

DR. WALTER TITHRIDGE
(after the etching by Veerbluergen)

mental capacity, and he was now assailed by the excusable suspicion that she was perhaps not exactly bright. He talked rapidly, apprehensively, of many things. Among the things he talked about were the St. Louis Cardinals (a baseball club).

From there it was but an easy associative step for his wife to go back to the bluebirds again.

"Aren't you going to get any bluebirds?" she persisted.

"I don't know where the hell I'd get any bluebirds to-night," he said, rather irritably, "me not being Bo-Peep."

The nuclear complex was made right then and there. There was a long tense silence, after which the bride burst into bitter tears.

"Now, dear," said her husband, more reasonably, "let's try to get this thing straightened out. What are you talking about, anyway?"

"Sex—if you want to know!" she blurted out, and swooned.

Instead of getting her a glass of water, he excitedly phoned the room clerk, but became embarrassed once he had got him, and merely asked that a couple of blankets be sent up. It was, unfortunately, as I have said, June—and warmish. Thus when the wife revived sufficiently to become aware of her surroundings, the husband was standing above her holding a pair of blankets, and looking pale and warm.

"What are those for?" she demanded, suspiciously, for the notion had now formed in her own mind (Dr. Tithridge feels, and I agree) that she very likely had married a dementia

"Mutual suspicions of mental inadequacy are common during the first year of any marriage."

præcox case. These mutual suspicions of mental inadequacy are common during the first year of any marriage, but rarely are they aggravated by factors so clearly calculated to upset the mental equilibrium as bluebirds at midnight and blankets in June. This husband and wife were drifting farther and farther apart. The solution to their problem was becoming more and more remote, what with this setting up of involved artificial barriers, this almost fantastical beclouding of the issue. Dr. Tithridge tells me that he believes the young man's reason would have been permanently dethroned had he (Dr. Tithridge) tweeted or chirped like a bird* on the occasion of the husband's first visit to him.

When the wife beheld her husband standing there with the blankets, she demanded, again, "What are you doing with those blankets?"

"I get cold," he mumbled, and he proceeded to put the blankets on the shelf of a closet which already held several extra pair. He was, furthermore, decidedly warm, and kept patting his brow with a handkerchief.

"Let's go out and take a walk," suggested his wife, apprehensively. To this her husband very readily agreed. They were getting afraid to stay in the same room with each other, than which there is no other condition in the world more certain to break up a marriage. Out in the street, among people, they both felt safer, and they wandered to a bench in a fairly crowded park, and sat down.

"Where did you get the idea that birds have anything to do with us?" demanded the bridegroom.

"My mumsy,"† she said.

"Well," he said, "she deceived you."

"About what?"

"About what you're talking about."

---

*Experiments of this sort, calculated to determine the possible effects of tweeting, or chirping, in the case of a Birds Fixation, fall, of course, outside the province of the psycho-analyst, and not only is the legality of their practice questionable, but the value of the results obtained is highly doubtful.

†Young women who allude to their mothers as "mumsy" almost invariably present difficult problems in adjustment. The word is a sentimentalization of the more common "mamma" and indicates a greater dependence upon maternal direction and supervision than may be expected in the case of young women who use the more familiar term.

"Sex?" she asked.

"That isn't sex, honey," he told her. "Birds and flowers are simply . . . they do not . . . that is, we could live all our life without them."

"I couldn't," she said, and, after a pause, "I always feared *you* didn't want children."

"I do want children. I want you. You want me. Everything is going to be all right."

"How is it?" she demanded.

"In the first place," he began, pulling at his collar, "it's this way. Now here's the way it is. Now you take me . . . or take you, say. In the first place the girl, that is Woman . . . why, Woman* . . ." He lapsed into a profound silence.

"Well, go on," she prompted.

"Well," he said, "you know how women are, don't you?"

"Yes," she said, doubtfully.

"That's fine," he said, brightening. "Now women are that way, then——"

"What way?" she asked.

"Why, the way you are . . . from me . . . than I am, I mean." He made a vague gesture.

"I don't see what you mean," she said. Her husband gave a light laugh.

"Hell's bells, it's simple enough," he cried, suddenly, giving the light laugh again; "it's certainly simple enough. Now, here. We'll take Adam and Eve. There they were, all alone, see?"

"There were two bluebirds," said his wife.

"Not till after the flood, there weren't," he corrected her. "Well, he found out that there were certain essential differences—what you might call on purpose. I mean there must have been some reason. You can count on it that things like that just don't happen. Well, then, he simply figured it out— figured out the reason."

"For what?"

"For all this discrepancy. Obviously it just didn't happen. It couldn't just have happened. It had to make some sense—

*Explanations of natural phenomena in terms of the collective noun, particularly where the noun becomes capitalized in the mind of the person striving to explain, are almost never successful.

nature is like that. So he—so he finally—ah—what he did was tell her, see? I mean he asked her."

"Asked her what?"

DR. KARL ZANER

"He simply asked her," said her husband in calm, almost cold tones,—"he simply asked her why she thought this was. Is there anything wrong in that? And so gradually they understood why it was. It's as simple as that!" He looked at her triumphantly.

"What *are* you talking about?" she demanded.

"Listen," he said at last, firmly. "Both of us speak a little French, and we might try it that way. I think I could explain better in French. Why, even little children, tiny girls, sing *Auprès de ma blonde* in France, and think nothing of it. It's just a nice, wholesome idea—*auprès de ma blonde*—and it sounds like poetry—but take it in English and what do you get?"

" 'Quite close to my blonde' . . ." answered his wife.

". . . *'Qu'il fait bon dormir,'* " her husband hurried on.

" 'How good it is to sleep,' " she translated.

"Fine! Now you're talking."

"Go on," she said, "*you're* talking."

"Well, all right, but first I wanted you to see that there is no reason to get embarrassed, because everything is lovely in French. So don't mind my frankness."

"I don't," said the bride.

"All right," he began again, *"Alors,* now, *il y a quelque chose que vous avez que je n'en ai pas, n'est-ce pas?"*

"Oui," she said.

"Bon," he said. *"Alors, ça c'est naturel—ah—ça c'est bien naturel . . ."*

"Par exemple," put in his wife, a little illogically.

"Dites," he said, and after a great pause, *"Dites donc—dites vous——"*

"You should really use 'tu' and 'toi' and not 'vous,'" said his wife; "it's more intimate."

"All right," he responded. "Now, *tu as quelque chose, tu as . . . toi."*

"Comment?" she demanded.

"I just don't know enough words," said the bridegroom, wretchedly. The bride put her hand on his arm.

"Let's try 'thee' and 'thou' in English," she suggested.

"That's not a bad idea," he said. "Well, all right. Now thee has——"

"Hath," she corrected.

"Thee hath certain—ah——"

"Differences," she supplied. "But isn't it 'thou hath'—or is it 'thee hath'?"

"To hell with it!" cried her husband. "In all thy life hast never been around, for Pete's sake?"

"Certainly, and thou—and you have no right to talk to me like that!"

"I'm *sorry*," said the young man. *"I'm sorry."* He rose to his feet. "Ye gods! to think this had to happen to me! Ah, well. Listen. I tell you what, I'll write it out for you. How about that? And if you don't like the idea, why, all right, I suppose."

It was the next day that the young husband, who had sat up all night in the hotel lobby, thinking and writing, visited Dr. Tithridge. I am happy to report that, as not infrequently

EMOTIONAL CHARADES.
PLATE I.
"One young man every night tenderly placed, with much strange cluck-ing, a basket near the hearth into which he had some expectation that a baby would be deposited by a stork."

happens in such cases, a solution was finally arrived at. However, in a great number of cases the difficulty is never overcome. The home becomes a curious sort of hybrid, with overtones of the botanical garden and the aviary. The husband grows morose and snappish, the wife cross and pettish. Very often she takes up lacrosse and he goes in for raising rabbits. If allowed to go on, the situation can become so involved and intricate that not all the analysts from the time of Joan of Arc down could unravel it.

The problem is by no means any simpler where the wife is cognizant of things as they are and the husband is ignorant. I know of one young man who every night tenderly placed, with much strange clucking, a basket near the hearth into which he had some expectation that a baby would be deposited by a stork. (Plate I.) Another young husband constructed at considerable expense a water-lily pond in his back yard and fondly rowed about in it, twilight after twilight, searching for infants, laying his finger to his lip, making "tchk, tchk" noises at his wife, who watched him in profound amazement. In both these cases the wives were fine women of strong character, with a background of sturdy pioneer stock, and they soon put a stop to such charades, once they divined the curiously entangled Wish Motives behind them. It may be said, indeed, that young wives are more candid and direct in their explanations of natural phenomena than young husbands, when they have to be.

The existence of such deplorable ignorance is a sad commentary on the sentimentality of a nation which sets itself up to be frankly sexual. There is much reason to be hopeful, however. The future parents of the land will doubtless come straight to the point in matters of this sort, when talking with their children. The children of today will be the parents of tomorrow, and you know how the children of today are.

FROM

THE OWL IN THE ATTIC

AND OTHER PERPLEXITIES

Mr. Monroe Holds the Fort

THE COUNTRY HOUSE, on this particular wintry afternoon, was most enjoyable. Night was trudging up the hill and the air was sharp. Mr. Monroe had already called attention several times to the stark beauty of the black tree branches limned, as he put it, against the sky. The wood fire had settled down to sleepy glowing in the grate.

"It *is* a little lonely, though," said Mrs. Monroe. (The nearest house was far away.)

"I love it," said her husband, darkly. At moments and in places like this, he enjoyed giving the impression of a strong, silent man wrapped in meditation. He stared, brooding, into the fire. Mrs. Monroe, looking quite tiny and helpless, sat on the floor at his feet and leaned against him. He gave her shoulder two slow, reflective pats.

"I really don't mind staying here when Germaine is here— just we two," said Mrs. Monroe, "but I think I would be terrified if I were alone." Germaine, the maid, a buxom, fearless woman, was in town on shopping leave. The Monroes had thought it would be fun to spend the weekend alone and get their own meals, the way they used to.

"There's nothing in the world to be afraid of," said Mr. Monroe.

"Oh, it gets so terribly black outside, and you hear all kinds of funny noises at night that you don't hear during the day." Mr. Monroe explained to her why that was—expansion (said he) of woodwork in the cold night air, and so on. From there he somehow went into a discussion of firearms, which would have betrayed to practically anyone that his knowledge of guns was limited to a few impressive names like Colt and Luger. They were one of those things he was always going to read up on but never did. He mentioned quietly, however, that he was an excellent shot.

"Mr. Farrington left his pistol here, you know," said Mrs. Monroe, "but I've never touched it—ugh!"

"He did?" cried her husband. "Where is it? I'd like to take

a look at it." Mr. Farrington was the man from whom they had taken, on long lease, the Connecticut place.

"It's upstairs in the chest of drawers in the back room," said Mrs. Monroe. Her husband, despite her protests, went up and got it and brought it down. "Please put it away!" said his wife. "Is it loaded? Oh, don't do that! Please!" Mr. Monroe, looking grim and competent, was aiming the thing, turning it over, scowling at it.

"It's loaded all right," he said, "all five barrels."

"Chambers," said his wife.

"Yes," he said. "Let me show you how to use it—after all, you can never tell when you're going to need a gun."

"Oh, I'd never use it—even if one of those convicts that escaped yesterday came right up the stairs and I could shoot him, I'd just stand there. I'd be *paralyzed*!"

"Nonsense!" said Mr. Monroe. "You don't have to shoot a man. Get the drop on him, stand him up with his face against a wall, and phone the police. Look here—" he covered an imaginary figure, backed him against the wall, and sat down at the phone table. "Always keep your eye on him; don't look into the transmitter." Mr. Monroe glared at his man, lifted up the receiver, holding the hook down with his finger, and spoke quietly to the phone. In the midst of this the phone rang. Mr. Monroe started sharply.

"It's for you, dear," he said presently. His wife took the receiver.

How curiously things happen! That is what Mr. Monroe thought, an hour later, as he drove back from the station after taking his wife there to catch the 7:10. Imagine her mother getting one of those fool spells at this time! Imagine expecting a grown daughter to come running every time you felt a little dizzy! Imagine—well, the ways of women were beyond him. He turned into the drive of the country house. Judas, but it was dark! Dark and silent. Mr. Monroe didn't put the machine in the garage. He got out and stood still, listening. Off toward the woods somewhere he heard a thumping noise. Partridge drumming, thought Mr. Monroe. But partridge didn't thump, they whirred—didn't they? Oh, well, they probably thumped at this time of year.

It was good to get inside the house. He built up the fire, and turned on the overhead lights—his wife never allowed them turned on. Then he went into a couple of other rooms and turned on more lights. He wished he had gone in town with her. Of course she'd be back in the morning on the 10:10, and they'd have the rest of that day—Sunday—together.

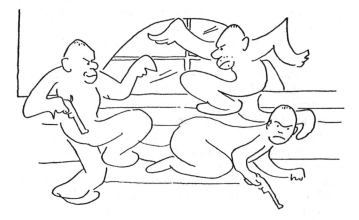

Burglars Flitting About in the Attic of a House in Which the Master Is Home Alone

Still . . . he went to the drawer where he had put the revolver and got it out. He fell to wondering whether the thing would work. Long-unused guns often jammed, or exploded. He went out into the kitchen, carrying the pistol. His wife had told him to be sure and get himself a snack. He opened the refrigerator door, looked in, decided he wasn't hungry, and closed it again. He went back to the living-room and began to pace up and down. He decided to put the pistol on the mantel, butt toward him. Then he practiced making quick grabs for it. Presently he sat down in a chair, picked up a *Nation* and began to read, at random: "Two men are intimately connected with the killing of striking workers at Marion, North Carolina. . . ." Where had those convicts his wife mentioned escaped from? Dannemora? Matteawan? How far were those places from this house? Maybe having all the lights on was a bad idea. He got up and turned the upper lights off; and then turned them on again. . . . There was a step outside. Crunch! crunch! . . . Mr. Monroe hurried to the mantel, knocked the gun on to the floor, fumbled for it, and stuck it in a hip pocket just as a knock sounded at the door.

"Wha-" began Mr. Monroe, and was surprised to find he couldn't say anything else. The knocking continued. He stepped to the door, stood far to one side, and said, "Yeh?" A cheery voice responded. Reassured, Mr. Monroe opened the door. A motorist wanted to know how to get to the Wilton road. Mr. Monroe told him, speaking quite loudly. Afterwards, lifted up by this human contact, he went back to his reading in the *Nation*: "Around 1:30 A.M. one of the foremen approached young Luther Bryson, 22, one of the victims, and harangued him: 'If you strike this time, you ——, we will shoot it out with you.' . . ." Mr. Monroe put the magazine down. He got up and went to the victrola, selected a jazz record, and began to play it. It occurred to him that if there were steps outside, he couldn't hear them. He shut the machine off. The abrupt silence made him stand still, listening. He heard all kinds of noises. One of them came from upstairs—a quick, sliding noise, like a convict slipping into a clothes closet . . . the fellow had a beard and a blue-steel gun . . . a man in the dark had the advantage. Mr. Monroe's mouth began to feel stuffy. "Damn it! This can't go on!" he said aloud, and felt bucked up. Then someone put his heel down sharply on the floor just above. Mr. Monroe tentatively picked up a flashlight, and pulled the pistol from his pocket. The phone rang sharply. "Good God!" said Mr. Monroe, backing against a wall. He slid on to the chair in front of the phone, with the gun in his right hand, and took up the receiver with his left. When he spoke into the transmitter his eyes kept roving around the room. "H'lo," he said. It was Mrs. Monroe. Her mother was all right. Was he all right? He was fine. What was he doing? Oh, reading. (He kept the gun trained on the foot of the steps leading upstairs.) Well, what would he think if she came back out on that midnight train? Her mother was all right. Would he be too sleepy to wait up and meet her? Hell, no! That was fine! Do that! . . .

Mr. Monroe hung up the receiver with a profound sigh of relief. He looked at his watch. Hm, wouldn't have to leave for the station for nearly two hours. Whistling, he went out to the refrigerator (still carrying the gun) and fetched out the butter and some cold meat. He made a couple of sandwiches (laying the gun on the kitchen table) and took them into the living-room (putting the gun in his pocket). He turned off the overhead lights, sat down, picked up a *Harper's* and began to read. Abruptly, that flitting, clothes-closety sound came from upstairs again. Mr. Monroe finished his sandwiches hurriedly, with the gun on his lap, got up, went from room to room turning off the extra lights, put on his hat and overcoat, locked several doors, went out and got into his car. After all, he could read just as well at the station, and he would be sure of being there on time—might fall asleep otherwise. He started the engine, and whirled out of the drive. He felt for the pistol, which was in his overcoat pocket. He would slip it back into the chest of drawers upstairs later on. Mr. Monroe came to a crossroads and a light. He began to whistle.

The Pet Department

Q. I enclose a sketch of the way my dog, William, has been lying for two days now. I think there must be something wrong with him. Can you tell me how to get him out of this?

Mrs. L. L. G.

A. I should judge from the drawing that William is in a trance. Trance states, however, are rare with dogs. It may just be ecstasy. If at the end of another twenty-four hours he doesn't seem to be getting anywhere, I should give him up. The position of the ears leads me to believe that he may be enjoying himself in a quiet way, but the tail is somewhat alarming.

Q. Our cat, who is thirty-five, spends all of her time in bed. She follows every move I make, and this is beginning to get to me. She never seems sleepy nor particularly happy. Is there anything I could give her?

Miss L. Mc.

A. There are no medicines which can safely be given to induce felicity in a cat, but you might try lettuce, which is a soporific, for the wakefulness. I would have to see the cat watching you to tell whether anything could be done to divert her attention.

Q. My husband, who is an amateur hypnotizer, keeps trying to get our bloodhound under his control. I contend that this is not doing the dog any good. So far he has not yielded to my husband's influence, but I am afraid that if he once got under, we couldn't get him out of it.

A. A. T.

A. Dogs are usually left cold by all phases of psychology, mental telepathy, and the like. Attempts to hypnotize this particular breed, however, are likely to be fraught with a definite menace. A bloodhound, if stared at fixedly, is liable to gain the impression that it is under suspicion, being followed, and so on. This upsets a bloodhound's life, by completely reversing its whole scheme of behavior.

Q. My wife found this owl in the attic among a lot of ormolu clocks and old crystal chandeliers. We can't tell whether it's stuffed or only dead. It is sitting on a strange and almost indescribable sort of iron dingbat.

MR. MOLLEFF

A. What your wife found is a museum piece—a stuffed cockatoo. It looks to me like a rather botchy example of taxidermy. This is the first stuffed bird I have ever seen with its eyes shut, but whoever had it stuffed probably wanted it stuffed that way. I couldn't say what the thing it is sitting on is supposed to represent. It looks broken.

Q. Our gull cannot get his head down any farther than this, and bumps into things.

H. L. F.

A. You have no ordinary gull to begin with. He looks to me a great deal like a rabbit backing up. If he *is* a gull, it is impossible to keep him in the house. Naturally he will bump into things. Give him his freedom.

Q. My police dog has taken to acting very strange, on account of my father coming home from work every night for the past two years and saying to him, "If you're a police dog, where's your badge?", after which he laughs (my father).

Ella R.

A. The constant reiteration of any piece of badinage sometimes has the same effect on present-day neurotic dogs that it has on people. It is dangerous and thoughtless to twit a police dog on his powers, authority, and the like. From the way your dog seems to hide behind tables, large vases, and whatever that thing is that looks like a suitcase, I should imagine that your father has carried this thing far enough—perhaps even too far.

Q. My husband's seal will not juggle, although we have tried everything.

GRACE H.

A. Most seals will not juggle; I think I have never known one that juggled. Seals balance things, and sometimes toss objects (such as the large ball in your sketch) from one to another. This last will be difficult if your husband has but one seal. I'd try him in plain balancing, beginning with a billiard cue or something. It may be, of course, that he is a non-balancing seal.

Q. We have a fish with ears and wonder if it is valuable.

JOE WRIGHT

A. I find no trace in the standard fish books of any fish with ears. Very likely the ears do not belong to the fish, but to some mammal. They look to me like a mammal's ears. It would be pretty hard to say what species of mammal, and almost impossible to determine what particular member of that species. They may merely be hysterical ears, in which case they will go away if you can get the fish's mind on something else.

Q. How would you feel if every time you looked up from your work or anything, here was a horse peering at you from behind something? He prowls about the house at all hours of the day and night. Doesn't seem worried about anything, merely wakeful. What should I do to discourage him?

MRS. GRACE VOYNTON

A. The horse is probably sad. Changing the flowered decorations of your home to something less like open meadows might discourage him, but then I doubt whether it is a good idea to discourage a sad horse. In any case speak to him quietly when he turns up from behind things. Leaping at a horse in a house and crying "Roogie, roogie!" or "Whoosh!" would only result in breakage and bedlam. Of course you might finally get used to having him around, if the house is big enough for both of you.

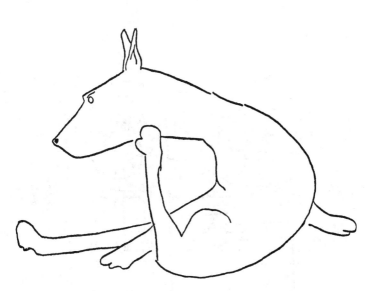

Q. The fact that my dog sits this way so often leads me to believe that something is preying on his mind. He seems always to be studying. Would there be any way of finding out what this is?

ARTHUR

A. Owing to the artificially complex life led by city dogs of the present day, they tend to lose the simpler systems of intuition which once guided all breeds, and frequently lapse into what comes very close to mental perplexity. I myself have known some very profoundly thoughtful dogs. Usually, however, their problems are not serious and I should judge that your dog has merely mislaid something and wonders where he put it.

Q. We have cats the way most people have mice.

Mrs. C. L. Footloose

A. I see you have. I can't tell from your communication, however, whether you wish advice or are just boasting.

Q. No one has been able to tell us what kind of dog we have. I am enclosing a sketch of one of his two postures. He only has two. The other one is the same as this except he faces in the opposite direction.

MRS. EUGENIA BLACK

A. I think that what you have is a cast-iron lawn dog. The expressionless eye and the rigid pose are characteristic of metal lawn animals. And that certainly is a cast-iron ear. You could, however, remove all doubt by means of a simple test with a hammer and a cold chisel, or an acetylene torch. If the animal chips, or melts, my diagnosis is correct.

Q. My oldest boy, Ford Maddox Ford Griswold, worked this wooden horse loose from a merry-go-round one night when he and some other young people were cutting up. Could you suggest any use for it in a family of five?

MRS. R. L. S. GRISWOLD

A. I cannot try the patience of my public nor waste my own time dealing with the problems of insensate animals. Already I have gone perhaps too far afield in the case of stuffed birds and cast-iron lawn dogs. Pretty soon I should be giving advice on wire-haired fox terrier weather-vanes.

Q. Mr. Jennings bought this beast when it was a pup in Montreal for a St. Bernard, but I don't think it is. It's grown enormously and is stubborn about letting you have anything, like the bath towel it has its paws on, and the hat, both of which belong to Mr. Jennings. He got it that bowling ball to play with but it doesn't seem to like it. Mr. Jennings is greatly attached to the creature.

MRS. FANNY EDWARDS JENNINGS

A. What you have is a bear. While it isn't my bear, I should recommend that you dispose of it. As these animals grow older they get more and more adamant about letting you have anything, until finally there might not be anything in the house you could call your own—except possibly the bowling ball. Zoos use bears. Mr. Jennings could visit it.

Q. Sometimes my dog does not seem to know me. I think he must be crazy. He will draw away, or show his fangs, when I approach him.

H. M. MORGAN, JR.

A. So would I, and I'm not crazy. If you creep up on your dog the way you indicate in the drawing, I can understand his viewpoint. Put your shirt in and straighten up; you look as if you had never seen a dog before, and that is undoubtedly what bothers the animal. These maladjustments can often be worked out by the use of a little common sense.

Q. After a severe storm we found this old male raven in the study of my father, the Hon. George Morton Bodwell, for many years head of the Latin Department at Tufts, sitting on a bust of Livy which was a gift to him from the class of '92. All that the old bird will say is "Grawk." Can ravens be taught to talk or was Poe merely "romancing"?

MRS. H. BODWELL COLWETHER

A. I am handicapped by an uncertainty as to who says "Grawk," the raven or your father. It just happens that "Arrk" is what ravens say. I have never known a raven that said anything but "Arrk."

Q. I have three Scotch terriers which take things out of closets and down from shelves, etc. My veterinarian advised me to gather together all the wreckage, set them down in the midst of it, and say "ba-ad Scotties!" This, however, merely seems to give them a kind of pleasure. If I spank one, the other two jump me—playfully, but they jump me.

MRS. O. S. PROCTOR

A. To begin with, I question the advisability of having three Scotch terriers. They are bound to get you down. However, it seems to me that you are needlessly complicating your own problem. The Scotties probably think that you are trying to enter into the spirit of their play. Their inability to comprehend what you are trying to get at will in the end make them melancholy, and you and the dogs will begin to drift farther and farther apart. I'd deal with each terrier, and each object, separately, beginning with the telephone, the disconnection of which must inconvenience you sorely.

Q. My husband paid a hundred and seventy-five dollars for this moose to a man in Dorset, Ontario, who said he had trapped it in the woods. Something is wrong with his antlers, for we have to keep twisting them back into place all the time. They're loose.

MRS. OLIPHANT BEATTY

A. You people are living in a fool's paradise. The animal is obviously a horse with a span of antlers strapped onto his head. If you really want a moose, dispose of the horse; if you want to keep the horse, take the antlers off. Their constant pressure on his ears isn't a good idea.

THE SEAL IN THE BEDROOM

& OTHER PREDICAMENTS

PART ONE

Women and Men

"All Right, Have It Your Way—You Heard a Seal Bark!"

"Have You People Got Any .38 Cartridges?"

"I'm Helping Mr. Gorley with His Novel, Darling"

*"When I Realize That I Once Actually Loved You
I Go Cold All Over"*

"Everybody Noticed It. You Gawked at Her All Evening"

"You're the Only Woman That Ever Let Me Alone"

"With You I Have Known Peace, Lida, and Now You Say You're
Going Crazy"

"Mamma! Come Quick! I Think Granpa Is Folding Up"

"Perhaps a Woman's Intuition Could Solve Your Problem, Mr. Barr"

"So I Says to Him, 'Don't Take That Tone with Me, Mr. Gebholtz'"

"Mamma Always Gets Sore and Spoils the Game for Everybody"

"It's in de Bag for de Little Guy, Bobby"

*"I Wouldn't Be Uneasy—One of My Husbands Was Gone
for Three Weeks"*

"Here's a Study for You, Doctor—He Faints"

"Well, What's Come Over You Suddenly?"

"She Was Crazy about Him, but He Interfered with
Her Novel"

"The Father Belonged to Some People Who Were Driving Through in
a Packard"

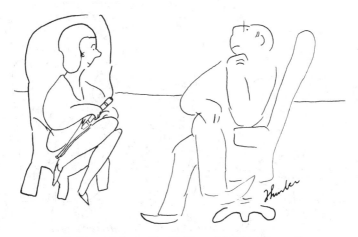

"I Keep Toying with the Idea of Suicide, Doctor"

"Stop me!"

"I Understand She Kills Herself in the Next Act and He Goes Back to His Wife"

"Will You Be Good Enough to Dance This Outside?"

"Your Wife Seems Terribly Smart, Mr. Bruce"

"He Got Aphasia and Forgot Where I Lived"

"Why Don't You Get Dressed, Then, and Go to Pieces Like a Man?"

*"Your Ailment Is on the Tip of My Tongue, Mrs. Cartright—
Let Me Think"*

"*I Told the Analyst Everything Except My Experience with Mr. Rinesfoos*"

"*For the Last Time—You and Your Horsie Get Away from Me and Stay Away!*"

"Lookit, Herman—Flars!"

"He Claims Something Keeps Following Him, Doctor"

"They're Playing 'Bolero,' Mr. Considine—It Drives Me Mad!"

"I Can Tell You Right Now That Isn't Going to Work"

"Here's to the Old-time Saloon, Stranger!"

"I Don't Know. George Got It Somewhere"

"Have You Fordotten Our Ittle Suicide Pact?"

"I Yielded, Yes—but I Never Led Your Husband On,
Mrs. Fisher!"

*"What Kind of Woman Is It, I Ask You, That Goes Gallivating
Around in a Foreign Automobile?"*

*"No Son of Mine Is Going to Stand There and Tell Me He's Scared
of the Woods"*

"Two Best Falls Out of Three—Okay, Mr. Montague?"

"Hello, Dear!—How's Everything in the Marts of Trade?"

"Get a Load of This Sunset, Babe!"

"They Say He Has No Weakness"

*"Then He Wrote Me from Detroit That He Couldn't Get Married
because There Was Crazy People in His Ancestors"*

"Are You the Young Man That Bit My Daughter?"

"Charlie Evans!—or Am I Crazy?"

"You Keep Your Wife's Name Out of This, Ashby!"

"If I'm a Fake, Officer, How Do You Account for This?"

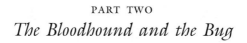

PART TWO
The Bloodhound and the Bug

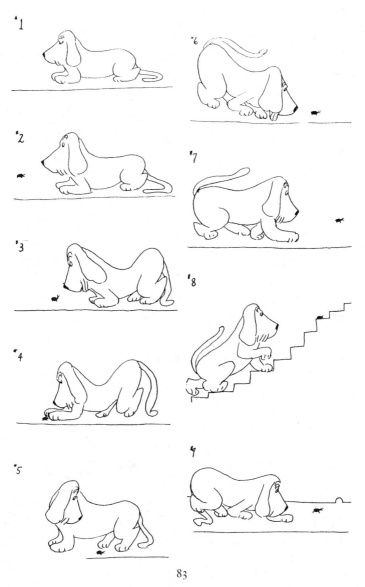

PART THREE

The Race of Life

A PARABLE

THIS SEQUENCE of thirty-five drawings represents the life story of a man and his wife; or several days, a month, or a year in their life and in that of their child; or their alternately interflowing and diverging streams of consciousness over any given period. It seems to lend itself to a wide variety of interpretations. Anything may be read into it, or left out of it, without making a great deal of difference. Two or three previewers were brought up short by this picture or that—mainly the Enormous Rabbit—and went back and started over again from the beginning. This mars the flow of the sequence by interrupting the increasing tempo of the action. It is better to skip pictures, or tear them out, rather than to begin over again and try to fit them in with some preconceived idea of what is going on.

The Enormous Rabbit, which brought two engravers and a receptionist up short, perhaps calls for a few words of explanation. It can be an Uncrossed Bridge which seems, at first glance, to have been burned behind somebody, or it can be Chickens Counted Too Soon, or a ringing phone, or a thought in the night, or a faint hissing sound. More than likely it is an Unopened Telegram which when opened (see Panel 12) proves not to contain the dreadful news one had expected by merely some such innocuous query as: "Did you find my silver-rimmed glasses in brown case after party Saturday?"

The snow in which the bloodhounds are caught may be either real snow or pieces of paper torn up.

The Start

Swinging Along

Neck and Neck

Accident

Water Jump

The Beautiful Stranger

The Quarrel

The Pacemaker

Spring Dance

Faster

The Enormous Rabbit

Escape

Top Speed

Winded

Quand Même

Breathing Spell

The Dive

Dog Trot

Down Hill

Menace

Up Hill

Dogs in the Blizzard

Out of the Storm

The Skull

The Water Hole

The Laggard

Indians!

War Dance

Gone!

The Bear

Sunset

On Guard

Dawn: Off Again

Final Sprint

The Goal

PART FOUR

Miscellany

"A Penny For Your Thoughts, Mr. Griscom"

Mrs. Cortez

Bar

"A Penny for Your Thoughts, Mr. Gardiner"

Fifty-second Street Interior

Mating-Time

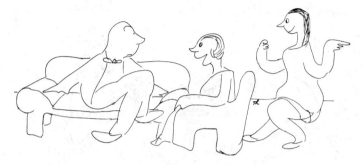

"A Penny for Your Thoughts, Mr. Jaffe"

"He's Finally Got Me So That I Think I See It, Too"

Youth

"A Penny for Your Thoughts, Mr. Speaks"

Scylla

Speakeasy

"A Penny for Your Thoughts, Dr. Garber"

The Furies

"A Penny for Your Thoughts, Mr. Coates"

Footie-Footie

Ad Astra

End of Paved Road

The Bloodhound and the Hare

Tennis

Waiting for Service

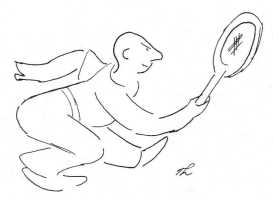

Drop Shot

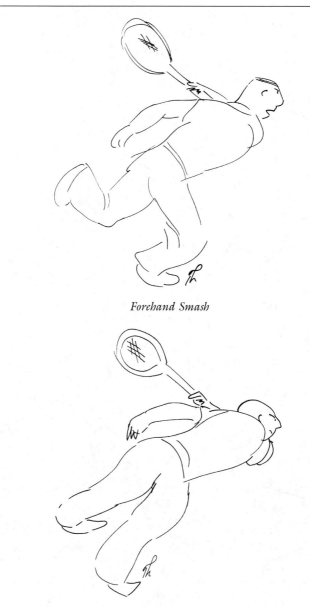

Forehand Smash

Placement

Cross Court

The Kill

PART SEVEN
Parties

First Husband Down

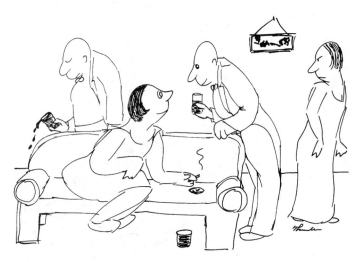

Love

"When I Wore a Tulip"

The Brawl

Berserk

The Bawling Out

The Fog

Four o'Clock in the Morning

PART EIGHT

The Collapse of Civilization

The Flirt

Street Scene

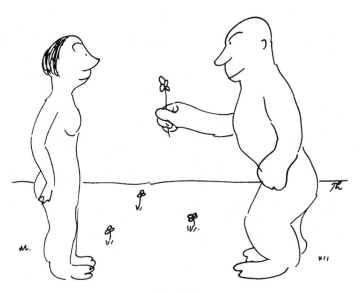

The Suitor

The Good Provider: I

The Good Provider: II

The Argument

The Storm

Spring

"My Man!"

The Prude

The Story-Teller

MY LIFE AND HARD TIMES

For
Mary A. Thurber

Contents

Preface to a Life

BENVENUTO CELLINI said that a man should be at least forty years old before he undertakes so fine an enterprise as that of setting down the story of his life. He said also that an autobiographer should have accomplished something of excellence. Nowadays nobody who has a typewriter pays any attention to the old master's quaint rules. I myself have accomplished nothing of excellence except a remarkable and, to some of my friends, unaccountable expertness in hitting empty ginger ale bottles with small rocks at a distance of thirty paces. Moreover, I am not yet forty years old. But the grim date moves toward me apace; my legs are beginning to go, things blur before my eyes, and the faces of the rose-lipped maids I knew in my twenties are misty as dreams.

At forty my faculties may have closed up like flowers at evening, leaving me unable to write my memoirs with a fitting and discreet inaccuracy or, having written them, unable to carry them to the publisher's. A writer verging into the middle years lives in dread of losing his way to the publishing house and wandering down to the Bowery or the Battery, there to disappear like Ambrose Bierce. He has sometimes also the kindred dread of turning a sudden corner and meeting himself sauntering along in the opposite direction. I have known writers at this dangerous and tricky age to phone their homes from their offices, or their offices from their homes, ask for themselves in a low tone, and then, having fortunately discovered that they were "out", to collapse in hard-breathing relief. This is particularly true of writers of light pieces running from a thousand to two thousand words.

The notion that such persons are gay of heart and carefree is curiously untrue. They lead, as a matter of fact, an existence of jumpiness and apprehension. They sit on the edge of the chair of Literature. In the house of Life they have the feeling that they have never taken off their overcoats. Afraid of losing themselves in the larger flight of the two-volume novel, or even the one-volume novel, they stick to short accounts of their misadventures because they never get so deep into them but that they feel they can get out. This type of writing is not a joyous form of self-expression but the manifestation of a twitchiness at once cosmic and mundane. Authors of such pieces have, nobody knows why, a genius for getting into minor difficulties: they walk into the wrong apartments, they drink furniture polish for stomach bitters, they drive their cars into the prize tulip beds of haughty neighbors, they playfully slap gangsters, mistaking them for old school friends. To call such persons "humorists," a loose-fitting and ugly word, is to miss the nature of their dilemma and the dilemma of their nature. The little wheels of their invention are set in motion by the damp hand of melancholy.

Such a writer moves about restlessly wherever he goes, ready to get the hell out at the drop of a pie-pan or the lift of a skirt. His gestures are the ludicrous reflexes of the maladjusted; his repose is the momentary inertia of the nonplussed. He pulls the blinds against the morning and creeps into smokey corners at night. He talks largely about small matters and smally about great affairs. His ears are shut to the ominous rumblings of the dynasties of the world moving toward a cloudier chaos than ever before, but he hears with an acute perception the startling sounds that rabbits make twisting in the bushes along a country road at night and a cold chill comes upon him when the comic supplement of a Sunday newspaper blows unexpectedly out of an areaway and envelopes his knees. He can sleep while the commonwealth crumbles but a strange sound in the pantry at three in the morning will strike terror into his stomach. He is not afraid, or much aware, of the menaces of empire but he keeps looking behind him as he walks along darkening streets out of the fear that he is being softly followed by little men padding along in single file, about a foot and a half high, large-eyed, and whiskered.

It is difficult for such a person to conform to what Ford Madox Ford in his book of recollections has called the sole reason for writing one's memoirs: namely, to paint a picture of one's time. Your short-piece writer's time is not Walter Lippmann's time, or Stuart Chase's time, or Professor Einstein's time. It is his own personal time, circumscribed by the short boundaries of his pain and his embarrassment, in which what happens to his digestion, the rear axle of his car, and the confused flow of his relationships with six or eight persons and two or three buildings is of greater importance than what goes on in the nation or in the universe. He knows vaguely that the nation is not much good any more; he has read that the crust of the earth is shrinking alarmingly and that the universe is growing steadily colder, but he does not believe that any of the three is in half as bad shape as he is.

Enormous strides are made in star-measurement, theoretical economics, and the manufacture of bombing planes, but he usually doesn't find out about them until he picks up an old copy of "Time" on a picnic grounds or in the summer house of a friend. He is aware that billions of dollars are stolen every year by bankers and politicians, and that thousands of people are out of work, but these conditions do not worry him a tenth as much as the conviction that he has wasted three months on a stupid psychoanalyst or the suspicion that a piece he has been working on for two long days was done much better and probably more quickly by Robert Benchley in 1924.

The "time" of such a writer, then, is hardly worth reading about if the reader wishes to find out what was going on in the world while the writer in question was alive and at what might be laughingly called "his best". All that the reader is going to find out is what happened to the writer. The compensation, I suppose, must lie in the comforting feeling that one has had, after all, a pretty sensible and peaceful life, by comparison. It is unfortunate, however, that even a well-ordered life can not lead anybody safely around the inevitable doom that waits in the skies. As F. Hopkinson Smith long ago pointed out, the claw of the sea-puss gets us all in the end.

J. T.

Sandy Hook,
Connecticut,
September 25, 1933.

CHAPTER ONE

The Night the Bed Fell

I SUPPOSE that the high-water mark of my youth in Columbus, Ohio, was the night the bed fell on my father. It
makes a better recitation (unless, as some friends of mine have
said, one has heard it five or six times) than it does a piece of
writing, for it is almost necessary to throw furniture around,
shake doors, and bark like a dog, to lend the proper atmosphere and verisimilitude to what is admittedly a somewhat
incredible tale. Still, it did take place.

It happened, then, that my father had decided to sleep in
the attic one night, to be away where he could think. My
mother opposed the notion strongly because, she said, the old
wooden bed up there was unsafe: it was wobbly and the heavy
headboard would crash down on father's head in case the bed
fell, and kill him. There was no dissuading him, however, and
at a quarter past ten he closed the attic door behind him and
went up the narrow twisting stairs. We later heard ominous
creakings as he crawled into bed. Grandfather, who usually
slept in the attic bed when he was with us, had disappeared
some days before. (On these occasions he was usually gone
six or eight days and returned growling and out of temper,
with the news that the federal Union was run by a passel of
blockheads and that the Army of the Potomac didn't have any
more chance than a fiddler's bitch.)

We had visiting us at this time a nervous first cousin of mine
named Briggs Beall, who believed that he was likely to cease
breathing when he was asleep. It was his feeling that if he
were not awakened every hour during the night, he might die
of suffocation. He had been accustomed to setting an alarm
clock to ring at intervals until morning, but I persuaded him
to abandon this. He slept in my room and I told him that I
was such a light sleeper that if anybody quit breathing in the
same room with me, I would wake instantly. He tested me
the first night—which I had suspected he would—by holding
his breath after my regular breathing had convinced him I was
asleep. I was not asleep, however, and called to him. This

seemed to allay his fears a little, but he took the precaution of putting a glass of spirits of camphor on a little table at the head of his bed. In case I didn't arouse him until he was almost gone, he said, he would sniff the camphor, a powerful reviver. Briggs was not the only member of his family who had his crotchets. Old Aunt Melissa Beall (who could whistle like a man, with two fingers in her mouth) suffered under the premonition that she was destined to die on South High Street, because she had been born on South High Street and married on South High Street. Then there was Aunt Sarah Shoaf, who never went to bed at night without the fear that a burglar was going to get in and blow chloroform under her door through a tube. To avert this calamity—for she was in greater dread of anesthetics than of losing her household goods—she always piled her money, silverware, and other valuables in a neat stack just outside her bedroom, with a note reading: "This is all I have. Please take it and do not use your chloroform, as this is all I have." Aunt Gracie Shoaf also had a burglar phobia, but she met it with more fortitude. She was confident that burglars had been getting into her house every night for forty years. The fact that she never missed anything was to her no proof to the contrary. She always claimed that she scared them off before they could take anything, by throwing shoes down the hallway. When she went to bed she piled, where she could get at them handily, all the shoes there were about her house. Five minutes after she had turned off the light, she would sit up in bed and say "Hark!" Her husband, who had learned to ignore the whole situation as long ago as 1903, would either be sound asleep or pretend to be sound asleep. In either case he would not respond to her tugging and pulling, so that presently she would arise, tiptoe to the door, open it slightly and heave a shoe down the hall in one direction, and its mate down the hall in the other direction. Some nights she threw them all, some nights only a couple of pair.

But I am straying from the remarkable incidents that took place during the night that the bed fell on father. By midnight we were all in bed. The layout of the rooms and the disposition of their occupants is important to an understanding of what later occurred. In the front room upstairs (just under

Some nights she threw them all.

father's attic bedroom) were my mother and my brother Herman, who sometimes sang in his sleep, usually "Marching Through Georgia" or "Onward, Christian Soldiers." Briggs Beall and myself were in a room adjoining this one. My brother Roy was in a room across the hall from ours. Our bull terrier, Rex, slept in the hall.

My bed was an army cot, one of those affairs which are made wide enough to sleep on comfortably only by putting up, flat with the middle section, the two sides which ordinarily hang down like the sideboards of a drop-leaf table. When these sides are up, it is perilous to roll too far toward the edge, for then the cot is likely to tip completely over, bringing the whole bed down on top of one, with a tremendous banging crash. This, in fact, is precisely what happened, about two o'clock in the morning. (It was my mother who, in recalling the scene later, first referred to it as "the night the bed fell on your father.")

Always a deep sleeper, slow to arouse (I had lied to Briggs), I was at first unconscious of what had happened when the iron cot rolled me onto the floor and toppled over on me. It left me still warmly bundled up and unhurt, for the bed rested above me like a canopy. Hence I did not wake up, only reached the edge of consciousness and went back. The racket, however, instantly awakened my mother, in the next room, who came to the immediate conclusion that her worst dread was realized: the big wooden bed upstairs had fallen on father. She therefore screamed, "Let's go to your poor father!" It was this shout, rather than the noise of my cot falling, that awakened Herman, in the same room with her. He thought that mother had become, for no apparent reason, hysterical. "You're all right, Mamma!" he shouted, trying to calm her. They exchanged shout for shout for perhaps ten seconds: "Let's go to your poor father!" and "You're all right!" That woke up Briggs. By this time I was conscious of what was going on, in a vague way, but did not yet realize that I was under my bed instead of on it. Briggs, awakening in the midst of loud shouts of fear and apprehension, came to the quick conclusion that he was suffocating and that we were all trying to "bring him out." With a low moan, he grasped the glass of camphor at the head of his bed and instead of sniffing it poured it over himself. The room reeked of camphor. "Ugf, ahfg," choked Briggs, like a drowning man, for he had almost succeeded in stopping his breath under the deluge of pungent spirits. He leaped out of bed and groped toward the open window, but he came up against one that was closed. With his hand, he beat out the glass, and I could hear it crash and tinkle on the alleyway below. It was at this juncture that I, in trying to get up, had the uncanny sensation of feeling my bed above me! Foggy with sleep, I now suspected, in my turn,

He came to the conclusion that he was suffocating.

that the whole uproar was being made in a frantic endeavor to extricate me from what must be an unheard-of and perilous situation. "Get me out of this!" I bawled. "Get me out!" I think I had the nightmarish belief that I was entombed in a mine. "Gugh," gasped Briggs, floundering in his camphor.

By this time my mother, still shouting, pursued by Herman, still shouting, was trying to open the door to the attic, in order to go up and get my father's body out of the wreckage.

The door was stuck, however, and wouldn't yield. Her frantic pulls on it only added to the general banging and confusion. Roy and the dog were now up, the one shouting questions, the other barking.

Father, farthest away and soundest sleeper of all, had by this time been awakened by the battering on the attic door. He decided that the house was on fire. "I'm coming, I'm coming!" he wailed in a slow, sleepy voice—it took him many minutes to regain full consciousness. My mother, still believing he was caught under the bed, detected in his "I'm coming!" the mournful, resigned note of one who is preparing to meet his Maker. "He's dying!" she shouted.

Roy had to throw Rex.

"I'm all right!" Briggs yelled to reassure her. "I'm all right!" He still believed that it was his own closeness to death that was worrying mother. I found at last the light switch in my room, unlocked the door, and Briggs and I joined the others at the attic door. The dog, who never did like Briggs, jumped for him—assuming that he was the culprit in whatever was going on—and Roy had to throw Rex and hold him. We could hear father crawling out of bed upstairs. Roy pulled the attic door open, with a mighty jerk, and father came down the stairs, sleepy and irritable but safe and sound. My mother began to weep when she saw him. Rex began to howl. "What in the name of God is going on here?" asked father.

The situation was finally put together like a gigantic jigsaw puzzle. Father caught a cold from prowling around in his bare feet but there were no other bad results. "I'm glad," said mother, who always looked on the bright side of things, "that your grandfather wasn't here."

CHAPTER TWO

The Car We Had to Push

MANY autobiographers, among them Lincoln Steffens and Gertrude Atherton, describe earthquakes their families have been in. I am unable to do this because my family was never in an earthquake, but we went through a number of things in Columbus that were a great deal like earthquakes. I remember in particular some of the repercussions of an old Reo we had that wouldn't go unless you pushed it for quite a way and suddenly let your clutch out. Once, we had been able to start the engine easily by cranking it, but we had had the car for so many years that finally it wouldn't go unless you pushed it and let your clutch out. Of course, it took more than one person to do this; it took sometimes as many as five or six, depending on the grade of the roadway and conditions underfoot. The car was unusual in that the clutch and brake were on the same pedal, making it quite easy to stall the engine after it got started, so that the car would have to be pushed again.

My father used to get sick at his stomach pushing the car, and very often was unable to go to work. He had never liked the machine, even when it was good, sharing my ignorance

It took sometimes as many as five or six.

and suspicion of all automobiles of twenty years ago and longer. The boys I went to school with used to be able to identify every car as it passed by: Thomas Flyer, Firestone-Columbus, Stevens Duryea, Rambler, Winton, White Steamer, etc. I never could. The only car I was really interested in was one that the Get-Ready Man, as we called him, rode around town in: a big Red Devil with a door in the back. The Get-Ready Man was a lank unkempt elderly gentleman with wild eyes and a deep voice who used to go about shouting at people through a megaphone to prepare for the end of the world. "GET READY! GET READ-Y!" he would bellow. "THE WORLLLD IS COMING TO AN END!" His startling exhortations would come up, like summer thunder, at the most unexpected times and in the most surprising places. I remember once during Mantell's production of "King Lear" at the Colonial Theatre, that the Get-Ready Man added his bawlings

The Get-Ready Man.

to the squealing of Edgar and the ranting of the King and the mouthing of the Fool, rising from somewhere in the balcony to join in. The theatre was in absolute darkness and there were rumblings of thunder and flashes of lightning offstage. Neither father nor I, who were there, ever completely got over the scene, which went something like this:

Edgar: Tom's a-cold.—O, do de, do de, do de!—Bless thee

from whirlwinds, star-blasting, and taking . . . the foul fiend
vexes!

(*Thunder off.*

Lear: What! Have his daughters brought him to this pass?—
Get-Ready Man: Get ready! Get ready!
Edgar: Pillicock sat on Pillicock-hill:—

Halloo, halloo, loo, loo!

(*Lightning flashes.*

Get-Ready Man: The Worllld is com-ing to an End!
Fool: This cold night will turn us all to fools and madmen!
Edgar: Take heed o' the foul fiend: obey thy paren——
Get-Ready Man: Get *Rea*-dy!
Edgar: Tom's a-*cold*!
Get-Ready Man: The *Worr*-uld is coming to an end! . . .

They found him finally, and ejected him, still shouting. The
Theatre, in our time, has known few such moments.

But to get back to the automobile. One of my happiest
memories of it was when, in its eighth year, my brother Roy
got together a great many articles from the kitchen, placed
them in a square of canvas, and swung this under the car with
a string attached to it so that, at a twitch, the canvas would
give way and the steel and tin things would clatter to the
street. This was a little scheme of Roy's to frighten father,
who had always expected the car might explode. It worked
perfectly. That was twenty-five years ago, but it is one of the
few things in my life I would like to live over again if I could.
I don't suppose that I can, now. Roy twitched the string in
the middle of a lovely afternoon, on Bryden Road near Eigh-
teenth Street. Father had closed his eyes and, with his hat off,
was enjoying a cool breeze. The clatter on the asphalt was
tremendously effective: knives, forks, can-openers, pie pans,
pot lids, biscuit-cutters, ladles, egg-beaters fell, beautifully together, in a lingering, clamant crash. "Stop the *car*!" shouted
father. "I can't," Roy said. "The engine fell out." "God Almighty!" said father, who knew what *that* meant, or knew
what it sounded as if it might mean.

It ended unhappily, of course, because we finally had to
drive back and pick up the stuff and even father knew the
difference between the works of an automobile and the equipment of a pantry. My mother wouldn't have known, however,

nor *her* mother. My mother, for instance, thought—or, rather, knew—that it was dangerous to drive an automobile without gasoline: it fried the valves, or something. "Now don't you dare drive all over town without gasoline!" she would say to us when we started off. Gasoline, oil, and water were much the same to her, a fact that made her life both confusing and perilous. Her greatest dread, however, was the Victrola—we had a very early one, back in the "Come Josephine in My Flying Machine" days. She had an idea that the Victrola might blow up. It alarmed her, rather than reassured her, to explain that the phonograph was run neither by gasoline nor by electricity. She could only suppose that it was propelled by some newfangled and untested apparatus which was likely to let go at any minute, making us all the victims and martyrs of the wild-eyed Edison's dangerous experiments. The telephone she was comparatively at peace with, except, of course, during storms, when for some reason or other she always took the receiver off the hook and let it hang. She came naturally by her confused and groundless fears, for her own mother lived the latter years of her life in the horrible suspicion that electricity was dripping invisibly all over the house. It leaked, she contended, out of empty sockets if the wall switch had been left on. She would go around screwing in bulbs, and if they lighted up she would hastily and fearfully turn off the wall switch and go back to her *Pearson's* or *Everybody's*, happy in the satisfaction that she had stopped not only a costly but a dangerous leakage. Nothing could ever clear this up for her.

Our poor old Reo came to a horrible end, finally. We had parked it too far from the curb on a street with a car line. It was late at night and the street was dark. The first streetcar that came along couldn't get by. It picked up the tired old automobile as a terrier might seize a rabbit and drubbed it unmercifully, losing its hold now and then but catching a new grip a second later. Tires booped and whooshed, the fenders queeled and graked, the steering-wheel rose up like a spectre and disappeared in the direction of Franklin Avenue with a melancholy whistling sound, bolts and gadgets flew like sparks from a Catherine wheel. It was a splendid spectacle but, of course, saddening to everybody (except the motorman of the streetcar, who was sore). I think some of us broke down and

wept. It must have been the weeping that caused grandfather to take on so terribly. Time was all mixed up in his mind; automobiles and the like he never remembered having seen. He apparently gathered, from the talk and excitement and weeping, that somebody had died. Nor did he let go of this delusion. He insisted, in fact, after almost a week in which we strove mightily to divert him, that it was a sin and a shame and a disgrace on the family to put the funeral off any longer. "Nobody is dead! The automobile is smashed!" shouted my father, trying for the thirtieth time to explain the situation to the old man. "Was he drunk?" demanded grandfather, sternly. "Was who drunk?" asked father. "Zenas," said grandfather. He had a name for the corpse now: it was his brother Zenas, who, as it happened, *was* dead, but not from driving an automobile while intoxicated. Zenas had died in 1866. A sensitive, rather poetical boy of twenty-one when the Civil War broke out, Zenas had gone to South America—"just," as he wrote back, "until it blows over." Returning after the war had blown over, he caught the same disease that was killing off the chestnut trees in those years, and passed away. It was the only case in history where a tree doctor had to be called in to spray a person, and our family had felt it very keenly; nobody else in the United States caught the blight. Some of us have looked upon Zenas' fate as a kind of poetic justice.

Now that grandfather knew, so to speak, who was dead, it became increasingly awkward to go on living in the same house with him as if nothing had happened. He would go into towering rages in which he threatened to write to the Board of Health unless the funeral were held at once. We realized that something had to be done. Eventually, we persuaded a friend of father's, named George Martin, to dress up in the manner and costume of the eighteen-sixties and pretend to be Uncle Zenas, in order to set grandfather's mind at rest. The impostor looked fine and impressive in sideburns and a high beaver hat, and not unlike the daguerreotypes of Zenas in our album. I shall never forget the night, just after dinner, when this Zenas walked into the living-room. Grandfather was stomping up and down, tall, hawk-nosed, round-oathed. The newcomer held out both his hands. "Clem!" he cried to

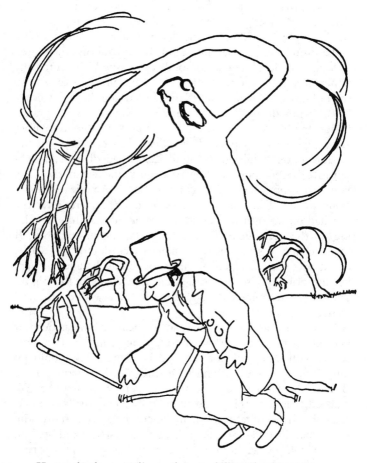

He caught the same disease that was killing the chestnut trees.

grandfather. Grandfather turned slowly, looked at the intruder, and snorted. "Who air *you*?" he demanded in his deep, resonant voice. "I'm Zenas!" cried Martin. "Your brother Zenas, fit as a fiddle and sound as a dollar!" "Zenas, my foot!" said grandfather. "Zenas died of the chestnut blight in '66!"

Grandfather was given to these sudden, unexpected, and extremely lucid moments; they were generally more embarrassing than his other moments. He comprehended before he went to bed that night that the old automobile had been destroyed and that its destruction had caused all the turmoil in the house. "It flew all to pieces, Pa," my mother told him, in graphically describing the accident. "I knew 'twould," growled grandfather. "I allus told ye to git a Pope-Toledo."

CHAPTER THREE

The Day the Dam Broke

M Y MEMORIES of what my family and I went through during the 1913 flood in Ohio I would gladly forget. And yet neither the hardships we endured nor the turmoil and confusion we experienced can alter my feeling toward my native state and city. I am having a fine time now and wish Columbus were here, but if anyone ever wished a city was in hell it was during that frightful and perilous afternoon in 1913 when the dam broke, or, to be more exact, when everybody in town *thought* that the dam broke. We were both ennobled and demoralized by the experience. Grandfather especially rose to magnificent heights which can never lose their splendor for me, even though his reactions to the flood were based upon a profound misconception; namely, that Nathan Bedford Forrest's cavalry was the menace we were called upon to face. The only possible means of escape for us was to flee the house, a step which grandfather sternly forbade, brandishing his old army sabre in his hand. "Let the sons — —— come!" he roared. Meanwhile hundreds of people were streaming by our house in wild panic, screaming "Go east! Go east!" We had to stun grandfather with the ironing board. Impeded as we were by the inert form of the old gentleman—he was taller than six feet and weighed almost a hundred and seventy pounds—we were passed, in the first half-mile, by practically everybody else in the city. Had grandfather not come to, at the corner of Parsons Avenue and Town Street, we would unquestionably have been overtaken and engulfed by the roaring waters—that is, if there had *been* any roaring waters. Later, when the panic had died down and people had gone rather sheepishly back to their homes and their offices, minimizing the distances they had run and offering various reasons for running, city engineers pointed out that even if the dam had broken, the water level would not have risen more than two additional inches in the West Side. The West Side was, at the time of the dam scare, under thirty feet of water—as, indeed, were all Ohio river towns during the great spring floods of twenty years ago. The East Side (where we lived and where all the running occurred) had never been in any danger at all. Only a rise of some ninety-five feet could have caused the flood waters to flow over High Street—the thoroughfare that divided the east side of town from the west—and engulf the East Side.

The fact that we were all as safe as kittens under a cookstove did not, however, assuage in the least the fine despair and the grotesque desperation which seized upon the residents of the

Two thousand people were in full flight

East Side when the cry spread like a grass fire that the dam had given way. Some of the most dignified, staid, cynical, and clear-thinking men in town abandoned their wives, stenographers, homes, and offices and ran east. There are few alarms in the world more terrifying than "The dam has broken!" There are few persons capable of stopping to reason when that clarion cry strikes upon their ears, even persons who live in towns no nearer than five hundred miles to a dam.

The Columbus, Ohio, broken-dam rumor began, as I recall it, about noon of March 12, 1913. High Street, the main canyon of trade, was loud with the placid hum of business and the buzzing of placid businessmen arguing, computing, wheedling, offering, refusing, compromising. Darius Conningway, one of the foremost corporation lawyers in the Middle-West, was telling the Public Utilities Commission in the language of Julius Caesar that they might as well try to move the Northern star as to move him. Other men were making their little boasts and their little gestures. Suddenly somebody began to run. It may be that he had simply remembered, all of a moment, an engagement to meet his wife, for which he was now frightfully late. Whatever it was, he ran east on Broad Street (probably toward the Maramor Restaurant, a favorite place for a man to meet his wife). Somebody else began to run, perhaps a newsboy in high spirits. Another man, a portly gentleman of affairs, broke into a trot. Inside of ten minutes, everybody on High Street, from the Union Depot to the Courthouse was running. A loud mumble gradually crystallized into the dread word "dam." "The dam has broke!" The fear was put into words by a little old lady in an electric, or by a traffic cop, or by a small boy: nobody knows who, nor does it now really matter. Two thousand people were abruptly in full flight. "Go east!" was the cry that arose—east away from the river, east to safety. "Go east! Go east! Go east!"

Black streams of people flowed eastward down all the streets leading in that direction; these streams, whose headwaters were in the dry-goods stores, office buildings, harness shops, movie theatres, were fed by trickles of housewives, children, cripples, servants, dogs, and cats, slipping out of the houses past which the main streams flowed, shouting and screaming. People ran out leaving fires burning and food cooking and doors wide open. I remember, however, that my mother turned out all the fires and that she took with her a dozen eggs and two loaves of bread. It was her plan to make Memorial Hall, just two blocks away, and take refuge somewhere in the top of it, in one of the dusty rooms where war veterans met and where old battle flags and stage scenery were stored. But the seething throngs, shouting "Go east!," drew her along and the rest of us with her. When grandfather regained full consciousness, at Parsons Avenue, he turned upon the retreating mob like a vengeful prophet and exhorted the men to form ranks and stand off the Rebel dogs, but at length he, too, got the idea that the dam had broken and, roaring "Go east!" in his powerful voice, he caught up in one arm a small child and in the other a slight clerkish man of perhaps forty-two and we slowly began to gain on those ahead of us.

A scattering of firemen, policemen, and army officers in dress uniforms—there had been a review at Fort Hayes, in the northern part of town—added color to the surging billows of people. "Go east!" cried a little child in a piping voice, as she ran past a porch on which drowsed a lieutenant-colonel of infantry. Used to quick decisions, trained to immediate obedience, the officer bounded off the porch and, running at full tilt, soon passed the child, bawling "Go east!" The two of them emptied rapidly the houses of the little street they were on. "What is it? What is it?" demanded a fat, waddling man who intercepted the colonel. The officer dropped behind and asked the little child what it was. "The dam has broke!" gasped the girl. "The dam has broke!" roared the colonel. "Go east! Go east! Go east!" He was soon leading, with the exhausted child in his arms, a fleeing company of three hundred persons who had gathered around him from living-rooms, shops, garages, backyards, and basements.

Nobody has ever been able to compute with any exactness how many people took part in the great rout of 1913, for the panic, which extended from the Winslow Bottling Works in the south end to Clintonville, six miles north, ended as abruptly as it began and the bobtail and ragtag and velvet-gowned groups of refugees melted away and slunk home, leaving the streets peaceful and deserted. The shouting, weeping, tangled evacuation of the city lasted not more than two hours in all. Some few people got as far east as Reynoldsburg, twelve miles away; fifty or more reached the Country Club, eight miles away; most of the others gave up, exhausted, or climbed trees in Franklin Park, four miles out. Order was restored and fear dispelled finally by means of militiamen riding about in motor lorries bawling through megaphones: "The dam has *not* broken!" At first this tended only to add to the confusion and increase the panic, for many stampeders thought the soldiers were bellowing "The dam has now broken!," thus setting an official seal of authentication on the calamity.

All the time, the sun shone quietly and there was nowhere any sign of oncoming waters. A visitor in an airplane, looking down on the straggling, agitated masses of people below, would have been hard put to it to divine a reason for the phenomenon. It must have inspired, in such an observer, a peculiar kind of terror, like the sight of the *Marie Celeste*, abandoned at sea, its galley fires peacefully burning, its tranquil decks bright in the sunlight.

An aunt of mine, Aunt Edith Taylor, was in a movie theatre on High Street when, over and above the sound of the piano in the pit (a W. S. Hart picture was being shown), there rose the steadily increasing tromp of running feet. Persistent shouts rose above the tromping. An elderly man, sitting near my aunt, mumbled something, got out of his seat, and went up the aisle at a dogtrot. This started everybody. In an instant the audience was jamming the aisles. "Fire!" shouted a woman who always expected to be burned up in a theatre; but now the shouts outside were louder and coherent. "The dam has broke!" cried somebody. "Go east!" screamed a small woman in front of my aunt. And east they went, pushing and shoving and clawing, knocking women and children down, emerging finally into the street, torn and sprawling. Inside the theatre, Bill Hart was calmly calling some desperado's bluff and the brave girl at the piano played "Row! Row! Row!" loudly and then "In My Harem." Outside, men were streaming across the Statehouse yard, others were climbing trees, a woman managed to get up onto the "These Are My Jewels" statue, whose bronze figures of Sherman, Stanton, Grant, and Sheridan watched with cold unconcern the going to pieces of the capital city.

"I ran south to State Street, east on State to Third, south on Third to Town, and out east on Town," my Aunt Edith has written me. "A tall spare woman with grim eyes and a determined chin ran past me down the middle of the street. I was still uncertain as to what was the matter, in spite of all the shouting. I drew up alongside the woman with some effort, for although she was in her late fifties, she had a beautiful easy running form and seemed to be in excellent condition.

'What is it?' I puffed. She gave me a quick glance and then looked ahead again, stepping up her pace a trifle. 'Don't ask me, ask God!' she said.

"When I reached Grant Avenue, I was so spent that Dr. H. R. Mallory—you remember Dr. Mallory, the man with the white beard who looks like Robert Browning?—well, Dr. Mallory, whom I had drawn away from at the corner of Fifth and Town, passed me. 'It's got us!' he shouted, and I felt sure that whatever it was *did* have us, for you know what conviction Dr. Mallory's statements always carried. I didn't know at the time what he meant, but I found out later. There was a

"It's got us!" he shouted.

boy behind him on roller-skates, and Dr. Mallory mistook the swishing of the skates for the sound of rushing water. He eventually reached the Columbus School for Girls, at the corner of Parsons Avenue and Town Street, where he collapsed, expecting the cold frothing waters of the Scioto to sweep him into oblivion. The boy on the skates swirled past him and Dr. Mallory realized for the first time what he had been running from. Looking back up the street, he could see no signs of water, but nevertheless, after resting a few minutes, he jogged on east again. He caught up with me at Ohio Avenue, where we rested together. I should say that about seven hundred people passed us. A funny thing was that all of them were on foot. Nobody seemed to have had the courage to stop and start his car; but as I remember it, all cars had to be cranked in those days, which is probably the reason."

The next day, the city went about its business as if nothing had happened, but there was no joking. It was two years or more before you dared treat the breaking of the dam lightly. And even now, twenty years after, there are a few persons, like Dr. Mallory, who will shut up like a clam if you mention the Afternoon of the Great Run.

CHAPTER FOUR

The Night the Ghost Got In

T HE GHOST that got into our house on the night of November 17, 1915, raised such a hullabaloo of misunder-
standings that I am sorry I didn't just let it keep on walking,
and go to bed. Its advent caused my mother to throw a shoe
through a window of the house next door and ended up with
my grandfather shooting a patrolman. I am sorry, therefore,
as I have said, that I ever paid any attention to the footsteps.

They began about a quarter past one o'clock in the morning, a rhythmic, quick-cadenced walking around the dining-
room table. My mother was asleep in one room upstairs, my
brother Herman in another; grandfather was in the attic, in
the old walnut bed which, as you will remember, once fell on
my father. I had just stepped out of the bathtub and was busily
rubbing myself with a towel when I heard the steps. They
were the steps of a man walking rapidly around the dining-
room table downstairs. The light from the bathroom shone
down the back steps, which dropped directly into the dining-
room; I could see the faint shine of plates on the plate-rail; I
couldn't see the table. The steps kept going round and round
the table; at regular intervals a board creaked, when it was
trod upon. I supposed at first that it was my father or my
brother Roy, who had gone to Indianapolis but were expected
home at any time. I suspected next that it was a burglar. It
did not enter my mind until later that it was a ghost.

After the walking had gone on for perhaps three minutes,
I tiptoed to Herman's room. "Psst!" I hissed, in the dark,
shaking him. "Awp," he said, in the low, hopeless tone of a
despondent beagle—he always half suspected that something
would "get him" in the night. I told him who I was. "There's
something downstairs!" I said. He got up and followed me
to the head of the back staircase. We listened together. There
was no sound. The steps had ceased. Herman looked at me
in some alarm: I had only the bath towel around my waist.
He wanted to go back to bed, but I gripped his arm. "There's
something down there!" I said. Instantly the steps began

again, circled the dining-room table like a man running, and started up the stairs toward us, heavily, two at a time. The light still shone palely down the stairs; we saw nothing coming; we only heard the steps. Herman rushed to his room and slammed the door. I slammed shut the door at the stairs top and held my knee against it. After a long minute, I slowly opened it again. There was nothing there. There was no sound. None of us ever heard the ghost again.

He always half suspected that something would get him.

The slamming of the doors had aroused mother: she peered out of her room. "What on earth are you boys doing?" she demanded. Herman ventured out of his room. "Nothing," he said, gruffly, but he was, in color, a light green. "What was all that running around downstairs?" said mother. So she had heard the steps, too! We just looked at her. "Burglars!" she shouted, intuitively. I tried to quiet her by starting lightly downstairs.

"Come on, Herman," I said.

"I'll stay with mother," he said. "She's all excited."

I stepped back onto the landing.

"Don't either of you go a step," said mother. "We'll call the police." Since the phone was downstairs, I didn't see how we were going to call the police—nor did I want the police—but mother made one of her quick, incomparable decisions. She flung up a window of her bedroom which faced the bedroom windows of the house of a neighbor, picked up a shoe, and whammed it through a pane of glass across the narrow space that separated the two houses. Glass tinkled into the bedroom occupied by a retired engraver named Bodwell and his wife. Bodwell had been for some years in rather a bad way and was subject to mild "attacks." Most everybody we knew or lived near had *some* kind of attacks.

It was now about two o'clock of a moonless night; clouds hung black and low. Bodwell was at the window in a minute, shouting, frothing a little, shaking his fist. "We'll sell the house and go back to Peoria," we could hear Mrs. Bodwell saying. It was some time before Mother "got through" to Bodwell. "Burglars!" she shouted. "Burglars in the house!" Herman and I hadn't dared to tell her that it was not burglars but ghosts, for she was even more afraid of ghosts than of burglars. Bodwell at first thought that she meant there were burglars in his house, but finally he quieted down and called the police for us over an extension phone by his bed. After he had disappeared from the window, mother suddenly made as if to throw another shoe, not because there was further need of it but, as she later explained, because the thrill of heaving a shoe through a window glass had enormously taken her fancy. I prevented her.

The police were on hand in a commendably short time: a Ford sedan full of them, two on motorcycles, and a patrol wagon with about eight in it and a few reporters. They began banging at our front door. Flashlights shot streaks of gleam up and down the walls, across the yard, down the walk between our house and Bodwell's. "Open up!" cried a hoarse voice. "We're men from Headquarters!" I wanted to go down and let them in, since there they were, but mother wouldn't hear of it. "You haven't a stitch on," she pointed out. "You'd catch your death." I wound the towel around me again. Finally the cops put their shoulders to our big heavy front door with its thick beveled glass and broke it in: I could hear a rending of wood and a splash of glass on the floor of the hall. Their lights played all over the living-room and crisscrossed nervously in the dining-room, stabbed into hallways, shot up the front stairs and finally up the back. They caught me standing in my towel at the top. A heavy policeman bounded up the steps. "Who are you?" he demanded. "I live here," I said. "Well, whattsa matta, ya hot?" he asked. It was, as a matter of fact, cold; I went to my room and pulled on some trousers. On my way out, a cop stuck a gun into my ribs. "Whatta you doin' here?" he demanded. "I live here," I said.

The officer in charge reported to mother. "No sign of nobody, lady," he said. "Musta got away—whatt'd he look like?" "There were two or three of them," mother said, "whooping and carrying on and slamming doors." "Funny," said the cop. "All ya windows and doors was locked on the inside tight as a tick."

Downstairs, we could hear the tromping of the other police. Police were all over the place; doors were yanked open, drawers were yanked open, windows were shot up and pulled down, furniture fell with dull thumps. A half-dozen policemen emerged out of the darkness of the front hallway upstairs. They began to ransack the floor: pulled beds away from walls, tore clothes off hooks in the closets, pulled suitcases and boxes off shelves. One of them found an old zither that Roy had won in a pool tournament. "Looky here, Joe," he said, strumming it with a big paw. The cop named Joe took it and turned it over. "What is it?" he asked me. "It's an old zither our guinea pig used to sleep on," I said. It was true that a pet guinea pig we once had would never sleep anywhere except on the zither, but I should never have said so. Joe and the other cop looked at me a long time. They put the zither back on a shelf.

"No sign o' nuthin'," said the cop who had first spoken to mother. "This guy," he explained to the others, jerking a thumb at me, "was nekked. The lady seems historical." They all nodded, but said nothing; just looked at me. In the small silence we all heard a creaking in the attic. Grandfather was turning over in bed. "What's 'at?" snapped Joe. Five or six cops sprang for the attic door before I could intervene or explain. I realized that it would be bad if they burst in on grandfather unannounced, or even announced. He was going through a phase in which he believed that General Meade's men, under steady hammering by Stonewall Jackson, were beginning to retreat and even desert.

When I got to the attic, things were pretty confused. Grandfather had evidently jumped to the conclusion that the police were deserters from Meade's army, trying to hide away in his attic. He bounded out of bed wearing a long flannel

Police were all over the place.

nightgown over long woolen underwear, a nightcap, and a leather jacket around his chest. The cops must have realized at once that the indignant white-haired old man belonged in the house, but they had no chance to say so. "Back, ye cowardly dogs!" roared grandfather. "Back t' the lines, ye goddam lily-livered cattle!" With that, he fetched the officer who found the zither a flat-handed smack alongside his head that sent him sprawling. The others beat a retreat, but not fast enough; grandfather grabbed Zither's gun from its holster and let fly. The report seemed to crack the rafters; smoke filled the attic. A cop cursed and shot his hand to his shoulder. Somehow, we all finally got downstairs again and locked the door against the old gentleman. He fired once or twice more in the darkness and then went back to bed. "That was grandfather," I explained to Joe, out of breath. "He thinks you're deserters." "I'll say he does," said Joe.

The cops were reluctant to leave without getting their hands on somebody besides grandfather; the night had been distinctly a defeat for them. Furthermore, they obviously didn't like the "layout"; something looked—and I can see their viewpoint—phony. They began to poke into things again. A reporter, a thin-faced, wispy man, came up to me. I had put on one of mother's blouses, not being able to find anything else. The reporter looked at me with mingled suspicion and interest. "Just what the hell is the real lowdown here, Bud?" he asked. I decided to be frank with him. "We had ghosts," I said. He gazed at me a long time as if I were a slot machine into which he had, without results, dropped a nickel. Then he walked away. The cops followed him, the one grandfather shot holding his now-bandaged arm, cursing and blaspheming. "I'm gonna get my gun back from that old bird," said the zither-cop. "Yeh," said Joe. "You—and who else?" I told them I would bring it to the station house the next day.

"What was the matter with that one policeman?" mother asked, after they had gone. "Grandfather shot him," I said. "What for?" she demanded. I told her he was a deserter. "Of all things!" said mother. "He was such a nice-looking young man."

Grandfather was fresh as a daisy and full of jokes at breakfast next morning. We thought at first he had forgotten all about what had happened, but he hadn't. Over his third cup of coffee, he glared at Herman and me. "What was the idee of all them cops tarryhootin' round the house last night?" he demanded. He had us there.

as he later explained it, some "fun." He got out of bed and, going to my father's room, shook him and said, "Buck, your time has come!" My father's name was not Buck but Charles, nor had he ever been called Buck. He was a tall, mildly nervous, peaceable gentleman, given to quiet pleasures, and eager that everything should run smoothly. "Hmm?" he said, with drowsy bewilderment. "Get up, Buck," said my brother, coldly, but with a certain gleam in his eyes. My father leaped out of bed, on the side away from his son, rushed from the room, locked the door behind him, and shouted us all up.

We were naturally enough reluctant to believe that Roy, who was quiet and self-contained, had threatened his father with any such abracadabra as father said he had. My older brother, Herman, went back to bed without any comment. "You've had a bad dream," my mother said. This vexed my father. "I tell you he called me Buck and told me my time had come," he said. We went to the door of his room, unlocked it, and tiptoed through it to Roy's room. He lay in his bed, breathing easily, as if he were fast asleep. It was apparent at a glance that he did not have a high fever. My mother gave my father a look. "I tell you he did," whispered father.

Our presence in the room finally seemed to awaken Roy and he was (or rather, as we found out long afterward, pretended to be) astonished and bewildered. "What's the matter?" he asked. "Nothing," said my mother. "Just your father had a nightmare." "I did not have a nightmare," said father, slowly and firmly. He wore an old-fashioned, "side-slit" nightgown which looked rather odd on his tall, spare figure. The situation, before we let it drop and everybody went back to bed again, became, as such situations in our family usually did, rather more complicated than ironed out. Roy demanded to know what had happened, and my mother told him, in considerably garbled fashion, what father had told her. At this a light dawned in Roy's eyes. "Dad's got it backward," he said. He then explained that he had heard father get out of bed and had called to him. "I'll handle this," his father had answered. "Buck is downstairs." "Who is this Buck?" my mother demanded of father. "I don't know any Buck and I never said that," father contended, irritably. None of us (except Roy, of course) believed him. "You had a dream," said mother. "People have these dreams." "I did not have a dream," father said. He was pretty well nettled by this time, and he stood in front of a bureau mirror, brushing his hair with a pair of military brushes; it always seemed to calm father to brush his hair. My mother declared that it was "a sin and a shame" for a grown man to wake up a sick boy simply because he (the grown man: father) had got on his back and had a bad dream. My father, as a matter of fact, *had* been known to have nightmares, usually about Lillian Russell and President Cleveland, who chased him.

We argued the thing for perhaps another half-hour, after which mother made father sleep in her room. "You're all safe now, boys," she said, firmly, as she shut her door. I could hear father grumbling for a long time, with an occasional monosyllable of doubt from mother.

It was some six months after this that father went through a similar experience with me. He was at that time sleeping in the room next to mine. I had been trying all afternoon, in vain, to think of the name Perth Amboy. It seems now like a very simple name to recall and yet on the day in question I thought of every other town in the country, as well as such words and names and phrases as terra cotta, Walla-Walla, bill of lading, vice versa, hoity-toity, Pall Mall, Bodley Head, Schumann-Heink, etc., without even coming close to Perth Amboy. I suppose terra cotta was the closest I came, although it was not very close.

Long after I had gone to bed, I was struggling with the problem. I began to indulge in the wildest fancies as I lay there in the dark, such as that there was no such town, and even that there was no such state as New Jersey. I fell to repeating the word "Jersey" over and over again, until it became idiotic and meaningless. If you have ever lain awake at night and repeated one word over and over, thousands and millions and hundreds of thousands of millions of times, you know the disturbing mental state you can get into. I got to thinking that there was nobody else in the world but me, and various other wild imaginings of that nature. Eventually, lying there thinking these outlandish thoughts, I grew slightly alarmed. I began to suspect that one might lose one's mind over some such trivial mental tic as a futile search for terra

firma Piggly Wiggly Gorgonzola Prester John Arc de Tri-
omphe Holy Moses Lares and Penates. I began to feel the
imperative necessity of human contact. This silly and alarming
tangle of thought and fancy had gone far enough. I might get
into some kind of mental aberrancy unless I found out the
name of that Jersey town and could go to sleep. Therefore, I
got out of bed, walked into the room where father was sleeping, and shook him. "Um?" he mumbled. I shook him more
fiercely and he finally woke up, with a glaze of dream and
apprehension in his eyes. "What's matter?" he asked, thickly.
I must, indeed, have been rather wild of eye, and my hair,
which is unruly, becomes monstrously tousled and snarled at
night. "Wha's it?" said my father, sitting up, in readiness to
spring out of bed on the far side. The thought must have been
going through his mind that all his sons were crazy, or on the
verge of going crazy. I see that now, but I didn't then, for I
had forgotten the Buck incident and did not realize how similar my appearance must have been to Roy's the night he
called father Buck and told him his time had come. "Listen,"
I said. "Name some towns in New Jersey quick!" It must have
been around three in the morning. Father got up, keeping the
bed between him and me, and started to pull his trousers on.
"Don't bother about dressing," I said. "Just name some
towns in New Jersey." While he hastily pulled on his clothes—
I remember he left his socks off and put his shoes on his bare
feet—father began to name, in a shaky voice, various New
Jersey cities. I can still see him reaching for his coat without
taking his eyes off me. "Newark," he said, "Jersey City, Atlantic City, Elizabeth, Paterson, Passaic, Trenton, Jersey City,
Trenton, Paterson—" "It has two names," I snapped. "Elizabeth and Paterson," he said. "No, no!" I told him, irritably.
"This is one town with one name, but there are two words
in it, like helter-skelter." "Helter-skelter," said my father,
moving slowly toward the bedroom door and smiling in a
faint, strained way which I understand now—but didn't
then—was meant to humor me. When he was within a few
paces of the door, he fairly leaped for it and ran out into the
hall, his coat-tails and shoelaces flying. The exit stunned me.
I had no notion that he thought I had gone out of my senses;
I could only believe that he had gone out of *his* or that, only

partially awake, he was engaged in some form of running in his sleep. I ran after him and I caught him at the door of mother's room and grabbed him, in order to reason with him. I shook him a little, thinking to wake him completely. "Mary! Roy! Herman!" he shouted. I, too, began to shout for my brothers and my mother. My mother opened her door instantly, and there we were at 3:30 in the morning grappling and shouting, father partly dressed, but without socks or shirt, and I in pajamas.

"*Now*, what?" demanded my mother, grimly, pulling us apart. She was capable, fortunately, of handling any two of us and she never in her life was alarmed by the words or actions of any one of us.

"Look out for Jamie!" said father. (He always called me Jamie when excited.) My mother looked at me.

"What's the matter with your father?" she demanded. I said I didn't know; I said he had got up suddenly and dressed and ran out of the room.

"Where did you think you were going?" mother asked him, coolly. He looked at me. We looked at each other, breathing hard, but somewhat calmer.

"He was babbling about New Jersey at this infernal hour of the night," said father. "He came to my room and asked me to name towns in New Jersey." Mother looked at me.

"I just asked him," I said. "I was trying to think of one and couldn't sleep."

"You see?" said father, triumphantly. Mother didn't look at him.

"Get to bed, both of you," she said. "I don't want to hear any more out of you tonight. Dressing and tearing up and down the hall at this hour in the morning!" She went back into the room and shut her door. Father and I went back to bed. "Are you all right?" he called to me. "Are you?" I asked. "Well, good night," he said. "Good night," I said.

Mother would not let the rest of us discuss the affair next morning at breakfast. Herman asked what the hell had been the matter. "We'll go on to something more elevating," said mother.

CHAPTER SIX

A Sequence of Servants

W HEN I look back on the long line of servants my mother
hired during the years I lived at home, I remember
clearly ten or twelve of them (we had about a hundred and
sixty-two, all told, but few of them were memorable). There
was, among the immortals, Dora Gedd, a quiet, mousy girl of
thirty-two who one night shot at a man in her room, throwing
our household into an uproar that was equalled perhaps only
by the goings-on the night the ghost got in. Nobody knew
how her lover, a morose garage man, got into the house, but
everybody for two blocks knew how he got out. Dora had
dressed up in a lavender evening gown for the occasion and
she wore a mass of jewelry, some of which was my mother's.
She kept shouting something from Shakespeare after the
shooting—I forget just what—and pursued the gentleman
downstairs from her attic room. When he got to the second
floor he rushed into my father's room. It was this entrance,
and not the shot or the shouting, that aroused father, a deep
sleeper always. "Get me out of here!" shouted the victim.
This situation rapidly developed, from then on, into one of
those bewildering involvements for which my family had, I
am afraid, a kind of unhappy genius. When the cops arrived
Dora was shooting out the Welsbach gas mantles in the living
room, and her gentleman friend had fled. By dawn everything
was quiet once more.

There were others. Gertie Straub: big, genial, and ruddy, a
collector of pints of rye (we learned after she was gone), who
came in after two o'clock one night from a dancing party at
Buckeye Lake and awakened us by bumping into and knocking over furniture. "Who's down there?" called mother from
upstairs. "It's me, dearie," said Gertie, "Gertie Straub."
"What are you *doing*?" demanded mother. "Dusting," said
Gertie.

Juanemma Kramer was one of my favorites. Her mother
loved the name Juanita so dearly that she had worked the first
part of it into the names of all her daughters—they were (in

174

addition to a Juanita) Juanemma, Juanhelen, and Juangrace. Juanemma was a thin, nervous maid who lived in constant dread of being hypnotized. Nor were her fears unfounded, for she was so extremely susceptible to hypnotic suggestion that one evening at B. F. Keith's theatre when a man on the stage was hypnotized, Juanemma, in the audience, was hypnotized too and floundered out into the aisle making the same cheeping sound that the subject on the stage, who had been told he was a chicken, was making. The act was abandoned and some xylophone players were brought on to restore order. One night, when our house was deep in quiet slumber, Juanemma became hypnotized in her sleep. She dreamed that a man "put her under" and then disappeared without "bringing her out." This was explained when, at last, a police surgeon whom we called in—he was the only doctor we could persuade to come out at three in the morning—slapped her into consciousness. It got so finally that any buzzing or whirring sound or any flashing object would put Juanemma under, and we had to let her go. I was reminded of her recently when, at a performance of the movie "Rasputin and the Empress," there came the scene in which Lionel Barrymore as the unholy priest hypnotizes the Czarevitch by spinning before his eyes a glittering watch. If Juanemma sat in any theatre and witnessed that scene she must, I am sure, have gone under instantly. Happily, she seems to have missed the picture, for otherwise Mr. Barrymore might have had to dress up again as Rasputin (which God forbid) and journey across the country to get her out of it—excellent publicity but a great bother.

Before I go on to Vashti, whose last name I forget, I will look in passing at another of our white maids (Vashti was colored). Belle Giddin distinguished herself by one gesture which fortunately did not result in the bedlam occasioned by Juanemma's hypnotic states or Dora Gedd's shooting spree. Belle burned her finger grievously, and purposely, one afternoon in the steam of a boiling kettle so that she could find out whether the pain-killer she had bought one night at a tent-show for fifty cents was any good. It was only fair.

Vashti turned out, in the end, to be partly legendary. She was a comely and sombre negress who was always able to find things my mother lost. "I don't know what's become of my garnet brooch," my mother said one day. "Yassum," said Vashti. In half an hour she had found it. "Where in the world was it?" asked mother. "In de yahd," said Vashti. "De dog mussa drug it out."

Vashti was in love with a young colored chauffeur named Charley, but she was also desired by her stepfather, whom none of us had ever seen but who was, she said, a handsome but messin' round gentleman from Georgia who had come north and married Vashti's mother just so he could be near Vashti. Charley, her fiancé, was for killing the stepfather but we counselled flight to another city. Vashti, however, would burst into tears and hymns and vow she'd never leave us; she got a certain pleasure out of bearing her cross. Thus we all lived in jeopardy, for the possibility that Vashti, Charley, and her stepfather might fight it out some night in our kitchen did not, at times, seem remote. Once I went into the kitchen at midnight to make some coffee. Charley was standing at a window looking out into the backyard; Vashti was rolling her eyes. "Heah he come! Heah he come!" she moaned. The stepfather didn't show up, however.

Charley finally saved up twenty-seven dollars toward taking Vashti away but one day he impulsively bought a .22 revolver with a mother-of-pearl handle and demanded that Vashti tell him where her mother and stepfather lived. "Doan go up dere, doan go *up* dere!" said Vashti. "Mah mothah is just as rarin' as he is!" Charley, however, insisted. It came out then that Vashti didn't have any stepfather; there was no such person. Charley threw her over for a yellow gal named Nancy: he never forgave Vashti for the vanishing from his life of a menace that had come to mean more to him than Vashti herself. Afterwards, if you asked Vashti about her stepfather or about Charley she would say, proudly, and with a woman-of-the-world air, "Neither one ob 'em is messin' round *me* any mo'."

Mrs. Doody, a huge, middle-aged woman with a religious taint, came into and went out of our house like a comet. The second night she was there she went berserk while doing the dishes and, under the impression that father was the Antichrist, pursued him several times up the backstairs and down the front. He had been sitting quietly over his coffee in the living room when she burst in from the kitchen waving a bread knife. My brother Herman finally felled her with a piece of Libby's cut-glass that had been a wedding present of mother's. Mother, I remember, was in the attic at the time, trying to find some old things, and, appearing on the scene in the midst of it all, got the quick and mistaken impression that father was chasing Mrs. Doody.

Mrs. Robertson, a fat and mumbly old colored woman, who might have been sixty and who might have been a hundred, gave us more than one turn during the many years that she did our washing. She had been a slave down South and she remembered having seen the troops marching—"a mess o' blue, den a mess o' gray." "What," my mother asked her once, "were they fighting about?" "Dat," said Mrs. Robertson, "Ah don't know." She had a feeling, at all times, that something was going to happen. I can see her now, staggering up from the basement with a basketful of clothes and coming abruptly to a halt in the middle of the kitchen. "Hahk!" she would say, in a deep, guttural voice. We would all hark; there was never anything to be heard. Neither, when she shouted "Look yondah!" and pointed a trembling hand at a window, was there ever anything to be seen. Father protested time and again that he couldn't stand Mrs. Robertson around, but mother always refused to let her go. It seems that she was a jewel. Once she walked unbidden, a dishpan full of wrung-out clothes under her arm, into father's study, where he was engrossed in some figures. Father looked up. She regarded him for a moment in silence. Then—"Look out!" she said, and withdrew. Another time, a murky winter afternoon, she came flubbering up the cellar stairs and bounced, out of breath, into the kitchen. Father was in the kitchen sipping some black coffee; he was in a jittery state of nerves from the effects of having had a tooth out, and had been in bed most of the day. "Dey is a death watch downstaihs!" rumbled the old colored lady. It developed that she had heard a strange "chipping" noise back of the furnace. "That was a cricket," said father. "Um-*hm*," said Mrs. Robertson. "Dat was uh death watch!" With that she put on her hat and went home, poising just long enough at the back door to observe darkly to father, *"Dey ain't no way!"* It upset him for days.

"One night while doing the dishes . . ."

Mrs. Robertson had only one great hour that I can think of—Jack Johnson's victory over Mistah Jeffries on the Fourth of July, 1910. She took a prominent part in the colored parade through the South End that night, playing a Spanish fandango on a banjo. The procession was led by the pastor of her church who, Mrs. Robertson later told us, had 'splained that the victory of Jack over Mistah Jeffries proved "de 'speriority ob de race." "What," asked my mother, "did he mean by that?" "Dat," said Mrs. Robertson, "Ah don't know."

Our other servants I don't remember so clearly, except the one who set the house on fire (her name eludes me), and Edda Millmoss. Edda was always slightly morose but she had gone along for months, all the time she was with us, quietly and efficiently attending to her work, until the night we had Carson Blair and F. R. Gardiner to dinner—both men of importance to my father's ambitions. Then suddenly, while serving the entrée, Edda dropped everything and, pointing a quivering finger at father, accused him in a long rigamarole of having done her out of her rights to the land on which Trinity Church in New York stands. Mr. Gardiner had one of his "attacks" and the whole evening turned out miserably.

mother, and he made a pass at her once but missed. That was during the month when we suddenly had mice, and Muggs refused to do anything about them. Nobody ever had mice exactly like the mice we had that month. They acted like pet mice, almost like mice somebody had trained. They were so friendly that one night when mother entertained at dinner the Friraliras, a club she and my father had belonged to for twenty years, she put down a lot of little dishes with food in them on the pantry floor so that the mice would be satisfied with that and wouldn't come into the dinning room. Muggs stayed out in the pantry with the mice, lying on the floor, growling to himself—not at the mice, but about all the people in the next room that he would have liked to get at. Mother slipped out into the pantry once to see how everything was going. Everything was going fine. It made her so mad to see Muggs lying there, oblivious of the mice—they came running up to her—that she slapped him and he slashed at her, but didn't make it. He was sorry immediately, mother said. He was always sorry, she said, after he bit someone, but we could not understand how she figured this out. He didn't act sorry.

Mother used to send a box of candy every Christmas to the people the Airedale bit. The list finally contained forty or more names. Nobody could understand why we didn't get rid of the dog. I didn't understand it very well myself, but we didn't get rid of him. I think that one or two people tried to poison Muggs—he acted poisoned once in a while—and old Major Moberly fired at him once with his service revolver near the Seneca Hotel in East Broad Street—but Muggs lived to be almost eleven years old and even when he could hardly get around he bit a Congressman who had called to see my father on business. My mother had never liked the Congressman— she said the signs of his horoscope showed he couldn't be trusted (he was Saturn with the moon in Virgo)—but she sent him a box of candy that Christmas. He sent it right back, probably because he suspected it was trick candy. Mother persuaded herself it was all for the best that the dog had bitten him, even though father lost an important business association because of it. "I wouldn't be associated with such a man," mother said, "Muggs could read him like a book."

We used to take turns feeding Muggs to be on his good

One time my mother went to the Chittenden Hotel to call on a woman mental healer who was lecturing in Columbus on the subject of "Harmonious Vibrations." She wanted to find out if it was possible to get harmonious vibrations into a dog. "He's a large tan-colored Airedale," mother explained. The woman said that she had never treated a dog but she advised my mother to hold the thought that he did not bite and would not bite. Mother was holding the thought the very next morning when Muggs got the iceman but she blamed that slip-up on the iceman. "If you didn't think he would bite you, he wouldn't," mother told him. He stomped out of the house in a terrible jangle of vibrations.

One morning when Muggs bit me slightly, more or less in passing, I reached down and grabbed his short stumpy tail and hoisted him into the air. It was a foolhardy thing to do and the last time I saw my mother, about six months ago, she said she didn't know what possessed me. I don't either, except that I was pretty mad. As long as I held the dog off the floor by his tail he couldn't get at me, but he twisted and jerked so, snarling all the time, that I realized I couldn't hold him that way very long. I carried him to the kitchen and flung him onto the floor and shut the door on him just as he crashed against it. But I forgot about the backstairs. Muggs went up the backstairs and down the frontstairs and had me cornered in the living room. I managed to get up onto the mantelpiece above the fireplace, but it gave way and came down with a tremendous crash throwing a large marble clock, several vases, and myself heavily to the floor. Muggs was so alarmed by the racket that when I picked myself up he had disappeared. We couldn't find him anywhere, although we whistled and shouted, until old Mrs. Detweiler called after dinner that night. Muggs had bitten her once, in the leg, and she came into the living room only after we assured her that Muggs had run away. She had just seated herself when, with a great growling and scratching of claws, Muggs emerged from under a davenport where he had been quietly hiding all the time, and bit her again. Mother examined the bite and put arnica on it and told Mrs. Detweiler that it was only a bruise. "He just bumped you," she said. But Mrs. Detweiler left the house in a nasty state of mind.

Lots of people reported our Airedale to the police but my father held a municipal office at the time and was on friendly terms with the police. Even so, the cops had been out a couple of times—once when Muggs bit Mrs. Rufus Sturtevant and again when he bit Lieutenant-Governor Malloy—but mother told them that it hadn't been Muggs' fault but the fault of

Lots of people reported our dog to the police.

the people who were bitten. "When he starts for them, they scream," she explained, "and that excites him." The cops suggested that it might be a good idea to tie the dog up, but mother said that it mortified him to be tied up and that he wouldn't eat when he was tied up.

Muggs at his meals was an unusual sight. Because of the fact that if you reached toward the floor he would bite you, we usually put his food plate on top of an old kitchen table with a bench alongside the table. Muggs would stand on the bench and eat. I remember that my mother's Uncle Horatio, who boasted that he was the third man up Missionary Ridge, was splutteringly indignant when he found out that we fed the dog on a table because we were afraid to put his plate on the floor. He said he wasn't afraid of any dog that ever lived and that he would put the dog's plate on the floor if we would give it to him. Roy said that if Uncle Horatio had fed Muggs on the ground just before the battle he would have been the first man up Missionary Ridge. Uncle Horatio was furious. "Bring him in! Bring him in now!" he shouted. "I'll feed the —— on the floor!" Roy was all for giving him a chance, but

Muggs at his meals was an unusual sight.

my father wouldn't hear of it. He said that Muggs had already been fed. "I'll feed him again!" bawled Uncle Horatio. We had quite a time quieting him.

In his last year Muggs used to spend practically all of his time outdoors. He didn't like to stay in the house for some

reason or other—perhaps it held too many unpleasant memories for him. Anyway, it was hard to get him to come in and
as a result the garbage man, the iceman, and the laundryman
wouldn't come near the house. We had to haul the garbage
down to the corner, take the laundry out and bring it back,
and meet the iceman a block from home. After this had gone
on for some time we hit on an ingenious arrangement for
getting the dog in the house so that we could lock him up
while the gas meter was read, and so on. Muggs was afraid of
only one thing, an electrical storm. Thunder and lightning
frightened him out of his senses (I think he thought a storm
had broken the day the mantelpiece fell). He would rush into
the house and hide under a bed or in a clothes closet. So we
fixed up a thunder machine out of a long narrow piece of
sheet iron with a wooden handle on one end. Mother would
shake this vigorously when she wanted to get Muggs into the
house. It made an excellent imitation of thunder, but I suppose it was the most roundabout system for running a household that was ever devised. It took a lot out of mother.

A few months before Muggs died, he got to "seeing
things." He would rise slowly from the floor, growling low,
and stalk stiff-legged and menacing toward nothing at all.
Sometimes the Thing would be just a little to the right or left
of a visitor. Once a Fuller Brush salesman got hysterics. Muggs
came wandering into the room like Hamlet following his father's ghost. His eyes were fixed on a spot just to the left of the
Fuller Brush man, who stood it until Muggs was about three
slow, creeping paces from him. Then he shouted. Muggs wavered on past him into the hallway grumbling to himself but
the Fuller man went on shouting. I think mother had to throw
a pan of cold water on him before he stopped. That was the
way she used to stop us boys when we got into fights.

Muggs died quite suddenly one night. Mother wanted to
bury him in the family lot under a marble stone with some
such inscription as "Flights of angels sing thee to thy rest"
but we persuaded her it was against the law. In the end we
just put up a smooth board above his grave along a lonely
road. On the board I wrote with an indelible pencil "Cave
Canem." Mother was quite pleased with the simple classic
dignity of the old Latin epitaph.

CHAPTER EIGHT

University Days

I PASSED all the other courses that I took at my University, but I could never pass botany. This was because all botany students had to spend several hours a week in a laboratory looking through a microscope at plant cells, and I could never see through a microscope. I never once saw a cell through a microscope. This used to enrage my instructor. He would wander around the laboratory pleased with the progress all the students were making in drawing the involved and, so I am told, interesting structure of flower cells, until he came to me. I would just be standing there. "I can't see anything," I would say. He would begin patiently enough, explaining how anybody can see through a microscope, but he would always end up in a fury, claiming that I could *too* see through a microscope but just pretended that I couldn't. "It takes away from the beauty of flowers anyway," I used to tell him. "We are not concerned with beauty in this course," he would say. "We are concerned solely with what I may call the *mechanics* of flars." "Well," I'd say, "I can't see anything." "Try it just once again," he'd say, and I would put my eye to the microscope and see nothing at all, except now and again a nebulous milky substance—a phenomenon of maladjustment. You were supposed to see a vivid, restless clockwork of sharply defined plant cells. "I see what looks like a lot of milk," I would tell him. This, he claimed, was the result of my not having adjusted the microscope properly, so he would readjust it for me, or rather, for himself. And I would look again and see milk.

I finally took a deferred pass, as they called it, and waited a year and tried again. (You had to pass one of the biological sciences or you couldn't graduate.) The professor had come back from vacation brown as a berry, bright-eyed, and eager to explain cell-structure again to his classes. "Well," he said to me, cheerily, when we met in the first laboratory hour of the semester, "we're going to see cells this time, aren't we?" "Yes, sir," I said. Students to right of me and to left of me

He was beginning to quiver all over like Lionel Barrymore.

and in front of me were seeing cells; what's more, they were quietly drawing pictures of them in their notebooks. Of course, I didn't see anything.

"We'll try it," the professor said to me, grimly, "with every adjustment of the microscope known to man. As God is my witness, I'll arrange this glass so that you see cells through it or I'll give up teaching. In twenty-two years of botany, I—" He cut off abruptly for he was beginning to quiver all over, like Lionel Barrymore, and he genuinely wished to hold onto his temper; his scenes with me had taken a great deal out of him.

So we tried it with every adjustment of the microscope known to man. With only one of them did I see anything but blackness or the familiar lacteal opacity, and that time I saw, to my pleasure and amazement, a variegated constellation of flecks, specks, and dots. These I hastily drew. The instructor, noting my activity, came back from an adjoining desk, a smile on his lips and his eyebrows high in hope. He looked at my cell drawing. "What's that?" he demanded, with a hint of a squeal in his voice. "That's what I saw," I said. "You didn't, you didn't, you *did*n't!" he screamed, losing control of his temper instantly, and he bent over and squinted into the microscope. His head snapped up. "That's your eye!" he shouted. "You've fixed the lens so that it reflects! You've drawn your eye!"

Another course that I didn't like, but somehow managed to pass, was economics. I went to that class straight from the botany class, which didn't help me any in understanding either subject. I used to get them mixed up. But not as mixed up as another student in my economics class who came there direct from a physics laboratory. He was a tackle on the football team, named Bolenciecwcz. At that time Ohio State University had one of the best football teams in the country, and Bolenciecwcz was one of its outstanding stars. In order to be eligible to play it was necessary for him to keep up in his studies, a very difficult matter, for while he was not dumber than an ox he was not any smarter. Most of his professors were lenient and helped him along. None gave him more hints, in answering questions, or asked him simpler ones than the economics professor, a thin, timid man named Bassum.

One day when we were on the subject of transportation and distribution, it came Bolenciecwcz's turn to answer a question. "Name one means of transportation," the professor said to him. No light came into the big tackle's eyes. "Just any means of transportation," said the professor. Bolenciecwcz sat

Bolenciecwcz was trying to think.

staring at him. "That is," pursued the professor, "any medium, agency, or method of going from one place to another." Bolenciecwcz had the look of a man who is being led into a trap. "You may choose among steam, horse-drawn, or electrically propelled vehicles," said the instructor. "I might suggest the one which we commonly take in making long journeys across land." There was a profound silence in which everybody stirred uneasily, including Bolenciecwcz and Mr. Bassum. Mr. Bassum abruptly broke this silence in an amazing manner. "Choo-choo-choo," he said, in a low voice, and turned instantly scarlet. He glanced appealingly around the room. All of us, of course, shared Mr. Bassum's desire that Bolenciecwcz should stay abreast of the class in economics, for the Illinois game, one of the hardest and most important of the season, was only a week off. "Toot, toot, too-toooooot!" some student with a deep voice moaned, and we all looked encouragingly at Bolenciecwcz. Somebody else gave a fine imitation of a locomotive letting off steam. Mr. Bassum himself rounded off the little show. "Ding, dong, ding, dong," he said, hopefully. Bolenciecwcz was staring at the floor now, trying to think, his great brow furrowed, his huge hands rubbing together, his face red.

"How did you come to college this year, Mr. Bolenciecwcz?" asked the professor. "*Chu*ffa chuffa, *chu*ffa chuffa."

"M'father sent me," said the football player.

"What on?" asked Bassum.

"I git an 'lowance," said the tackle, in a low, husky voice, obviously embarrassed.

"No, no," said Bassum. "Name a means of transportation. What did you *ride* here on?"

"Train," said Bolenciecwcz.

"Quite right," said the professor. "Now, Mr. Nugent, will you tell us——"

If I went through anguish in botany and economics—for different reasons—gymnasium work was even worse. I don't even like to think about it. They wouldn't let you play games or join in the exercises with your glasses on and I couldn't see with mine off. I bumped into professors, horizontal bars, agricultural students, and swinging iron rings. Not being able to see, I could take it but I couldn't dish it out. Also, in order to pass gymnasium (and you had to pass it to graduate) you had to learn to swim if you didn't know how. I didn't like the swimming pool, I didn't like swimming, and I didn't like the swimming instructor, and after all these years I still don't. I never swam but I passed my gym work anyway, by having another student give my gymnasium number (978) and swim across the pool in my place. He was a quiet, amiable blonde youth, number 473, and he would have seen through a microscope for me if we could have got away with it, but we couldn't get away with it. Another thing I didn't like about gymnasium work was that they made you strip the day you registered. It is impossible for me to be happy when I am stripped and being asked a lot of questions. Still, I did better than a lanky agricultural student who was cross-examined just before I was. They asked each student what college he was in—that is, whether Arts, Engineering, Commerce, or Agriculture. "What college are you in?" the instructor snapped at the youth in front of me. "Ohio State University," he said promptly.

It wasn't that agricultural student but it was another a whole lot like him who decided to take up journalism, possibly on the ground that when farming went to hell he could fall back on newspaper work. He didn't realize, of course, that that would be very much like falling back full-length on a kit of carpenter's tools. Haskins didn't seem cut out for journalism, being too embarrassed to talk to anybody and unable to use a typewriter, but the editor of the college paper assigned him to the cow barns, the sheep house, the horse pavilion, and the animal husbandry department generally. This was a genuinely big "beat," for it took up five times as much ground and got ten times as great a legislative appropriation as the College of Liberal Arts. The agricultural student knew animals, but nevertheless his stories were dull and colorlessly written. He took all afternoon on each of them, on account of having to hunt for each letter on the typewriter. Once in a while he had to ask somebody to help him hunt. "C" and "L," in particular, were hard letters for him to find. His editor finally got pretty much annoyed at the farmer-journalist because his pieces were so uninteresting. "See here, Haskins," he snapped at him one day, "why is it we never have anything hot from you on the horse pavilion? Here we have two hundred head of horses on this campus—more than any other university in the Western Conference except Purdue—and yet you never get any real low down on them. Now shoot over to the horse barns and dig up something lively." Haskins shambled out and came back in about an hour; he said he had something. "Well, start it off snappily," said the editor. "Something people will read." Haskins set to work and in a couple of hours brought a sheet of typewritten paper to the desk; it was a two-hundred word story about some disease that had broken out among the horses. Its opening sentence was simple but arresting. It read: "Who has noticed the sores on the tops of the horses in the animal husbandry building?"

Ohio State was a land grant university and therefore two years of military drill was compulsory. We drilled with old Springfield rifles and studied the tactics of the Civil War even though the World War was going on at the time. At 11 o'clock each morning thousands of freshmen and sophomores used to deploy over the campus, moodily creeping up on the old chemistry building. It was good training for the kind of warfare that was waged at Shiloh but it had no connection with what was going on in Europe. Some people used to think there was German money behind it, but they didn't dare say so or they would have been thrown in jail as German spies. It was a period of muddy thought and marked, I believe, the decline of higher education in the Middle West.

As a soldier I was never any good at all. Most of the cadets were glumly indifferent soldiers, but I was no good at all. Once General Littlefield, who was commandant of the cadet corps, popped up in front of me during regimental drill and snapped, "You are the main trouble with this university!" I think he meant that my type was the main trouble with the university but he may have meant me individually. I was mediocre at drill, certainly—that is, until my senior year. By that time I had drilled longer than anybody else in the Western Conference, having failed at military at the end of each preceding year so that I had to do it all over again. I was the only senior still in uniform. The uniform which, when new, had made me look like an interurban railway conductor, now that it had become faded and too tight made me look like Bert Williams in his bellboy act. This had a definitely bad effect on my morale. Even so, I had become by sheer practise little short of wonderful at squad manoeuvres.

One day General Littlefield picked our company out of the whole regiment and tried to get it mixed up by putting it through one movement after another as fast as we could execute them: squads right, squads left, squads on right into line, squads right about, squads left front into line, etc. In about three minutes one hundred and nine men were marching in one direction and I was marching away from them at an angle of forty degrees, all alone. "Company, halt!" shouted General Littlefield. "That man is the only man who has it right!" I was made a corporal for my achievement.

The next day General Littlefield summoned me to his office. He was swatting flies when I went in. I was silent and he was silent too, for a long time. I don't think he remembered me or why he had sent for me, but he didn't want to admit it. He swatted some more flies, keeping his eyes on them narrowly before he let go with the swatter. "Button up your coat!" he snapped. Looking back on it now I can see that he meant me although he was looking at a fly, but I just stood there. Another fly came to rest on a paper in front of the general and began rubbing its hind legs together. The general lifted the swatter cautiously. I moved restlessly and the fly flew away. "You startled him!" barked General Littlefield, looking at me severely. I said I was sorry. "That won't help the situation!" snapped the General, with cold military logic. I didn't see what I could do except offer to chase some more flies toward his desk, but I didn't say anything. He stared out the window at the faraway figures of co-eds crossing the campus toward the library. Finally, he told me I could go. So I went. He either didn't know which cadet I was or else he forgot what he wanted to see me about. It may have been that he wished to apologize for having called me the main trouble with the university; or maybe he had decided to compliment me on my brilliant drilling of the day before and then at the last minute decided not to. I don't know. I don't think about it much any more.

CHAPTER NINE

Draft Board Nights

I LEFT the University in June, 1918, but I couldn't get into the army on account of my sight, just as grandfather couldn't get in on account of his age. He applied several times and each time he took off his coat and threatened to whip the men who said he was too old. The disappointment of not getting to Germany (he saw no sense in everybody going to France) and the strain of running around town seeing influential officials finally got him down in bed. He had wanted to lead a division and his chagrin at not even being able to enlist as a private was too much for him. His brother Jake, some fifteen years younger than he was, sat up at night with him after he took to bed, because we were afraid he might leave the house without even putting on his clothes. Grandfather was against the idea of Jake watching over him—he thought it was a lot of tomfoolery—but Jake hadn't been able to sleep at night for twenty-eight years, so he was the perfect person for such a vigil.

On the third night, grandfather was wakeful. He would open his eyes, look at Jake, and close them again, frowning. He never answered any question Jake asked him. About four o'clock that morning, he caught his brother sound asleep in the big leather chair beside the bed. When once Jake did fall asleep he slept deeply, so that grandfather was able to get up, dress himself, undress Jake, and put him in bed without waking him. When my Aunt Florence came into the room at seven o'clock, grandfather was sitting in the chair reading the *Memoirs of U.S. Grant* and Jake was sleeping in the bed. "He watched while I slept," said grandfather, "so now I'm watchin' while he sleeps." It seemed fair enough.

One reason we didn't want grandfather to roam around at night was that he had said something once or twice about going over to Lancaster, his old home town, and putting his problem up to "Cump"—that is, General William Tecumseh Sherman, also an old Lancaster boy. We knew that his inability to find Sherman would be bad for him and we were afraid that he might try to get there in the little electric runabout that had been bought for my grandmother. She had become, surprisingly enough, quite skilful at getting around town in it. Grandfather was astonished and a little indignant when he saw her get into the contraption and drive off smoothly and easily. It was her first vehicular triumph over him in almost fifty years of married life and he determined to learn to drive the thing himself. A famous old horseman, he approached it

About four o'clock he caught his brother asleep.

as he might have approached a wild colt. His brow would darken and he would begin to curse. He always leaped into it quickly, as if it might pull out from under him if he didn't get into the seat fast enough. The first few times he tried to run the electric, he went swiftly around in a small circle, drove over the curb, across the sidewalk, and up onto the lawn. We all tried to persuade him to give up, but his spirit was aroused.

"Git that goddam buggy back in the road!" he would say, imperiously. So we would manoeuver it back into the street and he would try again. Pulling too savagely on the guiding-bar—to teach the electric a lesson—was what took him around in a circle, and it was difficult to make him understand that it was best to relax and not get mad. He had the notion that if you didn't hold her, she would throw you. And a man who (or so he often told us) had driven a four-horse McCormick reaper when he was five years old did not intend to be thrown by an electric runabout.

There was a tremendous to-do.

Since there was no way of getting him to give up learning to operate the electric, we would take him out to Franklin Park, where the roadways were wide and unfrequented, and spend an hour or so trying to explain the differences between driving a horse and carriage and driving an electric. He would keep muttering all the time; he never got it out of his head that when he took the driver's seat the machine flattened its ears on him, so to speak. After a few weeks, nevertheless, he got so he could run the electric for a hundred yards or so along a fairly straight line. But whenever he took a curve, he invariably pulled or pushed the bar too quickly and too hard and headed for a tree or a flower bed. Someone was always with him and we would never let him take the car out of the park.

One morning when grandmother was all ready to go to market, she called the garage and told them to send the electric around. They said that grandfather had already been there and taken it out. There was a tremendous to-do. We telephoned Uncle Will and he got out his Lozier and we started off to hunt for grandfather. It was not yet seven o'clock and there was fortunately little traffic. We headed for Franklin Park, figuring that he might have gone out there to try to break the car's spirit. One or two early pedestrians had seen a tall old gentleman with a white beard driving a little electric and cussing as he drove. We followed a tortuous trail and found them finally on Nelson Road, about four miles from the town of Shepard. Grandfather was standing in the road shouting, and the back wheels of the electric were deeply entangled in a barbed-wire fence. Two workmen and a farmhand were trying to get the thing loose. Grandfather was in a state of high wrath about the electric. "The —— — – —— backed up on me!" he told us.

But to get back to the war. The Columbus draft board never called grandfather for service, which was a lucky thing for them because they would have had to take him. There were stories that several old men of eighty or ninety had been summoned in the confusion, but somehow or other grandfather was missed. He waited every day for the call, but it never came. My own experience was quite different. I was called almost every week, even though I had been exempted from service the first time I went before the medical examiners. Either they were never convinced that it was me or else there was some clerical error in the records which was never cleared up. Anyway, there was usually a letter for me on Monday ordering me to report for examination on the second floor of Memorial Hall the following Wednesday at 9 P.M. The second time I went up, I tried to explain to one of the doctors that I had already been exempted. "You're just a blur to me," I said, taking off my glasses. "You're absolutely nothing to me," he snapped, sharply.

I had to take off all my clothes each time and jog around the hall with a lot of porters and bank presidents' sons and clerks and poets. Our hearts and lungs would be examined, and then our feet; and finally our eyes. That always came last. When the eye specialist got around to me, he would always say, "Why, you couldn't get into the service with sight like that!" "I know," I would say. Then a week or two later I would be summoned again and go through the same rigmarole. The ninth or tenth time I was called, I happened to pick up one of several stethoscopes that were lying on a table and suddenly, instead of finding myself in the line of draft men, I found myself in the line of examiners. "Hello, doctor," said one of them, nodding. "Hello," I said. That, of course, was before I took my clothes off; I might have managed it naked, but I doubt it. I was assigned, or rather drifted, to the chest-and-lung section, where I began to examine every other man, thus cutting old Dr. Ridgeway's work in two. "I'm glad to have you here, doctor," he said.

I passed most of the men that came to me, but now and then I would exempt one just to be on the safe side. I began by making each of them hold his breath and then say "mi, mi, mi, mi," until I noticed Ridgeway looking at me curiously. He, I discovered, simply made them say "ah," and some times he didn't make them say anything. Once I got hold of a man who, it came out later, had swallowed a watch—to make the doctors believe there was something wrong with him inside (it was a common subterfuge: men swallowed nails, hairpins, ink, etc., in an effort to be let out). Since I didn't know what you were supposed to hear through a stethoscope, the ticking of the watch at first didn't surprise me, but I decided to call Dr. Ridgeway into consultation, because nobody else had ticked. "This man seems to tick," I said to him. He looked at me in surprise but didn't say anything. Then he thumped the man, laid his ear to his chest, and finally tried the stethoscope. "Sound as a dollar," he said. "Listen lower down," I told him. The man indicated his stomach. Ridgeway gave him a haughty, indignant look. "That is for the abdominal men to worry about," he said, and moved off. A few minutes later, Dr. Blythe Ballomy got around to the man and listened,

An abdominal man worrying.

but he didn't blink an eye; his grim expression never changed. "You have swallowed a watch, my man," he said, crisply. The draftee reddened in embarrassment and uncertainty. "On *purpose?*" he asked. "That I can't say," the doctor told him, and went on.

I served with the draft board for about four months. Until the summonses ceased, I couldn't leave town and as long as I stayed and appeared promptly for examination, even though I did the examining, I felt that technically I could not be convicted of evasion. During the daytime, I worked as publicity agent for an amusement park, the manager of which was a tall, unexpected young man named Byron Landis. Some years before, he had dynamited the men's lounge in the statehouse annex for a prank; he enjoyed pouring buckets of water on sleeping persons, and once he had barely escaped arrest for jumping off the top of the old Columbus Transfer Company building with a homemade parachute.

He asked me one morning if I would like to take a ride in the new Scarlet Tornado, a steep and wavy roller-coaster. I didn't want to but I was afraid he would think I was afraid, so I went along. It was about ten o'clock and there was nobody at the park except workmen and attendants and concessionaires in their shirtsleeves. We climbed into one of the long gondolas of the roller-coaster and while I was looking around for the man who was going to run it, we began to move off. Landis, I discovered, was running it himself. But it was too late to get out; we had begun to climb, clickety-clockety, up the first steep incline, down the other side of which we careened at eighty miles an hour. "I didn't know you could run this thing!" I bawled at my companion, as we catapulted up a sixty-degree arch and looped headlong into space. "I didn't either!" he bawled back. The racket and the rush of air were terrific as we roared into the pitch-black Cave of Darkness and came out and down Monohan's Leap, so called because a workman named Monohan had been forced to jump from it when caught between two approaching experimental cars while it was being completed. That trip, although it ended safely, made a lasting impression on me. It is not too much to say that it has flavored my life. It is the reason I shout in my sleep, refuse to ride on the elevated, keep jerking the emergency brake in cars other people are driving, have the sensation of flying like a bird when

I first lie down, and in certain months can't keep anything on my stomach.

During my last few trips to the draft board, I went again as a draft prospect, having grown tired of being an examiner. None of the doctors who had been my colleagues for so long recognized me, not even Dr. Ridgeway. When he examined my chest for the last time, I asked him if there hadn't been another doctor helping him. He said there had been. "Did he look anything like me?" I asked. Dr. Ridgeway looked at me. "I don't think so," he said, "he was taller." (I had my shoes off while he was examining me.) "A good pulmonary man," added Ridgeway. "Relative of yours?" I said yes. He sent me on to Dr. Quimby, the specialist who had examined my eyes twelve or fifteen times before. He gave me some simple reading tests. "You could never get into the army with eyes like that," he said. "I know," I told him.

Late one morning, shortly after my last examination, I was awakened by the sound of bells ringing and whistles blowing. It grew louder and more insistent and wilder. It was the Armistice.

A Note at the End

THE HARD TIMES of my middle years I pass over, leaving the ringing bells of 1918, with all their false promise, to mark the end of a special sequence. The sharp edges of old reticences are softened in the autobiographer by the passing of time—a man does not pull the pillow over his head when he wakes in the morning because he suddenly remembers some awful thing that happened to him fifteen or twenty years ago, but the confusions and the panics of last year and the year before are too close for contentment. Until a man can quit talking loudly to himself in order to shout down the memories of blunderings and gropings, he is in no shape for the painstaking examination of distress and the careful ordering of event so necessary to a calm and balanced exposition of what, exactly, was the matter. The time I fell out of the gun room in Mr. James Stanley's house in Green Lake, New York, is for instance, much too near for me to go into with

A hotel room in Louisville.

any peace of mind, although it happened in 1925, the ill-fated year of "Horses, Horses, Horses" and "Valencia." There is now, I understand, a porch to walk out onto when you open the door I opened that night, but there wasn't then.

The mistaken exits and entrances of my thirties have moved me several times to some thought of spending the rest of my days wandering aimlessly around the South Seas, like a character out of Conrad, silent and inscrutable. But the necessity for frequent visits to my oculist and dentist has prevented this. You can't be running back from Singapore every few months to get your lenses changed and still retain the proper mood for wandering. Furthermore, my horn-rimmed glasses and my

They tried to sell me baskets.

Ohio accent betray me, even when I sit on the terrasses of little tropical cafes, wearing a pith helmet, staring straight ahead, and twitching a muscle in my jaw. I found this out when I tried wandering around the West Indies one summer. Instead of being followed by the whispers of men and the glances of women, I was followed by bead salesmen and native women with postcards. Nor did any dark girl, looking at all like Tondelaya in "White Cargo," come forward and offer to go to pieces with me. They tried to sell me baskets.

Under these circumstances it is impossible to be inscrutable and a wanderer who isn't inscrutable might just as well be back at Broad and High Streets in Columbus sitting in the Baltimore Dairy Lunch. Nobody from Columbus has ever made a first rate wanderer in the Conradean tradition. Some of them have been fairly good at disappearing for a few days to turn up in a hotel in Louisville with a bad headache and no recollection of how they got there, but they always scurry back to their wives with some cock-and-bull story of having lost their memory or having gone away to attend the annual convention of the Fraternal Order of Eagles.

There was, of course, even for Conrad's Lord Jim, no running away. The cloud of his special discomfiture followed him like a pup, no matter what ships he took or what wildernesses he entered. In the pathways between office and home and home and the houses of settled people there are always, ready to snap at you, the little perils of routine living, but there is no escape in the unplanned tangent, the sudden turn. In Martinique, when the whistle blew for the tourists to get back on the ship, I had a quick, wild, and lovely moment when I decided I wouldn't get back on the ship. I did, though. And I found that somebody had stolen the pants to my dinner jacket.

THE MIDDLE-AGED MAN
ON THE
FLYING TRAPEZE

The Departure of Emma Inch

E MMA INCH looked no different from any other middle-
aged, thin woman you might glance at in the subway or
deal with across the counter of some small store in a country
town, and then forget forever. Her hair was drab and un-
abundant, her face made no impression on you, her voice I
don't remember—it was just a voice. She came to us with a
letter of recommendation from some acquaintance who knew
that we were going to Martha's Vineyard for the summer and
wanted a cook. We took her because there was nobody else,
and she seemed all right. She had arrived at our hotel in Forty-
fifth Street the day before we were going to leave and we got
her a room for the night, because she lived way uptown somewhere. She said she really ought to go back and give up her
room, but I told her I'd fix that.

Emma Inch had a big scuffed brown suitcase with her, and
a Boston bull terrier. His name was Feely. Feely was seventeen
years old and he grumbled and growled and snuffled all the
time, but we needed a cook and we agreed to take Feely along
with Emma Inch, if she would take care of him and keep him
out of the way. It turned out to be easy to keep Feely out of
the way because he would lie grousing anywhere Emma put
him until she came and picked him up again. I never saw him
walk. Emma had owned him, she said, since he was a pup. He
was all she had in the world, she told us, with a mist in her
eyes. I felt embarrassed but not touched. I didn't see how
anybody could love Feely.

I didn't lose any sleep about Emma Inch and Feely the
night of the day they arrived, but my wife did. She told me
next morning that she had lain awake a long time thinking
about the cook and her dog, because she felt kind of funny
about them. She didn't know why. She just had a feeling that
they were kind of funny. When we were all ready to leave—
it was about three o'clock in the afternoon, for we had kept
putting off the packing—I phoned Emma's room, but she
didn't answer. It was getting late and we felt nervous—the
Fall River boat would sail in about two hours. We couldn't

understand why we hadn't heard anything from Emma and
Feely. It wasn't until four o'clock that we did. There was a
small rap on the door of our bedroom and I opened it and
Emma and Feely were there, Feely in her arms, snuffing and
snaffling, as if he had been swimming a long way.

My wife told Emma to get her bag packed, we were leaving
in a little while. Emma said her bag *was* packed, except for
her electric fan, and she couldn't get that in. "You won't need
an electric fan at the Vineyard," my wife told her. "It's cool
there, even during the day, and it's almost cold at night. Besides, there is no electricity in the cottage we are going to."
Emma Inch seemed distressed. She studied my wife's face.
"I'll have to think of something else then," she said. "Mebbe
I could let the water run all night." We both sat down and
looked at her. Feely's asthmatic noises were the only sounds
in the room for a while. "Doesn't that dog ever stop that?"

I asked, irritably. "Oh, he's just talking," said Emma. "He talks all the time, but I'll keep him in my room and he won't bother you none." "Doesn't he bother you?" I asked. "He *would* bother me," said Emma, "at night, but I put the electric fan on and keep the light burning. He don't make so much noise when it's light, because he don't snore. The fan kind of keeps me from noticing him. I put a piece of cardboard, like, where the fan hits it and then I don't notice Feely so much. Mebbe I could let the water run in my room all night instead of the fan." I said "Hmmm" and got up and mixed a drink for my wife and me—we had decided not to have one till we got on the boat, but I thought we'd better have one now. My wife didn't tell Emma there would be no running water in her room at the Vineyard.

"We've been worried about you, Emma," I said. "I phoned your room but you didn't answer." "I never answer the phone," said Emma, "because I always get a shock. I wasn't there anyways. I couldn't sleep in that room. I went back to Mrs. McCoy's on Seventy-eighth Street." I lowered my glass. "You went back to Seventy-eighth Street last *night*?" I demanded. "Yes, sir," she said. "I had to tell Mrs. McCoy I was going away and wouldn't be there any more for a while—Mrs. McCoy's the landlady. Anyways, I never sleep in a hotel." She looked around the room. "They burn down," she told us.

It came out that Emma Inch had not only gone back to Seventy-eighth Street the night before but had walked all the way, carrying Feely. It had taken her an hour or two, because Feely didn't like to be carried very far at a time, so she had had to stop every block or so and put him down on the sidewalk for a while. It had taken her just as long to walk back to our hotel, too; Feely, it seems, never got up before afternoon—that's why she was so late. She was sorry. My wife and I finished our drinks, looking at each other, and at Feely.

Emma Inch didn't like the idea of riding to Pier 14 in a taxi, but after ten minutes of cajoling and pleading she finally got in. "Make it go slow," she said. We had enough time, so I asked the driver to take it easy. Emma kept getting to her feet and I kept pulling her back onto the seat. "I never been in an automobile before," she said. "It goes awful fast." Now and then she gave a little squeal of fright. The driver turned his head and grinned. "You're O.K. wit' me, lady," he said. Feely growled at him. Emma waited until he had turned away again, and then she leaned over to my wife and whispered. "They all take cocaine," she said. Feely began to make a new sound—a kind of high, agonized yelp. "He's singing," said Emma. She gave a strange little giggle, but the expression of her face didn't change. "I wish you had put the Scotch where we could get at it," said my wife.

If Emma Inch had been afraid of the taxicab, she was terrified by the *Priscilla* of the Fall River Line. "I don't think I can go," said Emma. "I don't think I could get on a boat. I didn't know they were so big." She stood rooted to the pier, clasping Feely. She must have squeezed him too hard, for he screamed—he screamed like a woman. We all jumped. "It's his ears," said Emma. "His ears hurt." We finally got her on the boat, and once aboard, in the salon, her terror abated somewhat. Then the three parting blasts of the boat whistle rocked lower Manhattan. Emma Inch leaped to her feet and began to run, letting go of her suitcase (which she had refused to give up to a porter) but holding onto Feely. I caught her just as she reached the gangplank. The ship was on its way when I let go of her arm.

It was a long time before I could get Emma to go to her stateroom, but she went at last. It was an inside stateroom, and she didn't seem to mind it. I think she was surprised to find that it was like a room, and had a bed and a chair and a washbowl. She put Feely down on the floor. "I think you'll have to do something about the dog," I said. "I think they put them somewhere and you get them when you get off." "No, they don't," said Emma. I guess, in this case, they didn't. I don't know. I shut the door on Emma Inch and Feely, and went away. My wife was drinking straight Scotch when I got to our stateroom.

The next morning, cold and early, we got Emma and Feely off the *Priscilla* at Fall River and over to New Bedford in a taxi and onto the little boat for Martha's Vineyard. Each move was as difficult as getting a combative drunken man out of the night club in which he fancies he has been insulted. Emma sat in a chair on the Vineyard boat, as far away from sight of the water as she could get, and closed her eyes and held onto Feely. She had thrown a coat over Feely, not only to keep him warm but to prevent any of the ship's officers from taking him away from her. I went in from the deck at intervals to see how she was. She was all right, or at least all right for her, until five minutes before the boat reached the dock at Woods Hole, the only stop between New Bedford and the Vineyard. Then Feely got sick. Or at any rate Emma said he was sick. He didn't seem to me any different from what he always was— his breathing was just as abnormal and irregular. But Emma said he was sick. There were tears in her eyes. "He's a very sick dog, Mr. Thurman," she said. "I'll have to take him home." I knew by the way she said "home" what she meant. She meant Seventy-eighth Street.

The boat tied up at Woods Hole and was motionless and we could hear the racket of the deckhands on the dock loading freight. "I'll get off here," said Emma, firmly, or with more firmness, anyway, than she had shown yet. I explained to her that we would be home in half an hour, that everything would be fine then, everything would be wonderful. I said Feely would be a new dog. I told her people sent sick dogs to Martha's Vineyard to be cured. But it was no good. "I'll have to take him off here," said Emma. "I always have to take him home when he is sick." I talked to her eloquently about the loveliness of Martha's Vineyard and the nice houses and the nice people and the wonderful accommodations for dogs. But I knew it was useless. I could tell by looking at her. She was going to get off the boat at Woods Hole.

"You really can't do this," I said, grimly, shaking her arm. Feely snarled weakly. "You haven't any money and you don't know where you are. You're a long way from New York. Nobody ever got from Woods Hole to New York alone." She didn't seem to hear me. She began walking toward the stairs leading to the gangplank, crooning to Feely. "You'll have to go all the way back on boats," I said, "or else take a train, and you haven't any money. If you are going to be so stupid and leave us now, I can't give you any money." "I don't want any money, Mr. Thurman," she said. "I haven't earned any money." I walked along in irritable silence for a moment; then I gave her some money. I made her take it. We got to the gangplank. Feely snaffled and gurgled. I saw now that his eyes were a little red and moist. I knew it would do no good to summon my wife—not when Feely's health was at stake. "How do you expect to get home from here?" I almost shouted at Emma Inch as she moved down the gangplank. "You're way out on the end of Massachusetts." She stopped and turned around. "We'll walk," she said. "We like to walk, Feely and me." I just stood still and watched her go.

When I went up on deck, the boat was clearing for the Vineyard. "How's everything?" asked my wife. I waved a hand in the direction of the dock. Emma Inch was standing there, her suitcase at her feet, her dog under one arm, waving goodbye to us with her free hand. I had never seen her smile before, but she was smiling now.

There's an Owl in My Room

I saw Gertrude Stein on the screen of a newsreel theatre one afternoon and I heard her read that famous passage of hers about pigeons on the grass, alas (the sorrow is, as you know, Miss Stein's). After reading about the pigeons on the grass alas, Miss Stein said, "This is a simple description of a landscape I have seen many times." I don't really believe that that is true. Pigeons on the grass alas may be a simple description of Miss Stein's own consciousness, but it is not a simple description of a plot of grass on which pigeons have alighted, are alighting, or are going to alight. A truly simple description of the pigeons alighting on the grass of the Luxembourg Gardens (which, I believe, is where the pigeons alighted) would say of the pigeons alighting there only that they were pigeons alighting. Pigeons that alight anywhere are neither sad pigeons nor gay pigeons, they are simply pigeons.

It is neither just nor accurate to connect the word alas with pigeons. Pigeons are definitely not alas. They have nothing to do with alas and they have nothing to do with hooray (not even when you tie red, white, and blue ribbons on them and let them loose at band concerts); they have nothing to do with mercy me or isn't that fine, either. White rabbits, yes, and Scotch terriers, and bluejays, and even hippopotamuses, but not pigeons. I happen to have studied pigeons very closely and carefully, and I have studied the effect, or rather the lack of effect, of pigeons very carefully. A number of pigeons alight from time to time on the sill of my hotel window when I am eating breakfast and staring out the window. They never alas me, they never make me feel alas; they never make me feel anything.

Nobody and no animal and no other bird can play a scene so far down as a pigeon can. For instance, when a pigeon on my window ledge becomes aware of me sitting there in a chair in my blue polka-dot dressing-gown, worrying, he pokes his head far out from his shoulders and peers sideways at me, for all the world (Miss Stein might surmise) like a timid man peering around the corner of a building trying to ascertain whether

215

he is being followed by some hoofed fiend or only by the echo of his own footsteps. And yet it is *not* for all the world like a timid man peering around the corner of a building trying to ascertain whether he is being followed by a hoofed fiend or only by the echo of his own footsteps, And that is because there is no emotion in the pigeon and no power to arouse emotion. A pigeon looking is just a pigeon looking. When it comes to emotion, a fish, compared to a pigeon, is practically beside himself.

A pigeon peering at me doesn't make me sad or glad or apprehensive or hopeful. With a horse or a cow or a dog it would be different. It would be especially different with a dog. Some dogs peer at me as if I had just gone completely crazy

or as if they had just gone completely crazy. I can go so far as to say that most dogs peer at me that way. This creates in the consciousness of both me and the dog a feeling of alarm or downright terror and legitimately permits me to work into a description of the landscape, in which the dog and myself are figures, a note of emotion. Thus I should not have minded if Miss Stein had written: dogs on the grass, look out, dogs on the grass, look out, look out, dogs on the grass, look out Alice. That would be a simple description of dogs on the grass. But when any writer pretends that a pigeon makes him sad, or makes him anything else, I must instantly protest that this is a highly specialized fantastic impression created in an individual consciousness and that therefore it cannot fairly be presented as a simple description of what actually was to be seen.

People who do not understand pigeons—and pigeons can be understood only when you understand that there is nothing to understand about them—should not go around describing pigeons or the effect of pigeons. Pigeons come closer to a zero of impingement than any other birds. Hens embarrass me the way my old Aunt Hattie used to when I was twelve and she still insisted I wasn't big enough to bathe myself; owls disturb me; if I am with an eagle I always pretend that I am not with an eagle; and so on down to swallows at twilight who scare the hell out of me. But pigeons have absolutely no effect on me. They have absolutely no effect on anybody. They couldn't even startle a child. That is why they are selected from among all birds to be let loose, with colored ribbons attached to them, at band concerts, library dedications, and christenings of new dirigibles. If any body let loose a lot of owls on such an occasion there would be rioting and catcalls and whistling and fainting spells and throwing of chairs and the Lord only knows what else.

From where I am sitting now I can look out the window and see a pigeon being a pigeon on the roof of the Harvard Club. No other thing can be less what it is not than a pigeon can, and Miss Stein, of all people, should understand that simple fact. Behind the pigeon I am looking at, a blank wall of tired gray bricks is stolidly trying to sleep off oblivion; underneath the pigeon the cloistered windows of the Harvard Club are staring in horrified bewilderment at something they have seen across the street. The pigeon is just there on the roof being a pigeon, having been, and being, a pigeon and, what is more, always going to be, too. Nothing could be simpler than that. If you read that sentence aloud you will instantly see what I mean. It is a simple description of a pigeon on a roof. It is only with an effort that I am conscious of the pigeon, but I am acutely aware of a great sulky red iron pipe that is creeping up the side of the building intent on sneaking up on a slightly tipsy chimney which is shouting its head off.

There is nothing a pigeon can do or be that would make me feel sorry for it or for myself or for the people in the world, just as there is nothing I could do or be that would make a pigeon feel sorry for itself. Even if I plucked his feathers out it would not make him feel sorry for himself and it would not make me feel sorry for myself or for him. But try plucking the quills out of a porcupine or even plucking the fur out of a jackrabbit. There is nothing a pigeon could be, or can be, rather, which could get into my consciousness like a fumbling hand in a bureau drawer and disarrange my mind or pull anything out of it. I bar nothing at all. You could dress up a pigeon in a tiny suit of evening clothes and put a tiny silk hat on his head and a tiny gold-headed cane under his wing and send him walking into my room at night. It would make no impression on me. I would not shout, "Good god amighty, the birds are in charge!" But you could send an owl into my room, dressed only in the feathers it was born with, and no monkey business, and I would pull the covers over my head and scream.

No other thing in the world falls so far short of being able to do what it cannot do as a pigeon does. Of being *unable* to do what it *can* do, too, as far as that goes.

The Topaz Cufflinks Mystery

WHEN the motorcycle cop came roaring up, unexpectedly, out of Never-Never Land (the way motorcycle cops do), the man was on his hands and knees in the long grass beside the road, barking like a dog. The woman was driving slowly along in a car that stopped about eighty feet away; its headlights shone on the man: middle-aged, bewildered, sedentary. He got to his feet.

"What's goin' on here?" asked the cop. The woman giggled. "Cock-eyed," thought the cop. He did not glance at her.

"I guess it's gone," said the man. "I—ah—could not find it."

"What was it?"

"What I lost?" The man squinted, unhappily. "Some—some cufflinks; topazes set in gold." He hesitated: the cop didn't seem to believe him. "They were the color of a fine Moselle," said the man. He put on a pair of spectacles which he had been holding in his hand. The woman giggled.

"Hunt things better with ya glasses off?" asked the cop. He pulled his motorcycle to the side of the road to let a car pass. "Better pull over off the concrete, lady," he said. She drove the car off the roadway.

"I'm nearsighted," said the man. "I can hunt things at a distance with my glasses on, but I do better with them off if I am close to something." The cop kicked his heavy boots through the grass where the man had been crouching.

"He was barking," ventured the lady in the car, "so that I could see where he was." The cop pulled his machine up on its standard; he and the man walked over to the automobile.

"What I don't get," said the officer, "is how you lose ya cufflinks a hunderd feet in front of where ya car is; a person usually stops his car *past* the place he loses somethin', not a hunderd feet before he gits *to* the place."

The lady laughed again; her husband got slowly into the car, as if he were afraid the officer would stop him any moment. The officer studied them.

"Been to a party?" he asked. It was after midnight.

"We're not drunk, if that's what you mean," said the woman, smiling. The cop tapped his fingers on the door of the car.

"You people didn't lose no topazes," he said.

"Is it against the law for a man to be down on all fours beside a road, barking in a perfectly civil manner?" demanded the lady.

"No, ma'am," said the cop. He made no move to get on his motorcycle, however, and go on about his business. There

was just the quiet chugging of the cycle engine and the auto engine, for a time.

"I'll tell you how it was, Officer," said the man, in a crisp, new tone. "We were settling a bet. O.K.?"

"O.K.," said the cop. "Who win?" There was another pulsing silence.

"The lady bet," said her husband, with dignity, as though he were explaining some important phase of industry to a newly hired clerk, "the lady bet that my eyes would shine like a cat's do at night, if she came upon me suddenly close to the ground alongside the road. We had passed a cat, whose eyes gleamed. We had passed several persons, whose eyes did *not* gleam——"

"Simply because they were above the light and not under it," said the lady. "A man's eyes would gleam like a cat's if people were ordinarily caught by headlights at the same angle as cats are." The cop walked over to where he had left his motorcycle, picked it up, kicked the standard out, and wheeled it back.

"A cat's eyes," he said, "are different than yours and mine. Dogs, cats, skunks, it's all the same. They can see in a dark room."

"Not in a *totally* dark room," said the lady.

"Yes, they can," said the cop.

"No, they can't; not if there is no light at all in the room, not if it's absolutely *black*," said the lady. "The question came up the other night; there was a professor there and he said there must be at least a ray of light, no matter how faint."

"That may be," said the cop, after a solemn pause, pulling at his gloves. "But people's eyes don't shine—I go along these roads every night an' pass hunderds of cats and hunderds of people."

"The people are never close to the ground," said the lady.

"*I* was close to the ground," said her husband.

"Look at it this way," said the cop. "I've seen wildcats in *trees* at night and *their* eyes shine."

"There you are!" said the lady's husband. "That proves it."

"I don't see how," said the lady. There was another silence.

"Because a wildcat in a tree's eyes are higher than the level of a man's," said her husband. The cop may possibly have followed this, the lady obviously did not; neither one said anything. The cop got on his machine, raced his engine, seemed to be thinking about something, and throttled down. He turned to the man.

"Took ya glasses off so the headlights wouldn't make ya glasses shine, huh?" he asked.

"That's right," said the man. The cop waved his hand, triumphantly, and roared away. "Smart guy," said the man to his wife, irritably.

"I still don't see where the wildcat proves anything," said his wife. He drove off slowly.

"Look," he said. "You claim that the whole thing depends on how *low* a *cat's* eyes are; I——"

"I didn't say that; I said it all depends on how *high* a *man's* eyes . . ."

A Preface to Dogs

As soon as a wife presents her husband with a child, her capacity for worry becomes acuter: she hears more burglars, she smells more things burning, she begins to wonder, at the theatre or the dance, whether her husband left his service revolver in the nursery. This goes on for years and years. As the child grows older, the mother's original major fear—that the child was exchanged for some other infant at the hospital—gives way to even more magnificent doubts and suspicions: she suspects that the child is not bright, she doubts that it will be happy, she is sure that it will become mixed up with the wrong sort of people.

This insistence of parents on dedicating their lives to their children is carried on year after year in the face of all that dogs have done, and are doing, to prove how much happier the parent-child relationship can become, if managed without sentiment, worry, or dedication. Of course, the theory that dogs have a saner family life than humans is an old one, and it was in order to ascertain whether the notion is pure legend or whether it is based on observable fact that I have for four years made a careful study of the family life of dogs. My conclusions entirely support the theory that dogs have a saner family life than people.

In the first place, the husband leaves on a woodchuck-hunting expedition just as soon as he can, which is very soon, and never comes back. He doesn't write, makes no provision for the care or maintenance of his family, and is not liable to prosecution because he doesn't. The wife doesn't care where he is, never wonders if he is thinking about her, and although she may start at the slightest footstep, doesn't do so because she is hoping against hope that it is he. No lady dog has ever been known to set her friends against her husband, or put detectives on his trail.

This same lack of sentimentality is carried out in the mother dog's relationship to her young. For six weeks—but only six weeks—she looks after them religiously, feeds them (they come clothed), washes their ears, fights off cats, old women, and wasps that come nosing around, makes the bed, and rescues the puppies when they crawl under the floor boards of the barn or get lost in an old boot. She does all these things, however, without fuss, without that loud and elaborate show of solicitude and alarm which a woman displays in rendering some exaggerated service to her child.

At the end of six weeks, the mother dog ceases to lie awake at night harking for ominous sounds; the next morning she snarls at the puppies after breakfast, and routs them all out of the house. "This is forever," she informs them, succinctly. "I have my own life to live, automobiles to chase, grocery boys' shoes to snap at, rabbits to pursue. I can't be washing and feeding a lot of big six-weeks-old dogs any longer. That phase is definitely over." The family life is thus terminated, and the mother dismisses the children from her mind—frequently as many as eleven at one time—as easily as she did her husband. She is now free to devote herself to her career and to the novel and astonishing things of life.

In the case of one family of dogs that I observed, the mother, a large black dog with long ears and a keen zest for living, tempered only by an immoderate fear of toads and turtles, kicked ten puppies out of the house at the end of six weeks to the day—it was a Monday. Fortunately for my observations, the puppies had no place to go, since they hadn't made any plans, and so they just hung around the barn, now and again trying to patch things up with their mother. She refused, however, to entertain any proposition leading to a resumption of home life, pointing out firmly that she was, by inclination, a chaser of bicycles and a hearth-fire watcher, both of which activities would be insupportably cluttered up by the presence of ten helpers. The bicycle-chasing field was overcrowded, anyway, she explained, and the hearth-fire-watching field even more so. "We could chase parades together," suggested one of the dogs, but she refused to be touched, snarled, and drove him off.

It is only for a few weeks that the cast-off puppies make overtures to their mother in regard to the reëstablishment of a home. At the end of that time, by some natural miracle that I am unable clearly to understand, the puppies suddenly one day don't recognize their mother any more, and she doesn't recognize them. It is as if they had never met, and is a fine idea, giving both parties a clean break and a chance for a fresh start. Once, some months after this particular family had broken up and the pups had been sold, one of them, named Liza, was brought back to "the old nest" for a visit. The mother

dog of course didn't recognize the puppy and promptly bit her in the hip. They had to be separated, each grumbling something about you never know what kind of dogs you're going to meet. Here was no silly, affecting reunion, no sentimental tears, no bitter intimations of neglect, or forgetfulness, or desertion.

If a pup is not sold or given away, but is brought up in the same household with its mother, the two will fight bitterly, sometimes twenty or thirty times a day, for maybe a month. This is very trying to whoever owns the dogs, particularly if they are sentimentalists who grieve because mother and child don't know each other. The condition finally clears up: the two dogs grow to tolerate each other and, beyond growling a little under their breath about how it takes all kinds of dogs to make up a world, get along fairly well together when their paths cross. I know of one mother dog and her half-grown daughter who sometimes spend the whole day together hunting woodchucks, although they don't speak. Their association is not sentimental, but practical, and is based on the fact that it is safer to hunt woodchucks in pairs than alone. These two dogs start out together in the morning, without a word, and come back together in the evening, when they part, without saying good night, whether they have had any luck or not. Avoidance of farewells, which are always stuffy and sometimes painful, is another thing in which it seems to me dogs have better sense than people.

Well, one day the daughter, a dog about ten months old, seemed, by some prank of nature which again I am unable clearly to understand, for a moment or two, to recognize her mother, after all those months of oblivion. The two had just started out after a fat woodchuck who lives in the orchard. Something got wrong with the daughter's ear—a long, floppy ear. "Mother," she said, "I wish you'd look at my ear." Instantly the other dog bristled and growled. "I'm not your mother," she said, "I'm a woodchuck-hunter." The daughter grinned. "Well," she said, just to show that there were no hard feelings, "that's not my ear, it's a motorman's glove."

The Private Life of Mr. Bidwell

F ROM where she was sitting, Mrs. Bidwell could not see her husband, but she had a curious feeling of tension: she knew he was up to something.

"What are you doing, George?" she demanded, her eyes still on her book.

"Mm?"

"What's the matter with you?"

"Pahhhhh-h-h," said Mr. Bidwell, in a long, pleasurable exhale. "I was holding my breath."

Mrs. Bidwell twisted creakingly in her chair and looked at him; he was sitting behind her in his favorite place under the parchment lamp with the street scene of old New York on it. "I was just holding my breath," he said again.

"Well, please don't do it," said Mrs. Bidwell, and went back to her book. There was silence for five minutes.

"George!" said Mrs. Bidwell.

"Bwaaaaaa," said Mr. Bidwell. "What?"

"Will you please *stop* that?" she said. "It makes me nervous."

"I don't see how that bothers you," he said. "Can't I breathe?"

"You can breathe without holding your breath like a goop," said Mrs. Bidwell. "Goop" was a word that she was fond of using; she rather lazily applied it to everything. It annoyed Mr. Bidwell.

"Deep breathing," said Mr. Bidwell, in the impatient tone he used when explaining anything to his wife, "is good exercise. You ought to take more exercise."

"Well, please don't do it around me," said Mrs. Bidwell, turning again to the pages of Mr. Galsworthy.

At the Cowans' party, a week later, the room was full of chattering people when Mrs. Bidwell, who was talking to Lida Carroll, suddenly turned around as if she had been summoned. In a chair in a far corner of the room, Mr. Bidwell was holding his breath. His chest was expanded, his chin drawn in; there was a strange stare in his eyes, and his face was slightly empurpled. Mrs. Bidwell moved into the line of his vision and gave him a sharp, penetrating look. He deflated slowly and looked away.

Later, in the car, after they had driven in silence a mile or more on the way home, Mrs. Bidwell said, "It seems to me you might at least have the kindness not to hold your breath in other people's houses."

"I wasn't hurting anybody," said Mr. Bidwell.

"You looked silly!" said his wife. "You looked perfectly crazy!" She was driving and she began to speed up, as she always did when excited or angry. "What do you suppose

people thought—you sitting there all swelled up, with your eyes popping out?"

"I wasn't all swelled up," he said, angrily.

"You looked like a goop," she said. The car slowed down, sighed, and came to a complete, despondent stop.

"We're out of gas," said Mrs. Bidwell. It was bitterly cold and nastily sleeting. Mr. Bidwell took a long, deep breath.

The breathing situation in the Bidwell family reached a critical point when Mr. Bidwell began to inhale in his sleep, slowly, and exhale with a protracted, growling "wooooooooo." Mrs. Bidwell, ordinarily a sound sleeper (except on nights when she was sure burglars were getting in), would wake up and reach over and shake her husband. "George!" she would say.

"Hawwwwww," Mr. Bidwell would say, thickly. "Wahs maa nah, hm?"

After he had turned over and gone back to sleep, Mrs. Bidwell would lie awake, thinking.

One morning at breakfast she said, "George, I'm not going to put up with this another day. If you can't stop blowing up like a grampus, I'm going to leave you." There was a slight, quick lift in Mr. Bidwell's heart, but he tried to look surprised and hurt.

"All right," he said. "Let's not talk about it."

Mrs. Bidwell buttered another piece of toast. She described to him the way he sounded in his sleep. He read the paper.

With considerable effort, Mr. Bidwell kept from inflating his chest for about a week, but one night at the McNallys' he hit on the idea of seeing how many seconds he could hold his breath. He was rather bored by the McNallys' party, anyway. He began timing himself with his wrist-watch in a remote corner of the living-room. Mrs. Bidwell, who was in the kitchen talking children and clothes with Bea McNally, left her abruptly and slipped back into the living-room. She stood quietly behind her husband's chair. He knew she was there, and tried to let out his breath imperceptibly.

"I see you," she said, in a low, cold tone. Mr. Bidwell jumped up.

"Why don't you let me alone?" he demanded.

"Will you please lower your voice?" she said, smiling so that if anyone were looking he wouldn't think the Bidwells were arguing.

"I'm getting pretty damned tired of this," said Bidwell in a low voice.

"You've ruined my evening!" she whispered.

"You've ruined mine, too!" he whispered back. They knifed each other, from head to stomach, with their eyes.

"Sitting here like a goop, holding your breath," said Mrs. Bidwell. "People will think you are an idiot." She laughed, turning to greet a lady who was approaching them.

Mr. Bidwell sat in his office the next afternoon, a black, moist afternoon, tapping a pencil on his desk, and scowling. "All right, then, get out, get out!" he muttered. "What do I care?" He was visualizing the scene when Mrs. Bidwell would walk out on him. After going through it several times, he returned to his work, feeling vaguely contented. He made up his mind to breathe any way he wanted to, no matter what she did. And, having come to this decision, he oddly enough, and quite without effort, lost interest in holding his breath.

Everything went rather smoothly at the Bidwells' for a month or so. Mr. Bidwell didn't do anything to annoy his wife beyond leaving his razor on her dressing-table and forgetting to turn out the hall light when he went to bed. Then there came the night of the Bentons' party.

Mr. Bidwell, bored as usual, was sitting in a far corner of the room, breathing normally. His wife was talking animatedly with Beth Williamson about negligees. Suddenly her voice slowed and an uneasy look came into her eyes: George was up to something. She turned around and sought him out. To anyone but Mrs. Bidwell he must have seemed like any husband sitting in a chair. But his wife's lips set tightly. She walked casually over to him.

"What are you doing?" she demanded.

"Hm?" he said, looking at her vacantly.

"What are you *doing*?" she demanded, again. He gave her a harsh, venomous look, which she returned.

"I'm multiplying numbers in my head," he said, slowly and evenly, "if you must know." In the prolonged, probing examination that they silently, without moving any muscles save those of their eyes, gave each other, it became solidly, frozenly apparent to both of them that the end of their endurance had arrived. The curious bond that held them together snapped— rather more easily than either had supposed was possible. That night, while undressing for bed, Mr. Bidwell calmly multiplied numbers in his head. Mrs. Bidwell stared coldly at him for a few moments, holding a stocking in her hand; she didn't bother to berate him. He paid no attention to her. The thing was simply over.

George Bidwell lives alone now (his wife remarried). He

never goes to parties any more, and his old circle of friends rarely sees him. The last time that any of them did see him, he was walking along a country road with the halting, uncertain gait of a blind man: he was trying to see how many steps he could take without opening his eyes.

Mr. Preble Gets Rid of His Wife

M R. P REBLE was a plump middle-aged lawyer in Scarsdale. He used to kid with his stenographer about running away with him. "Let's run away together," he would say, during a pause in dictation. "All righty," she would say.

One rainy Monday afternoon, Mr. Preble was more serious about it than usual.

"Let's run away together," said Mr. Preble.

"All righty," said his stenographer. Mr. Preble jingled the keys in his pocket and looked out the window.

"My wife would be glad to get rid of me," he said.

"Would she give you a divorce?" asked the stenographer.

"I don't suppose so," he said. The stenographer laughed.

"You'd have to get rid of your wife," she said.

Mr. Preble was unusually silent at dinner that night. About half an hour after coffee, he spoke without looking up from his paper.

"Let's go down in the cellar," Mr. Preble said to his wife.

"What for?" she said, not looking up from her book.

"Oh, I don't know," he said. "We never go down in the cellar any more. The way we used to."

"We never did go down in the cellar that I remember," said Mrs. Preble. "I could rest easy the balance of my life if I never went down in the cellar." Mr. Preble was silent for several minutes.

"Supposing I said it meant a whole lot to me," began Mr. Preble.

"What's come over you?" his wife demanded. "It's cold down there and there is absolutely nothing to do."

"We could pick up pieces of coal," said Mr. Preble. "We might get up some kind of a game with pieces of coal."

"I don't want to," said his wife. "Anyway, I'm reading."

"Listen," said Mr. Preble, rising and walking up and down. "Why won't you come down in the cellar? You can read down there, as far as that goes."

"There isn't a good enough light down there," she said, "and anyway, I'm not going to go down in the cellar. You may as well make up your mind to that."

"Gee whiz!" said Mr. Preble, kicking at the edge of a rug. "Other people's wives go down in the cellar. Why is it you never want to do anything? I come home worn out from the office and you won't even go down in the cellar with me. God knows it isn't very far—it isn't as if I was asking you to go to the movies or some place."

"I don't want to *go*!" shouted Mrs. Preble. Mr. Preble sat down on the edge of a davenport.

"All right, all *right*," he said. He picked up the newspaper again. "I wish you'd let me tell you more about it. It's—kind of a surprise."

"Will you quit harping on that subject?" asked Mrs. Preble.

"Listen," said Mr. Preble, leaping to his feet. "I might as well tell you the truth instead of beating around the bush. I want to get rid of you so I can marry my stenographer. Is there anything especially wrong about that? People do it every day. Love is something you can't control——"

"We've been all over that," said Mrs. Preble. "I'm not going to go all over that again."

"I just wanted you to know how things are," said Mr. Preble. "But you have to take everything so literally. Good Lord, do you suppose I really wanted to go down in the cellar and make up some silly game with pieces of coal?"

"I never believed that for a minute," said Mrs. Preble. "I knew all along you wanted to get me down there and bury me."

"You can say that now—after I told you," said Mr. Preble. "But it would never have occurred to you if I hadn't."

"You didn't tell me; I got it out of you," said Mrs. Preble. "Anyway, I'm always two steps ahead of what you're thinking."

"You're never within a mile of what I'm thinking," said Mr. Preble.

"Is that so? I knew you wanted to bury me the minute you set foot in this house tonight." Mrs. Preble held him with a glare.

"Now that's just plain damn exaggeration," said Mr. Preble, considerably annoyed. "You knew nothing of the sort. As a matter of fact, I never thought of it till just a few minutes ago."

"It was in the back of your mind," said Mrs. Preble. "I suppose this filing woman put you up to it."

"You needn't get sarcastic," said Mr. Preble. "I have plenty of people to file without having her file. She doesn't know

anything about this. She isn't in on it. I was going to tell her you had gone to visit some friends and fell over a cliff. She wants me to get a divorce."

"That's a laugh," said Mrs. Preble. "*That's* a laugh. You may bury me, but you'll never get a divorce."

"She knows that! I told her that," said Mr. Preble. "I mean—I told her I'd never get a divorce."

"Oh, you probably told her about burying me, too," said Mrs. Preble.

"That's not true," said Mr. Preble, with dignity. "That's between you and me. I was never going to tell a soul."

"You'd blab it to the whole world; don't tell me," said Mrs. Preble. "I know you." Mr. Preble puffed at his cigar.

"I wish you were buried now and it was all over with," he said.

"Don't you suppose you would get caught, you crazy thing?" she said. "They always get caught. Why don't you go to bed? You're just getting yourself all worked up over nothing."

"I'm not going to bed," said Mr. Preble. "I'm going to bury you in the cellar. I've got my mind made up to it. I don't know how I could make it any plainer."

"Listen," cried Mrs. Preble, throwing her book down, "will you be satisfied and shut up if I go down in the cellar? Can I have a little peace if I go down in the cellar? Will you let me alone then?"

"Yes," said Mr. Preble. "But you spoil it by taking that attitude."

"Sure, sure, I always spoil everything. I stop reading right in the middle of a chapter. I'll never know how the story comes out—but that's nothing to you."

"Did I make you start reading the book?" asked Mr. Preble. He opened the cellar door. "Here, you go first."

"Brrr," said Mrs. Preble, starting down the steps. "It's *cold* down here! You *would* think of this, at this time of year! Any other husband would have buried his wife in the summer."

"You can't arrange those things just whenever you want to," said Mr. Preble. "I didn't fall in love with this girl till late fall."

"Anybody else would have fallen in love with her long before that. She's been around for years. Why is it you always let other men get in ahead of you? Mercy, but it's dirty down here! What have you got there?"

"I was going to hit you over the head with this shovel," said Mr. Preble.

"You were, huh?" said Mrs. Preble. "Well, get that out of your mind. Do you want to leave a great big clue right here in the middle of everything where the first detective that comes snooping around will find it? Go out in the street and find some piece of iron or something—something that doesn't belong to you."

"Oh, all right," said Mr. Preble. "But there won't be any piece of iron in the street. Women always expect to pick up a piece of iron anywhere."

"If you look in the right place you'll find it," said Mrs. Preble. "And don't be gone long. Don't you dare stop in at the cigarstore. I'm not going to stand down here in this cold cellar all night and freeze."

"All right," said Mr. Preble. "I'll hurry."

"And shut that *door* behind you!" she screamed after him. "Where were you born—in a barn?"

A Portrait of Aunt Ida

MY MOTHER'S Aunt Ida Clemmens died the other day out West. She was ninety-one years old. I remember her clearly, although I haven't thought about her in a long time and never saw her after I was twenty. I remember how dearly she loved catastrophes, especially those of a national or international importance. The sinking of the *Titanic* was perhaps the most important tragedy of the years in which I knew her. She never saw in such things, as her older sisters, Emma and Clara, did, the vengeance of a Deity outraged by Man's lust for speed and gaiety; she looked for the causes deep down in the dark heart of the corporate interests. You could never make her believe that the *Titanic* hit an iceberg. Whoever *heard* of such a thing! It was simply a flimsy prevarication devised to cover up the real cause. The real cause she could not, or would not, make plain, but somewhere in its black core was a monstrous secret of treachery and corrupt goings-on—men were like that. She came later on to doubt the courage of the brave gentlemen on the sinking ship who at the last waved goodbye smilingly and smoked cigarettes. It was her growing conviction that most of them had to be shot by the ship's officers in order to prevent them from crowding into the lifeboats ahead of the older and less attractive women passengers. Eminence and wealth in men Aunt Ida persistently attributed to deceit, trickery, and impiety. I think the only famous person she ever trusted in her time was President Mc-Kinley.

The disappearance of Judge Crater, the Hall-Mills murder, the Starr Faithfull case, and similar mysteries must have made Aunt Ida's last years happy. She loved the unsolvable and the unsolved. Mysteries that were never cleared up were brought about, in her opinion, by the workings of some strange force in the world which we do not thoroughly understand and which God does not intend that we ever shall understand. An invisible power, a power akin to electricity and radio (both of which she must have regarded as somehow or other blasphemous), but never to be isolated or channelled. Out of this power came murder, disappearances, and supernatural phenomena. All persons connected in any way whatever with celebrated cases were tainted in Aunt Ida's sight—and that went for prosecuting attorneys, too (always "tricky" men). But she would, I'm sure, rather have had a look at Willie Stevens than at President Roosevelt, at Jafsie than at the King of England, just as she would rather have gone through the old Wendel house than the White House.

Surgical operations and post-mortems were among Aunt Ida's special interests, although she did not believe that any operation was ever necessary and she was convinced that post-mortems were conducted to cover up something rather than to find something out. It was her conviction that doctors were in the habit of trying to obfuscate or distort the true facts about illness and death. She believed that many of her friends and relatives had been laid away without the real causes of their deaths being entered on the "city books." She was fond of telling a long and involved story about the death of one of her first cousins, a married woman who had passed away at twenty-five. Aunt Ida for thirty years contended that there was something "behind it." She believed that a certain physician, a gentleman of the highest reputation, would some day "tell the truth about Ruth," perhaps on his deathbed. When he died (without confessing, of course), she said after reading the account in the newspaper that she had dreamed of him a few nights before. It seemed that he had called to her and wanted to tell her something but couldn't.

Aunt Ida believed that she was terribly psychic. She had warnings, premonitions, and "feelings." They were invariably intimations of approaching misfortune, sickness, or death. She never had a premonition that everything was going to be all right. It was always that Grace So-and-So was not going to marry the man she was engaged to, or that Mr. Hollowell, who was down in South America on business, would never return, or that old Mrs. Hutchins would not last out the year (she missed on old Mrs. Hutchins for twenty-two years but finally made it). Most all of Aunt Ida's forewarnings of financial ruin and marital tragedy came in the daytime while she was marketing or sitting hulling peas; most all of her intimations of death appeared to her in dreams. Dreams of Ohio women of Aunt Ida's generation were never Freudian; they were purely prophetic. They dealt with black hearses and white hearses rolling soundlessly along through the night, and with coffins being carried out of houses, and with tombstones bearing names and dates, and with tall, faceless women in black veils and gloves. Most of Aunt Ida's dreams foretold the fate of women, for what happened to women was of much greater importance to Aunt Ida than what happened to men.

Men usually "brought things on themselves"; women, on the other hand, were usually the victims of dark and devious goings-on of a more or less supernatural nature.

Birth was, in some ways, as dark a matter to Aunt Ida as death. She felt that most babies, no matter what you said or anybody else said, were "not wanted." She believed that the children of famous people, brilliant people, and of first, second, or third cousins would be idiotic. If a child died young, she laid it to the child's parentage, no matter what the immediate cause of death might have been. "There is something in that family," Aunt Ida used to say, in her best funeral voice. This something was a vague, ominous thing, both far off and close at hand, misty and ready to spring, compounded of nobody could guess exactly what. One of Aunt Ida's favorite predictions was "They'll never raise that baby, you mark my words." The fact that they usually did never shook her confidence in her "feelings." If she was right once in twenty times, it proved that she knew what she was talking about. In foretelling the sex of unborn children, she was right about half the time.

Life after death was a source of speculation, worry, and exhilaration to Aunt Ida. She firmly believed that people could "come back" and she could tell you of many a house that was haunted (barrels of apples rolled down the attic steps of one of them, I remember, but it was never clear why they did). Aunt Ida put no faith in mediums or séances. The dead preferred to come back to the houses where they had lived and to go stalking through the rooms and down the halls. I think Aunt Ida always thought of them as coming back in the flesh, fully clothed, for she always spoke of them as "the dead," never as ghosts. The reason they came back was that they had left something unsaid or undone that must be corrected. Although a descendant of staunch orthodox Methodists, some of them ministers, Aunt Ida in her later years dabbled a little in various religions, superstitions, and even cults. She found astrology, New Thought, and the theory of reincarnation comforting. The people who are bowed down in this life, she grew to believe, will have another chance.

Aunt Ida was confident that the world was going to be destroyed almost any day. When Halley's comet appeared in 1910, she expected to read in the papers every time she picked them up the news that Paris had gone up in flames and that New York City had slid into the ocean. Those two cities, being horrible dens of vice, were bound to go first; the smaller towns would be destroyed in a more leisurely fashion with some respectable and dignified ending for the pious and the kindly people.

Two of Aunt Ida's favorite expressions were "I never heard of such a thing" and "If I never get up from this chair. . . ." She told all stories of death, misfortune, grief, corruption, and disaster with vehemence and exaggeration. She was hampered in narration by her inability to think of names, particularly simple names, such as Joe, Earl, Ned, Harry, Louise, Ruth, Bert. Somebody usually had to prompt her with the name of the third cousin, or whomever, that she was trying to think of, but she was unerring in her ability to remember difficult names the rest of us had long forgotten. "He used to work in the old Schirtzberger & Wallenheim saddle store in Naughton Street," she would say. "What *was* his name?" It would turn out that his name was Frank Butler.

Up to the end, they tell me, Aunt Ida could read without her glasses, and none of the commoner frailties of senility affected her. She had no persecution complex, no lapses of memory, no trailing off into the past, no unfounded bitternesses—unless you could call her violent hatred of cigarettes unfounded bitterness, and I don't think it was, because she actually knew stories of young men and even young women who had become paralyzed to the point of losing the use of both legs through smoking cigarettes. She tended to her begonias and wrote out a check for the rent the day she took to her bed for the last time. It irked her not to be up and about, and she accused the doctor the family brought in of not knowing his business. There was marketing to do, and friends to call on, and work to get through with. When friends and relatives began calling on her, she was annoyed. Making out that she was really sick! Old Mrs. Kurtz, who is seventy-two, visited her on the last day, and when she left, Aunt Ida looked after her pityingly. "Poor Cora," she said, "she's failin', ain't she?"

The Luck of Jad Peters

AUNT EMMA PETERS, at eighty-three—the year she died—still kept in her unused front parlor, on the table with Jad Peters's collection of lucky souvenirs, a large rough fragment of rock weighing perhaps twenty pounds. The rock stood in the centre of a curious array of odds and ends: a piece of tent canvas, a chip of pine wood, a yellowed telegram, some old newspaper clippings, the cork from a bottle, a bill from a surgeon. Aunt Emma never talked about the strange collection except once, during her last days, when somebody asked her if she wouldn't feel better if the rock were thrown away. "Let it stay where Lisbeth put it," she said. All that I know about the souvenirs I have got from other members of the family. A few of them didn't think it was "decent" that the rock should have been part of the collection, but Aunt Lisbeth, Emma's sister, had insisted that it should be. In fact, it was Aunt Lisbeth Banks who hired a man to lug it to the house and put it on the table with the rest of the things. "It's as much God's doing as that other clutter-trap," she would say. And she would rock back and forth in her rocking chair with a grim look. "You can't taunt the Lord," she would add. She was a very religious woman. I used to see her now and again at funerals, tall, gaunt, grim, but I never talked to her if I could help it. She liked funerals and she liked to look at corpses, and that made me afraid of her.

Just back of the souvenir table at Aunt Emma's, on the wall, hung a heavy-framed, full-length photograph of Aunt Emma's husband, Jad Peters. It showed him wearing a hat and overcoat and carrying a suitcase. When I was a little boy in the early nineteen-hundreds and was taken to Aunt Emma's house near Sugar Grove, Ohio, I used to wonder about that photograph (I didn't wonder about the rock and the other objects, because they weren't put there till much later). It seemed so funny for anyone to be photographed in a hat and overcoat and carrying a suitcase, and even funnier to have the photograph enlarged to almost life size and put inside so elaborate a frame. When we children would sneak into the front parlor to look at the picture, Aunt Emma would hurry us out again. When we asked her about the picture, she would say, "Never you mind." But when I grew up, I learned the story of the big photograph and of how Jad Peters came to be known as Lucky Jad. As a matter of fact, it was Jad who began calling himself that; once when he ran for a county office (and lost) he had "Lucky Jad Peters" printed on his campaign cards. Nobody else took the name up except in a scoffing way.

It seems that back in 1888, when Jad Peters was about thirty-five, he had a pretty good business of some kind or other which caused him to travel around quite a lot. One week he went to New York with the intention of going on to Newport, later, by ship. Something turned up back home, however, and one of his employees sent him a telegram reading "Don't go to Newport. Urgent you return here." Jad's story was that he was on the ship, ready to sail, when the telegram was delivered; it had been sent to his hotel, he said, a few minutes after he had checked out, and an obliging clerk had hustled the messenger boy on down to the dock. That was Jad's story. Most people believed, when they heard the story, that Jad had got the wire at his hotel, probably hours before the ship sailed, for he was a great one at adorning a tale. At any rate, whether or not he rushed off the ship just before the gangplank was hauled up, it sailed without him and some eight or nine hours out of the harbor sank in a storm with the loss of everybody on board. That's why he had the photograph taken and enlarged: it showed him just as he was when he got off the ship, he said. And that is how he came to start his collection of lucky souvenirs. For a few years he kept the telegram, and newspaper clippings of the ship disaster, tucked away in the family Bible, but one day he got them out and put them on the parlor table under a big glass bell.

From 1888 up until 1920, when Jad died, nothing much happened to him. He is remembered in his later years as a garrulous, boring old fellow whose business slowly went to pieces because of his lack of industry and who finally settled down on a small farm near Sugar Grove and barely scraped out an existence. He took to drinking in his sixties, and from then on made Aunt Emma's life miserable. I don't know how she managed to keep up the payments on his life-insurance policy, but some way or other she did. Some of her relatives said among themselves that it would be a blessing if Jad died in one of his frequent fits of nausea. It was pretty well known that Aunt Emma had never liked him very much—she married him because he asked her to twice a week for seven years and because there had been nobody else she cared about; she stayed married to him on account of their children and because her people always stayed married. She grew, in spite of Jad, to be a quiet, kindly old lady as the years went on, although her mouth would take on a strained, tight look when Jad showed up at dinner time from wherever he had been

during the day—usually from down at Prentice's store in the village, where he liked to sit around telling about the time he just barely got off the doomed boat in New York harbor in '88 and adding tales, more or less fantastic, of more recent close escapes he had had. There was his appendicitis operation, for one thing: he had come out of the ether, he would say, just when they had given him up. Dr. Benham, who had performed the operation, was annoyed when he heard this, and once met Jad in the street and asked him to quit repeating the preposterous story, but Jad added the doctor's bill to his collection of talismans, anyway. And there was the time when he had got up in the night to take a swig of stomach bitters for a bad case of heartburn and had got hold of the carbolic-acid bottle by mistake. Something told him, he would say, to take a look at the bottle before he uncorked it, so he carried it to a lamp, lighted the lamp, and he'd be gol-dam if it wasn't carbolic acid! It was then that he added the cork to his collection.

Old Jad got so that he could figure out lucky escapes for himself in almost every disaster and calamity that happened in and around Sugar Grove. Once, for example, a tent blew down during a wind storm at the Fairfield County Fair, killing two people and injuring a dozen others. Jad hadn't gone to the fair that year for the first time in nine or ten years. Something told him, he would say, to stay away from the fair that year. The fact that he always went to the fair, when he did go, on a Thursday and that the tent blew down on a Saturday didn't make any difference to Jad. He hadn't been there and the tent blew down and two people were killed. After the accident, he went to the fair grounds and cut a piece of canvas from the tent and put it on the parlor table next to the cork from the carbolic-acid bottle. Lucky Jad Peters!

I think Aunt Emma got so that she didn't hear Jad when he was talking, except on evenings when neighbors dropped in, and then she would have to take hold of the conversation and steer it away from any opening that might give Jad a chance to tell of some close escape he had had. But he always got his licks in. He would bide his time, creaking back and forth in his chair, clicking his teeth, and not listening much to the talk about crops and begonias and the latest reports on the Spencers' feeble-minded child, and then, when there was a long pause, he would clear his throat and say that that reminded him of the time he had had a mind to go down to Pullen's lumber yard to fetch home a couple of two-by-fours to shore up the chicken house. Well, sir, he had pottered around the house a little while and was about to set out for Pullen's when something told him not to go a step. And it was that very day that a pile of lumber in the lumber yard let go and crushed Grant Pullen's leg so's it had to be amputated. Well, sir, he would say—but Aunt Emma would cut in on him at this point. "Everybody's heard that old chestnut," she would say, with a forced little laugh, fanning herself in quick strokes with an old palm-leaf fan. Jad would go sullen and rock back and forth in his chair, clicking his teeth. He wouldn't get up when the guests rose to go—which they always did at this juncture. The memento of his close escape from the Pullen lumber-yard disaster was, of course, the chip of pine wood.

I think I have accounted for all of Jad's souvenirs that I remember except the big rough fragment of rock. The story of the rock is a strange one. In August, 1920, county engineers were widening the channel of the Hocking River just outside of Sugar Grove and had occasion to do considerable blasting out of river-bed rock. I have never heard Clem Warden tell the story himself, but it has been told to me by people who have. It seems that Clem was walking along the main street of Sugar Grove at about a quarter to four when he saw Jad coming along toward him. Clem was an old crony of Jad's—one of the few men of his own generation who could tolerate Jad—and the two stopped on the sidewalk and talked. Clem figured later that they had talked for about five minutes, and then either he or Jad said something about getting on, so they separated, Jad going on toward Prentice's store, slowly, on account of his rheumatic left hip, and Clem going in the other direction. Clem had taken about a dozen steps when suddenly he heard Jad call to him. "Say, Clem!" Jad said. Clem stopped and turned around, and here was Jad walking back toward him. Jad had taken about six steps when suddenly he was flung up against the front of Matheny's harness store "like a sack o' salt," as Clem put it. By the time Clem could reach him, he was gone. He never knew what hit him, Clem said, and for quite a few minutes nobody else knew what hit him, either. Then somebody in the crowd that gathered found the big muddy rock lying in the road by the gutter. A particularly big shot of dynamite, set off in the river bed, had hurtled the fragment through the air with terrific force. It had come flying over the four-story Jackson Building like a cannon ball and had struck Jad Peters squarely in the chest.

I suppose old Jad hadn't been in his grave two days before the boys at Prentice's quit shaking their heads solemnly over the accident and began making funny remarks about it. Cal Gregg's was the funniest. "Well, sir," said Cal, "I don't suppose none of us will ever know what it was now, but somethin' must of told Jad to turn around."

I Went to Sullivant

I WAS reminded the other morning—by what, I don't remember and it doesn't matter—of a crisp September morning last year when I went to the Grand Central to see a little boy of ten get excitedly on a special coach that was to take him to a boys' school somewhere north of Boston. He had never been away to school before. The coach was squirming with youngsters; you could tell, after a while, the novitiates, shining and tremulous and a little awed, from the more aloof boys, who had been away to school before, but they were all very much alike at first glance. There was for me (in case you thought I was leading up to that) no sharp feeling of old lost years in the tense atmosphere of that coach, because I never went away to a private school when I was a little boy. I went to Sullivant School in Columbus. I thought about it as I walked back to my hotel.

Sullivant was an ordinary public school, and yet it was not like any other I have ever known of. In seeking an adjective to describe the Sullivant School of my years—1900 to 1908—I can only think of "tough." Sullivant School was tough. The boys of Sullivant came mostly from the region around Central Market, a poorish district with many colored families and many white families of the laboring class. The school district also included a number of homes of the upper classes because, at the turn of the century, one or two old residential streets still lingered near the shouting and rumbling of the market, reluctant to surrender their fine old houses to the encroaching rabble of commerce, and become (as, alas, they now have) mere vulgar business streets.

I remember always, first of all, the Sullivant baseball team. Most grammar-school baseball teams are made up of boys in the seventh and eighth grades, or they were in my day, but with Sullivant it was different. Several of its best players were in the fourth grade, known to the teachers of the school as the Terrible Fourth. In that grade you first encountered fractions and long division, and many pupils lodged there for years, like logs in a brook. Some of the more able baseball-players had been in the fourth grade for seven or eight years. Then, too, there were a number of boys, most of them colored (about half of the pupils at Sullivant were colored), who had not been in the class past the normal time but were nevertheless deep in their teens. They had avoided starting to school—by eluding the truant officer—until they were ready to go into long pants, but he always got them in the end. One or two of these fourth-graders were seventeen or eighteen years old, but the dean of the squad was a tall, husky young man of twenty-two who was in the fifth grade (the

teachers of the third and fourth had got tired of having him around as the years rolled along and had pushed him on). His name was Dana Waney and he had a mustache. Don't ask me why his parents allowed him to stay in school so long. There were many mysteries at Sullivant that were never cleared up. All I know is why he kept on in school and didn't go to work: he liked playing on the baseball team, and he had a pretty easy time in class, because the teachers had given up asking him any questions at all years before. The story was that he had answered but one question in the seventeen years he had been going to classes at Sullivant and that was "What is one use of the comma?" "The commy," said Dana, embarrassedly unsnarling his long legs from beneath a desk much too low for him, "is used to shoot marbles with." ("Commies" was our word for those cheap, ten-for-a-cent marbles, in case it wasn't yours.)

The Sullivant School baseball team of 1905 defeated several high-school teams in the city and claimed the high-school championship of the state, to which title it had, of course, no technical right. I believe the boys could have proved their moral right to the championship, however, if they had been allowed to go out of town and play all the teams they challenged, such as the powerful Dayton and Toledo nines, but their road season was called off after a terrific fight that occurred during a game in Mt. Sterling, or Piqua, or Zenia—I can't remember which. Our first baseman—Dana Waney—crowned the umpire with a bat during an altercation over a called strike and the fight was on. It took place in the fourth inning, so of course the game was never finished (the battle continued on down into the business section of the town and raged for hours, with much destruction of property), but since Sullivant was ahead at the time 17 to 0 there could have been no doubt as to the outcome. Nobody was killed. All of us boys were sure our team could have beaten Ohio State University that year, but they wouldn't play us; they were scared.

Waney was by no means the biggest or toughest guy on the grammar-school team; he was merely the oldest, being about a year the senior of Floyd, the colored centre-fielder, who could jump five feet straight into the air without taking a running start. Nobody knew—not even the Board of Education, which once tried to find out—whether Floyd was Floyd's first name or his last name. He apparently only had one. He didn't have any parents, and nobody, including himself, seemed to know where he lived. When teachers insisted that he must have another name to go with Floyd, he would grow sullen and ominous and they would cease questioning him, because he was a dangerous scholar in a schoolroom brawl, as Mr. Harrigan, the janitor, found out one morning when he was called in by a screaming teacher (all our teachers were women) to get Floyd under control after she had tried to whip him and he had begun to take the room apart, beginning with the desks. Floyd broke into small pieces the switch she had used on him (some said he also ate it; I don't know, because I was home sick at the time with mumps or something). Harrigan was a burly, iron-muscled janitor, a man come from a long line of coal-shovellers, but he was no match for Floyd, who had, to be sure, the considerable advantage of being more aroused than Mr. Harrigan when their fight started. Floyd had him down and was sitting on his chest in no time, and Harrigan had to promise to be good and to say "Dat's what Ah get" ten times before Floyd would let him up.

I don't suppose I would ever have got through Sullivant School alive if it hadn't been for Floyd. For some reason he appointed himself my protector, and I needed one. If Floyd was known to be on your side, nobody in the school would dare be "after" you and chase you home. I was one of the ten or fifteen male pupils in Sullivant School who always, or almost always, knew their lessons, and I believe Floyd admired the mental prowess of a youngster who knew how many continents there were and whether or not the sun was inhabited.

Also, one time when it came my turn to read to the class—
we used to take turns reading American history aloud—I came
across the word "Duquesne" and knew how to pronounce it.
That charmed Floyd, who had been slouched in his seat idly
following the printed page of his worn and pencilled textbook.
"How you know dat was Dukane, boy?" he asked me after
class. "I don't know," I said. "I just knew it." He looked at
me with round eyes. "Boy, dat's sump'n," he said. After that,
word got around that Floyd would beat the tar out of anybody that messed around me. I wore glasses from the time I
was eight and I knew my lessons, and both of those things
were considered pretty terrible at Sullivant. Floyd had one
idiosyncrasy. In the early nineteen-hundreds, long warm furry
gloves that came almost to your elbows were popular with
boys, and Floyd had one of the biggest pairs in school. He
wore them the year around.

Dick Peterson, another colored boy, was an even greater
figure on the baseball team and in the school than Floyd was.
He had a way in the classroom of blurting out a long deep
rolling "beee—eee—ahhhh!" for no reason at all. Once he
licked three boys his own size single-handed, really single-
handed, for he fought with his right hand and held a mandolin
in his left hand all the time. It came out uninjured. Dick and
Floyd never met in mortal combat, so nobody ever knew
which one could "beat," and the scholars were about evenly
divided in their opinions. Many a fight started among them
after school when that argument came up. I think school
never let out at Sullivant without at least one fight starting
up, and sometimes there were as many as five or six raging
between the corner of Oak and Sixth Streets and the corner
of Rich and Fourth Streets, four blocks away. Now and again
virtually the whole school turned out to fight the Catholic
boys of the Holy Cross Academy in Fifth Street near Town,
for no reason at all—in winter with snowballs and iceballs, in
other seasons with fists, brickbats, and clubs. Dick Peterson
was always in the van, yelling, singing, beeee-ahing, whirling
all the way around when he swung with his right or (if he
hadn't brought his mandolin) his left and missed. He made
himself the pitcher on the baseball team because he was the
captain. He was the captain because everybody was afraid to

challenge his self-election, except Floyd. Floyd was too lazy to pitch and he didn't care who was captain, because he didn't fully comprehend what that meant. On one occasion, when Earl Battec, a steam-fitter's son, had shut out Mound Street School for six innings without a hit, Dick took him out of the pitcher's box and went in himself. He was hit hard and the other team scored, but it didn't make much difference, because the margin of Sullivant's victory was so great. The team didn't lose a game for five years to another grammar school. When Dick Peterson was in the sixth grade, he got into a saloon brawl and was killed.

When I go back to Columbus I always walk past Sullivant School. I have never happened to get there when classes were letting out, so I don't know what the pupils are like now. I am sure there are no more Dick Petersons and no more Floyds, unless Floyd is still going to school there. The play yard is still entirely bare of grass and covered with gravel, and the sycamores still line the curb between the schoolhouse fence and the Oak Street car line. A street-car line running past a schoolhouse is a dangerous thing as a rule, but I remember no one being injured while I was attending Sullivant. I do remember, however, one person who came very near being injured. He was a motorman on the Oak Street line, and once when his car stopped at the corner of Sixth to let off passengers, he yelled at Chutey Davidson, who played third base on the ball team, and was a member of the Terrible Fourth, to get out of the way. Chutey was a white boy, fourteen years old, but huge for his age, and he was standing on the tracks, taking a chew of tobacco. "Come ahn down offa that car an' I'll knock your block off!" said Chutey, in what I can only describe as a Sullivant tone of voice. The motorman waited until Chutey moved slowly off the tracks; then he went on about his business. I think it was lucky for him that he did. There were boys in those days.

If Grant Had Been Drinking
at Appomattox

(*Scribner's Magazine* published a series of three articles: "If Booth Had Missed Lincoln," "If Lee Had Not Won The Battle of Gettysburg," and "If Napoleon Had Escaped to America." This is the fourth.)

THE MORNING of the ninth of April, 1865, dawned beautifully. General Meade was up with the first streaks of crimson in the eastern sky. General Hooker and General Burnside were up, and had breakfasted, by a quarter after eight. The day continued beautiful. It drew on toward eleven o'clock. General Ulysses S. Grant was still not up. He was asleep in his famous old navy hammock, swung high above the floor of his headquarters' bedroom. Headquarters was distressingly disarranged: papers were strewn on the floor; confidential notes from spies scurried here and there in the breeze from an open window; the dregs of an overturned bottle of wine flowed pinkly across an important military map.

Corporal Shultz, of the Sixty-fifth Ohio Volunteer Infantry, aide to General Grant, came into the outer room, looked around him, and sighed. He entered the bedroom and shook the General's hammock roughly. General Ulysses S. Grant opened one eye.

"Pardon, sir," said Corporal Shultz, "but this is the day of surrender. You ought to be up, sir."

"Don't swing me," said Grant, sharply, for his aide was making the hammock sway gently. "I feel terrible," he added, and he turned over and closed his eye again.

"General Lee will be here any minute now," said the Corporal firmly, swinging the hammock again.

"Will you cut that out?" roared Grant. "D'ya want to make me sick, or what?" Shultz clicked his heels and saluted. "What's he coming here for?" asked the General.

"This is the day of surrender, sir," said Shultz. Grant grunted bitterly.

"Three hundred and fifty generals in the Northern armies,"

said Grant, "and he has to come to *me* about this. What time is it?"

"You're the Commander-in-Chief, that's why," said Corporal Shultz. "It's eleven twenty-five, sir."

"Don't be crazy," said Grant. "Lincoln is the Commander-in-Chief. Nobody in the history of the world ever surrendered before lunch. Doesn't he know that an army surrenders on its stomach?" He pulled a blanket up over his head and settled himself again.

"The generals of the Confederacy will be here any minute now," said the Corporal. "You really ought to be up, sir."

Grant stretched his arms above his head and yawned.

"All right, all right," he said. He rose to a sitting position and stared about the room. "This place looks awful," he growled.

"You must have had quite a time of it last night, sir," ventured Shultz.

"Yeh," said General Grant, looking around for his clothes. "I was wrassling some general. Some general with a beard."

Shultz helped the commander of the Northern armies in the field to find his clothes.

"Where's my other sock?" demanded Grant. Shultz began to look around for it. The General walked uncertainly to a table and poured a drink from a bottle.

"I don't think it wise to drink, sir," said Shultz.

"Nev' mind about me," said Grant, helping himself to a second, "I can take it or let it alone. Didn' ya ever hear the story about the fella went to Lincoln to complain about me drinking too much? 'So-and-So says Grant drinks too much,' this fella said. 'So-and-So is a fool,' said Lincoln. So this fella went to What's-His-Name and told him what Lincoln said and he came roarin' to Lincoln about it. 'Did you tell So-and-So I was a fool?' he said. 'No,' said Lincoln, 'I thought he knew it.'" The General smiled, reminiscently, and had another drink. "*That's* how I stand with Lincoln," he said, proudly.

The soft thudding sound of horses' hooves came through the open window. Shultz hurriedly walked over and looked out.

"Hoof steps," said Grant, with a curious chortle.

"It is General Lee and his staff," said Shultz.

"Show him in," said the General, taking another drink. "And see what the boys in the back room will have."

Shultz walked smartly over to the door, opened it, saluted, and stood aside. General Lee, dignified against the blue of the April sky, magnificent in his dress uniform, stood for a moment framed in the doorway. He walked in, followed by his staff. They bowed, and stood silent. General Grant stared at them. He only had one boot on and his jacket was unbuttoned.

"I know who you are," said Grant. "You're Robert Browning, the poet."

"This is General Robert E. Lee," said one of his staff, coldly.

"Oh," said Grant. "I thought he was Robert Browning. He certainly looks like Robert Browning. There was a poet for you, Lee: Browning. Did ja ever read 'How They Brought the Good News from Ghent to Aix'? 'Up Derek, to saddle, up Derek, away; up Dunder, up Blitzen, up Prancer, up Dancer, up Bouncer, up Vixen, up——'"

"Shall we proceed at once to the matter in hand?" asked General Lee, his eyes disdainfully taking in the disordered room.

"Some of the boys was wrassling here last night," explained Grant. "I threw Sherman, or some general a whole lot like Sherman. It was pretty dark." He handed a bottle of Scotch to the commanding officer of the Southern armies, who stood holding it, in amazement and discomfiture. "Get a glass, somebody," said Grant, looking straight at General Longstreet. "Didn't I meet you at Cold Harbor?" he asked. General Longstreet did not answer.

"I should like to have this over with as soon as possible," said Lee. Grant looked vaguely at Shultz, who walked up close to him, frowning.

"The surrender, sir, the surrender," said Corporal Shultz in a whisper.

"Oh sure, sure," said Grant. He took another drink. "All right," he said. "Here we go." Slowly, sadly, he unbuckled his sword. Then he handed it to the astonished Lee. "There you are, General," said Grant. "We dam' near licked you. If I'd been feeling better we *would* of licked you."

How to See a Bad Play

ONE of my friends, who is a critic of the drama, invited me to accompany him last season to all the plays which he suspected were not going to be good enough or interesting enough to take his girl to. His suspicions were right in each instance, and there were dozens of instances. I don't know why I kept accepting his invitations to first nights of dubious promise, but I did. Perhaps it was sheer fascination. I know a man, an inveterate smoker of five-cent cigars, who once refused my offer of a Corona: he said he just couldn't go the things. Bad plays can get that kind of hold on you; anyway, they did on me. (I'm not going to go to *any* plays this season; I'm going to ski, and play lotto.)

I still brood about some of the situations, characters, tactics, and strategies I ran into last season in the more awful plays. I thank whatever gods may be that very few lines of dialogue, however, come back at night to roost above my chamber door. As a matter of fact, the only line that haunts me is one from "Reprise," during the first scene of the first act of which a desperate young man is prevented from jumping off the balustrade of a penthouse (all plays set in penthouses are terrible) by another young man. The desperate young man then has three or four shots of what he describes as "excellent brandy" and the other man asks him if he still wants to jump. "No," says the desperate young man. "Your brandy has taken my courage." That marked the first time in the history of the world when three or four slugs of excellent brandy took a desperate man's courage. I find myself thinking about it.

It was in this very same play, "Reprise" (or was it "Yesterday's Orchids"?), that the double-wing-back formation and triple lateral pass reached a new height. I have drawn a little diagram (Fig. 1) to illustrate what I mean. There was really no business in the play, only a great deal of talk, and the director must have found out early—probably during the first rehearsal—that the way the play was written the characters were just going to sit in chairs or on chaise longues and talk to each other, so he got them to moving around. After all, there has to be action of some kind in every play. Fig. 1 shows one of the more intricate moves that were made, as accurately as I can remember it now (I may have left out a couple of shifts, but it's close enough). Character A, to begin with, is standing at the right (A 1) of the handsome chair, centre rear, and Character B is sitting (B 1) on the chaise longue. A moves over (A 2) and sits on the foot of the chaise longue, whereupon B gets up and moves to position B 2 and then around the chaise longue (B 3) to the same place he had been sitting, as A reverses his field (A 3), circles around the big chair (A 4), and goes to the little chair (A 5). B now moves to the foot of the chaise longue (B 4), and then goes over and sits in the big chair (B 5). As he does so, A moves over and sits on the foot of the chaise longue again (A 6), then B crosses to the

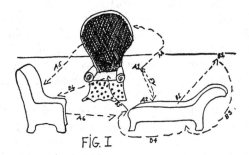

FIG. I

little chair (B 6), thus completing a full circle, with variations. All this time a lot of dialogue was going on, dealing with some brand-new angle on sex, but I was so engrossed in following the maze of crisscrosses that I didn't take in any of it, and hence, as far as sex knowledge goes, I am just where I was before I went to the play. There were a great many other involved crossings and recrossings, and what are known on the gridiron as Statue of Liberty plays, in this drama, but the one I have presented here was my favorite.

Another formation that interested me in several of the plays I studied was what I call the back-to-back emotional scene (Fig. 2). The two characters depicted here are, strange as it

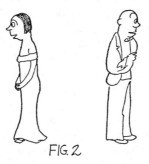

FIG. 2

may seem, "talking it out." In some plays in which this formation occurred they were declaring their love for each other;
in others she was telling him that she was in love with
someone else, or he was telling her that he had to go to South
America because he was in love with her sister or because he
thought she was in love with his brother, or his father-in-law,
or something of the sort. I have witnessed a number of emotional scenes in real life, but I have just happened to miss any
in which the parties involved moved past each other and faced
things out back to back. Apparently I don't get around as
much as playwrights do.

Fig. 3 illustrates another position that was frequently to be
seen on our stage last season: the woman, standing, comforting the man, sitting. In this curious entanglement, so different
from anything that has ever happened to me, the position of
the arms is always just as I have shown it in the picture and
the woman's head is always lifted, as if she were studying a

FIG. 3

cobweb in a far corner of the ceiling. Sometimes she closes her eyes, whereupon the man opens his. When they break away, it is quite simple to go into the back-to-back formation. Some years ago, along about the time of "Merton of the Movies," the comforting scene was done in quite a different manner: the woman sat on the chair, and the man got down on his knees and put his head in her lap. But times have changed.

In Fig. 4, we take up the character who bobbed up (and down) oftenest in last year's bad plays (she bobbed up and down in some of the better plays, too, but mostly in the bad plays); namely, the elderly lady who is a good sport, a hard drinker, and an authority on sex. There was one such lady in the forgettable "Yesterday's Reprise" (or was it "Orchids"?).

FIG 4

She could get away with half a quart of brandy between dinner time and bedtime (3 A.M.), and when she went to bed finally she took the bottle with her—"I'm going to put a nipple on this thing and go to bed," she announced as she made her exit. This type of old lady was also given to a stream of epigrams, such as: "At twenty, one is in love with love; at thirty, love is in love with one; at forty, one is in love with two; at fifty, one does not care what two are in love with one; and at sixty," etc., etc. It doesn't have to make a great deal of sense; the sophisticates in the audience always laugh, and one or two who have been through a lot applaud.

There were a lot of other trick moves, positions, and characters in last year's plays, but I have neither the time nor the inclination to remind you of all of them. In winding up the season, I might mention two postures that were very prevalent. It was customary, in the theatre of 1934–35, for juveniles to sit down backward, or wrong-side-out, in straight chairs—that is, facing the back of the chair with their arms crossed on the top of it and their chins on their arms. This position indicated nonchalance and restless energy. Of course, it has been resorted to for years (and years), but last season was the biggest season for it that I can recall; almost no man under forty-five sat down with his back to the chair back. Another popular position—for juveniles and ingénues—was sitting on the extreme edge of a davenport or chaise longue. It seems that nowadays a young couple in love never relax and lean back against anything; they must sit (and it is one of the few face-to-face postures in the modern theatre) on the very edge of whatever they are sitting on, their legs thrust backward, their bodies inclined sharply forward, their eyes sparkling, and their words coming very fast. From this position, as from the standing-sitting position (Fig. 3), it is easy to stand up, work the double-crossing maneuver, and go into the back-to-back emotional scene. Apparently young people no longer meet on their feet, face to face, and engage in the obsolete practice of putting their arms around each other. As I say, times have changed. Or maybe it's only the theatre that has changed.

The Funniest Man You Ever Saw

EVERYBODY seemed surprised that I had never met Jack Klohman.

"Judas, I didn't know there was anybody who didn't know Jack Klohman," said Mr. Potter, who was big and heavy, of body and mind. "He's funnier'n hell." Mr. Potter laughed and slapped his knee. "He's the funniest man you ever saw."

"He certainly is funny," said somebody else.

"He's marvellous," drawled a woman I didn't like. Looking around the group I discovered I didn't like any of them much, except Joe Mayer. This was undoubtedly unfair, for Joe was the only one I knew very well. The others had come over to the table where we were sitting. Somebody had mentioned Jack Klohman and everybody had begun to laugh.

"Do you know him, Joe?" I asked.

"I know him," said Joe, without laughing.

"Judas," went on Potter, "I'll never forget one night at Jap Rudolph's. Klohman was marvellous that night. This was a couple years ago, when Ed Wynn was here in a new show—let's see, what the devil was it? Not 'The Crazy Fool.'"

"'The Perfect Fool,'" said somebody else.

"Yes. But it wasn't that," said Potter. "What the dickens was it? Well, never mind; anyway there was a scene in it where——"

"Was it 'Simple Simon'?" asked the blonde girl who was with Creel.

"No. It was a couple years before that," said Potter.

"Oh, I know," said the blonde girl. "It was—now wait—it was 'The Manhatters'!"

"Ed Wynn wasn't in that," said Creel. "Wynn wasn't in that show."

"Well, it doesn't make much difference," said Potter. "Anyway, in this scene he has a line where——"

"'Manhattan Mary'!" cried Griswold.

"That's it!" said Potter, slapping his knee. "Well, in this scene he comes on with a rope, kind of a lariat——"

"Halter," said Griswold. "It was a halter."

262

"Yes, that's right," said Potter. "Anyway, he comes on with this halter——"

"Who comes on?" asked Joe Mayer. "Klohman?"

"No, no," said Potter. "Wynn comes on with the halter and walks up to the footlights and some guy asks him what he's got the rope for, what he's doing with the halter. 'Well,' says Wynn, 'I've either lost a horse or found a piece of rope——' "

"I think he said: 'I've either found a piece of rope or lost a horse,' " said Griswold. "Losing the horse coming last is funnier."

"Well, anyway," said Potter, "Jack Klohman used to elaborate on the idea and this night at Jap Rudolph's I thought we'd all pass away."

"I nearly did," said Joe Mayer.

"What did this Klohman do?" I asked finally, cutting in on the general laughter.

"Well," said Potter, "he'd go out into the kitchen, see, and come in with a Uneeda biscuit and he'd say: 'Look, I've either lost a biscuit box or found a cracker'—that's the right order, Gris—'I've either lost a biscuit box or lost'—I mean found—'a cracker.' "

"I guess you're right," said Griswold.

"It sounds right," said Joe Mayer.

"Then he'd do the same thing with everything he picked up, no matter what," said Potter. "Finally he went out of the room and was gone half an hour or so and then he comes down the stairs and holds up this faucet and says: 'I've either lost a bathtub or found a faucet.' He'd unscrewed a faucet from the bathtub and comes downstairs with this faucet—see what I mean? Laugh? I thought I'd pass away."

Everybody who had been at Jap Rudolph's that night roared with laughter.

"But that wasn't anything," said Potter. "Wait'll you hear. Along about two in the morning he slips out again, see?—all the way out of the house this time. Well, I'll be doggoned if that guy didn't come back carrying part of an honest-to-God chancel rail! He did! I'm telling you! Son-of-a-gun had actually got into a church somehow and wrenched part of this chancel rail loose and there he was standing in the door and he says: 'I've either lost a church or found a chancel rail.' It was rich. It was the richest thing I ever saw. Helen Rudolph had gone to bed, I remember—she wasn't very well—but we got her up and he did it again. It was rich."

"Sounds like a swell guy to have around," I said.

"You'd darn near pass away," said Potter.

"You really would," said Joe Mayer.

"He's got a new gag now," said one of the women. "He's got a new gag that's as funny as the dickens. He keeps taking things out of his pockets or off of a table or something and says that he's just invented them. He always takes something that's been invented for *years*, say like a lead pencil or something, and goes into this long story about how he thought it up one night. I remember he did it with about twenty different things one night at Jap's——"

"Jap Rudolph's?" I asked.

"Yes," said the woman. "He likes to drop in on them, so you can usually find him there, so we usually drop in on them too. Well, this night he took out a package of those Life Savers and handed us each one of the mints and——"

"Oh, yes, I remember that!" said Potter, slapping his knee and guffawing.

"Gave us each one of these mints," went on the woman, "and asked us what we thought of them—asked us whether we thought they'd go or not. 'It's a little thing I thought up one day,' he said. Then he'd go on with a long rigmarole about how he happened to think of the idea, and——"

"And then he'd take a pencil out of his pocket," cut in Potter, "and ask you what you thought of the eraser on the end of it. 'Just a little gadget I thought up the other night,' he'd say. Then he says he'll show you what it's for, so he makes everybody take a piece of paper and he says: 'Now everybody make some pencil marks on the paper; any kind— I won't look,' so then he goes into another room and says to let him know when you're ready. So we all make marks on the pieces of paper and somebody goes and gets him out of the other room——"

"They always go and get him out of the other room," Joe Mayer said to me.

"Sure," said Potter. "So he comes out with his sleeves rolled up, like a magician, and——"

"But the *funniest* thing he does," began the woman whom Potter had interrupted.

"And he gathers up the papers and erases the marks with the eraser and he says: 'Oh, it's just a novelty; I'm not going to try to market it.' Laugh? I thought I'd pass away. Of course you really ought to see him do it; the way he does it is a big part of it—solemn and all; he's always solemn, always acts solemn about it."

"The *funniest* thing he does," began the interrupted woman again, loudly, "is fake card tricks. He——"

"Oh, yes!" cried Potter, roaring and slapping his knee. "He does these fake card tricks. He—" Here the recollection of the funny man's antics proved too much for Potter and he laughed until he cried. It was several minutes before he could control himself. "He'll take a pack of cards," he finally began again. "He'll take a pack of cards—" Once more the image of Klohman taking a pack of cards was too much for the narrator and he went off into further gales of laughter. "He'll take this pack of cards," Potter eventually said once more, wiping his eyes, "and ask you to take any card and you take one and then he says: 'Put it anywhere in the deck' and you do and then he makes a lot of passes and so on——"

"Like a magician," said Joe Mayer.

"Yes," said Potter. "And then he draws out the wrong card, or maybe he *looks* at your card first and then goes through the whole deck till he finds it and shows it to you or——"

"Sometimes he just lays the pack down and acts as if he'd never started any trick," said Griswold.

"Does he do imitations?" I asked. Joe Mayer kicked my shins under the table.

"Does he do *imitations?*" bellowed Potter. "Wait'll I tell you——"

The Black Magic of Barney Haller

I T WAS one of those hot days on which the earth is unin-
habitable; even as early as ten o'clock in the morning, even
on the hill where I live under the dark maples. The long porch
was hot and the wicker chair I sat in complained hotly. My
coffee was beginning to wear off and with it the momentary
illusion it gives that things are Right and life is Good. There
were sultry mutterings of thunder. I had a quick feeling that
if I looked up from my book I would see Barney Haller. I
looked up, and there he was, coming along the road, lightning
playing about his shoulders, thunder following him like a dog.

Barney is (or was) my hired man. He is strong and amiable,
sweaty and dependable, slowly and heavily competent. But he
is also eerie: he trafficks with the devil. His ears twitch when
he talks, but it isn't so much that as the things he says. Once
in late June, when all of a moment sabres began to flash
brightly in the heavens and bowling balls rumbled, I took
refuge in the barn. I always have a feeling that I am going to
be struck by lightning and either riven like an old apple tree
or left with a foot that aches in rainy weather and a habit of
fainting. Those things happen. Barney came in, not to escape
the storm to which he is, or pretends to be, indifferent, but
to put the scythe away. Suddenly he said the first of those
things that made me, when I was with him, faintly creepy. He
pointed at the house. "Once I see dis boat come down de
rock," he said. It is phenomena like that of which I stand in
constant dread: boats coming down rocks, people being
teleported, statues dripping blood, old regrets and dreams in
the form of Luna moths fluttering against the windows at
midnight.

Of course I finally figured out what Barney meant—or what
I comforted myself with believing he meant: something about
a bolt coming down the lightning rod on the house; a commonplace, an utterly natural thing. I should have dismissed
it, but it had its effect on me. Here was a stolid man, smelling
of hay and leather, who talked like somebody out of Charles
Fort's books, or like a traveller back from Oz. And all the
time the lightning was zigging and zagging around him.

On this hot morning when I saw Barney coming along with his faithful storm trudging behind him, I went back frowningly to my copy of "Swann's Way." I hoped that Barney, seeing me absorbed in a book, would pass by without saying anything. I read: ". . . I myself seemed actually to have become the subject of my book: a church, a quartet, the rivalry between Francis I and Charles V . . ." I could feel Barney standing looking at me, but I didn't look at him.

"Dis morning bime by," said Barney, "I go hunt grotches in de voods."

"That's fine," I said, and turned a page and pretended to be engrossed in what I was reading. Barney walked on; he had wanted to talk some more, but he walked on. After a paragraph or two, his words began to come between me and the words in the book. "Bime by I go hunt grotches in de voods." If you are susceptible to such things, it is not difficult to visualize grotches. They fluttered into my mind: ugly little creatures, about the size of whippoorwills, only covered with blood and honey and the scrapings of church bells. Grotches . . . Who and what, I wondered, really was this thing in the form of a hired man that kept anointing me ominously, in passing, with abracadabra?

Barney didn't go toward the woods at once; he weeded the corn, he picked apple boughs up off the lawn, he knocked a yellow jacket's nest down out of a plum tree. It was raining now, but he didn't seem to notice it. He kept looking at me out of the corner of his eye, and I kept looking at him out of the corner of my eye. "Vot dime is it, blease?" he called to me finally. I put down my book and sauntered out to him. "When you go for those grotches," I said, firmly, "I'll go with you." I was sure he wouldn't want me to go. I was right; he protested that he could get the grotches himself. "I'll go with you," I said, stubbornly. We stood looking at each other. And then, abruptly, just to give *him* something to ponder over, I quoted:

> "I'm going out to clean the pasture spring;
> I'll only stop to rake the leaves away
> (And wait to watch the water clear, I may):
> I shan't be gone long.—You come too."

It wasn't, I realized, very good abracadabra, but it served: Barney looked at me in a puzzled way. "Yes," he said, vaguely.

"It's five minutes of twelve," I said, remembering he had asked.

"Den we go," he said, and we trudged through the rain over to the orchard fence and climbed that, and opened a gate and went out into the meadow that slopes up to the woods. I had a prefiguring of Barney, at some proper spot deep in the woods, prancing around like a goat, casting off his false nature, shedding his hired man's garments, dropping his Teutonic accent, repeating diabolical phrases, conjuring up grotches.

There was a great slash of lightning and a long bumping of thunder as we reached the edge of the woods.

I turned and fled. Glancing over my shoulder, I saw Barney standing and staring after me. . . .

It turned out (on the face of it) to be as simple as the boat that came down the rock. Grotches were "crotches": crotched saplings which he cut down to use as supports under the peach boughs, because in bearing time they became so heavy with fruit that there was danger of the branches snapping off. I saw Barney later, putting the crotches in place. We didn't have much to say to each other. I can see now that he was beginning to suspect me too.

About six o'clock next evening, I was alone in the house and sleeping upstairs. Barney rapped on the door of the front porch. I knew it was Barney because he called to me. I woke up slowly. It was dark for six o'clock. I heard rumblings and saw flickerings. Barney was standing at the front door with his storm at heel! I had the conviction that it wasn't storming anywhere except around my house. There couldn't, without the intervention of the devil or one of his agents, be so many lightning storms in one neighborhood.

I had been dreaming of Proust and the church at Combray and *madeleines* dipped in tea, and the rivalry between Francis I and Charles V. My head whirled and I didn't get up. Barney kept on rapping. He called out again. There was a flash, followed by a sharp splitting sound. I leaped up. This time, I thought, he is here to get me. I had a notion that he was standing at the door barefooted, with a wreath of grape leaves around his head, and a wild animal's skin slung over his shoulder. I didn't want to go down, but I did.

He was as usual, solid, amiable, dressed like a hired man. I went out on the porch and looked at the improbable storm, now on in all its fury. "This is getting pretty bad," I said, meaningly. Barney looked at the rain placidly. "Well," I said, irritably, "what's up?" Barney turned his little squinty blue eyes on me.

"We go to the garrick now and become warbs," he said.

"The hell we do!" I thought to myself, quickly. I was uneasy—I was, you might even say, terrified—but I determined not to show it. If he began to chant incantations or to make obscene signs or if he attempted to sling me over his shoulder, I resolved to plunge right out into the storm, lightning and all, and run to the nearest house. I didn't know what they would think at the nearest house when I burst in upon them, or what I would tell them. But I didn't intend to accompany this amiable-looking fiend to any garrick and become a warb. I tried to persuade myself that there was some simple explanation, that warbs would turn out to be as innocuous as boats on rocks and grotches in the woods, but the conviction gripped me (in the growling of the thunder) that here at last was the Moment when Barney Haller, or whoever he was, had chosen to get me. I walked toward the steps that lead to the lawn, and turned and faced him, grimly.

"Listen!" I barked, suddenly. "Did you know that even when it isn't brillig I can produce slithy toves? Did you happen to know that the mome rath never lived that could outgrabe me? Yeah and furthermore I can become anything I want to; even if I were a warb, I wouldn't have to keep on being one if I didn't want to. I can become a playing card at will, too; once I was the jack of clubs, only I forgot to take my glasses off and some guy recognized me. I . . ."

Barney was backing slowly away, toward the petunia box at one end of the porch. His little blue eyes were wide. He saw that I had him. "I think I go now," he said. And he walked out into the rain. The rain followed him down the road.

I have a new hired man now. Barney never came back to work for me after that day. Of course I figured out finally what he meant about the garrick and the warbs: he had simply got horribly mixed up in trying to tell me that he was going up to the garret and clear out the wasps, of which I have thousands. The new hired man is afraid of them. Barney could have scooped them up in his hands and thrown them out a window without getting stung. I am sure he trafficked with the devil. But I am sorry I let him go.

Something to Say

Hugh Kingsmill and I stimulated each other to such a pitch that after the first meeting he had a brain storm and I lay sleepless all night and in the morning was on the brink of a nervous breakdown.—*William Gerhardi's "Memoirs of a Polyglot."*

ELLIOT VEREKER was always coming into and going out of my life. He was the only man who ever continuously stimulated me to the brink of a nervous breakdown. I met him first at a party in Amawalk, New York, on the Fourth of July, 1927. He arrived about noon in an old-fashioned horse cab, accompanied by a lady in black velvet whom he introduced as "my niece, Olga Nethersole." She was, it turned out, neither his niece nor Olga Nethersole. Vereker was a writer; he was gaunt and emaciated from sitting up all night talking; he wore an admiral's hat which he had stolen from an admiral. Usually he carried with him an old Gladstone bag filled with burned-out electric-light bulbs which it was his pleasure to throw, unexpectedly, against the sides of houses and the walls of rooms. He loved the popping sound they made and the tinkling sprinkle of fine glass that followed. He had an inordinate fondness for echoes. "Halloooo!" he would bawl, wherever he was, in a terrific booming voice that could have conjured up an echo on a prairie. At the most inopportune and inappropriate moments he would snap out frank four-letter words, such as when he was talking to a little child or the sister of a vicar. He had no reverence and no solicitude. He would litter up your house, burn bedspreads and carpets with lighted cigarette stubs, and as likely as not depart with your girl and three or four of your most prized books and neckties. He was enamored of breaking phonograph records and phonographs; he liked to tear sheets and pillowcases in two; he would unscrew the doorknobs from your doors so that if you were in you couldn't get out and if you were out you couldn't get in. His was the true artistic fire, the rare gesture of genius. When I first met him, he was working on a novel entitled "Sue You Have Seen." He had worked it out, for some obscure reason, from the familiar expression "See

272

you soon." He never finished it, nor did he ever finish, or indeed get very far with, any writing, but he was nevertheless, we all felt, one of the great original minds of our generation. That he had "something to say" was obvious in everything he did.

Vereker could converse brilliantly on literary subjects: Proust, Goethe, Voltaire, Whitman. Basically he felt for them a certain respect, but sometimes, and always when he was drunk, he would belittle their powers and their achievements in strong and pungent language. Proust, I later discovered, he

had never read, but he made him seem more clear to me, and less important, than anybody else ever has. Vereker always liked to have an electric fan going while he talked and he would stick a folded newspaper into the fan so that the revolving blades scuttered against it, making a noise like the rattle of machine-gun fire. This exhilarated him and exhilarated me, too, but I suppose that it exhilarated him more than it did me. He seemed, at any rate, to get something out of it that I missed. He would raise his voice so that I could hear him above the racket. Sometimes, even then, I couldn't make out what he was saying. "What?" I would shout. "You heard me!" he would yell, his good humor disappearing in an instant.

I had, of course, not heard him at all. There was no reasoning with him, no convincing him. I can still hear the musketry of those fans in my ears. They have done, I think, something to me. But for Vereker, and his great promise, one could endure a great deal. He would talk about the interests implicated in life, the coincidence of desire and realization, the symbols behind art and reality. He was fond of quoting Santayana when he was sober.

"Santayana," he would say when he was drinking, "has weight; he's a ton of feathers." Then he would laugh roaringly; if he was at Tony's, he would flounder out into the kitchen, insulting some movie critic on the way, and repeat his line to whoever was there, and come roaring back.

Vereker had a way of flinging himself at a sofa, kicking one end out of it; or he would drop into a fragile chair like a tired bird dog and something would crack. He never seemed to notice. You would invite him to dinner, or, what happened oftener, he would drop in for dinner uninvited, and while you were shaking up a cocktail in the kitchen he would disappear. He might go upstairs to wrench the bathtub away from the wall ("Breaking lead pipe is one of the truly enchanting adventures in life," he said once), or he might simply leave for good in one of those inexplicable huffs of his which were a sign of his peculiar genius. He was likely, of course, to come back around two in the morning bringing some awful woman with him, stirring up the fire, talking all night long, knocking things off tables, singing, or counting. I have known him to lie back on a sofa, his eyes closed, and count up to as high as twenty-four thousand by ones, in a bitter, snarling voice. It was his protest against the regularization of a mechanized age. "Achievement," he used to say, "is the fool's gold of idiots." He never believed in doing anything or in having anything done, either for the benefit of mankind or for individuals. He would have written, but for his philosophical indolence, very great novels indeed. We all knew that, and we treated him with a deference for which, now that he is gone, we are sincerely glad.

Once Vereker invited me to a house which a lady had turned over to him when she went to Paris for a divorce. (She expected to marry Vereker afterward but he would not marry her, nor would he move out of her house until she took legal action. "American women," Vereker would say, "are like American colleges: they have dull, half-dead faculties.") When I arrived at the house, Vereker chose to pretend that he did not remember me. It was rather difficult to carry the situation off, for he was in one of his black moods. It was then that he should have written, but never did; instead he would gabble brilliantly about other authors. "Goethe," he would say, "was a wax figure stuffed with hay. When you say that Proust was sick, you have said everything. Shakespeare was a dolt. If there had been no Voltaire, it would not have been necessary to create one." Etc. I had been invited for the weekend and I intended to stay; none of us ever left Vereker alone when we came upon him in one of his moods. He frequently threatened suicide and six or seven times attempted it but, in every case, there was someone on hand to prevent him. Once, I remember, he got me out of bed late at night at my own apartment. "I'm going through with it this time," he said, and darted into the bathroom. He was fumbling around for some poison in the medicine chest, which fortunately contained none, when I ran in and pleaded with him. "You have so many things yet to do," I said to him. "Yes," he said, "and so many people yet to insult." He talked brilliantly all night long, and drank up a bottle of cognac that I had got to send to my father.

I had gone to the bathroom for a shower, the time he invited me to his lady's house, when he stalked into the room. "Get out of that tub, you common housebreaker," he said, "or I shall summon the police!" I laughed, of course, and went on bathing. I was rubbing myself with a towel when the police arrived—he had sent for them! Vereker would have made an excellent actor; he convinced the police that he had never seen me before in his life. I was arrested, taken away, and locked up for the night. A few days later I got a note from Vereker. "I shall never ask you to my house again," he wrote, "after the way I acted last Saturday." His repentances, while whimsical, were always as complete as the erratic charades which called them forth. He was unpredictable and, at times, difficult, but he was always stimulating. Sometimes he keyed you up to a point beyond which, you felt, you could not go.

Vereker had a close escape from death once which I shall never forget. A famous American industrialist had invited a number of American writers and some visiting English men of letters out to his Long Island place. We were to make the trip in a huge bus that had been chartered for the purpose. Vereker came along and insisted, when we reached Long Island, on driving the bus. It was an icy night and he would put on the brakes at a curve, causing the heavy vehicle to skid ponderously. Several times we surged perilously near to a ditch and once the bus snapped off a big tree like a match. I remember that H. G. Bennett was along, and Arnold Wells, the three Sitwells, and four or five Waughs. One of them finally shut off the ignition and another struck Vereker over the head with a crank. His friends were furious. When the car stopped, we carried him outside and put him down on the hard, cold ground. Marvin Deane, the critic, held Vereker's head, which was bleeding profusely, in his lap, looked up at the busload of writers, and said: "You might have killed him! And he is a greater genius than any of you!" It was superb. Then the amazing Vereker opened his eyes. "That goes for me, too," he said, and closed them again.

We hurried him to a hospital, where, in two days, he was on his feet again; he left the hospital without a word to anybody, and we all chipped in to pay the bill. Vereker had some money at the time which his mother had given him but, as he said, he needed it. "I am glad he is up and out," I said to the nurse who had taken care of him. "So am I," she said. Vereker affected everybody the same way.

Some time after this we all decided to make up a fund and send Vereker to Europe to write. His entire output, I had discovered, consisted of only twenty or thirty pages, most of them bearing the round stain of liquor glasses; one page was the beginning of a play done more or less in the style of Gertrude Stein. It seemed to me as brilliant as anything of its kind.

We got together about fifteen hundred dollars and I was delegated to approach Vereker, as tactfully as possible. We knew that it was folly for him to go on the way he was, dissipating his talent; for weeks he had been in one of his blackest moods: he would call on people, drink up their rye, wrench light-brackets off the walls, hurl scintillating gibes at his friends and at the accepted literary masters of all time, through whose superficiality Vereker saw more clearly, I think, than anybody else I have ever known. He would end up by bursting into tears. "Here, but for the gracelessness of God," he would shout, "stands the greatest writer in the history of the world!" We felt that, despite Vereker's drunken exaggeration, there was more than a grain of truth in what he said: certainly nobody else we ever met had, so utterly, the fire of genius that blazed in Vereker, if outward manifestations meant anything.

He would never try for a Guggenheim fellowship. "Guggenheim follow-sheep!" he would snarl. "Fall in line, all you little men! Don't talk to me about Good-in-time fellowships!" He would go on that way, sparklingly, for an hour, his tirade finally culminating in one of those remarkable fits of temper in which he could rip up any apartment at all, no matter whose, in less than fifteen minutes.

Vereker, much to my surprise and gratification, took the fifteen hundred dollars without making a scene. I had suspected that he might denounce us all, that he might go into one of his brilliant philippics against Money, that he might even threaten again to take his life, for it had been several months since he had attempted suicide. But no; he snarled a bit, it is true, but he accepted the money. "I'm cheap at twice the price," he said.

It was the most money Vereker had ever had in his life and of course we should have known better than to let him have it all at once. The night of the day I gave it to him he cut a wide swath in the cheaper West Side night clubs and in Harlem, spent three hundred dollars, insulted several women, and figured in fist fights with a policeman, two taxi-drivers, and two husbands, all of whom won. We instantly decided to arrange his passage on a ship that was sailing for Cherbourg three nights later. Somehow or other we kept him out of trouble until the night of the sailing, when we gave a going-away party for him at Marvin Deane's house. Everybody was there: Gene Tunney, Sir Hubert Wilkins, Count von Luckner, Edward Bernays, and the literary and artistic crowd generally. Vereker got frightfully drunk. He denounced everybody at the party and also Hugh Walpole, Joseph Conrad, Crane, Henry James, Hardy, and Meredith. He dwelt on the subject of "Jude the Obscure." "Jude the Obscure," he would shout, "Jude the Obscene, June the Obscude, Obs the June Moon." He combined with his penetrating critical evaluations and his rare creative powers a certain unique fantasy not unlike that of Lewis Carroll. I once told him so. "Not unlike your god-dam grandmother!" he screamed. He was sensitive; he hated to be praised to his face; and then of course he held the works of Carroll in a certain disesteem.

Thus the party went on. Everybody was speechless, spell-bound, listening to Elliot Vereker. You could not miss his force. He was always the one person in a room. When it got to be eleven o'clock, I felt that we had better round up Vere-ker and start for the docks, for the boat sailed at midnight. He was nowhere to be found. We were alarmed. We searched every room, looked under beds, and into closets, but he was gone. Some of us ran downstairs and out into the street, ask-ing cabdrivers and passersby if they had seen him, a gaunt, tall, wild man with his hair in his eyes. Nobody had. It was almost eleven-thirty when somebody thought to look on the roof, to which there was access by a ladder through a trap-door. Vereker was there. He lay sprawled on his face, the back of his head crushed in by a blow from some heavy instrument, probably a bottle. He was quite dead. "The world's loss," murmured Deane, as he looked down at the pitiful dust so lately the most burning genius we had ever been privileged to know, "is Hell's gain."

I think we all felt that way.

Snapshot of a Dog

I RAN ACROSS a dim photograph of him the other day, going through some old things. He's been dead twenty-five years. His name was Rex (my two brothers and I named him when we were in our early teens) and he was a bull terrier. "An American bull terrier," we used to say, proudly; none of your English bulls. He had one brindle eye that sometimes made him look like a clown and sometimes reminded you of a politician with derby hat and cigar. The rest of him was white except for a brindle saddle that always seemed to be slipping off and a brindle stocking on a hind leg. Nevertheless, there was a nobility about him. He was big and muscular and beautifully made. He never lost his dignity even when trying to accomplish the extravagant tasks my brothers and myself used to set for him. One of these was the bringing of a ten-foot wooden rail into the yard through the back gate. We would throw it out into the alley and tell him to go get it. Rex was as powerful as a wrestler, and there were not many things that he couldn't manage somehow to get hold of with his great jaws and lift or drag to wherever he wanted to put them, or wherever we wanted them put. He would catch the rail at the balance and lift it clear of the ground and trot with great confidence toward the gate. Of course, since the gate was only four feet wide or so, he couldn't bring the rail in broadside. He found that out when he got a few terrific jolts, but he wouldn't give up. He finally figured out how to do it, by dragging the rail, holding onto one end, growling. He got a great, wagging satisfaction out of his work. We used to bet kids who had never seen Rex in action that he could catch a baseball thrown as high as they could throw it. He almost never let us down. Rex could hold a baseball with ease in his mouth, in one cheek, as if it were a chew of tobacco.

He was a tremendous fighter, but he never started fights. I don't believe he liked to get into them, despite the fact that he came from a line of fighters. He never went for another dog's throat but for one of its ears (that teaches a dog a lesson), and he would get his grip, close his eyes, and hold on.

He could hold on for hours. His longest fight lasted from dusk until almost pitch-dark, one Sunday. It was fought in East Main Street in Columbus with a large, snarly nondescript that belonged to a big colored man. When Rex finally got his ear grip, the brief whirlwind of snarling turned to screeching. It was frightening to listen to and to watch. The Negro boldly picked the dogs up somehow and began swinging them around his head, and finally let them fly like a hammer in a hammer throw, but although they landed ten feet away with a great plump, Rex still held on.

The two dogs eventually worked their way to the middle of the car tracks, and after a while two or three streetcars were held up by the fight. A motorman tried to pry Rex's jaws open with a switch rod; somebody lighted a fire and made a torch of a stick and held that to Rex's tail, but he paid no attention. In the end, all the residents and storekeepers in the neighborhood were on hand, shouting this, suggesting that. Rex's joy of battle, when battle was joined, was almost tranquil. He had a kind of pleasant expression during fights, not a vicious one, his eyes closed in what would have seemed to be sleep had it not been for the turmoil of the struggle. The Oak Street Fire Department finally had to be sent for—I don't know why nobody thought of it sooner. Five or six pieces of apparatus arrived, followed by a battalion chief. A hose was attached and a powerful stream of water was turned on the dogs. Rex held on for several moments more while the torrent buffeted him about like a log in a freshet. He was a hundred yards away from where the fight started when he finally let go.

The story of that Homeric fight got all around town, and some of our relatives looked upon the incident as a blot on the family name. They insisted that we get rid of Rex, but we were very happy with him, and nobody could have made us give him up. We would have left town with him first, along any road there was to go. It would have been different, perhaps, if he had ever started fights, or looked for trouble. But he had a gentle disposition. He never bit a person in the ten strenuous years that he lived, nor ever growled at anyone except prowlers. He killed cats, that is true, but quickly and neatly and without especial malice, the way men kill certain

cheap piece that somebody had abandoned on a trash heap. Still, it was something he wanted, probably because it presented a nice problem in transportation. It tested his mettle. We first knew about his achievement when, deep in the night, we heard him trying to get the chest up onto the porch. It sounded as if two or three people were trying to tear the house down. We came downstairs and turned on the porch light. Rex was on the top step trying to pull the thing up, but it had caught somehow and he was just holding his own. I suppose he would have held his own till dawn if we hadn't helped him. The next day we carted the chest miles away and threw it out. If we had thrown it out in a nearby alley, he would have brought it home again, as a small token of his integrity in such matters. After all, he had been taught to carry heavy wooden objects about, and he was proud of his prowess.

I am glad Rex never saw a trained police dog jump. He was just an amateur jumper himself, but the most daring and tenacious I have ever seen. He would take on any fence we pointed out to him. Six feet was easy for him, and he could do eight by making a tremendous leap and hauling himself over finally by his paws, grunting and straining; but he lived and died without knowing that twelve- and sixteen-foot walls were too much for him. Frequently, after letting him try to go over one for a while, we would have to carry him home. He would never have given up trying.

There was in his world no such thing as the impossible. Even death couldn't beat him down. He died, it is true, but only, as one of his admirers said, after "straight-arming the death angel" for more than an hour. Late one afternoon he wandered home, too slowly and too uncertainly to be the Rex that had trotted briskly homeward up our avenue for ten years. I think we all knew when he came through the gate that he was dying. He had apparently taken a terrible beating, probably from the owner of some dog that he had got into a fight with. His head and body were scarred. His heavy collar with the teeth marks of many a battle on it was awry; some of the big brass studs in it were sprung loose from the leather. He licked at our hands and, staggering, fell, but got up again. We could see that he was looking for someone. One of his three masters was not home. He did not get home for an hour. During that hour the bull terrier fought against death as he had fought against the cold, strong current of Alum Creek, as he had fought to climb twelve-foot walls. When the person he was waiting for did come through the gate, whistling, ceasing to whistle, Rex walked a few wabbly paces toward him, touched his hand with his muzzle, and fell down again. This time he didn't get up.

The Evening's at Seven

H E HADN'T lighted the upper light in his office all afternoon and now he turned out the desk lamp. It was a
quarter of seven in the evening and it was dark and raining.
He could hear the rattle of taxicabs and trucks and the sound
of horns. Very far off a siren screamed its frenzied scream and
he thought: it's a little like an anguish dying with the years.
When it gets to Third Avenue, or Ninety-fifth Street, he
thought, I won't hear it any more.

I'll be home, he said to himself, as he got up slowly and
slowly put on his hat and overcoat (the overcoat was damp),
by seven o'clock, if I take a taxicab, I'll say hello, my dear,
and the two yellow lamps will be lighted and my papers will
be on my desk, and I'll say I guess I'll lie down a few minutes
before dinner, and she will say all right and ask two or three
small questions about the day and I'll answer them.

When he got outside of his office, in the street, it was dark
and raining and he lighted a cigarette. A young man went by
whistling loudly. Two girls went by talking gaily, as if it were
not raining, as if this were not a time for silence and for remembering. He called to a taxicab and it stopped and he got
in, and sat there, on the edge of the seat, and the driver finally
said where to? He gave a number he was thinking about.

She was surprised to see him and, he believed, pleased. It
was very nice to be in her apartment again. He faced her,
quickly, and it seemed to him as if he were facing somebody
in a tennis game. She would want to know (but wouldn't ask)
why he was, so suddenly, there, and he couldn't exactly say:
I gave a number to a taxi-driver and it was your number. He
couldn't say that; and besides, it wasn't that simple.

It was dark in the room and still raining outside. He lighted
a cigarette (not wanting one) and looked at her. He watched
her lovely gestures as of old and she said he looked tired and
he said he wasn't tired and he asked her what she had been
doing and she said oh, nothing much. He talked, sitting awkwardly on the edge of a chair, and she talked, lying gracefully

284

on a chaise-longue, about people they had known and hadn't cared about. He was mainly conscious of the rain outside and of the soft darkness in the room and of other rains and other darknesses. He got up and walked around the room looking at pictures but not seeing what they were, and realizing that some old familiar things gleamed darkly, and he came abruptly face to face with something he had given her, a trivial and comic thing, and it didn't seem trivial or comic now, but very large and important and embarrassing, and he turned away from it and asked after somebody else he didn't care about. Oh, she said, and this and that and so and such (words he wasn't listening to). Yes, he said, absently, I suppose so. Very much, he said (in answer to something else), very much. Oh, she said, laughing at him, not *that* much! He didn't have any idea what they were talking about.

She asked him for a cigarette and he walked over and gave her one, not touching her fingers but very conscious of her fingers. He was remembering a twilight when it had been raining and dark, and he thought of April and kissing and laughter. He noticed a clock on the mantel and it was ten after seven. She said you never used to believe in clocks. He laughed and looked at her for a time and said I have to be at the hotel by seven-thirty, or I don't get anything to eat; it's that sort of hotel. Oh, she said.

He walked to a table and picked up a figurine and set it down again with extreme care, looking out of the corner of his eye at the trivial and comic and gigantic present he had given her. He wondered if he would kiss her and when he would kiss her and if she wanted to be kissed and if she were thinking of it, but she asked him what he would have to eat tonight at his hotel. He said clam chowder. Thursday, he said, they always have clam chowder. Is that the way you know it's Thursday, she said, or is that the way you know it's clam chowder?

He picked up the figurine and put it down again, so that he could look (without her seeing him look) at the clock. It was eighteen minutes after seven and he had the mingled thoughts clocks gave him. You mustn't, she said, miss your meal. (She remembered he hated the word meal.) He turned around quickly and went over quickly and sat beside her and took hold of one of her fingers and she looked at the finger and not at him and he looked at the finger and not at her, both of them as if it were a new and rather remarkable thing.

He got up suddenly and picked up his hat and coat and as suddenly put them down again and took two rapid determined steps toward her, and her eyes seemed a little wider. A bell rang. Oh that, she said, will be Clarice. And they relaxed. He looked a question and she said: my sister; and he said oh, of course. In a minute it was Clarice like a small explosion in the dark and rainy day talking rapidly of this and that: my dear he and this awful and then of all people so nothing loth and I said and he said, if you can imagine that! He picked up his hat and coat and Clarice said hello to him and he said hello and looked at the clock and it was almost twenty-five after seven.

She went to the door with him looking lovely, and it was lovely and dark and raining outside and he laughed and she laughed and she was going to say something but he went out into the rain and waved back at her (not wanting to wave back at her) and she closed the door and was gone. He lighted a cigarette and let his hand get wet in the rain and the cigarette get wet and rain dripped from his hat. A taxicab drove up and the driver spoke to him and he said: what? and: oh, sure. And now he was going home.

He was home by seven-thirty, almost exactly, and he said good evening to old Mrs. Spencer (who had the sick husband), and good evening to old Mrs. Holmes (who had the sick Pomeranian), and he nodded and smiled and presently he was sitting at his table and the waitress spoke to him. She said: the Mrs. will be down, won't she? and he said yes, she will. And the waitress said clam chowder tonight, and consommé: you always take the clam chowder, ain't I right? No, he said, I'll have the consommé.

The Greatest Man in the World

LOOKING BACK on it now, from the vantage point of 1940, one can only marvel that it hadn't happened long before it did. The United States of America had been, ever since Kitty Hawk, blindly constructing the elaborate petard by which, sooner or later, it must be hoist. It was inevitable that some day there would come roaring out of the skies a national hero of insufficient intelligence, background, and character successfully to endure the mounting orgies of glory prepared for aviators who stayed up a long time or flew a great distance. Both Lindbergh and Byrd, fortunately for national decorum and international amity, had been gentlemen; so had our other famous aviators. They wore their laurels gracefully, withstood the awful weather of publicity, married excellent women, usually of fine family, and quietly retired to private life and the enjoyment of their varying fortunes. No untoward incidents, on a worldwide scale, marred the perfection of their conduct on the perilous heights of fame. The exception to the rule was, however, bound to occur and it did, in July, 1937, when Jack ("Pal") Smurch, erstwhile mechanic's helper in a small garage in Westfield, Iowa, flew a second-hand, single-motored Bresthaven Dragon-Fly III monoplane all the way around the world, without stopping.

Never before in the history of aviation had such a flight as Smurch's ever been dreamed of. No one had even taken seriously the weird floating auxiliary gas tanks, invention of the mad New Hampshire professor of astronomy, Dr. Charles Lewis Gresham, upon which Smurch placed full reliance. When the garage worker, a slightly built, surly, unprepossessing young man of twenty-two, appeared at Roosevelt Field early in July, 1937, slowly chewing a great quid of scrap tobacco, and announced "Nobody ain't seen no flyin' yet," the newspapers touched briefly and satirically upon his projected twenty-five-thousand-mile flight. Aëronautical and automotive experts dismissed the idea curtly, implying that it was a hoax, a publicity stunt. The rusty, battered, second-hand

287

plane wouldn't go. The Gresham auxiliary tanks wouldn't work. It was simply a cheap joke.

Smurch, however, after calling on a girl in Brooklyn who worked in the flap-folding department of a large paper-box factory, a girl whom he later described as his "sweet patootie," climbed nonchalantly into his ridiculous plane at dawn of the memorable seventh of July, 1937, spit a curve of tobacco juice into the still air, and took off, carrying with him only a gallon of bootleg gin and six pounds of salami.

When the garage boy thundered out over the ocean the papers were forced to record, in all seriousness, that a mad, unknown young man—his name was variously misspelled— had actually set out upon a preposterous attempt to span the world in a rickety, one-engined contraption, trusting to the long-distance refuelling device of a crazy schoolmaster. When, nine days later, without having stopped once, the tiny plane appeared above San Francisco Bay, headed for New York, spluttering and choking, to be sure, but still magnificently and miraculously aloft, the headlines, which long since had crowded everything else off the front page—even the shooting of the Governor of Illinois by the Vileti gang—swelled to unprecedented size, and the news stories began to run to twenty-five and thirty columns. It was noticeable, however, that the accounts of the epoch-making flight touched rather lightly upon the aviator himself. This was not because facts about the hero as a man were too meagre, but because they were too complete.

Reporters, who had been rushed out to Iowa when Smurch's plane was first sighted over the little French coast town of Serly-le-Mer, to dig up the story of the great man's life, had promptly discovered that the story of his life could not be printed. His mother, a sullen short-order cook in a shack restaurant on the edge of a tourists' camping ground near Westfield, met all inquiries as to her son with an angry "Ah, the hell with him; I hope he drowns." His father appeared to be in jail somewhere for stealing spotlights and laprobes from tourists' automobiles; his young brother, a weak-minded lad, had but recently escaped from the Preston, Iowa, Reformatory and was already wanted in several Western towns for the theft of money-order blanks from post offices. These alarming discoveries were still piling up at the very time that Pal Smurch, the greatest hero of the twentieth century, blear-eyed, dead for sleep, half-starved, was piloting his crazy junk-heap high above the region in which the lamentable story of his private life was being unearthed, headed for New York and a greater glory than any man of his time had ever known.

The necessity for printing some account in the papers of the young man's career and personality had led to a remarkable predicament. It was of course impossible to reveal the facts, for a tremendous popular feeling in favor of the young hero had sprung up, like a grass fire, when he was halfway across Europe on his flight around the globe. He was, therefore, described as a modest chap, taciturn, blond, popular with his friends, popular with girls. The only available snapshot of Smurch, taken at the wheel of a phony automobile in a cheap photo studio at an amusement park, was touched up so that the little vulgarian looked quite handsome. His twisted leer was smoothed into a pleasant smile. The truth was, in this way, kept from the youth's ecstatic compatriots; they did not dream that the Smurch family was despised and feared by its neighbors in the obscure Iowa town, nor that the hero himself, because of numerous unsavory exploits, had come to be regarded in Westfield as a nuisance and a menace. He had, the reporters discovered, once knifed the principal of his high school—not mortally, to be sure, but he had knifed him; and on another occasion, surprised in the act of stealing an altarcloth from a church, he had bashed the sacristan over the head with a pot of Easter lilies; for each of these offences he had served a sentence in the reformatory.

Inwardly, the authorities, both in New York and in Washington, prayed that an understanding Providence might, however awful such a thing seemed, bring disaster to the rusty, battered plane and its illustrious pilot, whose unheard-of flight had aroused the civilized world to hosannas of hysterical praise. The authorities were convinced that the character of the renowned aviator was such that the limelight of adulation was bound to reveal him, to all the world, as a congenital hooligan mentally and morally unequipped to cope with his own prodigious fame. "I trust," said the Secretary of State, at one of many secret Cabinet meetings called to consider the national dilemma, "I trust that his mother's prayer will be answered," by which he referred to Mrs. Emma Smurch's wish that her son might be drowned. It was, however, too late for that—Smurch had leaped the Atlantic and then the Pacific as if they were millponds. At three minutes after two o'clock on the afternoon of July 17, 1937, the garage boy brought his idiotic plane into Roosevelt Field for a perfect three-point landing.

It had, of course, been out of the question to arrange a modest little reception for the greatest flier in the history of the world. He was received at Roosevelt Field with such elaborate and pretentious ceremonies as rocked the world. Fortunately, however, the worn and spent hero promptly swooned, had to be removed bodily from his plane, and was spirited from the field without having opened his mouth once. Thus he did not jeopardize the dignity of this first reception, a reception illumined by the presence of the Secretaries of War and the Navy, Mayor Michael J. Moriarity of New York, the Premier of Canada, Governors Fanniman, Groves, McFeely, and Critchfield, and a brilliant array of European diplomats. Smurch did not, in fact, come to in time to take part in the gigantic hullabaloo arranged at City Hall for the next day. He was rushed to a secluded nursing home and confined in bed. It was nine days before he was able to get up, or to be more exact, before he was permitted to get up. Meanwhile the greatest minds in the country, in solemn assembly, had arranged a secret conference of city, state, and government officials, which Smurch was to attend for the purpose of being instructed in the ethics and behavior of heroism.

On the day that the little mechanic was finally allowed to get up and dress and, for the first time in two weeks, took a great chew of tobacco, he was permitted to receive the newspapermen—this by way of testing him out. Smurch did not wait for questions. "Youse guys," he said—and the *Times* man winced—"youse guys can tell the cock-eyed world dat I put it over on Lindbergh, see? Yeh—an' made an ass o' them two frogs." The "two frogs" was a reference to a pair of gallant French fliers who, in attempting a flight only halfway round the world, had, two weeks before, unhappily been lost at sea. The *Times* man was bold enough, at this point, to sketch out for Smurch the accepted formula for interviews in cases of this kind; he explained that there should be no arrogant statements belittling the achievements of other heroes, particularly heroes of foreign nations. "Ah, the hell with that," said Smurch. "I did it, see? I did it, an' I'm talkin' about it." And he did talk about it.

None of this extraordinary interview was, of course, printed. On the contrary, the newspapers, already under the disciplined direction of a secret directorate created for the occasion and composed of statesmen and editors, gave out to a panting and restless world that "Jacky," as he had been arbitrarily nicknamed, would consent to say only that he was very happy and that anyone could have done what he did. "My achievement has been, I fear, slightly exaggerated," the *Times* man's article had him protest, with a modest smile. These newspaper stories were kept from the hero, a restriction which did not serve to abate the rising malevolence of his temper. The situation was, indeed, extremely grave, for Pal Smurch was, as he kept insisting, "rarin' to go." He could not much longer be kept from a nation clamorous to lionize him. It was the most desperate crisis the United States of America had faced since the sinking of the *Lusitania*.

On the afternoon of the twenty-seventh of July, Smurch was spirited away to a conference-room in which were gathered mayors, governors, government officials, behaviorist psychologists, and editors. He gave them each a limp, moist paw and a brief unlovely grin. "Hah ya?" he said. When Smurch was seated, the Mayor of New York arose and, with obvious pessimism, attempted to explain what he must say and how he must act when presented to the world, ending his talk with a high tribute to the hero's courage and integrity. The Mayor was followed by Governor Fanniman of New York, who, after a touching declaration of faith, introduced Cameron Spottiswood, Second Secretary of the American Embassy in Paris, the gentleman selected to coach Smurch in the amenities of public ceremonies. Sitting in a chair, with a soiled yellow tie in his hand and his shirt open at the throat, unshaved, smoking a rolled cigarette, Jack Smurch listened with a leer on his lips. "I get ya, I get ya," he cut in, nastily. "Ya want me to ack like a softy, huh? Ya want me to ack like that —— —— baby-face Lindbergh, huh? Well, nuts to that, see?" Everyone took in his breath sharply; it was a sigh and a hiss. "Mr. Lindbergh," began a United States Senator, purple with rage, "and Mr. Byrd—" Smurch, who was paring his nails with a jackknife, cut in again. "Byrd!" he exclaimed. "Aw fa God's sake, *dat* big—" Somebody shut off his blasphemies with a sharp word. A newcomer had entered the room. Everyone stood up, except Smurch, who, still busy with his nails, did not even glance up. "Mr. Smurch," said someone, sternly, "the President of the United States!" It had been thought that the presence of the Chief Executive might have a chastening effect upon the young hero, and the former had been, thanks to the remarkable coöperation of the press, secretly brought to the obscure conference-room.

A great, painful silence fell. Smurch looked up, waved a

hand at the President. "How ya comin'?" he asked, and began rolling a fresh cigarette. The silence deepened. Someone coughed in a strained way. "Geez, it's hot, ain't it?" said Smurch. He loosened two more shirt buttons, revealing a hairy chest and the tattooed word "Sadie" enclosed in a stencilled heart. The great and important men in the room, faced by the most serious crisis in recent American history, exchanged worried frowns. Nobody seemed to know how to proceed. "Come awn, come awn," said Smurch. "Let's get the hell out of here! When do I start cuttin' in on de parties, huh? And what's they goin' to be *in* it?" He rubbed a thumb and forefinger together meaningly. "Money!" exclaimed a state senator, shocked, pale. "Yeh, money," said Pal, flipping his cigarette out of a window. "An' big money." He began rolling a fresh cigarette. "Big money," he repeated, frowning over the rice paper. He tilted back in his chair, and leered at each gentleman, separately, the leer of an animal that knows its power, the leer of a leopard loose in a bird-and-dog shop. "Aw fa God's sake, let's get some place where it's cooler," he said. "I been cooped up plenty for three weeks!"

Smurch stood up and walked over to an open window, where he stood staring down into the street, nine floors below. The faint shouting of newsboys floated up to him. He made out his name. "Hot dog!" he cried, grinning, ecstatic. He leaned out over the sill. "You tell 'em, babies!" he shouted down. "Hot diggity dog!" In the tense little knot of men standing behind him, a quick, mad impulse flared up. An unspoken word of appeal, of command, seemed to ring through the room. Yet it was deadly silent. Charles K. L. Brand, secretary to the Mayor of New York City, happened to be standing nearest Smurch; he looked inquiringly at the President of the United States. The President, pale, grim, nodded shortly. Brand, a tall, powerfully built man, once a tackle at Rutgers, stepped forward, seized the greatest man in the world by his left shoulder and the seat of his pants, and pushed him out the window.

"My God, he's fallen out the window!" cried a quick-witted editor.

"Get me out of here!" cried the President. Several men sprang to his side and he was hurriedly escorted out of a door toward a side-entrance of the building. The editor of the Associated Press took charge, being used to such things. Crisply he ordered certain men to leave, others to stay; quickly he outlined a story which all the papers were to agree on, sent two men to the street to handle that end of the tragedy, commanded a Senator to sob and two Congressmen to go to pieces nervously. In a word, he skillfully set the stage for the gigantic task that was to follow, the task of breaking to a grief-stricken world the sad story of the untimely, accidental death of its most illustrious and spectacular figure.

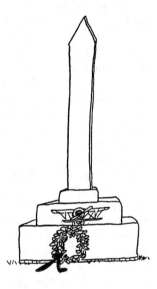

The funeral was, as you know, the most elaborate, the finest, the solemnest, and the saddest ever held in the United States of America. The monument in Arlington Cemetery, with its clean white shaft of marble and the simple device of a tiny plane carved on its base, is a place for pilgrims, in deep reverence, to visit. The nations of the world paid lofty tributes to little Jacky Smurch, America's greatest hero. At a given hour there were two minutes of silence throughout the nation. Even the inhabitants of the small, bewildered town of

Westfield, Iowa, observed this touching ceremony; agents of the Department of Justice saw to that. One of them was especially assigned to stand grimly in the doorway of a little shack restaurant on the edge of the tourists' camping ground just outside the town. There, under his stern scrutiny, Mrs. Emma Smurch bowed her head above two hamburger steaks sizzling on her grill—bowed her head and turned away, so that the Secret Service man could not see the twisted, strangely familiar, leer on her lips.

One Is a Wanderer

THE WALK up Fifth Avenue through the slush of the side-walks and the dankness of the air had tired him. The dark was coming quickly down, the dark of a February Sunday evening, and that vaguely perturbed him. He didn't want to go "home," though, and get out of it. It would be gloomy and close in his hotel room, and his soiled shirts would be piled on the floor of the closet where he had been flinging them for weeks, where he had been flinging them for months, and his papers would be disarranged on the tops of the tables and on the desk, and his pipes would be lying around, the pipes he had smoked determinedly for a while only to give them up, as he always did, to go back to cigarettes. He turned into the street leading to his hotel, walking slowly, trying to decide what to do with the night. He had had too many nights alone. Once he had enjoyed being alone. Now it was hard to be alone. He couldn't read any more, or write, at night. Books he tossed aside after nervously flipping through them; the writing he tried to do turned into spirals and circles and squares and empty faces.

I'll just stop in, he thought, and see if there are any messages; I'll see if there have been any phone calls. He hadn't been back to the hotel, after all, for—let's see—for almost five hours; just wandering around. There might be some messages. I'll just stop in, he thought, and see; and maybe I'll have one brandy. I don't want to sit there in the lobby again and drink brandy; I don't want to do that.

He didn't go through the revolving doors of the hotel, though. He went on past the hotel and over to Broadway. A man asked him for some money. A shabbily dressed woman walked by, muttering. She had what he called the New York Mouth, a grim, set mouth, a strained, querulous mouth, a mouth that told of suffering and discontent. He looked in the window of a cane-and-umbrella shop and in the window of a cheap restaurant, a window holding artificial pie and cake, a cup of cold coffee, a plate of artificial vegetables. He got into the shoving and pushing and halting and slow flowing of

Broadway. A big cop with a red face was striking his hands together and kidding with a couple of girls whom he had kept from crossing the street against a red light. A thin man in a thin overcoat watched them out of thin, emotionless eyes.

It was a momentary diversion to stand in front of the book counter in the drugstore at Forty-fifth Street and Broadway and look at the books, cheap editions of ancient favorites, movie editions of fairly recent best-sellers. He picked up some of the books and opened them and put them down again, but there was nothing he wanted to read. He walked over to the soda counter and sat down and asked for hot chocolate. It warmed him up a little and he thought about going to the movie at the Paramount; it was a movie with action and guns and airplanes, and Myrna Loy, the kind of movie that didn't bother you. He walked down to the theatre and stood there a minute, but he didn't buy a ticket. After all, he had been to one movie that day. He thought about going to the office. It would be quiet there, nobody would be there; maybe he could get some work done; maybe he could answer some of the letters he had been putting off for so long.

It was too gloomy, it was too lonely. He looked around the office for a while, sat down at his typewriter, tapped out the alphabet on a sheet of paper, took a paper-clip, straightened it, cleaned the "e" and the "o" on the typewriter, and put the cover over it. He never remembered to put the cover over the typewriter when he left in the evening. I never, as a matter of fact, remember anything, he thought. It is because I keep trying not to; I keep trying not to remember anything. It is an empty and cowardly thing, not to remember. It might lead you anywhere; no, it might stop you, it might stop you from getting anywhere. Out of remembrance comes everything; out of remembrance comes a great deal, anyway. You can't do anything if you don't let yourself remember things. He began to whistle a song because he found himself about to remember things, and he knew what things they would be, things that would bring a grimace to his mouth and to his eyes, disturbing fragments of old sentences, old scenes and gestures, hours, and rooms, and tones of voice, and the sound of a voice crying. All voices cry differently; there are no two voices in the whole world that cry alike; they're like footsteps and finger-prints and the faces of friends . . .

He became conscious of the song he was whistling. He got up from the chair in front of his covered typewriter, turned out the light, and walked out of the room to the elevator, and there he began to sing the last part of the song, waiting for the elevator. "Make my bed and light the light, for I'll be home late tonight, blackbird, bye bye." He walked over to his hotel through the slush and the damp gloom and sat down in a chair in the lobby, without taking off his overcoat. He didn't want to sit there long.

"Good evening, sir," said the waiter who looked after the guests in the lobby. "How are you?"

"I'm fine, thank you," he said. "I'm fine. I'll have a brandy, with water on the side."

He had several brandies. Nobody came into the lobby that he knew. People were gone to all kinds of places Sunday night. He hadn't looked at his letter box back of the clerk's desk when he came in, to see if there were any messages there. That was a kind of game he played, or something. He never looked for messages until after he had had a brandy. He'd look now after he had another brandy. He had another brandy and looked. "Nothing," said the clerk at the desk, looking too.

He went back to his chair in the lobby and began to think about calling up people. He thought of the Graysons. He saw the Graysons, not as they would be, sitting in their apartment, close together and warmly, but as he and Lydia had seen them in another place and another year. The four had shared a bright vacation once. He remembered various attitudes and angles and lights and colors of that vacation. There is something about four people, two couples, that like each other and get along; that have a swell time; that grow in intimacy and understanding. One's life is made up of twos, and of fours. The Graysons understood the nice little arrangements of living, the twos and fours. Two is company, four is a party, three is a crowd. One is a wanderer.

No, not the Graysons. Somebody would be there on Sunday night, some couple, some two; somebody he knew, somebody they had known. That is the way life is arranged. One arranges one's life—no, two arrange their life—in terms of

twos, and fours, and sixes. Marriage does not make two people
one, it makes two people two. It's sweeter that way, and simpler. All this, he thought, summoning the waiter, is probably
very silly and sentimental. I must look out that I don't get to
that state of tipsiness where all silly and lugubrious things
seem brilliant divinations of mine, sound and original ideas
and theories. What I must remember is that such things are
sentimental and tiresome and grow out of not working
enough and out of too much brandy. That's what I must remember. It is no good remembering that it takes four to make
a party, two to make a house.

People living alone, after all, have made a great many
things. Let's see, what have people living alone made? Not
love, of course, but a great many other things: money, for
example, and black marks on white paper. "Make this one a
double brandy," he told the waiter. Let's see, who that I *know*
has made something alone, who that I know *of* has made
something alone? Robert Browning? No, not Robert Browning. Odd, that Robert Browning would be the first person he
thought of. "And had you only heard me play one tune, or
viewed me from a window, not so soon with you would such
things fade as with the rest." He had written that line of
Browning's in a book once for Lydia, or Lydia had written it
in a book for him; or they had both written it in a book for
each other. "Not so soon with you would such things fade as
with the rest." Maybe he didn't have it exactly right; it was
hard to remember now, after so long a time. It didn't matter.
"Not so soon with you would such things fade as with the
rest." The fact is that all things do fade; with twos, and with
fours; all bright things, all attitudes and angles and lights and
colors, all growing in intimacy and understanding.

I think maybe I'll call the Bradleys, he thought, getting up
out of his chair. And don't, he said to himself, standing still
a moment, don't tell me you're not cockeyed now, because
you are cockeyed now, just as you said you wouldn't be when
you got up this morning and had orange juice and coffee and
determined to get some work done, a whole lot of work done;
just as you said you wouldn't be but you knew you would be,
all right. You knew you would be, all right.

The Bradleys, he thought, as he walked slowly around the lobby, avoiding the phone booths, glancing at the headlines of the papers on the newsstand, the Bradleys have that four-square thing, that two-square thing—that two-square thing, God damn them! Somebody described it once in a short story that he had read: an intimacy that you could feel, that you could almost take hold of, when you went into such a house, when you went into where such people were, a warming thing, a nice thing to be in, like being in warm sea water; a little embarrassing, too, yes, damned embarrassing, too. He would only take a damp blanket into that warmth. That's what I'd take into that warmth, he told himself, a damp blanket. They know it, too. Here comes old Kirk again with his damp blanket. It isn't because I'm so damned unhappy—I'm not so damned unhappy—it's because they're so damned happy, damn them. Why don't they know that? Why don't they do something about it? What right have they got to flaunt it at me, for God's sake? . . . Look here now, he told himself, you're getting too cockeyed now; you're getting into one of those states, you're getting into one of those states that Marianne keeps telling you about, one of those states when people don't like to have you around . . . Marianne, he thought. He went back to his chair, ordered another brandy, and thought about Marianne.

She doesn't know how I start my days, he thought, she only knows how I end them. She doesn't even know how I started my life. She only knows me when night gets me. If I could only be the person she wants me to be, why, then I would be fine, I would be the person she wants me to be. Like ordering a new dress from a shop, a new dress that nobody ever wore, a new dress that nobody's ever going to wear but you. I wouldn't get mad suddenly, about nothing. I wouldn't walk out of places suddenly, about nothing. I wouldn't snarl at nice people. About what she says is nothing. I wouldn't be "unbearable." Her word, "unbearable." A female word, female as a cat. Well, she's right, to. I am unbearable. "George," he said to the waiter, "I am unbearable, did you know that?" "No, sir, I did not, sir," said the waiter. "I would not call you unbearable, Mr. Kirk." "Well, you don't know, George," he said. "It just happens that I am unbearable. It just happened that way. It's a long story." "Yes, sir," said the waiter.

I could call up the Mortons, he thought. They'll have twos and fours there, too, but they're not so damned happy that they're unbearable. The Mortons are all right. Now look, the Mortons had said to him, if you and Marianne would only stop fighting and arguing and forever analyzing yourselves and forever analyzing everything, you'd be fine. You'd be fine if you got married and just shut up, just shut up and got married. That would be fine. Yes, sir, that would be fine. Everything would work out all right. You just shut up and get married, you just get married and shut up. Everybody knows that. It is practically the simplest thing in the world. . . . Well, it would be, too, if you were twenty-five maybe; it would be if you were twenty-five, and not forty.

"George," he said, when the waiter walked over for his empty glass, "I will be forty-one next November." "But that's not old, sir, and that's a long way off," said George. "No, it isn't," he said. "It's almost here. So is forty-two and forty-three and fifty, and here I am trying to be—do you know what I'm trying to be, George? I'm trying to be happy." "We all want to be happy, sir," said George. "I would like to see you happy, sir." "Oh, you will," he said. "You will, George. There's a simple trick to it. You just shut up and get married. But you see, George, I am an analyzer. I am also a rememberer. I have a pocketful of old used years. You put all those things together and they sit in a lobby getting silly and old." "I'm very sorry, sir," said George.

"And I'll have one more drink, George," he called after the waiter.

He had one more drink. When he looked up at the clock in the lobby it was only 9:30. He went up to his room and, feeling sleepy, he lay down on his bed without turning out the overhead light. When he woke up it was 12:30 by his wristwatch. He got up and washed his face and brushed his teeth and put on a clean shirt and another suit and went back down into the lobby, without looking at the disarranged papers on the tables and on the desk. He went into the dining-room and had some soup and a lamb chop and a glass of milk. There was nobody there he knew. He began to realize that he had to see somebody he knew. He paid his check and went out and got into a cab and gave the driver an address on Fifty-third Street.

There were several people in Dick and Joe's that he knew. There were Dick and Joe, for two—or, rather, for one, because he always thought of them as one; he could never tell them apart. There were Bill Vardon and Mary Wells. Bill Vardon and Mary Wells were a little drunk and gay. He didn't know them very well, but he could sit down with them. . . .

It was after three o'clock when he left the place and got into a cab. "How are you tonight, Mr. Kirk?" asked the driver. The driver's name was Willie. "I'm fine tonight, Willie," he said. "You want to go on somewheres else?" asked Willie. "Not tonight, Willie," he said. "I'm going home." "Well," said Willie, "I guess you're right there, Mr. Kirk. I guess you're right about that. These places is all right for what they are—you know what I mean—it's O.K. to kick around in 'em for a while and maybe have a few drinks with your friends, but when you come right down to it, home is the best place there is. Now, you take me, I'm hackin' for ten years, mostly up around here—because why? Because all these places know me; you know that, Mr. Kirk. I can get into 'em you might say the same way you do, Mr. Kirk—I have me a couple drinks in Dick and Joe's maybe or in Tony's or anywheres else I want to go into—hell, I've had drinks in 'em with you, Mr. Kirk—like on Christmas night, remember? But I got a home over in Brooklyn and a wife and a couple kids and, boy, I'm tellin' you that's the best place, you know what I mean?"

"You're right, Willie," he said. "You're absolutely right, there."

"You're darn tootin' I am," said Willie. "These joints is all right when a man wants a couple drinks or maybe even get a little tight with his friends, that's O.K. with me——"

"Getting tight with friends is O.K. with me, too," he said to Willie.

"But when a man gets fed up on that kind of stuff, a man wants to go home. Am I right, Mr. Kirk?"

"You're absolutely right, Willie," he said. "A man wants to go home."

"Well, here we are, Mr. Kirk. Home it is."

He got out of the cab and gave the driver a dollar and told him to keep the change and went into the lobby of the hotel. The night clerk gave him his key and then put two fingers into the recesses of the letter box. "Nothing," said the night clerk.

When he got to his room, he lay down on the bed a while and smoked a cigarette. He found himself feeling drowsy and he got up. He began to take his clothes off, feeling drowsily contented, mistily contented. He began to sing, not loudly, because the man in 711 would complain. The man in 711 was a gray-haired man, living alone . . . an analyzer . . . a re-memberer . . .

"Make my bed and light the light, for I'll be home late tonight . . ."

A Box to Hide In

I WAITED till the large woman with the awful hat took up her sack of groceries and went out, peering at the tomatoes and lettuce on her way. The clerk asked me what mine was.

"Have you got a box," I asked, "a large box? I want a box to hide in."

"You want a box?" he asked.

"I want a box to hide in," I said.

"Whatta you mean?" he said. "You mean a big box?"

I said I meant a big box, big enough to hold me.

"I haven't got any boxes," he said. "Only cartons that cans come in."

I tried several other groceries and none of them had a box big enough for me to hide in. There was nothing for it but to face life out. I didn't feel strong, and I'd had this over-powering desire to hide in a box for a long time.

"Whatta you mean you want to hide in this box?" one grocer asked me.

"It's a form of escape," I told him, "hiding in a box. It circumscribes your worries and the range of your anguish. You don't see people, either."

"How in the hell do you eat when you're in this box?" asked the grocer. "How in the hell do you get anything to eat?" I said I had never been in a box and didn't know, but that that would take care of itself.

"Well," he said, finally, "I haven't got any boxes, only some pasteboard cartons that cans come in."

It was the same every place. I gave up when it got dark and the groceries closed, and hid in my room again. I turned out the light and lay on the bed. You feel better when it gets dark. I could have hid in a closet, I suppose, but people are always opening doors. Somebody would find you in a closet. They would be startled and you'd have to tell them why you were in the closet. Nobody pays any attention to a big box lying on the floor. You could stay in it for days and nobody'd think to look in it, not even the cleaning-woman.

. . .

My cleaning-woman came the next morning and woke me up. I was still feeling bad. I asked her if she knew where I could get a large box.

"How big a box you want?" she asked.

"I want a box big enough for me to get inside of," I said. She looked at me with big, dim eyes. There's something wrong with her glands. She's awful but she has a big heart, which makes it worse. She's unbearable, her husband is sick and her children are sick and she is sick too. I got to thinking how pleasant it would be if I were in a box now, and didn't have to see her. I would be in a box right there in the room and she wouldn't know. I wondered if you have a desire to bark or laugh when someone who doesn't know walks by the

box you are in. Maybe she would have a spell with her heart, if I did that, and would die right there. The officers and the elevatorman and Mr. Gramadge would find us. "Funny dog-gone thing happened at the building last night," the doorman would say to his wife. "I let in this woman to clean up 10-F and she never come out, see? She's never there more'n an hour, but she never come out, see? So when it got to be time for me to go off duty, why I says to Crennick, who was on the elevator, I says what the hell you suppose has happened to that woman cleans 10-F? He says he didn't know; he says he never seen her after he took her up. So I spoke to Mr. Gramadge about it. 'I'm sorry to bother you, Mr. Gramadge,'

I says, 'but there's something funny about that woman cleans 10-F.' So I told him. So he said we better have a look and we all three goes up and knocks on the door and rings the bell, see, and nobody answers so he said we'd have to walk in so Crennick opened the door and we walked in and here was this woman cleans the apartment dead as a herring on the floor and the gentleman that lives there was in a box." . . .

The cleaning-woman kept looking at me. It was hard to realize she wasn't dead. "It's a form of escape," I murmured. "What say?" she asked, dully.

"You don't know of any large packing boxes, do you?" I asked.

"No, I don't," she said.

I haven't found one yet, but I still have this overpowering urge to hide in a box. Maybe it will go away, maybe I'll be all right. Maybe it will get worse. It's hard to say.

FROM

LET YOUR MIND ALONE!

AND OTHER MORE OR LESS
INSPIRATIONAL PIECES

LET YOUR MIND ALONE!

1. Pythagoras and the Ladder

IT WAS in none other than the black, memorable year 1929 that the indefatigable Professor Walter B. Pitkin rose up with the announcement that "for the first time in the career of mankind happiness is coming within the reach of millions of people." Happy living, he confidently asserted, could be attained by at least six or seven people out of every ten, but he figured that not more than one person in a thousand was actually attaining it. However, all the external conditions required for happy living were present, he said, just waiting to be used. The only obstacle was a psychological one. Figuring on a basis of 130,000,000 population in this country and reducing the Professor's estimates to round numbers, we find that in 1929 only 130,000 people were happy, but that between 78,000,000 and 91,000,000 could have been happy, leaving only 52,000,000, at the outside, doomed to discontent. The trouble with all the unhappy ones (except the 52,000,000) was that they didn't Know Themselves, they didn't understand the Science of Happiness, they had no Technique of Thinking. Professor Pitkin wrote a book on the subject; he is, in fact, always writing a book on the subject. So are a number of other people. I have devoted myself to a careful study of as many of these books as a man of my unsteady eyesight and wandering attention could be expected to encompass. And I decided to write a series of articles of my own on the subject, examining what the Success Experts have to say and offering some ideas of my own, the basic one of which is, I think, that man will be better off if he quits monkeying with his mind and just lets it alone. In this, the first of the series, I shall abandon Professor Pitkin to his percentages and his high hopes and consider the author of a best-seller published last summer (an alarming number of these books reach the best-seller list). Let us plunge right into Dr. James L. Mursell's "Streamline Your Mind" and see what he has to contribute to the New Happiness, as Professor Pitkin has called it.

In Chapter VI, which is entitled "Using What You've Got," Dr. Mursell deals with the problem of how to learn and how to make use of what you have learned. He believes, to begin with, that you should learn things by doing them, not by just reading up on them. In this connection he presents the case of a young man who wanted to find out "how to conduct a lady to a table in a restaurant." Although I have been gored by a great many dilemmas in my time, that particular problem doesn't happen to have been one of them. I must have just stumbled onto the way to conduct a lady to a table in a res-

Conducting a Lady to a Table in a Restaurant

taurant. I don't remember, as a young man, ever having given the matter much thought, but I know that I frequently worried about whether I would have enough money to pay for the dinner and still tip the waiter. Dr. Mursell does not touch on the difficult problem of how to maintain your poise as you depart from a restaurant table on which you have left no tip. I constantly find these mental authorities avoiding the larger issues in favor of something which seems comparatively trivial. The plight of the Doctor's young man, for instance, is as nothing compared to my own plight one time in a restaurant in Columbus when I looked up to find my cousin Wilmer Thurber standing beside me flecked with buttermilk and making a sound which was something between the bay of a beagle and the cry of a large bird.

I had been having lunch in the outer of two small rooms which comprised a quiet basement restaurant known as the Hole in the Wall, opposite the State House grounds, a place much frequented by elderly clerks and lady librarians, in spite of its raffish name. Wilmer, it came out, was in the other room; neither of us knew the other was there. The Hole in the Wall was perhaps the calmest restaurant I have ever known; the studious people who came there for lunch usually lunched alone; you rarely heard anybody talk. The aged proprietor of the place, because of some defect, spoke always in whispers, and this added to an effect of almost monasterial quiet. It was upon this quiet that there fell suddenly, that day, the most unearthly sound I have ever heard. My back was to the inner room and I was too disconcerted to look around. But from the astonished eyes of those who sat in front of me facing the doorway to that room I became aware that the Whatever-It-Was had entered our room and was approaching my table. It wasn't until a cold hand was laid on mine that I looked up and beheld Wilmer, who had, it came out, inhaled a draught of buttermilk as one might inhale cigarette smoke, and was choking. Having so fortunately found me, he looked at me with wide, stricken eyes and, still making that extraordinary sound, a low, canine *how-ooo* that rose to a high, bird-like *yeee-eep*, he pointed to the small of his back as who should say "Hit me!" There I was, faced with a restaurant problem which, as I have said, makes that of Dr. Mursell's young man seem very unimportant indeed. What I did finally, after an awful, frozen moment, was to get up and dash from the place, without even paying for my lunch. I sent the whispering old man a check, but I never went back to his restaurant. Many of our mental authorities, most of whom are psychologists of one school or another, will say that my dreadful experience must have implanted in me a fear of restaurants (Restauphobia). It did nothing of the sort; it simply implanted in me a wariness of Wilmer. I never went into a restaurant after that without first making sure that this inveterate buttermilk-drinker was not there.

But let us get back to Dr. Mursell and his young man's peculiar quandary. I suppose this young man must have got to worrying about who went first, the lady or himself. These things, as we know, always work out; if the young man doesn't work them out, the lady will. (If she wants him to go first, she will say, "You go first.") What I am interested in here is not the correct procedure but Dr. Mursell's advice to the young man in question. He writes, "Do not merely learn it in words. Try it over with your sister." In that second sentence he reveals, it seems to me, what these inspirationalists so frequently reveal, a lack of understanding of people; in this case, brothers and sisters. Ninety-nine brothers out of a hundred who were worrying about how to conduct a lady to a table in a restaurant would starve before they would go to their sisters and ask them how the thing is done. They would as lief go to their mothers and have a good, frank talk about sex. But let us, for the sake of the argument, try Dr. Mursell's system.

Sister, who is twenty-one, and who goes around with a number of young men whom her brother frankly regards as pussycats, is sitting by the fire one evening reading André Gide, or *Photoplay*, or something. Brother, who is eighteen, enters. "Where's Mom?" he asks. "How should I know?" she snaps. "Thought you might know that, Stupid. Y'ought to know something," he snaps back. Sister continues to read, but she is obviously annoyed by the presence of her brother; he is chewing gum, making a strange, cracking noise every fifth chew, and this gets on her nerves. "Why don't you spit out that damn gum?" she asks, finally. "Aw, nuts," says her brother, in a falsetto singsong. "Nuts to you, Baby, nuts." There is a long, tense silence; he rustles and re-rustles the evening paper. "Where's Itsy Bitsy Dicky tonight?" he asks, suddenly. "Ditch you for a live gal?" By Itsy Bitsy Dicky, he refers to one Richard Warren, a beau of his sister's, whom he considers a hollyhock. "Why don't you go to hell?" asks his sister, coldly. Brother reads the sports page and begins to whistle "Horses," a song which has annoyed his sister since she was ten and he was seven, and which he is whistling for that reason. "*Stop* that!" she screams, at last. He stops for about five seconds and then bursts out, loudly, "*Cra*-zy over *hor*-ses, *hor*-ses, *hor*-ses, she's a little wi-i-i-ld!" Here we have, I think, a typical meeting between brother and sister. Now, out of it, somehow, we have to arrive at a *tableau vivant* in which the brother asks the sister to show him how to conduct a lady to a table in a restaurant. Let us attempt to work that out. "Oh, say, Sis," the brother begins, after a long pause. "Shut up, you lout!" she says. "No, listen, I want to ask you a favor." He begins walking around the room, blushing. "I've asked Greta Dearing out to dinner tomorrow night and I'm not sure how to get her to the table. I mean whether—I mean I don't know how we both get to the table. Come on out in the hall with me and we'll pretend this room is the restaurant. You show me how to get you over to that table in the corner." The note of falsity is so apparent in this that I need not carry out the embarrassing fiction any longer. Obviously the young man is going to have to read up on the subject or, what is much simpler, just take his girl to the restaurant. This acting-out of things falls down of its own stuffiness.

There is a curious tendency on the part of the How-to-Live men to make things hard. It recurs time and again in the thought-technique books. In this same Chapter VI there is a classic example of it. Dr. Mursell recounts the remarkable experience of a professor and his family who were faced with the necessity of reroofing their country house. They decided, for some obscure reason, to do the work themselves, and they intended to order the materials from Sears, Roebuck. The first thing, of course, was to find out how much roofing material they needed. "Here," writes Dr. Mursell, "they struck a snag." They didn't, he points out, have a ladder, and since the roof was too steep to climb, they were at their wits' end as to how they were going to go about measuring it. You and I have this problem solved already: we would get a ladder. But not, it wonderfully turns out, Dr. Mursell's professor and his family. "For several days," writes Dr. Mursell, "they were completely stumped." Nobody thought of getting a ladder. It is impossible to say how they would have solved their problem had not a guest come finally to visit them. This guest noticed that the angle formed by the two sides of the roof

2. Destructive Forces in Life

THE MENTAL efficiency books go into elaborate detail about how to attain Masterful Adjustment, as one of them calls it, but it seems to me that the problems they set up, and knock down, are in the main unimaginative and pedestrian: the little fusses at the breakfast table, the routine troubles at the office, the familiar anxieties over money and health—the welter of workaday annoyances which all of us meet with and usually conquer without extravagant wear and tear. Let us examine, as a typical instance, a brief case history presented by the learned Mr. David Seabury, author of "What Makes Us Seem So Queer," "Unmasking Our Minds," "Keep Your Wits," "Growing Into Life," and "How to Worry Successfully." I select it at random. "Frank Fulsome," writes Mr. Seabury, "flung down the book with disgust and growled an insult at his wife. That little lady put her hands to her face and fled from the room. She was sure Frank must hate her to speak so cruelly. Had she known it, he was not really speaking to her at all. The occasion merely gave vent to a pent-up desire to 'punch his fool boss in the jaw.'" This is, I believe, a characteristic Seabury situation. Many of the women in his treatises remind you of nobody so much as Ben Bolt's Alice, who "wept with delight when you gave her a smile, and trembled with fear at your frown." The little ladies most of us know would, instead of putting their hands to their faces and fleeing from the room, come right back at Frank Fulsome. Frank would perhaps be lucky if he didn't get a punch in the jaw himself. In any case, the situation would be cleared up in approximately three minutes. This "had she known" business is not as common among wives today as Mr. Seabury seems to think it is. The Latent Content (as the psychologists call it) of a husband's mind is usually as clear to the wife as the Manifest Content, frequently much clearer.

I could cite a dozen major handicaps to Masterful Adjustment which the thought technicians never touch upon, a dozen situations not so easy of analysis and solution as most of theirs. I will, however, content myself with one. Let us consider the case of a man of my acquaintance who had accomplished Discipline of Mind, overcome the Will to Fail, mastered the Technique of Living—had, in a word, practically attained Masterful Adjustment—when he was called on the phone one afternoon about five o'clock by a man named Bert Scursey. The other man, whom I shall call Harry Conner, did not answer the phone, however; his wife answered it. As Scursey told me the story later, he had no intention when he dialled the Conners' apartment at the Hotel Graydon of doing more than talk with Harry. But, for some strange reason, when Louise Conner answered, Bert Scursey found himself pretending to be, and imitating the voice of, a colored

A Mentally Disciplined Husband with Mentally Undisciplined Wife

woman. This Scursey is by way of being an excellent mimic, and a colored woman is one of the best things he does.

"Hello," said Mrs. Conner. In a plaintive voice, Scursey said, "Is dis heah Miz Commah?" "Yes, this is Mrs. Conner," said Louise. "Who is speaking?" "Dis heah's Edith Rummum," said Scursey. "Ah used wuck fo yo frens was nex doah yo place a Sou Norwuck." Naturally, Mrs. Conner did not follow this, and demanded rather sharply to know who was calling and what she wanted. Scursey, his voice soft with feigned tears, finally got it over to his friend's wife that he was one Edith Rummum, a colored maid who had once worked for some friends of the Conners' in South Norwalk, where they had lived some years before. "What is it you want,

Edith?" asked Mrs. Conner, who was completely taken in by the imposter (she could not catch the name of the South Norwalk friends, but let that go). Scursey—or Edith, rather—explained in a pitiable, hesitant way that she was without work or money and that she didn't know what she was going to do; Rummum, she said, was in the jailhouse because of a cutting scrape on a roller-coaster. Now, Louise Conner happened to be a most kind-hearted person, as Scursey well knew, so she said that she could perhaps find some laundry work for Edith to do. "Yessum," said Edith. "Ah laundas." At this point, Harry Conner's voice, raised in the room behind his wife, came clearly to Scursey, saying, "Now, for God's sake, Louise, don't go giving our clothes out to somebody you never saw or heard of in your life." This interjection of Conner's was in firm keeping with a theory of logical behavior which he had got out of the Mind and Personality books. There was no Will to Weakness here, no Desire to Have His Shirts Ruined, no False Sympathy for the Colored Woman Who Has Not Organized Her Life.

But Mrs. Conner who often did not listen to Mr. Conner, in spite of his superior mental discipline, prevailed.* "Where are you now, Edith?" she asked. This disconcerted Scursey for a moment, but he finally said, "Ah's jes rounda corna, Miz Commah." "Well, you come over to the Hotel Graydon," said Mrs. Conner. "We're in Apartment 7-A on the seventh floor." "Yessm," said Edith. Mrs. Conner hung up and so did Scursey. He was now, he realized, in something of a predicament. Since he did not possess a streamlined mind, as Dr. Mursell has called it, and had definitely a Will to Confuse, he did not perceive that his little joke had gone far enough. He wanted to go on with it, which is a characteristic of woolgatherers, pranksters, wags, wish-fulfillers, and escapists generally. He enjoyed fantasy as much as reality, probably even more, which is a sure symptom of Regression, Digression, and Analogical Redintegration. What he finally did, therefore, was to call back the Conners and get Mrs. Conner on the phone again. "Jeez, Miz Commah," he said, with a hint of panic in his voice, "Ah cain' fine yo apottoman!" "Where are you,

*This sometimes happens even when the husband is mentally disciplined and the wife is not.

Edith?" she asked. "Lawd, Ah doan know," said Edith. "Ah's on *some* floah in de Hotel Graydon." "Well, listen, Edith, you took the elevator, didn't you?" "Dass whut Ah took," said Edith, uncertainly. "Well, you go back to the elevator and tell the boy you want off at the seventh floor. I'll meet you at the elevator." "Yessm," said Edith, with even more uncertainty. At this point, Conner's loud voice, speaking to his wife, was again heard by Scursey. "Where in the hell is she calling from?" demanded Conner, who had developed Logical Reasoning. "She must have wandered into somebody else's apartment if she is calling you from this building, for God's sake!" Whereupon, having no desire to explain where Edith was calling from, Scursey hung up.

After an instant of thought, or rather Disintegrated Phantasmagoria, Scursey rang the Conners again. He wanted to prevent Louise from going out to the elevator and checking up with the operator. This time, as Scursey had hoped, Harry Conner answered, having told his wife that he would handle this situation. "Hello!" shouted Conner, irritably. "Who is this?" Scursey now abandoned the rôle of Edith and assumed a sharp, fussy, masculine tone. "Mr. Conner," he said, crisply, "this is the office. I am afraid we shall have to ask you to remove this colored person from the building. She is blundering into other people's apartments, using their phones. We cannot have that sort of thing, you know, at the Graydon." The man's words and his tone infuriated Conner. "There are a lot of sort of things I'd like to see you not have at the Graydon!" he shouted. "Well, please come down to the lobby and do something about this situation," said the man, nastily. "You're damned right I'll come down!" howled Conner. He banged down the receiver.

Bert Scursey sat in a chair and gloated over the involved state of affairs which he had created. He decided to go over to the Graydon, which was just up the street from his own apartment, and see what was happening. It promised to have all the confusion which his disorderly mind so deplorably enjoyed. And it did have. He found Conner in a tremendous rage in the lobby, accusing an astonished assistant manager of having insulted him. Several persons in the lobby watched the curious scene. "But, Mr. Conner," said the assistant manager, a Mr. Bent, "I have no idea what you are talking about." "If you listen, you'll find out!" bawled Harry Conner. "In the first place, this colored woman's coming to the hotel was no idea of mine. I've never seen her in my life and I don't want to see her! I want to go to my *grave* without seeing her!" He had forgotten what the Mind and Personality books had taught him: never raise your voice in anger, always stick to the point. Naturally, Mr. Bent could only believe that his guest had gone out of his mind. He decided to humor him. "Where is this—ah—colored woman, Mr. Conner?" he asked, warily. He was somewhat pale and was fiddling with a bit of paper. A dabbler in psychology books himself, he knew that colored women are often Sex Degradation symbols, and he wondered if Conner had not fallen out of love with his wife without realizing it. (This theory, I believe, Mr. Bent has clung to ever since, although the Conners are one of the happiest couples in the country.) "I don't know where she is!" cried Conner. "She's up on some other floor phoning my wife! *You* seemed to know all about it! I had nothing to do with it! I opposed it from the start! But I want no insults from you no matter *who* opposed it!" "Certainly not, certainly not," said Mr. Bent, backing slightly away. He began to wonder what he was going to do with this maniac.

At this juncture Scursey, who had been enjoying the scene at a safe distance, approached Conner and took him by the arm. "What's the matter, old boy?" he asked. "H'lo, Bert," said Conner, sullenly. And then, his eyes narrowing, he began to examine the look on Scursey's face. Scursey is not good at dead-panning; he is only good on the phone. There was a guilty grin on his face. "You ——," said Conner, bitterly, remembering Scursey's pranks of mimicry, and he turned on his heel, walked to the elevator, and, when Scursey tried to get in too, shoved him back into the lobby. That was the end of the friendship between the Conners and Bert Scursey. It was more than that. It was the end of Harry Conner's stay at the Graydon. It was, in fact, the end of his stay in New York City. He and Louise live in Oregon now, where Conner accepted a less important position than he had held in New York because the episode of Edith had turned him against Scursey, Mr. Bent, the Graydon, and the whole metropolitan area.

Anybody can handle the Frank Fulsomes of the world, but is there anything to be done about the Bert Scurseys? Can we so streamline our minds that the antics of the Scurseys roll off them like water off a duck's back? I don't think so. I believe the authors of the inspirational books don't think so, either, but are afraid to attack the subject. I imagine they have been hoping nobody would bring it up. Hardly anybody goes through life without encountering his Bert Scursey and having his life—and his mind—accordingly modified. I have known a dozen Bert Scurseys. I have often wondered what happened to some of their victims. There was, for example, the man who rang up a waggish friend of mine by mistake, having got a wrong number. "Is this the Shu-Rite Shoestore?" the caller asked, querulously. "Shu-Rite Shoestore, good morning!" said my friend, brightly. "Well," said the other, "I just called up to say that the shoes I bought there a week ago are shoddy. They're made, by God, of cardboard. I'm going to bring them in and show you. I want satisfaction!" "And you shall have it!" said my friend. "Our shoes are, as you say, shoddy. There have been many complaints, many complaints. Our shoes, I am afraid, simply go to pieces on the foot. We shall, of course, refund your money." I know another man who was always being roused out of bed by people calling a certain railroad which had a similar phone number. "When can I get a train to Buffalo?" a sour-voiced woman demanded one morning about seven o'clock. "Not till two A.M. tomorrow, Madam," said this man. "But that's ridiculous!" cried the woman. "I know," said the man, "and we realize that. Hence we include, in the regular fare, a taxi which will call for you in plenty of time to make the train. Where do you live?" The lady, slightly mollified, told him an address in the Sixties. "We'll have a cab there at one-thirty, Madam," he said. "The driver will handle your baggage." "Now I can count on that?" she said. "Certainly, Madam," he told her. "One-thirty, sharp."

Just what changes were brought about in that woman's character by that call, I don't know. But the thing might have altered the color and direction of her life, the pattern of her mind, the whole fabric of her nature. Thus we see that a person might build up a streamlined mind, a mind awakened to a new life, a new discipline, only to have the whole works shot to pieces by so minor and unpredictable a thing as a wrong telephone number. On the other hand, the undisciplined mind would never have the fortitude to consider a trip to Buffalo at two in the morning, nor would it have the determination to seek redress from a shoestore which had sold it a faulty pair of shoes. Hence the undisciplined mind runs far less chance of having its purposes thwarted, its plans distorted, its whole scheme and system wrenched out of line. The undisciplined mind, in short, is far better adapted to the confused world in which we live today than the streamlined mind. This is, I am afraid, no place for the streamlined mind.

3. The Case for the Daydreamer

ALL THE BOOKS in my extensive library on training the mind agree that realism, as against fantasy, reverie, daydreaming, and woolgathering, is a highly important thing. "Be a realist," says Dr. James L. Mursell, whose "Streamline Your Mind" I have already discussed. "Take a definite step to turn a dream into a reality," says Mrs. Dorothea Brande, the "Wake-Up-and-Live!" woman. They allow you a certain amount of reverie and daydreaming (no woolgathering), but only when it is purposeful, only when it is going to lead to realistic action and concrete achievement. In this insistence on reality I do not see as much profit as these Shapers of Success do. I have had a great deal of satisfaction and benefit out of daydreaming which never got me anywhere in their definition of getting somewhere. I am reminded, as an example, of an incident which occurred this last summer.

I had been travelling about the country attending dog shows. I was writing a series of pieces on these shows. Not being in the habit of carrying press cards, letters of introduction, or even, in some cases, the key to my car or the tickets to a show which I am on my way to attend, I had nothing by which to identify myself. I simply paid my way in, but at a certain dog show I determined to see if the officials in charge would give me a pass. I approached a large, heavy-set man who looked somewhat like Victor McLaglen. His name was Bustard. Mr. Bustard. "You'll have to see Mr. Bustard," a ticket-taker had told me. This Mr. Bustard was apparently very busy trying to find bench space for old Miss Emily Van Winkle's Pomeranians, which she had entered at the last minute, and attending to a number of other matters. He glanced at me, saw that he outweighed me some sixty pounds, and decided to make short shrift of whatever it was I wanted. I explained I was writing an article about the show and would like a pass to get in. "Why, that's impossible!" he cried. "That's ridiculous! If I gave you a pass, I'd have to give a pass to everyone who came up and asked me for a pass!" I was pretty much overwhelmed. I couldn't, as is usual in these cases, think of anything to say except "I see." Mr. Bustard delivered a brief, snarling lecture on the subject of people who expect to get into dog shows free, unless they are showing dogs, and ended with "Are you showing dogs?" I tried to think of something sharp and well-turned. "No, I'm not showing any dogs," I said, coldly. Mr. Bustard abruptly turned his back on me and walked away.

As soon as Mr. Bustard disappeared, I began to think of things I should have said. I thought of a couple of sharp cracks on his name, the least pointed of which was Buzzard. Finely edged comebacks leaped to mind. Instead of going into the

Child Making Flat Statements about a Gentleman's Personal Appearance

dog show—or following Mr. Bustard—I wandered up and down the streets of the town, improving on my retorts. I fancied a much more successful encounter with Mr. Bustard. In this fancied encounter, I, in fact, enraged Mr. Bustard. He lunged at me, whereupon, side-stepping agilely, I led with my left and floored him with a beautiful right to the jaw. "Try that one!" I cried aloud. "Mercy!" murmured an old lady who was passing me at the moment. I began to walk more rapidly; my heart took a definite lift. Some people, in my dream, were bending over Bustard, who was out cold. "Better take him home and let the other bustards pick his bones," I said. When I got back to the dog show, I was in high fettle.

After several months I still feel, when I think of Mr. Bustard, that I got the better of him. In a triumphant daydream, it seems to me, there is felicity and not defeat. You can't just take a humiliation and dismiss it from your mind, for it will crop up in your dreams, but neither can you safely carry a dream into reality in the case of an insensitive man like Mr. Bustard who outweighs you by sixty pounds. The thing to do is to visualize a triumph over the humiliator so vividly and insistently that it becomes, in effect, an actuality. I went on with my daydreams about Mr. Bustard. All that day at the dog show I played tricks on him in my imagination, I outgeneralled him, I made him look silly, I had him on the run. I would imagine myself sitting in a living room. It was late at night. Outside it was raining heavily. The doorbell rang. I went to the door and opened it, and a man was standing there. "I wonder if you would let me use your phone?" he asked. "My car has broken down." It was, of all people, Mr. Bustard. You can imagine my jibes, my sarcasm, my repartee, my shutting the door in his face at the end. After a whole afternoon of this kind of thing, I saw Mr. Bustard on my way out of the show. I actually felt a little sorry about the tossing around I had given him. I gave him an enigmatic, triumphant smile which must have worried him a great deal. He must have wondered what I had been up to, what superior of his I had seen, what I had done to get back at him—who, after all, I was.

Now, let us figure Dr. Mursell in my place. Let us suppose that Dr. Mursell went up to Mr. Bustard and asked him for a pass to the dog show on the ground that he could streamline the dog's intuition. I fancy that Mr. Bustard also outweighs Dr. Mursell by sixty pounds and is in better fighting trim; we men who write treatises on the mind are not likely to be in as good shape as men who run dog shows. Dr. Mursell, then, is rebuffed, as I was. If he tries to get back at Mr. Bustard right there and then, he will find himself saying "I see" or "Well, I didn't know" or, at best, "I just asked you." Even the streamlined mind runs into this Blockage, as the psychologists call it. Dr. Mursell, like myself, will go away and think up better things to say, but, being a realist dedicated to carrying a dream into actuality, he will perforce have to come back and tackle Mr. Bustard again. If Mr. Bustard's patience gives out, or if he is truly stung by some crack of the Doctor's he is likely to begin shoving, or snap his fingers, or say *"'Raus!,"* or even tweak the Doctor's nose. Dr. Mursell, in that case, would get into no end of trouble. Realists are always getting into trouble. They miss the sweet, easy victories of the daydreamer.

I do not pretend that the daydream cannot be carried too far. If at this late date, for instance, I should get myself up to look as much like Mr. Bustard as possible and then, gazing into the bathroom mirror, snarl "Bustard, you dog!," that would be carrying the daydream too far. One should never run the risk of identifying oneself with the object of one's scorn. I have no idea what complexes and neuroses might lie that way. The mental experts could tell you—or, if they couldn't, they would anyway.

Now let us turn briefly to the indomitable Mrs. Brande, eight of whose precious words of advice have, the ads for her book tell us, changed the lives of 860,000 people, or maybe it is 86,000,000—Simon & Schuster published her book. (These words are "act as if it were impossible to fail," in case your life hasn't been changed.) Discussing realistic action as against the daydream, she takes up the case of a person, any person, who dreams about going to Italy but is getting nowhere. The procedure she suggests for such a person is three-fold: (1) read a current newspaper in Italian, buy some histories, phrase books, and a small grammar; (2) put aside a small coin each day; (3) do something in your spare time to make money—"if it is nothing more than to sit with children while their parents are at parties." (I have a quick picture of the parents reeling from party to party, but that is beside the point.)

I can see the newspaper and the books intensifying the dream, but I can't somehow see them getting anybody to Italy. As for putting a small coin aside each day, everybody who has tried it knows that it does not work out. At the end of three weeks you usually have $2.35 in the pig bank or the cooky jar, a dollar and a half of which you have to use for something besides Italy, such as a C.O.D. package. At that rate, all that you would have in the bank or the jar at the end of six years would be about $87.45. Within the next six years Italy will probably be at war, and even if you were well enough to travel after all that time, you couldn't get into the country. The disappointment of a dream nursed for six years, with a reality in view that did not eventuate, would be enough to embitter a person for life. As for this business of sitting with children while their parents are at parties, anybody who has done it knows that no trip to anywhere, even Utopia, would be worth it. Very few people can sit with children, especially children other than their own, more than an hour and a half without having their dispositions and even their characters badly mauled about. In fifteen minutes the average child whose parents are at a party can make enough flat statements of fact about one's personal appearance and ask enough pointed questions about one's private life to send one away feeling that there is little, if any, use in going on with anything at all, let alone a trip to Italy.

The long and hard mechanics of reality which these inspirationalists suggest are, it seems to me, far less satisfactory than the soft routine of a dream. The dreamer builds up for himself no such towering and uncertain structure of hope; he has no depleted cooky jar to shake his faith in himself. It is significant that the line "Oh, to be in England now that April's there," which is a definite dream line, is better known than any line the poet wrote about actually being in England. (I guess *that* will give the inspirationalists something to think about.) You can sit up with children if you want to, you can put a dime a day in an empty coffee tin, you can read the Fascist viewpoint in an Italian newspaper, but when it comes to a choice between the dream and the reality of present-day Italy, I personally shall sit in a corner by the fire and read "The Ring and the Book." And in the end it will probably be me who sends you a postcard from Italy, which you can put between the pages of the small grammar or the phrase book.

4. A Dozen Disciplines

Mrs. Dorothea Brande, whose theory of how to get to Italy I discussed in the preceding pages, has a chapter in her "Wake Up and Live!" which suggests twelve specific disciplines. The purpose of these disciplines, she says, is to make our minds keener and more flexible. I'll take them up in order and show why it is no use for Mrs. Brande to try to sharpen and limber up my mind, if these disciplines are all she has to offer. I quote them as they were quoted in a Simon & Schuster advertisement for the book, because the advertisement puts them more succinctly than Mrs. Brande does herself.

"1. Spend one hour a day without speaking except in answer to direct questions."

No hour of the day goes by that I am not in some minor difficulty which could easily become major if I did not shout for help. Just a few hours ago, for example, I found myself in a dilemma that has become rather familiar about my house: I had got tied up in a typewriter ribbon. The whole thing had come unwound from the spool and was wound around me. What started as an unfortunate slip of the hand slowly grew into an enormous involvement. To have gone a whole hour waiting for someone to show up and ask me a question could not conceivably have improved my mind. Two minutes of silence now and then is all right, but that is as far as I will go.

"2. Think one hour a day about one subject exclusively."

Such as what, for example? At forty-two, I have spent a great many hours thinking about all sorts of subjects, and there is not one of them that I want to go back to for a whole solid hour. I can pretty well cover as much of any subject as I want to in fifteen minutes. Sometimes in six. Furthermore, it would be impossible for me, or for Mrs. Brande, or for Simon & Schuster to think for an hour exclusively on one subject. What is known as "psychological association" would be bound to come into the thing. For instance, let us say that I decide to think for a solid hour about General Grant's horse (as good a subject as any at a time when practically all subjects

are in an unsettled state). The fact that it is General Grant's
horse would remind me of General Grant's beard and that
would remind me of Charles Evans Hughes and that would
remind me of the NRA. And so it would go. If I resolutely
went back to General Grant's horse again, I would, by association, begin thinking about General Lee's horse, which was
a much more famous horse, a horse named Traveller. I doubt
if Mrs. Brande even knows the name of General Grant's horse,
much less enough about it to keep her mind occupied for sixty
minutes. I mean sixty minutes of real constructive thinking

American Male Tied up in Typewriter Ribbon

that would get her somewhere. Sixty minutes of thinking of
any kind is bound to lead to confusion and unhappiness.

"3. Write a letter without using the first person singular."

What for? To whom? About what? All I could possibly think
of to write would be a letter to a little boy telling him how
to build a rabbit hutch, and I don't know how to build a
rabbit hutch very well. I never knew a little boy who couldn't
tell me more about building a rabbit hutch than I could tell
him. Nobody in my family was ever good at building rabbit
hutches, although a lot of us raised rabbits. I have sometimes

wondered how we managed it. I remember the time that my father offered to help me and my two brothers build a rabbit hutch out of planks and close-meshed chicken wire. Somehow or other he got inside of the cage after the wire had been put up around the sides and over the top, and he began to monkey with the stout door. I don't know exactly what happened, but he shut the door and it latched securely and he was locked in with the rabbits. The place was a shambles before he got out, because nobody was home at the time and he couldn't get his hand through the wire to unlatch the door. He had his derby on in the hutch all during his captivity and that added to his discomfiture. I remember, too, that we boys (we were not yet in our teens) didn't at first know what the word "hutch" meant, but we had got hold of a pamphlet on the subject, which my brother Herman read with great care. One sentence in the pamphlet read, "The rabbits' hutches should be cleaned thoroughly once a week." It was this admonition which caused my brother one day to get each of the astonished rabbits down in turn and wash its haunches thoroughly with soap and water.

No, I do not think that anybody can write a letter without using the first person singular. Even if it could be done, I see no reason to do it.

"4. Talk for fifteen minutes without using the first person."

No can do. No going to *try* to do, either. You can't teach an old egoist new persons.

"5. Write a letter in a placid, successful tone, sticking to facts about yourself."

Now we're getting somewhere, except that nothing is more stuffy and conceited-sounding than a "placid, successful tone." The way to write about yourself is to let yourself go. Build it up, exaggerate, make yourself out a person of importance. Fantasy is the food for the mind, not facts. Are we going to wake up and live or are we going to sit around writing factual letters in a placid, successful tone?

"6. Pause before you enter any crowded room and consider your relations with the people in it."

Now, Mrs. Brande, if I did that there would be only about one out of every thirty-two crowded rooms I approached that I would ever enter. I always shut my mind and plunge into a crowded room as if it were a cold bath. That gives me and everybody in the room a clean break, a fresh starting point. There is no good in rehashing a lot of old relations with people. The longer I paused outside a crowded room and thought about my relations with the people in it, the more inclined I would be to go back to the checkroom and get my hat and coat and go home. That's the best place for a person, anyway—home.

"7. Keep a new acquaintance talking, exclusively about himself."

And then tiptoe quietly away. He'll never notice the difference.

"8. Talk exclusively about yourself for fifteen minutes."

And see what happens.

"9. Eliminate the phrases 'I mean' and 'As a matter of fact' from your conversation."

Okie-dokie.

"10. Plan to live two hours a day according to a rigid time schedule."

Well, I usually wake up at nine in the morning and lie there till eleven, if that would do. Of course, I could *plan* to do a lot of different things over a period of two hours, but if I actually started out to accomplish them I would instantly begin to worry about whether I was going to come out on the dot in the end and I wouldn't do any of them right. It would be like waiting for the pistol shot during the last quarter of a close football game. This rule seems to me to be devised simply to make men irritable and jumpy.

"11. Set yourself twelve instructions on pieces of paper, shuffle them, and follow the one you draw. Here are a few samples: 'Go twelve hours without food.' 'Stay up all night and work.' 'Say nothing all day except in answer to questions.' "

In that going twelve hours without food, do you mean I can have drinks? Because if I can have drinks, I can do it easily. As for staying up all night and working, I know all about that: that simply turns night into day and day into night. I once got myself into such a state staying up all night that I was always having orange juice and boiled eggs at twilight and was just ready for lunch after everybody had gone to bed. I had to go away to a sanitarium to get turned around. As for saying nothing all day except in answer to questions, what am I to do if a genial colleague comes into my office and says, "I think your mother is one of the nicest people I ever met" or "I was thinking about giving you that twenty dollars you lent me"? Do I just stare at him and walk out of the room? I lose enough friends, and money, the way it is.

"12. Say 'Yes' to every reasonable request made of you in the course of one day."

All right, start making some. I can't think of a single one offhand. The word "reasonable" has taken a terrible tossing around in my life—both personal and business. If you mean watering the geraniums, I'll do that. If you mean walking around Central Park with you for the fresh air and exercise, you are crazy.

Has anybody got any more sets of specific disciplines? If anybody has, they've got to be pretty easy ones if I am going to wake up and live. It's mighty comfortable dozing here and waiting for the end.

5. How to Adjust Yourself to Your Work

I FIND that the inspirational books are frequently disposed to touch, with pontifical cheerfulness or owlish mysticism, on the problem of how to get along in the business world, how to adjust yourself to your employer and to your fellow-worker. It seems to me that in this field the trainers of the mind, both lady and gentleman, are at their unhappiest. Let us examine, in this our fourth lesson, what Mrs. Dorothea Brande, who is reputedly changing the lives of almost as many people as the Oxford Group, has to say on the subject. She presents the case of a man (she calls him "you") who is on the executive end of an enterprise and feels he should be on the planning end. "In that case," she writes, "your problem is to bring your talents to the attention of your superior officers with as little crowding and bustling as possible. Learn to write clear, short, definite memoranda and present them to your immediate superior until you are perfectly certain that he will never act upon them. In no other circumstances are you justified in going over his head." Very well, let us start from Mrs. Brande's so-called point of justification in going over your superior's head, and see what happens.

Let us suppose that you have presented your favorite memoranda to your immediate superior, Mr. Sutphen, twice and nothing has happened. You are still not perfectly certain that he will never act upon them. To be sure, he has implied, or perhaps even said in so many words, that he never will, but you think that maybe you have always caught him at the wrong moment. So you get up your memoranda a third time. Mr. Sutphen, glancing at your paper and noting that it is that same old plan for tearing out the west wall, or speeding up the out-of-town truck deliveries, or substituting colored lights for bells, is pretty well convinced that all you do in your working hours is write out memoranda. He figures that you are probably suffering from a mild form of monomania and determines to dispense with your services if you submit any memoranda again. After waiting a week and hearing nothing from Mr. Sutphen, you decide, in accordance with Mrs.

Brande's suggestion, to go over his head and take the matter up with Mr. Leffley. In doing so, you will not be stringing along with me. I advise you not to go over Mr. Sutphen's head to Mr. Leffley; I advise you to quit writing memoranda and get to work.

The Mr. Leffleys of this country have enough to do the way it is, or think they have, and they do not like to have you come to them with matters which should be taken up with the Mr. Sutphens. They are paying the Mr. Sutphens to keep you and your memoranda from suddenly bobbing up in front of them. In the first place, if you accost the Mr. Leffleys personally, you become somebody else in the organization whose name and occupation they are supposed to know. Already they know who too many people are. In the second place, the Mr. Leffleys do not like to encounter unexpected memoranda. It gives them a suspicion that there is a looseness somewhere; it destroys their confidence that things are going all right; it shakes their faith in the Mr. Sutphens—and in the Mr. Bairds, the Mr. Crowfuts, and the old Miss Bendleys who are supposed to see that every memorandum has been filed away, or is being acted on. I know of one young man who was always sending to his particular Mr. Leffley, over Mr. Sutphen's head, memoranda done up in limp-leather covers and tied with ribbon, this to show that he was not only clear, short, and definite, but neat. Mr. Leffley did not even glance between the leather covers; he simply told Miss Bendley to turn the thing over to Mr. Sutphen, who had already seen it. The young man was let go and is now a process-server. Keep, I say, your clear, short, and definite memoranda to yourself. If Mr. Sutphen has said no, he means no. If he has taken no action, no action is going to be taken. People who are all the time submitting memoranda are put down as jealous, disgruntled, and vaguely dangerous. Employers do not want them around. Sooner or later Mr. Sutphen, or Mr. Leffley himself, sees to it that a printed slip, clear, short, and definite, is put in their pay envelopes.

My own experience, and the experience of many of my friends, in dealing with superiors has covered a wide range of crucial situations of which these success writers appear to be oblivious and for which they therefore have no recommended course of action (which is probably just as well). I am reminded of the case of Mr. Russell Soames, a friend of mine, who worked for a man whom we shall call Mr. B. J. Winfall. This Winfall, some five or six years ago, in the days when Capone was at large and wholesale shootings were common in Chicago, called Soames into his office and said, "Soames, I'm going out to Chicago on that Weltmer deal and I want you to go along with me." "All right, Mr. Winfall," said Soames. They went to Chicago and had been there only four or five hours when they were calling each other Russell and B. J. and fighting for the check at the bar. On the third day, B. J. called Russell into his bedroom (B. J. had not left his bedroom in thirty-six hours) and said, "Russell, before we go back to New York, I want to see a dive, a hideout, a joint. I want to see these gangsters in their haunts. I want to see them in action, by God, if they ever get into action. I think most of it is newspaper talk. Your average gangster is a yellow cur." B. J. poured himself another drink from a bottle on his bedside table and repeated, "A yellow cur." Drink, as you see, made B. J. pugnacious (he had already gone through his amorous phase). Russell Soames tried to argue his chief out of this perilous plan, but failed. When Russell would not contact the right parties to arrange for B. J.'s little expedition, B. J. contacted them himself, and finally got hold of a man who knew a man who could get them into a regular hangout of gorillas and finger men.

Along about midnight of the fourth day in Chicago, B. J. Winfall was ready to set out for the dive. He wore a cap, which covered his bald spot, and he had somehow got hold of a cheap, ill-fitting suit, an ensemble which he was pleased to believe gave him the effect of a hardboiled fellow; as a matter of fact, his nose glasses, his pink jowls, and his paunch betrayed him instantly for what he was, a sedentary businessman. Soames strove to dissuade his boss, even in the taxi on their way to the tough spot, but Winfall pooh-poohed him. "Pooh pooh, Russell," he snarled out of the corner of his mouth, unfamiliarly. "These kind of men are rats." He had brought a flask with him and drank copiously from it. "Rats," he said, "of the first order. The first order, Russell, my boy." Soames kept repeating that he felt B. J. was underrating the dangerousness of the Chicago gangster and begged him to be on his good behavior when they got to the joint, if only for the sake of B. J.'s wife and children and his (Russell's) old mother. He exacted a reluctant promise that B. J. would behave himself, but he was by no means easy in his mind when their taxi finally stopped in front of a low, dark building in a far, dark street. "Leave it to me, Russell, my boy," said B. J. as they got out of the cab. "Leave it to me." Their driver refused to wait, and Russell, who paid him off, was just in time to restrain his employer from beating on the door of the place with both fists. Russell himself knocked, timidly. A thin Italian with deadly eyes opened the door a few inches, Russell mentioned a name, falteringly, and the man admitted them.

As Russell described it to me later, it was a dingy, smoky place with a rough bar across the back attended by a liver-faced barman with a dirty rag thrown over one shoulder, and only one eye. Leaning on the bar and sitting at tables were a lot of small tough-faced men. They all looked up sullenly when Russell and B. J. walked in. Russell felt that there was a movement of hands in pockets. Smiling amiably, blinking nervously, Russell took his companion's arm, but the latter broke away, strode to the bar, and shouted for whiskey. The bartender fixed his one eye on B. J. with the glowering, steady gaze Jack Dempsey used to give his opponents in the ring. He took his time slamming glasses and a bottle down on the bar. B. J. filled a glass, tossed it off, turned heavily, and faced the roomful of men. "I'm Two-Gun Winfall from New York City!" he shouted. "Anybody *want* anything?"

By the most cringing, obsequious explanations and apologies, Russell Soames managed to get himself and his boss out of the place alive. The secret of accomplishing such a feat as he accomplished that night is not to be found in any of the inspirational books. Not a single one of their impressive bits of advice would get you anywhere. Take Mrs. Brande's now famous italicized exhortation, *"Act as if it were impossible to fail."* Wasn't B. J. Winfall doing exactly that? And was that any way to act in this particular situation? It was not. It was Russell Soames' craven apologies, his abject humility, his (as he told me later) tearful admission that he and B. J. were just drunken bums with broken hearts, that got them out of there imagination." Here again I cannot hold with the dear lady. The nature of imagination, as she describes it, would merely terrify the average man. The idea of bringing such a distorted viewpoint of himself into his relation with his fellow-workers would twist his personality laboriously out of shape and, in the end, appall his fellow-workers. Men who catch an unfamiliar view of a room from the top of a stepladder are neither amused nor enlightened; they have a quick, gasping moment of vertigo which turns rapidly into plain terror. No man likes to see a familiar thing at an unfamiliar angle, or in an unfamiliar light, and this goes, above all things, for his own face. The glimpses that men get of themselves in mirrors set at angles to each other upset them for days. Frequently they shave in the dark for weeks thereafter. To ask a man to steadily contemplate this thing he has seen fleetingly in a mirror and to figure it as dealing with his fellow-workers day by day is to ask him to abandon his own character and to step into another, which he both disowns and dislikes. Split personality could easily result, leading to at least fifteen of the thirty-three "varieties of obliquity" which Mr. David Seabury lists in his "How to Worry Successfully," among them Cursory Enumeration, Distortion of Focus, Nervous Hesitation (superinduced by Ambivalence), Pseudo-Practicality, Divergency, Retardation, Emotionalized Compilation, Negative Dramatization, Rigidism, Secondary Adaptation, False Externalization, Non-Validation, Closure, and Circular Brooding.

I don't know why I am reminded at this point of my Aunt Kate Obetz, but I am. She was a woman without any imaginative la-di-da, without any working code save that of direct action, who ran a large dairy farm near Sugar Grove, Ohio, after her husband's death, and ran it successfully. One day something went wrong with the cream separator, and one of her hands came to her and said nobody on the farm could fix it. Should they send to town for a man? "No!" shouted my Aunt Kate. "I'll fix it myself!" Shouldering her way past a number of dairy workers, farm hands and members of her family, she grasped the cream separator and began monkeying with it. In a short time she had reduced it to even more pieces than it had been in when she took hold of it. She couldn't fix it. She was just making things worse. At length, she turned

6. Anodynes for Anxieties

I SHOULD like to begin this lesson with a quotation from Mr. David Seabury's "How to Worry Successfully." When things get really tough for me, I always turn to this selection and read it through twice, the second time backward, and while it doesn't make me feel fine, exactly, it makes me feel better. Here it is:

"If you are indulging in gloomy fears which follow each other round and round until the brain reels, there are two possible procedures:

"First, quit circling. It doesn't matter where you cease whirling, as long as you stop.

"Second, if you cannot find a constant, think of something as different from the fact at which you stopped as you possibly can. Imagine what would happen if you mixed that contrast into your situation. If nothing results to clarify your worry, try another set of opposites and continue the process until you do get a helpful answer. If you persist, you will soon solve any ordinary problem."

I first read this remarkable piece of advice two months ago and I vaguely realized then that in it, somewhere, was a strangely familiar formula, not, to be sure, a formula that would ever help me solve anything, but a formula for something or other. And one day I hit on it. It is the formula by which the Marx brothers construct their dialogue. Let us take their justly famous scene in which Groucho says to Chico, "It is my belief that the missing picture is hidden in the house next door." Here Groucho has ceased whirling, or circling, and has stopped at a fact, that fact being his belief that the picture is hidden in the house next door. Now Chico, in accordance with Mr. Seabury's instructions, thinks of something as different from that fact as he possibly can. He says, "There isn't any house next door." Thereupon Groucho "mixes that contrast into his situation." He says, "Then we'll build one!" Mr. Seabury says, "If you persist you will soon solve any ordinary problem." He underestimates the power of his formula. If you persist, you will soon solve anything at all, no matter how impossible. That way, of course, lies madness, but I would be the last person to say that madness is not a solution.

It will come as no surprise to you, I am sure, that throughout the Mentality Books with which we have been concerned there runs a thin, wavy line of this particular kind of Marxist philosophy. Mr. Seabury's works are heavily threaded with it, but before we continue with him, let us turn for a moment to dear Dorothea Brande, whose "Wake Up and Live!" has changed the lives of God knows how many people by this time. Writes Mrs. Brande, "One of the most famous men in America constantly sends himself postcards, and occasionally

The Filing-card System

notes. He explained the card sending as being his way of relieving his memory of unnecessary details. In his pocket he carries a few postals addressed to his office. I was with him one threatening day when he looked out the restaurant window, drew a card from his pocket, and wrote on it. Then he threw it across the table to me with a grin. It was addressed to himself at his office, and said. 'Put your raincoat with your hat.' At the office he had other cards addressed to himself at home."

We have here a muzziness of thought so enormous that it is difficult to analyze. First of all, however, the ordinary mind is struck by the obvious fact that the famous American in question has, to relieve his memory of unnecessary details, burdened that memory with the details of having to have postcards at his office, in his pockets, and at his home all the time. If it isn't harder to remember always to take self-addressed postcards with you wherever you go than to remember to put your raincoat with your hat when the weather looks threatening, then you and I will eat the postcards or even the raincoat. Threatening weather itself is a natural sharp reminder of one's raincoat, but what is there to remind one that one is running out of postcards? And supposing the famous man does run out of postcards, what does he do—hunt up a Western Union and send himself a telegram? You can see how monstrously wrapped up in the coils of his own little memory system this notable American must soon find himself. There is something about this system of buying postcards, addressing them to oneself, writing messages on them, and then mailing them that is not unlike one of those elaborate Rube Goldberg contraptions taking up a whole room and involving bicycles, shotguns, parrots, and little colored boys, all set up for the purpose of eliminating the bother of, let us say, setting an alarm clock. Somehow, I can just see Mrs. Brande's famous man at his desk. On it there are two phones, one in the Bryant exchange, the other in the Vanderbilt exchange. When he wants to remind himself of something frightfully urgent, he picks up the Bryant phone and calls the Vanderbilt number, and when that phone rings, he picks it up and says hello and then carries on a conversation with himself. "Remember tomorrow is wifey's birthday!" he shouts over one phone. "O.K.!" he bawls back into the other. This, it seems to me, is a fair enough extension of the activities of our famous gentleman. There is no doubt, either, but that the two-phone system would make the date stick more sharply in his mind than if he just wrote it down on a memo pad. But to intimate that all this shows a rational disciplining of the mind, a development of the power of the human intellect, an approach to the Masterful Adjustment of which our Success Writers are so enamored, is to intimate that when Groucho gets the house built next door, the missing picture will be found in it.

When it comes to anxieties and worries, Mr. Seabury's elaborate systems for their relief or solution make the device of

Mrs. Brande's famous American look childishly simple. Mr. Seabury knows, and apparently approves of, a man "who assists himself by fancied interviews with wise advisers. If he is in money difficulties, he has mental conversations with a banker; when business problems press, he seeks the aid of a great industrialist and talks his problems over with this ghostly friend until he comes to a definite conclusion." Here, unless I am greatly mistaken, we have wish fulfillment, fantasy, reverie, and woolgathering at their most perilous. This kind of goings-on with a ghostly banker or industrialist is an escape mechanism calculated to take a man so far from reality he might never get back. I tried it out myself one night just before Christmas when I had got down to $60 in the bank and hadn't bought half my presents yet. I went to bed early that night and had Mr. J. P. Morgan call on me. I didn't have to go to his office; he heard I was in some difficulty and called on me, dropping everything else. He came right into my bedroom and sat on the edge of the bed. "Well, well, well," he said, "what's this I hear about you being down?" "I'm not so good, J. P.," I said, smiling wanly. "We'll have the roses back in those cheeks in no time," he said. "I'm not really sick," I told him. "I just need money." "Well, well, well," he exclaimed, heartily, "is *that* all we need?" "Yes, sir," I said. He took out a checkbook. "How'd a hundred thousand dollars do?" he asked, jovially. "That would be all right," I said. "Could you give it to me in cash, though—in tens and twenties?" "Why, certainly, my boy, certainly," said Mr. Morgan, and he gave me the money in tens and twenties. "Thank you very much, J. P.," I said. "Not at all, Jim, not at all!" cried my ghostly friend. "What's going on in there?" shouted my wife, who was in the next room. It seems that I had got to talking out loud, first in my own voice and then louder, and with more authority, in Mr. Morgan's. "Nothing, darling," I answered. "Well, cut it out," she said. The depression that settled over me when I realized that I was just where I had been when I started to talk with Mr. Morgan was frightful. I haven't got completely over it yet.

This mental-conversation business is nothing, however, compared to what Mr. Seabury calls "picture-puzzle making in worry." To employ this aid in successful thinking, you have to have fifty or sixty filing cards, or blank cards of some kind or other. To show you how it works, let us follow the case history of one Frank Fordson as Mr. Seabury relates it. It seems that this Fordson, out of work, is walking the streets. "He enters store after store with discouraged, pessimistic proprietors. There are poor show windows and dusty sidewalks. They make Frank morbid. His mind feels heavy. He wishes he could happen on a bright idea." He does, as you shall see. Frank consults a psychologist. This psychologist tells him to take fifty filing cards and write on each of them a fact connected with his being out of work. So he writes on one "out of work" and on another "dusty sidewalks" and on another "poor show windows," etc. You and I would not be able to write down more than fifteen things like that before getting off onto something else, like "I hate Joe Grubig" or "Now is the time for all good men," but Frank can do fifty in his stride, all about how tough things are. This would so depress the ordinary mind that it would go home to bed, but not Frank. Frank puts all of the fifty cards on the floor of the psychologist's office and begins to couple them up at random, finally bringing into accidental juxtaposition the one saying "out of work" and one saying "dull sign." Well, out of this haphazard arrangement of the cards, Frank, Mr. Seabury says, got an idea. He went to a hardware store the next day and offered to shine the store's dull sign if the proprietor would give him a can of polish and let him keep what was left. Then he went around shining other signs, for money, and made $3 that day. Ten days later he got a job as a window-dresser and, before the year was out, a "position in advertising."

"Take one of your own anxieties," writes Mr. Seabury. "Analyze it so as to recall all the factors. Write three score of these on separate cards. Move the cards about on the floor into as many different relations as possible. Study each combination." Mr. Seabury may not know it, but the possible different relations of sixty cards would run into the millions. If a man actually studied each of these combinations, it would at least keep him off the streets and out of trouble—and also out of the advertising business, which would be something, after all. Toy soldiers, however, are more fun.

Now, if this kind of playing with filing cards doesn't strike your fancy, there is the "Worry Play." Let me quote Mr. Seabury again. "You should write out a description of your worry," he says, "divide it into three acts and nine scenes, as if it were a play, and imagine it on the stage, or in the movies, with various endings. Look at it as impersonally as you would look at a comedy and you might be surprised at the detachment you would gain." I have tried very hard to do this. I try out all these suggestions. They have taken up most of my time and energy for the past six months and got me into such a state that my doctor says I can do only three more of these articles at the outside before I go to a sanitarium. A few years ago I had an old anxiety and I was reminded of it by this "Worry Play" idea. Although this old anxiety has been dead and gone for a long time, it kept popping up in my mind because, of all the worries I ever had, it seemed to lend itself best to the drama. I tried not to think about it, but there it was, and I finally realized I would have to write it out and imagine it on the stage before I could dismiss it from my consciousness and get back to work. Well, it ran almost as long as "Mourning Becomes Electra" and took me a little over three weeks to dramatize. Then, when I thought I was rid of it, I dreamed one night I had sold the movie rights, and so I had to adapt it to the movies (a Mr. Sam Maschino, a movie agent, kept bobbing up in my dreams, hectoring me). This took another two weeks. I could not, however, attain this detachment that Mr. Seabury talks about. Since the old anxiety was my own anxiety, I was the main character in it. Sometimes, for as many as fifteen pages of the play script and the movie continuity, I was the only person on the set. I visualized myself in the main rôle, naturally—having rejected Leslie Howard, John Gielgud, and Lionel Barrymore for one reason or another. I was lousy in the part, too, and that worried me. Hence I advise you not to write out your worries in the form of a play. It is simpler to write them out on sixty pieces of paper and juggle them around. Or talk about them to J. P. Morgan. Or send postcards to yourself about them. There are a number of solutions for anxieties which I believe are better than any of these, however: go out and skate, or take in a basketball game, or call on a girl. Or burn up a lot of books.

7. The Conscious vs. The Unconscious

It is high time that we were getting around to a consideration of the magnum opus of Louis E. Bisch, M.D., Ph.D., formerly Professor of Neuropsychiatry at the New York Polyclinic Medical School and Hospital, and Associate in Educational Psychology at Columbia University, and the author of "Be Glad You're Neurotic." Some of the reassuring chapter titles of his popular treatise are "I'm a Neurotic Myself and Delighted," "You Hate Yourself. No Wonder!," "No, You're Not Going Insane Nor Will Any of Your Fears Come True," "Are Your Glands on Friendly Terms?," and "Of Course Your Sex Life Is Far from Satisfactory." Some of you will be satisfied with just these titles and will not go on to the book itself, on the ground that you have a pretty good idea of it already. I should like, however, to have you turn with me to Chapter VII, one of my favorite chapters in all psychomentology, "Your Errors and Compulsions Are Calls for Help."

The point of this chapter, briefly, is that the unconscious mind often opposes what the conscious mind wants to do or say, and frequently trips it up with all kinds of evasions, deceits, gags, and kicks in the pants. Our popular psychiatrists try to make these mysteries clear to the layman by the use of simple, homely language, and I am trying to do the same. Dr. Bisch relates a lot of conflicts and struggles that take place between the Hercules of the Conscious and the Augean Stables of the Unconscious (that is my own colorful, if somewhat labored, metaphor and I don't want to see any of the other boys swiping it). "I myself," writes Dr. Bisch, "forgot the number of a hospital where I was to deliver a lecture when I was about to apologize for my delay. I had talked to that particular hospital perhaps a hundred times before. This was the first time, however, that I was consciously trying to do what unconsciously I did not want to do." If you want unconsciously as well as consciously to call a hospital one hundred times out of one hundred and one, I say your conscious and unconscious are on pretty friendly terms. I say you are doing fine. This little experience of Dr. Bisch's is merely to give you a general idea of the nature of the chapter and to ease you into the discussion gently. There are many more interesting examples of conflict and error, of compulsion and obsession, to come. "A colleague," goes on Dr. Bisch, "told me that when he decided to telephone his wife to say he could not be home for dinner he dialled three wrong numbers before he got his own. 'It's because she always flares up when I'm detained at the office,' he explained." This shows that psychiatrists are just as scared of their wives as anybody else. Of course, I believe that this particular psychiatrist dialled the

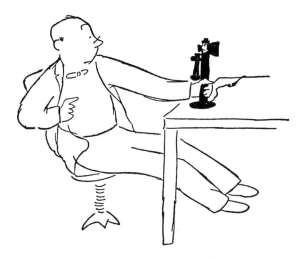

Psychiatrist about to Phone His Wife

three wrong numbers on purpose. In the case of all husbands, both neurotic and normal, this is known as sparring for time and has no real psychological significance.

I almost never, I find in going slowly and carefully through Dr. Bisch's chapter, taking case histories in their order, agree with him. He writes, "The appearance of persons whom one dislikes or is jealous of, who have offended in some way or whom one fears, tend to be blotted from the mind." Well, some twelve years ago I knew, disliked, was jealous of, feared, and had been offended by a man whom I shall call Philip

Vause. His appearance has not only not been blotted from my mind, it hasn't even tended to be. I can call it up as perfectly as if I were holding a photograph of the man in my hand. In nightmares I still dream of Philip Vause. When, in these dreams, I get on subways, he is the guard; when I fly through the air, the eagle that races with me has his face; when I climb the Eiffel Tower, there he is at the top, his black hair roached back, the mole on the left cheek, the thin-lipped smile, and all. Dr. Bisch goes on to say that "the more disagreeable an incident, the deeper is it finally repressed." To which he adds, "The recollection of the pain attending child-birth never lingers long." He has me there.

Dr. Bisch proceeds from that into this: "A man who mislays his hat either dislikes it, wants a new one, experienced unpleasantness when last he wore it, or he does not want to go out. And what you lose you may be sure you do not value, even if it be your wedding ring. Psychologists claim that we lose things because we want to be rid of them or the association they carry, but that we are unwilling to admit the fact to ourselves and actually throw the thing away." This shows you pretty clearly, I think, the point psychologists have reached. I call it mysticism, but I am a polite fellow; you can call it anything you want to. Under any name, it isn't getting us anywhere. Every husband whose tearful wife has lost her wedding ring will now begin to brood, believing (if he strings along with the psychologists instead of with me) that the little darling threw it away, because she is really in love with Philip Vause, and that her tears over her loss are as phony as the plight of a panhandler's family. Let us leave all the sad young couples on the point of separating and go on to Dr. Bisch's analysis of a certain man.

"A certain man," writes Dr. Bisch, "forgot to wind the alarm on several occasions, in consequence of which he was late for work. He also forgot his keys on two occasions and had to wake up his wife in the early hours of the morning. Twice he forgot the furnace at night with the result that there was no heat the next day. In this case the unconscious was trying to tell him that he did not like living in the country although consciously he maintained that he did, for the good of the children." There are, from the standpoint of my own school of psychology, so many fallacies in this piece of analysis that I hardly know where to begin. But let us begin at the beginning, with the failure to wind the alarm clock. Now, a man who does not want to stay home winds the clock so that it will wake him and he can get the hell out and go to the office. There is surely nothing sounder than this. Hence the failure to wind the alarm clock shows that his unconscious was trying to tell him that he did not want to go to the office any more but wanted to stay at his house in the country all the time. The key-forgetting business I simply do not believe. A man who has had to rout out his wife once in the early hours of the morning is not going to forget his key a second time. This is known as Thurber's Empirical Law No. 1. If Dr. Bisch had lived in the country as long and as happily as I have, he would know this simple and unmystical fact: any man can forget to fix the clock and the furnace; especially the furnace, because the clock is usually right where it can be seen, whereas the furnace isn't. Some husbands "forget" to bank the furnace because they have kept hearing funny noises in the cellar all evening and are simply scared to go down there. Hundreds of simple little conscious motives enter into life, Dr. Bisch, hundreds of them.

"A woman," goes on Dr. Bisch, "who wished to consult an attorney about a divorce wrote to him: 'I have been married 22 years.' But the second 2 had evidently been added afterward, indicating that probably she was embarrassed to admit not being able to make a go of it after living with the man so long." How's that again, Doctor? I may be dumb, but I don't exactly catch all that. Couldn't the woman have really been married only 2 years, and couldn't she have added the second 2 indicating that probably she was embarrassed to admit that she was giving up trying to make a go of it after living with the man so *short* a time? Maybe we better just drop this one.

"A woman," continues Dr. Bisch (this is another woman), "who was talking to me about an intended trip to the lakes of northern Italy said: 'I don't wish to visit Lavonia Bay.' She, herself, was surprised, as no such place exists. Inasmuch as the trip was to be a honeymoon, it was 'love, honor, and obey' that really was bothering her." I take off my hat to the Doctor's astonishing powers of divination here, because I never would have figured it out. Now that he has given me the key, I get it, of course. "Love, honor, and obey," love-honor-obey, Lavonia Bay. I wonder if he knows the one about the woman who asked the librarian for a copy of "In a Garden." What she really wanted was "Enoch Arden." I like Lavonia Bay better, though, because it is psycho-neurotic, whereas there was nothing the matter with the other poor woman; she just thought that the name of the book was "In a Garden." Dr. Bisch might very likely see something more in this, but the way I've always heard it was that she just thought the name was "In a Garden."

"When a usually efficient secretary," writes Dr. Bisch, "makes errors in typing or shorthand, the excuse of fatigue or indisposition should be taken with a grain of salt. Resentment may have developed toward the employer or the work, or something may unconsciously be bothering her. Some years ago my own secretary often hit the *t* key by mistake. I discovered a young man by the name of Thomas was courting her." That doesn't explain the mistakes of a secretary I had five or six years ago. I had never had a secretary before, and had, indeed, never dictated a letter up to that time. We got some strange results. One of these, in a letter to a man I hoped I would never hear from again, was this sentence: "I feel that the cuneo has, at any rate, garbled the deig." This was not owing to fatigue or indisposition, or to resentment, although there *was* a certain resentment—or even to a young man named Cuneo or Deig. It was simply owing to the fact that my secretary, an Eastern girl, could only understand part of what I, a Middle-Westerner, was saying. In those days, I talked even more than I do now as if I had steel wool in my mouth, and the young lady just did not "get" me. Being afraid to keep asking me what I was trying to say, she simply put down what it sounded like. I signed this particular letter, by the way, just as she wrote it, and I never heard again from the man I sent it to, which is what I had hoped would happen. Psychiatrists would contend that I talked unintelligibly because of that very hope, but this is because they don't know that in Ohio, to give just one example, the word "officials" is pronounced "fishuls," no matter what anybody hopes.

We now go on to the case of a gentleman who deviated from the normal, or uninteresting. "In dressing for a formal dinner," says Dr. Bisch, "a man put on a bright red bow tie. His enthusiasm was self-evident." That is all our psychiatrist says about this one, and I think he is letting it go much too easily; I sense a definite drop here. If I were to say to you that in dressing for a formal dinner last night I put on a bright red bow tie and you were to say merely, "Your enthusiasm was self-evident," I would give you a nasty look and go on to somebody else who would get a laugh out of it, or at least ask what the hell was the idea. For the purpose of analysis in this particular case, I think you would have to know who the man was, anyway. If it was Ernest Boyd, that's one thing; if it was Jack Dempsey, that's another thing; if it was Harpo Marx or Dave Chasen, that's still another thing, or two other things. I think you really have to know who the man was. If the idea was to get a laugh, I don't think it was so very good. As for Dr. Bisch's notion that the man was enthusiastic, I don't see that at all. I just don't see it. Enthusiastic about what?

Our psychiatrist, in this meaty chapter, takes up a great many more cases, many more than I can disagree with in the space at my disposal, but I can't very well leave out the one about the man and the potatoes, because it is one of my favorites. It seems that there kept running through this unfortunate gentleman's mind the words "mashed potatoes, boiled potatoes, mashed potatoes, boiled potatoes"—*that* old line. This went on for days, and the poor fellow, who had a lot of other things he wanted to keep repeating, could only keep repeating that. "Here," says Dr. Bisch, "the difficulty lay in the fact that the man had previously received a reprimand from his employer regarding his easy-going ways with the men who were under him in his department. 'Don't be too soft!' the employer had shouted. 'Be hard!' That very evening his wife served French fried potatoes that were burnt. 'I should be hard with her, too,' he mused. The next day the 'mashed potatoes, boiled potatoes' had been born." Now my own analysis is that the fellow really wanted to kill (mash) his wife and then go out and get fried or boiled. My theory brings in the fried potatoes and Dr. Bisch's doesn't, or not so well, anyway. I might say, in conclusion, that I don't like fellows who muse about getting hard with their wives and then take it out in repeating some silly line over and over. If I were a psychiatrist, I would not bother with them. There are so many really important ailments to attend to.

8. Sex ex Machina

WITH the disappearance of the gas mantle and the advent of the short circuit, man's tranquillity began to be threatened by everything he put his hand on. Many people believe that it was a sad day indeed when Benjamin Franklin tied that key to a kite string and flew the kite in a thunderstorm; other people believe that if it hadn't been Franklin, it would have been someone else. As, of course, it was in the case of the harnessing of steam and the invention of the gas engine. At any rate, it has come about that so-called civilized man finds himself today surrounded by the myriad mechanical devices of a technological world. Writers of books on how to control your nerves, how to conquer fear, how to cultivate calm, how to be happy in spite of everything, are of several minds as regards the relation of man and the machine. Some of them are prone to believe that the mind and body, if properly disciplined, can get the upper hand of this mechanized existence. Others merely ignore the situation and go on to the profitable writing of more facile chapters of inspiration. Still others attribute the whole menace of the machine to sex, and so confuse the average reader that he cannot always be certain whether he has been knocked down by an automobile or is merely in love.

Dr. Bisch, the Be-Glad-You're-Neurotic man, has a remarkable chapter which deals, in part, with man, sex, and the machine. He examines the case of three hypothetical men who start across a street on a red light and get in the way of an oncoming automobile. A dodges successfully; B stands still, "accepting the situation with calm and resignation," thus becoming one of my favorite heroes in modern belles-lettres; and C hesitates, wavers, jumps backward and forward, and finally runs head on into the car. To lead you through Dr. Bisch's complete analysis of what was wrong with B and C would occupy your whole day. He mentions what the Mc-Dougallians would say ("Instinct!"), what the Freudians would retort ("Complexes!"), and what the behaviorists would shout ("Conditioned reflexes!"). He also brings in what the physiologists would say—deficient thyroid, hypoadrenal functioning, and so on. The average sedentary man of our time who is at all suggestible must emerge from this chapter believing that his chances of surviving a combination of instinct, complexes, reflexes, glands, sex, and present-day traffic conditions are about equal to those of a one-legged blind man trying to get out of a labyrinth.

Let us single out what Dr. Bisch thinks the Freudians would say about poor Mr. C, who ran right into the car. He writes, " 'Sex hunger,' the Freudians would declare. 'Always keyed up and irritable because of it. Undoubtedly suffers from insomnia and when he does sleep his dream life must be productive, distorted, and possibly frightening. Automobile unquestionably has sex significance for him . . . to C the car is both enticing and menacing at one and the same time. . . . A thorough analysis is indicated. . . . It might take months. But then, the man needs an analysis as much as food. He is heading for a complete nervous collapse.' " It is my studied opinion, not to put too fine a point on it, that Mr. C is heading for a good mangling, and that if he gets away with only a nervous collapse, it will be a miracle.

I have not always, I am sorry to say, been able to go the whole way with the Freudians, or even a very considerable distance. Even though, as Dr. Bisch says, "One must admit that the Freudians have had the best of it thus far. At least they have received the most publicity." It is in matters like their analysis of men and machines, of Mr. C and the automobile, that the Freudians and I part company. Of course, the analysis above is simply Dr. Bisch's idea of what the Freudians would say, but I think he has got it down pretty well. Dr. Bisch himself leans toward the Freudian analysis of Mr. C, for he says in this same chapter, "An automobile bearing down upon you may be a sex symbol at that, you know, especially if you dream it." It is my contention, of course, that even if you dream it, it is probably not a sex symbol, but merely an automobile bearing down upon you. And if it bears down upon you in real life, I am sure it is an automobile. I have seen the same behavior that characterized Mr. C displayed by a squirrel (Mr. S) that lives in the grounds of my house in the country. He is a fairly tame squirrel, happily mated and not sex-hungry, if I am any judge, but nevertheless he frequently runs out toward my automobile when I start down the driveway, and then hesitates, wavers, jumps forward and backward, and occasionally would run right into the car except that he is awfully fast on his feet and that I always hurriedly put on the brakes of the 1935 V-8 Sex Symbol that I drive.

I have seen this same behavior in the case of rabbits (notoriously uninfluenced by any sex symbols save those of other rabbits), dogs, pigeons, a doe, a young hawk (which flew at my car), a blue heron that I encountered on a country road in Vermont, and once, near Paul Smiths in the Adirondacks,

Happily-mated Rabbit Terrified by Motor-car

a fox. They all acted exactly like Mr. C. The hawk, unhappily, was killed. All the others escaped with nothing worse, I suppose, than a complete nervous collapse. Although I cannot claim to have been conversant with the private life and the secret compulsions, the psychoneuroses and the glandular activities of all these animals, it is nevertheless my confident and unswervable belief that there was nothing at all the matter with any one of them. Like Mr. C, they suddenly saw a car swiftly bearing down upon them, got excited, and lost their heads. I do not believe, you see, there was anything the matter with Mr. C, either. But I do believe that, after a thorough analysis lasting months, with a lot of harping on the incident of the automobile, something might very well come to be the matter with him. He might even actually get to suffering from the delusion that he believes automobiles are sex symbols.

It seems to me worthy of note that Dr. Bisch, in reciting the reactions of three persons in the face of an oncoming car, selected three men. What would have happened had they been Mrs. A, Mrs. B, and Mrs. C? You know as well as I do: all three of them would have hesitated, wavered, jumped forward and backward, and finally run head on into the car if some man hadn't grabbed them. (I used to know a motorist who, every time he approached a woman standing on a curb pre-paring to cross the street, shouted, "Hold it, stupid!") It is not too much to say that, with a car bearing down upon them, ninety-five women out of a hundred would act like Mr. C— or Mr. S, the squirrel, or Mr. F, the fox. But it is certainly too much to say that ninety-five out of every hundred women look upon an automobile as a sex symbol. For one thing, Dr. Bisch points out that the automobile serves as a sex symbol because of the "mechanical principle involved." But only one woman in a thousand really knows anything about the me-chanical principle involved in an automobile. And yet, as I have said, ninety-five out of a hundred would hesitate, waver, and jump, just as Mr. C did. I think we have the Freudians here. If we haven't proved our case with rabbits and a blue heron, we have certainly proved it with women.

To my notion, the effect of the automobile and of other mechanical contrivances on the state of our nerves, minds, and spirits is a problem which the popular psychologists whom I have dealt with know very little about. The sexual explanation of the relationship of man and the machine is not good enough. To arrive at the real explanation, we have to begin very far back, as far back as Franklin and the kite, or at least as far back as a certain man and woman who appear in a book of stories written more than sixty years ago by Max Adeler. One story in this book tells about a housewife who bought a combination ironing board and card table, which some New England genius had thought up in his spare time. The hus-band, coming home to find the devilish contraption in the parlor, was appalled. "What is that thing?" he demanded. His wife explained that it was a card table, but that if you pressed a button underneath, it would become an ironing board. Whereupon she pushed the button and the table leaped a foot into the air, extended itself, and became an ironing board. The story goes on to tell how the thing finally became so finely sensitized that it would change back and forth if you merely touched it—you didn't have to push the button. The husband stuck it in the attic (after it had leaped up and struck him a couple of times while he was playing euchre), and on windy nights it could be heard flopping and banging around, changing from a card table to an ironing board and back. The story serves as one example of our dread heritage of annoyance, shock, and terror arising out of the nature of mechanical contrivances *per se*. The mechanical principle involved in this damnable invention had, I believe, no relationship to sex whatsoever. There are certain analysts who see sex in anything, even a leaping ironing board, but I think we can ignore these scientists.

No man (to go on) who has wrestled with a self-adjusting card table can ever be quite the man he once was. If he arrives at the state where he hesitates, wavers, and jumps at every mechanical device he encounters, it is not, I submit, because he recognizes the enticements of sex in the device, but only because he recognizes the menace of the machine as such. There might very well be, in every descendant of the man we have been discussing, an inherited desire to jump at, and conquer, mechanical devices before they have a chance to turn into something twice as big and twice as menacing. It is not reasonable to expect that his children and their children will have entirely escaped the stigma of such traumata. I myself will never be the man I once was, nor will my descendants probably ever amount to much, because of a certain experience I had with an automobile.

I had gone out to the barn of my country place, a barn which was used both as a garage and a kennel, to quiet some large black poodles. It was 1 A.M. of a pitch-dark night in winter and the poodles had apparently been terrified by some kind of a prowler, a tramp, a turtle, or perhaps a fiend of some sort. Both my poodles and I myself believed, at the time, in fiends, and still do. Fiends who materialize out of nothing and nowhere, like winged pigweed or Russian thistle. I had quite a time quieting the dogs, because their panic spread to me and mine spread back to them again, in a kind of vicious circle. Finally, a hush as ominous as their uproar fell upon them, but they kept looking over their shoulders, in a kind of apprehensive way. "There's nothing to be afraid of," I told them as firmly as I could, and just at that moment the klaxon of my car, which was just behind me, began to shriek. Everybody has heard a klaxon on a car suddenly begin to sound; I understand it is a short circuit that causes it. But very few people have heard one scream behind them while they were quieting six or eight alarmed poodles in the middle of the night in an old barn. I jump now whenever I hear a klaxon, even the klaxon on my own car when I push the button intentionally. The experience has left its mark. Everybody, from the day of the jumping card table to the day of the screaming klaxon, has had similar shocks. You can see the result, entirely unsuperinduced by sex, in the strained faces and muttering lips of people who pass you on the streets of great, highly mechanized cities. There goes a man who picked up one of those trick matchboxes that whir in your hands; there goes a woman who tried to change a fuse without turning off the current; and yonder toddles an ancient who cranked an old Reo with the spark advanced. Every person carries in his consciousness the old scar, or the fresh wound, of some harrowing misadventure with a contraption of some sort. I know people who would not deposit a nickel and a dime in a cigarette-vending machine and push the lever even if a diamond necklace came out. I know dozens who would not climb into an airplane even if it didn't move off the ground. In none of these people have I discerned what I would call a neurosis, an "exaggerated" fear; I have discerned only a natural caution in a world made up of gadgets that whir and whine and whiz and shriek and sometimes explode.

I should like to end with the case history of a friend of mine in Ohio named Harvey Lake. When he was only nineteen, the steering bar of an old electric runabout broke off in his hand, causing the machine to carry him through a fence and into the grounds of the Columbus School for Girls. He developed

9. Sample Intelligence Test

THE FUZZINESS that creeps into the thought processes of those inspirationalists who seek to clarify the human scene reaches an interesting point in Chapter XIV of "How to Develop Your Personality," by Sadie Myers Shellow, Ph.D. Dr. Shellow was formerly psychologist with the Milwaukee Electric Railway & Light Company. These things happen in a world of endless permutations. I myself was once connected with the Central Ohio Optical Company. I was hired because I had a bicycle, although why an optical company would want a bicycle might appear on the face of it as inexplicable as why a railway-and-light company would want a psychologist. My experience of motormen leads me to believe that they are inarticulate to the point of never saying anything at all, and I doubt if there is a motorman in all Wisconsin who would reveal the story of his early childhood to a psychologist. Dr. Shellow, of course, may have proceeded along some other line, but most psychologists start with your childhood. Or with your sex life. I somehow have never thought of motormen as having sex lives, but this doesn't mean that they don't have them. I feel that this speculation is not getting us anywhere.

Let us return to Dr. Shellow's book. It was first published five years ago, but her publishers have just brought out a dollar edition, which puts the confusion in Chapter XIV within reach of everyone. In 1932, the book went into six printings. The present edition was printed from the original plates, which means that the mistakes which appear in it have gone on and on through the years. The book begins with a prefatory note by Albert Edward Wiggam, a foreword by Morris S. Viteles, and an introduction by Dr. Shellow herself. In Chapter I, first paragraph, Dr. Shellow gives the dictionary definition of "personality" as follows: "The sum total of traits necessary to describe what is to be a person." Unless I have gone crazy reading all these books, and I think I have, that sentence defines personality as the sum total of traits necessary to describe an unborn child. If Dr. Shellow's error here is typographical, it looms especially large in a book containing a chapter that tells how to acquire reading skill and gives tests for efficiency in reading. Dr. Shellow tells of a young woman who "was able to take in a whole page at a glance, and through concentrated attention relate in detail what she had read as the words flashed by." If Dr. Shellow used this system in reading the proofs of her book, the system is apparently no good. It certainly *sounds* as if it were no good. I have started out with an admittedly minor confusion—the definition of

Motorman Concealing His Sex Life from a Woman Psychologist

personality—but let us go on to something so mixed up that it becomes almost magnificent.

Chapter XIV is called "Intelligence Tests," and under the heading "Sample Intelligence Test" twelve problems are posed. There are some pretty fuzzy goings-on in the explanation of No. 11, but it is No. 12 that interests me most; what the Milwaukee motormen made of it I can't imagine. No. 12 is stated as follows: "Cross out the *one* word which makes this sentence absurd and substitute one that is correct: A pound of feathers is lighter than a pound of lead." Let us now proceed to Dr. Shellow's explanation of how to arrive at the solution of this toughy. She writes, "In 12 we get at the critical ability of the mind. Our first impulse is to agree that a pound of feathers is lighter than a pound of lead, since feathers are lighter than lead, but if we look back, we will see that a *pound* of feathers could be no lighter than a *pound* of lead since a pound is always the same. What one word, then, makes the whole sentence absurd? We might cross out the second pound and substitute ounce, in which case we would have: A pound of feathers is heavier than an ounce of lead, and that would be correct. Or we might cross out the word heavier and substitute bulkier, in which case we would have eliminated the absurdity."

We have here what I can only call a paradise of errors. I find, in Dr. Shellow's presentation of the problem and her solution of it, Transference, Wishful Thinking, Unconscious Substitution, Psychological Dissociation, Gordian Knot Cutting, Cursory Enumeration, Distortion of Focus, Abandonment of Specific Gravity, Falsification of Premise, Divergence from Consistency, Overemphasis on Italics, Rhetorical Escapism, and Disregard of the Indefinite Article. Her major error—the conjuring up of the word "heavier" out of nowhere—is enough to gum up any problem beyond repair, but there are other interesting pieces of woolly reasoning in No. 12. Dr. Shellow gets off on the wrong foot in her very presentation of the problem. She begins, "Cross out the *one* word which makes this sentence absurd." That means there is *only* one word which can be changed and restricts the person taking the test to that one word, but Dr. Shellow goes on, in her explanation, to change first one and then another. As a matter of fact, there are five words in the sentence any one of which can be changed to give the sentence meaning. Thus we are all balled up at the start. If Dr. Shellow had written, "Cross out one word which makes this sentence absurd," that would have been all right. I think I know how she got into trouble. I imagine that she originally began, "Cross out one of the words," and found herself face to face with that ancient stumbling block in English composition, whether to say "which *makes* this sentence absurd" or "which *make* this sentence absurd." (I don't like to go into italics, but to straighten Dr. Shellow out you got to go into italics.) I have a notion that Dr. Shellow decided that "make" was right, which of course it is, but that she was dissatisfied with "Cross out one of the words which make this sentence absurd" because here "words" dominates "one." Since she wanted to emphasize "one," she italicized it and then, for good measure, put the definite article "the" in front of it. That would have given her "Cross out the *one* of the words which make this sentence absurd." From there she finally arrived at what she arrived at, and the problem began slowly to close in on her.

I wouldn't dwell on this at such length if Dr. Shellow's publishers had not set her up as a paragon of lucidity, precision, and logical thought. (Come to think that over, I believe I would dwell on it at the same length even if they hadn't.) Some poor fellows may have got inferiority complexes out of being unable to see through Dr. Shellow's authoritative explanation of No. 12, and I would like to restore their confidence in their own minds. You can't just go batting off any old sort of answer to an intelligence test in this day when every third person who reads these books has a pretty firm idea that his mind is cracking up.

Let us go on to another interesting fuzziness in the Doctor's explanation. Take her immortal sentence: "We might cross out the second pound and substitute ounce," etc. What anybody who followed those instructions would arrive at is: "A pound of feathers is lighter than *a* ounce of lead." Even leaving the matter of weight out of it (which I am reluctant to do, since weight is the main point), you can't substitute "ounce" for "pound" without substituting "an" for "a," thus changing two words. If "an" and "a" are the same word, then things have come to a pretty pass, indeed. If such slipshoddery were allowed, you could solve the problem with "A pound of feathers is lighter than two pound of lead." My own way out was to change "is" to "ain't," if anybody is interested.

Let us close this excursion into the wonderland of psychology with a paragraph of Dr. Shellow's which immediately follows her explanation of No. 12: "If the reader went through this test quickly before reading the explanation, he may have discovered some things about himself. A more detailed test would be even more revealing. Everyone should at some time or other take a good comprehensive intelligence test and analyze his own defects so that he may know into what errors his reasoning takes him and of what faulty habits of thought he must be aware." I want everybody to file out quietly, now, without any wisecracks.

10. Miscellaneous Mentation

IN GOING back over the well-thumbed pages of my library of recent books on mental technique, I have come upon a number of provocative passages which I marked with a pencil but, for one reason or another, was unable to fit into any of my preceding chapters. I have decided to take up this group of miscellaneous matters here, treating the various passages in the order in which I come to them. First, then, there is a paragraph from Dr. Louis E. ("Be Glad You're Neurotic") Bisch, on Overcompensation. He writes, "To overcome a handicap and overcompensate is much the same as consciously and deliberately setting out to overcome a superstition. We will say that you are afraid to pass under a ladder. But suppose you defy the superstition and do it anyway? You may feel uneasy for a few hours or a few days. To your surprise, perhaps, nothing dreadful happens to you. This gives you courage. You try the ladder stunt again. Still you find yourself unharmed. After a while you look for ladders; you delight in walking under them; your ego has been pepped up and you defy all the demons that may be!"

Of course, the most obvious comment to be made here is that if you keep looking for and walking under ladders long enough, something *is* going to happen to you, in the very nature of things. Then, since your defiance of "all the demons that may be" proves you still believe in them, you will be right back where you were, afraid to walk under a ladder again. But what interests me most in Dr. Bisch's study of how to "pep up the ego" is its intensification of the very kind of superstition which the person in this case sets out to defy and destroy. To substitute walking under ladders for not walking under ladders is a distinction without a difference. For here we have, in effect, a person who was afraid to walk under ladders, and is now afraid not to. In the first place he avoided ladders because he feared the very fear that that would put into him. This the psychologists call phobophobia (they really do). But *now* he is afraid of the very fear he had of being afraid and hence is a victim of what I can only call phobophobophobia, and is in even deeper than he was before. Let us leave him in this perfectly frightful mess and turn to our old authority, Mr. David Seabury, and a quite different kind of problem.

"A young woman," writes Mr. Seabury, "remarked recently that she had not continued her literary career because she found her work commonplace. 'And,' she went on, 'I don't want to fill the world with more mediocre writing.' 'What sort of finished product do you expect a girl of twenty-two to produce?' I asked. 'You are judging what you can be in the future by what you are doing in the present. Would you have

Ladder Phobia

a little elm tree a year old compare itself with a giant tree and get an inferiority feeling? An elm tree of one year is a measly little thing, but given time it shades a whole house.'" Mr. Seabury does not take into consideration that, given time, a lady writer shades a whole house, too, and that whereas a little elm tree is bound to grow up to be a giant elm tree, a lady writer who at twenty-two is commonplace and mediocre is bound to grow to be a giant of commonplaceness and mediocrity. I think that this young woman is the only young woman writer in the history of the United States who thought that she ought not to go on with her writing because it was mediocre. If ever a psychologist had it in his power to pluck a brand from the burning, Mr. Seabury had it here. But what did he do? He made the young writer of commonplace things believe she would grow to be a veritable elm in the literary world. I hope she didn't listen to him, but I am afraid she probably did. Still, she sounds like a smart girl, and maybe she saw the weakness in Mr. Seabury's "You are judging what you can be in the future by what you are doing in the present." I can think of no sounder judgment to make.

Let us now look at something from Dr. James L. ("Streamline Your Mind") Mursell. In a chapter on "Mastering and Using Language," he brings out that most people do not know how to read. Dr. Mursell would have them get a precise and dogmatic meaning out of everything they read, thus leaving nothing to the fantasy and the imagination. This is particularly unfortunate, it seems to me, when applied to poetry, as Dr. Mursell applies it. He writes, "A large group of persons *seemed* to read the celebrated stanza beginning

> The Assyrian came down like the wolf on the fold
> And his cohorts were gleaming in purple and gold,

and ending

> Where the blue wave rolls nightly on deep Galilee.

"But when a suspicious-minded investigator tested them, quite a number turned out to suppose that the Assyrian's cohorts were an article of wearing apparel and that the last line referred to the astronomical discoveries of Galileo. Is this reading?"

Well, yes. What the second line means is simply that the *cohorts'* articles of wearing apparel were gleaming in purple and gold, so nothing much is distorted except the number of people who came down like the wolf on the fold. The readers who got it wrong had, it seems to me, as deep a poetic feeling (which is the main thing) as those who knew that a cohort was originally one of the ten divisions of a Roman legion and had, to begin with, three hundred soldiers, later five hundred to six hundred. Furthermore, those who got it wrong had a fine flaring image of one Assyrian coming down valiantly all alone, instead of with a couple of thousand soldiers to help him, the big coward. As for "Where the blue wave rolls nightly on deep Galilee," the reading into this of some vague association with the far, lonely figure of Galileo lends it a misty poetic enchantment which, to my way of thinking, the line can very well put up with. Dr. Mursell should be glad that some of the readers didn't think "the blue wave" meant the Yale football team. And even if they had, it would be all right with me. There is no person whose spirit hasn't at one time or another been enriched by some cherished transfiguring of meanings. Everybody is familiar with the youngster who thought the first line of the Lord's Prayer was "Our Father, who art in heaven, Halloween be thy Name." There must have been for him, in that reading, a thrill, a delight, and an exaltation that the exact sense of the line could not possibly have created. I once knew of a high-school teacher in a small town in Ohio who for years had read to his classes a line that actually went "She was playing coquette in the garden below" as if it were "She was playing croquet in the garden below." When, one day, a bright young scholar raised his hand and pointed out the mistake, the teacher said, grimly, "I have read that line my way for seventeen years and I intend to go on reading it my way." I am all for this point of view. I remember that, as a boy of eight, I thought "Post No Bills" meant that the walls on which it appeared belonged to one Post No Bill, a man of the same heroic proportions as Buffalo Bill. Some suspicious-minded investigator cleared this up for me, and a part of the glamour of life was gone.

We will now look at a couple of items from the very latest big-selling inspirational volume, no less a volume than Mr. Dale Carnegie's "How to Win Friends and Influence People." Writes Mr. Carnegie, "The New York Telephone Company conducts a school to train its operators to say 'Number please' in a tone that means 'Good morning, I am happy to be of service to you.' Let's remember that when we answer the telephone tomorrow." Now it seems to me that if this is something we have deliberately to remember, some thing we have to be told about, then obviously the operators aren't getting their message over. And I don't think they are. What I have always detected in the voices of telephone operators is a note of peremptory willingness. Their tone always conveys to me "What number do you want? And don't mumble!" If it is true, however, that the operator's tone really means "Good morning, I am happy to be of service to you," then it is up to the subscriber to say, unless he is a curmudgeon, "Thank you. How are you this morning?" If Mr. Carnegie doesn't know what the operator would say to that, I can tell him. She would say, "I am sorry, sir, but we are not allowed to give out that information." And the subscriber and the operator would be right back where they are supposed to be, on a crisp, businesslike basis, with no genuine "good morning" and no real happiness in it at all.

I also want to examine one of Mr. Carnegie's rules for behavior in a restaurant. He writes, "You don't have to wait until you are Ambassador to France or chairman of the Clambake Committee of the Elk's Club before you use this philosophy of appreciation. You can work magic with it every day. If, for example, the waitress brings us mashed potatoes when we ordered French fried, let's say 'I'm sorry to trouble you, but I prefer French fried.' She'll reply. 'No trouble at all,' and will be glad to do it because you have shown respect for her." Now, it is my belief that if we said to the waitress, "I'm sorry to trouble you, but I prefer French fried," she would say, "Well, make up ya mind." The thing to say to her is simply, "I asked for French fried potatoes, not mashed potatoes." To which, of course, she might reply, under her breath, "Well, take the marbles outa ya mouth when ya talkin'." There is no way to make a waitress really glad to do anything. Service is all a matter of business with her, as it is with the phone operators, and Mr. Carnegie might as well face the fact. Anyway, I do not see any "philosophy of appreciation" in saying to a waitress, "I'm sorry to trouble you, but I prefer French fried." Philosophy and appreciation are both capable of higher flights than that. "How are you, Beautiful?" is a higher form of appreciation than what Mr. Carnegie recommends, and it is not very high. But at least it isn't stuffy, and "I'm sorry to trouble you, but I prefer French fried" is; waitresses hate men who hand them that line.

For a final example of mistaken observation of life and analysis of people, I must turn again to the prolific Mr. Seabury. He writes that once, at a dinner, he sat opposite "a tall, lanky man with restless fingers" who was telling the lady on his right about his two dogs and their four puppies. "It was obvious," says Mr. Seabury, "that he had identified himself with the mother dog and was accustomed to spend a good deal of his time in conversation with her about the welfare of her young." Having been a dog man myself for a great many years, I feel that I am on sounder ground there than Mr. Seabury. I know that no dog man ever identifies himself with the mother dog. There is a type of dog man who sometimes wistfully identifies himself with the father dog, or would like to, at any rate, because of the comparative freedom, lack of responsibility, and general carefree attitude that marks the family life of all father dogs. But no dog man, as I have said, ever identifies himself with the mother dog. He may, to be sure, spend a good deal of his time in conversation with her, but this conversation is never about the welfare of her young. Every dog man knows that there is nothing he can say to any mother dog about the welfare of her young that will make the slightest impression on her. This is partly because she does not know enough English to carry on a conversation that would get very far, and partly because, even if she did, she would not let any suggestions or commands, coaxings or wheedlings, influence her in the least.

Every dog man, when his mother dog has had her first pups, has spent a long time fixing up a warm bed in a nice, airy corner for the mother dog to have her pups in, only to discover that she prefers to have them under the barn, in a hollow log, or in the dark and inaccessible reaches of a storeroom amidst a lot of overshoes, ice skates, crokinole boards, and ball bats. Every dog man has, at the risk of his temper and his limbs, grimly and resolutely dug the mother dog and her pups out from among the litter of debris that she prefers, stepping on the ball bats, kneeling on the ice skates, and put her firmly into the bassinet he has prepared for her, only to have her carry the pups back to the nest among the overshoes and the crokinole boards during the night. In the end, every dog man

The Breaking Up of the Winships

T HE TROUBLE that broke up the Gordon Winships seemed to me, at first, as minor a problem as frost on a window-pane. Another day, a touch of sun, and it would be gone. I was inclined to laugh it off, and, indeed, as a friend of both Gordon and Marcia, I spent a great deal of time with each of them, separately, trying to get them to laugh it off, too—with him at his club, where he sat drinking Scotch and smoking too much, and with her in their apartment, that seemed so large and lonely without Gordon and his restless moving around and his quick laughter. But it was no good; they were both adamant. Their separation has lasted now more than six months. I doubt very much that they will ever go back to-gether again.

It all started one night at Leonardo's, after dinner, over their Bénédictine. It started innocently enough, amiably even, with laughter from both of them, laughter that froze finally as the clock ran on and their words came out sharp and flat and stinging. They had been to see "Camille." Gordon hadn't liked it very much. Marcia had been crazy about it because she is crazy about Greta Garbo. She belongs to that consid-erable army of Garbo admirers whose enchantment borders almost on fanaticism and sometimes even touches the edges of frenzy. I think that, before everything happened, Gordon admired Garbo, too, but the depth of his wife's conviction that here was the greatest figure ever seen in our generation on sea or land, on screen or stage, exasperated him that night. Gordon hates (or used to) exaggeration, and he respects (or once did) detachment. It was his feeling that detachment is a necessary thread in the fabric of a woman's charm. He didn't like to see his wife get herself "into a sweat" over anything and, that night at Leonardo's, he unfortunately used that ex-pression and made that accusation.

Marcia responded, as I get it, by saying, a little loudly (they had gone on to Scotch and soda), that a man who had no abandon of feeling and no passion for anything was not altogether a man, and that his so-called love of detachment simply covered up a lack of critical appreciation and understanding of the arts in general. Her sentences were becoming long and wavy, and her words formal. Gordon suddenly began to pooh-pooh her; he kept saying "Pooh!" (an annoying mannerism of his, I have always thought). He wouldn't answer her arguments or even listen to them. That, of course, infuriated her. "Oh, pooh to you, too!" she finally more or less shouted. He snapped at her, "Quiet, for God's sake! You're yelling like a prizefight manager!" Enraged at that, she had recourse to her eyes as weapons and looked steadily at him for a while with the expression of one who is viewing a

Cocktail Party, 1937

small and horrible animal, such as a horned toad. They then sat in moody and brooding silence for a long time, without moving a muscle, at the end of which, getting a hold on herself, Marcia asked him, quietly enough, just exactly what actor on the screen or on the stage, living or dead, he considered greater than Garbo. Gordon thought a moment and then said, as quietly as she had put the question, "Donald Duck." I don't believe that he meant it at the time, or even thought that he meant it. However that may have been, she looked at him scornfully and said that that speech just about perfectly represented the shallowness of his intellect and the small range of his imagination. Gordon asked her not to make a spectacle of herself—she had raised her voice slightly—and went on to say that her failure to see the genius of Donald Duck proved conclusively to him that she was a woman without humor. That, he said, he had always suspected; now, he said, he knew it. She had a great desire to hit him, but instead she sat back and looked at him with her special Mona Lisa smile, a smile rather more of contempt than, as in the original, of mystery. Gordon hated that smile, so he said that Donald Duck happened to be exactly ten times as great as Garbo would ever be and that anybody with a brain in his head would admit it instantly. Thus the Winships went on and on, their resentment swelling, their sense of values blurring, until it ended up with her taking a taxi home alone (leaving her vanity bag and one glove behind her in the restaurant) and with him making the rounds of the late places and rolling up to his club around dawn. There, as he got out, he asked his taxi-driver which he liked better, Greta Garbo or Donald Duck, and the driver said he liked Greta Garbo best. Gordon said to him, bitterly, "Pooh to you, too, my good friend!" and went to bed.

The next day, as is usual with married couples, they were both contrite, but behind their contrition lay sleeping the ugly words each had used and the cold glances and the bitter gestures. She phoned him, because she was worried. She didn't want to be, but she was. When he hadn't come home, she was convinced he had gone to his club, but visions of him lying in a gutter or under a table, somehow horribly mangled, haunted her, and so at eight o'clock she called him up. Her heart lightened when he said, "Hullo," gruffly: he was alive, thank God! His heart may have lightened a little, too, but not very much, because he felt terrible. He felt terrible and he felt that it was her fault that he felt terrible. She said that she was sorry and that they had both been very silly, and he growled something about he was glad she realized *she'd* been silly, anyway. That attitude put a slight edge on the rest of her words. She asked him shortly if he was coming home. He said sure he was coming home; it was his home, wasn't it? She told him to go back to bed and not be such an old bear, and hung up.

The next incident occurred at the Clarkes' party a few days later. The Winships had arrived in fairly good spirits to find themselves in a buzzing group of cocktail-drinkers that more or less revolved around the tall and languid figure of the guest of honor, an eminent lady novelist. Gordon late in the evening won her attention and drew her apart for one drink together and, feeling a little high and happy at that time, as is the way with husbands, mentioned lightly enough (he wanted to get it out of his subconscious), the argument that he and his wife had had about the relative merits of Garbo and Duck. The tall lady, lowering her cigarette-holder, said, in the spirit of his own gaiety, that he could count her in on his side. Unfortunately, Marcia Winship, standing some ten feet away, talking to a man with a beard, caught not the spirit but only a few of the words of the conversation, and jumped to the conclusion that her husband was deliberately reopening the old wound, for the purpose of humiliating her in public. I think that in another moment Gordon might have brought her over, and put his arm around her, and admitted his "defeat"—he was feeling pretty fine. But when he caught her eye, she gazed through him, freezingly, and his heart went down. And then his anger rose.

Their fight, naturally enough, blazed out again in the taxi they took to go home from the party. Marcia wildly attacked the woman novelist (Marcia had had quite a few cocktails), defended Garbo, excoriated Gordon, and laid into Donald Duck. Gordon tried for a while to explain exactly what had happened, and then he met her resentment with a resentment that mounted even higher, the resentment of the misunderstood husband. In the midst of it all she slapped him. He looked at her for a second under lowered eyelids and then said, coldly, if a bit fuzzily, "This is the end, but I want you to go to your grave knowing that Donald Duck is *twenty times* the artist Garbo will ever be, the longest day you, or she, ever live, if you *do*—and I can't understand, with so little to live for, why you should!" Then he asked the driver to stop the car, and he got out, in wavering dignity. "Caricature! Cartoon!" she screamed after him. "You and Donald Duck both, you—" The driver drove on.

The last time I saw Gordon—he moved his things to the club the next day, forgetting the trousers to his evening clothes and his razor—he had convinced himself that the point at issue between him and Marcia was one of extreme importance involving both his honor and his integrity. He said that now it could never be wiped out and forgotten. He said that he sincerely believed Donald Duck was as great a creation as any animal in all the works of Lewis Carroll, probably even greater, perhaps much greater. He was drinking and there was a wild light in his eye. I reminded him of his old love of detachment, and he said to the hell with detachment. I laughed at him, but he wouldn't laugh. "If," he said, grimly, "Marcia persists in her silly belief that that Swede is great and that Donald Duck is merely a caricature, I cannot conscientiously live with her again. I believe that he is great, that the man who created him is a genius, probably our only genius. I believe, further, that Greta Garbo is just another actress. As God is my judge, I believe that! What does she expect me to do, go whining back to her and pretend that I think Garbo is wonderful and that Donald Duck is simply a cartoon? Never!" He gulped down some Scotch straight. "Never!" I could not ridicule him out of his obsession. I left him and went over to see Marcia.

I found Marcia pale, but calm, and as firm in her stand as Gordon was in his. She insisted that he had deliberately tried to humiliate her before that gawky so-called novelist, whose clothes were the dowdiest she had ever seen and whose affectations obviously covered up a complete lack of individuality and intelligence. I tried to convince her that she was wrong about Gordon's attitude at the Clarkes' party, but she said she knew him like a book. Let him get a divorce and marry that creature if he wanted to. They can sit around all day, she said, and all night, too, for all I care, and talk about their precious Donald Duck, the damn comic strip! I told Marcia that she shouldn't allow herself to get so worked up about a trivial and nonsensical matter. She said it was not silly and nonsensical to her. It might have been once, yes, but it wasn't now. It had made her see Gordon clearly for what he was, a cheap, egotistical, resentful cad who would descend to ridiculing his wife in front of a scrawny, horrible stranger who could not write and never would be able to write. Furthermore, her belief in Garbo's greatness was a thing she could not deny and would not deny, simply for the sake of living under the same roof with Gordon Winship. The whole thing was part and

Nine Needles

O NE OF the more spectacular minor happenings of the
past few years which I am sorry that I missed took place
in the Columbus, Ohio, home of some friends of a friend of
mine. It seems that a Mr. Albatross, while looking for something in his medicine cabinet one morning, discovered a bottle of a kind of patent medicine which his wife had been taking
for a stomach ailment. Now, Mr. Albatross is one of those
apprehensive men who are afraid of patent medicines and of
almost everything else. Some weeks before, he had encountered a paragraph in a Consumers' Research bulletin which
announced that this particular medicine was bad for you. He
had thereupon ordered his wife to throw out what was left of
her supply of the stuff and never buy any more. She had promised, and here now was another bottle of the perilous liquid.
Mr. Albatross, a man given to quick rages, shouted the conclusion of the story at my friend: "I threw the bottle out the
bathroom window and the medicine chest after it!" It seems
to me that must have been a spectacle worth going a long
way to see.

I am sure that many a husband has wanted to wrench the
family medicine cabinet off the wall and throw it out the window, if only because the average medicine cabinet is so filled
with mysterious bottles and unidentifiable objects of all kinds
that it is a source of constant bewilderment and exasperation
to the American male. Surely the British medicine cabinet and
the French medicine cabinet and all the other medicine cabinets must be simpler and better ordered than ours. It may be
that the American habit of saving everything and never throwing anything away, even empty bottles, causes the domestic
medicine cabinet to become as cluttered in its small way as
the American attic becomes cluttered in its major way. I have
encountered few medicine cabinets in this country which were
not pack-jammed with something between a hundred and fifty
and two hundred different items, from dental floss to boracic
acid, from razor blades to sodium perborate, from adhesive
tape to coconut oil. Even the neatest wife will put off clearing

out the medicine cabinet on the ground that she has something else to do that is more important at the moment, or
more diverting. It was in the apartment of such a wife and her
husband that I became enormously involved with a medicine
cabinet one morning not long ago.

I had spent the weekend with this couple—they live on East
Tenth Street near Fifth Avenue—such a weekend as left me
reluctant to rise up on Monday morning with bright and shining face and go to work. They got up and went to work, but
I didn't. I didn't get up until about two-thirty in the afternoon. I had my face all lathered for shaving and the washbowl
was full of hot water when suddenly I cut myself with the
razor. I cut my ear. Very few men cut their ears with razors,
but I do, possibly because I was taught the old Spencerian
free-wrist movement by my writing teacher in the grammar
grades. The ear bleeds rather profusely when cut with a razor
and is difficult to get at. More angry than hurt, I jerked open
the door of the medicine cabinet to see if I could find a styptic
pencil and out fell, from the top shelf, a little black paper
packet containing nine needles. It seems that this wife kept a
little paper packet containing nine needles on the top shelf of
the medicine cabinet. The packet fell into the soapy water of
the washbowl, where the paper rapidly disintegrated, leaving
nine needles at large in the bowl. I was, naturally enough, not
in the best condition, either physical or mental, to recover
nine needles from a washbowl. No gentleman who has lather
on his face and whose ear is bleeding is in the best condition
for anything, even something involving the handling of nine
large blunt objects.

It did not seem wise to me to pull the plug out of the
washbowl and let the needles go down the drain. I had visions
of clogging up the plumbing system of the house, and also a
vague fear of causing short circuits somehow or other (I know
very little about electricity and I don't want to have it explained to me). Finally, I groped very gently around the bowl
and eventually had four of the needles in the palm of one hand
and three in the palm of the other—two I couldn't find. If I
had thought quickly and clearly, I wouldn't have done that.
A lathered man whose ear is bleeding and who has four wet
needles in one hand and three in the other may be said to

have reached the lowest known point of human efficiency. There is nothing he can do but stand there. I tried transferring the needles in my left hand to the palm of my right hand, but I couldn't get them off my left hand. Wet needles cling to you. In the end, I wiped the needles off onto a bathtowel

"And the Medicine Chest After It!"

which was hanging on a rod above the bathtub. It was the only towel that I could find. I had to dry my hands afterward on the bathmat. Then I tried to find the needles in the towel. Hunting for seven needles in a bathtowel is the most tedious occupation I have ever engaged in. I could find only five of them. With the two that had been left in the bowl, that meant there were four needles in all missing—two in the washbowl and two others lurking in the towel or lying in the bathtub under the towel. Frightful thoughts came to me of what might happen to anyone who used that towel or washed his face in the bowl or got into the tub, if I didn't find the missing needles. Well, I didn't find them. I sat down on the edge of the tub to think, and I decided finally that the only thing to do was wrap up the towel in a newspaper and take it away with me. I also decided to leave a note for my friends explaining as clearly as I could that I was afraid there were two needles in the bathtub and two needles in the washbowl, and that they better be careful.

I looked everywhere in the apartment, but I could not find a pencil, or a pen, or a typewriter. I could find pieces of paper, but nothing with which to write on them. I don't know what gave me the idea—a movie I had seen, perhaps, or a story I had read—but I suddenly thought of writing a message with a lipstick. The wife might have an extra lipstick lying around and, if so, I concluded it would be in the medicine cabinet. I went back to the medicine cabinet and began poking around in it for a lipstick. I saw what I thought looked like the metal tip of one, and I got two fingers around it and began to pull gently—it was under a lot of things. Every object in the medicine cabinet began to slide. Bottles broke in the washbowl and on the floor; red, brown, and white liquids spurted; nail files, scissors, razor blades, and miscellaneous objects sang and clattered and tinkled. I was covered with perfume, peroxide, and cold cream.

It took me half an hour to get the debris all together in the middle of the bathroom floor. I made no attempt to put anything back in the medicine cabinet. I knew it would take a steadier hand than mine and a less shattered spirit. Before I went away (only partly shaved) and abandoned the shambles, I left a note saying that I was afraid there were needles in the bathtub and the washbowl and that I had taken their towel and that I would call up and tell them everything—I wrote it in iodine with the end of a toothbrush. I have not yet called up, I am sorry to say. I have neither found the courage nor thought up the words to explain what happened. I suppose my friends believe that I deliberately smashed up their bathroom and stole their towel. I don't know for sure, because they have not yet called me up, either.

A Couple of Hamburgers

IT HAD been raining for a long time, a slow, cold rain falling out of iron-colored clouds. They had been driving since morning and they still had a hundred and thirty miles to go. It was about three o'clock in the afternoon. "I'm getting hungry," she said. He took his eyes off the wet, winding road for a fraction of a second and said, "We'll stop at a dog-wagon." She shifted her position irritably. "I wish you wouldn't call them *dog*-wagons," she said. He pressed the klaxon button and went around a slow car. "That's what they are," he said. "Dog-wagons." She waited a few seconds. "*Decent* people call them *diners*," she told him, and added, "Even if you call them diners, I don't like them." He speeded up a hill. "They have better stuff than most restaurants," he said. "Anyway, I want to get home before dark and it takes too long in a restaurant. We can stay our stomachs with a couple hamburgers." She lighted a cigarette and he asked her to light one for him. She lighted one deliberately and handed it to him. "I wish you wouldn't say 'stay our stomachs,'" she said. "You know I hate that. It's like 'sticking to your ribs.' You say that all the time." He grinned. "Good old American expressions, both of them," he said. "Like sow belly. Old pioneer term, sow belly." She sniffed. "My ancestors were pioneers, too. You don't have to be vulgar just because you were a pioneer." "Your ancestors never got as far west as mine did," he said. "The real pioneers travelled on their sow belly and got somewhere." He laughed loudly at that. She looked out at the wet trees and signs and telephone poles going by. They drove on for several miles without a word; he kept chortling every now and then.

"What's that funny sound?" she asked, suddenly. It invariably made him angry when she heard a funny sound. "What funny sound?" he demanded. "You're always hearing funny sounds." She laughed briefly. "That's what you said when the bearing burned out," she reminded him. "You'd never have noticed it if it hadn't been for me." "I noticed it, all right," he said. "Yes," she said. "When it was too late." She enjoyed bringing up the subject of the burned-out bearing whenever he got to chortling. "It was too late when *you* noticed it, as far as that goes," he said. Then, after a pause, "Well, what does it sound like *this* time? All engines make a noise running, you know." "I know all about that," she answered. "It sounds like—it sounds like a lot of safety pins being jiggled around in a tumbler." He snorted. "That's your imagination. Nothing gets the matter with a car that sounds like a lot of safety pins. I happen to know that." She tossed away her cigarette. "Oh, sure," she said. "You always happen to know everything." They drove on in silence.

"I want to stop somewhere and get something to *eat!*" she said loudly. "All right, all right!" he said. "I been watching for a dog-wagon, haven't I? There hasn't been any. I can't make you a dog-wagon." The wind blew rain in on her and she put up the window on her side all the way. "I won't stop at just any old diner," she said. "I won't stop unless it's a cute one." He looked around at her. "Unless it's a *what* one?" he shouted. "You know what I mean," she said. "I mean a decent, clean one where they don't slosh things at you. I hate to have a lot of milky coffee sloshed at me." "All right," he said. "We'll find a cute one, then. You pick it out. I wouldn't know. I might find one that was cunning but not cute." That struck him as funny and he began to chortle again. "Oh, shut up," she said.

Five miles farther along they came to a place called Sam's Diner. "Here's one," he said, slowing down. She looked it over. "I don't want to stop there," she said. "I don't like the ones that have nicknames." He brought the car to a stop at one side of the road. "Just what's the matter with the ones that have nicknames?" he asked with edgy, mock interest. "They're always Greek ones," she told him. "They're always Greek ones," he repeated after her. He set his teeth firmly together and started up again. After a time, "Good old Sam, the Greek," he said, in a singsong. "Good old Connecticut Sam Beardsley, the Greek." "You didn't see his name," she snapped. "Winthrop, then," he said. "Old Samuel Cabot Winthrop, the Greek dog-wagon man." He was getting hungry.

On the outskirts of the next town she said, as he slowed down, "It looks like a factory kind of town." He knew that she meant she wouldn't stop there. He drove on through the place. She lighted a cigarette as they pulled out into the open again. He slowed down and lighted a cigarette for himself. "Factory kind of town than *I* am!" he snarled. It was ten miles before they came to another town. "Torrington," he growled. "Happen to know there's a dog-wagon here because I stopped in it once with Bob Combs. Damn cute place, too, if you ask me." "I'm not asking you anything," she said, coldly. "You think you're *so* funny. I think I know the one you mean," she said, after a moment. "It's right in the town and it sits at an angle from the road. They're never so good, for some reason." He glared at her and almost ran up against the curb. "What the hell do you mean 'sits at an angle from the road'?" he cried. He was very hungry now. "Well, it isn't silly," she said, calmly. "I've noticed the ones that sit at an angle. They're cheaper, because they fitted them into funny little pieces of ground. The big ones parallel to the road are the best." He drove right through Torrington, his lips compressed. "Angle from the *road*, for God's sake!" he snarled, finally. She was looking out her window.

On the outskirts of the next town there was a diner called The Elite Diner. "This looks—" she began. "I see it, I see it!" he said. "It doesn't happen to look any cuter to me than any goddam—" she cut him off. "Don't be such a sorehead, for Lord's sake," she said. He pulled up and stopped beside the diner, and turned on her. "Listen," he said, grittingly, "I'm going to put down a couple of hamburgers in this place even if there isn't one single inch of chintz or cretonne in the whole—" "Oh, be still," she said. "You're just hungry and mean like a child. Eat your old hamburgers, what do I care?" Inside the place they sat down on stools and the counterman walked over to them, wiping up the counter top with a cloth as he did so. "What'll it be, folks?" he said. "Bad day, ain't it? Except for ducks." "I'll have a couple of—" began the husband, but his wife cut in. "I just want a pack of cigarettes," she said. He turned around slowly on his stool and stared at her as she put a dime and a nickel in the cigarette machine and ejected a package of Lucky Strikes. He turned to the counterman again. "I want a couple of hamburgers," he said. "With mustard and lots of onion. *Lots* of onion!" She hated onions. "I'll wait for you in the car," she said. He didn't answer and she went out.

He finished his hamburgers and his coffee slowly. It was terrible coffee. Then he went out to the car and got in and drove off, slowly humming "Who's Afraid of the Big Bad Wolf?" After a mile or so, "Well," he said, "what was the matter with the Elite Diner, milady?" "Didn't you *see* that cloth the man was wiping the counter with?" she demanded. "Ugh!" She shuddered. "I didn't happen to want to eat any of the counter," he said. He laughed at that comeback. "You didn't even notice it," she said. "You never notice anything. It was filthy." "I noticed they had some damn fine coffee in there," he said. "It was swell." He knew she loved good coffee. He began to hum his tune again; then he whistled it; then he began to sing it. She did not show her annoyance, but she knew that he knew she was annoyed. "Will you be kind enough to tell me what time it is?" she asked. "Big *bad* wolf, big *bad* wolf—five minutes o' five—tum-dee-*doo*-dee-dum-m-m." She settled back in her seat and took a cigarette from her case and tapped it on the case. "I'll wait till we get home," she said. "If you'll be kind enough to speed up a little." He drove on at the same speed. After a time he gave up the "Big Bad Wolf" and there was deep silence for two miles. Then suddenly he began to sing, very loudly, "*H*-A-double-R-*I*-G-A-*N spells Harr*-i-gan—" She gritted her teeth. She hated that worse than any of his songs except "Barney Google." He would go on to "Barney Google" pretty soon, she knew. Suddenly she leaned slighty forward. The straight line of her lips began to curve up ever so slightly. She heard the safety pins in the tumbler again. Only now they were louder, more insistent, ominous. He was singing too loud to hear them. "Is a *name* that *shame* has never been con-*nec*-ted with—*Harr*-i-gan, that's *me!*" She relaxed against the back of the seat, content to wait.

Aisle Seats in the Mind

I FOLLOW as closely as anyone, probably more closely than most people, the pronouncements on life, death, and the future of the movies as given out from time to time by Miss Mary Pickford. Some friends of mine think that it has even become a kind of obsession with me. I wouldn't go so far as to say that, but I do admit that many times when I would ordinarily sit back and drink my brandy and smoke a cigar and become a little drowsy mentally and a little sodden intellectually, something that Mary Pickford has just said engages my inner attention so that instead of dozing off, I am kept as bright-eyed and alert as a hunted deer. Often I wake up at night, too, and lie there thinking about life, and death, and the future of the movies. Miss Pickford's latest arresting observation came in an interview with a *World-Telegram* correspondent out in Beverly Hills. Said Miss Pickford, in part, "Any type of salaciousness is as distasteful to Mr. Lasky as it is to me. There will be no salaciousness at all in our films. Not one little bit! We will consider only those stories which will insure wholesome, healthy, yet vital entertainment. *Be a guardian, not an usher, at the portal of your thought.*"

Miss Pickford has a way which I can only call intriguing, much as I hate the word, of throwing out little rounded maxims, warnings, and morals at the ends of her paragraphs. I had a great-aunt who did the same thing, and in my teens she fascinated and frightened me; perhaps that is why Miss Pickford's exhortations so engross me, and keep me from the dicing tables, the dens of vice, and the more salacious movies, poems, and novels. Miss Pickford's newest precept has occupied a great many of my waking hours since I read it, and quite a few of my sleeping ones. In the first place, it has brought me sharply up against the realization that I am not a guardian at the portal of my thought and that, what is more, being now forty-two years of age, I probably never will be. What I am like at the portal of my thought is one of those six-foot-six ushers who used to stand around the lobby of the Hippodrome during performances of "Jumbo." (They were not really ushers, but doormen, I think, but let us consider them as ushers for the sake of the argument.) What I want to convey is that I am *all* usher, as far as the portal of my thought goes, terribly usher. But I am unlike the "Jumbo" ushers or any other ushers in that I show any and all thoughts to their seats whether they have tickets or not. They can be under-age and without their parents, or they can be completely cock-eyed, or they can show up without a stitch on; I let them in and show them to the best seats in my mind (the ones in the royal arena and the gold boxes).

I don't want you to think that all I do is let in *salacious* thoughts. Salacious thoughts can get in along with any others,

A Trio of Thoughts

including those that are under-age and those that are cock-eyed, but my mental audience is largely made up of thoughts that are, I am sorry to say, idiotic. For days a thought has been running around in the aisles of my mind, singing and shouting, a thought that, if I were a guardian, I would certainly have barred at the portal or thrown out instantly as soon as it got in. This thought is one without reason or motivation, but it keeps singing, over and over, to a certain part of the tune of "For He's a Jolly Good Fellow," these words:

> A message for Captain Bligh,
> And a greeting to Franchot Tone.

I hope it doesn't slip by the guardian at your own portal of thought, but, whether it does or not, it is sung to that part of the aforementioned tune the words of which go "Which nobody can deny, which nobody can deny." And it is pretty easy, if you are the usher type, to let it into your mind, where it is likely to get all your other thoughts to singing the same thing, just as Donald Duck did to the orchestra in "The Band Concert." Where it came from I don't know. Thoughts like that can spot the usher type of mind a mile away, and they seek it out as tramps seek out the backdoors of generous farm wives.

Just last Sunday another vagrant thought came up to the portal of my mind, or, rather, was shown up to the portal of my mind, and I led it instantly to a seat down front, where much to my relief, it has been shouting even more loudly than the Captain Bligh-Franchot Tone thought and is, in fact, about to cause that thought to leave the theatre. This new thought was introduced at my portal by my colored maid, Margaret, who, in seeking to describe a certain part of the electric refrigerator which she said was giving trouble, called it "doom-shaped." Since Margaret pronounced that wonderful word, everything in my mind and everything in the outside world has taken on the shape of doom. If I were a true guardian of the portal of my thought, I would have refused that expression admittance, because it is too provocative, too edgy, and too dark, for comfort, but then I would have missed the unique and remarkable experience that I had last Sunday, when, just as night was falling, I walked down a doom-shaped street under a doom-shaped sky and up a doom-shaped staircase to my doom-shaped apartment. Like Miss Pickford, I am all for the wholesome, the healthy, and the vital, but sometimes I think one's mind can become, if one is the guardian type, too wholesome, healthy, and vital to be much fun. Any mind, I say boldly here and now, which would not let a doom-shaped thought come in and take a seat is not a mind that I want around.

As in all my discourses about Miss Pickford and her philosophy, I am afraid I have drifted ever so slightly from the main point, which, in this case, I suppose, is the question of keeping salacious thoughts out of the mind, and not doom-shaped ones, or Franchot Tone. Miss Pickford, however, is to blame for my inability to stick to the exact point, because of her way of following up some specific thought, such as the unanimity of her and Mr. Lasky's feelings about salaciousness, with an extremely challenging and all-encompassing injunction, such as that everybody should be a guardian at the portal of his thought, and not an usher.

I have brooded for a long time about the origin of Miss Pickford's injunction. I am not saying that she did not think it up herself. It's hers and she's welcome to it, as far as I am concerned (I'd rather have "doom-shaped" for my own). But I somehow feel that she was quoting someone and that the only reason she didn't add "as the poet has it" or "as the fella said" is that she naturally supposes that everybody would know who wrote the line. I don't happen to know; I don't happen ever to have heard it before. It may be that it is a product of one of the immortal minds, but somehow I doubt that. To me it sounds like Eddie Guest or the late Ella Wheeler Wilcox. It may have been tossed off, of course, in a bad moment, by John Cowper Powys, or Gene Tunney, or Senator Victor Donahey of Ohio, but I am inclined to think not. If you should happen to know, for certain, that it is the work of Shakespeare or Milton, there is no use in your calling me up about it, or sending a telegram. By the time I could hear from you, I would have got it out of my mind, and only "doom-shaped" would be there, sitting in a darkened theatre. I would like that, so please let us alone.

Mrs. Phelps

WHEN I went to Columbus, Ohio, on a visit recently, I called one afternoon on Mrs. Jessie Norton, an old friend of my mother's. Mrs. Norton is in her seventies, but she is in bright possession of all her faculties (except that she does not see very well without her spectacles and is forever mislaying them). She always has a story to tell me over the teacups. She reads my fortune in the tea leaves, too, before I go, and for twenty years has told me that a slim, blonde woman is going to come into my life and that I should beware of the sea. Strange things happen to Mrs. Norton. She is psychic. My mother once told me that Mrs. Norton had been psychic since she was seven years old. Voices speak to her in the night, cryptically, persons long dead appear to her in dreams, and even her waking hours are sometimes filled with a mystic confusion.

Mrs. Norton's story this time dealt with a singular experience she had had only a few months before. It seems that she had gone to bed late on a blowy night, the kind of night on which the wind moans in the wires, and telephone bells ring without benefit of human agency, and there are inexplicable sounds at doors and windows. She had felt, as she got into bed, that something was going to happen. Mrs. Norton has never in her life had the feeling that something was going to happen that something hasn't happened. Once it was the Columbus flood, another time it was the shooting of McKinley, still another time the disappearance forever of her aged cat, Flounce.

On the occasion I am telling about, Mrs. Norton, who lives alone in a vast old graystone apartment building known as Hampton Court, was awakened three hours after midnight by a knocking on her back door. Her back door leads out into a treeless and rather dreary courtyard, as do all the other back doors in the building. It is really four buildings joined together and running around a whole block, with the courtyard in the center. Mrs. Norton looked out her bedroom window and saw two women standing at her door below—there was

that he was dead—there was no need to call a doctor; but would Mrs. Norton telephone for an—an undertaker?

Mrs. Norton, not yet fully awake, suggested that it might be a good idea to make the ladies some tea. Tea was a quieting thing and the brewing of it would give Mrs. Norton a while to think. Mrs. Phelps said that she would take pleasure in a cup of tea. So Mrs. Norton made the tea and the three ladies each drank a cup of it, slowly, talking of other things than the tragedy. Mrs. Phelps seemed to feel much better. Mrs. Norton then wanted to know if there was any particular undertaker that Mrs. Phelps would like to call in and Mrs. Phelps named one, whom I shall call Bellinger. So Mrs. Norton phoned Bellinger's, and a sleepy voice answered and said a man would be right over to Mrs. Phelps' apartment. At this Mrs. Phelps said, "I think I would like to go back to father alone for a moment. Would you ladies be kind enough to come over in a little while?" Mrs. Norton said they would be over as soon as she got dressed, and Mrs. Phelps left. "She seems very sweet," said Mrs. Stokes. "It's the first time I've really talked to her. It's very sad. And at this time of the night, too." Mrs. Norton said that it was a terrible thing, but that, of course, it was to be expected, since Mrs. Phelps' father must have been a very old man, for Mrs. Phelps looked to be sixty-five at least.

When Mrs. Norton was dressed, the two ladies went out into the bleak courtyard and made their way slowly across it and knocked at the back door of Mrs. Phelps' apartment. There was no answer. They knocked more loudly, taking turns, and then together, and there was still no answer. They could see a light inside, but they heard no sound. Bewildered and alarmed (for Mrs. Phelps had not seemed deaf), the two ladies went through Mrs. Stokes' apartment, which was right next door, and around to Mrs. Phelps' front door and rang the bell. It rang loudly and they rang it many times, but no one came to the door. There was a light on in the hall. They could not hear anyone moving inside.

It was at this juncture that Bellinger's man arrived, a small, grumpy man whose overcoat was too large for him. He took over the ringing of the bell and rang it many times, insistently, but without success. Then, grumbling to himself, he turned the doorknob and the door opened and the three walked into the hallway. Mrs. Norton called and then Mrs. Stokes called and then Bellinger's man shouted, but there was no other sound. The ladies looked at Bellinger's man in frank twittery fright. He said he would take a look around. They heard him going from room to room, opening and closing doors, first downstairs and then upstairs, now and then calling out "Madam!" He came back downstairs into the hallway where the ladies were and said there was nobody in the place, dead or alive. He was angry. After all, he had been roused out of his sleep. He said he believed the whole thing was a practical joke, and a damned bad practical joke, if you asked him. The ladies assured him it was not a joke, but he said "Bah" and walked to the door. There he turned and faced them with his hand on the knob and announced that in thirty-three years with Bellinger this was the first and only time he had ever been called out on a case in which there was no corpse, the first and only time. Then he strode out the door, jumped into his car, and drove off. The ladies hurried out of the apartment after him.

They went back to Mrs. Norton's apartment and made some more tea and talked in excited whispers about the curious happenings of the night. Mrs. Stokes said she did not know Mrs. Phelps very well but that she seemed to be a pleasant and kindly neighbor. Mrs. Norton said that she had known her only to nod to but that she had seemed very nice. Mrs. Stokes wondered whether they should call the police, but Mrs. Norton said that the police would be of no earthly use on what was obviously a psychic case. The ladies would go to bed and get some sleep and go over to Mrs. Phelps' apartment when it was daylight. Mrs. Stokes said she didn't feel like going back to her apartment—she would have to pass Mrs. Phelps' apartment on the way—so Mrs. Norton said she could sleep in her extra bed.

The two women, worn out by their experience, fell asleep shortly and did not wake up until almost ten o'clock. They hurriedly got up and dressed and went over to Mrs. Phelps' back door, on which Mrs. Norton knocked. The door opened and Mrs. Phelps stood there, smiling. She was fully dressed and did not look grief-stricken or tired. "Well!" she said. "This *is* nice! Do come in!" They went in. Mrs. Phelps led them into the living room, a neat and well-ordered room, and asked them to take chairs. They sat down, each on the edge of her chair, and waited. Mrs. Phelps talked pleasantly of this and that. Did they ever see anything grow like her giant begonia in the window? She had grown it from a slip that a Mrs. Bricker had given her. Had they heard that the Chalmers child was down with the measles? The other ladies murmured responses now and then and finally rose and said that they must be going. Mrs. Phelps asked them to run in any time; it had been so sweet of them to call. They went out into the courtyard and walked all the way to Mrs. Norton's door without a word, and there they stopped and stared at each other.

That, aggravatingly enough, is where Mrs. Norton's story ended—except for the bit of information that Mrs. Stokes, frightened of Mrs. Phelps, had moved away from Hampton Court a week after the night of alarm. Mrs. Norton does not believe in probing into the psychic. One must take, gratefully, such glimpses of the psychic as are presented to one, and seek no further. She had no theories as to what happened to Mrs. Phelps after Mrs. Phelps "went back to her father." The disappearance fitted snugly into the whole pattern of the night and she let it go at that. Mrs. Norton and Mrs. Phelps have become quite good friends now, and Mrs. Phelps frequently drops in for tea. They have had no further adventures. Mrs. Phelps has not mentioned her father since that night. All that Mrs. Norton really knows about her is that she was born in Bellefontaine, Ohio, and sometimes wishes that she were back there. I took the story for what it was, fuzzy edges and all: an almost perfect example of what goes on in the life that moves slowly about the lonely figure of Mrs. Jessie Norton, reading the precarious future in her tea leaves, listening to the whisperings and knockings of the ominous present at her door. Before I left her she read my fortune in the teacup I had drunk from. It seems that a slight, blonde woman is going to come into my life and that I should beware of the sea.

Wild Bird Hickok and His Friends

IN ONE of the many interesting essays that make up his book called "Abinger Harvest," Mr. E. M. Forster, discussing what he sees when he is reluctantly dragged to the movies in London, has set down a sentence that fascinates me. It is: "American women shoot the hippopotamus with eyebrows made of platinum." I have given that remarkable sentence a great deal of study, but I still do not know whether Mr. Forster means that American women have platinum eyebrows or that the hippopotamus has platinum eyebrows or that American women shoot platinum eyebrows into the hippopotamus. At any rate, it faintly stirred in my mind a dim train of elusive memories which were brightened up suddenly and brought into sharp focus for me when, one night, I went to see "The Plainsman," a hard-riding, fast-shooting movie dealing with warfare in the Far West back in the bloody seventies. I knew then what Mr. Forster's curious and tantalizing sentence reminded me of. It was like nothing in the world so much as certain sentences which appeared in a group of French paperback dime (or, rather, twenty-five-centime) novels that I collected a dozen years ago in France. "The Plainsman" brought up these old pulp thrillers in all clarity for me because, like that movie, they dealt mainly with the stupendous activities of Buffalo Bill and Wild Bill Hickok; but in them were a unique fantasy, a special inventiveness, and an imaginative abandon beside which the movie treatment of the two heroes pales, as the saying goes, into nothing. In moving from one apartment to another some years ago, I somehow lost my priceless collection of *contes héroïques du Far-Ouest*, but happily I find that a great many of the deathless adventures of the French Buffalo Bill and Wild Bill Hickok remain in my memory. I hope that I shall recall them, for anodyne, when with eyes too dim to read, I pluck finally at the counterpane.

In the first place, it should perhaps be said that in the eighteen-nineties the American dime-novel hero who appears to have been most popular with the French youth—and adult—given to such literature was Nick Carter. You will find somewhere in one of John L. Stoddard's published lectures—there used to be a set in almost every Ohio bookcase—an anecdote about how an American tourist, set upon by *apaches* in a dark *rue* in Paris in the nineties, caused them to scatter in terror merely by shouting, *"Je suis Nick Carter!"* But at the turn of the century, or shortly thereafter, Buffalo Bill became the favorite. Whether he still is or not, I don't know—perhaps Al Capone or John Dillinger has taken his place. Twelve years ago, however, he was going great guns—or perhaps I should say great dynamite, for one of the things I most clearly remember about the Buffalo Bill of the French authors was that he always carried with him sticks of dynamite which, when he

"Vous vous Promenez Très Tard ce Soir, Mon Vieux!"

was in a particularly tough spot—that is, surrounded by more than two thousand Indians—he hurled into their midst, destroying them by the hundred. Many of the most inspired paperbacks that I picked up in my quest were used ones I found in those little stalls along the Seine. It was there, for instance, that I came across one of my favorites, "Les Aventures du Wild Bill dans le Far-Ouest."

Wild Bill Hickok was, in this wonderful and beautiful tale, an even more prodigious manipulator of the six-gun than he seems to have been in real life, which, as you must know, is saying a great deal. He frequently mowed down a hundred or two hundred Indians in a few minutes with his redoubtable pistol. The French author of this masterpiece for some mysterious but delightful reason referred to Hickok sometimes as Wild Bill and sometimes as Wild Bird. *"Bonjour, Wild Bill!"* his friend Buffalo Bill often said to him when they met, only to shout a moment later, *"Regardez, Wild Bird! Les Peaux-Rouges!"* The two heroes spent a great deal of their time, as in "The Plainsman," helping each other out of dreadful situations. Once, for example, while hunting Seminoles in Florida, Buffalo Bill fell into a tiger trap that had been set for him by the Indians—he stepped onto what turned out to be sticks covered with grass, and plunged to the bottom of a deep pit. At this point our author wrote, *" 'Mercy me!' s'écria Buffalo Bill."* The great scout was rescued, of course, by none other than Wild Bill, or Bird, who, emerging from the forest to see his old comrade in distress, could only exclaim *"My word!"*

It was, I believe, in another volume that one of the most interesting characters in all French fiction of the Far West appeared, a certain Major Preston, alias Preeton, alias Preslon (the paperbacks rarely spelled anyone's name twice in succession the same way). This hero, we were told when he was introduced, "had distinguished himself in the Civil War by capturing Pittsburgh," a feat which makes Lee's invasion of Pennsylvania seem mere child's play. Major Preeton (I always preferred that alias) had come out West to fight the Indians with cannon, since he believed it absurd that nobody had thought to blow them off the face of the earth with cannon before. How he made out with his artillery against the forest skulkers I have forgotten, but I have an indelible memory of a certain close escape that Buffalo Bill had in this same book. It seems that, through an oversight, he had set out on a scouting trip without his dynamite—he also carried, by the way, cheroots and a flashlight—and hence, when he stumbled upon a huge band of redskins, he had to ride as fast as he could for the nearest fort. He made it just in time. "Buffalo Bill," ran the story, "clattered across the drawbridge and into the fort just ahead of the Indians, who, unable to stop in time, plunged into the moat and were drowned." It may have been in this same tale that Buffalo Bill was once so hard pressed that he had to send for Wild Bird to help him out. Usually, when one was in trouble, the other showed up by a kind of instinct, but this time Wild Bird was nowhere to be found. It was a long time, in fact, before his whereabouts were discovered. You will never guess where he was. He was "taking the baths at Atlantic City under orders of his physician." But he came riding across the country in one day to Buffalo Bill's side, and all was well. Major Preeton, it sticks in my mind, got bored with the service in the Western hotels and went "back to Philadelphia" (Philadelphia appears to have been the capital city of the United States at this time). The Indians in all these tales—and this is probably what gave Major Preeton his great idea—were seldom seen as individuals or in pairs or small groups, but prowled about in well-ordered columns of squads. I recall, however, one drawing (the paperbacks were copiously illustrated) which showed two *Peaux-Rouges* leaping upon and capturing a scout who had wandered too far from his drawbridge one night. The picture represented one of the Indians as smilingly taunting his captive, and the caption read, *"Vous vous promenez très tard ce soir, mon vieux!"* This remained my favorite line until I saw one night in Paris an old W. S. Hart movie called "Le Roi du Far-Quest," in which Hart, insulted by a drunken ruffian, turned upon him and said, in his grim, laconic way, *"Et puis, après?"*

I first became interested in the French tales of the Far West when, one winter in Nice, a French youngster of fifteen, who, it turned out, devoted all his spending money to them, asked me if I had ever seen a "wishtonwish." This meant nothing to me, and I asked him where he had heard about the wishtonwish. He showed me a Far West paperback he was reading. There was a passage in it which recounted an adventure of Buffalo Bill and Wild Bill during the course of which Buffalo Bill signalled to Wild Bird "in the voice of the wishtonwish." Said the author in a parenthesis which at that time gave me as much trouble as Mr. Forster's sentence about the platinum eyebrows does now, "The wishtonwish was seldom heard west of Philadelphia." It was some time—indeed, it was not until I got back to America—that I traced the wishtonwish to its lair, and in so doing discovered the influence of James Fenimore Cooper on all these French writers of Far West tales. Cooper, in his novels, frequently mentioned the wishtonwish, which was a Caddoan Indian name for the prairie dog. Cooper erroneously applied it to the whippoorwill. An animal called the "ouapiti" also figured occasionally in the French stories, and this turned out to be the wapiti, or American elk, also mentioned in Cooper's tales. The French writer's parenthetical note on the habitat of the wishtonwish only added to the delightful confusion and inaccuracy which threaded these wondrous stories.

There were, in my lost and lamented collection, a hundred other fine things, which I have forgotten, but there is one that will forever remain with me. It occurred in a book in which, as I remember it, Billy the Kid, alias Billy the Boy, was the central figure. At any rate, two strangers had turned up in a small Western town and their actions had aroused the suspicions of a group of respectable citizens, who forthwith called on the sheriff to complain about the newcomers. The sheriff listened gravely for a while, got up and buckled on his gun belt, and said, *"Alors, je vais demander ses cartes d'identité!"* There are few things, in any literature, that have ever given me a greater thrill than coming across that line.

Doc Marlowe

I WAS too young to be other than awed and puzzled by Doc Marlowe when I knew him. I was only sixteen when he died. He was sixty-seven. There was that vast difference in our ages and there was a vaster difference in our backgrounds. Doc Marlowe was a medicine-show man. He had been a lot of other things, too: a circus man, the proprietor of a concession at Coney Island, a saloon-keeper; but in his fifties he had traveled around with a tent-show troupe made up of a Mexican named Chickalilli, who threw knives, and a man called Professor Jones, who played the banjo. Doc Marlowe would come out after the entertainment and harangue the crowd and sell bottles of medicine for all kinds of ailments. I found out all this about him gradually, toward the last, and after he died. When I first knew him, he represented the Wild West to me, and there was nobody I admired so much.

I met Doc Marlowe at old Mrs. Willoughby's rooming house. She had been a nurse in our family, and I used to go and visit her over week-ends sometimes, for I was very fond of her. I was about eleven years old then. Doc Marlowe wore scarred leather leggings, a bright-colored bead vest that he said he got from the Indians, and a ten-gallon hat with kitchen matches stuck in the band, all the way around. He was about six feet four inches tall, with big shoulders, and a long, drooping mustache. He let his hair grow long, like General Custer's. He had a wonderful collection of Indian relics and six-shooters, and he used to tell me stories of his adventures in the Far West. His favorite expressions were "Hay, boy!" and "Hay, boy-gie!," which he used the way some people now use "Hot dog!" or "Doggone!" He told me once that he had killed an Indian chief named Yellow Hand in a tomahawk duel on horseback. I thought he was the greatest man I had ever seen. It wasn't until he died and his son came on from New Jersey for the funeral that I found out he had never been in the Far West in his life. He had been born in Brooklyn.

Doc Marlowe had given up the road when I knew him, but he still dealt in what he called "medicines." His stock in trade

ities in the ointment, my friend," Doc Marlowe told him, suavely. He always called the liniment ointment.

News of his miracles got around by word of mouth among the poorer classes of town—he was not able to reach the better people (the "tony folks," he called them)—but there was never a big enough sale to give Doc a steady income. For one thing, people thought there was more magic in Doc's touch than in his liniment, and, for another, the ingredients of Blackhawk cost so much that his profits were not very great. I know, because I used to go to the wholesale chemical company once in a while for him and buy his supplies. Everything that went into the liniment was standard and expensive (and well-known, not secret). A man at the company told me he didn't see how Doc could make much money on it at thirty-five cents a bottle. But even when he was very low in funds Doc never cut out any of the ingredients or substituted cheaper ones. Mrs. Willoughby had suggested it to him once, she told me, when she was helping him "put up a batch," and he had got mad. "He puts a heap of store by that liniment being right up to the mark," she said.

Doc added to his small earnings, I discovered, by money he made gambling. He used to win quite a few dollars on Saturday nights at Freck's saloon, playing poker with the marketmen and the railroaders who dropped in there. It wasn't for several years that I found out Doc cheated. I had never heard about marked cards until he told me about them and showed me his. It was one rainy afternoon, after he had played seven-up with Mrs. Willoughby and old Mr. Peiffer, another roomer of hers. They had played for small stakes (Doc wouldn't play cards unless there was some money up, and Mrs. Willoughby wouldn't play if very much was up). Only twenty or thirty cents had changed hands in the end. Doc had won it all. I remember my astonishment and indignation when it dawned on me that Doc had used the marked cards in playing the old lady and the old man. "You didn't cheat *them*, did you?" I asked him. "Jimmy, my boy," he told me, "the man that calls the turn wins the money." His eyes twinkled and he seemed to enjoy my anger. I was outraged, but I was helpless. I knew I could never tell Mrs. Willoughby about how Doc had cheated her at seven-up. I liked her, but I liked him, too. Once he had given me a whole dollar to buy fireworks with on the Fourth of July.

I remember once, when I was staying at Mrs. Willoughby's, Doc Marlowe was roused out of bed in the middle of the night by a poor woman who was frantic because her little girl was sick. This woman had had the sciatica driven out of her by his liniment, she reminded Doc. He placed her then. She had never been able to pay him a cent for his liniment or his "treatments," and he had given her a great many. He got up and dressed, and went over to her house. The child had colic, I suppose. Doc couldn't have had any idea what was the matter, but he sopped on liniment; he sopped on a whole bottle. When he came back home, two hours later, he said he had "relieved the distress." The little girl had gone to sleep and was all right the next day, whether on account of Doc Marlowe or in spite of him I don't know. "I want to thank you, Doctor," said the mother, tremulously, when she called on him that afternoon. He gave her another bottle of liniment, and he didn't charge her for it or for his "professional call." He used to massage, and give liniment to, a lot of sufferers who were too poor to pay. Mrs. Willoughby told him once that he was too generous and too easily taken in. Doc laughed—and winked at me, with the twinkle in his eye that he had had when he told me how he had cheated the old lady at cards.

Once I went for a walk with him out Town Street on a Saturday afternoon. It was a warm day, and after a while I said I wanted a soda. Well, he said, he didn't care if he took something himself. We went into a drugstore, and I ordered a chocolate soda and he had a lemon phosphate. When we had finished, he said, "Jimmy, my son, I'll match you to see who pays for the drinks." He handed me a quarter and he told me to toss the quarter and he would call the turn. He called heads and won. I paid for the drinks. It left me with a dime.

I was fifteen when Doc got out his pamphlets, as he called them. He had eased the misery of the wife of a small-time printer and the grateful man had given him a special price on two thousand advertising pamphlets. There was very little in them about Blackhawk Liniment. They were mostly about

Doc himself and his "Life in the Far West." He had gone out to Franklin Park one day with a photographer—another of his numerous friends—and there the photographer took dozens of pictures of Doc, a lariat in one hand, a six-shooter in the other. I had gone along. When the pamphlets came out, there were the pictures of Doc, peering around trees, crouching behind bushes, whirling the lariat, aiming the gun. "Dr. H. M. Marlowe Hunting Indians" was one of the captions. "Dr. H. M. Marlowe after Hoss-Thieves" was another one. He was very proud of the pamphlets and always had a sheaf with him. He would pass them out to people on the street.

Two years before he died Doc got hold of an ancient, wheezy Cadillac somewhere. He aimed to start traveling around again, he said, but he never did, because the old automobile was so worn out it wouldn't hold up for more than a mile or so. It was about this time that a man named Hardman and his wife came to stay at Mrs. Willoughby's. They were farm people from around Lancaster who had sold their place. They got to like Doc because he was so jolly, they said, and they enjoyed his stories. He treated Mrs. Hardman for an old complaint in the small of her back and wouldn't take any money for it. They thought he was a fine gentleman. Then there came a day when they announced that they were going to St. Louis, where they had a son. They talked some of settling in St. Louis. Doc Marlowe told them they ought to buy a nice auto cheap and drive out, instead of going by train—it wouldn't cost much and they could see the country, give themselves a treat. Now, he knew where they could pick up just such a car.

Of course, he finally sold them the decrepit Cadillac—it had been stored away somewhere in the back of a garage whose owner kept it there for nothing because Doc had relieved his mother of a distress in the groins, as Doc explained it. I don't know just how the garage man doctored up the car, but he did. It actually chugged along pretty steadily when Doc took the Hardmans out for a trial spin. He told them he hated to part with it, but he finally let them have it for a hundred dollars. I knew, of course, and so did Doc, that it couldn't last many miles.

Doc got a letter from the Hardmans in St. Louis ten days

later. They had had to abandon the old junk pile in West
Jefferson, some fifteen miles out of Columbus. Doc read the
letter aloud to me, peering over his glasses, his eyes twinkling,
every now and then punctuating the lines with "Hay, boy!"
and "Hay, boy-gie!" "I just want you to know, Dr. Marlowe," he read, "what I think of low-life swindlers like you
[Hay, boy!] and that it will be a long day before I put my
trust in a two-faced lyer and imposture again [Hay, boy-gie!].
The garrage man in W. Jefferson told us your old rattle-trap
had been doctored up just to fool us. It was a low down dirty
trick as no swine would play on a white man [Hay, boy!]."
Far from being disturbed by the letter, Doc Marlowe was
plainly amused. He took off his glasses, after he finished it and
laughed, his hand to his brow and his eyes closed. I was pretty
mad, because I had liked the Hardmans, and because they had
liked him. Doc Marlowe put the letter carefully back into its
envelope and tucked it away in his inside coat pocket, as if it
were something precious. Then he picked up a pack of cards
and began to lay out a solitaire hand. "Want to set in a little
seven-up game, Jimmy?" he asked me. I was furious. "Not
with a cheater like you!" I shouted, and stamped out of the
room, slamming the door. I could hear him chuckling to himself behind me.

The last time I saw Doc Marlowe was just a few days before
he died. I didn't know anything about death, but I knew that
he was dying when I saw him. His voice was very faint and
his face was drawn; they told me he had a lot of pain. When
I got ready to leave the room, he asked me to bring him a tin
box that was on his bureau. I got it and handed it to him.
He poked around in it for a while with unsteady fingers and
finally found what he wanted. He handed it to me. It was a
quarter, or rather it looked like a quarter, but it had heads on
both sides. "Never let the other fella call the turn, Jimmy, my
boy," said Doc, with a shadow of his old twinkle and the echo
of his old chuckle. I still have the two-headed quarter. For a
long time I didn't like to think about it, or about Doc Marlowe, but I do now.

The Admiral on the Wheel

WHEN the colored maid stepped on my glasses the other morning, it was the first time they had been broken since the late Thomas A. Edison's seventy-ninth birthday. I remember that day well, because I was working for a newspaper then and I had been assigned to go over to West Orange that morning and interview Mr. Edison. I got up early and, in reaching for my glasses under the bed (where I always put them), I found that one of my more sober and reflective Scotch terriers was quietly chewing them. Both tortoiseshell temples (the pieces that go over your ears) had been eaten and Jeannie was toying with the lenses in a sort of jaded way. It was in going over to Jersey that day, without my glasses, that I realized that the disadvantages of defective vision (bad eyesight) are at least partially compensated for by its peculiar advantages. Up to that time I had been in the habit of going to bed when my glasses were broken and lying there until they were fixed again. I had believed I could not go very far without them, not more than a block, anyway, on account of the danger of bumping into things, getting a headache, losing my way. None of those things happened, but a lot of others did. I saw the Cuban flag flying over a national bank, I saw a gay old lady with a gray parasol walk right through the side of a truck, I saw a cat roll across a street in a small striped barrel, I saw bridges rise lazily into the air, like balloons.

I suppose you have to have just the right proportion of sight to encounter such phenomena: I seem to remember that oculists have told me I have only two-fifths vision without what one of them referred to as "artificial compensation" (glasses). With three-fifths vision or better, I suppose the Cuban flag would have been an American flag, the gay old lady a garbage man with a garbage can on his back, the cat a piece of butcher's paper blowing in the wind, the floating bridges smoke from tugs, hanging in the air. With perfect vision, one is extricably trapped in the workaday world, a prisoner of reality, as lost in the commonplace America of 1937 as Alexander Selkirk was lost on his lonely island. For the hawk-eyed person life has none of those soft edges which for me blur into fantasy; for such a person an electric welder is merely an electric welder, not a radiant fool setting off a sky-rocket by day. The kingdom of the partly blind is a little like Oz, a little like Wonderland, a little like Poictesme. Anything you can think of, and a lot you never would think of, can happen there.

For three days after the maid, in cleaning the apartment, stepped on my glasses—I had not put them far enough under the bed—I worked at home and did not go uptown to have them fixed. It was in this period that I made the acquaintance of a remarkable Chesapeake spaniel. I looked out my window and after a moment spotted him, a noble, silent dog lying on a ledge above the entrance to a brownstone house in lower Fifth Avenue. He lay there, proud and austere, for three days and nights, sleepless, never eating, the perfect watchdog. No ordinary dog could have got up on the high ledge above the doorway, to begin with; no ordinary people would have owned such an animal. The ordinary people were the people who walked by the house and did not see the dog. Oh, I got my glasses fixed finally and I know that now the dog has gone, but I haven't looked to see what prosaic object occupies the spot where he so staunchly stood guard over one of the last of the old New York houses on Fifth Avenue; perhaps an unpainted flowerbox or a cleaning cloth dropped from an upper window by a careless menial. The moment of disenchantment would be too hard; I never look out that particular window any more.

Sometimes at night, even with my glasses on, I see strange and unbelievable sights, mainly when I am riding in an automobile which somebody else is driving (I never drive myself at night out of fear that I might turn up at the portals of some mystical monastery and never return). Only last summer I was riding with someone along a country road when suddenly I cried at him to look out. He slowed down and asked me sharply what was the matter. There is no worse experience than to have someone shout at you to look out for something you don't see. What this driver didn't see and I did see (two-fifths vision works a kind of magic in the night) was a little old admiral in full-dress uniform riding a bicycle at right angles to the car I was in. He might have been starlight behind a tree, or a billboard advertising Moxie; I don't know—we were quickly past the place he rode out of; but I would recognize him if I saw him again. His beard was blowing in the breeze and his hat was set at a rakish angle, like Admiral Beatty's. He was having a swell time. The gentleman who was driving the car has been, since that night, a trifle stiff and distant with me. I suppose you can hardly blame him.

To go back to my daylight experiences with the naked eye, it was me, in case you have heard the story, who once killed fifteen white chickens with small stones. The poor beggars never had a chance. This happened many years ago when I was living at Jay, New York. I had a vegetable garden some seventy feet behind the house, and the lady of the house had asked me to keep an eye on it in my spare moments and to chase away any chickens from neighboring farms that came pecking around. One morning, getting up from my typewriter, I wandered out behind the house and saw that a flock of white chickens had invaded the garden. I had, to be sure, misplaced my glasses for the moment, but I could still see well enough to let the chickens have it with ammunition from a pile of stones that I kept handy for the purpose. Before I could be stopped, I had riddled all the tomato plants in the garden, over the tops of which the lady of the house had, the twilight before, placed newspapers and paper bags to ward off the effects of frost. It was one of the darker experiences of my dimmer hours.

Some day, I suppose, when the clouds are heavy and the rain is coming down and the pressure of realities is too great, I shall deliberately take my glasses off and go wandering out into the streets. I daresay I may never be heard of again (I have always believed it was Ambrose Bierce's vision and not his whim that caused him to wander into oblivion). I imagine I'll have a remarkable time, wherever I end up.

THE LAST FLOWER

A PARABLE IN PICTURES

FOR ROSEMARY

IN THE WISTFUL HOPE THAT HER WORLD
WILL BE BETTER THAN MINE

WORLD WAR XII, AS EVERYBODY KNOWS,

BROUGHT ABOUT THE COLLAPSE OF CIVILIZATION

TOWNS, CITIES, AND VILLAGES DISAPPEARED
FROM THE EARTH

ALL THE GROVES AND FORESTS WERE
DESTROYED

AND ALL THE GARDENS

AND ALL THE WORKS OF ART

MEN, WOMEN, AND CHILDREN BECAME LOWER
THAN THE LOWER ANIMALS

DISCOURAGED AND DISILLUSIONED, DOGS DESERTED
THEIR FALLEN MASTERS

EMBOLDENED BY THE PITIFUL CONDITION
OF THE FORMER LORDS OF THE EARTH,
RABBITS DESCENDED UPON THEM

BOOKS, PAINTINGS, AND MUSIC DISAPPEARED
FROM THE EARTH, AND HUMAN BEINGS
JUST SAT AROUND, DOING NOTHING

YEARS AND YEARS WENT BY

EVEN THE FEW GENERALS WHO WERE LEFT
FORGOT WHAT THE LAST WAR HAD DECIDED

BOYS AND GIRLS GREW UP TO STARE AT EACH OTHER
BLANKLY, FOR LOVE HAD PASSED FROM THE EARTH

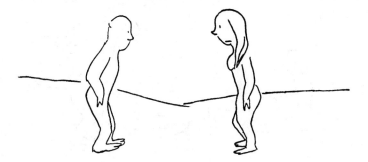

ONE DAY A YOUNG GIRL WHO HAD NEVER
SEEN A FLOWER CHANCED TO COME
UPON THE LAST ONE IN THE WORLD

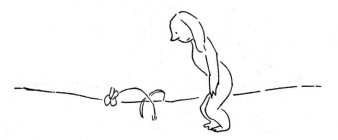

SHE TOLD THE OTHER HUMAN BEINGS
THAT THE LAST FLOWER WAS DYING

THE ONLY ONE WHO PAID ANY ATTENTION
TO HER WAS A YOUNG MAN SHE
FOUND WANDERING ABOUT

TOGETHER THE YOUNG MAN AND THE GIRL
NURTURED THE FLOWER AND IT BEGAN
TO LIVE AGAIN

ONE DAY A BEE VISITED THE FLOWER,
AND A HUMMINGBIRD

BEFORE LONG THERE WERE TWO FLOWERS, AND
THEN FOUR, AND THEN A GREAT MANY

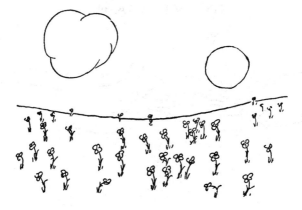

GROVES AND FORESTS FLOURISHED AGAIN

THE YOUNG GIRL BEGAN TO TAKE
AN INTEREST IN HOW SHE LOOKED

THE YOUNG MAN DISCOVERED THAT
TOUCHING THE GIRL WAS PLEASURABLE

LOVE WAS REBORN INTO THE WORLD

THEIR CHILDREN GREW UP STRONG AND HEALTHY
AND LEARNED TO RUN AND LAUGH

DOGS CAME OUT OF THEIR EXILE

THE YOUNG MAN DISCOVERED, BY PUTTING ONE
STONE UPON ANOTHER, HOW TO BUILD A SHELTER

PRETTY SOON EVERYBODY WAS BUILDING SHELTERS

TOWNS, CITIES, AND VILLAGES SPRANG UP

SONG CAME BACK INTO THE WORLD

AND TROUBADOURS AND JUGGLERS

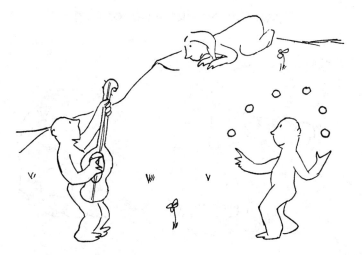

AND TAILORS AND COBBLERS

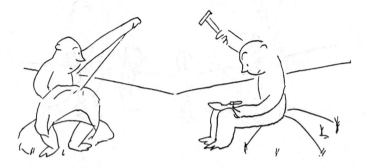

AND PAINTERS AND POETS

AND SCULPTORS AND WHEELWRIGHTS

AND SOLDIERS

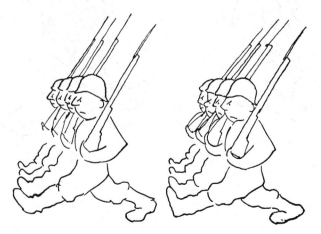

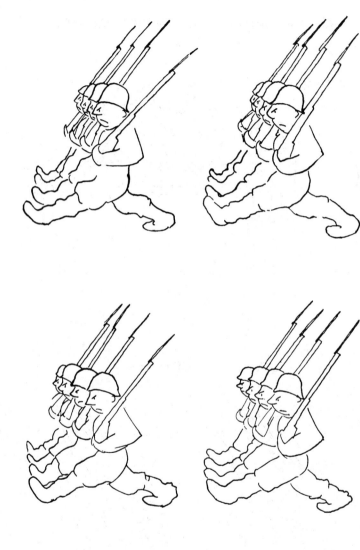

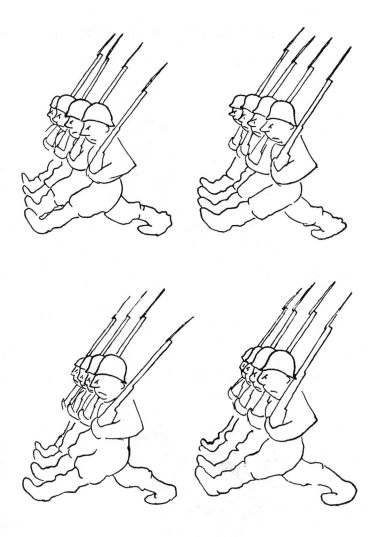

AND LIEUTENANTS AND CAPTAINS

AND GENERALS AND MAJOR·GENERALS

AND LIBERATORS

SOME PEOPLE WENT ONE PLACE TO LIVE,
AND SOME ANOTHER

BEFORE LONG, THOSE WHO WENT TO LIVE IN THE VALLEYS
WISHED THEY HAD GONE TO LIVE IN THE HILLS

AND THOSE WHO HAD GONE TO LIVE IN THE HILLS
WISHED THEY HAD GONE TO LIVE IN THE VALLEYS

THE LIBERATORS, UNDER THE GUIDANCE OF GOD,
SET FIRE TO THE DISCONTENT

SO PRESENTLY THE WORLD WAS AT WAR AGAIN

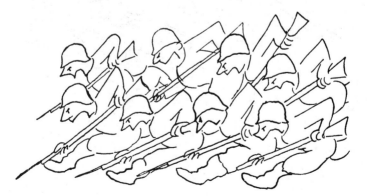

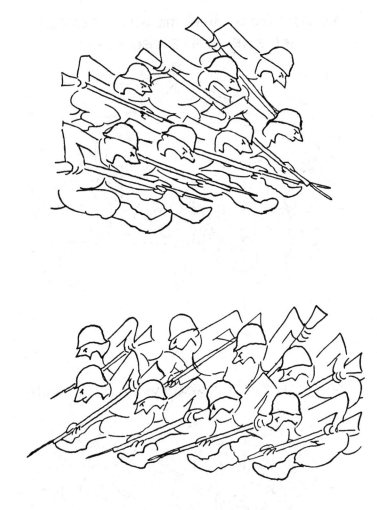

THIS TIME THE DESTRUCTION WAS SO COMPLETE...

EXCEPT ONE MAN

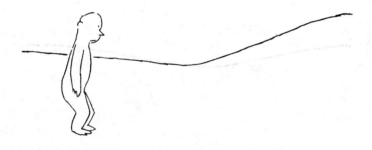

AND ONE WOMAN

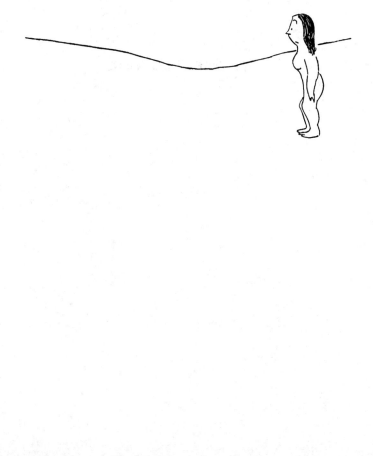

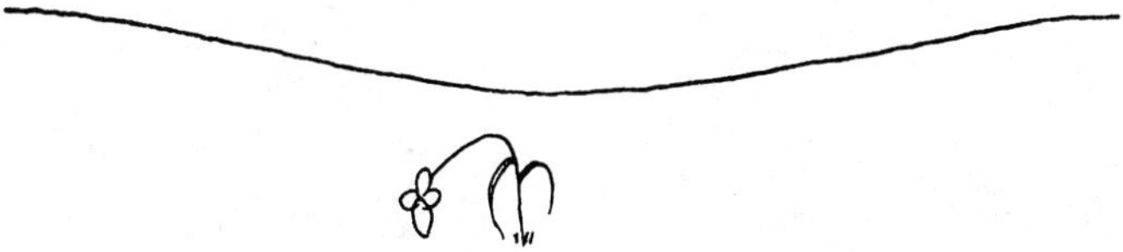

FABLES FOR OUR TIME
AND
FAMOUS POEMS
ILLUSTRATED

The Mouse Who Went
to the Country

ONCE upon a Sunday there was a city mouse who went
to visit a country mouse. He hid away on a train the
country mouse had told him to take, only to find that on
Sundays it did not stop at Beddington. Hence the city mouse
could not get off at Beddington and catch a bus for Sibert's
Junction, where he was to be met by the country mouse. The
city mouse, in fact, was carried on to Middleburg, where he
waited three hours for a train to take him back. When he got
back to Beddington he found that the last bus for Sibert's
Junction had just left, so he ran and he ran and he ran and
he finally caught the bus and crept aboard, only to find that
it was not the bus for Sibert's Junction at all, but was going
in the opposite direction through Pell's Hollow and Grumm
to a place called Wimberby. When the bus finally stopped, the
city mouse got out into a heavy rain and found that there
were no more buses that night going anywhere. "To the hell
with it," said the city mouse, and he walked back to the city.
   Moral: Stay where you are, you're sitting pretty.

447

The Little Girl and the Wolf

ONE AFTERNOON a big wolf waited in a dark forest for a little girl to come along carrying a basket of food to her grandmother. Finally a little girl did come along and she was carrying a basket of food. "Are you carrying that basket to your grandmother?" asked the wolf. The little girl said yes, she was. So the wolf asked her where her grandmother lived and the little girl told him and he disappeared into the wood.

When the little girl opened the door of her grandmother's house she saw that there was somebody in bed with a nightcap and nightgown on. She had approached no nearer than twenty-five feet from the bed when she saw that it was not her grandmother but the wolf, for even in a nightcap a wolf does not look any more like your grandmother than the Metro-Goldwyn lion looks like Calvin Coolidge. So the little girl took an automatic out of her basket and shot the wolf dead.

Moral: It is not so easy to fool little girls nowadays as it used to be.

The Two Turkeys

ONCE upon a time there were two turkeys, an old turkey and a young turkey. The old turkey had been cock of the walk for many years and the young turkey wanted to take his place. "I'll knock that old buzzard cold one of these days," the young turkey told his friends. "Sure you will, Joe, sure you will," his friends said, for Joe was treating them to some corn he had found. Then the friends went and told the old turkey what the young turkey had said. "Why, I'll have his gizzard!" said the old turkey, setting out some corn for his visitors. "Sure you will, Doc, sure you will," said the visitors.

One day the young turkey walked over to where the old turkey was telling tales of his prowess in battle. "I'll bat your teeth into your crop," said the young turkey. "You and who else?" said the old turkey. So they began to circle around each other, sparring for an opening. Just then the farmer who owned the turkeys swept up the young one and carried him off and wrung his neck.

Moral: Youth will be served, frequently stuffed with chestnuts.

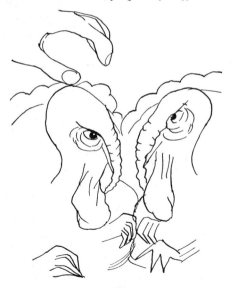

The Tiger Who Understood People

ONCE upon a time there was a tiger who escaped from a zoo in the United States and made his way back to the jungle. During his captivity the tiger had learned a great deal about how men do things and he thought he would apply their methods to life in the jungle. The first day he was home he met a leopard and he said, "There's no use in you and me hunting for food; we'll make the other animals bring it to us." "How will we do that?" asked the leopard. "Easy," said the tiger, "you and I will tell everybody that we are going to put on a fight and that every animal will have to bring a freshly killed boar in order to get in and see the fight. Then we will just spar around and not hurt each other. Later you can say you broke a bone in your paw during the second round and I will say I broke a bone in my paw during the first round. Then we will announce a return engagement and they'll have to bring us more wild boars." "I don't think this will work," said the leopard. "Oh, yes it will," said the tiger. "You just go around saying that you can't help winning because I am a big palooka and I will go around saying I can't lose because you are a big palooka, and everybody will want to come and see the fight."

So the leopard went around telling everybody that he couldn't help winning because the tiger was a big palooka and the tiger went around telling everybody he couldn't lose because the leopard was a big palooka. The night of the fight came and the tiger and the leopard were very hungry because they hadn't gone out and done any hunting at all; they wanted to get the fight over as soon as possible and eat some of the freshly killed wild boars which all the animals would bring to the fight. But when the hour of the combat came none of the animals at all showed up. "The way I look at it," a fox had told them, "is this: if the leopard can't help winning and the tiger can't lose, it will be a draw and a draw is a very dull thing to watch, particularly when fought by fighters who are both big palookas." The animals all saw the logic of this and stayed away from the arena. When it got to be midnight and it was obvious that none of the animals would appear and that there wouldn't be any wild-boar meat to devour, the tiger and the leopard fell upon each other in a rage. They were both injured so badly and they were both so worn out by hunger that a couple of wild boars who came wandering along attacked them and killed them easily.

Moral: If you live as humans do, it will be the end of you.

The Fairly Intelligent Fly

A LARGE spider in an old house built a beautiful web in which to catch flies. Every time a fly landed on the web and was entangled in it the spider devoured him, so that when another fly came along he would think the web was a safe and quiet place in which to rest. One day a fairly intelligent fly buzzed around above the web so long without lighting that the spider appeared and said, "Come on down." But the fly was too clever for him and said, "I never light where I don't see other flies and I don't see any other flies in your house." So he flew away until he came to a place where there were a great many other flies. He was about to settle down among them when a bee buzzed up and said, "Hold it, stupid, that's flypaper. All those flies are trapped." "Don't be silly," said the fly, "they're dancing." So he settled down and became stuck to the flypaper with all the other flies.

Moral: There is no safety in numbers, or in anything else.

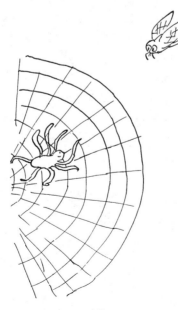

The Lion Who Wanted to Zoom

THERE was once a lion who coveted an eagle's wings. So he sent a message to the eagle asking him to call, and when the eagle came to the lion's den the lion said, "I will trade you my mane for your wings." "Keep talking, brother," said the eagle. "Without my wings I could no longer fly." "So what?" said the lion. "I can't fly now, but that doesn't keep me from being king of beasts. I became king of beasts on account of my magnificent mane." "All right," said the eagle, "but give me your mane first." "Just approach a little nearer," said the lion, "so that I can hand it to you." The eagle came closer and the lion clapped a huge paw on him, pinning him to the ground. "Come across with those wings!" he snarled.

So the lion took the eagle's wings but kept his own mane. The eagle was very despondent for a while and then he had an idea. "I bet you can't fly off the top of that great rock yonder," said the eagle. "Who, me?" said the lion, and he walked to the top of the rock and took off. His weight was too great for the eagle's wings to support, and besides he did not know how to fly, never having tried it before. So he crashed at the foot of the rock and burst into flames. The eagle hastily climbed down to him and regained his wings and took off the lion's mane, which he put about his own neck and shoulders. Flying back to the rocky nest where he lived with his mate, he decided to have some fun with her. So, covered with the lion's mane, he poked his head into the nest and in a deep, awful voice said *"Harrrooo!"* His mate, who was very nervous anyway, grabbed a pistol from a bureau drawer and shot him dead, thinking he was a lion.

Moral: Never allow a nervous female to have access to a pistol, no matter what you're wearing.

The Very Proper Gander

Not so very long ago there was a very fine gander. He was strong and smooth and beautiful and he spent most of his time singing to his wife and children. One day somebody who saw him strutting up and down in his yard and singing remarked, "There is a very proper gander." An old hen overheard this and told her husband about it that night in the roost. "They said something about propaganda," she said. "I have always suspected that," said the rooster, and he went around the barnyard next day telling everybody that the very fine gander was a dangerous bird, more than likely a hawk in gander's clothing. A small brown hen remembered a time when at a great distance she had seen the gander talking with some hawks in the forest. "They were up to no good," she said. A duck remembered that the gander had once told him he did not believe in anything. "He said to hell with the flag, too," said the duck. A guinea hen recalled that she had once seen somebody who looked very much like the gander throw something that looked a great deal like a bomb. Finally everybody snatched up sticks and stones and descended on the gander's house. He was strutting in his front yard, singing to his children and his wife. "There he is!" everybody cried. "Hawk-lover! Unbeliever! Flag-hater! Bomb-thrower!" So they set upon him and drove him out of the country.

Moral: Anybody who you or your wife thinks is going to overthrow the government by violence must be driven out of the country.

The Moth and the Star

A YOUNG and impressionable moth once set his heart on a certain star. He told his mother about this and she counselled him to set his heart on a bridge lamp instead. "Stars aren't the thing to hang around," she said; "lamps are the thing to hang around." "You get somewhere that way," said the moth's father. "You don't get anywhere chasing stars." But the moth would not heed the words of either parent. Every evening at dusk when the star came out he would start flying toward it and every morning at dawn he would crawl back home worn out with his vain endeavor. One day his father said to him, "You haven't burned a wing in months, boy, and it looks to me as if you were never going to. All your brothers have been badly burned flying around street lamps and all your sisters have been terribly singed flying around house lamps. Come on, now, get out of here and get yourself scorched! A big strapping moth like you without a mark on him!"

The moth left his father's house, but he would not fly around street lamps and he would not fly around house lamps. He went right on trying to reach the star, which was four and one-third light years, or twenty-five trillion miles, away. The moth thought it was just caught in the top branches of an elm. He never did reach the star, but he went right on trying, night after night, and when he was a very, very old moth he began to think that he really had reached the star and he went around saying so. This gave him a deep and lasting pleasure, and he lived to a great old age. His parents and his brothers and his sisters had all been burned to death when they were quite young.

Moral: Who flies afar from the sphere of our sorrow is here today and here tomorrow.

The Shrike and the Chipmunks

O NCE upon a time there were two chipmunks, a male and a female. The male chipmunk thought that arranging nuts in artistic patterns was more fun than just piling them up to see how many you could pile up. The female was all for piling up as many as you could. She told her husband that if he gave up making designs with the nuts there would be room in their large cave for a great many more and he would soon become the wealthiest chipmunk in the woods. But he would not let her interfere with his designs, so she flew into a rage and left him. "The shrike will get you," she said, "because you are helpless and cannot look after yourself." To be sure, the female chipmunk had not been gone three nights before the male had to dress for a banquet and could not find his studs or shirt or suspenders. So he couldn't go to the banquet, but that was just as well, because all the chipmunks who did go were attacked and killed by a weasel.

The next day the shrike began hanging around outside the chipmunk's cave, waiting to catch him. The shrike couldn't get in because the doorway was clogged up with soiled laundry and dirty dishes. "He will come out for a walk after breakfast and I will get him then," thought the shrike. But the chipmunk slept all day and did not get up and have breakfast until after dark. Then he came out for a breath of air before beginning work on a new design. The shrike swooped down to snatch up the chipmunk, but could not see very well on account of the dark, so he batted his head against an alder branch and was killed.

A few days later the female chipmunk returned and saw the awful mess the house was in. She went to the bed and shook her husband. "What would you do without me?" she demanded. "Just go on living, I guess," he said. "You wouldn't last five days," she told him. She swept the house and did the dishes and sent out the laundry, and then she made the chipmunk get up and wash and dress. "You can't be healthy if you lie in bed all day and never get any exercise," she told him. So she took him for a walk in the bright sunlight and

460

they were both caught and killed by the shrike's brother, a shrike named Stoop.

Moral: Early to rise and early to bed makes a male healthy and wealthy and dead.

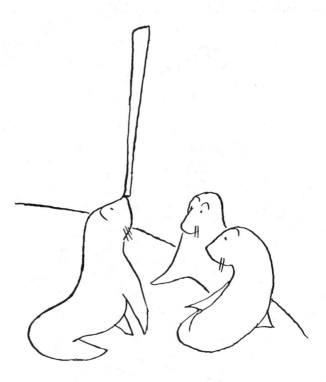

The Seal Who Became Famous

A SEAL who lay basking on a large, smooth rock said to himself: all I ever do is swim. None of the other seals can swim any better than I can, he reflected, but, on the other hand, they can all swim just as well. The more he pondered the monotony and uniformity of his life, the more depressed he became. That night he swam away and joined a circus.

Within two years the seal had become a great balancer. He could balance lamps, billiard cues, medicine balls, hassocks, taborets, dollar cigars, and anything else you gave him. When he read in a book a reference to the Great Seal of the United States, he thought it meant him. In the winter of his third year as a performer he went back to the large, smooth rock to visit his friends and family. He gave them the Big Town stuff right away: the latest slang, liquor in a golden flask, zippers, a gardenia in his lapel. He balanced for them everything there was on the rock to balance, which wasn't much. When he had run through his repertory, he asked the other seals if they could do what he had done and they all said no. "O.K.," he said. "Let's see you do something I can't do." Since the only thing they could do was swim, they all plunged off the rock into the sea. The circus seal plunged right after them, but he was so hampered by his smart city clothes, including a pair of seventeen-dollar shoes, that he began to founder at once. Since he hadn't been in swimming for three years, he had forgot what to do with his flippers and tail, and he went down for the third time before the other seals could reach him. They gave him a simple but dignified funeral.

Moral: Whom God has equipped with flippers should not monkey around with zippers.

The Hunter and the Elephant

ONCE upon a time there was a hunter who spent the best years of his life looking for a pink elephant. He looked in Cathay and he looked in Africa; he looked in Zanzibar and he looked in India; but he couldn't find one. The longer he looked, the more he wanted a pink elephant. He would trample black orchids and he would walk right past purple cows, so intent was he on his quest. Then one day in a far corner of the world he came upon a pink elephant and he spent ten days digging a trap for it and he hired forty natives to help him drive the elephant into the trap. The pink elephant was finally captured and tied up and taken back to America.

When the hunter got home, he found that his farm was really no place for an elephant. It trampled his wife's dahlias and peonies, it broke his children's toys, it crushed the smaller animals around the place, and it smashed pianos and kitchen cabinets as if they were berry boxes. One day, when the hunter had had the elephant for about two years, he woke up to find that his wife had left his bed and his children had left his board and all the animals on the estate were dead except the elephant. The elephant was the same as ever except that it had faded. It wasn't pink any more. It was white.

Moral: A burden in the bush is worth two on your hands.

The Scotty Who Knew Too Much

SEVERAL summers ago there was a Scotty who went to the country for a visit. He decided that all the farm dogs were cowards, because they were afraid of a certain animal that had a white stripe down its back. "You are a pussy-cat and I can lick you," the Scotty said to the farm dog who lived in the house where the Scotty was visiting. "I can lick the little animal with the white stripe, too. Show him to me." "Don't you want to ask any questions about him?" said the farm dog. "Naw," said the Scotty. "*You* ask the questions."

So the farm dog took the Scotty into the woods and showed him the white-striped animal and the Scotty closed in on him, growling and slashing. It was all over in a moment and the Scotty lay on his back. When he came to, the farm dog said, "What happened?" "He threw vitriol," said the Scotty, "but he never laid a glove on me."

A few days later the farm dog told the Scotty there was another animal all the farm dogs were afraid of. "Lead me to him," said the Scotty. "I can lick anything that doesn't wear horseshoes." "Don't you want to ask any questions about him?" said the farm dog. "Naw," said the Scotty. "Just show me where he hangs out." So the farm dog led him to a place in the woods and pointed out the little animal when he came along. "A clown," said the Scotty, "a pushover," and he closed in, leading with his left and exhibiting some mighty fancy footwork. In less than a second the Scotty was flat on his back, and when he woke up the farm dog was pulling quills out of him. "What happened?" said the farm dog. "He pulled a knife on me," said the Scotty, "but at least I have learned how you fight out here in the country, and now I am going to beat *you* up." So he closed in on the farm dog, holding his nose with one front paw to ward off the vitriol and covering his eyes with the other front paw to keep out the knives. The Scotty couldn't see his opponent and he couldn't smell his opponent and he was so badly beaten that he had to be taken back to the city and put in a nursing home.

Moral: It is better to ask some of the questions than to know all the answers.

The Bear Who Let It Alone

IN THE WOODS of the Far West there once lived a brown bear who could take it or let it alone. He would go into a bar where they sold mead, a fermented drink made of honey, and he would have just two drinks. Then he would put some money on the bar and say, "See what the bears in the back room will have," and he would go home. But finally he took to drinking by himself most of the day. He would reel home at night, kick over the umbrella stand, knock down the bridge lamps, and ram his elbows through the windows. Then he would collapse on the floor and lie there until he went to sleep. His wife was greatly distressed and his children were very frightened.

At length the bear saw the error of his ways and began to reform. In the end he became a famous teetotaller and a persistent temperance lecturer. He would tell everybody that came to his house about the awful effects of drink, and he would boast about how strong and well he had become since he gave up touching the stuff. To demonstrate this, he would stand on his head and on his hands and he would turn cartwheels in the house, kicking over the umbrella stand, knocking down the bridge lamps, and ramming his elbows through the windows. Then he would lie down on the floor, tired by his healthful exercise, and go to sleep. His wife was greatly distressed and his children were very frightened.

Moral: You might as well fall flat on your face as lean over too far backward.

The Owl Who Was God

ONCE upon a starless midnight there was an owl who sat on the branch of an oak tree. Two ground moles tried to slip quietly by, unnoticed. "You!" said the owl. "Who?" they quavered, in fear and astonishment, for they could not believe it was possible for anyone to see them in that thick darkness. "You two!" said the owl. The moles hurried away and told the other creatures of the field and forest that the owl was the greatest and wisest of all animals because he could see in the dark and because he could answer any question. "I'll see about that," said a secretary bird, and he called on the owl one night when it was again very dark. "How many claws am I holding up?" said the secretary bird. "Two," said the owl, and that was right. "Can you give me another expression for 'that is to say' or 'namely'?" asked the secretary bird. "To wit," said the owl. "Why does a lover call on his love?" asked the secretary bird. "To woo," said the owl.

The secretary bird hastened back to the other creatures and reported that the owl was indeed the greatest and wisest animal in the world because he could see in the dark and because he could answer any question. "Can he see in the daytime, too?" asked a red fox. "Yes," echoed a dormouse and a French poodle. "Can he see in the daytime, too?" All the other creatures laughed loudly at this silly question, and they set upon the red fox and his friends and drove them out of the region. Then they sent a messenger to the owl and asked him to be their leader.

When the owl appeared among the animals it was high noon and the sun was shining brightly. He walked very slowly, which gave him an appearance of great dignity, and he peered about him with large, staring eyes, which gave him an air of tremendous importance. "He's God!" screamed a Plymouth Rock hen. And the others took up the cry "He's God!" So they followed him wherever he went and when he began to bump into things they began to bump into things, too. Finally he came to a concrete highway and he started up the middle of it and all the other creatures followed him. Presently a hawk, who was acting as outrider, observed a truck coming toward them at fifty miles an hour, and he reported to the secretary bird and the secretary bird reported to the owl. "There's danger ahead," said the secretary bird. "To wit?" said the owl. The secretary bird told him. "Aren't you afraid?" he asked. "Who?" said the owl calmly, for he could not see the truck. "He's God!" cried all the creatures again, and they were still crying "He's God!" when the truck hit them and ran them down. Some of the animals were merely injured, but most of them, including the owl, were killed.

Moral: You can fool too many of the people too much of the time.

The Sheep in Wolf's Clothing

NOT very long ago there were two sheep who put on wolf's clothing and went among the wolves as spies, to see what was going on. They arrived on a fete day, when all the wolves were singing in the taverns or dancing in the street. The first sheep said to his companion, "Wolves are just like us, for they gambol and frisk. Every day is fete day in Wolfland." He made some notes on a piece of paper (which a spy should never do) and he headed them "My Twenty-Four Hours in Wolfland," for he had decided not to be a spy any longer but to write a book on Wolfland and also some articles for the *Sheep's Home Companion*. The other sheep guessed what he was planning to do, so he slipped away and began to write a book called "My Ten Hours in Wolfland." The first sheep suspected what was up when he found his friend had gone, so he wired a book to his publisher called "My Five Hours in Wolfland," and it was announced for publication first. The other sheep immediately sold his manuscript to a newspaper syndicate for serialization.

Both sheep gave the same message to their fellows: wolves were just like sheep, for they gambolled and frisked, and every day was fete day in Wolfland. The citizens of Sheepland were convinced by all this, so they drew in their sentinels and they let down their barriers. When the wolves descended on them one night, howling and slavering, the sheep were as easy to kill as flies on a windowpane.

Moral: Don't get it right, just get it written.

The Stork Who Married a Dumb Wife

A DANISH stork was in the habit of spending six nights a
week out on the town with the boys, drinking and dicing
and playing the match game. His wife had never left their nest,
which was on a chimney top, since he married her, for he did
not want her to get wise to the ways of the male. When he
got home, which was usually at four o'clock in the morning—
unless the party had gone on to Reuben's—he always brought
her a box of candy and handed it to her together with a stork
story, which is the same as a cock-and-bull story. "I've been
out delivering babies," he would say. "It's killing me, but it
is my duty to go on." "Who do you deliver babies for?" she
asked one morning. "Human beings," he said. "A human
being cannot have a baby without help from someone. All the
other animals can, but human beings are helpless. They depend on the other animals for everything from food and clothing to companionship." Just then the phone rang and the
stork answered it. "Another baby on the way," he said when
he had hung up. "I'll have to go out again tonight." So that
night he went out again and did not get home until seven-
thirty in the morning. "Thish was very special case," he said,
handing his wife a box of candy. "Five girls." He did not add
that the five girls were all blondes in their twenties.

After a while the female stork got to thinking. Her husband
had told her never to leave the nest, because the world was
full of stork traps, but she began to doubt this. So she flew
out into the world, looking and listening. In this way she
learned to tell time and to take male talk with a grain of salt;
she found out that candy is dandy, as the poet has said, but
that licker is quicker; she discovered that the offspring of the
human species are never brought into the world by storks.
This last discovery was a great blow to her, but it was a greater
blow to Papa when he came home the next morning at a
quarter to six. "Hello, you phony obstetrician," said his wife
coldly. "How are all the blonde quintuplets today?" And she
crowned him with a chimney brick.

*Moral: The male was made to lie and roam, but woman's
place is in the home.*

The Green Isle in the Sea

ONE sweet morning in the Year of Our Lord, Nineteen hundred and thirty-nine, a little old gentleman got up and threw wide the windows of his bedroom, letting in the living sun. A black widow spider, who had been dozing on the balcony, slashed at him, and although she missed, she did not miss very far. The old gentleman went downstairs to the dining-room and was just sitting down to a splendid breakfast when his grandson, a boy named Burt, pulled the chair from under him. The old man's hip was strained but it was fortunately not broken.

Out in the street, as he limped toward a little park with many trees, which was to him a green isle in the sea, the old man was tripped up by a gaily-colored hoop sent rolling at him, with a kind of disinterested deliberation, by a grim little girl. Hobbling on a block farther, the old man was startled, but not exactly surprised, when a bold daylight robber stuck a gun in his ribs. "Put 'em up, Mac," said the robber, "and come across." Mac put them up and came across with his watch and money and a gold ring his mother had given him when he was a boy.

When at last the old gentleman staggered into the little park, which had been to him a fountain and a shrine, he saw that half the trees had been killed by a blight, and the other half by a bug. Their leaves were gone and they no longer afforded any protection from the skies, so that the hundred planes which appeared suddenly overhead had an excellent view of the little old gentleman through their bombing-sights.

Moral: The world is so full of a number of things, I am sure we should all be as happy as kings, and you know how happy kings are.

The Crow and the Oriole

ONCE upon a time a crow fell in love with a Baltimore oriole. He had seen her flying past his nest every spring on her way North and every autumn on her way South, and he had decided that she was a tasty dish. He had observed that she came North every year with a different gentleman, but he paid no attention to the fact that all the gentlemen were Baltimore orioles. "Anybody can have that mouse," he said to himself. So he went to his wife and told her that he was in love with a Baltimore oriole who was as cute as a cuff link. He said he wanted a divorce, so his wife gave him one simply by opening the door and handing him his hat. "Don't come crying to me when she throws you down," she said. "That fly-by-season hasn't got a brain in her head. She can't cook or sew. Her upper register sounds like a streetcar taking a curve. You can find out in any dictionary that the crow is the smartest and most capable of birds—or was till you became one." "Tush!" said the male crow. "Pish! You are simply a jealous woman." He tossed her a few dollars. "Here," he said, "go buy yourself some finery. You look like the bottom of an old teakettle." And off he went to look for the oriole.

This was in the springtime and he met her coming North with an oriole he had never seen before. The crow stopped the female oriole and pleaded his cause—or should we say cawed his pleas? At any rate, he courted her in a harsh, grating voice, which made her laugh merrily. "You sound like an old window shutter," she said, and she snapped her fingers at him. "I am bigger and stronger than your gentleman friend," said the crow. "I have a vocabulary larger than his. All the orioles in the country couldn't even lift the corn I own. I am a fine sentinel and my voice can be heard for miles in case of danger." "I don't see how that could interest anybody but another crow," said the female oriole, and she laughed at him and flew on toward the North. The male oriole tossed the crow some coins. "Here," he said, "go buy yourself a blazer or something. You look like the bottom of an old coffeepot."

The crow flew back sadly to his nest, but his wife was not there. He found a note pinned to the front door. "I have gone away with Bert," it read. "You will find some arsenic in the medicine chest."

Moral: Even the llama should stick to mamma.

The Elephant Who Challenged the World

AN ELEPHANT who lived in Africa woke up one morning with the conviction that he could defeat all the other animals in the world in single combat, one at a time. He wondered that he hadn't thought of it before. After breakfast he called first on the lion. "You are only the King of Beasts," bellowed the elephant, "whereas I am the Ace!" and he demonstrated his prowess by knocking the lion out in fifteen minutes, no holds barred. Then in quick succession he took on the wild boar, the water buffalo, the rhinoceros, the hippopotamus, the giraffe, the zebra, the eagle, and the vulture, and he conquered them all. After that the elephant spent most of his time in bed eating peanuts, while the other animals, who were now his slaves, built for him the largest house any animal in the world had ever had. It was five stories high, solidly made of the hardest woods to be found in Africa. When it was finished, the Ace of Beasts moved in and announced that he could pin back the ears of any animal in the world. He challenged all comers to meet him in the basement of the big house, where he had set up a prize ring ten times the regulation size.

Several days went by and then the elephant got an anonymous letter accepting his challenge. "Be in your basement tomorrow afternoon at three o'clock," the message read. So at three o'clock the next day the elephant went down to the basement to meet his mysterious opponent, but there was no one there, or at least no one he could see. "Come out from behind whatever you're behind!" roared the elephant. "I'm not behind anything," said a tiny voice. The elephant tore around the basement, upsetting barrels and boxes, banging his head against the furnace pipes, rocking the house on its foundations, but he could not find his opponent. At the end of an hour the elephant roared that the whole business was a trick and a deceit—probably ventriloquism—and that he would never come down to the basement again. "Oh, yes you will," said the tiny voice. "You will be down here at three o'clock tomorrow and you'll end up on your back." The elephant's laughter shook the house. "We'll see about that," he said.

The next afternoon the elephant, who slept on the fifth floor of the house, woke up at two-thirty o'clock and looked at his wristwatch. "Nobody I can't see will ever get me down to the basement again," he growled, and went back to sleep. At exactly three o'clock the house began to tremble and quiver as if an earthquake had it in its paws. Pillars and beams bent and broke like reeds, for they were all drilled full of tiny holes. The fifth floor gave way completely and crashed down upon the fourth, which fell upon the third, which fell upon the second, which carried away the first as if it had been the floor of a berry basket. The elephant was precipitated into the basement, where he fell heavily upon the concrete floor and lay there on his back, completely unconscious. A tiny voice began to count him out. At the count of ten the elephant came to, but he could not get up. "What animal are you?" he demanded of the mysterious voice in a quavering tone which had lost its menace. "I am the termite," answered the voice.

The other animals, straining and struggling for a week, finally got the elephant lifted out of the basement and put him in jail. He spent the rest of his life there, broken in spirit and back.

Moral: The battle is sometimes to the small, for the bigger they are the harder they fall.

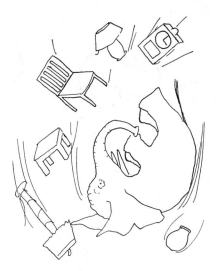

The Birds and the Foxes

ONCE upon a time there was a bird sanctuary in which hundreds of Baltimore orioles lived together happily. The refuge consisted of a forest entirely surrounded by a high wire fence. When it was put up, a pack of foxes who lived nearby protested that it was an arbitrary and unnatural boundary. However, they did nothing about it at the time because they were interested in civilizing the geese and ducks on the neighboring farms. When all the geese and ducks had been civilized, and there was nothing else left to eat, the foxes once more turned their attention to the bird sanctuary. Their leader announced that there had once been foxes in the sanctuary but that they had been driven out. He proclaimed that Baltimore orioles belonged in Baltimore. He said, furthermore, that the orioles in the sanctuary were a continuous menace to the peace of the world. The other animals cautioned the foxes not to disturb the birds in their sanctuary.

So the foxes attacked the sanctuary one night and tore down the fence that surrounded it. The orioles rushed out and were instantly killed and eaten by the foxes.

The next day the leader of the foxes, a fox from whom God was receiving daily guidance, got upon the rostrum and addressed the other foxes. His message was simple and sublime. "You see before you," he said, "another Lincoln. We have liberated all those birds!"

Moral: Government of the orioles, by the foxes, and for the foxes, must perish from the earth.

The Courtship of Arthur and Al

ONCE upon a time there was a young beaver named Al and an older beaver named Arthur. They were both in love with a pretty little female. She looked with disfavor upon the young beaver's suit because he was a harum-scarum and a ne'er-do-well. He had never done a single gnaw of work in his life, for he preferred to eat and sleep and to swim lazily in the streams and to play Now-I'll-Chase-You with the girls. The older beaver had never done anything but work from the time he got his first teeth. He had never played anything with anybody.

When the young beaver asked the female to marry him, she said she wouldn't think of it unless he amounted to something. She reminded him that Arthur had built thirty-two dams and was working on three others, whereas he, Al, had never even made a bread-board or a pin tray in his life. Al was very sorry, but he said he would never go to work just because a woman wanted him to. Thereupon she offered to be a sister to him, but he pointed out that he already had seventeen sisters. So he went back to eating and sleeping and swimming in the streams and playing Spider-in-the-Parlor with the girls. The female married Arthur one day at the lunch hour—he could never get away from work for more than one hour at a time. They had seven children and Arthur worked so hard supporting them he wore his teeth down to the gum line. His health broke in two before long and he died without ever having had a vacation in his life. The young beaver continued to eat and sleep and swim in the streams and play Unbutton-Your-Shoe with the girls. He never Got Anywhere, but he had a long life and a Wonderful Time.

Moral: It is better to have loafed and lost than never to have loafed at all.

The Hen Who Wouldn't Fly

IN ONE of the Midwestern states there lived a speckled hen who was opposed to aviation. In her youth, watching a flight of wild geese going north, she had seen two fall (shot by hunters), go into a nose dive, and crash into the woods. So she went about the countryside saying that flying was very dangerous and that any fowl with any sense would stick to the solid earth. Every time she had to cross a concrete highway near her farm she ran on foot, screaming and squawking; sometimes she made it easily, at other times she was almost tagged by passing cars. Five of her sisters and three of her daughters' husbands were killed trying to cross the road in one month (July).

Before long an enterprising wood duck set up an airways service across the road and back. He charged five grains of corn to take a hen or a rooster across, two grains for a chick. But the speckled hen, who was a power in the community, went around clucking and cut-cutting and cadawcutting and telling everybody that air travel was not safe and never would be. She persuaded the chickens not to ride on the duck's back, and he failed in business and returned to the forests. Before the year was out, the speckled hen, four more of her sisters, three of her sons-in-law, four aunts, and a grandfather had been killed trying to cross the road on foot.

Moral: Use the wings God gave you, or nothing can save you.

The Glass in the Field

A SHORT time ago some builders, working on a studio in Connecticut, left a huge square of plate glass standing upright in a field one day. A goldfinch flying swiftly across the field struck the glass and was knocked cold. When he came to he hastened to his club, where an attendant bandaged his head and gave him a stiff drink. "What the hell happened?" asked a sea gull. "I was flying across a meadow when all of a sudden the air crystallized on me," said the goldfinch. The sea gull and a hawk and an eagle all laughed heartily. A swallow listened gravely. "For fifteen years, fledgling and bird, I've flown this country," said the eagle, "and I assure you there is no such thing as air crystallizing. Water, yes; air, no." "You were probably struck by a hailstone," the hawk told the goldfinch. "Or he may have had a stroke," said the sea gull. "What do you think, swallow?" "Why, I—I think maybe the air crystallized on him," said the swallow. The large birds laughed so loudly that the goldfinch became annoyed and bet them each a dozen worms that they couldn't follow the course he had flown across the field without encountering the hardened atmosphere. They all took his bet; the swallow went along to watch. The sea gull, the eagle, and the hawk decided to fly together over the route the goldfinch indicated. "You come, too," they said to the swallow. "I—I—well, no," said the swallow. "I don't think I will." So the three large birds took off together and they hit the glass together and they were all knocked cold.

Moral: He who hesitates is sometimes saved.

The Tortoise and the Hare

THERE was once a wise young tortoise who read in an ancient book about a tortoise who had beaten a hare in a race. He read all the other books he could find but in none of them was there any record of a hare who had beaten a tortoise. The wise young tortoise came to the natural conclusion that he could outrun a hare, so he set forth in search of one. In his wanderings he met many animals who were willing to race him: weasels, stoats, dachshunds, badger-boars, short-tailed field mice and ground squirrels. But when the tortoise asked if they could outrun a hare, they all said no, they couldn't (with the exception of a dachshund named Freddy, and nobody paid any attention to him). "Well, I can," said the tortoise, "so there's no use wasting my time on you." And he continued his search.

After many days, the tortoise finally encountered a hare and challenged him to a race. "What are you going to use for legs?" asked the hare. "Never mind that," said the tortoise. "Read this." He showed the hare the story in the ancient book, complete with moral about the swift not always being so terribly fast. "Tosh," said the hare. "You couldn't go fifty feet in an hour and a half, whereas I can go fifty feet in one and a fifth seconds." "Posh," said the tortoise. "You probably won't even finish second." "We'll see about that," said the hare. So they marked off a course fifty feet long. All the other animals gathered around. A bull-frog set them on their marks, a gun dog fired a pistol, and they were off.

When the hare crossed the finish line, the tortoise had gone approximately eight and three-quarter inches.

Moral: A new broom may sweep clean, but never trust an old saw.

The Patient Bloodhound

IN MAY, 1937, a bloodhound who lived in Wapokoneta Falls,
Ohio, was put on the trail of a man suspected of a certain
crime. The bloodhound followed him to Akron, Cleveland,
Buffalo, Syracuse, Rochester, Albany, and New York. The
Westminster dog show was going on at the time but the
bloodhound couldn't get to the garden because the man got
on the first ship for Europe. The ship landed at Cherbourg
and the bloodhound followed the man to Paris, Beauvais, Ca-
lais, Dover, London, Chester, Llandudno, Bettws-y-Coed,
and Edinburgh, where the dog wasn't able to take in the international sheep trials. From Edinburgh, the bloodhound
trailed the man to Liverpool, but since the man immediately
got on a ship for New York, the dog didn't have a chance to
explore the wonderful Liverpool smells.

In America again, the bloodhound traced the man to Tea-
neck, Tenafly, Nyack, and Peapack—where the dog didn't
have time to run with the Peapack beagles. From Peapack the
hound followed the man to Cincinnati, St. Louis, Kansas City,
St. Louis, Cincinnati, Columbus, Akron, and finally back to
Wapokoneta Falls. There the man was acquitted of the crime
he had been followed for.

The bloodhound had developed fallen paw-pads and he was
so worn out he could never again trail anything that was faster
than a turtle. Furthermore, since he had gone through the
world with his eyes and nose to the ground, he had missed
all its beauty and excitement.

*Moral: The paths of glory at least lead to the Grave, but the
paths of duty may not get you Anywhere.*

The Unicorn in the Garden

Once upon a sunny morning a man who sat in a breakfast nook looked up from his scrambled eggs to see a white unicorn with a golden horn quietly cropping the roses in the garden. The man went up to the bedroom where his wife was still asleep and woke her. "There's a unicorn in the garden," he said. "Eating roses." She opened one unfriendly eye and looked at him. "The unicorn is a mythical beast," she said, and turned her back on him. The man walked slowly downstairs and out into the garden. The unicorn was still there; he was now browsing among the tulips. "Here, unicorn," said the man, and he pulled up a lily and gave it to him. The unicorn ate it gravely. With a high heart, because there was a unicorn in his garden, the man went upstairs and roused his wife again. "The unicorn," he said, "ate a lily." His wife sat up in bed and looked at him, coldly. "You are a booby," she said, "and I am going to have you put in the booby-hatch." The man, who had never liked the words "booby" and "booby-hatch," and who liked them even less on a shining morning when there was a unicorn in the garden, thought for a moment. "We'll see about that," he said. He walked over to the door. "He has a golden horn in the middle of his forehead," he told her. Then he went back to the garden to watch the unicorn; but the unicorn had gone away. The man sat down among the roses and went to sleep.

As soon as the husband had gone out of the house, the wife got up and dressed as fast as she could. She was very excited and there was a gloat in her eye. She telephoned the police and she telephoned a psychiatrist; she told them to hurry to her house and bring a strait-jacket. When the police and the psychiatrist arrived they sat down in chairs and looked at her, with great interest. "My husband," she said, "saw a unicorn this morning." The police looked at the psychiatrist and the psychiatrist looked at the police. "He told me it ate a lily," she said. The psychiatrist looked at the police and the police looked at the psychiatrist. "He told me it had a golden horn in the middle of its forehead," she said. At a solemn signal

493

from the psychiatrist, the police leaped from their chairs and seized the wife. They had a hard time subduing her, for she put up a terrific struggle, but they finally subdued her. Just as they got her into the strait-jacket, the husband came back into the house.

"Did you tell your wife you saw a unicorn?" asked the police. "Of course not," said the husband. "The unicorn is a mythical beast." "That's all I wanted to know," said the psychiatrist. "Take her away. I'm sorry, sir, but your wife is as crazy as a jay bird." So they took her away, cursing and screaming, and shut her up in an institution. The husband lived happily ever after.

Moral: Don't count your boobies until they are hatched.

The Rabbits Who Caused All the Trouble

WITHIN the memory of the youngest child there was a family of rabbits who lived near a pack of wolves. The wolves announced that they did not like the way the rabbits were living. (The wolves were crazy about the way they themselves were living, because it was the only way to live.) One night several wolves were killed in an earthquake and this was blamed on the rabbits, for it is well known that rabbits pound on the ground with their hind legs and cause earthquakes. On another night one of the wolves was killed by a bolt of lightning and this was also blamed on the rabbits, for it is well known that lettuce-eaters cause lightning. The wolves threatened to civilize the rabbits if they didn't behave, and the rabbits decided to run away to a desert island. But the other animals, who lived at a great distance, shamed them, saying,

"You must stay where you are and be brave. This is no world for escapists. If the wolves attack you, we will come to your aid, in all probability." So the rabbits continued to live near the wolves and one day there was a terrible flood which drowned a great many wolves. This was blamed on the rabbits, for it is well known that carrot-nibblers with long ears cause floods. The wolves descended on the rabbits, for their own good, and imprisoned them in a dark cave, for their own protection.

When nothing was heard about the rabbits for some weeks, the other animals demanded to know what had happened to them. The wolves replied that the rabbits had been eaten and since they had been eaten the affair was a purely internal matter. But the other animals warned that they might possibly unite against the wolves unless some reason was given for the destruction of the rabbits. So the wolves gave them one. "They were trying to escape," said the wolves, "and, as you know, this is no world for escapists."

Moral: Run, don't walk, to the nearest desert island.

The Hen and the Heavens

ONCE upon a time a little red hen was picking up stones and worms and seeds in a barnyard when something fell on her head. "The heavens are falling down!" she shouted, and she began to run, still shouting, "The heavens are falling down!" All the hens that she met and all the roosters and turkeys and ducks laughed at her, smugly, the way you laugh at one who is terrified when you aren't. "What did you say?" they chortled. "The heavens are falling down!" cried the little red hen. Finally a very pompous rooster said to her, "Don't be silly, my dear, it was only a pea that fell on your head." And he laughed and laughed and everybody else except the little red hen laughed. Then suddenly with an awful roar great chunks of crystallized cloud and huge blocks of icy blue sky began to drop on everybody from above, and everybody was killed, the laughing rooster and the little red hen and everybody else in the barnyard, for the heavens actually *were* falling down.

Moral: It wouldn't surprise me a bit if they did.

Excelsior

By HENRY WADSWORTH LONGFELLOW

The shades of night were falling fast,
As through an Alpine village passed
A youth, who bore, 'mid snow and ice,
A banner with the strange device—
    Excelsior!

"Try not the pass," the old man said;
"Dark lowers the tempest overhead;
The roaring torrent is deep and wide!"
And loud that clarion voice replied,
        Excelsior!

"O stay," the maiden said, "and rest
Thy weary head upon this breast!"
A tear stood in his bright blue eye,
But still he answered, with a sigh,
                    Excelsior!

"Beware the pine-tree's withered branch!
Beware the awful avalanche!"
This was the peasant's last good night:
A voice replied, far up the height,
            Excelsior!

At break of day, as heavenward
The pious monks of Saint Bernard
Uttered the oft-repeated prayer,
A voice cried through the startled air,
        Excelsior!

A traveller, by the faithful hound,
Half-buried in the snow was found,
Still grasping in his hand of ice
That banner with the strange device,
                Excelsior!

There in the twilight cold and gray,
Lifeless, but beautiful, he lay,
And from the sky, serene and far,
A voice fell, like a falling star—
                Excelsior!

Lochinvar

By SIR WALTER SCOTT

O, young Lochinvar is come out of the west,
Through all the wide Border his steed was the best;
And, save his good broadsword, he weapon had none,
He rode all unarmed, and he rode all alone.
So faithful in love, and so dauntless in war,
There never was knight like the young Lochinvar.

But, ere he alighted at Netherby gate,
The bride had consented, the gallant came late;
For a laggard in love, and a dastard in war,
Was to wed the fair Ellen of brave Lochinvar.

So boldly he entered the Netherby Hall,
Among bridesmen, and kinsmen, and brothers, and all.
Then spoke the bride's father, his hand on his sword
(For the poor craven bridegroom said never a word),
"O come ye in peace here, or come ye in war,
Or to dance at our bridal, young Lord Lochinvar?"

"I long wooed your daughter, my suit you denied—
Love swells like the Solway, but ebbs like its tide—
And now I am come, with this lost love of mine,
To lead but one measure, drink one cup of wine.
There are maidens in Scotland more lovely by far,
That would gladly be bride to the young Lochinvar."

The bride kissed the goblet; the knight took it up,
He quaffed off the wine, and threw down the cup.
She looked down to blush, and she looked up to sigh.
With a smile on her lips, and a tear in her eye.
He took her soft hand, ere her mother could bar—
"Now tread we a measure," said young Lochinvar.

So stately his form, and so lovely her face,
That never a hall such a galliard did grace;
While her mother did fret, and her father did fume,
And the bridegroom stood dangling his bonnet and
    plume . . .

One touch to her hand, and one word in her ear,
When they reached the hall door, and the charger stood near;
So light to the croupe the fair lady he swung,
So light to the saddle before he sprung;
"She is won! we are gone! Over bank, bush, and scaur;
They'll have fleet steeds that follow," quoth young Lochinvar.

There was mounting 'mong Graemes of the Netherby clan;
Forsters, Fenwicks, and Musgraves, they rode and they ran;
There was racing and chasing on Cannobie Lee,
But the lost bride of Netherby ne'er did they see.
So daring in love, and so dauntless in war,
Have ye e'er heard of gallant like young Lochinvar?

Curfew Must Not Ring To-night

By Rose Hartwick Thorpe

"Sexton," Bessie's white lips faltered, pointing to the prison
    old,
With its turrets tall and gloomy, with its walls dark, damp,
    and cold,
"I've a lover in that prison, doomed this very night to die,
At the ringing of the Curfew, and no earthly help is nigh;
Cromwell will not come till sunset," and her lips grew
    strangely white
As she breathed the husky whisper:—
                "Curfew must not ring to-night."

"Bessie," calmly spoke the sexton—every word pierced her
    young heart
Like the piercing of an arrow, like a deadly poisoned dart—
"Long, long years I've rung the Curfew from that gloomy,
    shadowed tower;
Every evening, just at sunset, it has told the twilight hour;
I have done my duty ever, tried to do it just and right,
Now I'm old I will not falter—
                 Curfew, it must ring to-night."

With quick step she bounded forward, sprang within the old
    church door,
Left the old man threading slowly paths so oft he'd trod
    before;
Not one moment paused the maiden, but with eye and
    cheek aglow
Mounted up the gloomy tower, where the bell swung to
    and fro:
As she climbed the dusty ladder, on which fell no ray of
    light,
Up and up—her white lips saying:—
                    "Curfew must not ring to-night."

She has reached the topmost ladder; o'er her hangs the
    great dark bell;
Awful is the gloom beneath her, like the pathway down to
    hell.
Lo, the ponderous tongue is swinging—'tis the hour of
    Curfew now,
And the sight has chilled her bosom, stopped her breath,
    and paled her brow.
Shall she let it ring? No, never! flash her eyes with sudden
    light,
As she springs and grasps it firmly—
                    "Curfew shall not ring to-night!"

Out she swung—far out; the city seemed a speck of light
    below,
There 'twixt heaven and earth suspended as the bell swung
    to and fro,
And the sexton at the bell rope, old and deaf, heard not the
    bell,
Sadly thought, "That twilight Curfew rang young Basil's
    funeral knell."
Still the maiden clung more firmly and with trembling lips
    so white,
Said to hush her heart's wild throbbing:—
                                "Curfew shall not ring to-night!"

O'er the distant hills came Cromwell; Bessie sees him, and
    her brow,
Lately white with fear and anguish, has no anxious traces
    now.
At his feet she tells her story, shows her hands all bruised
    and torn;
And her face so sweet and pleading, yet with sorrow pale
    and worn,
Touched his heart with sudden pity, lit his eyes with misty
    light:
"Go! your lover lives," said Cromwell,
                                "Curfew shall not ring to-night."

Wide they flung the massive portal; led the prisoner forth to
    die—
All his bright young life before him. 'Neath the darkening
    English sky
Bessie comes with flying footsteps, eyes aglow with love-
    light sweet;
Kneeling on the turf beside him, lays his pardon at his feet.
In his brave, strong arms he clasped her, kissed the face up-
    turned and white,
Whispered, "Darling, you have saved me—
                    Curfew will not ring to-night."

Barbara Frietchie

By JOHN GREENLEAF WHITTIER

On the pleasant morn of the early fall
When Lee marched over the mountain wall;

Over the mountains winding down,
Horse and foot, into Frederick town,

Forty flags with their silver stars,
Forty flags with their crimson bars,

Flapped in the morning wind . . .

. . . the sun
Of noon looked down, and saw not one.

Up rose old Barbara Frietchie then,
Bowed with her fourscore years and ten;

Bravest of all in Frederick town,
She took up the flag the men hauled down;

In her attic window the staff she set,
To show that one heart was loyal yet.

Up the street came the rebel tread,
Stonewall Jackson riding ahead.

Under his slouched hat left and right
He glanced; the old flag met his sight.

"Halt!"—the dust-brown ranks stood fast;
"Fire!"—out blazed the rifle-blast.

It shivered the window, pane and sash;
It rent the banner with seam and gash.

Quick, as it fell, from the broken staff
Dame Barbara snatched the silken scarf.

She leaned far out on the window-sill,
And shook it forth with a royal will.

"Shoot, if you must, this old gray head,
But spare your country's flag," she said.

A shade of sadness, a blush of shame,
Over the face of the leader came;

The nobler nature within him stirred
To life at that woman's deed and word;

"Who touches a hair of yon gray head
Dies like a dog! March on!" he said.

All day long through Frederick street
Sounded the tread of marching feet:

All day long that free flag tossed
Over the heads of the rebel host.

Ever its torn fold rose and fell
On the loyal winds that loved it well;

And through the hill-gaps sunset light
Shone over it with a warm good-night . . .

MY WORLD—
AND WELCOME TO IT

The Whip-Poor-Will

T HE NIGHT had just begun to get pale around the edges when the whip-poor-will began. Kinstrey, who slept in a back room on the first floor, facing the meadow and the strip of woods beyond, heard a blind man tapping and a bugle calling and a woman screaming "Help! Police!" The sergeant in gray was cutting open envelopes with a sword. "Sit down there, sit down there, sit down there!" he chanted at Kinstrey. "Sit down there, cut your throat, cut your throat, whip-poor-will, whip-poor-will, whip-poor-will!" And Kinstrey woke up.

He opened his eyes, but lay without moving for several minutes, separating the fantastic morning from the sounds and symbols of his dream. There was the palest wash of light in the room. Kinstrey scowled through tousled hair at his wristwatch and saw that it was ten minutes past four. "Whip-poor-will, whip-poor-will, whip-poor-will!" The bird sounded very near—in the grass outside the window, perhaps. Kinstrey got up and went to the window in his bare feet and looked out. You couldn't tell where the thing was. The sound was all around you, incredibly loud and compelling and penetrating. Kinstrey had never heard a whip-poor-will so near at hand before. He had heard them as a boy in Ohio in the country, but he remembered their call as faint and plaintive and far-away, dying before long somewhere between the hills and the horizon. You didn't hear the bird often in Ohio, it came back to him, and it almost never ventured as close to a house or barn as this brazen-breasted bird murdering sleep out there along the fence line somewhere. "Whip-poor-will, whip-poor-will, whip-poor-will!" Kinstrey climbed back into bed and began to count; the bird did twenty-seven whips without pausing. His lungs must be built like a pelican's pouch, or a puffin or a penguin or pemmican or a paladin. . . . It was bright daylight when Kinstrey fell asleep again.

At breakfast, Madge Kinstrey, looking cool and well rested in her white piqué house coat, poured the coffee with steady authority. She raised her eyebrows slightly in mild surprise when Kinstrey mentioned the whip-poor-will the second time (she had not listened the first time, for she was lost in exploring with long, sensitive finger an infinitesimal chip on the rim of her coffee cup).

"Whip-poor-will?" she said, finally. "No, I didn't hear it. Of course, my room is on the front of the house. You must have been slept out and ready to wake up anyway, or you wouldn't have heard it."

"Ready to wake up?" said Kinstrey. "At four o'clock in the morning? I hadn't slept three hours."

"Well, I didn't hear it," said Mrs. Kinstrey. "I don't listen for night noises; I don't even hear the crickets or the frogs."

"Neither do I," said Kinstrey. "It's not the same thing. This thing is loud as a fire bell. You can hear it for a mile."

"I didn't hear it," she said, buttering a piece of thin toast.

Kinstrey gave it up and turned his scowling attention to the headlines in the *Herald Tribune* of the day before. The vision of his wife sleeping quietly in her canopied four-poster came between his eyes and the ominous headlines. Madge always slept quietly, almost without moving, her arms straight and still outside the covers, her fingers relaxed. She did not believe anyone had to toss and turn. "It's a notion," she would tell Kinstrey. "Don't let your nerves get the best of you. Use your will power."

"Um, hm," said Kinstrey aloud, not meaning to.

"Yes, sir?" said Arthur, the Kinstrey's colored butler, offering Kinstrey a plate of hot blueberry muffins.

"Nothing," said Kinstrey, looking at his wife. "Did you hear the whip-poor-will, Arthur?"

"No, sir, I didn't," said Arthur.

"Did Margaret?"

"I don't think she did, sir," said Arthur. "She didn't say anything about it."

The next morning the whip-poor-will began again at the same hour, rolling out its loops and circles of sound across the new day. Kinstrey, in his dreams, was beset by trios of little bearded men rolling hoops at him. He tried to climb up onto a gigantic Ferris wheel whose swinging seats were rumpled beds. The round cop with wheels for feet rolled toward him shouting, "Will power will, will power will, whip-poor-will!"

Kinstrey opened his eyes and stared at the ceiling and began to count the whips. At one point the bird did fifty-three straight, without pausing. I suppose, like the drops of water or the bright light in the third degree, this could drive you nuts, Kinstrey thought. Or make you confess. He began to think of things he hadn't thought of for years: the time he took the quarter from his mother's pocketbook, the time he steamed open a letter addressed to his father; it was from his teacher in the eighth grade. Miss—let's see—Miss Willpool, Miss Whippoor, Miss Will Power, Miss Wilmott—that was it.

He had reached the indiscretions of his middle twenties when the whip-poor-will suddenly stopped, on "poor," not on "will." Something must have frightened it. Kinstrey sat up on the edge of the bed and lighted a cigarette and listened. The bird was through calling, all right, but Kinstrey couldn't go back to sleep. The day was as bright as a flag. He got up and dressed.

"I thought you weren't going to smoke cigarettes before breakfast any more," said Madge later. "I found four stubs in the ashtray in your bedroom."

It was no use telling her he had smoked them before going to bed; you couldn't fool Madge; she always knew. "That goddam bird woke me up again," he said, "and this time I couldn't get back to sleep." He passed her his empty coffee cup. "It did fifty-three without stopping this morning," he added. "I don't know how the hell it breathes."

His wife took his coffee cup and set it down firmly. "Not three cups," she said. "Not with you sleeping so restlessly the way it is."

"You didn't hear it, I suppose?" he said.

She poured herself some more coffee. "No," she said, "I didn't hear it."

Margaret hadn't heard it, either, but Arthur had. Kinstrey talked to them in the kitchen while they were clearing up after breakfast. Arthur said that it "wuk" him but he went right back to sleep. He said he slept like a log—must be the air off the ocean. As for Margaret, she always slept like a log; only thing ever kept her awake was people a-hoopin' and a-hollerin'. She was glad she didn't hear the whip-poor-will. Down where she came from, she said, if you heard a whip-poor-will singing near the house, it meant there was going to be a death. Arthur said he had heard about that, too; must have been his grandma told him, or somebody.

If a whip-poor-will singing near the house meant death, Kinstrey told them, it wouldn't really make any difference whether you heard it or not. "It doesn't make any difference whether you see the ladder you're walking under," he said, lighting a cigarette and watching the effect of his words on Margaret. She turned from putting some plates away, and her eyes widened and rolled a little.

"Mr. Kinstrey is just teasin' you, Mag," said Arthur, who smiled and was not afraid. Thinks he's pretty smart, Kinstrey thought. Just a little bit too smart, maybe. Kinstrey remembered Arthur's way of smiling, almost imperceptibly, at things Mrs. Kinstrey sometimes said to her husband when Arthur was just coming into the room or just going out—little things that were none of his business to listen to. Like "Not three cups of coffee if a bird keeps you awake." Wasn't that what she had said?

"Is there any more coffee?" he asked, testily. "Or did you throw it out?" He knew they had thrown it out; breakfast had been over for almost an hour.

"We can make you some fresh," said Arthur.

"Never mind," said Kinstrey. "Just don't be so sure of yourself. There's nothing in life to be sure about."

When, later in the morning, he started out the gate to walk down to the post office, Madge called to him from an upstairs window. "Where are you going?" she asked, amiably enough. He frowned up at her. "To the taxidermist's," he said, and went on.

He realized, as he walked along in the warm sunlight, that he had made something of a spectacle of himself. Just because he hadn't had enough sleep—or enough coffee. It wasn't his fault, though. It was that infernal bird. He discovered, after a quarter of a mile, that the imperative rhythm of the whip-poor-will's call was running through his mind, but the words of the song were new: fatal bell, fatal bell, fa-tal bell. Now, where had that popped up from? It took him some time to place it; it was a fragment from "Macbeth." There was something about the fatal bellman crying in the night. "The fatal bellman cried the livelong night"—something like that. It was an owl that cried the night Duncan was murdered. Funny thing to call up after all these years; he hadn't read the play since college. It was that fool Margaret, talking about the whip-poor-will and the old superstition that if you hear the whip-poor-will singing near the house, it means there is going to be a death. Here it was 1942, and people still believed in stuff like that.

The next dawn the dream induced by the calling of the whip-poor-will was longer and more tortured—a nightmare filled with dark perils and heavy hopelessness. Kinstrey woke up trying to cry out. He lay there breathing hard and listening to the bird. He began to count: one, two, three, four, five . . .

Then, suddenly, he leaped out of bed and ran to the window and began yelling and pounding on the windowpane and running the blind up and down. He shouted and cursed until his voice got hoarse. The bird kept right on going. He slammed the window down and turned away from it, and there was Arthur in the doorway.

"What is it, Mr. Kinstrey?" said Arthur. He was fumbling with the end of a faded old bathrobe and trying to blink the sleep out of his eyes. "Is anything the matter?"

Kinstrey glared at him. "Get out of here!" he shouted. "And put some coffee on. Or get me a brandy or something."

"I'll put some coffee on," said Arthur. He went shuffling away in his slippers, still half asleep.

"Well," said Madge Kinstrey over her coffee cup at breakfast, "I hope you got your tantrum over and done with this morning. I never heard such a spectacle—squalling like a spoiled brat."

"You can't hear spectacles," said Kinstrey, coldly. "You see them."

"I'm sure I don't know what you're talking about," she said.

No, you don't, thought Kinstrey, you never have; never have, nev-er have, nev-er have. Would he ever get that damned rhythm out of his head? It struck him that perhaps Madge had no subconscious. When she lay on her back, her eyes closed; when she got up, they opened, like a doll's. The mechanism of her mind was as simple as a cigarette box; it was either open or it was closed, and there was nothing else, nothing else, nothing else . . .

The whole problem turns on a very neat point, Kinstrey thought as he lay awake that night, drumming on the headboard with his fingers. William James would have been interested in it; Henry, too, probably. I've got to ignore this thing, get adjusted to it, become oblivious of it. I mustn't fight it, I mustn't build it up. If I get to screaming at it, I'll be running across that wet grass out there in my bare feet, charging that bird as if it were a trench full of Germans, throwing rocks at it, giving the Rebel yell or something, for God's sake. No, I mustn't build it up. I'll think of something else every time it pops into my mind. I'll name the Dodger infield to myself, over and over: Camilli, Herman, Reese, Vaughan, Camilli, Herman, Reese . . .

Kinstrey did not succeed in becoming oblivious of the whip-poor-will. Its dawn call pecked away at his dreams like a vulture at a heart. It slowly carved out a recurring nightmare in which Kinstrey was attacked by an umbrella whose handle, when you clutched it, clutched right back, for the umbrella was not an umbrella at all but a raven. Through the gloomy hallways of his mind rang the Thing's dolorous cry: nevermore, nevermore, nevermore, whip-poor-will, whip-poor-will . . .

One day, Kinstrey asked Mr. Tetford at the post office if the whip-poor-wills ever went away. Mr. Tetford squinted at him. "Don't look like the sun was brownin' you up none," he said. "I don't know as they ever go away. They move around. I like to hear 'em. You get used to 'em."

"Sure," said Kinstrey. "What do people do when they can't get used to them, though—I mean old ladies or sick people?"

"Only one's been bothered was old Miss Purdy. She darn near set fire to the whole island tryin' to burn 'em out of her woods. Shootin' at 'em might drive 'em off, or a body could trap 'em easy enough and let 'em loose somewheres else. But people get used to 'em after a few mornings."

"Oh, sure," said Kinstrey. "Sure."

That evening in the living room, when Arthur brought in the coffee, Kinstrey's cup cackled idiotically in its saucer when he took it off the tray.

Madge Kinstrey laughed. "Your hand is shaking like a leaf," she said.

He drank all his coffee at once and looked up savagely. "If I could get one good night's sleep, it might help," he said. "That damn bird! I'd like to wring its neck."

"Oh, come, now," she said, mockingly. "You wouldn't hurt a fly. Remember the mouse we caught in the Westport house? You took it out in the field and let it go."

"The trouble with you—" he began, and stopped. He opened the lid of a cigarette box and shut it, opened and shut it again, reflectively. "As simple as that," he said.

She dropped her amused smile and spoke shortly. "You're acting like a child about that silly bird," she said. "Worse than a child. I was over at the Barrys' this afternoon. Even their little Ann didn't make such a fuss. A whip-poor-will frightened her the first morning, but now she never notices them."

"I'm not frightened, for God's sake!" shouted Kinstrey. "Frightened or brave, asleep or awake, open or shut—you make everything black or white."

"Well," she said, "I like that."

"I think the bird wakes you up, too," he said. "I think it wakes up Arthur and Margaret."

"And we just pretend it doesn't?" she asked. "Why on earth should we?"

"Oh, out of some fool notion of superiority, I suppose. Out of—I don't know."

"I'll thank you not to class me with the servants," she said coldly. He lighted a cigarette and didn't say anything. "You're being ridiculous and childish," she said, "fussing about nothing at all, like an invalid in a wheel chair." She got up and started from the room.

"Nothing at all," he said, watching her go.

She turned at the door. "Ted Barry says he'll take you on at tennis if your bird hasn't worn you down too much." She went on up the stairs, and he heard her close the door of her room.

He sat smoking moodily for a long time, and fell to wondering whether the man's wife in "The Raven" had seen what the man had seen perched on the pallid bust of Pallas just above the chamber door. Probably not, he decided. When he went to bed, he lay awake a long while trying to think of the last line of "The Raven." He couldn't get any farther than "Like a demon that is dreaming," and this kept running through his head. "Nuts," he said at last, aloud, and he had the oddly disturbing feeling that it wasn't he who had spoken but somebody else.

Kinstrey was not surprised that Madge was a little girl in pigtails and a play suit. The long gray hospital room was filled with poor men in will chairs, running their long, sensitive fingers around the rims of empty coffee cups. "Poor Will, poor Will," chanted Madge, pointing her finger at him. "Here are your spectacles, here are your spectacles." One of the sick men was Arthur, grinning at him, grinning at him and holding him with one hand, so that he was powerless to move his arms or legs. "Hurt a fly, hurt a fly," chanted Madge. "Whip him now, whip him now!" she cried, and she was the umpoor in the high chair beside the court, holding a black umbrella over her head: love thirty, love forty, forty-one, forty-two, forty-three, forty-four. His feet were stuck in the wet concrete on his side of the net and Margaret peered over the net at him, holding a skillet for a racquet. Arthur was pushing him down now, and he was caught in the concrete from head to foot. It was Madge laughing and counting over him: refer-three, refer-four, refer-five, refer-will, repoor-will, whip-poor-will, whip-poor-will, whip-poor-will . . .

The dream still clung to Kinstrey's mind like a cobweb as he stood in the kitchen in his pajamas and bare feet, wondering what he wanted, what he was looking for. He turned on the cold water in the sink and filled a glass, but only took a sip, and put it down. He left the water running. He opened the breadbox and took out half a loaf wrapped in oiled paper, and pulled open a drawer. He took out the bread knife and then put it back and took out the long, sharp carving knife. He was standing there holding the knife in one hand and the bread in the other when the door to the dining room opened.

It was Arthur. "Who do you do first?" Kinstrey said to him, hoarsely. . . .

The Barrys, on their way to the beach in their station wagon, drove into the driveway between the house and the barn. They were surprised to see that, at a quarter to eleven in the morning, the Kinstrey servants hadn't taken in the milk. The bottle, standing on the small back porch, was hot to Barry's touch. When he couldn't rouse anyone, pounding and calling, he climbed up on the cellar door and looked in the kitchen window. He told his wife sharply to get back in the car. . . .

The local police and the state troopers were in and out of the house all day. It wasn't every morning in the year that you got called out on a triple murder and suicide.

It was just getting dark when Troopers Baird and Lennon came out of the front door and walked down to their car, pulled up beside the road in front of the house. Out in back, probably in the little strip of wood there, Lennon figured, a whip-poor-will began to call. Lennon listened a minute. "You ever hear the old people say a whip-poor-will singing near the house means death?" he asked.

Baird grunted and got in under the wheel. Lennon climbed in beside him. "Take more'n a whip-poor-will to cause a mess like that," said Trooper Baird, starting the car.

The Macbeth Murder Mystery

"IT WAS a stupid mistake to make," said the American woman I had met at my hotel in the English lake country, "but it was on the counter with the other Penguin books—the little sixpenny ones, you know, with the paper covers—and I supposed of course it was a detective story. All the others were detective stories. I'd read all the others, so I bought this one without really looking at it carefully. You can imagine how mad I was when I found it was Shakespeare." I murmured something sympathetically. "I don't see why the Penguin-books people had to get out Shakespeare's plays in the same size and everything as the detective stories," went on my companion. "I think they have different-colored jackets," I said. "Well, I didn't notice that," she said. "Anyway, I got real comfy in bed that night and all ready to read a good mystery story and here I had 'The Tragedy of Macbeth'—a book for high-school students. Like 'Ivanhoe.' " "Or 'Lorna Doone,' " I said. "Exactly," said the American lady. "And I was just crazy for a good Agatha Christie, or something. Hercule Poirot is my favorite detective." "Is he the rabbity one?" I asked. "Oh, no," said my crime-fiction expert. "He's the Belgian one. You're thinking of Mr. Pinkerton, the one that helps Inspector Bull. He's good, too."

Over her second cup of tea my companion began to tell the plot of a detective story that had fooled her completely—it seems it was the old family doctor all the time. But I cut in on her. "Tell me," I said. "Did you read 'Macbeth'?" "I *had* to read it," she said. "There wasn't a scrap of anything else to read in the whole room." "Did you like it?" I asked. "No, I did not," she said, decisively. "In the first place, I don't think for a moment that Macbeth did it." I looked at her blankly. "Did what?" I asked. "I don't think for a moment that he killed the King," she said. "I don't think the Macbeth woman was mixed up in it, either. You suspect them the most, of course, but those are the ones that are never guilty—or shouldn't be, anyway." "I'm afraid," I began, "that I—" "But don't you see?" said the American lady. "It would spoil

536

everything if you could figure out right away who did it. Shakespeare was too smart for that. I've read that people never *have* figured out 'Hamlet,' so it isn't likely Shakespeare would have made 'Macbeth' as simple as it seems." I thought this over while I filled my pipe. "Who do you suspect?" I asked, suddenly. "Macduff," she said, promptly. "Good God!" I whispered, softly.

"Oh, Macduff did it, all right," said the murder specialist. "Hercule Poirot would have got him easily." "How did you figure it out?" I demanded. "Well," she said, "I didn't right away. At first I suspected Banquo. And then, of course, he was the second person killed. That was good right in there, that part. The person you suspect of the first murder should always be the second victim." "Is that so?" I murmured. "Oh, yes," said my informant. "They have to keep surprising you. Well, after the second murder I didn't know *who* the killer was for a while." "How about Malcolm and Donalbain, the King's sons?" I asked. "As I remember it, they fled right after the first murder. That looks suspicious." "Too suspicious," said the American lady. "Much too suspicious. When they flee, they're never guilty. You can count on that." "I believe," I said, "I'll have a brandy," and I summoned the waiter. My companion leaned toward me, her eyes bright, her teacup quivering. "Do you know who discovered Duncan's body?" she demanded. I said I was sorry, but I had forgotten. "Macduff discovers it," she said, slipping into the historical present. "Then he comes running downstairs and shouts, 'Confusion has broke open the Lord's anointed temple' and 'Sacrilegious murder has made his masterpiece' and on and on like that." The good lady tapped me on the knee. "All that stuff was *rehearsed*," she said. "You wouldn't say a lot of stuff like that, offhand, would you—if you had found a body?" She fixed me with a glittering eye. "I—" I began. "You're right!" she said. "You wouldn't! Unless you had practiced it in advance. 'My God, there's a body in here!' is what an innocent man would say." She sat back with a confident glare.

I thought for a while. "But what do you make of the Third Murderer?" I asked. "You know, the Third Murderer has puzzled 'Macbeth' scholars for three hundred years." "That's because they never thought of Macduff," said the American lady. "It was Macduff, I'm certain. You couldn't have one of the victims murdered by two ordinary thugs—the murderer always has to be somebody important." "But what about the banquet scene?" I asked, after a moment. "How do you account for Macbeth's guilty actions there, when Banquo's ghost came in and sat in his chair?" The lady leaned forward and tapped me on the knee again. "There wasn't any ghost," she said. "A big, strong man like that doesn't go around seeing ghosts—especially in a brightly lighted banquet hall with dozens of people around. Macbeth was *shielding somebody!*" "Who was he shielding?" I asked. "Mrs. Macbeth, of course," she said. "He thought she did it and he was going to take the rap himself. The husband always does that when the wife is suspected." "But what," I demanded, "about the sleep-walking scene, then?" "The same thing, only the other way around," said my companion. "That time *she* was shielding *him*. She wasn't asleep at all. Do you remember where it says, 'Enter Lady Macbeth with a taper'?" "Yes," I said. "Well, people who walk in their sleep *never carry lights!*" said my fellow-traveler. "They have a second sight. Did you ever hear of a sleepwalker carrying a light?" "No," I said, "I never did." "Well, then, she wasn't asleep. She was acting guilty to shield Macbeth." "I think," I said, "I'll have another brandy," and I called the waiter. When he brought it, I drank it rapidly and rose to go. "I believe," I said, "that you have got hold of something. Would you lend me that 'Macbeth'? I'd like to look it over tonight. I don't feel, somehow, as if I'd ever really read it." "I'll get it for you," she said. "But you'll find that I am right."

I read the play over carefully that night, and the next morning, after breakfast, I sought out the American woman. She was on the putting green, and I came up behind her silently and took her arm. She gave an exclamation. "Could I see you alone?" I asked, in a low voice. She nodded cautiously and followed me to a secluded spot. "You've found out something?" she breathed. "I've found out," I said, triumphantly, "the name of the murderer!" "You mean it wasn't Macduff?" she said. "Macduff is as innocent of those murders," I said, "as Macbeth and the Macbeth woman." I opened the copy of the play, which I had with me, and turned to Act II, Scene 2. "Here," I said, "you will see where Lady Macbeth says, 'I laid their daggers ready. He could not miss 'em. Had he not resembled my father as he slept, I had done it.' Do you see?" "No," said the American woman, bluntly, "I don't." "But it's simple!" I exclaimed. "I wonder I didn't see it years ago. The reason Duncan resembled Lady Macbeth's father as he slept is that *it actually was her father!*" "Good God!" breathed my companion, softly. "Lady Macbeth's father killed the King," I said, "and, hearing someone coming, thrust the body under the bed and crawled into the bed himself." "But," said the lady, "you can't have a murderer who only appears in the story once. You can't have that." "I know that," I said, and I turned to Act II, Scene 4. "It says here, 'Enter Ross with an old Man.' Now, that old man is never identified and it is my contention he was old Mr. Macbeth, whose ambition it was to make his daughter Queen. There you have your motive." "But even then," cried the American lady, "he's still a minor character!" "Not," I said, gleefully, "when you realize that he was also *one of the weird sisters in disguise!*" "You mean one of the three witches?" "Precisely," I said. "Listen to this speech of the old man's. 'On Tuesday last, a falcon towering in her pride of place, was by a mousing owl hawk'd at and kill'd.' Who does that sound like?" "It sounds like the way the three witches talk," said my companion, reluctantly. "Precisely!" I said again. "Well," said the American woman, "maybe you're right, but—" "I'm sure I am," I said. "And do you know what I'm going to do now?" "No," she said. "What?" "Buy a copy of 'Hamlet,'" I said, "and solve *that!*" My companion's eyes brightened. "Then," she said, "you don't think Hamlet did it?" "I am," I said, "absolutely positive he didn't." "But who," she demanded, "do you suspect?" I looked at her cryptically. "Everybody," I said, and disappeared into a small grove of trees as silently as I had come.

The Man Who Hated Moonbaum

A FTER they had passed through the high, grilled gate they walked for almost a quarter of a mile, or so it seemed to Tallman. It was very dark; the air smelled sweet; now and then leaves brushed against his cheek or forehead. The little, stout man he was following had stopped talking, but Tallman could hear him breathing. They walked on for another minute. "How we doing?" Tallman asked, finally. "Don't ask me questions!" snapped the other man. "Nobody asks me questions! You'll learn." The hell I will, thought Tallman, pushing through the darkness and the fragrance and the mysterious leaves; the hell I will, baby; this is the last time you'll ever see me. The knowledge that he was leaving Hollywood within twenty-four hours gave him a sense of comfort.

There was no longer turf or gravel under his feet; there was something that rang flatly: tile, or flagstones. The little man began to walk more slowly and Tallman almost bumped into him. "Can't we have a light?" said Tallman. "There you go!" shouted his guide. "Don't get me screaming! What are you trying to do to me?" "I'm not trying to do anything to you," said Tallman. "I'm trying to find out where we're going."

The other man had come to a stop and seemed to be groping around. "First it's wrong uniforms," he said, "then it's red fire—red fire in Scotland, red fire three hundred years ago! I don't know why I ain't crazy!" Tallman could make out the other man dimly, a black, gesturing blob. "You're doing all right," said Tallman. Why did I ever leave the Brown Derby with this guy? he asked himself. Why did I ever let him bring me to his house—if he has a house? Who the hell does he think he is?

Tallman looked at his wristwatch; the dial glowed wanly in the immense darkness. He was a little drunk, but he could see that it was half past three in the morning. "Not trying to do anything to me, he says!" screamed the little man. "Wasn't his fault! It's never anybody's fault! They give me ten thousand dollars' worth of Sam Browne belts for Scotch Highlanders and it's nobody's fault!" Tallman was beginning to get his hangover headache. "I want a light!" he said. "I want a drink! I want to know where the hell I am!" "That's it! Speak out!" said the other. "Say what you think! I like a man who knows where he is. We'll get along." "Contact!" said Tallman. "Camera! Lights! Get out that hundred-year-old brandy you were talking about."

The response to this was a soft flood of rose-colored radiance; the little man had somehow found a light switch in the dark. God knows where, thought Tallman; probably on a tree. They were in a courtyard paved with enormous flagstones which fitted together with mosaic perfection. The light revealed the dark stones of a building which looked like the Place de la Concorde side of the Crillon. "Come on, you people!" said the little man. Tallman looked behind him, half expecting to see the shadowy forms of Scottish Highlanders, but there was nothing but the shadows of trees and of oddly shaped plants closing in on the courtyard. With a key as small as a dime, the little man opened a door that was fifteen feet high and made of wood six inches thick.

Marble stairs tumbled down like Niagara into a grand canyon of a living room. The steps of the two men sounded sharp and clear on the stairs, died in the soft depths of an immensity of carpet in the living room. The ceiling towered above them. There were highlights on dark wood medallions, on burnished shields, on silver curves and edges. On one wall a forty-foot tapestry hung from the ceiling to within a few feet of the floor. Tallman was looking at this when his companion grasped his arm. "The second rose!" he said. "The second rose from the right!" Tallman pulled away. "One of us has got to snap out of this, baby," he said. "How about that brandy?" "Don't interrupt me!" shouted his host. "That's what Whozis whispers to What's-His-Name—greatest love story in the world, if I do say so myself—king's wife mixed up in it—knights riding around with spears—Whozis writes her a message made out of twigs bent together to make words: 'I love you'—sends it floating down a stream past her window—they got her locked in—goddamnedest thing in the history of pictures. Where was I? Oh—'Second rose from the right,' she says. Why? Because she seen it twitch, she seen it move. What's-His-Name is bending over her, kissing her maybe. He whirls around and shoots an arrow at the rose—second from the right, way up high there—down comes the whole tapestry, weighs eleven hundred pounds, and out rolls this spy, shot through the heart. What's-His-Name sent him to watch the lovers." The little man began to pace up and down the deep carpet. Tallman lighted a fresh cigarette from his glowing stub and sat down in an enormous chair. His host came to a stop in front of the chair and shook his finger at its occupant.

"Look," said the little man. "I don't know who you are and I'm telling you this. You could ruin me, but I got to tell you. I get Moonbaum here—I get Moonbaum himself here—you can ask Manny or Sol—I get the best arrow shot in the world here to fire that arrow for What's-His-Name—"

"Tristram," said Tallman. "Don't prompt me!" bellowed the little man. "For Tristram. What happens? Do I know he's got arrows you shoot bears with? Do I know he ain't got caps on 'em? If I got to know that, why do I have Mitnik? Moonbaum is sitting right there—the tapestry comes down and out rolls this guy, shot through the heart—only the arrow is in his stomach. So what happens? So Moonbaum laughs! That makes Moonbaum laugh! The greatest love story in the history of pictures, and Moonbaum laughs!" The little man raced over to a large chest, opened it, took out a cigar, stuck it in his mouth, and resumed his pacing. "How do you like it?" he shouted. "I love it," said Tallman. "I love every part of it. I always have." The little man raised his hands above his head. "He loves it! He hears one—maybe two—scenes, and he loves every part of it! Even Moonbaum don't know how it comes out, and you love every part of it!" The little man was standing before Tallman's chair again, shaking his cigar at him. "The story got around," said Tallman. "These things leak out. Maybe you talk when you're drinking. What about that brandy?"

The little man walked over and took hold of a bell rope on the wall, next to the tapestry. "Moonbaum laughs like he's dying," he said. "Moonbaum laughs like he's seen Chaplin." He dropped the bell rope. "I hope you really got that hundred-year-old brandy," said Tallman. "Don't keep telling me what you hope!" howled the little man. "Keep listening to what I hope!" He pulled the bell rope savagely. "Now we're getting somewhere," said Tallman. For the first time the little man went to a chair and sat down; he chewed on his unlighted cigar. "Do you know what Moonbaum wants her called?" he demanded, lowering his heavy lids. "I can guess," said Tallman. "Isolde." "Birds of a feather!" shouted his host. "Horses of the same color! Isolde! Name of God, man, you can't call a woman Isolde! What do I want her called?" "You have me there," said Tallman. "I want her called Dawn," said the little man, getting up out of his chair. "It's short, ain't it? It's sweet, ain't it? You can say it, can't you?" "To get back to that brandy," said Tallman, "who is supposed to answer that bell?" "Nobody is supposed to answer it," said the little man. "That don't ring, that's a fake bell rope; it don't ring anywhere. I got it to remind me of an idea Moonbaum ruined. Listen: Louisiana mansion—guy with seven daughters—old-Southern-colonel stuff—Lionel Barrymore could play it—we open on a room that looks like a million dollars—Barrymore crosses and pulls the bell rope. What happens?" "Nothing," said Tallman. "You're crazy!" bellowed the little man. "Part of the wall falls in! Out flies a crow—in walks a goat, maybe—the place has gone to seed, see? It's just a hulk of its former self, it's a shallows!" He turned and walked out of the room. It took him quite a while.

When he came back, he was carrying a bottle of brandy and two huge brandy glasses. He poured a great deal of brandy into each glass and handed one to Tallman. "You and Mitnik!" he said, scornfully. "Pulling walls out of Southern mansions. Crows you give me, goats you give me! What the hell kind of effect is that?" "I could have a bad idea," said Tallman, raising his glass. "Here's to Moonbaum. May he maul things over in his mind all night and never get any spontanuity into 'em." "I drink nothing to Moonbaum," said the little man. "I hate Moonbaum. You know where they catch that crook—that guy has a little finger off one hand and wears a glove to cover it up? What does Moonbaum want? Moonbaum wants the little finger to *flap*! What do I want? I want it stuffed. What do I want it stuffed with? Sand. Why?" "I know," said Tallman. "So that when he closes his hand over the head of his cane, the little finger sticks out stiffly, giving him away." The little man seemed to leap into the air; his brandy splashed out of his glass. "Suitcase!" he screamed. "Not cane! Suitcase! He grabs hold of a suitcase!" Tallman didn't say anything; he closed his eyes and sipped his brandy; it was wonderful brandy. He looked up presently to find his host staring at him with a resigned expression in his eyes. "All right, then, suitcase," the little man said. "Have it suitcase. We won't fight about details. I'm trying to tell you my story. I don't tell my stories to everybody." "Richard Harding Davis stole that finger gag—used it in 'Gallegher,'" said Tallman. "You could sue him." The little man walked over to his chair and flopped into it. "He's beneath me," he said. "He's beneath me like the dirt. I ignore him."

Tallman finished his brandy slowly. His host's chin sank upon his chest; his heavy eyelids began to close. Tallman waited several minutes and then tiptoed over to the marble stairs. He took off his shoes and walked up the stairs, carefully. He had the heavy door open when the little man shouted at him. "Birds of a feather, all of you!" he shouted. "You can tell Moonbaum I said so! Shooting guys out of tapestries!" "I'll tell him," said Tallman. "Good night. The brandy was wonderful." The little man was not listening. He was pacing the floor again, gesturing with an empty brandy glass in one hand and the unlighted cigar in the other. Tallman stepped out into the cool air of the courtyard and put on one shoe and laced it. The heavy door swung shut behind him with a terrific crash. He picked up the other shoe and ran wildly toward the trees and the oddly shaped plants. It was daylight now. He could see where he was going.

The Secret Life of Walter Mitty

W E'RE going through!" The Commander's voice was like thin ice breaking. He wore his full-dress uniform, with the heavily braided white cap pulled down rakishly over one cold gray eye. "We can't made it, sir. It's spoiling for a hurricane, if you ask me." "I'm not asking you, Lieutenant Berg," said the Commander. "Throw on the power lights! Rev her up to 8,500! We're going through!" The pounding of the cylinders increased: ta-pocketa-pocketa-pocketa-*pocketa-pocketa*. The Commander stared at the ice forming on the pilot window. He walked over and twisted a row of complicated dials. "Switch on No. 8 auxiliary!" he shouted. "Switch on No. 8 auxiliary!" repeated Lieutenant Berg. "Full strength in No. 3 turret!" shouted the Commander. "Full strength in No. 3 turret!" The crew, bending to their various tasks in the huge, hurtling eight-engined Navy hydroplane, looked at each other and grinned. "The Old Man'll get us through," they said to one another. "The Old Man ain't afraid of Hell!" . . .

"Not so fast! You're driving too fast!" said Mrs. Mitty. "What are you driving so fast for?"

"Hmm?" said Walter Mitty. He looked at his wife, in the seat beside him, with shocked astonishment. She seemed grossly unfamiliar, like a strange woman who had yelled at him in a crowd. "You were up to fifty-five," she said. "You know I don't like to go more than forty. You were up to fifty-five." Walter Mitty drove on toward Waterbury in silence, the roaring of the SN202 through the worst storm in twenty years of Navy flying fading in the remote, intimate airways of his mind. "You're tensed up again," said Mrs. Mitty. "It's one of your days. I wish you'd let Dr. Renshaw look you over."

Walter Mitty stopped the car in front of the building where his wife went to have her hair done. "Remember to get those overshoes while I'm having my hair done," she said. "I don't need overshoes," said Mitty. She put her mirror back into her bag. "We've been all through that," she said, getting out of the car. "You're not a young man any longer." He raced the engine a little. "Why don't you wear your gloves? Have you lost your gloves?" Walter Mitty reached in a pocket and brought out the gloves. He put them on, but after she had turned and gone into the building and he had driven on to a red light, he took them off again. "Pick it up, brother!" snapped a cop as the light changed, and Mitty hastily pulled on his gloves and lurched ahead. He drove around the streets aimlessly for a time, and then he drove past the hospital on his way to the parking lot.

. . . "It's the millionaire banker, Wellington McMillan," said the pretty nurse. "Yes?" said Walter Mitty, removing his gloves slowly. "Who has the case?" "Dr. Renshaw and Dr. Benbow, but there are two specialists here, Dr. Remington from New York and Mr. Pritchard-Mitford from London. He flew over." A door opened down a long, cool corridor and Dr. Renshaw came out. He looked distraught and haggard. "Hello, Mitty," he said. "We're having the devil's own time with McMillan, the millionaire banker and close personal friend of Roosevelt. Obstreosis of the ductal tract. Tertiary. Wish you'd take a look at him." "Glad to," said Mitty.

In the operating room there were whispered introductions: "Dr. Remington, Dr. Mitty. Mr. Pritchard-Mitford, Dr. Mitty." "I've read your book on streptothricosis," said Pritchard-Mitford, shaking hands. "A brilliant performance, sir." "Thank you," said Walter Mitty. "Didn't know you were in the States, Mitty," grumbled Remington. "Coals to Newcastle, bringing Mitford and me up here for a tertiary." "You are very kind," said Mitty. A huge, complicated machine, connected to the operating table, with many tubes and wires, began at this moment to go pocketa-pocketa-pocketa. "The new anesthetizer is giving way!" shouted an interne. "There is no one in the East who knows how to fix it!" "Quiet, man!" said Mitty, in a low, cool voice. He sprang to the machine, which was now going pocketa-pocketa-queep-pocketa-queep. He began fingering delicately a row of glistening dials. "Give me a fountain pen!" he snapped. Someone handed him a fountain pen. He pulled a faulty piston out of the machine and inserted the pen in its place. "That will hold for ten minutes," he said. "Get on with the operation." A nurse hurried over and whispered to Renshaw, and Mitty saw the man turn pale. "Coreopsis has set in," said Renshaw nervously. "If

you would take over, Mitty?" Mitty looked at him and at the
craven figure of Benbow, who drank, and at the grave, uncertain faces of the two great specialists. "If you wish," he
said. They slipped a white gown on him; he adjusted a mask
and drew on thin gloves; nurses handed him shining . . .

"Back it up, Mac! Look out for that Buick!" Walter Mitty
jammed on the brakes. "Wrong lane, Mac," said the parking-
lot attendant, looking at Mitty closely. "Gee. Yeh," muttered
Mitty. He began cautiously to back out of the lane marked
"Exit Only." "Leave her sit there," said the attendant. "I'll
put her away." Mitty got out of the car. "Hey, better leave
the key." "Oh," said Mitty, handing the man the ignition
key. The attendant vaulted into the car, backed it up with
insolent skill, and put it where it belonged.

They're so damn cocky, thought Walter Mitty, walking
along Main Street; they think they know everything. Once he
had tried to take his chains off, outside New Milford, and he
had got them wound around the axles. A man had had to
come out in a wrecking car and unwind them, a young, grinning garageman. Since then Mrs. Mitty always made him drive
to a garage to have the chains taken off. The next time, he
thought, I'll wear my right arm in a sling; they won't grin at
me then. I'll have my right arm in a sling and they'll see I
couldn't possibly take the chains off myself. He kicked at the
slush on the sidewalk. "Overshoes," he said to himself, and
he began looking for a shoe store.

When he came out into the street again, with the overshoes
in a box under his arm, Walter Mitty began to wonder what
the other thing was his wife had told him to get. She had told
him, twice, before they set out from their house for Waterbury. In a way he hated these weekly trips to town—he was
always getting something wrong. Kleenex, he thought,
Squibb's, razor blades? No. Toothpaste, toothbrush, bicar-
bonate, carborundum, initiative and referendum? He gave it
up. But she would remember it. "Where's the what's-its-
name?" she would ask. "Don't tell me you forgot the what's-
its-name." A newsboy went by shouting something about the
Waterbury trial.

. . . "Perhaps this will refresh your memory." The District
Attorney suddenly thrust a heavy automatic at the quiet figure

on the witness stand. "Have you ever seen this before?" Walter Mitty took the gun and examined it expertly. "This is my Webley-Vickers 50.80," he said calmly. An excited buzz ran around the courtroom. The Judge rapped for order. "You are a crack shot with any sort of firearms, I believe?" said the District Attorney, insinuatingly. "Objection!" shouted Mitty's attorney. "We have shown that the defendant could not have fired the shot. We have shown that he wore his right arm in a sling on the night of the fourteenth of July." Walter Mitty raised his hand briefly and the bickering attorneys were stilled. "With any known make of gun," he said evenly, "I could have killed Gregory Fitzhurst at three hundred feet *with my left hand*." Pandemonium broke loose in the courtroom. A woman's scream rose above the bedlam and suddenly a lovely, dark-haired girl was in Walter Mitty's arms. The District Attorney struck at her savagely. Without rising from his chair, Mitty let the man have it on the point of the chin. "You miserable cur!" . . .

"Puppy biscuit," said Walter Mitty. He stopped walking and the buildings of Waterbury rose up out of the misty courtroom and surrounded him again. A woman who was passing laughed. "He said 'Puppy biscuit,'" she said to her companion. "That man said 'Puppy biscuit' to himself." Walter Mitty hurried on. He went into an A. & P., not the first one he came to but a smaller one farther up the street. "I want some biscuit for small, young dogs," he said to the clerk. "Any special brand, sir?" The greatest pistol shot in the world thought a moment. "It says 'Puppies Bark for It' on the box," said Walter Mitty.

His wife would be through at the hairdresser's in fifteen minutes, Mitty saw in looking at his watch, unless they had trouble drying it; sometimes they had trouble drying it. She didn't like to get to the hotel first; she would want him to be there waiting for her as usual. He found a big leather chair in the lobby, facing a window, and he put the overshoes and the puppy biscuit on the floor beside it. He picked up an old copy of *Liberty* and sank down into the chair. "Can Germany Conquer the World Through the Air?" Walter Mitty looked at the pictures of bombing planes and of ruined streets.

. . . "The cannonading has got the wind up in young Raleigh, sir," said the sergeant. Captain Mitty looked up at him through touseled hair. "Get him to bed," he said wearily. "With the others. I'll fly alone." "But you can't, sir," said the sergeant anxiously. "It takes two men to handle that bomber and the Archies are pounding hell out of the air. Von Richtman's circus is between here and Saulier." "Somebody's got to get that ammunition dump," said Mitty. "I'm going over. Spot of brandy?" He poured a drink for the sergeant and one for himself. War thundered and whined around the dugout and battered at the door. There was a rending of wood and splinters flew through the room. "A bit of a near thing," said Captain Mitty carelessly. "The box barrage is closing in," said the sergeant. "We only live once, Sergeant," said Mitty, with his faint, fleeting smile. "Or do we?" He poured another brandy and tossed it off. "I never see a man could hold his brandy like you, sir," said the sergeant. "Begging your pardon, sir." Captain Mitty stood up and strapped on his huge Webley-Vickers automatic. "It's forty kilometers through hell, sir," said the sergeant. Mitty finished one last brandy. "After all," he said softly, "what isn't?" The pounding of the cannon increased; there was the rat-tat-tatting of machine guns, and from somewhere came the menacing pocketa-pocketa-pocketa of the new flame-throwers. Walter Mitty walked to the door of the dugout humming "Auprès de Ma Blonde." He turned and waved to the sergeant. "Cheerio!" he said. . . .

Something struck his shoulder. "I've been looking all over this hotel for you," said Mrs. Mitty. "Why do you have to hide in this old chair? How did you expect me to find you?" "Things close in," said Walter Mitty vaguely. "What?" Mrs. Mitty said. "Did you get the what's-its-name? The puppy biscuit? What's in that box?" "Overshoes," said Mitty. "Couldn't you have put them on in the store?" "I was thinking," said Walter Mitty. "Does it ever occur to you that I am sometimes thinking?" She looked at him. "I'm going to take your temperature when I get you home," she said.

They went out through the revolving doors that made a faintly derisive whistling sound when you pushed them. It was two blocks to the parking lot. At the drugstore on the corner

Interview with a Lemming

THE WEARY scientist, tramping through the mountains of northern Europe in the winter weather, dropped his knapsack and prepared to sit on a rock.

"Careful, brother," said a voice.

"Sorry," murmured the scientist, noting with some surprise that a lemming which he had been about to sit on had addressed him. "It is a source of considerable astonishment to me," said the scientist, sitting down beside the lemming, "that you are capable of speech."

"You human beings are always astonished," said the lemming, "when any other animal can do anything you can. Yet there are many things animals can do that you cannot, such as stridulate, or chirr, to name just one. To stridulate, or chirr, one of the minor achievements of the cricket, your species is dependent on the intestines of the sheep and the hair of the horse."

"We are a dependent animal," admitted the scientist.

"You are an amazing animal," said the lemming.

"We have always considered you rather amazing, too," said the scientist. "You are perhaps the most mysterious of creatures."

"If we are going to indulge in adjectives beginning with 'm,'" said the lemming, sharply, "let me apply a few to your species—murderous, maladjusted, maleficent, malicious and muffle-headed."

"You find our behavior as difficult to understand as we do yours?"

"You, as you would say, said it," said the lemming. "You kill, you mangle, you torture, you imprison, you starve each other. You cover the nurturing earth with cement, you cut down elm trees to put up institutions for people driven insane by the cutting down of elm trees, you—"

"You could go on all night like that," said the scientist, "listing our sins and our shames."

"I could go on all night and up to four o'clock tomorrow afternoon," said the lemming. "It just happens that I have made a lifelong study of the self-styled higher animal. Except for one thing, I know all there is to know about you, and a singularly dreary, dolorous and distasteful store of information it is, too, to use only adjectives beginning with 'd.' "

"You say you have made a lifelong study of my species—" began the scientist.

"Indeed I have," broke in the lemming. "I know that you are cruel, cunning and carnivorous, sly, sensual and selfish, greedy, gullible and guileful—"

"Pray don't wear yourself out," said the scientist, quietly. "It may interest you to know that I have made a lifelong study of lemmings, just as you have made a lifelong study of people. Like you, I have found but one thing about my subject which I do not understand."

"And what is that?" asked the lemming.

"I don't understand," said the scientist, "why you lemmings all rush down to the sea and drown yourselves."

"How curious," said the lemming. "The one thing I don't understand is why you human beings don't."

You Could Look It Up

IT ALL begun when we dropped down to C'lumbus, Ohio, from Pittsburgh to play a exhibition game on our way out to St. Louis. It was gettin' on into September, and though we'd been leadin' the league by six, seven games most of the season, we was now in first place by a margin you could 'a' got it into the eye of a thimble, bein' only a half a game ahead of St. Louis. Our slump had given the boys the leapin' jumps, and they was like a bunch a old ladies at a lawn fete with a thunderstorm comin' up, runnin' around snarlin' at each other, eatin' bad and sleepin' worse, and battin' for a team average of maybe .186. Half the time nobody'd speak to nobody else, without it was to bawl 'em out.

Squawks Magrew was managin' the boys at the time, and he was darn near crazy. They called him "Squawks" 'cause when things was goin' bad he lost his voice, or perty near lost it, and squealed at you like a little girl you stepped on her doll or somethin'. He yelled at everybody and wouldn't listen to nobody, without maybe it was me. I'd been trainin' the boys for ten year, and he'd take more lip from me than from anybody else. He knowed I was smarter'n him, anyways, like you're goin' to hear.

This was thirty, thirty-one year ago; you could look it up, 'cause it was the same year C'lumbus decided to call itself the Arch City, on account of a lot of iron arches with electric-light bulbs into 'em which stretched acrost High Street. Thomas Albert Edison sent 'em a telegram, and they was speeches and maybe even President Taft opened the celebration by pushin' a button. It was a great week for the Buckeye capital, which was why they got us out there for this exhibition game.

Well, we just lose a double-header to Pittsburgh, 11 to 5 and 7 to 3, so we snarled all the way to C'lumbus, where we put up at the Chittaden Hotel, still snarlin'. Everybody was tetchy, and when Billy Klinger took a sock at Whitey Cott at breakfast, Whitey threw marmalade all over his face.

"Blind each other, whatta I care?" says Magrew. "You can't see nothin' anyways."

553

C'lumbus win the exhibition game, 3 to 2, whilst Magrew set in the dugout, mutterin' and cursin' like a fourteen-year-old Scotty. He bad-mouthed everybody on the ball club and he bad-mouthed everybody offa the ball club, includin' the Wright brothers, who, he claimed, had yet to build a airship big enough for any of our boys to hit it with a ball bat.

"I wisht I was dead," he says to me. "I wisht I was in heaven with the angels."

I told him to pull hisself together, 'cause he was drivin' the boys crazy, the way he was goin' on, sulkin' and bad-mouthin' and whinin'. I was older'n he was and smarter'n he was, and he knowed it. I was ten times smarter'n he was about this Pearl du Monville, first time I ever laid eyes on the little guy, which was one of the saddest days of my life.

Now, most people name of Pearl is girls, but this Pearl du Monville was a man, if you could call a fella a man who was only thirty-four, thirty-five inches high. Pearl du Monville was a midget. He was part French and part Hungarian, and maybe even part Bulgarian or somethin'. I can see him now, a sneer on his little pushed-in pan, swingin' a bamboo cane and smokin' a big cigar. He had a gray suit with a big black check into it, and he had a gray felt hat with one of them rainbow-colored hatbands onto it, like the young fellas wore in them days. He talked like he was talkin' into a tin can, but he didn't have no foreign accent. He might a been fifteen or he might a been a hundred, you couldn't tell. Pearl du Monville.

After the game with C'lumbus, Magrew headed straight for the Chittaden bar—the train for St. Louis wasn't goin' for three, four hours—and there he set, drinkin' rye and talkin' to this bartender.

"How I pity me, brother," Magrew was tellin' this bartender. "How I pity me." That was alwuz his favorite tune. So he was settin' there, tellin' this bartender how heart-breakin' it was to be manager of a bunch a blindfolded circus clowns, when up pops this Pearl du Monville outa nowheres.

It give Magrew the leapin' jumps. He thought at first maybe the D.T.'s had come back on him; he claimed he'd had 'em once, and little guys had popped up all around him, wearin' red, white and blue hats.

"Go on, now!" Magrew yells. "Get away from me!"

But the midget clumb up on a chair acrost the table from Magrew and says, "I seen that game today, Junior, and you ain't got no ball club. What you got there, Junior," he says, "is a side show."

"Whatta ya mean, 'Junior'?" says Magrew, touchin' the little guy to satisfy hisself he was real.

"Don't pay him no attention, mister," says the bartender. "Pearl calls everybody 'Junior,' 'cause it alwuz turns out he's a year older'n anybody else."

"Yeh?" says Magrew. "How old is he?"

"How old are you, Junior?" says the midget.

"Who, me? I'm fifty-three," says Magrew.

"Well, I'm fifty-four," says the midget.

Magrew grins and asts him what he'll have, and that was the beginnin' of their beautiful friendship, if you don't care what you say.

Pearl du Monville stood up on his chair and waved his cane around and pretended like he was ballyhooin' for a circus. "Right this way, folks!" he yells. "Come on in and see the greatest collection of freaks in the world! See the armless pitchers, see the eyeless batters, see the infielders with five thumbs!" and on and on like that, feedin' Magrew gall and handin' him a laugh at the same time, you might say.

You could hear him and Pearl du Monville hootin' and hollerin' and singin' way up to the fourth floor of the Chittaden, where the boys was packin' up. When it come time to go to the station, you can imagine how disgusted we was when we crowded into the doorway of that bar and seen them two singin' and goin' on.

"Well, well, well," says Magrew, lookin' up and spottin' us. "Look who's here. . . . Clowns, this is Pearl du Monville, a monseer of the old, old school. . . . Don't shake hands with 'em, Pearl, 'cause their fingers is made of chalk and would bust right off in your paws," he says, and he starts guffawin' and Pearl starts titterin' and we stand there givin' 'em the iron eye, it bein' the lowest ebb a ball-club manager'd got hisself down to since the national pastime was started.

Then the midget begun givin' us the ballyhoo. "Come on

in!" he says, wavin' his cane. "See the legless base runners,
see the outfielders with the butter fingers, see the southpaw
with the arm of a little chee-ild!"

Then him and Magrew begun to hoop and holler and
nudge each other till you'd of thought this little guy was the
funniest guy than even Charlie Chaplin. The fellas filed outa
the bar without a word and went on up to the Union Depot,
leavin' me to handle Magrew and his new-found crony.

Well, I got 'em outa there finely. I had to take the little guy
along, 'cause Magrew had a holt onto him like a vise and I
couldn't pry him loose.

"He's comin' along as masket," says Magrew, holdin' the
midget in the crouch of his arm like a football. And come
along he did, hollerin' and protestin' and beatin' at Magrew
with his little fists.

"Cut it out, will ya, Junior?" the little guy kept whinin'.
"Come on, leave a man loose, will ya, Junior?"

But Junior kept a holt onto him and begun yellin', "See
the guys with the glass arm, see the guys with the cast-iron
brains, see the fielders with the feet on their wrists!"

So it goes, right through the whole Union Depot, with
people starin' and catcallin', and he don't put the midget
down till he gets him through the gates.

"How'm I goin' to go along without no toothbrush?" the
midget asts. "What'm I goin' to do without no other suit?"
he says.

"Doc here," says Magrew, meanin' me—"doc here will
look after you like you was his own son, won't you, doc?"

I give him the iron eye, and he finely got on the train and
prob'ly went to sleep with his clothes on.

This left me alone with the midget. "Lookit," I says to him.
"Why don't you go on home now? Come mornin', Magrew'll
forget all about you. He'll prob'ly think you was somethin'
he seen in a nightmare maybe. And he ain't goin' to laugh so
easy in the mornin', neither," I says. "So why don't you go
on home?"

"Nix," he says to me. "Skiddoo," he says, "twenty-three
for you," and he tosses his cane up into the vestibule of the
coach and clam'ers on up after it like a cat. So that's the way
Pearl du Monville come to go to St. Louis with the ball club.

I seen 'em first at breakfast the next day, settin' opposite each other; the midget playin' "Turkey in the Straw" on a harmonium and Magrew starin' at his eggs and bacon like they was a uncooked bird with its feathers still on.

"Remember where you found this?" I says, jerkin' my thumb at the midget. "Or maybe you think they come with breakfast on these trains," I says, bein' a good hand at turnin' a sharp remark in them days.

The midget puts down the harmonium and turns on me. "Sneeze," he says; "your brains is dusty." Then he snaps a couple drops of water at me from a tumbler. "Drown," he says, tryin' to make his voice deep.

Now, both them cracks is Civil War cracks, but you'd of thought they was brand new and the funniest than any crack Magrew'd ever heard in his whole life. He started hoopin' and hollerin', and the midget started hoopin' and hollerin', so I walked on away and set down with Bugs Courtney and Hank Metters, payin' no attention to this weak-minded Damon and Phidias acrost the aisle.

Well, sir, the first game with St. Louis was rained out, and there we was facin' a double-header next day. Like maybe I told you, we lose the last three double-headers we play, makin' maybe twenty-five errors in the six games, which is all right for the intimates of a school for the blind, but is disgraceful for the world's champions. It was too wet to go to the zoo, and Magrew wouldn't let us go to the movies, 'cause they flickered so bad in them days. So we just set around, stewin' and frettin'.

One of the newspaper boys come over to take a pitture of Billy Klinger and Whitey Cott shakin' hands—this reporter'd heard about the fight—and whilst they was standin' there, toe to toe, shakin' hands, Billy give a back lunge and a jerk, and throwed Whitey over his shoulder into a corner of the room, like a sack a salt. Whitey come back at him with a chair, and Bethlehem broke loose in that there room. The camera was tromped to pieces like a berry basket. When we finely got 'em pulled apart, I heard a laugh, and there was Magrew and the midget standin' in the door and givin' us the iron eye.

"Wrasslers," says Magrew, cold-like, "that's what I got for

a ball club, Mr. Du Monville, wrasslers—and not very good wrasslers at that, you ast me."

"A man can't be good at everythin'," says Pearl, "but he oughta be good at somethin'."

This sets Magrew guffawin' again, and away they go, the midget taggin' along by his side like a hound dog and handin' him a fast line of so-called comic cracks.

When we went out to face that battlin' St. Louis club in a double-header the next afternoon, the boys was jumpy as tin toys with keys in their back. We lose the first game, 7 to 2, and are trailin', 4 to 0, when the second game ain't but ten minutes old. Magrew set there like a stone statue, speakin' to nobody. Then, in their half a the fourth, somebody singled to center and knocked in two more runs for St. Louis.

That made Magrew squawk. "I wisht one thing," he says. "I wisht I was manager of a old ladies' sewin' circus 'stead of a ball club."

"You are, Junior, you are," says a familyer and disagreeable voice.

It was that Pearl du Monville again, poppin' up outa nowheres, swingin' his bamboo cane and smokin' a cigar that's three sizes too big for his face. By this time we'd finely got the other side out, and Hank Metters slithered a bat acrost the ground, and the midget had to jump to keep both his ankles from bein' broke.

I thought Magrew'd bust a blood vessel. "You hurt Pearl and I'll break your neck!" he yelled.

Hank muttered somethin' and went on up to the plate and struck out.

We managed to get a couple runs acrost in our half a the sixth, but they come back with three more in their half a the seventh, and this was too much for Magrew.

"Come on, Pearl," he says. "We're gettin' outa here."

"Where you think you're goin'?" I ast him.

"To the lawyer's again," he says cryptly.

"I didn't know you'd been to the lawyer's once, yet," I says.

"Which that goes to show how much you don't know," he says.

With that, they was gone, and I didn't see 'em the rest of the day, nor know what they was up to, which was a God's blessin'. We lose the nightcap, 9 to 3, and that puts us into second place plenty, and as low in our mind as a ball club can get.

The next day was a horrible day, like anybody that lived through it can tell you. Practice was just over and the St. Louis club was takin' the field, when I hears this strange sound from the stands. It sounds like the nervous whickerin' a horse gives when he smells somethin' funny on the wind. It was the fans ketchin' sight of Pearl du Monville, like you have prob'ly guessed. The midget had popped up onto the field all dressed up in a minacher club uniform, sox, cap, little letters sewed onto his chest, and all. He was swingin' a kid's bat and the only thing kept him from lookin' like a real ballplayer seen through the wrong end of a microscope was this cigar he was smokin'.

Bugs Courtney reached over and jerked it outa his mouth and throwed it away. "You're wearin' that suit on the playin' field," he says to him, severe as a judge. "You go insultin' it and I'll take you out to the zoo and feed you to the bears."

Pearl just blowed some smoke at him which he still has in his mouth.

Whilst Whitey was foulin' off four or five prior to strikin' out, I went on over to Magrew. "If I was as comic as you," I says, "I'd laugh myself to death," I says. "Is that any way to treat the uniform, makin' a mockery out of it?"

"It might surprise you to know I ain't makin' no mockery outa the uniform," says Magrew. "Pearl du Monville here has been made a bone-of-fida member of this so-called ball club. I fixed it up with the front office by long-distance phone."

"Yeh?" I says. "I can just hear Mr. Dillworth or Bart Jenkins agreein' to hire a midget for the ball club. I can just hear 'em." Mr. Dillworth was the owner of the club and Bart Jenkins was the secretary, and they never stood for no monkey business. "May I be so bold as to inquire," I says, "just what you told 'em?"

"I told 'em," he says, "I wanted to sign up a guy they ain't no pitcher in the league can strike him out."

"Uh-huh," I says, "and did you tell 'em what size of a man he is?"

"Never mind about that," he says. "I got papers on me, made out legal and proper, constitutin' one Pearl du Monville a bone-of-fida member of this former ball club. Maybe that'll shame them big babies into gettin' in there and swingin', knowin' I can replace any one of 'em with a midget, if I have a mind to. A St. Louis lawyer I seen twice tells me it's all legal and proper."

"A St. Louis lawyer would," I says, "seein' nothin' could make him happier than havin' you makin' a mockery outa this one-time baseball outfit," I says.

Well, sir, it'll all be there in the papers of thirty, thirty-one year ago, and you could look it up. The game went along without no scorin' for seven innings, and since they ain't nothin' much to watch but guys poppin' up or strikin' out, the fans pay most of their attention to the goin's-on of Pearl du Monville. He's out there in front a the dugout, turnin' handsprings, balancin' his bat on his chin, walkin' a imaginary line, and so on. The fans clapped and laughed at him, and he ate it up.

So it went up to the last a the eighth, nothin' to nothin', not more'n seven, eight hits all told, and no errors on neither side. Our pitcher gets the first two men out easy in the eighth. Then up come a fella name of Porter or Billings, or some such name, and he lammed one up against the tobacco sign for three bases. The next guy up slapped the first ball out into left for a base hit, and in come the fella from third for the only run of the ball game so far. The crowd yelled, the look a death come onto Magrew's face again, and even the midget quit his tom-foolin'. Their next man fouled out back a third, and we come up for our last bats like a bunch a schoolgirls steppin' into a pool of cold water. I was lower in my mind than I'd been since the day in Nineteen-four when Chesbro throwed the wild pitch in the ninth inning with a man on third and lost the pennant for the Highlanders. I knowed something just as bad was goin' to happen, which shows I'm a clairvoyun, or was then.

When Gordy Mills hit out to second, I just closed my eyes. I opened 'em up again to see Dutch Muller standin' on second, dustin' off his pants, him havin' got his first hit in maybe twenty times to the plate. Next up was Harry Loesing, battin' for our pitcher, and he got a base on balls, walkin' on a fourth one you could a combed your hair with.

Then up come Whitey Cott, our lead-off man. He crotches down in what was prob'ly the most fearsome stanch in organized ball, but all he can do is pop out to short. That brung up Billy Klinger, with two down and a man on first and second. Billy took a cut at one you could a knocked a plug hat offa this here Carnera with it, but then he gets sense enough to wait 'em out, and finely he walks, too, fillin' the bases.

Yes, sir, there you are; the tyin' run on third and the winnin' run on second, first a the ninth, two men down, and Hank Metters comin' to the bat. Hank was built like a Pope-Hartford and he couldn't run no faster'n President Taft, but he had five home runs to his credit for the season, and that wasn't bad in them days. Hank was still hittin' better'n anybody else on the ball club, and it was mighty heartenin', seein' him stridin' up towards the plate. But he never got there.

"Wait a minute!" yells Magrew, jumpin' to his feet. "I'm sendin' in a pinch hitter!" he yells.

You could a heard a bomb drop. When a ball-club manager says he's sendin' in a pinch hitter for the best batter on the club, you know and I know and everybody knows he's lost his holt.

"They're goin' to be sendin' the funny wagon for you, if you don't watch out," I says, grabbin' a holt of his arm.

But he pulled away and run out towards the plate, yellin', "Du Monville battin' for Metters!"

All the fellas begun squawlin' at once, except Hank, and he just stood there starin' at Magrew like he'd gone crazy and was claimin' to be Ty Cobb's grandma or somethin'. Their pitcher stood out there with his hands on his hips and a disagreeable look on his face, and the plate umpire told Magrew to go on and get a batter up. Magrew told him again Du Monville was battin' for Metters, and the St. Louis manager finely got the idea. It brung him outa his dugout, howlin' and bawlin' like he'd lost a female dog and her seven pups.

Magrew pushed the midget towards the plate and he says to him, he says, "Just stand up there and hold that bat on your shoulder. They ain't a man in the world can throw three strikes in there 'fore he throws four balls!" he says.

"I get it, Junior!" says the midget. "He'll walk me and force in the tyin' run!" And he starts on up to the plate as cocky as if he was Willie Keeler.

I don't need to tell you Bethlehem broke loose on that there ball field. The fans got onto their hind legs, yellin' and whistlin', and everybody on the field begun wavin' their arms and hollerin' and shovin'. The plate umpire stalked over to Magrew like a traffic cop, waggin' his jaw and pointin' his finger, and the St. Louis manager kept yellin' like his house was on fire. When Pearl got up to the plate and stood there, the pitcher slammed his glove down onto the ground and started stompin' on it, and they ain't nobody can blame him. He's just walked two normal-sized human bein's, and now here's a guy up to the plate they ain't more'n twenty inches between his knees and his shoulders.

The plate umpire called in the field umpire, and they talked a while, like a couple doctors seein' the bucolic plague or somethin' for the first time. Then the plate umpire come over to Magrew with his arms folded acrost his chest, and he told him to go on and get a batter up, or he'd forfeit the game to St. Louis. He pulled out his watch, but somebody batted it outa his hand in the scufflin', and I thought there'd be a free-for-all, with everybody yellin' and shovin' except Pearl du Monville, who stood up at the plate with his little bat on his shoulder, not movin' a muscle.

Then Magrew played his ace. I seen him pull some papers outa his pocket and show 'em to the plate umpire. The umpire begun lookin' at 'em like they was bills for somethin' he not only never bought it, he never even heard of it. The other umpire studied 'em like they was a death warren, and all this time the St. Louis manager and the fans and the players is yellin' and hollerin'.

Well, sir, they fought about him bein' a midget, and they fought about him usin' a kid's bat, and they fought about where'd he been all season. They was eight or nine rule books brung out and everybody was thumbin' through 'em, tryin' to find out what it says about midgets, but it don't say nothin' about midgets, 'cause this was somethin' never'd come up in the history of the game before, and nobody'd ever dreamed about it, even when they has nightmares. Maybe you can't send no midgets in to bat nowadays, 'cause the old game's changed a lot, mostly for the worst, but you could then, it turned out.

The plate umpire finely decided the contrack papers was all legal and proper, like Magrew said, so he waved the St. Louis players back to their places and he pointed his finger at their manager and told him to quit hollerin' and get on back in the dugout. The manager says the game is percedin' under protest, and the umpire bawls, "Play ball!" over 'n' above the yellin' and booin', him havin' a voice like a hog-caller.

The St. Louis pitcher picked up his glove and beat at it with his fist six or eight times, and then got set on the mound and studied the situation. The fans realized he was really goin' to pitch to the midget, and they went crazy, hoopin' and hollerin' louder'n ever, and throwin' pop bottles and hats and cushions down onto the field. It took five, ten minutes to get the fans quieted down again, whilst our fellas that was on base set down on the bags and waited. And Pearl du Monville kept standin' up there with the bat on his shoulder, like he'd been told to.

So the pitcher starts studyin' the setup again, and you got to admit it was the strangest setup in a ball game since the players cut off their beards and begun wearin' gloves. I wisht I could call the pitcher's name—it wasn't old Barney Pelty nor Nig Jack Powell nor Harry Howell. He was a big right-hander, but I can't call his name. You could look it up. Even in a crotchin' position, the ketcher towers over the midget like the Washington Monument.

The plate umpire tries standin' on his tiptoes, then he tries crotchin' down, and he finely gets hisself into a stanch no-body'd ever seen on a ball field before, kinda squattin' down on his hanches.

Well, the pitcher is sore as a old buggy horse in fly time. He slams in the first pitch, hard and wild, and maybe two foot higher'n the midget's head.

"Ball one!" hollers the umpire over 'n' above the racket, 'cause everybody is yellin' worsten ever.

The ketcher goes on out towards the mound and talks to

the pitcher and hands him the ball. This time the big right-hander tried a undershoot, and it comes in a little closer, maybe no higher'n a foot, foot and a half above Pearl's head. It would a been a strike with a human bein' in there, but the umpire's got to call it, and he does.

"Ball two!" he bellers.

The ketcher walks on out to the mound again, and the whole infield comes over and gives advice to the pitcher about what they'd do in a case like this, with two balls and no strikes on a batter that oughta be in a bottle of alcohol 'stead of up there at the plate in a big-league game between the teams that is fightin' for first place.

For the third pitch, the pitcher stands there flat-footed and tosses up the ball like he's playin' ketch with a little girl.

Pearl stands there motionless as a hitchin' post, and the ball comes in big and slow and high—high for Pearl, that is, it bein' about on a level with his eyes, or a little higher'n a grown man's knees.

They ain't nothin' else for the umpire to do, so he calls, "Ball three!"

Everybody is onto their feet, hoopin' and hollerin', as the pitcher sets to throw ball four. The St. Louis manager is makin' signs and faces like he was a contorturer, and the infield is givin' the pitcher some more advice about what to do this time. Our boys who was on base stick right onto the bag, runnin' no risk of bein' nipped for the last out.

Well, the pitcher decides to give him a toss again, seein' he come closer with that than with a fast ball. They ain't nobody ever seen a slower ball throwed. It come in big as a balloon and slower'n any ball ever throwed before in the major leagues. It come right in over the plate in front of Pearl's chest, lookin' prob'ly big as a full moon to Pearl. They ain't never been a minute like the minute that followed since the United States was founded by the Pilgrim grandfathers.

Pearl du Monville took a cut at that ball, and he hit it! Magrew give a groan like a poleaxed steer as the ball rolls out in front a the plate into fair territory.

"Fair ball!" yells the umpire, and the midget starts runnin' for first, still carryin' that little bat, and makin' maybe ninety foot an hour. Bethlehem breaks loose on that ball field and in them stands. They ain't never been nothin' like it since creation was begun.

The ball's rollin' slow, on down towards third, goin' maybe eight, ten foot. The infield comes in fast and our boys break from their bases like hares in a brush fire. Everybody is standin' up, yellin' and hollerin', and Magrew is tearin' his hair outa his head, and the midget is scamperin' for first with all the speed of one of them little dashhounds carryin' a satchel in his mouth.

The ketcher gets to the ball first, but he boots it on out past the pitcher's box, the pitcher fallin' on his face tryin' to stop it, the shortstop sprawlin' after it full length and zaggin' it on over towards the second baseman, whilst Muller is scorin' with the tyin' run and Loesing is roundin' third with the winnin' run. Ty Cobb could a made a three-bagger outa that bunt, with everybody fallin' over theirself tryin' to pick the ball up. But Pearl is still maybe fifteen, twenty feet from the bag, toddlin' like a baby and yeepin' like a trapped rabbit, when the second baseman finely gets a holt of that ball and slams it over to first. The first baseman ketches it and stomps on the bag, the base umpire waves Pearl out, and there goes your old ball game, the craziest ball game ever played in the history of the organized world.

Their players start runnin' in, and then I see Magrew. He starts after Pearl, runnin' faster'n any man ever run before. Pearl sees him comin' and runs behind the base umpire's legs and gets a holt onto 'em. Magrew comes up, pantin' and roarin', and him and the midget plays ring-around-a-rosy with the umpire, who keeps shovin' at Magrew with one hand and tryin' to slap the midget loose from his legs with the other.

Finely Magrew ketches the midget, who is still yeepin' like a stuck sheep. He gets holt of that little guy by both his ankles and starts whirlin' him round and round his head like Magrew was a hammer thrower and Pearl was the hammer. Nobody can stop him without gettin' their head knocked off, so everybody just stands there and yells. Then Magrew lets the midget fly. He flies on out towards second, high and fast, like a human home run, headed for the soap sign in center field.

Their shortstop tries to get to him, but he can't make it, and I knowed the little fella was goin' to bust to pieces like a dollar watch on a asphalt street when he hit the ground. But it so happens their center fielder is just crossin' second, and he starts runnin' back, tryin' to get under the midget, who had took to spiralin' like a football 'stead of turnin' head over foot, which give him more speed and more distance.

I know you never seen a midget ketched, and you prob'ly never even seen one throwed. To ketch a midget that's been throwed by a heavy-muscled man and is flyin' through the air, you got to run under him and with him and pull your hands and arms back and down when you ketch him, to break the compact of his body, or you'll bust him in two like a matchstick. I seen Bill Lange and Willie Keeler and Tris Speaker make some wonderful ketches in my day, but I never seen nothin' like that center fielder. He goes back and back and still further back and he pulls that midget down outa the air like he was liftin' a sleepin' baby from a cradle. They wasn't a bruise onto him, only his face was the color of cat's meat and he ain't got no air in his chest. In his excitement, the base umpire, who was runnin' back with the center fielder when he ketched Pearl, yells, "Out!" and that give hysteries to the Bethlehem which was ragin' like Niagry on that ball field.

Everybody was hoopin' and hollerin' and yellin' and runnin', with the fans swarmin' onto the field, and the cops tryin' to keep order, and some guys laughin' and some of the women fans cryin', and six or eight of us holdin' onto Magrew to keep him from gettin' at that midget and finishin' him off. Some of the fans picks up the St. Louis pitcher and the center fielder, and starts carryin' 'em around on their shoulders, and they was the craziest goin's-on knowed to the history of organized ball on this side of the 'Lantic Ocean.

I seen Pearl du Monville strugglin' in the arms of a lady fan with a ample bosom, who was laughin' and cryin' at the same time, and him beatin' at her with his little fists and bawlin' and yellin'. He clawed his way loose finely and disappeared in the forest of legs which made that ball field look like it was Coney Island on a hot summer's day.

That was the last I ever seen of Pearl du Monville. I never seen hide nor hair of him from that day to this, and neither did nobody else. He just vanished into the thin of the air, as the fella says. He was ketched for the final out of the ball game and that was the end of him, just like it was the end of the ball game, you might say, and also the end of our losin' streak, like I'm goin' to tell you.

That night we piled onto a train for Chicago, but we wasn't snarlin' and snappin' any more. No, sir, the ice was finely broke and a new spirit come into that ball club. The old zip come back with the disappearance of Pearl du Monville out back a second base. We got to laughin' and talkin' and kiddin' together, and 'fore long Magrew was laughin' with us. He got a human look onto his pan again, and he quit whinin' and complainin' and wishtin' he was in heaven with the angels.

Well, sir, we wiped up that Chicago series, winnin' all four games, and makin' seventeen hits in one of 'em. Funny thing was, St. Louis was so shook up by that last game with us, they never did hit their stride again. Their center fielder took to misjudgin' everything that come his way, and the rest a the fellas followed suit, the way a club'll do when one guy blows up.

'Fore we left Chicago, I and some of the fellas went out and bought a pair of them little baby shoes, which we had 'em golded over and give 'em to Magrew for a souvenir, and he took it all in good spirit. Whitey Cott and Billy Klinger made up and was fast friends again, and we hit our home lot like a ton of dynamite and they was nothin' could stop us from then on.

I don't recollect things as clear as I did thirty, forty year ago. I can't read no fine print no more, and the only person I got to check with on the golden days of the national pastime, as the fella says, is my friend, old Milt Kline, over in Springfield, and his mind ain't as strong as it once was.

He gets Rube Waddell mixed up with Rube Marquard, for one thing, and anybody does that oughta be put away where he won't bother nobody. So I can't tell you the exact margin we win the pennant by. Maybe it was two and a half games, or maybe it was three and a half. But it'll all be there in the newspapers and record books of thirty, thirty-one year ago and, like I was sayin', you could look it up.

The Gentleman in 916

ONE OF my remarkable collection of colored maids wrote me a letter the other day. This girl, named Maisie, is the one who caused my hair to whiten over night a few years ago by telling me when I got home one gloomy November evening, tired and jumpy, that there was something wrong with the doom-shaped thing in the kitchen. This monstrous menace turned out, too late to save my reason, to be the dome- (to her) shaped thing on top of the electric icebox.

Maisie's letter went along quietly enough for two paragraphs, listing the physical woes of herself and her family, a rather staggering list, to be sure, but containing nothing to cause my white hair to stand on end. And then came an alarming sentence.

"I tried to see you in December," she wrote, "but the time-keeper said you were in Florida."

This was the first news I had had that there is a man holding a watch on me. All my doom-shaped fears came back with a rush. It is true that I was not in Florida at the time, but this did not comfort me. I could only guess that the man who is watching the sands run through my hour-glass is not really on the job.

"What difference does it make where this bird is?" he probably says to himself. "He hasn't got many hours left, so why should I bother following him around? I'll just sit here and watch the clock."

There are times, however, when I think he *is* keeping track, that he is right in the room with me. Since I have, for the time being, about one-fiftieth vision, I can't actually see him; but I can hear him. It is no illusion that the blind become equipped with the eardrums of an elk hound. I can hear a pin drop on a carpet. It makes two sounds—a sharp plop when it strikes the carpet and a somewhat smaller sound, a faint thip! when it bounces and strikes again. It is because of acute sharpness of ear that I hear, or think I hear, the time-keeper. This is always when I am alone in a room, or think

I am. I shut the radio off suddenly, and I hear him flitting across the carpet, making a sound about three times as loud as a pin.

"Hello," I say, but he never answers. Sometimes a waiter does, or a bell boy, or a maid who has crept into the room. On these occasions the timekeeper slips into a closet or under the bed. I never ask the waiter or the bell boy or the maid to look for the hiding man, for consider how it would sound. It would sound like this:

"Waiter?"

"Yes, sir?"

"Would you mind looking under the bed? I think there is a timekeeper there."

"A timekeeper, sir? I'm sorry, sir, but it sounds as if you said timekeeper, sir."

"That's right—timekeeper. There is a timekeeper hiding somewhere in this room, a chap who wears sneakers, and a suit of the same design as the wallpaper, probably."

"I'm very sorry. Shall I call your doctor?"

"No, never mind, it's all right. Let it go."

I haven't let anybody call the doctor yet, but I am planning to let one of the waiters do it one of these days, a waiter named Heyst. He not only always brings the wrong order to me, but he is also the man who distributes the menus, shoving them under the door. To some people a menu being shoved under a door would make only a faint moving sound, but to me it sounds like a man stepping on a market basket, and is very disconcerting.

So I am going to let Heyst call the doctor some day. You know what would happen to a man who phoned a doctor and said, "The gentleman in 916 hears timekeepers, sir." He would be put away before sundown.

I don't know who pays the timekeeper. I do, probably, without knowing it—I can't see my checkbook stubs. It is thoughtful of him, at least, to carry a watch that makes no sound at all. That would keep me awake at night when he sits in a chair at the foot of my bed. Even the sound of a wrist-watch prevents me from sleeping, because it sounds like two men trying to take a wheel off a locomotive. If I put stoppels in my ears, the racket is deadened somewhat. Then the ticking is fainter and farther away, a comparatively peaceful sound, like two men trying to take a rug away from a bulldog.

The Letters of James Thurber

> Adams was a great letter writer of the type that is now almost extinct . . . his circle of friends was larger perhaps and more distinguished than that of any other American of his generation.—*H. S. Commager on "Letters of Henry Adams."*

JAMES THURBER was a letter writer of the type that is now completely extinct. His circle of correspondents was perhaps no larger but it was easily more bewildered than that of any other American of his generation. Thurber laid the foundation for his voluminous correspondence during his Formative Period. In those years he wrote to many distinguished persons, none of whom ever replied, among them Admiral Schley, Young Barbarian, Senator Atlee Pomerene, June Caprice, and a man named Unglaub who played first base for the Washington Senators at the turn of the century. Unglaub, in Thurber's estimation, stood head and shoulders above all the rest of his correspondents and, indeed, he said so in his letter to McKinley. Thurber did not write as many letters as Henry Adams or John Jay Chapman or some of the other boys whose correspondence has been published lately, but that is because he never set pen to paper after his forty-third year.

The effect of Thurber's letters on his generation was about the same as the effect of anybody's letters on any generation; that is to say, nil. It is only when a man's letters are published after his death that they have any effect and this effect is usually only on literary critics. Nobody else ever reads a volume of letters and anybody who says he does is a liar. A person may pick up a volume of correspondence now and then and read a letter here and there, but he never gets any connected idea of what the man is trying to say and soon abandons the book for the poems of John Greenleaf Whittier. This is largely because every man whose letters have ever been published was in the habit of writing every third one to a Mrs. Cameron or a Mrs. Winslow or a Miss Betch, the confidante of a lifetime, with whom he shared any number of gaily obscure little secrets. These letters all read like this: "Dear Puttums: I love what you say about Mooey! It's so devastatingly true! B——

dropped in yesterday (Icky was out at the time) and gave some sort of report on Neddy but I am afraid I didn't listen (*ut ediendam aut debendo!*). He and Liddy are in Venice, I think I gathered, or Newport. What in the world do you suppose came over Buppa that Great Night? ? ? You, of course, were as splendidly consequent as ever (*in loco sporenti abadabba est*)—but I was deeply disappointed in Sig's reaction. All he can think of, poor fellow, is Margery's 'flight.' Remind me to tell you some day what Pet said about the Ordeal." These particular letters are sometimes further obscured by a series of explanatory editorial footnotes, such as "Probably Harry Boynton or his brother Norton," "A neighbor at Bar Harbor," "The late Edward J. Belcher," "Also sometimes lovingly referred to as Butty, a niece-in-law by his first marriage." In the end, as I say, one lays the book aside for "Snow-Bound" in order to get a feeling of reality before going to bed.

Thurber's letters from Europe during his long stay there in 1937 and 1938 (the European Phase) are perhaps the least interesting of all those he, or anybody else, ever wrote. He seems to have had at no time any idea at all, either clear or vague, as to what was going on. A certain Groping, to be sure, is discernible, but it doesn't appear to be toward anything. All this may have been due in great part to the fact that he took his automobile to Europe with him and spent most of his time worrying about running out of gas. The gasoline gauge of his car had got out of order and sometimes registered "empty" when the tank was half full and "full" when it contained only two or three gallons. A stronger character would have had the gauge fixed or carried a five-gallon can of *essence* in the back of the car, thus releasing the mind for more mature and significant preoccupations, but not Thurber.

I have been unable to find any one of Thurber's many correspondents who saved any of his letters (Thurber himself kept carbons, although this is not generally known or cared about). "We threw them out when we moved," people would tell me, or "We gave them to the janitor's little boy." Thurber gradually became aware of this on his return to America (the Final Phase) because of the embarrassed silence that always greeted him when, at his friends' homes, he would say, "Why don't we get out my letters to you and read them aloud?" After a painful pause the subject was quickly changed, usually by putting up the ping-pong table.

In his last years the once voluminous letter writer ceased writing letters altogether, and such communication as he maintained with the great figures of his time was over the telephone and consisted of getting prominent persons on the phone, making a deplorable sound with his lips, and hanging up. His continual but vain attempts to reach the former Barbara Hutton by phone clouded the last years of his life but at the same time gave him something to do. His last words, to his wife, at the fag end of the Final Phase, were "Before they put up the ping-pong table, tell them I am not running out of gas." He was as wrong, and as mixed up, in this particular instance as he was in most others. I am not sure that we should not judge him too harshly.

Here Lies Miss Groby

Miss Groby taught me English composition thirty years ago. It wasn't what prose said that interested Miss Groby; it was the way prose said it. The shape of a sentence crucified on a blackboard (parsed, she called it) brought a light to her eye. She hunted for Topic Sentences and Transitional Sentences the way little girls hunt for white violets in springtime. What she loved most of all were Figures of Speech. You remember her. You must have had her, too. Her influence will never die out of the land. A small schoolgirl asked me the other day if I could give her an example of metonymy. (There are several kinds of metonymies, you may recall, but the one that will come to mind most easily, I think, is Container for the Thing Contained). The vision of Miss Groby came clearly before me when the little girl mentioned the old, familiar word. I saw her sitting at her desk, taking the rubber band off the roll-call cards, running it back upon the fingers of her right hand, and surveying us all separately with quick little henlike turns of her head.

Here lies Miss Groby, not dead, I think, but put away on a shelf with the other T squares and rulers whose edges had lost their certainty. The fierce light that Miss Groby brought to English literature was the light of Identification. Perhaps, at the end, she could no longer retain the dates of the birth and death of one of the Lake poets. That would have sent her to the principal of the school with her resignation. Or perhaps she could not remember, finally, exactly how many Cornishmen there were who had sworn that Trelawny should not die, or precisely how many springs were left to Housman's lad in which to go about the woodlands to see the cherry hung with snow.

Verse was one of Miss Groby's delights because there was so much in both its form and content that could be counted. I believe she would have got an enormous thrill out of Wordsworth's famous lines about Lucy if they had been written this way:

A violet by a mossy stone
Half hidden from the eye,
Fair as a star when ninety-eight
Are shining in the sky.

It is hard for me to believe that Miss Groby ever saw any famous work of literature from far enough away to know what it meant. She was forever climbing up the margins of books and crawling between their lines, hunting for the little gold of phrase, making marks with a pencil. As Palamides hunted the Questing Beast, she hunted the Figure of Speech. She hunted it through the clangorous halls of Shakespeare and through the green forests of Scott.

Night after night, for homework, Miss Groby set us to searching in "Ivanhoe" and "Julius Caesar" for metaphors, similes, metonymies, apostrophes, personifications, and all the rest. It got so that figures of speech jumped out of the pages at you, obscuring the sense and pattern of the novel or play you were trying to read. "Friends, Romans, countrymen, lend me your ears." Take that, for instance. There is an unusual but perfect example of Container for the Thing Contained. If you read the funeral oration unwarily—that is to say, for its meaning—you might easily miss the C.F.T.T.C. Antony is, of course, not asking for their ears in the sense that he wants them cut off and handed over; he is asking for the function of those ears, for their power to hear, for, in a word, the thing they contain.

At first I began to fear that all the characters in Shakespeare and Scott were crazy. They confused cause with effect, the sign for the thing signified, the thing held for the thing holding it. But after a while I began to suspect that it was I myself who was crazy. I would find myself lying awake at night saying over and over, "The thinger for the thing contained." In a great but probably misguided attempt to keep my mind on its hinges, I would stare at the ceiling and try to think of an example of the Thing Contained for the Container. It struck me as odd that Miss Groby had never thought of that inversion. I finally hit on one, which I still remember. If a woman were to grab up a bottle of Grade A and say to her husband,

"Get away from me or I'll hit you with the milk," that would be a Thing Contained for the Container. The next day in class I raised my hand and brought my curious discovery straight out before Miss Groby and my astonished schoolmates. I was eager and serious about it and it never occurred to me that the other children would laugh. They laughed loudly and long. When Miss Groby had quieted them she said to me rather coldly, "That was not really amusing, James." That's the mixed-up kind of thing that happened to me in my teens.

In later years I came across another excellent example of this figure of speech in a joke long since familiar to people who know vaudeville or burlesque (or radio, for that matter). It goes something like this:

A: What's your head all bandaged up for?
B: I got hit with some tomatoes.
A: How could that bruise you up so bad?
B: These tomatoes were in a can.

I wonder what Miss Groby would have thought of that one.

I dream of my old English teacher occasionally. It seems that we are always in Sherwood Forest and that from far away I can hear Robin Hood winding his silver horn.

"Drat that man for making such a racket on his cornet!" cries Miss Groby. "He scared away a perfectly darling Container for the Thing Contained, a great, big, beautiful one. It leaped right back into its context when that man blew that cornet. It was the most wonderful Container for the Thing Contained I ever saw here in the Forest of Arden."

"This is Sherwood Forest," I say to her.

"That doesn't make any difference at all that I can see," she says to me.

Then I wake up, tossing and moaning.

A Ride with Olympy

OLYMPY SEMENTZOFF called me *"Monsieur"* because I was the master of the Villa Tamisier and he was the gardener, the Russian husband of the French caretaker, Maria. I called him *"Monsieur,"* too, because I could never learn to call any man Olympy and because there was a wistful air of *ancien régime* about him. He drank Bénédictine with me and smoked my cigarettes; he also, as you will see, drove my car. We conversed in French, a language alien to both of us, but more alien to me than to him. He said *"gauche"* for both "right" and "left" when he was upset, but when I was upset I was capable of flights that put the French people on their guard, wide-eyed and wary. Once, for instance, when I cut my wrist on a piece of glass I ran into the lobby of a hotel shouting in French, "I am sick with a knife!" Olympy would have known what to say (except that it would have been his left wrist in any case) but he wouldn't have shouted: his words ran softly together and sounded something like the burbling of water over stones. Often I did not know what he was talking about; rarely did he know what I was talking about. There was a misty, faraway quality about this relationship, in French, of Russia and Ohio. The fact that the accident Olympy and I were involved in fell short of catastrophe was, in view of everything, something of a miracle.

Olympy and Maria "came with" the villa my wife and I rented on Cap d'Antibes. Maria was a deep-bosomed, large-waisted woman, as persistently pleasant as Riviera weather in a good season; no mistral ever blew in the even climate of her temperament. She must have been more than forty-five but she was as strong as a root; once when I had trouble getting a tough cork out of a wine bottle she took hold and whisked it out as if it had been a maidenhair fern. On Sundays her son came over from the barracks in Antibes and we all had a glass of white Bordeaux together, sometimes the Sementzoffs' wine, sometimes our own. Her son was eighteen and a member of the Sixth Regiment of Chasseurs Alpins, a tall, somber boy, handsome in his uniform and cape. He was an *enfant du premier lit*, as the French say. Maria made her first bed with a sergeant of the army who was *cordonnier* for his regiment during the war and seemed somehow to have laid by quite a little money. After the war the sergeant-shoemaker resigned from the army, put his money in investments of some profoundly mysterious nature in Indo-China, and lost it all. *"Il est mort,"* Maria told us, *"de chagrin."* Grief over his ill-fortune brought on a decline; the *chagrin*, Maria said, finally reached his brain, and he died at the age of thirty-eight. Maria had to sell their house to pay the taxes, and go to work.

Olympy Sementzoff, Maria's second husband, was shy, not very tall, and wore a beard; in his working clothes you didn't notice much more than that. When he was dressed for Sunday—he wore a fine double-breasted jacket—you observed that his mouth was sensitive, his eyes attractively sad, and that he wore his shyness with a certain air. He worked in a boat factory over near Cannes—Maria said that he was a *spécialiste de bateaux*; odd jobs about the villa grounds he did on his off days. It was scarcely light when he got up in the morning, for he had to be at work at seven; it was almost dark when he got home. He was paid an incredibly small amount for what he did at the factory and a handful of sous each month for what he did about the grounds. When I gave him a hundred francs for some work he had done for me in the house—he could repair anything from a drain to a watch—he said, *"Oh, monsieur, c'est trop!"* *"Mais non, monsieur,"* said I. *"Ce n'est pas beaucoup."* He took it finally, after an exchange of bows and compliments.

The elderly wife of the Frenchman from whom we rented the villa told us, in a dark whisper, that Olympy was a White Russian and that there was perhaps a *petit mystère* about him, but we figured this as her own fanciful bourgeois alarm. Maria did not make a mystery out of her husband. There was the Revolution, most of Olympy's brothers and sisters were killed—one knew how that was—and he escaped. He was, of course, an exile and must not go back. If she knew just who he was in Russia and what he had done, she didn't make it very clear. He was in Russia and he escaped; she had married him thirteen years before; *et puis, voilà!* It would have been nice to believe that there was the blood of the Czars in

Olympy, but if there was anything to the ancient legend that all the stray members of the Imperial House took easily and naturally to driving a taxi, that let Olympy out. He was not a born chauffeur, as I found out the day I came back from our automobile ride on foot and—unhappily for Maria—alone.

Olympy Sementzoff rode to and from his work in one of those bastard agglomerations of wheels, motor and super-structure that one saw only in France. It looked at first glance like the cockpit of a cracked-up plane. Then you saw that there were two wheels in front and a single wheel in back. Except for the engine—which Maria said was a "Morgan *moteur*"—and the wheels and tires, it was handmade. Olympy's boss at the boat factory had made most of it, but Olympy himself had put on the *ailes*, or fenders, which were made of some kind of wood. The strange canopy that served as a top was Maria's proud handiwork; it seemed to have been made of canvas and kitchen aprons. The thing had a right-hand drive. When the *conducteur* was in his seat he was very low to the ground: you had to bend down to talk to him. There was a small space beside the driver in which another person could sit, or crouch. The whole affair was not much larger than an overturned cab-inet victrola. It got bouncingly under way with all the racket of a dog fight and in full swing was capable of perhaps thirty miles an hour. The contraption had cost Olympy three thou-sand francs, or about a hundred dollars. He had driven it for three years and was hand in glove with its mysterious mech-anism. The gadgets on the dash and on the floorboard, which he pulled or pushed to make the thing go, seemed to include fire tongs, spoons, and doorknobs. Maria miraculously man-aged to squeeze into the seat beside the driver in an emer-gency, but I could understand why she didn't want to drive to the Nice Carnival in the "Morgan." It was because she didn't that I suggested Olympy should take her over one day in my Ford sedan. Maria had given us to understand that her *mari* could drive any car—he could be a chauffeur if he wanted to, a *bon* chauffeur. All I would have to do, *voyez-vous*, was to take Olympy for a turn around the Cap so that he could get the hang of the big car. Thus it was that one day after lunch we set off.

Half a mile out of Antibes on the shore road, I stopped the

car and changed places with Olympy, letting the engine run. Leaning forward, he took a tense grip on a steering wheel much larger than he was used to and too far away from him. I could see that he was nervous. He put his foot on the clutch, tentatively, and said, *"Embrayage?"* He had me there. My knowledge of French automotive terms is inadequate and volatile. I was forced to say I didn't know. I couldn't remember the word for clutch in any of the three languages, French, Italian and German, in which it was given in my "Motorist's Guide" (which was back at the villa). Somehow *"embrayage"* didn't sound right for clutch (it is, though). I knew it wouldn't do any good for an American writer to explain in French to a Russian boat specialist the purpose that particular pedal served; furthermore, I didn't really know. I compromised by putting my left foot on the brake. *"Frein,"* I said. *"Ah,"* said Olympy, unhappily. This method of indicating what something might be by demonstrating what it wasn't had a disturbing effect. I shifted my foot to the accelerator—or rather pointed my toe at it—and suddenly the word for that, even the French for gasoline, left me. I was growing a little nervous myself. *"Benzina,"* I said, in Italian, finally. *"Ah?"* said Olympy. Whereas we had been one remove from reality to begin with, we were now two, or perhaps three, removes. A polyglot approach to the fine precision of a gas engine is roundabout and dangerous. We both lost a little confidence in each other. I suppose we should have given up right then, but we didn't.

Olympy decided the extra pedal was the *embrayage*, shifted into low from neutral, and the next thing I knew we were making a series of short forward bounds like a rabbit leaping out of a wheat field to see where he is. This form of locomotion takes a lot out of man and car. The engine complained in loud, rhythmic whines. And then Olympy somehow got his left foot on the starter and there was a familiar undertone of protest; this set his right foot to palpitating on the accelerator and the rabbit-jumps increased in scope. Abandoning my search for the word for starter, I grabbed his left knee and shouted *"Ça commence!"* Just what was commencing Olympy naturally couldn't figure—probably some habitual and ominous idiosyncrasy of the machinery. He gave me a quick, pale look. I shut off the ignition, and we discussed the starter situation, breathing a little heavily. He understood what it was, finally, and presently we were lurching ahead again, Olympy holding her in low gear, like a wrestler in a clinch, afraid to risk shifting into second. He tried it at last and with a jamming jolt and a roar we went into reverse: the car writhed like a tortured leopard and the engine quit.

I was puzzled and scared, and so was Olympy. Only a foolish pride in masculine fortitude kept us going. I showed him the little jog to the right you have to make to shift into second and he started the engine and we were off again, jolting and lurching. He made the shift, finally, with a noise like lightning striking a foundry—and veered swoopingly to the right. We barely missed a series of staunch granite blocks, set in concrete, that mark ditches and soft shoulders. We whisked past a pole. The leaves of a vine hanging on a wall slapped at me through the window. My voice left me. I was fascinated and paralyzed by the swift passes disaster was making at my head. At length I was able to grope blindly toward the ignition switch, but got my wrist on the klaxon button. When I jerked my arm away, Olympy began obediently sounding the horn. We were riding on the edge of a ditch. I managed somehow to shut off the ignition and we rolled to a stop. Olympy, unused to a left-hand drive, had forgotten there was a large portion of the car to his right, with me in it. I told him, *"A gauche, à gauche, toujours à gauche!"* *"Ah,"* said Olympy, but there was no comprehension in him. I could see he didn't know we had been up against the vines of villa walls: intent on the dark problem of gearshifting, he had been oblivious of where the car and I had been. There was a glint in his eye now. He was determined to get the thing into high on his next attempt; we had come about half a mile in the lower gears.

The road curved downhill as it passed Eden Roc and it was here that an elderly English couple, unaware of the fact that hell was loose on the highway, were walking. Olympy was in second again, leaning forward like a racing bicycle rider. I shouted at him to look out, he said *"Oui"*—and we grazed the old man and his wife. I glanced back in horror: they were staring at us, mouths and eyes wide, unable to move or make a sound. Olympy raced on to a new peril: a descending hairpin curve, which he negotiated in some far-fetched manner, with me hanging onto the emergency brake. The road straightened out, I let go the brake, and Olympy slammed into high with the desperate gesture of a man trying to clap his hat over a poised butterfly. We began to whiz: Olympy hadn't counted on a fast pickup. He whirled around a car in front of us with a foot to spare. *"Lentement!"* I shouted, and then *"Gauche!"* as I began to get again the whimper of poles and walls in my ears. *"Ça va mieux, maintenant,"* said Olympy, quietly. A wild thought ran through my head that maybe this was the way they used to drive in Russia in the old days.

Ahead of us now was one of the most treacherous curves on the Cap. The road narrowed and bent, like a croquet wicket, around a high stone wall that shut off your view of what was coming. What was coming was usually on the wrong side of the road, so it wouldn't do to shout *"Gauche!"* now. We made the turn all right. There was a car coming, but it was well over on its own side. Olympy apparently didn't think so. He whirled the wheel to the right, didn't take up the play fast enough in whirling it back, and there was a tremendous banging crash, like a bronze monument falling. I had a glimpse of Olympy's right hand waving around like the hand of a man hunting for something under a table. I didn't know what his feet were doing. We were still moving, heavily, with a ripping noise and a loud roar. *"Poussez le phare!"* I shouted, which means "push the headlight!" *"Ah-h-h-h,"* said Olympy. I shut off the ignition and pulled on the hand brake, but we had already stopped. We got out and looked at the pole we had sideswiped and at the car. The right front fender was crumpled and torn and the right back one banged up, but nothing else had been hurt. Olympy's face was so stricken when he looked at me that I felt I had to cheer him up. *"Il fait beau,"* I announced, which is to say that the weather is fine. It was all I could think of.

I started for a garage that Olympy knew about. At the first street we came to he said *"Gauche"* and I turned left. *"Ah, non,"* said Olympy. *"Gauche,"* and he pointed the other way. "You mean *droit*?" I asked, just that way. *"Ah!"* said Olympy. *"C'est bien ça!"* It was as if he had thought of something he hadn't been able to remember for days. That explained a great deal.

I left Olympy and the car at the garage; he said he would walk back. One of the garage men drove me into Juan-les-Pins and I walked home from there—and into a look of wild dismay in Maria's eyes. I hadn't thought about that: she had seen us drive away together and here I was, alone. *"Où est votre mari?"* I asked her, hurriedly. It was something of a failure as a reassuring beginning. I had taken the question out of her own mouth, so I answered it. "He has gone for a walk," I told her. Then I tried to say that her husband was *bon*, but I pronounced it *beau*, so that what I actually said was that her husband was handsome. She must have figured that he was not only dead but laid out. There was a *mauvais quart d'heure* for both of us before the drooping figure of Olympy finally appeared. He explained sadly to Maria that the mechanism of the Ford is strange and curious compared to the mechanism of the Morgan. I agreed with him. Of course, he protested, he would pay for the repairs to the car, but Maria and I both put down that suggestion. Maria's idea of my work was that I was paid by the City of New York and enjoyed a tremendous allowance. Olympy got forty francs a day at the boat factory.

That night, at dinner, Maria told us that her *mari* was pacing up and down in their little bedroom at the rear of the house. He was in a state. I didn't want an attack of *chagrin* to come on him as it had on the *cordonnier* and perhaps reach his brain. When Maria was ready to go we gave her a handful of cigarettes for Olympy and a glass of Bénédictine. The next day, at dawn, I heard the familiar *tintamarre* and *hurlement* and *brouhaha* of Olympy's wonderful contraption getting under way once more. He was off to the boat factory and his forty francs a day, his dollar and thirty cents. It would have cost him two weeks' salary to pay for the fenders, but he would have managed it somehow. When I went down to breakfast, Maria came in from the kitchen with a large volume, well fingered and full of loose pages, which she handed to me. It was called *Le Musée d'Art* and subtitled *Galerie des Chefs-d'œuvre et Précis de l'Histoire de l'Art au XIXᵉ Siècle, en France et à l'Etranger (1000 gravures, 58 planches hors texte)*. A

present to *Monsieur* from Olympy Sementzoff, with his compliments. The incident of the automobile was thus properly
rounded off with an exchange of presents: cigarettes, Bénédictine, and *Le Musée d'Art.* It seemed to me the way such
things should always end, but perhaps Olympy and I were
ahead of our day—or behind it.

MEN, WOMEN AND DOGS

"It's a naïve domestic Burgundy without any breeding, but I think you'll be amused by its presumption."

"You're going a bit far, Miss Blanchard."

587

"You gah dam pussy cats!"

"It's Lida Bascom's husband—he's frightfully unhappy."

"Touché!"

"There's no use you trying to save <u>me</u>, my good man."

"I come from haunts of coot and hern!"

"They're going to put you away if you don't quit acting like this."

"You and your premonitions!"

"You were wonderful at the Gardners' last night, Fred, when you turned on the charm."

"Here! Here! There's a place for that, sir!"

"What have you done with Dr. Millmoss?"

"One of you men in the kitchen give the officer another drink!"

"For Heaven's sake, why don't you go outdoors and trace something?"

"I think of you as being enormously alive."

"If you can keep a secret, I'll tell you how my husband died."

"He's been like this ever since Munich."

"Why did I ever marry below my emotional level!"

"I'd feel a great deal easier if her husband hadn't gone to bed."

"And this is Tom Weatherby, an old beau of your mother's. He never got to first base."

"Darling, I seem to have this rabbit."

*"I don't know them either, dear, but there may be some very simple
explanation."*

"I love the idea of there being two sexes, don't you?"

"Well, I'm disenchanted, too. We're all disenchanted."

"I don't want him to be comfortable if he's going to look too funny."

"This is like that awful afternoon we telephoned Mencken."

"Unhappy woman!"

*"I wouldn't rent this room to everybody, Mr. Spencer. This is where
my husband lost his mind."*

"I brought a couple of midgets—do you mind?"

"This gentleman was kind enough to see me home, darling."

"You said a moment ago that everybody you look at seems to be a rabbit. Now just what do you mean by that, Mrs. Sprague?"

"Well, who _made_ the magic go out of our marriage—you or me?"

"Well, if I called the wrong number, why did you answer the phone?"

"Now I'm going to go in over your horns!"

"Which you am I talking to now?"

"The party's breaking up, darling."

"Look out, Harry!"

"This is not the real me you're seeing, Mrs. Clisbie."

"And this is the little woman."

"That's my first wife up there, and this is the <u>present</u> Mrs. Harris."

"He's given up everything for a whole year."

"George! If that's you I'll never forgive you!"

"Perhaps this will refresh your memory."

"Hello, darling—woolgathering?"

"Why, I never dreamed your union had been blessed with issue!"

"It's Parkins, sir; we're 'aving a bit of a time below stairs."

The Masculine Approach

The Candy-and-Flowers Campaign

The I'm-Drinking-Myself-to-Death-and-Nobody-Can-Stop-Me Method

The Strong, Silent System

The Pawing System

The Strange-Fascination Technique

The You'll-Never-See-Me-Again Tactics

The Heroic, or Dangers-I-Have-Known, Method

The Let-'Em-Wait-and-Wonder Plan

The Unhappy-Childhood Story

The Indifference Attitude

The Letter-Writing Method

The Man-of-the-World, or Ordering-in-French, Maneuver

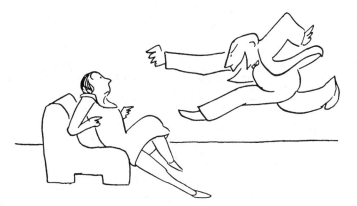

The Sweep-'Em-Off-Their-Feet Method

The Her-Two-Little-Hands-in-His-Huge-Ones Pass

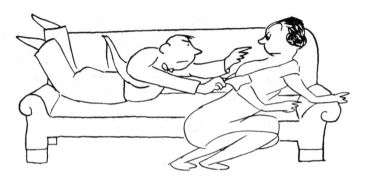

The Sudden Onslaught

The Continental-Manners Technique

The I'm-Not-Good-Enough-for-You Announcement

The Just-a-Little-Boy System

The Harpo Marx Attack

The I-May-Go-Away-for-a-Year-or-Two Move

The War Between Men and Women

I. The Overt Act

II. The Battle on the Stairs

III. The Fight in the Grocery

IV. Men's G.H.Q.

V. Women's G.H.Q.

VI. Capture of three physics professors

VII. Surrender of three blondes

VIII. The Battle of Labrador

IX. The Spy

X. Mrs. Pritchard's Leap

XI. Zero Hour—Connecticut

XII. The Sniper

XIII. Parley

XIV. Gettysburg

XV. Retreat

XVI. Rout

XVII. Surrender

FROM

THE THURBER CARNIVAL

The Catbird Seat

M R. Martin bought the pack of Camels on Monday night in the most crowded cigar store on Broadway. It was theater time and seven or eight men were buying cigarettes. The clerk didn't even glance at Mr. Martin, who put the pack in his overcoat pocket and went out. If any of the staff at F & S had seen him buy the cigarettes, they would have been astonished, for it was generally known that Mr. Martin did not smoke, and never had. No one saw him.

It was just a week to the day since Mr. Martin had decided to rub out Mrs. Ulgine Barrows. The term "rub out" pleased him because it suggested nothing more than the correction of an error—in this case an error of Mr. Fitweiler. Mr. Martin had spent each night of the past week working out his plan and examining it. As he walked home now he went over it again. For the hundredth time he resented the element of imprecision, the margin of guesswork that entered into the business. The project as he had worked it out was casual and bold, the risks were considerable. Something might go wrong anywhere along the line. And therein lay the cunning of his scheme. No one would ever see in it the cautious, painstaking hand of Erwin Martin, head of the filing department at F & S, of whom Mr. Fitweiler had once said, "Man is fallible but Martin isn't." No one would see his hand, that is, unless it were caught in the act.

Sitting in his apartment, drinking a glass of milk, Mr. Martin reviewed his case against Mrs. Ulgine Barrows, as he had every night for seven nights. He began at the beginning. Her quacking voice and braying laugh had first profaned the halls of F & S on March 7, 1941 (Mr. Martin had a head for dates). Old Roberts, the personnel chief, had introduced her as the newly appointed special adviser to the president of the firm, Mr. Fitweiler. The woman had appalled Mr. Martin instantly, but he hadn't shown it. He had given her his dry hand, a look of studious concentration, and a faint smile. "Well," she had said, looking at the papers on his desk, "are you lifting the oxcart out of the ditch?" As Mr. Martin recalled that moment, over his milk, he squirmed slightly. He must keep his mind on her crimes as a special adviser, not on her peccadillos as a personality. This he found difficult to do, in spite of entering an objection and sustaining it. The faults of the woman as a woman kept chattering on in his mind like an unruly witness. She had, for almost two years now, baited him. In the halls, in the elevator, even in his own office, into which she romped now and then like a circus horse, she was constantly shouting these silly questions at him. "Are you lifting the oxcart out of the ditch? Are you tearing up the pea patch? Are you hollering down the rain barrel? Are you scraping around the bottom of the pickle barrel? Are you sitting in the catbird seat?"

It was Joey Hart, one of Mr. Martin's two assistants, who had explained what the gibberish meant. "She must be a Dodger fan," he had said. "Red Barber announces the Dodger games over the radio and he uses those expressions—picked 'em up down South." Joey had gone on to explain one or two. "Tearing up the pea patch" meant going on a rampage; "sitting in the catbird seat" meant sitting pretty, like a batter with three balls and no strikes on him. Mr. Martin dismissed all this with an effort. It had been annoying, it had driven him near to distraction, but he was too solid a man to be moved to murder by anything so childish. It was fortunate, he reflected as he passed on to the important charges against Mrs. Barrows, that he had stood up under it so well. He had maintained always an outward appearance of polite tolerance. "Why, I even believe you like the woman," Miss Paird, his other assistant, had once said to him. He had simply smiled.

A gavel rapped in Mr. Martin's mind and the case proper was resumed. Mrs. Ulgine Barrows stood charged with willful, blatant, and persistent attempts to destroy the efficiency and system of F & S. It was competent, material, and relevant to review her advent and rise to power. Mr. Martin had got the story from Miss Paird, who seemed always able to find things out. According to her, Mrs. Barrows had met Mr. Fitweiler at a party, where she had rescued him from the embraces of a powerfully built drunken man who had mistaken the president of F & S for a famous retired Middle Western football coach. She had led him to a sofa and somehow worked upon him a monstrous magic. The aging gentleman had jumped to the conclusion there and then that this was a woman of singular attainments, equipped to bring out the best in him and in the firm. A week later he had introduced her into F & S as his special adviser. On that day confusion got its foot in the door. After Miss Tyson, Mr. Brundage, and Mr. Bartlett had been fired and Mr. Munson had taken his hat and stalked out, mailing in his resignation later, old Roberts had been emboldened to speak to Mr. Fitweiler. He mentioned that Mr. Munson's department had been "a little disrupted" and hadn't they perhaps better resume the old system there? Mr. Fitweiler had said certainly not. He had the greatest faith in Mrs. Barrow's ideas. "They require a little seasoning, a little seasoning, is all," he had added. Mr. Roberts had given it up. Mr. Martin reviewed in detail all the changes wrought by Mrs. Barrows. She had begun chipping at the cornices of the firm's edifice and now she was swinging at the foundation stones with a pickaxe.

Mr. Martin came now, in his summing up, to the afternoon of Monday, November 2, 1942—just one week ago. On that day, at 3 P.M., Mrs. Barrows had bounced into his office. "Boo!" she had yelled. "Are you scraping around the bottom of the pickle barrel?" Mr. Martin had looked at her from under his green eyeshade, saying nothing. She had begun to wander about the office, taking it in with her great, popping eyes. "Do you really need *all* these filing cabinets?" she had demanded suddenly. Mr. Martin's heart had jumped. "Each of these files," he had said, keeping his voice even, "plays an indispensable part in the system of F & S." She had brayed at him, "Well, don't tear up the pea patch!" and gone to the door. From there she had bawled, "But you sure have got a lot of fine scrap in here!" Mr. Martin could no longer doubt that the finger was on his beloved department. Her pickaxe was on the upswing, poised for the first blow. It had not come yet; he had received no blue memo from the enchanted Mr. Fitweiler bearing nonsensical instructions deriving from the obscene woman. But there was no doubt in Mr. Martin's mind that one would be forthcoming. He must act quickly. Already a precious week had gone by. Mr. Martin stood up in his living room, still holding his milk glass. "Gentlemen of the jury," he said to himself, "I demand the death penalty for this horrible person."

The next day Mr. Martin followed his routine, as usual. He polished his glasses more often and once sharpened an already sharp pencil, but not even Miss Paird noticed. Only once did he catch sight of his victim; she swept past him in the hall with a patronizing "Hi!" At five-thirty he walked home, as usual, and had a glass of milk, as usual. He had never drunk anything stronger in his life—unless you could count ginger ale. The late Sam Schlosser, the S of F & S, had praised Mr. Martin at a staff meeting several years before for his temperate habits. "Our most efficient worker neither drinks nor smokes," he had said. "The results speak for themselves." Mr. Fitweiler had sat by, nodding approval.

Mr. Martin was still thinking about that red-letter day as he walked over to the Schrafft's on Fifth Avenue near Forty-sixth Street. He got there, as he always did, at eight o'clock. He finished his dinner and the financial page of the *Sun* at a quarter to nine, as he always did. It was his custom after dinner to take a walk. This time he walked down Fifth Avenue at a casual pace. His gloved hands felt moist and warm, his forehead cold. He transferred the Camels from his overcoat to a jacket pocket. He wondered, as he did so, if they did not represent an unnecessary note of strain. Mrs. Barrows smoked only Luckies. It was his idea to puff a few puffs on a Camel (after the rubbing-out), stub it out in the ashtray holding her lipstick-stained Luckies, and thus drag a small red herring across the trail. Perhaps it was not a good idea. It would take time. He might even choke, too loudly.

Mr. Martin had never seen the house on West Twelfth Street where Mrs. Barrows lived, but he had a clear enough picture of it. Fortunately, she had bragged to everybody about her ducky first-floor apartment in the perfectly darling three-story red-brick. There would be no doorman or other attendants; just the tenants of the second and third floors. As he walked along, Mr. Martin realized that he would get there before nine-thirty. He had considered walking north on Fifth Avenue from Schrafft's to a point from which it would take him until ten o'clock to reach the house. At that hour people were less likely to be coming in or going out. But the procedure would have made an awkward loop in the straight thread of his casualness, and he had abandoned it. It was impossible to figure when people would be entering or leaving the house, anyway. There was a great risk at any hour. If he ran into anybody, he would simply have to place the rubbing-out of Ulgine Barrows in the inactive file forever. The same thing would hold true if there were someone in her apartment. In that case he would just say that he had been passing by, recognized her charming house and thought to drop in.

It was eighteen minutes after nine when Mr. Martin turned into Twelfth Street. A man passed him, and a man and a woman talking. There was no one within fifty paces when he came to the house, halfway down the block. He was up the steps and in the small vestibule in no time, pressing the bell under the card that said "Mrs. Ulgine Barrows." When the clicking in the lock started, he jumped forward against the door. He got inside fast, closing the door behind him. A bulb in a lantern hung from the hall ceiling on a chain seemed to give a monstrously bright light. There was nobody on the stair, which went up ahead of him along the left wall. A door opened down the hall in the wall on the right. He went toward it swiftly, on tiptoe.

"Well, for God's sake, look who's here!" bawled Mrs. Barrows, and her braying laugh rang out like the report of a shotgun. He rushed past her like a football tackle, bumping her. "Hey, quit shoving!" she said, closing the door behind them. They were in her living room, which seemed to Mr. Martin to be lighted by a hundred lamps. "What's after you?" she said. "You're as jumpy as a goat." He found he was unable to speak. His heart was wheezing in his throat. "I—yes," he finally brought out. She was jabbering and laughing as she started to help him off with his coat. "No, no," he said. "I'll put it here." He took it off and put it on a chair near the door. "Your hat and gloves, too," she said. "You're in a lady's house." He put his hat on top of the coat. Mrs. Barrows seemed larger than he had thought. He kept his gloves on. "I was passing by," he said. "I recognized—is there anyone here?" She laughed louder than ever. "No," she said, "we're all alone. You're as white as a sheet, you funny man. Whatever *has* come over you? I'll mix you a toddy." She started toward a door across the room. "Scotch-and-soda be all right? But say, you don't drink, do you?" She turned and gave him her amused look. Mr. Martin pulled himself together. "Scotch-and-soda will be all right," he heard himself say. He could hear her laughing in the kitchen.

Mr. Martin looked quickly around the living room for the weapon. He had counted on finding one there. There were andirons and a poker and something in a corner that looked like an Indian club. None of them would do. It couldn't be that way. He began to pace around. He came to a desk. On it lay a metal paper knife with an ornate handle. Would it be sharp enough? He reached for it and knocked over a small brass jar. Stamps spilled out of it and it fell to the floor with a clatter. "Hey," Mrs. Barrows yelled from the kitchen, "are you tearing up the pea patch?" Mr. Martin gave a strange laugh. Picking up the knife, he tried its point against his left wrist. It was blunt. It wouldn't do.

When Mrs. Barrows reappeared, carrying two highballs, Mr. Martin, standing there with his gloves on, became acutely conscious of the fantasy he had wrought. Cigarettes in his pocket, a drink prepared for him—it was all too grossly improbable. It was more than that; it was impossible. Somewhere in the back of his mind a vague idea stirred, sprouted. "For heaven's sake, take off those gloves," said Mrs. Barrows. "I always wear them in the house," said Mr. Martin. The idea began to bloom, strange and wonderful. She put the glasses on a coffee table in front of a sofa and sat on the sofa. "Come over here, you odd little man," she said. Mr. Martin went over and sat beside her. It was difficult getting a cigarette out of the pack of Camels, but he managed it. She held a match for him, laughing. "Well," she said, handing him his drink, "this is perfectly marvelous. You with a drink and a cigarette."

Mr. Martin puffed, not too awkwardly, and took a gulp of the highball. "I drink and smoke all the time," he said. He clinked his glass against hers. "Here's nuts to that old windbag, Fitweiler," he said, and gulped again. The stuff tasted awful, but he made no grimace. "Really, Mr. Martin," she said, her voice and posture changing, "you are insulting our employer." Mrs. Barrows was now all special adviser to the president. "I am preparing a bomb," said Mr. Martin, "which will blow the old goat higher than hell." He had only had a little of the drink, which was not strong. It couldn't be that. "Do you take dope or something?" Mrs. Barrows asked coldly. "Heroin," said Mr. Martin. "I'll be coked to the gills when I bump that old buzzard off." "Mr. Martin!" she shouted, getting to her feet. "That will be all of that. You must go at once." Mr. Martin took another swallow of his drink. He tapped his cigarette out in the ashtray and put the pack of Camels on the coffee table. Then he got up. She stood glaring at him. He walked over and put on his hat and coat. "Not a word about this," he said, and laid an index finger against his lips. All Mrs. Barrows could bring out was "Really!" Mr. Martin put his hand on the doorknob. "I'm sitting in the catbird seat," he said. He stuck his tongue out at her and left. Nobody saw him go.

Mr. Martin got to his apartment, walking, well before eleven. No one saw him go in. He had two glasses of milk after brushing his teeth, and he felt elated. It wasn't tipsiness, because he hadn't been tipsy. Anyway, the walk had worn off all effects of the whisky. He got in bed and read a magazine for a while. He was asleep before midnight.

Mr. Martin got to the office at eight-thirty the next morning, as usual. At a quarter to nine, Ulgine Barrows, who had never before arrived at work before ten, swept into his office. "I'm reporting to Mr. Fitweiler now!" she shouted. "If he turns you over to the police, it's no more than you deserve!" Mr. Martin gave her a look of shocked surprise. "I beg your pardon?" he said. Mrs. Barrows snorted and bounced out of the room, leaving Miss Paird and Joey Hart staring after her. "What's the matter with that old devil now?" asked Miss Paird. "I have no idea," said Mr. Martin, resuming his work. The other two looked at him and then at each other. Miss Paird got up and went out. She walked slowly past the closed door of Mr. Fitweiler's office. Mrs. Barrows was yelling inside, but she was not braying. Miss Paird could not hear what the woman was saying. She went back to her desk.

Forty-five minutes later, Mrs. Barrows left the president's office and went into her own, shutting the door. It wasn't until half an hour later that Mr. Fitweiler sent for Mr. Martin. The head of the filing department, neat, quiet, attentive, stood in front of the old man's desk. Mr. Fitweiler was pale and nervous. He took his glasses off and twiddled them. He made a small, bruffing sound in his throat. "Martin," he said, "you have been with us more than twenty years." "Twenty-two, sir," said Mr. Martin. "In that time," pursued the president, "your work and your—uh—manner have been exemplary." "I trust so, sir," said Mr. Martin. "I have understood, Martin," said Mr. Fitweiler, "that you have never taken a drink or smoked." "That is correct, sir," said Mr. Martin. "Ah, yes." Mr. Fitweiler polished his glasses. "You may describe what you did after leaving the office yesterday, Martin," he said. Mr. Martin allowed less than a second for his bewildered pause. "Certainly, sir," he said. "I walked home. Then I went to Schrafft's for dinner. Afterward I walked home again. I went to bed early, sir, and read a magazine for a while. I was asleep before eleven." "Ah, yes," said Mr. Fitweiler again. He was silent for a moment, searching for the proper words to say to the head of the filing department. "Mrs. Barrows," he said finally, "Mrs. Barrows has worked hard, Martin, very hard. It grieves me to report that she has suffered a severe breakdown. It has taken the form of a persecution complex accompanied by distressing hallucinations." "I am very sorry, sir," said Mr. Martin. "Mrs. Barrows is under the delusion," continued Mr. Fitweiler, "that you visited her last evening and behaved yourself in an—uh—unseemly manner." He raised his hand to silence Mr. Martin's little pained outcry. "It is the nature of these psychological diseases," Mr. Fitweiler said, "to fix upon the least likely and most innocent party as the—uh—source of persecution. These matters are not for the lay mind to grasp, Martin. I've just had my psychiatrist, Dr. Fitch, on the phone. He would not, of course, commit himself, but he made enough generalizations to substantiate my suspicions. I suggested to Mrs. Barrows when she had completed her—uh—story to me this morning, that she visit Dr. Fitch, for I suspected a condition at once. She flew, I regret to say, into a rage, and demanded—uh—requested that I call you on the carpet. You may not know, Martin, but Mrs. Barrows had planned a reorganization of your department—subject to my approval, of course, subject to my approval. This brought you, rather than anyone else, to her mind—but again that is a phenomenon for Dr. Fitch and not for us. So, Martin, I am afraid Mrs. Barrows' usefulness here is at an end." "I am dreadfully sorry, sir," said Mr. Martin.

It was at this point that the door to the office blew open with the suddenness of a gas-main explosion and Mrs. Barrows catapulted through it. "Is the little rat denying it?" she screamed. "He can't get away with that!" Mr. Martin got up and moved discreetly to a point beside Mr. Fitweiler's chair. "You drank and smoked at my apartment," she bawled at Mr. Martin, "and you know it! You called Mr. Fitweiler an old windbag and said you were going to blow him up when you got coked to the gills on your heroin!" She stopped yelling to catch her breath and a new glint came into her popping eyes. "If you weren't such a drab, ordinary little man," she said, "I'd think you'd planned it all. Sticking your tongue out, saying you were sitting in the catbird seat, because you thought no one would believe me when I told it! My God, it's really too perfect!" She brayed loudly and hysterically, and the fury was on her again. She glared at Mr. Fitweiler. "Can't you see how he has tricked us, you old fool? Can't you see his little game?" But Mr. Fitweiler had been surreptitiously pressing all the buttons under the top of his desk and employees of F & S began pouring into the room. "Stockton," said Mr. Fitweiler, "you and Fishbein will take Mrs. Barrows to her home. Mrs. Powell, you will go with them." Stockton, who had played a little football in high school, blocked Mrs. Barrows as she made for Mr. Martin. It took him and Fishbein together to force her out of the door into the hall, crowded with stenographers and office boys. She was still screaming imprecations at Mr. Martin, tangled and contradictory imprecations. The hubbub finally died out down the corridor.

"I regret that this has happened," said Mr. Fitweiler. "I shall ask you to dismiss it from your mind, Martin." "Yes, sir," said Mr. Martin, anticipating his chief's "That will be

The Cane in the Corridor

F UNNY THING about post-operative mental states," said
Joe Fletcher, rocking the big brandy glass between the
palms of his hands and studying the brown tides reflectively.
"They take all kinds of curious turns."

George Minturn moved restlessly in his chair, making a new
pattern of his long legs. "Let's go to Barney's," he said.
"Let's go to Barney's now."

Mrs. Minturn walked over and emptied an ashtray into the
fireplace as eloquently as if she were winding the clock. "It's
much too late," she said. "I'm sure everybody we'd want to
see has left there and gone home to bed."

Minturn finished his brandy and poured out some more.

"You remember Reginald Gardiner's imitation of wallpaper," continued Fletcher, "in which he presented a visual design as making a pattern of sound? Many post-operative cases
make those interesting transferences. I know one man who
kept drawing on a piece of paper what the ringing of a telephone *looks* like."

"I don't want to hear about him," said Minturn.

Fletcher drank the last of his brandy and held up his glass;
after a moment his host walked over and poured in a little
more.

Mrs. Minturn found herself finishing her own drink and
getting another one, although she seldom touched anything
after dinner. "Here's to the Washington Bridge," she said.
"Here's to some big dam or other. Let's talk about some big
dam. After all, you're an engineer, Joe."

Fletcher lighted a cigarette, holding his brandy glass between his knees. "Which brings up an interesting point," he
said. "I mean, if occupational experience gives a special shape
and color to the patient's perceptions, then the theory that it
is not really a hallucination but a deeper insight into reality
probably falls down. For instance, if the number eighteen
clangs for one patient and whistles for another—say for
George here—"

Minturn spilled ashes on the lapel of his dinner coat and

rubbed them into it. "I don't want to hear any numbers," he said thickly. "I don't want to hear any more about it."

His wife, who had been trying to get Fletcher's eye but couldn't, since he continued to study his brandy, spoke up sharply. "George is just getting over a frightful cold," she said, "and he's pretty easily shaken. He would worry frightfully about people, but he doesn't dare think about them. They upset him so." Fletcher did look at her now, and smiled. She realized she had not said what she had meant to say. Something oblique but cleverly phrased and nicely pointed had got lost on its way to her tongue. "You think you're so darn smart," she said.

Minturn got up and began to pace. The brandy had run out. He sat down and lighted a cigarette.

"Of course, the people that doctors refer to as squashes," pursued Fletcher, "the invertebrates, you might say, just lie there like vegetables. It is the high-strung cases that manifest the interesting—manifestations. As you just said, Nancy, you think you're so darn smart. I mean, hospitalization moves the mind toward a false simplification. A man gets the idea that he can hold processes in his hand, the way I'm holding this glass. He lies there, you might say, pulling the easy little meanings out of life as simply as if they were daisy petals."

"Daisy petals," said Minturn. "Where's brandy? Why isn't there any more brandy?"

"He gets the idea," Fletcher went on, "that he knows as much about life as Alfred North Whitehead or Carson McCullers."

Minturn said, "Oh, God."

"Carson McCullers makes George nervous," said Mrs. Minturn, "and you know it."

"I ask you to remember I have scarcely seen you people since Carson McCullers began to write," said Fletcher stiffly. "I know 'Sanctuary' upset George so he had to go away to the mountains. I *do* know that."

"He didn't go away to the mountains at all," said Mrs. Minturn. "So you *don't* know that."

"I want to go away to the mountains now," said Minturn. He began pacing around again, picking up things.

"There's more brandy in the kitchen, darling," said Mrs. Minturn. "In the kitchen," she repeated as he started upstairs.

"Oh," said Minturn. He went out to the kitchen.

Mrs. Minturn went over to Fletcher and stood looking down at him. "It's very sweet of you, Joe, to keep harping on hospitals and sick people and mental states," she said. "I know why you're doing it. You're doing it because George didn't come to see you when you were in the hospital. You know very well that George is too sensitive to visit people in the hospital."

Fletcher stood up, too. "Is that why *you* didn't come to see me?" he asked. She was taller than he was. He sat down again.

"Yes, it was, if you want to know so much," she said. "George would have sensed it and he would have worried about you all the time. As it was, he *did* worry about you all the time. But he can't stand things the way you can. You know how sensitive he's always been."

Fletcher tried to drink out of his empty glass. "He wasn't so goddam sensitive when we were both with the Cleveland Telephone Company. He wasn't so goddam sensitive then. No, he was practically a regular guy."

Mrs. Minturn drew herself up a little higher. "It is just quite possible, perhaps," she said, "that you were just not quite perceptious at that time." She went slowly back to her chair and sat down as Minturn came in with a bottle of brandy and a corkscrew.

"Here," he said, handing them to Fletcher. Fletcher put down his glass, inserted the corkscrew accurately into the center of the cork, twisted it competently, and pulled out the cork. "Wonderful thing, technology," said Minturn, "wonderful thing, wonderful thing. I want a drink." Fletcher poured a great splash of brandy into his host's glass and another into his own.

"He doesn't happen to mean he *believes* in it," said Mrs. Minturn. "The trouble with you is you can't tell when a person is allusive even."

"You're thinking of Technocracy," Fletcher told her, taking her glass and pouring a small quantity of brandy into it with studious precision.

"Maybe," said Mrs. Minturn, darkly, "and just maybe not."

"Why can't we go home now? Why can't we go home now, Nancy?" said Minturn from deep down in his chair.

"We *are* home, dear," said Mrs. Minturn. She turned to Fletcher. "Anybody that thinks I can't appreciate a game that two can play at is definitely," said Mrs. Minturn, hiccuping, "crazy." She held her breath and tried counting ten slowly.

"Why don't you try bending over and drinking out of the opposite side of your glass?" asked Fletcher.

Minturn sat up a little in his chair.

"Don't have to say things like that," he said, severely.

To compensate for her hiccups, Mrs. Minturn assumed a posture of strained dignity. Minturn slid farther down into his chair. They both watched Fletcher, who had set the brandy revolving in his glass and was studying it. He took a sip of his drink. "It is a common misconception," he said, "that post-operative mental states disappear on the patient's advent from the hospital. Out of the hospital, they might recur at any time, and some pretty strange phenomena could happen—as in the case of the hospitalization of a friend."

"If you're just trying to get George down, it's not going to be of the least consequence. I can assure you of that," said Mrs. Minturn. "He's stronger than you are in lots of more important ways."

"Phenomena," said Minturn.

"I'm talking of what *I* might do, not of what George might do," said Fletcher, "in case you consider the manifestation what you choose to call weakness."

"Well," said Mrs. Minturn, "I certainly do—that and meanness."

"I want to see Mrs. Trimingham," said Minturn. "I want to go to Bermuda."

"I suppose it would be too much to say that you can't very well disprove what I'm saying till I say it," said Fletcher.

"No, it wouldn't," said Mrs. Minturn. "I don't see why we can't talk about the Grand Coolidge Dam, or something." She laughed. "That's really frightfully funny. It really is." She laughed again.

Minturn had closed his eyes, but he opened them again. "Can't say I do," he said. "Can't say I do."

Fletcher went over and splashed some more brandy into Minturn's glass. "Let us say that George is lying in the hospital," he said. "Now, because of a recurring phenomena, I call on him every day."

"That's cheap," said Mrs. Minturn, "and that's pompous."

"It's no more pompous than it is predictable," said Fletcher, sharply. "It's a condition. It just so happens that it might take the turn of me calling on George every day, from the time he goes in until he gets out."

"You can't do that," said George. "There's such a thing as the law."

"Of course he can't," said Mrs. Minturn. "Besides, George is not going to the hospital."

"I'm not going to the hospital," said Minturn.

"Everybody goes to the hospital sooner or later," said Fletcher. His voice was rising.

"Nine hundred million people don't," said Mrs. Minturn, "all the time."

"I'm stating a pathological case!" shouted Fletcher. "Hypothetical. George has been lying there in that bed for six weeks!"

"No," said Minturn.

"You ought to be ashamed of yourself," said Mrs. Minturn.

"Why?" asked Fletcher. "I'm not saying there is anything the matter with him. He's convalescing, but he can't get up."

"Why can't I get up?" asked Minturn.

"Because you're too weak. You have no more strength than a house mouse. You feel as if you were coming apart like a cheap croquet mallet. If you tried to stand, your knees would bend the wrong way, like a flamingo's."

"I want to go home," mumbled Minturn.

"You *are* home," said his wife.

"He means from the hospital," Fletcher told her, "in the corridors of which, by the way, you hear my cane tapping practically all the time."

"What are *you* doing there?" said Minturn thickly.

"I come to see you every day," said Fletcher. "I have been

to see you every day since you got there." He had been moving around the room, and now he went back and sat down.

"Can't stand you calling on me every day," said Minturn. He finished his drink and poured a new one with some effort.

"Don't worry about it, George," said Mrs. Minturn. "We'll take you to the Mayo brothers or someplace and he'll never find out about it."

"I don't want to go to the Mayo brothers," said Minturn.

Fletcher sat forward in his chair. "And what's more," he said, "I bring you very strange things. That's part of it. That's part of the phenomena. I bring you puzzles that won't work, linked nails that won't come apart, pigs in clover in which the little balls are glued to the bottom of the box. I bring you mystery novels in Yiddish, and artificial flowers made of wire and beads, and horehound candy."

"Terrible, terrible rat," said Mrs. Minturn, "terrible rat Fletcher."

"Police find something to do about that," said Minturn. "Such a thing as law and order. Such a thing as malpractice."

"And licorice whips," continued Fletcher, "and the complete files of *Physical Culture* for 1931, and matchboxes that go broo-oo-oo, broo-oo-oo."

"Broo," said Minturn. "I want to go to Twenty-One."

"Terrible, terrible, terrible rat," said Mrs. Minturn.

"I see," said Fletcher. "You don't even feel sorry for poor old tap-tap. Tap, tap, tap, tap, tap."

"What's that?" said Minturn.

"That's my cane in the corridor," said Fletcher. "You are lying there, trying to unwrassle something I have brought you, when, tap, tap, tap, here I come again."

"Terrible rat, go home," said Mrs. Minturn.

Fletcher bowed to her gravely. "I'm going," he said. "It constitutes the first occasion on which I have ever been ejected from this or any other house, but that is as it should be, I presume."

"Don't throw anybody out," said Minturn. "Tap, tap, tap," he added.

Halfway to the hall door, Fletcher turned. "That's right, laugh," he said. "Tap, tap, tap, tap, tap, then."

"Tap, tap, tap," said Minturn from far down near the floor. A new attack of hiccups kept Mrs. Minturn speechless, but she stood up as her guest went out into the hall. Minturn was still saying "Tap, tap," and Mrs. Minturn was hiccuping, as Fletcher found his hat and coat and went out the front door into the melting snow, looking for a taxi.

FROM

THE BEAST IN ME

AND OTHER ANIMALS

The Princess and the Tin Box

ONCE upon a time, in a far country, there lived a king whose daughter was the prettiest princess in the world. Her eyes were like the cornflower, her hair was sweeter than the hyacinth, and her throat made the swan look dusty.

From the time she was a year old, the princess had been showered with presents. Her nursery looked like Cartier's window. Her toys were all made of gold or platinum or diamonds or emeralds. She was not permitted to have wooden blocks or china dolls or rubber dogs or linen books, because such materials were considered cheap for the daughter of a king.

When she was seven, she was allowed to attend the wedding of her brother and throw real pearls at the bride instead of rice. Only the nightingale, with his lyre of gold, was permitted to sing for the princess. The common blackbird, with his boxwood flute, was kept out of the palace grounds. She walked in silver-and-samite slippers to a sapphire-and-topaz bathroom and slept in an ivory bed inlaid with rubies.

On the day the princess was eighteen, the king sent a royal ambassador to the courts of five neighboring kingdoms to announce that he would give his daughter's hand in marriage to the prince who brought her the gift she liked the most.

The first prince to arrive at the palace rode a swift white stallion and laid at the feet of the princess an enormous apple made of solid gold which he had taken from a dragon who had guarded it for a thousand years. It was placed on a long ebony table set up to hold the gifts of the princess's suitors. The second prince, who came on a gray charger, brought her a nightingale made of a thousand diamonds, and it was placed beside the golden apple. The third prince, riding on a black horse, carried a great jewel box made of platinum and sapphires, and it was placed next to the diamond nightingale. The fourth prince, astride a fiery yellow horse, gave the princess a gigantic heart made of rubies and pierced by an emerald arrow. It was placed next to the platinum-and-sapphire jewel box.

Now the fifth prince was the strongest and handsomest of all the five suitors, but he was the son of a poor king whose realm had been overrun by mice and locusts and wizards and mining engineers so that there was nothing much of value left in it. He came plodding up to the palace of the princess on a plow horse and he brought her a small tin box filled with mica and feldspar and hornblende which he had picked up on the way.

The other princes roared with disdainful laughter when they saw the tawdry gift the fifth prince had brought to the princess. But she examined it with great interest and squealed with delight, for all her life she had been glutted with precious stones and priceless metals, but she had never seen tin before or mica or feldspar or hornblende. The tin box was placed next to the ruby heart pierced with an emerald arrow.

"Now," the king said to his daughter, "you must select the gift you like best and marry the prince that brought it."

The princess smiled and walked up to the table and picked up the present she liked the most. It was the platinum-and-sapphire jewel box, the gift of the third prince.

"The way I figure it," she said, "is this. It is a very large and expensive box, and when I am married, I will meet many admirers who will give me precious gems with which to fill it to the top. Therefore, it is the most valuable of all the gifts my suitors have brought me and I like it the best."

The princess married the third prince that very day in the midst of great merriment and high revelry. More than a hundred thousand pearls were thrown at her and she loved it.

Moral: All those who thought the princess was going to select the tin box filled with worthless stones instead of one of the other gifts will kindly stay after class and write one hundred times on the blackboard "I would rather have a hunk of aluminum silicate than a diamond necklace."

The Lady on the Bookcase

O NE DAY twelve years ago an outraged cartoonist, four of whose drawings had been rejected in a clump by *The New Yorker*, stormed into the office of Harold Ross, editor of the magazine. "Why is it," demanded the cartoonist, "that you reject my work and publish drawings by a fifth-rate artist like Thurber?" Ross came quickly to my defense like the true friend and devoted employer he is. "You mean third-rate," he said quietly, but there was a warning glint in his steady gray eyes that caused the discomfited cartoonist to beat a hasty retreat.

"With you I have known peace, Lida, and now you say you're going crazy."

With the exception of Ross, the interest of editors in what I draw has been rather more journalistic than critical. They want to know if it is true that I draw by moonlight, or under water, and when I say no, they lose interest until they hear the rumor that I found the drawings in an old trunk or that I do the captions while my nephew makes the sketches.

The other day I was shoving some of my originals around on the floor (I do not draw on the floor; I was just shoving the originals around) and they fell, or perhaps I pushed them, into five separate and indistinct categories. I have never wanted to write about my drawings, and I still don't want to, but it occurred to me that it might be a good idea to do it now, when everybody is busy with something else, and get it over quietly.

Home

Category No. 1, then, which may be called the Unconscious or Stream of Nervousness category, is represented by "With you I have known peace, Lida, and now you say you're going crazy" and the drawing entitled with simple dignity, "Home." These drawings were done while the artist was thinking of something else (or so he has been assured by experts) and hence his hand was guided by the Unconscious which, in turn, was more or less influenced by the Subconscious.

Students of Jung have instructed me that Lida and the House-Woman are representations of the *anima*, the female essence or directive which floats around in the ageless universal Subconscious of Man like a tadpole in a cistern. Less intellectual critics insist that the two ladies are actual persons I have consciously known. Between these two schools of thought lies a discouragingly large space of time extending roughly from 1,000,000 B.C. to the middle Nineteen Thirties.

Whenever I try to trace the true identity of the House-Woman, I get to thinking of Mr. Jones. He appeared in my office one day twelve years ago, said he was Mr. Jones, and asked me to lend him "Home" for reproduction in an art magazine. I never saw the drawing again. Tall, well-dressed, kind of sad-looking chap, and as well spoken a gentleman as you would want to meet.

Category No. 2 brings us to Freud and another one of those discouragingly large spaces—namely, the space between the Concept of the Purely Accidental and the Theory of Haphazard Determination. Whether chance is capricious or we are all prisoners of pattern is too long and cloudy a subject to go into here. I shall consider each of the drawings in Category No. 2, explaining what happened and leaving the definition

"All right, have it your way—you heard a seal bark."

of the forces involved up to you. The seal on top of the bed, then ("All right, have it your way—you heard a seal bark"), started out to be a seal on a rock. The rock, in the process of being drawn, began to look like the head of a bed, so I made a bed out of it, put a man and wife in the bed, and stumbled onto the caption as easily and unexpectedly as the seal had stumbled into the bedroom.

"That's my first wife up there, and this is the present *Mrs. Harris."*

The woman on top of the bookcase ("That's my first wife up there, and this is the *present* Mrs. Harris") was originally designed to be a woman crouched on the top step of a staircase, but since the tricks and conventions of perspective and planes sometimes fail me, the staircase assumed the shape of a bookcase and was finished as such, to the surprise and embarrassment of the first Mrs. Harris, the present Mrs. Harris, the lady visitor, Mr. Harris and me. Before *The New Yorker* would print the drawing, they phoned me long distance to inquire whether the first Mrs. Harris was alive or dead or stuffed. I replied that my taxidermist had advised me that you cannot stuff a woman, and that my physician had informed me that a dead lady cannot support herself on all fours. This meant, I said, that the first Mrs. Harris was unquestionably alive.

The man riding on the other man's shoulders in the bar ("For the last time, you and your horsie get away from me and stay away!") was intended to be standing alongside the irate speaker, but I started his head up too high and made it too small, so that he would have been nine feet tall if I had completed his body that way. It was but the work of thirty-

"For the last time, you and your horsie get away from me and stay away!"

two seconds to put him on another man's shoulders. As simple or, if you like, as complicated as that. The psychological factors which may be present here are, as I have indicated, elaborate and confused. Personally, I like Dr. Claude Thornway's theory of the Deliberate Accident or Conditioned Mistake.

Category No. 3 is perhaps a variant of Category No. 2; indeed, they may even be identical. The dogs in "The father belonged to some people who were driving through in a Packard" were drawn as a captionless spot, and the interior with

"The father belonged to some people who were driving through in a Packard."

figures just sort of grew up around them. The hippopotamus in "What have you done with Dr. Millmoss?" was drawn to amuse my small daughter. Something about the creature's ex-

"What have you done with Dr. Millmoss?"

pression when he was completed convinced me that he had recently eaten a man. I added the hat and pipe and Mrs. Millmoss, and the caption followed easily enough. Incidentally, my daughter, who was 2 years old at the time, identified the beast immediately. "That's a hippotomanus," she said. *The New Yorker* was not so smart. They described the drawing for their files as follows: "Woman with strange animal." *The New Yorker* was nine years old at the time.

Category No. 4 is represented by perhaps the best known of some fifteen drawings belonging to this special grouping, which may be called the Contributed Idea Category. This drawing ("Touché!") was originally done for *The New Yorker*

"Touché!"

by Carl Rose, caption and all. Mr. Rose is a realistic artist, and his gory scene distressed the editors, who hate violence. They asked Rose if he would let me have the idea, since there is obviously no blood to speak of in the people I draw. Rose graciously consented. No one who looks at "Touché!" believes that the man whose head is in the air is really dead. His opponent will hand it back to him with profuse apologies, and the discommoded fencer will replace it on his shoulders and say, "No harm done, forget it." Thus the old controversy as to whether death can be made funny is left just where it was before Carl Rose came along with his wonderful idea.

"Well, I'm disenchanted, too. We're all disenchanted."

Category No. 5, our final one, can be called, believe it or not, the Intentional or Thought-Up Category. The idea for each of these two drawings just came to me and I sat down and made a sketch to fit the prepared caption. Perhaps, in the case of "Well, I'm disenchanted, too. We're all disenchanted," another one of those Outside Forces played a part. That is, I may have overheard a husband say to his wife, on the street or at a party, "I'm disenchanted." I do not think this is true, however, in the case of the rabbit-headed doctor and his woman patient. I believe that scene and its caption came to me one night in bed. I *may* have got the idea in a doctor's office or a rabbit hutch, but I don't think so.

"You said a moment ago that everybody you look at seems to be a rabbit. Now just what do you mean by that, Mrs. Sprague?"

If you want to, you can cut these drawings out and push them around on the floor, making your own categories or applying your own psychological theories; or you can even invent some fresh rumors. I should think it would be more fun, though, to take a nap, or baste a roast, or run around the reservoir in Central Park.

A Call on Mrs. Forrester

(After rereading, in my middle years, Willa Cather's "A Lost
Lady" and Henry James's "The Ambassadors")

I DROPPED off a Burlington train at Sweet Water one afternoon last fall to call on Marian Forrester. It was a lovely
day. October stained the hills with quiet gold and russet, and
scarlet as violent as the blood spilled not far away so many
years ago along the banks of the Little Big Horn. It had been
just such a day as this when I was last in Sweet Water, fifteen
years before, but the glory of the earth affected me more
sharply now than it had when I was midway through my confident thirties. October weather, once a plentiful wine, had
become a rare and precious brandy and I took my time sa-
voring it as I walked out of the town toward the Forrester
house. Sweet Water has changed greatly since the days when
Frank Ellinger stepped down from the Burlington and everybody in the place knew about it. The town is large and wealthy
now and, it seemed to me, vulgar and preoccupied. I was
afflicted with the sense of having come into the presence of
an old uncle, declining in the increase of his fortune, who no
longer bothered to identify his visitors. It was a relief to leave
the town behind, but as I approached the Forrester house I
felt that the lines of my face were set in brave resolution rather
than in high anticipation. It was all so different from the free,
lost time of the lovely lady's "bright occasions" that I found
myself making a little involuntary gesture with my hand, like
one who wipes the tarnish from a silver spoon, searching for
a fine forgotten monogram.

I first met Marian Forrester when I was twenty-seven, and
then again when I was thirty-six. It is my vanity to believe that
Mrs. Forrester had no stauncher admirer, no more studious
appreciator. I took not only her smallest foible but her largest
sin in my stride; I was as fascinated by the glitter of her flaws
as by the glow of her perfections, if indeed I could tell one
radiance from the other. There was never anything reprehen-
sible to me in the lady's ardent adventures, and even in her
awfullest attachment I persisted in seeing only the further

666

flowering of a unique and privileged spirit. As I neared her home, I remembered a dozen florid charities I had invented to cover her multitude of frailties: her dependence on money and position, her admiration of an aristocracy, half false and half imaginary, her lack of any security inside herself, her easy loneliness. It was no use, I was fond of telling myself, to look for the qualities of the common and wholesome morning glory in the rare and wanton Nicotiana. From the darkest earth, I would add, springs ever the sweetest rose. A green isle in the sea, if it has the sparkling fountain, needs not the solemn shrine, and so forth and so on.

I had built the lady up very high, as you see. I had commanded myself to believe that emotional literacy, a lively spirit, and personal grace, so rarely joined in American females, particularly those who live between Omaha and Denver, were all the raiment a lady needed. As I crossed the bridge, with the Forrester house now in full view, I had, all of a sudden, a disturbing fancy. There flashed into my consciousness a vivid vision of the pretty lady, seated at her dressing table, practicing in secrecy her little arts, making her famous earrings gleam with small studied turnings of her head, revealing her teeth for a moment in a brief mocking smile, and, unhappiest picture of all, rehearsing her wonderful laughter.

I stopped on the bridge and leaned against the rail and felt old and tired. Black clouds had come up, obscuring the sun, and they seemed to take the mushroom shape of atomic dust, threatening all frail and ancient satisfactions. It began to rain.

I wondered what I would say to Marian Forrester if she appeared at the door in one of her famous, familiar postures, *en déshabillé*, her hair down her back, a brush in her hand, her face raised in warm, anachronistic gaiety. I tried to remember what we had ever talked about, and could think only of the dreadful topic of grasping women and eligible men. We had never discussed any book that I could recall, and she had never mentioned music. I had another of my ungallant fancies, a vision of the lovely lady at a concert in the town, sitting with bright eye and deaf ear, displaying a new bonnet and gown, striving, less subtly than of old, to capture the attention of worried and oblivious gentlemen. I recalled with sharp clarity a gown and bonnet she had once worn, but for the life of me I could not put a face between them. I caught the twinkle of earrings, and that was all.

The latest newspaper lying open on a chair, a note stuck in a milk bottle on the back porch, are enough to indicate the pulse of a living house, but there would not even be these faint signs of today and tomorrow in Marian Forrester's house, only the fibrillation of a yesterday that had died but would not stay dead. There would be an old copy of *Ainslee's* on the floor somewhere, a glitter of glass under a broken windowpane, springs leaking from a ruptured sofa, a cobweb in a chandelier, a dusty etching of Notre Dame unevenly hung on the wall, and a stopped clock on the marble mantel above a cold fireplace. I could see the brandy bottle, too, on a stained table, wearing its cork drunkenly.

Just to the left of the front door, the big hall closet would be filled with relics of the turn of the century, the canes and guns of Captain Forrester, a crokinole board, a diavolo, a frivolous parasol, a collection of McKinley campaign buttons, a broken stereopticon, a table tennis net, a toppled stack of blue poker chips and a scatter of playing cards, a woodburning set, and one of those large white artificial Easter eggs you put to your eye and, squinting into it, behold the light that never was, in a frosty fairyland. There would be a crack in the crusty shell, and common daylight would violate the sanctuary of the yellowed and tottery angels. You could find, in all the litter, as measuring sticks of calamity, nothing longer than an envelope firmly addressed in a gentleman's hand, a canceled check, a stern notice from the bank.

The shade of one upstairs window was pulled all the way down, and it suddenly had the effect of making the house appear to wink, as if it were about to whisper, out of the corner of its door, some piece of scandal. If I went in, I might be embarrassed by the ungainly sounds of someone moving about upstairs, after the lady had descended, sounds which she would cover by riffling nervously through a dozen frilly seasons of her faded past, trying a little shrilly to place me among the beaux in some half-remembered ballroom. I was afraid, too, that I might encounter in some dim and dusty mirror a young man frowning disapproval of an older self come to make a judgment on a poor lady not for her sake and salvation but, in some strange way, for his own. And what if she brought out, in the ruins of her famous laughter, what was left of the old disdain, and fixed me shrewdly for what I was, a frightened penitent, come to claim and take away and burn the old praises he had given her? I wouldn't succeed, of course, standing there in my unbecoming middle years, foolishly clutching reasons and arguments like a shopper's husband loaded down with bundles. She would gaily accuse me of being in love with another and, with the ghost of one of her poses of charming bewilderment, would claim a forfeit for my cruelty and insist that I sit down and have a brandy. I would have one—oh, several—and in the face of my suspicions of the presence of a man upstairs, my surrender would compromise the delicacy of my original cool intentions, and the lost individual would be, once again as always in this house, myself. I wondered, standing there in the rain, how it would all come out.

She would get the other lady's name out of me easily enough, when the brandy began to ebb in the bottle, and being Marian Forrester, for whom jealousy was as simple as a reflex, she would be jealous of the imaginary relations of a man she could not place, with a woman she had never heard of. I would then confess my love for Madame de Vionnet, the lady of the lilacs, of Gloriani's bright Sunday garden, of the stately house in the Boulevard Malsherbes, with its cool parlor and dark medallions. I would rise no doubt to the seedy grandiloquence of which I am capable when the cognac is flowing, and I could hear her pitiless comment. "One of those women who have something to *give*, for heaven's sake!" she would say. "One of those women who save men, a female whose abandon might possibly tiptoe to the point of tousling her lover's hair, a woman who at the first alarm of a true embrace would telephone the gendarmes." "Stop it!" I heard myself shout there in the rain. "I beg you to remember it was once said of Madame de Vionnet that when she touched a thing the ugliness, God knows how, went out of it." "How sweet!" I could hear Mrs. Forrester go on. "And yet, according to you, she lost her lover, for all her charm, and to a snippet of an applecheek from New England. Did the ugliness go out of *that*? And if it did, what did the poor lady do with all the prettiness?"

As I stood there in the darkening afternoon, getting soaked, I realized sharply that in my fantasy I had actually been handing Marian Forrester stones to throw at the house in Paris, and the confusion in my viewpoint of the two ladies, if up to that moment I had had a viewpoint, overwhelmed me. I figured what would happen as the shadows deepened in the Forrester house, and we drank what was left of the brandy out of ordinary tumblers—the ballons of the great days would long since have been shattered. Banter would take on the sharp edge of wrangling, and in the end she would stand above me, maintaining a reedy balance, and denounce the lady of the lilacs in the flat terms she had overheard gentlemen use so long ago over their cigars and coffee in the library. I would set my glass down on the sticky arm of the chair and get up and stalk out into the hall. But though she had the last word, she would not let me have the last silence, the gesture in conclusion. She would follow me to the door. In her house, by an ancient rule, Marian Forrester always had the final moment—standing on the threshold, her face lifted, her eyes shining, her hand raised to wave good-bye. Yes, she would follow me to the door, and in the hall—I could see it so clearly I shivered there on the bridge—something wonderful would happen. With the faintest of smiles and the slightest of murmurs I would bow to my hostess, open the door and walk, not out into the rain, but into that damn closet, with its junk and clutter, smashing the Easter egg with my shoe, becoming tangled in the table tennis net, and holding in my hand, when I regained my balance, that comic parasol. Madame de Vionnet would ignore such a calamity, she would pretend not to see it, on the ground that a hostess is blind—a convention that can leave a man sitting at table with an omelet in his lap, unable to mention it, forced to go on with the conversation. But Marian would laugh, the lost laugh of the bright occasions, of the day of her shameless passion in the snow, and it would light the house like candles, reducing the sounds upstairs, in some miraculous way, to what they really were, the innocent creaking of the old floor boards. "What's all this about saving men?" I would cry. "Look who's talking!" And, still holding the parasol, I would kiss her on the cheek, mumble something about coming back some day, and leave, this time by the right door, finding, as I went to rejoin myself at the bridge, a poker chip in the cuff of my trousers.

It seems like a long time ago, my call on Mrs. Forrester. I have never been back. I didn't even send her a Valentine last February. But I did send a pretty book of impeccable verses to Madame de Vionnet, writing in the inscription something polite and nostalgic about "ta voix dans le Bois de Boulogne." I did this, I suppose, out of some obscure guilt sense—these things are never very clear to any man, if the truth were told. I think the mental process goes like this, though. Drinking brandy out of a water glass in the amiable company of a lady who uses spirits for anodyne and not amenity, a timid gentleman promises his subconscious to make up for it later on by taking a single malaga before *déjeuner à midi* with a fastidious lady, toying with aspic, discussing Thornton Wilder, praising the silver point in the hall on the way out, and going home to lie down, exhausted but somehow purified.

I will carry lilacs, one of these summers, to the house in the Boulevard Malesherbes, and take Madame de Vionnet to a matinee of "Louise," have a white port with her at one of the little terraces at the quietest corner of the Parc Monceau, and drop her at her door well before the bold moon has begun to wink at the modest twilight. Since, in the best Henry James tradition, I will get nothing out of this for myself, it ought to make up for something. I could do worse than spend my last summers serenely, sipping wine, clop-clopping around town, listening to good music, kissing a lady's hand at her door, going to bed early and getting a good night's sleep. A man's a fool who walks in the rain, drinks too much brandy, risks his neck floundering around in an untidy closet. Besides, if you miss the 6:15, the eastbound Burlington that has a rendezvous with dusk in Sweet Water every day except Sundays and holidays, you have to wait till midnight for the next train east. A man could catch his death, dozing there in that cold and lonesome station.

The Hopeless Quandary.

CREATURES OF THE MEADOW

Left, the Aspic on a stalk of Visiting Fireman. Center, the Throttle. Right, a Ticket in a patch of Marry-in-Haste. Below, a 99-year lease working slowly toward the surface through the years.

A pair of Martinets.

*The Hoodwink on a spray of
Ragamuffin.*

The Bodkin (left) and the Chintz.

A GROUP OF RARE BLOSSOMS AND BUTTERFLIES

Flowers (left to right): Baker's Dozen, Shepherd's Pie, Sailor's Hornpipe, Stepmother's Kiss.
Butterflies (left to right): The Admirable Crichton, the Great Gatsby, The Magnificent Ambersons (male and female), the Beloved Vagabond.

The White-faced Rage (left) and the Blind Rage.

A GROUP OF MORE OR LESS PLEASANT BIRDS

Left to right: the Apothecary, the Night Watchman, the Scoutmaster,
and the Barred Barrister.

The Goad.

The male Wedlock (left) cautiously approaching a clump of Devil-May-Care; at right, the female.

A female Shriek (right) rising out of the Verbiage to attack a female Swoon.

The Lapidary in a clump of Merry-Go-Round.

A Garble with an Utter in its claws.

The Dudgeon.

*Two widely distributed rodents: the Barefaced Lie (left) and the
White Lie.*

The female Snarl (left) and the male Sulk.

*An Upstart rising from a clump of Johnny-Come-Lately. The small
rodent (right) is a Spouse.*

A GROUP OF BIRDS OF THE WESTERN HEMISPHERE

(Left to right) The Whited Sepulchre; the Misfit; the American Play-boy, or Spendthrift, also sometimes called (southern U. S. A.) the Common Blackguard; a Stuffed Shirt; and (above) a Termagant.

The Femur (left) and the Metatarsal.

A GROUP OF SEMI-EDIBLE VEGETABLES

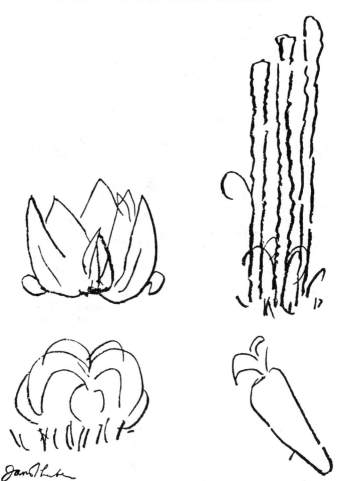

*Top: Quench (left) and Arpeggio. Bottom: Therapy (left) and
Scabbard.*

The Living, or Spitting, Image (left) and a Dead Ringer.

A female Volt with all her Ergs in one Gasket.

The male and female Tryst.

The Early and the Late Riser.

A TRIO OF PREHISTORIC CREATURES

Left to right: the Thesaurus, the Stereopticon, and the Hexameter.
The tree is a Sacroiliac.

A Scone (left) and a Crumpet, peering out of the Tiffin.

The Tantamount.

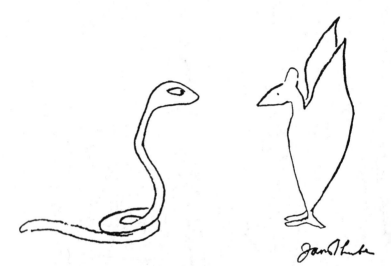

A Serenade (left) about to engage in combat with a Victual.

THREE FRESH-WATER CREATURES

The Qualm   The Glib   The Moot

FOUR PLANTS OF THE TEMPERATE ZONE

Left to right: Single Standard, False Witness, Double Jeopardy,
Heartburn.

A Gloat near a patch of
I-Told-You-So.

The Huff.

A Grope approaching, unaware, a Clinch in hiding.

The Peeve (or Pet Peeve).

The Troth, Plighted (right) and Unplighted.

The Common Carrier.

A GROUP OF DESTRUCTIVE INSECTS

The Coal Bin

The Door Latch

The Clock Tick (or Stop Watch)

The Tire Tool   *The Window Ledge*   *The Ball Bat*

THE 13 CLOCKS

I

O NCE upon a time, in a gloomy castle on a lonely hill, where there were thirteen clocks that wouldn't go, there lived a cold, aggressive Duke, and his niece, the Princess Saralinda. She was warm in every wind and weather, but he was always cold. His hands were as cold as his smile and almost as cold as his heart. He wore gloves when he was asleep, and he wore gloves when he was awake, which made it difficult for him to pick up pins or coins or the kernels of nuts, or to tear the wings from nightingales. He was six feet four, and forty-six, and even colder than he thought he was. One eye wore a velvet patch; the other glittered through a monocle, which made half his body seem closer to you than the other half. He had lost one eye when he was twelve, for he was fond of peering into nests and lairs in search of birds and animals to maul. One afternoon, a mother shrike had mauled him first. His nights were spent in evil dreams, and his days were given to wicked schemes.

Wickedly scheming, he would limp and cackle through the cold corridors of the castle, planning new impossible feats for the suitors of Saralinda to perform. He did not wish to give her hand in marriage, since her hand was the only warm hand in the castle. Even the hands of his watch and the hands of all the thirteen clocks were frozen. They had all frozen at the same time, on a snowy night, seven years before, and after that it was always ten minutes to five in the castle. Travelers and mariners would look up at the gloomy castle on the lonely hill and say, "Time lies frozen there. It's always Then. It's never Now."

The cold Duke was afraid of Now, for Now has warmth and urgency, and Then is dead and buried. Now might bring a certain knight of gay and shining courage— "But, no!" the cold Duke muttered. "The Prince will break himself against a new and awful labor: a place too high to reach, a thing too far to find, a burden too heavy to lift." The Duke was afraid of Now, but he tampered with the clocks to see if they would go, out of a strange perversity, praying that they wouldn't.

Tinkers and tinkerers and a few wizards who happened by tried to start the clocks with tools or magic words, or by shaking them and cursing, but nothing whirred or ticked. The clocks were dead, and in the end, brooding on it, the Duke decided he had murdered time, slain it with his sword, and wiped his bloody blade upon its beard and left it lying there, bleeding hours and minutes, its springs uncoiled and sprawling, its pendulum disintegrating.

The Duke limped because his legs were of different lengths. The right one had outgrown the left because, when he was young, he had spent his mornings place-kicking pups and punting kittens. He would say to a suitor, "What is the difference in the length of my legs?" and if the youth replied, "Why, one is shorter than the other," the Duke would run him through with the sword he carried in his swordcane and feed him to the geese. The suitor was supposed to say, "Why, one is longer than the other." Many a prince had been run through for naming the wrong difference. Others had been slain for offenses equally trivial: trampling the Duke's camellias, failing to praise his wines, staring too long at his gloves, gazing too long at his niece. Those who survived his scorn and sword were given incredible labors to perform in order to win his niece's hand, the only warm hand in the castle, where time had frozen to death at ten minutes to five one snowy night. They were told to cut a slice of moon, or change the ocean into wine. They were set to finding things that never were, and building things that could not be. They came and tried and failed and disappeared and never came again. And some, as I have said, were slain, for using names that start with X, or dropping spoons, or wearing rings, or speaking disrespectfully of sin.

The castle and the Duke grew colder, and Saralinda, as a princess will, even in a place where time lies frozen, became a little older, but only a little older. She was nearly twenty-one the day a prince, disguised as a minstrel, came singing to the town that lay below the castle. He called himself Xingu, which was not his name, and dangerous, since the name began with X—and still does. He was, quite properly, a thing of shreds and patches, a ragged minstrel, singing for pennies and the love of singing. Xingu, as he so rashly called himself, was the youngest son of a powerful king, but he had grown weary of rich attire and banquets and tournaments and the available princesses of his own realm, and yearned to find in a far land the maiden of his dreams, singing as he went, learning the life of the lowly, and possibly slaying a dragon here and there.

At the sign of the Silver Swan, in the town below the castle, where taverners, travelers, tale-tellers, tosspots, troublemakers, and other townspeople were gathered, he heard of Saralinda, loveliest princess on all the thousand islands of the ocean seas. "If you can turn the rain to silver, she is yours," a taverner leered.

"If you can slay the thorny Boar of Borythorn, she is yours," grinned a traveler. "But there is no thorny Boar of Borythorn, which makes it hard."

"What makes it even harder is her uncle's scorn and sword," sneered a tale-teller. "He will slit you from your guggle to your zatch."

"The Duke is seven feet, nine inches tall, and only twenty-eight years old, or in his prime," a tosspot gurgled. "His hand is cold enough to stop a clock, and strong enough to choke a bull, and swift enough to catch the wind. He breaks up minstrels in his soup, like crackers."

"Our minstrel here will warm the old man's heart with song, dazzle him with jewels and gold," a troublemaker simpered. "He'll trample on the Duke's camellias, spill his wine, and blunt his sword, and say his name begins with X, and in the end the Duke will say, 'Take Saralinda, with my blessing, O lordly Prince of Rags and Tags, O rider of the sun!'"

The troublemaker weighed eighteen stone, but the minstrel picked him up and tossed him in the air and caught him and set him down again. Then he paid his due and left the Swan.

"I've seen that youth before," the traveler mused, staring after Xingu, "but he was neither ragamuffin then, nor minstrel. Now let me see, where was it?"

"In his soup," the tosspot said, "like crackers."

II

Outside the tavern the night was lighted by a rocking yellow moon that held a white star in its horn. In the gloomy castle on the hill a lantern gleamed and darkened, came and went, as if the gaunt Duke stalked from room to room, stabbing bats and spiders, killing mice. "Dazzle the Duke with jewels," the minstrel said aloud. "There's something in it somewhere, but what it is and where, I cannot think." He wondered if the Duke would order him to cause a fall of purple snow, or make a table out of sawdust, or merely slit him from his guggle to his zatch, and say to Saralinda, "There he lies, your latest fool, a nameless minstrel. I'll have my varlets feed him to the geese." The minstrel shuddered in the moonlight, wondering where his zatch and guggle were. He wondered how and why and when he could invade the castle. A duke was never known to ask a ragged minstrel to his table, or set a task for him to do, or let him meet a princess. "I'll think of some way," thought the Prince. "I'll think of something."

The hour was late, and revelers began to reel and stagger home from inns and taverns, none in rags, and none in tags, and some in velvet gowns. One third of the dogs in town began to bark. The minstrel took his lute from his shoulder and improvised a song. He had thought of something.

> *"Hark, hark, the dogs do bark,*
> *But only one in three.*
> *They bark at those in velvet gowns,*
> *They never bark at me."*

A tale-teller, tottering home to bed, laughed at the song, and troublemakers and tosspots began to gather and listen.

> *"The Duke is fond of velvet gowns,*
> *He'll ask you all to tea.*
> *But I'm in rags, and I'm in tags,*
> *He'll never send for me."*

The townspeople crowded around the minstrel, laughing and cheering. "He's a bold one, Rags is, makin' songs about the Duke!" giggled a strutfurrow who had joined the crowd.

The minstrel went on singing.

> *"Hark, hark, the dogs do bark,*
> *The Duke is fond of kittens.*
> *He likes to take their insides out,*
> *And use their fur for mittens."*

The crowd fell silent in awe and wonder, for the towns-people knew the Duke had slain eleven men for merely staring at his hands, hands that were gloved in velvet gloves, bright with rubies and with diamonds. Fearing to be seen in the doomed and desperate company of the mad minstrel, the rev-elers slunk off to their homes to tell their wives. Only the traveler, who thought he had seen the singer some otherwhere and time, lingered to warn him of his peril. "I've seen you shining in the lists," he said, "or toppling knights in battle, or breaking men in two like crackers. You must be Tristram's son, or Lancelot's, or are you Tyne or Tora?"

"A wandering minstrel, I," the minstrel said, "a thing of shreds and zatches." He bit his tongue in consternation at the slip it made.

"Even if you were the mighty Zorn of Zorna," said the man, "you could not escape the fury of the Duke. He'll slit you from your guggle to your zatch, from here to here." He touched the minstrel's stomach and his throat.

"I now know what to guard," the minstrel sighed.

A black figure in velvet mask and hood and cloak disap-peared behind a tree. "The cold Duke's spy-in-chief," the traveler said, "a man named Whisper. Tomorrow he will die." The minstrel waited. "He'll die because, to name your sins, he'll have to mention mittens. I leave at once for other lands, since I have mentioned mittens." He sighed. "You'll never live to wed his niece. You'll only die to feed his geese. Good-bye, good night, and sorry."

The traveler vanished, like a fly in the mouth of a frog, and the minstrel was left alone in the dark, deserted street. Some-where a clock dropped a stony chime into the night. The min-strel began to sing again. A soft finger touched his shoulder and he turned to see a little man smiling in the moonlight. He wore an indescribable hat, his eyes were wide and aston-ished, as if everything were happening for the first time, and he had a dark, describable beard. "If you have nothing better than your songs," he said, "you are somewhat less than much, and only a little more than anything."

"I manage in my fashion," the minstrel said, and he strummed his lute and sang.

> *"Hark, hark, the dogs do bark,*
> *The cravens are going to bed.*
> *Some will rise and greet the sun,*
> *But Whisper will be dead."*

The old man lost his smile.

"Who are you?" the minstrel asked.

"I am the Golux," said the Golux, proudly, "the only Golux in the world, and not a mere Device."

"You resemble one," the minstrel said, "as Saralinda resembles the rose."

"I resemble only half the things I say I don't," the Golux said. "The other half resemble me." He sighed. "I must always be on hand when people are in peril."

"My peril is my own," the minstrel said.

"Half of it is yours and half is Saralinda's."

"I hadn't thought of that," the minstrel said. "I place my faith in you, and where you lead, I follow."

"Not so fast," the Golux said. "Half the places I have been to, never were. I make things up. Half the things I say are there cannot be found. When I was young I told a tale of buried gold, and men from leagues around dug in the woods. I dug myself."

"But why?"

"I thought the tale of treasure might be true."

"You said you made it up."

"I know I did, but then I didn't know I had. I forget things, too." The minstrel felt a vague uncertainty. "I make mistakes, but I am on the side of Good," the Golux said, "by accident and happenchance. I had high hopes of being Evil when I was two, but in my youth I came upon a firefly burning in a spider's web. I saved the victim's life."

"The firefly's?" said the minstrel.

"The spider's. The blinking arsonist had set the web on fire." The minstrel's uncertainty increased, but as he thought to slip away, a deep bell sounded in the castle and many lights appeared, and voices shouted orders and commands. A stream of lanterns started flowing down the darkness. "The Duke has heard your songs," the Golux said. "The fat is in the fire, the die is cast, the jig is up, the goose is cooked, and the cat is out of the bag."

"My hour has struck," the minstrel said. They heard a faint and distant rasping sound, as if a blade of steel were being sharpened on a stone.

"The Duke prepares to feed you to his geese," the Golux said. "We must invent a tale to stay his hand."

"What manner of tale?" the minstrel asked.

"A tale," the Golux said, "to make the Duke believe that slaying you would light a light in someone else's heart. He hates a light in people's hearts. So you must say a certain prince and princess can't be wed until the evening of the second day after the Duke has fed you to his geese."

"I wish that you would not keep saying that," the minstrel said.

"The tale sounds true," the Golux said, "and very like a witch's spell. The Duke has awe of witches' spells. I'm certain he will stay his hand, I think."

The sound of tramping feet came near and nearer. The iron guards of the Duke closed in, their lanterns gleaming and their spears and armor. "Halt!" There was a clang and clanking.

"Do not arrest my friend," the youth implored.

"What friend?" the captain growled.

The minstrel looked around him and about, but there was no one there. A guard guffawed and said, "Maybe he's seen the Golux."

"There isn't any Golux. I have been to school, and know," the captain said. The minstrel's uncertainty increased again. "Fall in!" the captain bawled. "Dress up that line."

"You heard him. Dress it up," the sergeant said. They marched the minstrel to the dungeon in the castle. A stream of lantern light flowed slowly up the hill.

III

It was morning. The cold Duke gazed out a window of the castle, as if he were watching flowers in bloom or flying birds. He was watching his varlets feeding Whisper to the geese. He turned away and took three limps and stared at the minstrel, standing in the great hall of the castle, both hands bound behind him. "What manner of prince is this you speak of, and what manner of maiden does he love, to use a word that makes no sense and has no point?" His voice sounded like iron dropped on velvet.

"A noble prince, a noble lady," the minstrel said. "When they are wed a million people will be glad."

The Duke took his sword out of his sword-cane and stared at it. He limped across and faced his captive, and touched his guggle softly with the point, and touched his zatch, and sighed and frowned, and put the sword away. "We shall think of some amusing task for you to do," he said. "I do not like your tricks and guile. I think there is no prince or maiden who would wed if I should slay you, but I am neither sure nor certain. He grinned and said again, "We'll think of some amusing task for you to do."

"But I am not a prince," the minstrel said, "and only princes may aspire to Saralinda's hand."

The cold Duke kept on grinning. "Why, then we'll make a prince of you," he said. "The prince of Rags and Jingles." He clapped his gloves together and two varlets appeared without a word or sound. "Take him to his dungeon," said the Duke. "Feed him water without bread, and bread without water."

The varlets were taking the minstrel out of the great hall when down the marble stairs the Princess Saralinda floated like a cloud. The Duke's eye gleamed like crystal. The minstrel gazed in wonder. The Princess Saralinda was tall, with freesias in her dark hair, and she wore serenity brightly like the rainbow. It was not easy to tell her mouth from the rose, or her brow from the white lilac. Her voice was faraway music, and her eyes were candles burning on a tranquil night. She moved across the room like wind in violets, and her laughter sparkled on the air, which, from her presence, gained a faint and undreamed fragrance. The Prince was frozen by her beauty, but not cold, and the Duke, who was cold but not frozen, held up the palms of his gloves, as if she were a fire at which to warm his hands. The minstrel saw the blood come warmly to the lame man's cheeks. "This thing of rags and tags and tatters will play our little game," he told his niece, his voice like iron on velvet.

"I wish him well," the Princess said.

The minstrel broke his bonds and took her hand in his, but it was slashed away by the swift cane of the Duke. "Take him to his dungeon now," he said. He stared coldly at the minstrel through his monocle. "You'll find the most amusing bats and spiders there."

"I wish him well," the Princess said again, and the varlets took the minstrel to his dungeon.

When the great iron door of the dungeon clanked behind the minstrel, he found himself alone in blackness. A spider, swinging on a strand of web, swung back and forth. The zickering of bats was echoed by the walls. The minstrel took a step, avoiding snakes, and something squirmed. "Take care," the Golux said, "you're on my foot."

"Why are you here?" the minstrel cried.

"I forgot something. I forgot about the task the Duke will set you."

The minstrel thought of swimming lakes too wide to swim, of turning liquids into stone, or finding boneless creatures made of bone. "How came you here?" he asked. "And can you leave?"

"I never know," the Golux said. "My mother was a witch, but rather mediocre in her way. When she tried to turn a thing to gold, it turned to clay; and when she changed her rivals into fish, all she ever got was mermaids." The minstrel's heart was insecure. "My father was a wizard," said his friend, "who often cast his spells upon himself, when he was in his cups. Strike a light or light a lantern! Something I have hold of has no head."

The minstrel shuddered. "The task," he said. "You came to tell me."

"I did? Oh, yes. My father lacked the power of concentration, and that is bad for monks and priests, and worse for wizards. Listen. Tell the Duke that you will hunt the Boar, or travel thrice around the moon, or turn November into June. Implore him not to send you out to find a thousand jewels."

"And then?"

"And then he'll send you out to find a thousand jewels."

"But I am poor!" the minstrel cried.

"Come, come," the Golux said. "You're Zorn of Zorna. I had it from a traveler I met. It came to him as he was leaving town. Your father's casks and coffers shine with rubies and with sapphires."

"My father lives in Zorna," said the Prince, "and it would take me nine and ninety days: three and thirty days to go, and three and thirty days to come back here."

"That's six and sixty."

"It always takes my father three and thirty days to make decisions," said the Prince. "In spells and labors a certain time is always set, and I might be at sea when mine expires."

"That's another problem for another day," the Golux said. "Time is for dragonflies and angels. The former live too little and the latter live too long."

Zorn of Zorna thought awhile and said, "The task seems strange and simple."

"There are no jewels," the Golux said, "within the reach and ranges of this island, except the gems here in this castle. The Duke knows not that you are Zorn of Zorna. He thinks you are a minstrel without a penny or a moonstone. He's fond of jewels. You've seen them on his gloves."

The Prince stepped on a turtle. "The Duke has spies," he said, "who may know who I am."

The Golux sighed. "I may be wrong," he said, "but we must risk and try it."

The Prince sighed in his turn. "I wish you could be surer."

"I wish I could," the Golux said. "My mother was born, I regret to say, only partly in a caul. I've saved a score of princes in my time. I cannot save them all." Something that would have been purple, if there had been light to see it by, scuttled across the floor. "The Duke might give me only thirty days, or forty-two, to find a thousand jewels," said Zorn of Zorna. "Why should he give me ninety-nine?"

"The way I figure it," the Golux said, "is this. The longer

the labor lasts, the longer lasts his gloating. He loves to gloat, you know."

The Prince sat down beside a toad. "My father may have lost his jewels," he said, "or given them away."

"I thought of that," the Golux said. "But I have other plans than one. Right now we have to sleep."

They found a corner without creatures and slept until the town clock struck the midnight hour.

Chains clanked and rattled, and the great iron door began to move. "The Duke has sent for you again," the Golux said. "Be careful what you say and what you do."

The great iron door began to open slowly. "When shall I see you next?" Zorn whispered. There was no answer. The Prince groped around in the dark and felt a thing very like a cat, and touched the thing without a head, but he could not find the Golux.

The great iron door was open wide now and the dungeon filled with lantern light.

"The Duke commands your presence," growled a guard. "What was *that*?"

"What was what?"

"I know not," said the guard. "I thought I heard the sound of someone laughing."

"Is the Duke afraid of laughter?" asked the Prince.

"The Duke is not afraid of anything. Not even," said the guard, "the Todal."

"The Todal?"

"The Todal."

"What's the Todal?"

A lock of the guard's hair turned white and his teeth began to chatter. "The Todal looks like a blob of glup," he said. "It makes a sound like rabbits screaming, and smells of old, unopened rooms. It's waiting for the Duke to fail in some endeavor, such as setting you a task that you can do."

"And if he sets me one, and I succeed?" the Prince inquired.

"The Blob will glup him," said the guard. "It's an agent of the devil, sent to punish evil-doers for having done less evil than they should. I talk too much. Come on. The Duke is waiting."

IV

The Duke sat at one end of a black oak table in the black oak room, lighted by flaming torches that threw red gleams on shields and lances. The Duke's gloves sparkled when he moved his hands. He stared moodily through his monocle at young Prince Zorn. The Duke sneered, which made him even colder. "So you would hunt the Boar," he said, "or travel thrice around the moon, or turn November into June." He laughed, and a torch went out. "Saralinda in November turns November into June. A cow can travel thrice around the moon, or even more. And *anyone* can merely *hunt* the Boar. I have another plan for you. I thought it up myself last night, while I was killing mice. I'll send you out to find a thousand jewels and bring them back."

The Prince turned pale, or tried to. "A wandering minstrel, I," he said, "a thing of—"

"Rubies and sapphires." The Duke's chuckle sounded like ice cackling in a cauldron. "For you are Zorn of Zorna," he whispered, softly. "Your father's casks and vaults and coffers shine with jewels. In six and sixty days you could sail to Zorna and return."

"It always takes my father three and thirty days to make decisions," cried the Prince.

The Duke grinned. "That is what I wanted to know, my naïve Prince," he said. "Then you would have me give you nine and ninety days?"

"That would be fair," the Prince replied. "But how do you know that I am Zorn?"

"I have a spy named Hark," the Duke explained, "who found your princely raiment in your quarters in the town and brought it here, with certain signs and seals and signatures, revealing who you are. Go put the raiment on." He pointed at a flight of iron stairs. "You'll find it in a chamber on whose door a star is turning black. Don it and return. I'll think of beetles while you're gone, and things like that." The Duke limped to his chair and sat down again, and the Prince started up the iron stairs, wondering where the Golux was. He stopped and turned and said, "You will not give me nine and ninety days. How many, then?" The Duke sneered. "I'll think of a lovely number," he said. "Go on."

When Zorn came back he wore his royal attire, but the Duke's spies had sealed his sword, so that he could not draw it. The Duke sat staring at a man who wore a velvet mask and cloak and hood. "This is Hark," he said, "and this is Listen." He gestured with his cane at nothing.

"There's no one there," said Zorn.

"Listen is invisible," the Duke explained. "Listen can be heard, but never seen. They are here to learn the mark and measure of your task. I give you nine and ninety hours, not nine and ninety days, to find a thousand jewels and bring them here. When you return, the clocks must all be striking five."

"The clocks here in the castle?" asked the Prince. "The thirteen clocks?"

"The clocks here in the castle," said the Duke, "the thirteen clocks."

The Prince looked at the two clocks on the walls. Their hands pointed to ten minutes of five. "The hands are frozen," said the Prince. "The clocks are dead."

"Precisely," said the Duke, "and what is more, which makes your task a charming one, there are no jewels that could be found within the space of nine and ninety hours, except those in my vaults, and these." He held his gloves up and they sparkled.

"A pretty task," said Hark.

"Ingenious," said the voice of Listen.

"I thought you'd like it," said the Duke. "Unseal his sword." Invisible hands unsealed the Prince's sword.

"And if I should succeed?" asked Zorn.

The Duke waved a gloved hand at the iron stairs, and Zorn saw Saralinda standing there. "I wish him well," she said, and her uncle laughed and looked at Zorn. "I hired a witch," he said, "to cast a tiny spell upon her. When she is in my presence, all that she can say is this: 'I wish him well.' You like it?"

"A clever spell," said Hark.

"An awful spell," the voice of Listen said.

The Prince and Princess spoke a silent language with their

eyes, until the Duke cried, "Go!" and Saralinda vanished up the stairs.

"And if I fail?" asked Zorn.

The Duke removed his sword from his sword-cane and ran his glove along the blade. "I'll slit you from your guggle to your zatch, and feed you to the Todal."

"I've heard of it," said Zorn.

The Duke smiled. "You've only heard of half of it," he said. "The other half is worse. It's made of lip. It feels as if it had been dead at least a dozen days, but it moves about like monkeys and like shadows." The Prince took out his sword and put it back. "The Todal can't be killed," the Duke said, softly.

"It gleeps," said Hark.

"What's gleeping?" asked the Prince.

The Duke and Hark and Listen laughed. "Time is wasting, Prince," the Duke reminded him. "Already you have only eight and ninety hours. I wish you every strangest kind of luck." A wide oak door suddenly opened at the end of the room, and the Prince saw lightning and midnight and falling rain. "One last word and warning," said the Duke. "I would not trust the Golux overfar. He cannot tell what can be from what can't. He seldom knows what should be from what is."

The Prince glanced at Hark and at the Duke, and at a spot where he thought Listen stood. "When all the clocks are striking five," he said, and left the room. The laughter of the Duke and Hark and Listen followed him out the door and down the stairs and into the darkness. When he had gone a few steps from the castle, he looked up at a lighted window and thought he saw the Princess Saralinda standing there. A rose fell at his feet, and as he picked it up, the laughter of the Duke and Hark and Listen increased inside the black oak room and died away.

V

The Prince had gone but a short way from the castle when he felt a gentle finger touch his elbow. "It is the Golux," said the Golux, proudly. "The only Golux in the world."

The Prince was in no mood for the old man's gaiety and cheer. The Golux did not seem wonderful to him now, and even his indescribable hat was suddenly describable. "The Duke thinks you are not so wise as he thinks you think you are," he said.

The Golux smiled. "I think he is not so wise as he thinks I think he is," he said. "I was there. I know the terms. I had thought that only dragonflies and angels think of time, never having been an angel or a dragonfly."

"How were you there?" the Prince said in surprise.

"I am Listen," the Golux said, "or at any rate, he thinks I am. Never trust a spy you cannot see. The Duke is lamer than I am old, and I am shorter than he is cold, but it comes to you with some surprise that I am wiser than he is wise."

The Prince's courage began to return. "I think you are the most remarkable man in the world," he said.

"Who thought not so a moment since, knows not the apple from the quince," the Golux said. He scowled. "We now have only eight and ninety *hours* to find a thousand gems," he said.

"You said that you had other plans than one," the Prince reminded him.

"What plans?" the Golux asked.

"You didn't say," said Zorn.

The Golux closed his eyes and clasped his hands. "There was a treasure ship that sank, not more than forty hours from here," he said. "But, come to think of it, the Duke ransacked the ship and stole the jewels."

"So much," sighed Zorn, "for that."

The Golux thought again. "If there were hail," he said, "and we could stain the hail with blood, it might turn into rubies."

"There is no hail," said Zorn.

The Golux sighed. "So much," he said, "for that."

"The task is hard," said Zorn, "and can't be done."

"I can do a score of things that can't be done," the Golux said. "I can find a thing I cannot see and see a thing I cannot find. The first is time, the second is a spot before my eyes. I can feel a thing I cannot touch and touch a thing I cannot feel. The first is sad and sorry, the second is your heart. What would you do without me? Say 'nothing.'"

"Nothing," said the Prince.

"Good. Then you're helpless and I'll help you. I said I had another plan than one, and I have just remembered what it is. There is a woman on this isle, who'd have some eight and eighty years, and she is gifted with the strangest gift of all. For when she weeps, what do you think she weeps?"

"Tears," said Zorn.

"Jewels," said the Golux.

The Prince stared at him. "But that is too remarkable to be," he said.

"I don't see why," the Golux said. "Even the lowly oyster makes his pearls without the use of eyes or hands or any tools, and pearls are jewels. The oyster is a blob of glup, but a woman is a woman."

The Prince thought of the Todal and felt a small cold feeling in his guggle. "Where does this wondrous woman dwell?" he asked.

The old man groaned. "Over mountain, over stream, by the way of storm and thunder, in a hut so high or deep—I never can remember which—the naked eye can't see it." He stood up. "We must be on our way," he said. "It will take us ninety hours, or more or less, to go and come. It's this way, or it's that way. Make up my mind."

"How can I?" asked the Prince. "You have a rose," the Golux said. "Hold it in your hand." The Prince took out the rose and held it in his hand, and its stem slowly turned and stopped. "It's this way," cried the Golux, and they started off in the direction the stem of the rose had pointed out. "I will tell you the tale of Hagga," said the Golux.

When Hagga was eleven (he began) and picking cherries in the woods one day, and asphodel, she came upon the good King Gwain of Yarrow with his foot caught in a wolf trap. "Weep for me, maiden," said the King, "for I am ludicrous and laughable, with my foot caught in this trap. I am no longer ert, for I have lost my ertia. By twiddling my fingers or clapping my hands, I have often changed the fate of men, but now I cannot get my foot loose from this thing."

"I have no time for tears," the maiden said. She knew the secret of the trap, and was about to free the fettered foot, when a farmer from a near-by farm began to laugh. The King beshrewed him and his wife, and turned them into grasshoppers, creatures that look as if their feet were caught in traps, even when they aren't.

"Lo, the maid has freed my foot," the King exulted, seeing that she had, "but it is numb, and feels like someone else's foot, not mine." The maiden took off his shoe and rubbed his foot, until it felt like his and he could put it down. And for her kindness the grateful King gave her the power to weep jewels when she wept, instead of tears. When the people learned of the strange gift the King had given Hagga, they came from leagues around, by night and day, in warm and winter weather, to make her sad and sorry. Nothing tragic happened but she heard of it and wept. People came with heavy hearts and left with pearls and rubies. Paths were paved with pearls, and rivers ran with rubies. Children played with sapphires in the streets, and dogs chewed opals. Every peacock had at least nine diamonds in its gizzard, and one, cut open on St. Wistow's Day, had thirty-eight. The price of stones and pebbles rose, the price of gems declined, until, by making Hagga weep, you could be hanged and fined. In the end, the jewels were melted, in a frightful fire, by order of the King. "I will make her weep myself, one day each year," the King decreed, "and thus and hence, the flow of gems will make some sense, and have some point and balance." But alas, and but alack, the maid could weep no more at any tale of tragedy or tribulation. Damsels killed by dragons left her cold, and broken hearts, and children lost, and love denied. She never wept by day or night, in warm or winter weather. She grew to be sixteen, and twenty-six, and thirty-four, and forty-eight, and fifty-two, and now she waits, at eighty-eight, for me and you. "I hope," the Golux said, "that this is true. I make things up, you know."

The young Prince sighed and said, "I know you do. If Hagga weeps no more, why should she weep for you?"

The Golux thought it over. "I feel that she is frail and fragile. I trust that she is sad and sorry. I hope that she is neither dead nor dying. I'll think of something very sad to tell her. Very sad and lonely. Take out your rose, I think we're lost."

They had become tangled in brambles by now, and the trees of the forest they had entered were tall and thick. Thorns began to tear the Prince's raiment. Lightning flashed and thunder rolled, and all paths vanished. The Prince took out the rose and held it in his hand. The stem began to turn and twist, and pointed.

"Around this way," the Golux said. "It's lighter here." He found a narrow path that led straight onward. As they walked along the path, the Golux leading, they met a Jackadandy, whose clothes were torn and tattered.

"I told my tales to Hagga," said the man; "but Hagga weeps no more. I told her tales of lovers lost in April. I told her tales of maidens dead in June. I told her tales of princes fed to geese. I even told her how I lost my youngest niece."

"This is sad," the Golux said, "and getting sadder."

"The way is long," the torn man said, "and getting longer. The road goes uphill all the way, and even farther. I wish you luck," he said. "You'll need it." He disappeared in brambles.

The only light in the forest came from lightning, and when it flashed they watched the rose and followed where it pointed. This brought them, on the second day, into a valley. They saw a Jack-o'-lent approaching, his clothes all torn and tattered. "I told my tales to Hagga," said the man, "but Hagga weeps no more. I told her tales of lovers lost at sea and drowned in fountains. I told her tales of babies lost in woods and lost on mountains. She wept not," said the Jack-o'-lent. "The way is dark, and getting darker. The hut is high and even higher. I wish you luck. There is none." He vanished in the briars.

The brambles and the thorns grew thick and thicker in a ticking thicket of bickering crickets. Farther along and stronger, bonged the gongs of a throng of frogs, green and vivid on their lily pads. From the sky came the crying of flies, and the pilgrims leaped over a bleating sheep creeping knee-deep in a sleepy stream, in which swift and slippery snakes slid and slithered silkily, whispering sinful secrets.

A comet whistled through the sky, and by its light they saw the hut of Hagga high on Hagga's hill. "If she is dead, there may be strangers there," the Golux said.

"How many hours do we have left?" the Prince demanded.

"If we can make her weep within the hour," the Golux said, "we'll barely make it."

"I hope that she's alive and sad," said Zorn.

"I feel that she has died," the Golux sighed. "I feel it in my stomach. You better carry me. I'm weary."

Zorn of Zorna picked the Golux up and carried him.

VI

It was cold on Hagga's hill, and fresh with furrows where the dragging points of stars had plowed the fields. A peasant in a purple smock stalked the smoking furrows, sowing seeds. There was a smell, the Golux thought, a little like Forever in the air, but mixed with something faint and less enduring, possibly the fragrance of a flower. "There's no light in her window," the Golux said, "and it is dark and getting darker."

"There's no smoke in her chimney," said the Prince, "and it is cold and getting colder."

The Golux barely breathed and said, "What worries me the most is that spider's web there on the door, that stretches from the hinges to the latch."

The young Prince felt a hollow feeling in his zatch. "Knock on her door," the Golux said, his voice so high it quavered. He crossed his fingers and kept them crossed, and Zorn knocked on the door. No one answered. "Knock again," the Golux cried, and Prince Zorn knocked again.

Hagga was there. She came to the door and stared at them, a woman neither dead nor dying, and clearly only thirty-eight or thirty-nine. The Golux had missed her age by fifty years, as old men often do. "Weep for us," the Golux cried, "or else this Prince will never wed his Princess."

"I have no tears," said Hagga. "Once I wept when ships were overdue, or brooks ran dry, or tangerines were overripe, or sheep got something in their eye. I weep no more," said Hagga. Her eyes were dry as deserts and her mouth seemed made of stone. "I have turned a thousand persons gemless from my door. Come in," she said. "I weep no more."

The room was dark and held a table and a chair, and in one corner something like a chest, made of oak and bound with brass. The Golux smiled and then looked sad, and said, "I have tales to make a hangman weep, and tales to bring a tear of sorrow to a monster's eye. I have tales that would disturb a dragon's sleep, and even make the Todal sigh."

At the mention of the Todal, Hagga's hair turned gray. "Once I wept when maids were married underneath the April moon. I weep no more when maids are buried, even in the month of June."

"You have the emotions of a fish," said the Golux, irritably. He sat on the floor and told her tales of the death of kings, and kindred things, and little children choked by rings.

"I have no tears," said Hagga.

He told her tales of the frogs in the forum, and the toads in the rice that destroyed the poppycockalorum and the cockahoopatrice.

"I weep no more," said Hagga.

"Look," the Golux said, "and listen! The Princess Saralinda will never wed this youth until the day he lays a thousand jewels upon a certain table."

"I would weep for Saralinda," Hagga sighed, "if I were able."

The Prince had wandered to the oaken chest. He seized its cover with his hand and threw it open. A radiance filled the room and lit the darkest corners. Inside the chest there were at least ten thousand jewels of the very sort and kind the Duke demanded. Diamonds flared and rubies glowed, and sapphires burned and emeralds seemed on fire. They looked at Hagga. "These are the jewels of laughter," Hagga said. "I woke up fourteen days ago to find them on my bed. I had laughed until I wept at something in my sleep." The Golux grabbed a gleaming handful of the gems, and then another, crowing with delight. "Put them back," said Hagga. "For there's a thing that you must know, concerning jewels of laughter. They always turn again to tears a fortnight after. It has been a fortnight, to the day and minute, since I took the pretties to this chest and put them in it."

Even as they watched, the light and color died. The diamonds dimmed, the emeralds went out, and the jewels of Hagga's laughter turned to tears, with a little sound like sighing. There was nothing in the chest but limpid liquid, leering up at them and winking. "You must think," the Golux cried. "You must think of what you laughed at in your sleep."

Hagga's eyes were blank. "I do not know, for this was fourteen days ago."

"Think!" the Golux said.

"Think!" said Zorn of Zorna.

Hagga frowned and said, "I never can remember dreams."

The Golux clasped his hands behind his back and thought it over. "As I remember and recall," he said, "the jewels of sorrow last forever. Such was the gift and power the good Gwain gave you. What was he doing, by the way, so many leagues from Yarrow?"

"Hunting," Hagga said. "Wolves, as I recall it."

The Golux scowled. "I am a man of logic, in my way. What happened on that awful day, to make him value sorrow over and above the gift of laughter? Why have these jewels turned to tears a fortnight after?"

"There was a farmer from a near-by farm, who laughed," said Hagga. " 'On second thought,' the good King said, 'I will amend and modify the gift I gave you. The jewels of sorrow will last beyond all measure, but may the jewels of laughter give you little pleasure.' "

The Golux groaned. "If there's one thing in the world I hate," he said, "it is amendments." His eyes turned bright and brighter, and he clapped his hands. "I will make her laugh until she weeps," he said.

The Golux told her funny tales of things that were and had been, but Hagga's eyes were dry as quartz and her mouth seemed made of agate. "I laugh at nothing that has been," she said, "or is."

The Golux smiled. "Then we will think of things that will be, and aren't now, and never were. I'll think of something," and he thought, and thought of something.

> *"A deboy who was terribly hobble,*
> *Cast only stones that were cobble*
> *And bats that were ding,*
> *From a shot that was sling,*
> *But never hit inks that were bobble."*

Hagga laughed until she wept, and seven moonstones trickled down her cheek and clattered on the floor. "She's weeping semiprecious stones!" the Golux wailed. He tried again:

> *"There was an old coddle so molly,*
> *He talked in a glot that was poly,*
> *His gaws were so gew*
> *That his laps became dew,*
> *And he ate only pops that were lolly."*

Hagga laughed until she wept, and seven brilliants trickled down her cheek and clattered on the floor. "Rhinestones!" groaned the Golux. "Now she's weeping costume jewelry!"

The young Prince tried his hand at telling tales of laughter, but for his pains he got a shower of tourmaline, a cat's-eye, and a flux of pearls. "The Duke hates pearls," the Golux moaned. "He thinks they're made by fish."

It grew darker in the room and they could scarcely see. The starlight and the moon were gone. They stood there, still as statues. The Golux cleared his throat. The Prince uncrossed his arms and crossed them. And then, without a rhyme or reason, out of time and out of season, Hagga laughed and kept on laughing. No one had said a word, no one had told a tale. It might have been the hooting of an owl. It might have been the crawling of a snail. But Hagga laughed and kept on laughing, and precious jewels twinkled down her cheek and sparkled on the floor, until the hut was ankle-deep in diamonds and in rubies. The Golux counted out a thousand and put them in a velvet sack that he had brought along. "I wish that she had laughed," he sighed, "at something I had said."

Zorn of Zorna took her hand. "God keep you warm in winter," said the Prince, "and cool in summer."

"Farewell," the Golux said, "and thank you."

Hagga laughed and kept on laughing, and sapphires burned upon the floor and lit the Golux toward the door.

"How many hours are left us now?" the young Prince cried. "It's odd," the Golux muttered to himself. "I could have sworn that she had died. This is the only time my stomach ever lied."

"How many hours are left us now?" the Prince implored.

Hagga sat upon the chest and kept on laughing.

"I should say," the Golux said, "that we have only forty left, but it is downhill all the way.

They went out into the moonless night and peered about them in the dark.

"I think it's this way," the Golux said, and they went the way he thought it was.

"What about the clocks?" demanded Zorn.

The Golux exhaled a sorry breath. "That's another problem for another hour," he said.

Inside the hut, something red and larger than a ruby glowed among the jewels and Hagga picked it up. "A rose," she said. "They must have dropped it."

VII

In the black oak room the yellow torches flared and crackled on the walls, and their fire burned on the lances and the shields. The Duke's gloves glittered. "How goes the night?" he gnarled.

"The moon is down," said Hark. "I have not heard the clocks."

"You'll never hear them!" screamed the Duke. "I slew time in this castle many a cold and snowy year ago."

Hark stared at him emptily and seemed to be chewing something. "Time froze here. Someone left the windows open."

"Bah!" The Duke sat down at the far end of the table, stood up again, and limped about. "It bled hours and minutes on the floor. I saw it with my eye." Hark kept on chewing something. Outside the Gothic windows thunder growled. An owl flew by.

"There are no jewels," roared the Duke. "They'll have to bring me pebbles from the sea or mica from the meadows." He gave his awful laugh. "How goes the night?" he asked again.

"I have been counting off and on," said Hark, "and I should say they have some forty minutes left."

"They'll never make it!" the cold Duke screamed. "I hope they drowned, or broke their legs, or lost their way." He came so close to Hark their noses almost touched. "Where were they going?" he whispered harshly.

Hark stepped backward seven steps. "I met a Jackadandy, some seven hours ago," he said. "They passed him on their way to Hagga's hill. Do you remember Hagga, and have you thought of her?"

The Duke's loud laughter rang the shields.

"Hagga weeps no more," he said. "Hagga has no tears. She did not even weep when she was told about the children locked up in my tower."

"I hated that," said Hark.

"I liked it," said the Duke. "No child can sleep in my camellias." He began to limp again and stared out at the night. "Where is Listen?" he demanded.

"He followed them," said Hark, "the Golux and the Prince."

"I do not trust him," growled the Duke. "I like a spy that I can see. Let me have men about me that are visible." He shouted "Listen!" up the stairs, and "Listen!" out the windows, but no one answered. "I'm cold," he rasped.

"You always are."

"I'm colder," snarled the Duke, "and never tell me what I always am!" He took his sword out and slashed at nothing and at silence. "I miss Whisper."

"You fed him to the geese," said Hark. "They seemed to like him."

"Silence! What was that?"

"What did it sound like?"

"Like princes stealing up the stairs, like Saralinda leaving." The Duke limped to the iron stairs and slashed again at silence and at nothing. "What does he feel like? Have you felt him?"

"Listen? He's five feet high," said Hark. "He has a beard, and something on his head I can't describe."

"The Golux!" shrieked the Duke. "You felt the Golux! I hired him as a spy and didn't know it."

A purple ball with gold stars on it came slowly bouncing down the iron stairs and winked and twinkled, like a naked child saluting priests. "What insolence is this?" the Duke demanded. "What *is* that thing?"

"A ball," said Hark.

"I know that!" screamed the Duke. "But why? What does its ghastly presence signify?"

"It looks to me," said Hark, "very like a ball the Golux and those children used to play with."

"They're on his side!" The Duke was apoplectic. "Their ghosts are on his side."

"He has a lot of friends," said Hark.

"Silence!" roared the Duke. "He knows not what is dead from what is dying, or where he's been from where he's going, or striking clocks from clocks that never strike."

"What makes me think he does?" The spy stopped chewing. Something very much like nothing anyone had seen before came trotting down the stairs and crossed the room.

"What is that?" the Duke asked, palely.

"I don't know what it is," said Hark, "but it's the only one there ever was."

The Duke's gloved hands shook and shimmered. "I'll throw them up for grabs betwixt the Todal and the geese! I'll lock them in the dungeon with the thing without a head!" At the mention of the Todal, Hark's velvet mask turned gray. The Duke's eye twisted upward in its socket. "I'll slay them all!" he said. "This sweetheart and her suitor, this cross-eyed clown! You hear me?"

"Yes," said Hark, "but there are rules and rites and rituals, older than the sound of bells and snow on mountains."

"Go on," the Duke said, softly, looking up the stairs.

"You must let them have their time and turn to make the castle clocks strike five."

"The castle clocks were murdered," said the Duke. "I killed time here myself one snowy morning. You still can see the old brown stains, where seconds bled to death, here on my sleeve." He laughed. "What else?" he asked.

"You know as well as I," said Hark. "The Prince must have his turn and time to lay a thousand jewels there on the table."

"And if he does?"

"He wins the hand of Princess Saralinda."

"The only warm hand in the castle," said the Duke. "Who

loses Saralinda loses fire. I mean the fire of the setting suns, and not the cold and cheerless flame of jewels. Her eyes are candles burning in a shrine. Her feet appear to me as doves. Her fingers bloom upon her breast like flowers."

"This is scarcely the way," said Hark, "to speak of one's own niece."

"She's not my niece! I stole her!" cried the Duke. "I stole her from the castle of a king! I snatched her from the bosom of a sleeping queen. I still bear on my hands the marks of where she bit me."

"The Queen?" asked Hark.

"The Princess," roared the Duke.

"Who was the King?" asked Hark.

His master scowled. "I never knew," he said. "My ship was beached upon an island in a storm. There was no moon or any star. No lights were in the castle."

"How could you find the Princess then?" asked Hark.

"She had a radiance," said the Duke. "She shone there like a star upon her mother's breast. I knew I had to have that splendor in my castle. I mean to keep her here till she is twenty-one. The day she is, I'll wed her, and that day is tomorrow."

"Why haven't you before?" asked Hark. "This castle is your kingdom."

The Duke smiled and showed his upper teeth. "Because her nurse turned out to be a witch who cast a spell upon me."

"What were its terms?" asked Hark.

"I cannot wed her till the day she's twenty-one, and that day is tomorrow."

"You said that once before."

"I must keep her in a chamber where she is safe from me. I've done that."

"I like that part," said Hark.

"I hate it," snarled the Duke. "I must give and grant the right to any prince to seek her hand in marriage. I've done that, too." He sat down at the table.

"In spells of this sort," Hark said, chewing, "one always finds a chink or loophole, by means of which the right and perfect prince can win her hand in spite of any task you set him. How did the witch announce that part of it?"

"Like this. 'She can be saved, and you destroyed, only by

a prince whose name begins with X and doesn't.' There is no prince whose name begins with X and doesn't."

Hark's mask slipped off and he put it back again, but not before the Duke saw laughter in his eyes. "This prince," said Hark, "is Zorn of Zorna, but to your terror and distaste, he once posed as a minstrel. His name was Xingu then and wasn't. This is the prince whose name begins with X and doesn't."

The Duke's sword had begun to shake. "Nobody ever tells me anything," he whispered to himself.

Another ball came bouncing down the stairs, a black ball stamped with scarlet owls. The cold Duke watched it roll across the floor. "What impudence is this?" he cried.

Hark walked to the stairs and listened, and turned and said, "There's someone up there."

"It's the children!" croaked the Duke.

"The children are dead," said Hark, "and the sound I heard was made by living feet."

"How much time is left them?" cried the Duke.

"Half an hour, I think," said Hark.

"I'll have their guggles on my sword for playing games with me!" The Duke started up the stairs and stopped. "They're up there, all of them. Call out the guards," he barked.

"The guards are guarding the clocks," said Hark. "You wanted it that way. There are eleven guards, and each one guards a clock. You and I are guarding *these*." He pointed at the two clocks on the walls. "You wanted it that way."

"Call out the guards," the Duke repeated, and his agent called the guards. They trooped into the room like engines. The Duke limped up the stairs, his drawn sword shining. "Follow me!" he cried. "Another game's afoot! I'll slay the Golux and the Prince, and marry Saralinda!" He led the way. The guards ramped up the stairs like engines. Hark smiled, and chewed again, and followed.

The black oak room was silent for a space of seven seconds. Then a secret door swung open in a wall. The Golux slipped into the room. The Princess followed. His hands were raw and red from climbing vines to Saralinda's chamber. "How could you find the castle in the dark without my rose?" she asked. "He would not let me burn a torch."

"You lighted up your window like a star, and we could see the castle from afar," the Golux said. "Our time is marked in minutes. Start the clocks!"

"I cannot start the clocks," the Princess said.

They heard the sound of fighting far above. "He faces thirteen men," she cried, "and that is hard."

"We face thirteen clocks," the Golux said, "and that is harder. Start the clocks!"

"How can I start the clocks?" the Princess wailed.

"Your hand is warmer than the snow is cold," the Golux said. "Touch the first clock with your hand." The Princess touched it. Nothing happened. "Again!" Saralinda held her hand against the clock and nothing happened. "We are ruined," said the Golux simply, and Saralinda's heart stood still.

She cried, "Use magic!"

"I have no magic to depend on," groaned the Golux. "Try the other clock."

The Princess tried the other clock and nothing happened. "Use logic, then!" she cried. In the secret walls they heard the Iron Guard pounding after Zorn, and coming close.

"Now let me see," the Golux said. "If you can touch the clocks and never start them, then you can start the clocks and never touch them. That's logic, as I know and use it. Hold your hand this far away. Now that far. Closer! Now a little farther back. A little farther. There! I think you have it! Do not move!"

The clogged and rigid works of the clock began to whir. They heard a tick and then a ticking. The Princess Saralinda fled from room to room, like wind in clover, and held her hand the proper distance from the clocks. Something like a vulture spread its wings and left the castle. "That was Then," the Golux said.

"It's Now!" cried Saralinda.

A morning glory that had never opened, opened in the courtyard. A cock that never crowed, began to crow. The light of morning stained the windows, and in the walls the cold Duke moaned, "I hear the sound of time. And yet I slew it, and wiped my bloody sword upon its beard." He thought that Zorn of Zorna had escaped the guards. His sword kept whin-

ing in the blackness, and once he slashed his own left knee—
he thought it was the Golux. "Come out, you crooning
knave!" he cried. "Stand forward, Zorn of Zorna!"

"He's not here," said the spy.

They heard the savage clash of swords. "They've got him!"
squealed the Duke. "Eleven men to one!"

"You may have heard of Galahad," said Hark, "whose
strength was as the strength of ten."

"That leaves one man to get him," cried the Duke. "I
count on Krang, the strongest guard I have, the finest fencer
in the world, save one. An unknown prince in armor van-
quished him a year ago, somewhere on an island. No one else
can do it."

"The unknown prince," said Hark, "was Zorn of Zorna."

"I'll slay him then myself!" The Duke's voice rose and
echoed down the dark and secret stairs. "I slew time with the
bloody hand that grips your arm, and time is greater far than
Zorn of Zorna!"

Hark began to chew again. "No mortal man can murder
time," he said, "and even if he could, there's something else:
a clockwork in a maiden's heart, that strikes the hours of
youth and love, and knows the southward swan from winter
snow, and summer afternoons from tulip time."

"You sicken me with your chocolate chatter," snarled the
Duke. "Your tongue is made of candy. I'll slay this ragged
prince, if Krang has missed him. If there were light, I'd show
you on my sleeves the old brown stains of seconds, where they
bled and died. I slew time in these gloomy halls, and wiped
my bloody blade—"

"Ah, shut up," said Hark. "You are the most aggressive
villain in the world. I always meant to tell you that. I said it
and I'm glad."

"Silence," roared the Duke. "Where are we?" They stumbled down the secret stairs.

"This is the hidden door," said Hark, "that leads into the
oak room."

"Open," roared the Duke, his sword gripped in his hand.
Hark groped and found the secret knob.

VIII

The black oak room was bright with flaming torches, but brighter with the light of Saralinda. The cold eye of the Duke was dazzled by the gleaming of a thousand jewels that sparkled on the table. His ears were filled with chiming as the clocks began to strike.

"One!" said Hark.

"Two!" cried Zorn of Zorna.

"Three!" the Duke's voice almost whispered.

"Four!" sighed Saralinda.

"Five!" the Golux crowed, and pointed at the table. "The task is done, the terms are met," he said.

The Duke's cold eye slowly moved around the room. "Where are my guards?" he croaked, "and where is Krang, the greatest of them all?"

"I lured them to the tower," said Zorn, "and locked them in. The one that's tied in knots is Krang."

The Duke glared at the jewels on the table. "They're false!" he said. "They must be colored pebbles!" He picked one up, and saw that it was real, and put it down again.

"The task is done," said Hark, "the terms are met."

"Not until I count them," said the Duke. "If there be only one that isn't here, I wed the Princess Saralinda on the morrow." The figures in the room were still and he could hear their breathing.

"What a gruesome way to treat one's niece," the Golux cried.

"She's not my niece," the lame man sneered. "I stole her from a king." He showed his lower teeth. "We all have flaws," he said, "and mine is being wicked." He sat down at the table and began to count the gems.

"Who is my father then?" the Princess cried.

The spy's black eyebrows rose. "I thought the Golux told you, but then, of course, he never could remember things."

"Especially," the Golux said, "the names of kings."

"Your father," said the spy, "is good King Gwain of Yarrow."

"I knew that once," the Golux said, "but I forgot it." He

turned to Saralinda. "Then the gift your father gave to Hagga has operated in the end to make you happy."

The Duke looked up and bared his teeth. "The tale is much too tidy for my taste," he snarled. "I hate it." He went on counting.

"It's neat," said Hark, "and, to *my* taste, refreshing." He removed his mask. His eyes were bright and jolly. "If I may introduce myself," he said, "I am a servant of the King, the good King Gwain of Yarrow."

"That," the Golux said, "I didn't know. You could have saved the Princess many years ago."

The servant of the King looked sad, and said, "This part I always hate to tell, but I was under a witch's spell."

"I weary of witches," the Golux said, "with due respect to Mother."

The Duke's smile showed his upper teeth. "I cannot even trust the spies I see," he muttered. His eye moved glassily around and saw the Golux. "You mere Device!" he gnarled. "You platitude! You Golux ex machina!"

"Quiet, please," the Golux said, "you gleaming thief."

"Nine hundred ninety-eight." The Duke was counting. "Nine hundred ninety-nine." He had counted all the jewels, and put them in a sack. There was none left on the table. He gave them all a look of horrid glee. "The Princess," said the Duke, "belongs to me."

A deathly silence filled the room. The Golux turned a little pale and his hand began to shake. He remembered something in the dark, coming down from Hagga's hill, that struck against his ankle, a sapphire or a ruby that had fallen from the sack. "One thousand," groaned the Duke, in a tone of vast surprise. A diamond had fallen from his glove, the left one, and no one but the Golux saw it fall. The Duke stood up and sneered. "What are you waiting for?" he shrieked. "Depart! If you be gone forever, it will not be long enough! If you return no more, then it will be too soon!" He slowly turned to Zorn. "What kind of knots?" he snarled.

"Turk's head," the young Prince said. "I learned them from my sister."

"Begone!" the cold Duke screamed again, and bathed his hands in rubies. "My jewels," he croaked, "will last forever."

The Golux, who had never tittered, tittered. The great doors of the oak room opened, and they left the cold Duke standing there, up to his wrists in diamonds.

"Yarrow," said the Prince, "is halfway on our journey." They stood outside the castle.

"You'll need these," said the Golux. He held the reins of two white horses. "Your ship lies in the harbor. It sails within the hour."

"It sails at midnight," Hark corrected him.

"I can't remember everything," the Golux said. "My father's clocks were always slow. He also lacked the power of concentration."

Zorn helped the Princess to her saddle. She gazed a last time at the castle. "A fair wind stands for Yarrow," said the Prince.

The Golux gazed a last time at the Princess. "Keep warm," he said. "Ride close together. Remember laughter. You'll need it even in the blessed isles of Ever After."

"There are no horses in the stables," mused the Prince. "Whence came these white ones?"

"The Golux has a lot of friends," said Hark. "I guess they give him horses when he needs them. But on the other hand, he may have made them up. He makes things up, you know."

"I know he does," sighed Zorn of Zorna. "You sail for Yarrow with us?"

"I must stay a fortnight longer," Hark replied. "So runs my witch's spell. It will give me time to tidy up, and untie Krang as well."

They looked around for the old Device, but he was there no longer. "Where has he gone?" cried Saralinda.

"Oh," said Hark, "he knows a lot of places."

"Give him," Saralinda said, "my love, and this." Hark took the rose.

The two white horses snorted snowy mist in the cool green glade that led down to the harbor. A fair wind stood for Yarrow and, looking far to sea, the Princess Saralinda thought she saw, as people often think they see, on clear and windless days, the distant shining shores of Ever After. Your guess is quite as good as mine (there are a lot of things that shine) but I have always thought she did, and I will always think so.

EPILOGUE

A fortnight later, the Duke was gloating over his jewels in the oak room when they suddenly turned to tears, with a little sound like sighing. The fringes of his glowing gloves were stained with Hagga's laughter. He staggered to his feet and drew his sword, and shouted, "Whisper!" In the courtyard of the castle six startled geese stopped hunting snails and looked up at the oak room. "What slish is *this*?" exclaimed the Duke, disgusted by the pool of melted gems leering on the table. His monocle fell, and he slashed his sword at silence and at nothing. Something moved across the room, like monkeys and like shadows. The torches on the walls went out, the two clocks stopped, and the room grew colder. There was a smell of old, unopened rooms and the sound of rabbits screaming. "Come on, you blob of glup," the cold Duke roared. "You may frighten octopi to death, you gibbous spawn of hate and thunder, but not the Duke of Coffin Castle!" He sneered. "Now that my precious gems have turned to thlup, living on, alone and cold, is not my fondest wish! On guard, you musty sofa!" The Todal gleeped. There was a stifled shriek and silence.

When Hark came into the room, holding a lighted lantern above his head, there was no one there. The Duke's sword lay gleaming on the floor, and from the table dripped the jewels of Hagga's laughter, that never last forever, like the jewels of sorrow, but turn again to tears a fortnight after. Hark stepped on something that squutched beneath his foot and flobbed against the wall. He picked it up and held it near the lantern. It was the small black ball stamped with scarlet owls. The last spy of the Duke of Coffin Castle, alone and lonely in the gloomy room, thought he heard, from somewhere far away, the sound of someone laughing.

FROM

THE THURBER ALBUM

Daguerreotype of a Lady

WHEN I FIRST became aware of Mrs. Albright in my world—at the age of three or four, I suppose—she was almost seventy, and a figure calculated to excite the retina and linger in the consciousness of any child. Aunt Margery, as everybody called her, was stout and round and, in the phrase of one of her friends, set close to the ground, like a cabbage. Her shortness was curiously exaggerated by the effect of an early injury. She had fractured her right kneecap in a fall on the ice when she was in her late teens, and the leg remained twisted, so that when she was standing, she bent over as if she were about to lean down and tie her shoelace, and her torso swayed from side to side when she walked, like the slow pendulum of an ancient clock, arousing sympathy in the old and wonder in the young. I used to marvel at the way she kept her balance, hobbling about in her garden after sundown, with a trowel in one hand and a sprinkling can in the other, her mouth tightening and her eyes closing every now and then when the misery seized her knee. She scorned the support of a cane; canes were for men, who were often feeble and tottery as early as their sixties. It took her a good ten minutes to mount the short staircase that led to the second floor of her home. She would grasp the banister with one hand and, with the other, pull her bad leg up beside her good one, pausing every few steps to catch her breath. She had to come downstairs backward, and this journey was even more laborious and painful. She got up before dawn every morning except Sunday the year around, and she rarely went to bed until after ten o'clock at night.

Aunt Margery was an active woman who got things done, and she did not always carry her cross with meekness and equanimity. She was capable of cursing her bad leg in good, round words that shocked women of more pious vocabulary. In her moments of repose, which were rare enough in a long and arduous lifetime, the gentleness of her face, enhanced by white hair smoothly parted in the middle, belied the energy of her body and the strength of her spirit, but her mouth grew firm, her eyes turned serious or severe, and her will overcame her handicap when she felt called upon, as she often did, to take up some burden too heavy for the shoulders of lesser women, or too formidable for mere menfolks to cope with. Her neighbors often summoned her in an hour of crisis, when there was illness in their homes, or a wife in labor, or a broken bone to set, for she was a natural nurse, renowned for her skill and wisdom and, as we shall see, for many an earthy remedy and forthright practice.

Mrs. Albright, born Margery Dangler more than a hundred and twenty years ago, in a time of stout-hearted and self-reliant women, came West in a covered wagon driven by her father, during the Presidency of Martin Van Buren, when she was only nine. The Danglers, before their westward venture, had lived in Long Branch, in New Jersey—she always used "in" before a state or county. The family settled for a time in Kokomo, in Indiana, and then retraced its steps to Ohio, to live in Lebanon, in Warren County, Degraff, in Logan County, and Arcanum and Greenville, in Darke County. (Judge Stacy Taylor also lingered awhile in Lebanon, but he had been gone for fifteen years when the Danglers reached that little town.) Shortly after the Civil War, Mrs. Albright came to Columbus, where she spent the last forty years of her life in the north half of a two-family frame house at the corner of Fifth Street and Walnut Alley. Her husband had died in Greenville the year the war ended, and she lived with her daughter Belle. When I first knew the neighborhood, at the turn of the century, Fifth Street was paved with cobblestones, and a genial City Council allowed a tall sycamore tree to stand squarely in the middle of the brick sidewalk in front of Mrs. Albright's house, dropping its puffballs in season. On the opposite side of the street, the deep-toned clock in the steeple of Holy Cross Church marked, in quarter hours, the passing of the four decades she lived there. It was a quiet part of town in those days, and the two-story frame house was one of the serene, substantial structures of my infancy and youth, for all its flimsy shabbiness.

Mrs. Albright and her daughter were poor. They took in sewing and washing and ironing, and there was always a roomer in the front room upstairs, but they often found it hard to scrape together ten dollars on the first of the month to pay Mr. Lisle, a landlord out of Horatio Alger, who collected his rents in person, and on foot. The sitting-room carpet was faded and, where hot coals from an iron stove had burned it, patched. There was no hot water unless you heated it on the coal stove in the dark basement kitchen, and light was supplied by what Mrs. Albright called coal-oil lamps. The old house was a firetrap, menaced by burning coal and by lighted lamps carried by ladies of dimming vision, but these perils, like economic facts, are happily lost on the very young. I spent a lot of time there as a child, and I thought it was a wonderful place, different from the dull formality of the ordinary home and in every difference enchanting. The floors were uneven, and various objects were used to keep the doors from closing: a fieldstone, a paving brick that Mrs. Albright had encased in a neat covering made of a piece of carpet, and a conch shell, in which you could hear the roaring of the sea when you held it to your ear. All the mirrors in the house were made of wavy glass, and reflected images in fascinating distortions. In the coal cellar, there was what appeared to be an outside toilet moved inside, miraculously connected with the city sewage system; and the lower sash of one of the windows in the sitting room was flush with the floor—a perfect place to sit and watch the lightning or the snow. Furthermore, the eastern wall of Jim West's livery stable rose less than fifteen feet away from Mrs. Albright's back stoop. Against this wall, there was a trellis of moonflowers, which popped open like small white parachutes at twilight in the summertime, and between the trellis and the stoop you could pull up water from a cistern in the veritable oaken bucket of the song. Over all this presided a great lady, fit, it seemed to me, to be the mother of King Arthur or, what was more, of Dick Slater and Bob Estabrook, captain and lieutenant, respectively, in the nickel novels, "Liberty Boys of '76."

I was reminded of Mrs. Albright not long ago when I ran across an old query of Emerson's: "Is it not an eminent convenience to have in your town a person who knows where arnica grows, or sassafras, or pennyroyal?" Mrs. Albright was skilled in using the pharmacopoeia of the woods and fields. She could have brought the great philosopher dozens of roots and leaves and barks, good for everything from ache to agony and from pukin' spells to a knotted gut. She could also have found in the countryside around Concord the proper plants for the treatment of asthma and other bronchial disturbances. She gathered belladonna, Jimson weed, and digitalis, made a mixture of them, added a solution of saltpetre, put the stuff in a bowl, and set it on fire. The patient simply bent over the bowl and inhaled the fumes. She knew where sour grass grew, which you chew for dyspepsy, and mint, excellent for the nau-shy, and the slippery elm, whose fragrant inner bark was the favorite demulcent of a hundred years ago—the thing to use for raw throat and other sore tishas.

Mrs. Albright's sitting room was often redolent of spirits of camphor, which could be applied to minor cuts (wet baking soda or cold mashed potato was the stuff for burns); rubbed on the forehead, for headache; used as a gargle or mouthwash, in a mild solution that was never mild enough for me; and sniffed, for attacks of dizzy spells or faintness. Such attacks in Mrs. Albright's own case might have been the result of lack of sleep or overwork, but they were never symptoms of the vapors or other feminine weaknesses. A dab of camphor on the back of each hand acted to break affectionate dogs of the habit of licking. Aunt Margery had owned a long line of af-fectionate dogs, the first of which, Tuney—named after her brother Tunis, who was later killed at Shiloh by a ramrod fired from a nervous Southern farmboy's musket—made the west-ward trip from Long Branch in the wagon with the Danglers. The last of the line, Cap, a brindle mongrel who looked like a worn carpetbag, caught the secret of vitality from his in-domitable mistress and lived to be sixteen, when Aunt Mar-gery, with heavy heart but steady hand, administered the ether that put a merciful end to the miserable burden of his years. That was the year Mrs. Albright adopted, fed, and reared a newborn mouse, whose mother had been annihilated in a trap set in the cellar to catch the largest rats I have ever seen. I say annihilated because it was surely the deadliest rat-trap in the world, made of a hickory plank, a powerful spring, and a heavy iron ring that could have killed a full-grown cat when it let

go. Once, Mrs. Albright cornered in the cellar the ugly patri-
arch of all rats, who had found a safe way to get at the cheese
in the trap, and she whammed its life out with a lump of coal.

Shelves in Mrs. Albright's sitting room, where they were
handy to get at, held alum, for canker sores; coca butter, for
the chest; paregoric, for colic and diarrhea; laudanum, for
pain; balsam apples, for poultices; bismuth, for the bowels;
magneeshy (carbonate of magnesium), a light, chalky substance, wrapped in blue paper, that was an antacid and a gentle
laxative; and calomel and blue mass, regarded by women of
Aunt Margery's generation as infallible regulators of the liver.
Blue mass came in the form of pills, and she made it by rubbing up metallic mercury with confection of roses. Blue mass
and calomel are no longer found in every house, as they were
in Mrs. Albright's day, and the free and easy use of paregoric
and laudanum, both tinctures of opium, has long been
frowned upon by doctors. Your druggist may have heard of
balsam apples, alias balsam pears, but unless he is an elderly
man, he has probably never seen one. The poultice of today
has no source so picturesque as the balsam apple, a warty,
oblong West Indian fruit, tropical red or orange in color. It
was used for decoration, too, a hundred years ago and more,
and looked nice on a window sill with love apples turning
from green to red. One legend has it, by the way, that the
first American tomato was eaten in 1820, by a gentleman of
Salem, in New Jersey, a town not far from Long Branch,
where Margery Albright was born ten years after this startling
and foolhardy act. I was pleased to find out from my pharmacist, Mr. Blakely, of Crutch & Macdonald's drugstore, in
Litchfield, Connecticut, that folks in small towns and rural
regions still favor slippery elm for sore throat. No housewife
actually strips the bark from the tree nowadays, the way Mrs.
Albright did, but slippery-elm lozenges, manufactured by the
Henry Thayer Company (founded 1847) from a formula more
than ninety years old, are bought by many people in wet or
wintry weather. I got a box of the lozenges from Mr. Blakely
myself and tried a couple. They smelled faintly like fertilizer
to my snobbish city nose, but their taste was bland enough
and inoffensive. I am sure they soothe the inflamed tishas of
the throat. Mr. Blakely also said that people from seventy to

a hundred years old drop in now and then for blue pills when their liver is kicking up. When I asked him about balsam apples, he told me he knew what they were, but he confessed that he had never seen one. It made me feel old and odd, suddenly, as if I were a contemporary of Aunt Margery's who had lived beyond his time.

Aunt Margery held that cold black coffee—not iced, just cold—was fine for torpor, depression of the spirits, and fatigue. She also used it to disguise the taste of castor oil for timid palates, but she drank the oil straight from the bottle herself, in great, gulping dollops that made me flinch and shudder when I was a boy. For gas on the stomach, and for gentlemen who had brought out the jugs the night before, she made a fizzing mixture of vinegar, sugar, and baking soda. Soda crackers soaked in water were excellent for thinning out the blood in cases that were not severe enough for leeches or the letting of a vein. If you fell down and broke the skin on your elbow or your knee, she kept a sharp lookout for the appearance of proud flesh. In the event of serious injuries, such as gunshot wounds or axe cuts, you had to beware of gangrum. It was easy enough to identify this awful disease as gangrene, but I was well out of my teens before I discovered what "blue boars" are, or, rather, is. Mrs. Albright had described it as a knotted groin, a symptom of the Black Death, at least one siege of which she had survived somewhere in her travels. The true name is "buboes," from which the word "bubonic" is derived, and Webster supports Mrs. Albright in her definition of the malady as a knotted groin. Then there was cholera morbus, which sounds Asiatic and deadly, but is really no more serious, I found in looking it up the other day, than summer complaint accompanied by green-apple bellyache. If you had the jumpin' toothache, there was nothing better than a large chaw of tobacco. Once, when she was sixteen, Margery Albright was out horseback-riding with a gallant of her acquaintance who bore the gloomy name of Aubrey Hogwood. A jumpin' toothache nearly knocked her from the saddle, and Hogwood, not knowing what the trouble was, paled and stammered when she demanded his tobacco pouch. ("I says to him, 'Hogwood,' says I, 'hand me your pouch.'") She took a man-sized helping of the weed and chewed it lustily. The toothache went away, and so did Hogwood. A pallid romantic of queasy stomach, he drifted out of the realistic maiden's life. In Greenville, in Darke County, not long afterward, she married one John Albright, a farmer, whom she was destined to pull out of what I will always think of as the Great Fever.

One day in Darke County, Albright—his wife always called him by his last name—staggered in from the fields, pale and ganted—this was her word for "gaunt"—and took to his bed with an imposing fever and fits of the shakes that rattled the china in the cupboard. She was not yet thirty at the time, but already a practical nurse of considerable experience, famous in her neighborhood for her cool presence at sickbeds and her competence as a midwife. She had nursed Albright through a bad case of janders—jaundice to you and me. Her celebrated chills-and-fever medicine, with which she dosed me more than once fifty years after Albright's extremity, failed to do any good. It was a fierce liquid, compounded of the bitterest roots in the world and heavily spiked with quinine, and it seared your throat, burned your stomach, and set your eyes to streaming, but several doses left Albright's forehead still as hot as the bottom of a flatiron. His wife was jubrous—her word for "dubious"—about his chances of pulling through this strange seizure. Albright tossed all night and moaned and whinkered—a verb she made up herself out of "whinny" and "whicker"—and in the morning his temperature had not gone down. She tested his forehead with the flat of her sensitive hand, for she held that thermometers were just pieces of glass used to keep patients' mouths closed while the doctors thought up something to say about conditions that baffled them. The average doctor, in her opinion, was an educated fool, who fussed about a sickroom, fretted the patient, and got in a body's way. The pontifical doctor was likely to be named, in her pungent idiom, a pus-gut, and the talkative doctor, with his fluent bedside manner, was nothing more than a whoop in a whirlwind.

In the afternoon of the second day of the Great Fever, John Albright's wife knew what she had to do. She went out into the pasture and gathered a pailful of sheep droppings, which she referred to in the flattest possible terms. Sheep droppings were not the only thing that Mrs. Albright looked for in the pasture and the barnyard to assist her ministrations as a natural nurse. Now and then, in the case of a stubborn pregnancy, she would cut a quill from a chicken feather, fill it with powdered tobacco, and blow the contents up one nostril of the expectant mother. This would induce a fit of sneezing that acted to dislodge the most reluctant baby. Albright, whinkering on his bed of pain, knew what she was up to this time, and he began to gag even before the terrible broth was brewing on the kitchen stove. She got it down him somehow, possibly with a firm hand behind his neck and one knee on his stomach. I heard the story of this heroic cure—for cure it was—a dozen times. Albright lay about the house for a day or two, retching and protesting, but before the week was out, he was back at his work in the fields. He died, a few years later, of what his widow called a jaggered kidney stone, and she moved, with her daughter, to Columbus, where she worked for a while as housekeeper of the old American House, a hotel that nobody now remembers. She liked to tell about the tidiest lodger she ever had to deal with, the Honorable Stephen A. Douglas, who kept his room neat as a pin and sometimes even made his own bed. He was a little absent-minded, though, and left a book behind him when he checked out. She could not remember the title of the book or what became of it.

Margery Albright was a woman's woman, who put little faith in the integrity and reliability of the average male. From farmhand to physician, men were the frequent object of her colorful scorn, especially the mealymouthed, and the lazy, the dull, and the stupid, who "sat around like Stoughton bottles"—a cryptic damnation that charmed me as a little boy. I am happy to report that Webster has a few words to say about Dr. Stoughton and the bottle that passed into the workaday idiom of the last century. Stoughton, an earlier Dr. Munyon or Father John, made and marketed an elixir of wormwood, germander, rhubarb, orange peel, cascarilla, and aloes. It was used to flavor alcoholic beverages and as a spring tonic for winter-weary folks. It came in a bottle that must have been squat, juglike, and heavy. Unfortunately, my Webster does not have a picture, or even a description, of the old container that became a household word. The dictionary merely says, "To sit, stand, etc., like a Stoughton bottle: to sit, stand, etc., stolidly and dumbly." Mrs. Albright's figure of speech gave the Stoughton bottle turgid action as well as stolid posture. Only a handful of the husbands and fathers she knew were alert or efficient enough to escape the name of Stoughton bottle.

Aunt Margery lived to be eighty-eight years old, surviving, I am constrained to say, the taking of too much blue mass and calomel. She was salivated, as she called it, at least once a year. This, according to my pharmacist, means that she suffered from mercurial poisoning, as the result of an incautious use of calomel. In spite of everything, her strength and vigor held out to the end, and I can remember no single time that she permitted a doctor to look after her. Her daughter Belle held the medical profession in less contempt, and once, in her fiftieth year, after ailing for several months, she went to see a physician in the neighborhood. He was greatly concerned about her condition and called a colleague into consultation. The result of their joint findings was a dark prognosis indeed. The patient was given not more than a year to live. When Mrs. Albright heard the news, she pushed herself out of her rocking chair and stormed about the room, damning the doctors with such violence that her right knee turned in on her like a flamingo's and she had to be helped back to her chair. Belle recovered from whatever it was that was wrong, and when she died, also at the age of eighty-eight, she had outlived by more than fifteen years the last of the two doctors who had condemned her to death. Mrs. Albright never forgave, or long forgot, the mistaken medical men. Every so often, apropos of little or nothing, she would mutter imprecations on their heads. I can remember only two doctors whom she treated with anything approaching respect. She would josh these doctors now and then, when their paths crossed in some sickroom, particularly on the subject of their silly theory that air and water were filled with invisible agencies of disease. This, to a natural nurse who had mastered the simple techniques of barnyard and pasture, was palpable nonsense. "How, then," Dr. Rankin asked her once, "do you account for the spread of an epidemic?" "It's just the contagion," said Mrs. Albright. The doctor gave this a moment of studious thought. "It's just possible," he said, "that we may both be right."

Dr. Dunham, one of her favorites—if I may use so strong a word—arrived late at a house on Parsons Avenue on the night of December 8, 1894. I had got there ahead of him, with the assistance of Mrs. Albright. "You might have spared your horse," she snapped when he finally showed up. "We managed all right without you." But she was jubrous about something, and she decided to take it up with the doctor. "He has too much hair on his head for a male child," she told him. "Ain't it true that they don't grow up to be bright?" Dr. Dunham gave the matter his usual grave consideration. "I believe that holds good only when the hair is thicker at the temples than this infant's," he said. "By the way, I wouldn't discuss the matter with the mother." Fortunately for my own peace of mind, I was unable to understand English at the time. It was a source of great satisfaction to Margery Albright, and not a little surprise, when it became evident, in apt season, that I was going to be able to grasp my mother tongue and add, without undue effort, two and two. I have had my own jubrous moments, however. There was the time when, at forty-three, I sweated and strained to shove an enormous bed nearer the lamp on a small table, instead of merely lifting the small table and placing it nearer the enormous bed. There have been other significant instances, too, but this is the story of Aunt Margery Albright.

I remember the time in 1905 when the doctors thought my father was dying, and the morning someone was wise enough to send for Aunt Margery. We went to get her in my grandfather's surrey. It was an old woodcut of a morning. I can see Mrs. Albright, dressed in her best black skirt and percale blouse (she pronounced it "percal"), bent over before the oval mirror of a cherrywood bureau, tying the velvet ribbons of an antique bonnet under her chin. People turned to stare at the lady out of Lincoln's day as we helped her to the curb. The carriage step was no larger than the blade of a hoe, and getting Aunt Margery, kneecap and all, into the surrey was an impressive operation. It was the first time she had been out of her own dooryard in several years, but she didn't enjoy the

April drive. My father was her favorite person in the world, and they had told her he was dying. Mrs. Albright's encounter with Miss Wilson, the registered nurse on the case, was a milestone in medical history—or, at least, it was for me. The meeting between the starched young lady in white and the bent old woman in black was the meeting of the present and the past, the newfangled and the old-fashioned, the ritualistic and the instinctive, and the shock of antagonistic schools of thought clashing sent out cold sparks. Miss Wilson was coolly disdainful, and Mrs. Albright plainly hated her crisp guts. The patient, ganted beyond belief, recognized Aunt Margery, and she began to take over, in her ample, accustomed way. The showdown came on the third day, when Miss Wilson returned from lunch to find the patient propped up in a chair before a sunny window, sipping, of all outrageous things, a cup of cold coffee, held to his lips by Mrs. Albright, who was a staunch believer in getting a patient up out of bed. All the rest of her life, Aunt Margery, recalling the scene that followed, would mimic Miss Wilson's indignation, crying in a shrill voice, "It shan't be done!" waving a clenched fist in the air, exaggerating the young nurse's wrath. "It shan't be done!" she would repeat, relaxing at last with a clutch at her protesting kneecap and a satisfied smile. For Aunt Margery won out, of course, as the patient, upright after many horizontal weeks, began to improve. The doctors were surprised and delighted, Miss Wilson tightly refused to comment, Mrs. Albright took it all in her stride. The day after the convalescent was able to put on his clothes and walk a little way by himself, she was hoisted into the surrey again and driven home. She enjoyed the ride this time. She asked the driver to stop for a moment in front of the marble house at Washington and Town, built by Dr. S. B. Hartman out of the profits of Peruna, a tonic far more popular than Dr. Stoughton's, even if the bottle it came in never did make Webster's dictionary.

The old frame house in Columbus and the old sycamore tree that shaded it disappeared a long time ago, and a filling station now stands on the northwest corner of Fifth Street and Walnut Alley, its lubricating pit about where Mrs. Albright's garden used to be. The only familiar landmark of my

youth is the church across the way, whose deep-toned clock
still marks the passing of the quarter hours as tranquilly as
ever. When Belle died in 1937, in another house on Fifth
Street, the family possessions were scattered among the friends
who had looked after her in her final years. I sometimes wonder who got the photograph album that had been promised
to me; the card table, bought for a dollar or two before the
Civil War, but now surely an antique of price and value; the
two brown plaster-of-Paris spaniels that stood on either end
of the mantel in Mrs. Albright's bedroom; and the muddy
color print that depicted the brave and sturdy Grace Darling
pulling away from a yellow lighthouse on her famous errand
of mercy. I have no doubt that some of the things were
thrown away: the carpet-covered brick, the fieldstone, the
green tobacco tin that Aunt Margery used for a button box,
and the ragbag filled with silk cuttings for the crazy quilts she
made. Who could have guessed that a writer living in the East
would cherish such objects as these, or that he would have
settled for one of the dark and wavy mirrors, or the window
sash in the sitting room that was flush with the floor?

I sometimes wonder, too, what has happened to the people
who used to call so often when Aunt Margery was alive. I can
remember all the tenants of the front room upstairs, who came
and went: Vernie, who clerked in a store; the fabulous Doc
Marlowe, who made and sold Sioux Liniment and wore a ten-
gallon hat with kitchen matches stuck in the band; the blonde
and mysterious Mrs. Lane, of the strong perfume and the
elegant dresses; Mr. Richardson, a guard at the penitentiary,
who kept a gun in his room; and a silent, thin, smiling man
who never revealed his business and left with his rent two
weeks in arrears. I remember Dora and Sarah Koontz, daughters of a laborer, who lived for many years in the other half
of the two-family house, and the visitors who dropped in from
time to time: Mr. Pepper and his daughter Dolly, who came
to play cards on summer evenings; Mrs. Straub, who babbled
of her children—her Clement and her Minna; Joe Chickalilli,
a Mexican rope thrower; and Professor Fields, a Stoughton
bottle if there ever was one, who played the banjo and helped
Doc Marlowe sell the liniment that Mrs. Albright and Belle
put up in bottles; and the Gammadingers and their brood,

who lived on a farm in the Hocking Valley. Most of them were beholden to Mrs. Albright for some service or other in time of trouble, and they all adored her.

When Margery Albright took to her bed for the last time—the bed in the front room downstairs, where she could hear people talking and life stirring in the street outside her window—she gave strict orders that she was not to be "called back." She had seen too much of that, at a hundred bedsides, and she wanted to die quietly, without a lot of unseemly fuss over the natural ending of a span of nearly ninety complete and crowded years. There was no call, she told her daughter, to summon anybody. There was nothing anybody could do. A doctor would just pester her, and she couldn't abide one now. Her greatest comfort lay in the knowledge that her plot in Green Lawn Cemetery had been paid for, a dollar at a time, through the years, and that there was money enough for a stone marker tucked away in a place her daughter knew about. Mrs. Albright made Belle repeat to her the location of this secret and precious cache. Then she gave a few more final instructions and turned over in bed, pulling her bad leg into a comfortable position. "Hush up!" she snapped when her daughter began to cry. "You give a body the fidgets."

Women who were marked for death, Aunt Margery had often told me, always manifested, sooner or later, an ominous desire to do something beyond the range of their failing strength. These ladies in the very act of dying fancied, like Verdi's Violetta, that life was returning in full and joyous tide. They wanted to sit up in bed and comb their hair, or alter a dress, or bathe the cat, or change the labels on the jam jars. It was an invariable sign that the end was not far off. Old Mrs. Dozier, who had insisted on going to the piano to play "Abide with Me," collapsed with a discordant jangle on the keys and was dead when they carried her back to the bed. Mrs. Albright's final urge, with which her ebbing sense no doubt sternly dealt, might easily have been to potter about in her garden, since it was coming summer and the flowers needed constant attention. It was a narrow plot, occasionally enlivened with soil from the country, that began with an elephant-ear near the rickety wooden fence in front and

extended to the trellis of moonflowers against the wall of Jim
West's stable. It was further shaded by her own house and the
Fenstermakers', and it caught only stingy glimpses of the sun,
but, to the wonder of the jubrous, it sustained for forty summers Canterbury bells and bluebells, bleeding hearts and fuch-
sias, asters and roses. There were tall stalks of asparagus, raised
for ornament, and castor-oil plants six feet high (I doubt that
she made the castor oil that she disguised in coffee for timid
palates and drank neat from the bottle herself, but I have no
doubt she could have). "This garden," said Dr. Sparks, pastor
of the old Third Street Methodist Church, one day, "is a tes-
tament of faith." "It takes faith, and it takes work, and it takes
a lot of good, rich manure," said Mrs. Albright, far and away
the most distinguished manurist of her time.

Since there had to be services of some kind, in accordance
with a custom that irked her, Mrs. Albright would have preferred a country parson, who rode a horse in any weather and
could lend a hand at homely chores, if need be. She liked what
she called a man of groin, who could carry his proper share
of the daily burden and knew how to tell a sow from a saw-
buck. City ministers, in her estimation, were delicate fellows,
given to tampering with the will of God, and with the mysteries of life after death, which the Almighty would have
cleared up for people Himself if He had had a mind to. It was
her fancy that urban reverends were inclined to insanity, because of their habit of studying. "Studying," in Mrs. Albright's language, meant that form of meditation in which the
eyes are lifted up. The worst cases let their gaze slowly follow,
about a room, the juncture of ceiling and walls, and once a
pastor developed this symptom, he was in imminent danger
of going off his worshipful rocker. Such parsons, whether they
studied or not, made Mrs. Albright uneasy, except for the
Reverend Stacy Matheny, a first cousin of my mother's. He
had been born on a farm in Fairfield County, and he knew
how to hitch a horse, split a rail, and tell a jaybird from a
bootjack. Mrs. Albright wanted him to read her funeral service
because he was a man of few words, and he would get it over
with and not whinker all afternoon, keeping people away from
their jobs. Aunt Margery never discussed religion with me or
with anyone else. She seemed to take it for granted that the

Lord would find a fitting place in Heaven for women who devoted their lives to good works, and she let it go at that. The men would have to save their own souls, and the Devil take the hindmost.

The Reverend Stacy Matheny compared the late Margery Albright to the virtuous woman of proverbs, who rose while it was yet night, worked willingly with her hands, and ate not the bread of idleness. The original lady of the tribute was, of course, far richer in wordly goods than Mrs. Albright, whose clothing was not silk and purple, but in trait and toil and temper they were rare and similar examples of that noble breed of women the French call *brave et travailleuse*. I wished that some closer student of Aunt Margery could have taken over those final rites, whose formality would have annoyed the great lady as much as the lugubrious faces of her friends and neighbors. Somebody should have told how she snatched up a pair of scissors one day and cut a hornet in two when it lighted on the head of a sleeping baby; and how she took an axe and chopped off the head of a savage outlaw cat that killed chickens, attacked children, and, blackest sin of all, disturbed the sleep of a woman patient; and about the time she whipped off her calico blouse, put it over the eyes of a frightened horse, and led him out of a burning barn while the menfolks, at a safe distance, laughed at her corset cover and cheered her courage. But it would have taken all afternoon to do even faint justice to the saga of Mrs. Albright, born Margery Dangler, more than a hundred and twenty years ago, in Long Branch, in New Jersey, who departed this earthly scene June 6, 1918, in the confident hope—as old epitaphs used to say— of the blessed resurrection and the life eternal. It seemed to me, standing there in the dim parlor of the old frame house, that something as important as rain had gone out of the land.

The services came to a close with the singing of "No Night There" by two tearful women, who sang it as only middle-aged Methodist females in Ohio can sing a hymn—upper register all the way, nasal, tremulous, and loud. Mrs. Albright, I reflected, would enjoy the absence of night in Paradise only because everlasting light would give her more time to look after people and to get things done. I still like to believe, after all these years, that chalcedony is subject to cleaning, and that a foolish angel falls now and then and breaks a wing, for glory, as mere reward of labors ended, would make Margery Albright uncomfortable and sad. I trust that Providence has kept this simple truth in mind.

Lavender with a Difference

BELINDA WOOLF telephoned my mother at the Southern Hotel in Columbus one morning three years ago, and apologized, in a faintly familiar voice, for never having run in to call on her. Something always seemed to turn up, she declared, to keep her from dropping by for a visit, and she was sorry. "I've thought of you, Mrs. Thurber," said Belinda. "I've thought of you every day since I worked for you on Champion Avenue. It's been a long time, hasn't it?" It certainly had. Belinda Woolf was only twenty-three years old when she came to work for us as cook in the Spring of 1899, and she was seventy-three when she finally got around to calling her former employer. Exactly half a century had gone by since my mother had heard her voice. Belinda had thought of telephoning for more than eighteen thousand days but, as she indicated, more than eighteen thousand things had turned up to prevent her.

About a year after Belinda's appearance out of the past, I went to Columbus, and my mother and I drove out to see her. She is now the wife of Joe Barlow, master carpenter of the Neil House, where Charles Dickens used to stay, during his western trips a hundred years ago. In fifty years Belinda had not wandered very far. She was living only two blocks from our old house on South Champion Avenue. The weather was warm and we sat on the verandah and talked about a night in 1899 that we all remembered. It was past midnight, according to an old clock in the attic of my memory, when Belinda suddenly flung open a window of her bedroom and fired two shots from a .32-calibre revolver at the shadowy figure of a man skulking about in our backyard. Belinda's shooting frightened off the prowler and aroused the family. I was five years old, going on six, at the time, and I had thought that only soldiers and policemen were allowed to have guns. From then on I stood in awe, but not in fear, of the lady who kept a revolver under her pillow. "It was a lonesome place, wasn't it?" said Belinda, with a sigh, "way out there at the end of nowhere." We sat for awhile without talking, thinking about the lonesome place at the end of nowhere.

No. 921 South Champion Avenue is just another house now, in a long row of houses, but when we lived there, in 1899 and 1900, it was the last house on the street. Just south of us the avenue dwindled to a wood road that led into a thick grove of oak and walnut trees, long since destroyed by the southward march of asphalt. Our nearest neighbor on the north was fifty yards away, and across from us was a country meadow that ticked with crickets in the summertime and turned yellow with goldenrod in the fall. Living on the edge of town, we rarely heard footsteps at night, or carriage wheels, but the darkness, in every season, was deepened by the lonely sound of locomotive whistles. I no longer wonder, as I did when I was six, that Aunt Mary Van York, arriving at dusk for her first visit to us, looked about her disconsolately, and said to my mother, "Why in the world do you want to live in this godforsaken place, Mary?"

Almost all my memories of the Champion Avenue house have as their focal point the lively figure of my mother. I remember her tugging and hauling at a burning mattress and finally managing to shove it out a bedroom window onto the roof of the front porch, where it smoldered until my father came home from work and doused it with water. When he asked his wife how the mattress happened to catch fire, she told him the peculiar truth (all truths in that house were peculiar)—that his youngest son, Robert, had set it on fire with a buggy whip. It seemed he had lighted the lash of the whip in the gas grate of the nursery and applied it to the mattress. I also have a vivid memory of the night my mother was alone in the house with her three small sons and set the oil-splashed bowl of a kerosene lamp on fire, trying to light the wick, and herded all of us out of the house, announcing that it was going to explode. We children waited across the street in high anticipation, but the spilled oil burned itself out and, to our bitter disappointment, the house did not go up like a sky-rocket to scatter colored balloons among the stars. My mother claims that my brother William, who was seven at the time, kept crying, "Try it again, Mama, try it again," but she is a famous hand at ornamenting a tale, and there is no way of telling whether he did or not.

My brightest remembrance of the old house goes back to the confused and noisy second and last visit of Aunt Mary, who had cut her first visit short because she hated our two dogs—Judge, an irritable old pug, and Sampson, a restless water spaniel—and they hated her. She had snarled at them and they had growled at her all during her stay with us, and not even my mother remembers how she persuaded the old lady to come back for a weekend, but she did, and, what is more, she cajoled Aunt Mary into feeding "those dreadful brutes" the evening she arrived.

In preparation for this seemingly simple act of household routine, my mother had spent the afternoon gathering up all the dogs of the neighborhood, in advance of Aunt Mary's appearance, and putting them in the cellar. I had been allowed to go with her on her wonderful forays, and I thought that we were going to keep all the sixteen dogs we rounded up. Such an adventure does not have to have logical point or purpose in the mind of a six-year-old, and I accepted as a remarkable but natural phenomenon my mother's sudden assumption of the stature of Santa Claus.

She did not always let my father in on her elaborate pranks, but he came home that evening to a house heavy with tension and suspense, and she whispered to him the peculiar truth that there were a dozen and a half dogs in the cellar, counting our Judge and Sampson. "What are you up to now, Mame?" he asked her, and she said she just wanted to see Aunt Mary's face when the dogs swarmed up into the kitchen. She could not recall where she had picked up all of the dogs, but I remembered, and still do, that we had imprisoned the Johnsons' Irish terrier, the Eiseles' shepherd, and the Mitchells' fox terrier, among others. "Well, let's get it over with, then," my father said nervously. "I want to eat dinner in peace, if that is possible."

The big moment finally arrived. My mother, full of smiles and insincerity, told Aunt Mary that it would relieve her of a tedious chore—and heaven knows, she added, there were a thousand steps to take in that big house—if the old lady would be good enough to set down a plate of dog food in the kitchen at the head of the cellar stairs and call Judge and Sampson to their supper. Aunt Mary growled and grumbled, and consigned all dogs to the fires of hell, but she grudgingly took the plate, and carried it to the kitchen, with the Thurber family on her heels. "Heavenly days!" cried Aunt Mary. "Do you make a ceremony out of feeding these brutes?" She put the plate down and reached for the handle of the door.

None of us has ever been able to understand why bedlam hadn't broken loose in the cellar long before this, but it hadn't. The dogs were probably so frightened by their unique predicament that their belligerence had momentarily left them. But when the door opened and they could see the light of freedom and smell the odor of food, they gave tongue like a pack of hunting hounds. Aunt Mary got the door halfway open and the bodies of three of the largest dogs pushed it the rest of the way. There was a snarling, barking, yelping swirl of yellow and white, black and tan, gray and brindle as the dogs tumbled into the kitchen, skidded on the linoleum, sent the food flying from the plate, and backed Aunt Mary into a corner. "Great God Almighty!" she screamed. "It's a dog factory!" She was only five feet tall, but her counterattack was swift and terrible. Grabbing a broom, she opened the back door and the kitchen windows, and began to beat and flail at the army of canines, engaged now in half a dozen separate battles over the scattered food. Dogs flew out the back door and leaped through the windows, but some of them ran up-stairs, and three or four others hid under sofas and chairs in the parlor. The indignant snarling and cursing of Judge and Sampson rose above even the laughter of my mother and the delighted squeals of her children. Aunt Mary whammed her way from room to room, driving dogs ahead of her. When the last one had departed and the upset house had been put back in order, my father said to his wife, "Well, Mame, I hope you're satisfied." She was.

Aunt Mary, toward the end of her long life, got the curious notion that it was my father and his sons, and not my mother, who had been responsible for the noisy flux of "all those brutes." Years later, when we visited the old lady on one of her birthdays, she went over the story again, as she always did, touching it up with distortions and magnifications of her own. Then she looked at the male Thurbers in slow, rueful turn, sighed deeply, gazed sympathetically at my mother, and said, in her hollowest tone, "Poor Mary!"

Only a few months after poor Mary borrowed the neighbors' dogs, she "bought" the Simonses' house. It was a cold, blocky house, not far from ours, and its owner had been trying to sell it for a long time. The thing had become a standing joke among the Frioleras, a club of young married couples to which the Simonses and my father and mother belonged. It was generally believed that Harry and Laura would never get the big, damp place off their hands. Then, late one dark afternoon, a strange and avid purchaser showed up. It was my mother, wearing dark glasses, her hair and eyebrows whitened with flour, her cheeks lightly shadowed with charcoal to make them look hollow, and her upper front teeth covered with the serrated edge of a soda cracker. On one side of her, as she pressed the doorbell of the Simonses' house, stood a giggling cousin of hers, named Belle Cook, and I was on her other side; we were there to prevent a prolonged scrutiny of the central figure of our trio. Belle was to pose as my mother's daughter, and I was to be Belle's son. Simons had never met Miss Cook, and my mother was confident that he wouldn't recognize me. His wife, Laura, would have penetrated her friend's disguise at once, or, failing that, she would surely have phoned the police, for the weird visitor seemed, because of her sharp, projecting teeth, both demented and about to spring, but my mother had found out that Laura would not be home. When she made herself up, an hour before, I had watched her transformation from mother to witch with a mixture of wonder and worry that lingered in my memory for years.

Harry Simons, opening his front door on that dark evening in the age of innocence, when trust flowered as readily as suspicion does today, was completely taken in by the sudden apparition of an eccentric elderly woman who babbled of her recently inherited fortune and said she had passed his house the day before and fallen in love with it. Simons was a big, jovial, sanguine man, expert at business deals in a lighted office but a setup for my mother's deviltry at dusk. When she praised every room she stumbled into and every object she bumped against—she wouldn't take off her dark glasses in the lamplit gloom—a wild hope must have glazed his eye, disarming his perception. He admitted later, when the cat was out of the bag, that Belle's idiotic laughter, and mine, at everything that was said had disturbed him, especially when it was provoked by my mother's tearful account of the sad death of her mythical husband, a millionaire oil man. But idiocy in a family is one thing, and money is another. Mrs. Prentice, or Douglas, or whatever she called herself, was rolling in money that day. She upped Simons' asking price for the house by several thousand dollars, on the ground that she wouldn't think of paying as little as ten thousand for such a lovely place. When she found out that the furniture was for sale, she upped the price on that, too, promising to send her check through her lawyers the next day. By this time, she was overacting with fine abandon, but the overwhelmed Simons was too far gone in her land of fantasy for reality to operate. On her way out of the house, she picked up small portable things—a vase, a travelling clock, a few books—remarking that, after all, they now belonged to her. Still Simons' wits did not rally, and all of a sudden the three of us were out in the street again—my mother who had been my grandmother, her cousin who had been my mother, and me. I feel that this twisted hour marked the occupation of my mind by a sense of confusion that has never left it.

My father was home from work when we got back, and he gasped at the sight of his wife, even though she had thrown away her cracker teeth. When these latest goings on were explained to him, he was all for taking his friend's possessions over to his unsold house and returning them, with nervous apologies. But my mother had another idea. That night she gift-wrapped, separately, the vase, the clock, and the books, and they were delivered to Simons' door the next morning, before he set out for his office, each "present" containing a card that read, "To Harry Simons from Mame Thurber with love." It was not my mother's most subdued performance, but it was certainly one of her outstanding triumphs. The Frioleras laughed about it for years. It is among my mother's major sorrows that of the fifty members of that merry club, founded in 1882, there are only three still alive. At one of their parties fifty years ago—they played pedro and euchre in the winter and went on picnics and bicycle trips in the summer— my father asked his wife, apropos of what prank I do not know, "How long do you expect to keep up this kind of thing, Mame?" She thought a moment and replied, "Why, until I'm eighty, I suppose."

Mary Agnes Thurber, eldest of the six children of William and Katherine Fisher, was eighty years old in January, 1946, and I went to Columbus for a birthday party that brought together scores of her relatives. The day after the event, a columnist in one of the Columbus papers recklessly described her as "a bit of lavender and old lace." She was indignant. "Why, he doesn't even know about the time I threw those eggs!" she exclaimed. I didn't know about it, either, but I found out. At a meeting, a few months before, of one of the several women's clubs she belongs to, she had gone to the kitchen of her hostess' house, carefully removed a dozen eggs from a cardboard container, and returned to the living room to reactivate a party that she felt was growing dull. Balancing the box on the palm of her hand, like a halfback about to let go a forward pass, she cried, "I've always wanted to throw a dozen eggs, and now I'm going to do it!" The ladies gathered in the room squealed and scattered as the carton sailed into the air. Then it drifted harmlessly to the floor. Lavender and old lace, in their conventional and symbolic sense, are not for Mary Thurber. It would be hard for me to say what is. Now, at eighty-six, she never wears black. "Black is for old ladies," she told me scornfully not long ago.

In 1884, when Mamie Fisher got out of high school, she wanted to go on the stage, but her unladylike and godless urge was discouraged by her family. Aunt Melissa warned her that young actresses were in peril not only of hellfire but of lewd Shakespearean actors, skilled in the arts of seduction, and she pointed out that there was too much talk about talent in the world, and not enough about virtue. She predicted that God's wrath would be visited, in His own time, upon all

theatres, beginning, like as not, with those in Paris, France.
Mamie Fisher listened with what appeared to be rapt and contrite attention. Actually, she was studying Aunt Melissa's voice,
so that she could learn to imitate it.

Deprived of a larger audience, the frustrated comedienne
performed for whoever would listen, and once distressed a
couple of stately guests in her father's home by descending
the front stairs in her dressing gown, her hair tumbling and
her eyes staring, to announce that she had escaped from the
attic, where she was kept because of her ardent and hapless
love for Mr. Briscoe, the postman. An entry in her diary of
that period, dated Monday, May 14, 1888, would have puzzled
the shocked visitors: "Went over to Flora's to talk over yesterday's visit. I tell you that Ira D. is cute, but I do not like
him very well—he is a perfect gentleman, only he will insist
on kissing me every time and I will not allow it. I can truth-
fully say I never kissed a fellow in all my life but once, and
that was Charlie Thurber at the depot a few years ago."

Those of her relatives who drew no sharp line between life
and art, the gifted and the mad, and consoled themselves with
the hope that marriage would settle her down, could not have
been more mistaken. Even the birth of her third son, in 1896,
had little effect on her merry inventions, and her aunts must
have been relieved when we left Champion Avenue and
moved to Washington, D.C., in 1901. They probably thought
of Washington, in those years, as a city of inviolable decorum,
but it was there that we met a young Cleveland newspaperman
named George Marvin, whose gaiety was to enrich our lives.
He was a superior wag, with a round, mobile face, a trick of
protruding his large eyeballs that entranced the Thurber boys,
and a gift of confusion that matched my mother's. Uncivil
clerks and supercilious shoppe proprietors in the nation's capital came to regret their refusal to sell Marvin and my mother
one dish of ice cream with two spoons, or a single glove for
the left hand, or one shoe. The mild, soft-spoken Jekylls from
the Middle West would be transformed into Mr. and Mrs.
Hyde, to the consternation of the management. "Senator
Beveridge will hear about this!" Marvin would shout, and
they would stalk out of the shoppe, in high and magnificent
dudgeon. But it was when we were all back in Columbus two

years later that these comics reached their heights. Their finest hour arrived one day at Memorial Hall, during a lecture given by a woman mental healer whose ability and sincerity my mother held in low esteem. She has always been a serious and devoted student of psychotherapy, even when it was known and practiced under foolish and flowery names, and she learned long ago to detect tommyrot. Arriving after the lecture had begun, our cutups found an empty wheelchair in the lobby, and my mother, bundled up in it, was rolled down the aisle by her confederate. The lady on the platform had reached a peroration of whoosh, during which she chanted that if you had done it before, you could do it again, whatever it was, and other candy-coated inspiration to that effect. At the peak of this marshmallow mentation, my mother leaped from the chair, crying that she had walked before and could do it again. Some ten or twenty persons of the two hundred present must have recognized her, but the others were caught between cheers and consternation. The lecturer shouted, "Hallelujah, sister!" and at this point Marvin increased the confusion by bulging out his eyes, dropping his jaw, and mumbling that what he had done before he was now doing again; namely, losing his grip on reality. The crisis ended when a querulous man shouted, "Hey, that's my wheelchair!" and the culprits made good their escape.

The career of almost any actress is marked by open dates and, in the end, a long period of retirement. Who heard of the late Julia Marlowe in her last twenty years? But my mother's crowded calendar shows no season of repose, and the biographer is overwhelmed by instances and can only select a few more. There was the time she went back to Washington, in her sixties, wearing a red rose so the woman she was going to meet could identify her; they hadn't seen each other for thirty years. The train being early, or her hostess late, she pinned the rose on a sleeping dowager, twenty years her senior, who was sitting on a bench in the railway terminal, and watched at a distance the dismay of her friend when she finally arrived and the irritability of the sleeper awakened by a cry of "Why, Mame Thurber, how are you? You're looking just fine." And there was the occasion, not long ago, when she deflated a pompous gentleman, overproud of his forebears, who made the mistake of asking her how far back she had traced her own ancestry. "Until I came to a couple of horse thieves," she said with a troubled sigh. "Do you mean a father and son?" the shocked man asked, "or was it a couple of brothers?" My mother sighed again. "It was much worse than that," she said. "A man and his wife. You see, it runs in both sides of the family." A hundred other hours and moments I leave to the record of another year.

With all this to take up her time, Mrs. Charles Thurber nevertheless managed to run her home like any other good housewife, hovering over the cook when we had one, following the cleaning woman around with pail and cloth of her own, and rearing three sons who were far from being mother's helpers. She was famous for her pastry and, after long study and practice, learned to make the best chocolate creams in the world. Two or three professional candy men tried to catch her secret, watching her at work like a child watching a magician, and with just about as little profit. She made her last twenty pounds of chocolates when she was eighty, and then turned to writing a cookbook of her own recipes, which she still works at, dropping it now and then to tinker with her play, whose plot and personae and provenance are another one of her secrets.

She still writes me, as she always has, fifty letters a year, and I found, going over them, that time hasn't dulled their sparkle. In one, dated December 26, 1949, she told, in fine full detail, the story of her 1933 search for Miss Bagley, which has become a family saga. Miss Annette Bagley, known to her intimates as Anna, wandered from her home in England more than sixty years ago to become a home-to-home sewing woman in Columbus. She and my mother became great friends, and then, one morning in the spring of 1895, Miss Bagley, at the age of thirty-four, took a train to Boston, where she planned to open a dressmaking shop. For several years my mother's fond letters were promptly answered, but about the turn of the century, two of them were returned by the Boston post office. Miss Bagley had dropped out of sight, leaving no forwarding address, and it wasn't until 1913 that she was heard from again. The floods of that year had inundated Columbus and she sent a worried telegram from Boston. My mother replied, by wire, that all her friends were safe, and Miss Bagley apparently received this telegram at the Western Union office in which she had dispatched her own, but a letter my mother instantly sent to the old address was returned, like the others. Twenty silent years went by.

In 1933, Mary Thurber took up the quest again, writing to the postmasters of Boston and surrounding towns, and inventing a story about the settlement of an estate. "Money," she wrote me in the 1949 letter, "always increases people's interest." It greatly increased the interest of an Anna Bagley in Malden, Massachusetts, who turned out to be the wrong one, and with whom my mother exchanged a brief and cloudy correspondence. Then she came East to take up the search in person. She was sixty-seven and she knew that Miss Bagley, if she was alive, was seventy-two. In Boston my mother set out on the old, dim trail like a trained researcher, looking up out-dated phone books and directories at the Chamber of Commerce. The most recent record of Annette Bagley she could find placed her friend in Malden in 1925, so she went to Malden. Miss Bagley was not at the address listed, and the woman who lived there had never heard of her. My mother did what any good reporter would have done; she looked up old residents of the neighborhood and called on the older druggists and grocers. She learned that Annette Bagley had left that Malden house about seven years before. Someone seemed to remember that the old lady had moved to Everett Street. This street turned out to be only a block long, and my mother rang all its doorbells without success. Nobody knew anything about Miss Bagley. Then a druggist suggested that her quarry might have moved not to Everett Street but to the town of Everett, which is only a few miles from Malden. My mother transferred her pattern of search to Everett, and it was in that Boston suburb that the trail became warm. She found Annette Bagley listed in a three-year-old directory, but the elusive dressmaker was no longer at the address given. Neighbors, however, thought she had not gone far away, so her tracer continued her questioning of druggists and grocers and elderly people she stopped on the street. At twilight of the second day of her search, she came upon a small dressmaking shop on a side street. "I looked through the window," my mother

wrote, "and there she was, sitting and sewing with her back
to me." Thirty-eight years had made a great difference in the
two friends, and it wasn't until my mother asked the old lady
if she had ever lived in Columbus, Ohio, that Annette Bagley
recognized her.

The reason for her years of hiding was simple enough. She
did not want her Columbus friends to know that her dream
of a big and flourishing dressmaking establishment of her own
had failed to come true. "I took her to dinner in Boston,"
my mother wrote, "and then to a movie. It was hard for her
to believe that my oldest son, William, was forty, for when
she had seen him last he was only two. I'm not sure about
the movie, but I think it was 'It Happened One Night,' or
'One Sunday Afternoon,' or something like that." It isn't often that my memory outdoes my mother's, but I have always
remembered the name of that movie since she first told me
the story of her celebrated search for Annette Bagley eighteen
years ago. It was called "I Loved You Wednesday."

Miss Bagley was ninety last year, and my mother still writes
to her, and the letters no longer come back. The little sewing
shop on the side street was closed years ago, of course, and
the dream forgotten, but my mother is sure that, big establishment or no big establishment, Annette Bagley was the finest dressmaker Boston and its suburbs ever had.

In New York, which my mother visits often, she likes to
escape from her sons and see the sights of the city on her
own. One morning some twenty years ago, she reached the
second floor of the famous Wendel house, on Fifth Avenue,
but her tour of inspection was interrupted. "I was just going
by and I thought I would drop in," she told me. On that visit
she made a tour of Greenwich Village by herself, but asked
me to take her to what she called "the Tony's" and "the 21,"
whose fame she had somehow heard about. At "the Tony's"
she was fortunate enough to meet one of her idols, the late
Heywood Broun, and she enchanted him by casting an offhand horoscope for him that turned out to be a recognizable
portrait, done in the bold colors of both virtue and short-
coming. She has always had a lot of fun monkeying around
with the inexact sciences—she corresponded with Evangeline

Adams, and once had Professor Coué out to dinner at our house in Columbus—and I am sure that she has already dipped into Dianetics. She embarrassed my father one time, in an impish numerology phase, by making him return a set of ominously numbered automobile license plates and exchange it for a safer one. Twelve years ago, when she entered Columbia Presbyterian Medical Center for a major operation that she took in her stride, she demanded to know the date of birth of her distinguished surgeon before she would let him operate. He solemnly gave it to her, and was pleased to learn that he had been engaged for thirty years in a profession for which his signs clearly fitted him. Later, he was astonished by her familiarity with medicine and surgery, and told her one day that she had the sound implementation of a nurse. "Of course," my mother said. "I'm Capricorn with the moon in Sagittarius."

The day she was discharged from the hospital, she decided to visit the World's Fair, and she did, in spite of heat and humidity. In a bus on the way back, she found that she had exceeded her strength, and she asked the bus driver to take her pulse. He took it with one hand, continuing to drive with the other, and reported that it was a little high but nothing to worry about. I have no doubt that she found out his birthday and still remembers it, for she rarely forgets a name or a date. She once sent me a clipping of an Earl Wilson column in which he had given Dorothy Parker's birthday as August 23rd. "Dorothy Parker's birthday is August 22nd," my mother wrote. "August 23rd is Helen Gude's birthday." A few days ago I phoned her in Columbus and asked her if she remembered her surgeon's birthday. "Why, certainly," she said. "He was born on the 30th of March. My Columbus surgeon is also Aries—April 1st."

In the recollections of a woman in her eighties whose mind and memory are as sharp as they ever were, the years are sometimes greatly foreshortened. When she came to New York in 1947, I found that she had made a date for tea at the Algonquin with an old friend of my father's, Charles Dewey Hilles. She said that she herself hadn't seen him for "a long time." Mr. Hilles, a celebrated Ohio Republican, died two years ago, and his long obituaries told of his having been, among many other things, an Assistant Secretary of the Treasury under Taft, Chairman of the Republican National Committee from 1912 to 1916, and a member of dozens of boards of directors. I had the good luck to be asked to the Ohio tea party, along with one John Aloysius McNulty, for many years a reporter on Columbus newspapers. We had a jolly time, and various ancient facts and forgotten dates were brought up. It came out that my mother was a year older than Mr. Hilles. "When was it," I finally asked, "that you two last met?" My mother thought about this and said, "Well, Mr. Hilles was secretary to the superintendent of the Boys' Industrial School at Lancaster, Ohio. Let me see—yes, it must have been in 1888." My mother was twenty-two in 1888, and Mr. Hilles, of course, was only twenty-one. Now, no elderly man of high and varied achievement likes to be reminded of his juvenile beginnings, and it was obvious to us all that my mother's grasp of her friend's later career was tenuous. McNulty saved the situation. "Eighteen-eighty-eight," he said, "was the year the owls were so bad."

When I was in Columbus a year ago, my mother said, "Would it be possible for you to take me to lunch at the Waldorf-Astoria the next time I'm in New York?" From the tentative way she put it, I could see why she had never asked me before to take her to lunch at the Waldorf-Astoria. She was afraid that I couldn't swing it, and she hadn't wanted to embarrass me. I had taken her to every place I could think of, from the old Lafayette to Tony's and "21," but the Waldorf had never crossed my mind. I have made a conspicuous note about it on a memorandum pad, and the next time she comes to New York, I will take her to lunch at the Waldorf-Astoria, in a Hispano-Suiza if she wants it that way. It is little enough to do for Mary Agnes Fisher Thurber.

FROM

THURBER COUNTRY

File and Forget

I WANT to thank my secretary, Miss Ellen Bagley, for putting the following letters in order. I was not up to the task myself, for reasons that will, I think, become clear to the reader.   J. T.

WEST CORNWALL, CONN.
NOVEMBER 2, 1949

Miss Alma Winege,
The Charteriss Publishing Co.,
132 East What Street,
New York, N.Y.
DEAR MISS WINEGE:

Your letter of October 25th, which you sent to me in care of The Homestead, Hot Springs, Ark., has been forwarded to my home in West Cornwall, Conn., by The Homestead, Hot Springs, Va. As you know, Mrs. Thurber and I sometimes visit this Virginia resort, but we haven't been there for more than a year. Your company, in the great tradition of publishers, has sent so many letters to me at Hot Springs, Ark., that the postmaster there has simply taken to sending them on to the right address, or what would be the right address if I were there. I explained to Mr. Cluffman, and also to Miss Lexy, when I last called at your offices, that all mail was to be sent to me at West Cornwall until further notice. If and when I go to The Homestead, I will let you know in advance. Meanwhile, I suggest that you remove from your files all addresses of mine except the West Cornwall one. Another publishing firm recently sent a letter to me at 65 West 11th Street, an address I vacated in the summer of 1930. It would not come as a surprise to me if your firm, or some other publishers, wrote me in care of my mother at 568 Oak Street, Columbus, Ohio. I was thirteen years old when we lived there, back in 1908.

As for the contents of your letter of the 25th, I did not order thirty-six copies of Peggy Peckham's book, "Grandma Was a Nudist." I trust that you have not shipped these books to me

761

in care of The Homestead, Hot Springs, Ark., or anywhere else.

Sincerely yours,

J. THURBER

P.S. Margaret Peckham, by the way, is not the author of this book. She is the distinguished New York psychiatrist whose "The Implications of Nudism" was published a couple of years ago. She never calls herself Peggy.　　　J. T.

WEST CORNWALL, CONN.
NOVEMBER 3, 1949

Miss Alma Winege,
The Charteriss Publishing Co.,
132 East What Street,
New York, N.Y.
DEAR MISS WINEGE:

In this morning's mail I received a card from the Grand Central branch of the New York Post Office informing me that a package of books had been delivered to me at 410 East 57th Street. The branch office is holding the package for further postage, which runs to a considerable amount. I am enclosing the notification card, since these must be the thirty-six copies of "Grandma Was a Nudist." I have not lived at 410 East 57th Street since the fall of 1944. Please see to it that this address is removed from your files, along with The Homestead address.

Whoever ordered those books, if anyone actually did, probably wonders where they are.

Sincerely yours,

J. THURBER

THE CHARTERISS PUBLISHING COMPANY
NEW YORK, N.Y.

November 5, 1949

Mr. James M. Thurber,
West Cornwall, Conn.
DEAR MR. THURBER:

I am dreadfully sorry about the mixup over Miss Peckham's book. We have been pretty much upset around here since the departure of Mr. Peterson and Mr. West, and several new girls came to us with the advent of Mr. Jordan. They have not yet got their "sea legs," I am afraid, but I still cannot understand from what file our shipping department got your address as 165 West 11th Street. I have removed the 57th Street address from the files and also the Arkansas address and I trust that we will not disturb your tranquillity further up there in Cornwall. It must be lovely this time of year in Virginia and I envy you and Mrs. Thurber. Have a lovely time at The Homestead.

Sincerely yours,
ALMA WINEGE

P.S. What you had to say about "Grandma" amused us all.   A. W.

COLUMBUS, OHIO
NOVEMBER 16, 1949

DEAR MR. THURBER:

I have decided to come right out with the little problem that was accidentally dumped in my lap yesterday. I hope you will forgive me for what happened, and perhaps you can suggest what I should do with the books. There are three dozen of them and, unfortunately, they arrived when my little son Donald was alone downstairs. By the time I found out about the books, he had torn off the wrappings and had built a cute little house out of them. I have placed them all on a shelf out of his reach while awaiting word as to where to send them. I presume I could ship them to you C.O.D. if I can get somebody to wrap them properly.

I heard from old Mrs. Winston next door that you and your family once lived here at 568 Oak Street. She remembers you and your brothers as cute little tykes who were very noisy and raised rabbits and guinea pigs. She says your mother was a wonderful cook. I am sorry about Donald opening the books and I hope you will forgive him.

Sincerely yours,
CLARA EDWARDS
(Mrs. J. C.)

WEST CORNWALL, CONN.
NOVEMBER 19, 1949

Mr. Leon Charteriss,
The Charteriss Publishing Co.,
132 East What Street,
New York, N.Y.

DEAR MR. CHARTERISS:

I am enclosing a letter from a Mrs. J. C. Edwards, of Columbus, Ohio, in the fervent hope that you will do something to stop this insane flux of books. I never ordered these books. I have not read "Grandma Was a Nudist." I do not intend to read it. I want something done to get these volumes off my trail and cut out of my consciousness.

I have written Miss Winege about the situation, but I am afraid to take it up with her again, because she might send them to me in care of the Department of Journalism at Ohio State University, where I was a student more than thirty years ago.

Sincerely yours,
J. THURBER

P.S. I never use my middle initial, but your firm seems to think it is "M." It is not. J. T.

THE CHARTERISS PUBLISHING COMPANY
NEW YORK, N.Y.

NOVEMBER 23, 1949

Mr. James M. Thurber,
West Cornwall, Conn.

DEAR MR. THURBER:

Mr. Charteriss has flown to California on a business trip and will be gone for several weeks. His secretary has turned your letter of the 19th over to me. I have asked Mr. Cluffman to write to Miss Clara Edwards in Columbus and arrange for the reshipment of the thirty-six copies of "Grandma Was a Nudist."

I find, in consulting the records, that you have three times ordered copies of your own book, "Thurber's Ark," to be shipped to you at West Cornwall, at the usual discount rate of forty per cent. I take it that what you really wanted was thirty-six copies of your own book and they are being sent out to you today with our regrets for the discomfit we have caused you. I hope you will be a little patient with us during this so trying period of reorganization.

Cordially yours,
JEANNETTE GAINES
Stock Order Dept.

P.S. You will be happy to know that we have traced down the gentleman who ordered those copies of "Grandma."

WEST CORNWALL, CONN.
NOVEMBER 25, 1949

Mr. Henry Johnson,
The Charteriss Pub. Co.,
New York, N.Y.
DEAR HARRY:

Since the reorganization at Charteriss, I have the forlorn and depressing feeling that I no longer know anybody down there except you. I know that this immediate problem of mine is not in your field, but I turn to you as a last resource. What I want, or rather what I don't want, is simple enough, Harry. God knows it is simple.

I don't want any more copies of my book. I don't want any more copies of my book. I don't want any more copies of my book.

As ever,
JIM

P.S. It has just occurred to me that I haven't seen you for more than two years. Let's have a drink one of these days. I'll give you a ring the next time I'm in the city.   J. T.

THE CHARTERISS PUBLISHING COMPANY
NEW YORK, N.Y.
NOVEMBER 26, 1949

Mr. James Grover Thurber,
Cornwall, Conn.
DEAR JIM THURBER:

I haven't had the pleasure of meeting you since I had the great good luck to join forces with Charteriss, but I look forward to our meeting with a high heart. Please let me know the next time you are in the city, as I should like to wine and dine you and perhaps discuss the new book that I feel confident you have in you. If you don't want to talk shop, we can discuss the record of our mutual football team. You were at Northwestern some years ahead of my time, I believe, but I want you to know that they still talk about Jimmy Thurber out there.

Your letter to Harry Johnson has just come to my attention, and I regret to say that Harry is no longer with us. He went to Simon and Schuster in the summer of 1948. I want you to feel, however, that every single one of us here is your friend, willing and eager to drop everything to do your slightest bidding. All of us feel very deeply about your having turned against your book "Thurber's Ark." I note that in your present mood you have the feeling that you never want to see it again. Well, Jim, let me assure you that this is just a passing fancy, derived from a moment of depression. When you put in your last order for thirty-six copies, you must surely have had some definite use in mind for them, and I am banking on twenty years' experience in the book-publishing game when I take the liberty of sending these twenty books off to you today. There is one thing I am something of an expert at, if I do say so myself, and that is the understanding of the "creative spirit."

We have a new system here, which is to send our authors not ten free copies, as of old, but fifteen. Therefore, five of the thirty-six copies will reach you with our compliments. The proper deductions will be made on the record.

Don't forget our dinner date.

Cordially,

CLINT JORDAN

P.S. I approve of your decision to resume the use of your middle name. It gives a book dignity and flavor to use all three names. I think it was old Willa Cather who started the new trend, when she dropped the Seibert.   C. J.

THE CHARTERISS PUBLISHING COMPANY
NEW YORK, N.Y.

DECEMBER 13, 1949

DEAR THURBER:

Just back at the old desk after a trip to California and a visit with my mother, who is eighty-nine now but as chipper as

ever. She would make a swell Profile. Ask me about her some-
day.

Need I say I was delighted to hear from the staff when I
got back about your keen interest in "Grandma Was a Nudist"? The book has been moving beautifully and its ceiling has
gone sky-high. We're planning a brief new advertising campaign and I'd be tickled pink if you would be good enough
to bat out a blurb for us.

Yours,
LEON

THE CHARTERISS PUBLISHING COMPANY
NEW YORK, N.Y.
DECEMBER 15, 1949

Mr. James M. Thurber,
West Cornwall, Conn.
DEAR MR. THURBER:

I hope you will forgive me—indeed, all of us—for having
inexcusably mislaid the address of the lady to whom the thirty-
six copies of "Grandma Was a Nudist" were sent by mistake.
I understand that we have already dispatched to you at your
home another thirty-six volumes of that book.

My apologies again.

Sincerely yours,
H. F. CLUFFMAN

WEST CORNWALL, CONN.
DECEMBER 19, 1949

Mr. H. F. Cluffman,
The Charteriss Publishing Co.,
132 East What Street,
New York, N.Y.
DEAR MR. CLUFFMAN:

The lady's name is Mrs. J. C. Edwards, and she lives at 568
Oak Street, Columbus, Ohio.

I have explained as clearly as I could in previous letters that
I did not order thirty-six copies of "Grandma Was a Nudist."
If you have actually shipped to me another thirty-six copies of
this book, it will make a total of seventy-two copies, none of
which I will pay for. The thirty-six copies of "Thurber's Ark"

that Mr. Jordan has written me he intends to send to West Cornwall would bring up to one hundred and eight the total number of books that your firm, by a conspiracy of confusion unique even in the case of publishers, has mistakenly charged to my account. You may advise Mr. Jordan that I do not wish to receive the five free copies he mentioned in his letter.

If your entire staff of employees went back to *Leslie's Weekly*, where they belong, it would set my mind at rest.

Sincerely yours,

J. THURBER

P.S. I notice that you use only my middle initial, "M." Mr. Jordan and I—or was it Mr. Charteriss?—have decided to resume the use of the full name, which is Murfreesboro.   J. T.

WEST CORNWALL, CONN.
DECEMBER 27, 1949

Mr. Leon Charteriss,
The Charteriss Publishing Co.,
132 East What Street,
New York, N.Y.
DEAR MR. CHARTERISS:

I am sure you will be sorry to learn that Mr. Thurber has had one of his spells as a result of the multiplication of books and misunderstanding that began with Miss Alma Winege's letter of October 25, 1949. Those of us around Mr. Thurber are greatly disturbed by the unfortunate circumstances that have caused him to give up writing, at least temporarily, just after he had resumed work following a long fallow period.

Thirty-six copies of Mr. Thurber's book and thirty-six copies of "Grandma Was a Nudist" have arrived at his home here, and he has asked me to advise you that he intends to burn all seventy-two. West Cornwall is scarcely the community for such a demonstration—he proposes to burn them in the middle of U.S. Highway No. 7—since the town regards with a certain suspicion any writer who has not won a Pulitzer Prize. I am enclosing copies of all the correspondence between your company and Mr. Thurber, in the hope that someone connected with your firm will read it with proper care and intelligence and straighten out this deplorable and inexcusable situation.

Mr. Thurber wishes me to tell you that he does not want to hear from any of you again.

Sincerely yours,
ELLEN BAGLEY
Secretary to Mr. Thurber

THE CHARTERISS PUBLISHING COMPANY
NEW YORK, N.Y.

DECEMBER 28, 1949

Mr. James Murfreesboro Thurber,
72 West,
Cornwall, Conn.
DEAR MR. THURBER:

I have at hand your letter of December 19th, the opening paragraph of which puzzles me. You send me the following name and address—Mrs. J. C. Edwards, 568 Oak Street, Columbus, Ohio—but it is not clear what use you wish me to make of this. I would greatly appreciate it if you would clear up this small matter for me.

Sincerely yours,
H. F. CLUFFMAN

P.S. *Leslie's Weekly* ceased publication many years ago. I could obtain the exact date if you so desire.

H. F. C.

THE CHARTERISS PUBLISHING COMPANY
NEW YORK, N.Y.

DECEMBER 29, 1949

Mr. James M. Thurber,
West Cornwall, Conn.
DEAR MR. THURBER:

You will be sorry to hear that Mr. Charteriss was taken suddenly ill with a virus infection. His doctor believes that he lost his immunity during his visit to the West Coast. He is now in the hospital, but his condition is not serious.

Since the departure of Miss Gaines, who was married last week, I have taken over the Stock Order Department for the time being. I did not take the liberty of reading your enclosures in the letter to Mr. Charteriss, but sent them directly to him at the hospital. I am sure that he will be greatly cheered up by them when he is well enough to read. Meanwhile, I want you to know that you can repose all confidence in the Stock Order Department to look after your needs, whatever they may be.

Sincerely yours,
GLADYS MACLEAN

P.S. I learned from Mr. Jordan that you were a friend of Willa Cather's. Exciting!

COLUMBUS, OHIO
JANUARY 3, 1950

DEAR JAMIE:

I don't understand the clipping from the Lakeville *Journal* Helen's mother sent me, about someone burning all those books of yours in the street. I never heard of such a thing, and don't understand how they could have taken the books without your knowing it, or what you were doing with so many copies of the novel about the naked grandmother. Imagine, at her age! She couldn't carry on like that in Columbus, let me tell you. Why, when I was a girl, you didn't dare walk with a man after sunset, unless he was your husband, and even then there was talk.

It's a good thing that state policeman came along in time to save most of the books from being completely ruined, and you must be thankful for the note Mr. Jordan put in one of the books, for the policeman would never have known who they belonged to if he hadn't found it.

A Mrs. Edwards phoned this morning and said that her son Donald collects your books and wants to send them to you—to be autographed, I suppose. Her son has dozens of your books and I told her you simply wouldn't have time to sign all of them, and she said she didn't care what you did with them. And then she said they weren't your books at all, and so I just hung up on her.

Be sure to bundle up when you go out.

With love,
MOTHER

P.S. This Mrs. Edwards says she lives at 568 Oak Street. I told her we used to live there and she said God knows she was aware of that. I don't know what she meant. I was afraid this little boy would send you all those books to sign and so I told his mother that you and Helen were at The Homestead, in Hot Springs. You don't suppose he would send them there, do you?

And here, gentle reader, I know you will be glad to leave all of us.

Do You Want to Make
Something Out of It?

(OR, IF YOU PUT AN "O" ON "UNDERSTO,"
YOU'LL RUIN MY "THUNDERSTORM")

I'M PROBABLY not the oldest word-game player in the country, and I know I'm not the ablest, but my friends will all
testify that I'm the doggedest. (We'll come back to the word
"doggedest" later on.) I sometimes keep on playing the
game, all by myself, after it is over and I have gone to bed.
On a recent night, tossing and spelling, I spent two hours
hunting for another word besides "phlox" that has "hlo" in
it. I finally found seven: "matchlock," "decathlon," "pen-
tathlon," "hydrochloric," "chlorine," "chloroform," and
"monthlong." There are more than a dozen others, beginning with "phlo," but I had to look them up in the dictionary
the next morning, and that doesn't count.

By "the game," I mean Superghosts, as some of us call it,
a difficult variation of the familiar parlor game known as
Ghosts. In Ghosts, as everybody knows, one of a group of
sedentary players starts with a letter, and the spelling proceeds
clockwise around the group until a player spells a word of
more than three letters, thus becoming "a third of a ghost,"
or two-thirds, or a whole ghost. The game goes on until
everyone but the winner has been eliminated. Superghosts
differs from the old game in one small, tricky, and often
exacerbating respect: The rules allow a player to *prefix* a letter
to the word in progress, thus increasing the flexibility of the
indoor sport. If "busines" comes to a player, he does not have
to add the final "s"; he can put an "n" in front, and the player
who has to add the "e" to "unbusinesslik" becomes part of
a ghost. In a recent game in my league, a devious gentleman
boldly stuck an "n" in front of "sobsiste," stoutly maintaining
the validity of "unsobsisterlike," but he was shouted down.
There is a lot of shouting in the game, especially when it is
played late at night.

Starting words in the middle and spelling them in both directions lifts the pallid pastime of Ghosts out of the realm of children's parties and ladies' sewing circles and makes it a game to test the mettle of the mature adult mind. As long ago as 1930, aficionados began to appear in New York parlors, and then the game waned, to be revived, in my circle, last year. The Superghost aficionado is a moody fellow, given to spelling to himself at table, not listening to his wife, and staring dully at his frightened children, wondering why he didn't detect, in yesterday's game, that "cklu" is the guts of "lacklustre," and priding himself on having stumped everybody with "nehe," the middle of "swineherd." In this last case, "bonehead" would have done, since we allow slang if it is in the dictionary, but "Stonehenge" is out, because we don't allow proper nouns. All compound and hyphenated words are privileged, even "jack-o'-lantern" and "love-in-a-mist," but the speller must indicate where a hyphen occurs.

Many people, who don't like word games and just want to sit around and drink and talk, hate Superghosts and wish it were in hell with Knock, Knock, Who's There? The game is also tough on bad spellers, poor visualizers, mediocre concentrators, ladies and gentlemen of small vocabulary, and those who are, to use a word presently popular with the younger drinking set, clobbered. I remember the night a bad speller, female, put an "m" on "ale," thinking, as she later confessed, that "salamander" is spelled with two "e"s. The next player could have gone to "alemb"—the word "alembic" turns up a lot—but he made it "alema" and was promptly challenged. (You can challenge a player if you think he is bluffing.) What the challenged player had in mind was "stalemate." The man who had challenged him got sore, because he hadn't thought of "stalemate," and went home. More than one game has ended in hard feelings, but I have never seen players come to blows, or friendships actually broken.

I said we would get back to "doggedest," and here we are. This word, if it is a word, caused a lot of trouble during one game, when a lady found "ogged" in her lap, refused to be bogged, dogged, fogged, jogged, or logged, and added an "e." She was challenged and lost, since Webster's unabridged dictionary is accepted as the final judge and authority, and while it gives "doggedly" and "doggedness," it doesn't give "doggedest." She could also have got out of "ogged" with an "r" in front, for "frogged" is a good word, and also what might be called a lady's word, but she stuck doggedly to "doggedest." Then there was the evening a dangerous and exasperating player named Bert Mitchell challenged somebody's "dogger." The challenged man had "doggerel" in mind, of course, but Mitchell said, in his irritating voice, "You have spelled a word. 'Dogger' is a word," and he flipped through the unabridged dictionary, which he reads for pleasure and always has on his lap during a game. "Dogger" is indeed a word, and quite a word. Look it up yourself.

When I looked up "dogger" the other day, I decided to have a look at "dog," a word practically nobody ever looks up, because everybody is smugly confident that he knows what a dog is. Here, for your amazement, are some dogs other than the carnivorous mammal:

The hammer in a gunlock. Any of various devices, usually of simple design, for holding, gripping, or fastening something; as: **a** Any of various devices consisting essentially of a spike, rod, or bar of metal, as of iron, with a ring, hook, claw, lug, or the like, at the end, used for gripping, clutching, or holding something, as by driving or embedding it in the object, hooking it to the object, etc. See RAFT DOG, TOE DOG. **b** Specif., either of the hooks or claws of a pair of sling dogs. See CRAMPON. **c** An iron for holding wood in a fireplace; a firedog; an andiron. **d** In a lathe, a clamp for gripping the piece of work and for communicating motion to it from the faceplate. A *clamp dog* consists of two parts drawn together by screws. A *bent-tail dog* has an L-shaped projection that enters a slot in the faceplate for communicating motion. A *straight-tail dog* has a projecting part that engages with a stud fastened to or forming part of the faceplate. A *safety dog* is one equipped with safety setscrews. **e** Any of the jaws in a lathe chuck. **f** A pair of nippers or forceps. **g** A wheeled gripping device for drawing the fillet from which coin blanks are stamped through the opening at the head of the drawbench. **h** Any of a set of adjusting screws for the bed tool of a punching machine. **i** A grapple for clutching and raising a pile-driver monkey or a well-boring tool. **j** A stop or detent; a click or ratchet. **k** A drag for the wheel of a vehicle. **l** A steel block attached to a locking bar or tappet of an interlocking machine, by which locking between bars is accomplished.

m A short, heavy, sharp-pointed, steel hook with a ring at one end.
n A steel toothlike projection on a log carriage or on the endless chain that conveys logs into the sawmill.

And now, unless you have had enough, we will get back to Superghosts, through the clanging and clatter of all those dogs. The game has a major handicap, or perhaps I should call it blockage. A player rarely gets the chance to stick the others with a truly tough word, because someone is pretty sure to simplify the word under construction. Mitchell tells me that he always hopes he can get around to "ug-ug" or "ach-ach" on his way to "plug-ugly" and "stomach-ache." These words are hyphenated in my Webster's, for the old boy was a great hyphenator. (I like his definition of "plug-ugly": "A kind of city rowdy, ruffian, or disorderly tough;—a term said to have been originated by a gang of such in Baltimore.") In the case of "ug," the simplifiers usually go to "bug," trying to catch someone with "buggies," or they add an "l" and the word ends in "ugliness." And "ach" often turns into "machinery," although it could go in half a dozen directions. Since the simplifiers dull the game by getting into easy words, the experts are fond of a variant that goes like this: Mitchell, for example, will call up a friend and say, "Get out of 'ightf' twenty ways." Well, I tossed in bed one night and got ten: "rightful," "frightful," "delightful," "nightfall," "lightfoot," "straightforward," "eightfold," "lightfingered," "tight-fisted," and "tight-fitting." The next day, I thought of "light-face," "right-footed," and "night-flowering," and came to a stop. "Right fielder" is neither compounded nor hyphenated by Webster, and I began to wonder about Mitchell's twenty "ightf"'s. I finally figured it out. The old devil was familiar with the ten or more fish and fowl and miscellaneous things that begin with "nightf."

It must have been about 1932 that an old player I know figured that nothing could be got out of "dke" except "handkerchief," and then, in a noisy game one night this year, he passed that combination on to the player at his left. This rascal immediately made it "dkee." He was challenged by the lady on *his* left and triumphantly announced that his word was "groundkeeper." It looked like an ingenious escape from "handkerchief," but old Webster let the fellow down. Webster accepts only "groundman" and "groundsman," thus implying that there is no such word as "groundkeeper."

Mitchell threw "abc" at me one night, and I couldn't get anything out of it and challenged him. "Dabchick," he said patronizingly, and added blandly, "It is the little grebe." Needless to say, it *is* the little grebe.

I went through a hundred permutations in bed that night without getting anything else out of "abc" except a word I made up, which is "grabcheck," one who quickly picks up a tab, a big spender, a generous fellow. I have invented quite a few other words, too, which I modestly bring to the attention of modern lexicographers, if there are any. I think of dictionary-makers as being rigidly conventional gentlemen who are the first to put the new aside. They probably won't even read my list of what I shall call bedwords, but I am going to set it down anyway. A young matron in Bermuda last spring told me to see what I could do with "sgra," and what I did with it occupied a whole weekend. Outside of "disgrace" and its variants, all I could find were "cross-grained" and "misgraff," which means to misgraft (obsolete). I found this last word while looking, in vain, for "misgrade" in the dictionary. Maybe you can think of something else, and I wish you luck. Here, then, in no special order, are my bedwords based on "sgra."

pussgrapple. A bickering, or minor disturbance; an argument or dispute among effeminate men. Also, less frequently, a physical struggle between, or among, women.

kissgranny. 1. A man who seeks the company of older women, especially older women with money; a designing fellow, a fortune hunter. 2. An overaffectionate old woman, a hugmoppet, a bunnytalker.

glassgrabber. 1. A woman who disapproves of, or interferes with, her husband's drinking; a kill-joy, a shush-laugh, a douselight. 2. A man who asks for another drink at a friend's house, or goes out and gets one in the kitchen.

blessgravy. A minister or cleric; the head of a family; one who says grace. Not to be confused with *praisegravy*, one who extols a woman's cooking, especially the cooking of a friend's wife; a gay fellow, a flirt, a seducer. *Colloq.*, a break-vow, a shrugholy.

cussgravy. A husband who complains of his wife's cooking, more especially a husband who complains of his wife's cooking in the presence of guests; an ill-tempered fellow, a curmudgeon. Also, sometimes, a peptic-ulcer case.

messgranter. An untidy housekeeper, a careless housewife. Said of a woman who admits, often proudly, that she has let herself go; a bragdowdy, a frumpess.

hissgrammar. An illiterate fellow, a user of slovenly rhetoric, a father who disapproves of booklearning. Also, more rarely, one who lisps, a twisttongue.

chorusgrable. *Orig.* a young actress, overconfident of her ability and her future; a snippet, a flappertigibbet. *Deriv.* Betty Grable, an American movie actress.

pressgrape. One who presses grapes, a grape presser. Less commonly, a crunchberry.

pressgrain. 1. A man who tries to make whiskey in his own cellar; hence, a secret drinker, a hidebottle, a sneakslug. 2. One who presses grain in a grain presser. *Arch.*

dressgrader. A woman who stares another woman up and down, a starefrock; hence, a rude female, a hobblede-hoyden.

fussgrape. 1. One who diets or toys with his food, a light eater, a person without appetite, a scornmuffin, a shuncabbage. 2. A man, usually American, who boasts of his knowledge of wines, a smugbottle.

bassgrave. 1. Cold-eyed, unemotional, stolid, troutsolemn. 2. The grave of a bass. *Obs.*

lassgraphic. Of, or pertaining to, the vivid description of females; as, the guest was so lassgraphic his host asked him to change the subject or get out. Also said of fathers of daughters, more rarely of mothers.

blissgray. Aged by marriage. Also, sometimes, discouraged by wedlock, or by the institution of marriage.

glassgrail. A large nocturnal moth. Not to be confused with *smackwindow*, the common June bug, or bangsash.

hossgrace. Innate or native dignity, similar to that of the thoroughbred hoss. *Southern U.S.*

bussgranite. Literally, a stonekisser; a man who persists in trying to win the favor or attention of cold, indifferent, or capricious women. Not to be confused with *snatchkiss*, a kitchen lover.

tossgravel. 1. A male human being who tosses gravel, usually at night, at the window of a female human being's bedroom, usually that of a young virgin; hence, a lover, a male sweetheart, and an eloper. 2. One who is suspected by the father of a daughter of planning an elopement with her, a grablass.

If you should ever get into a game of Superghosts with Mitchell, by the way, don't pass "bugl" on to him, hoping to send him into "bugling." He will simply add an "o," making the group "buglo," which is five-sevenths of "bugloss." The word means "hawkweed," and you can see what Mitchell would do if you handed him "awkw," expecting to make him continue the spelling of "awkward." Tough guy, Mitchell. Tough game, Superghosts. You take it from here. I'm tired.

A Final Note on Chanda Bell

(AFTER READING TWO OR THREE LITERARY
MEMORIALS, TO THIS OR THAT LAMENTED TALENT,
WRITTEN BY ONE CRITIC
OR ANOTHER)

THERE WERE only three of us around Chanda Bell at the end: Charles Vayne, her attorney; Hadley, the butler (if he was a butler); and myself. The others had departed with the beginning of the war, to new dedications, or old hideouts, and the obituaries in the journals after Miss Bell's death were erroneous in claiming that the great, dark house in the East Sixties was, up to the very last, bedlam and carnival. Chanda Bell's famous largess and laissez-faire had, naturally enough, attracted the strange and the sublimated from the nooks and crannies of Greenwich Village. I had been particularly pleased to witness the going away of the middle-aged man who rode the tricycle, the schoolteacher who had resigned from the human race to become a bird, and Miss Menta, the disturbingly nude Chilean transcendentalist.

Charles Vayne, as regular and as futile as a clock in an empty house, showed up once a week with important documents that Chanda Bell would never sign. Some of them were dated as far back as 1924. A year of my friendship with the gifted lady had passed (so long ago!) before I could be sure that I knew what she was trying not to say, but Vayne never knew. Her use of the triple negative, in such expressions as "not unmeaningless," and her habit of starting sentences in the middle bewildered him, and so did her fondness for surrogate words with ambiguous meanings, like the words in dreams: "rupture" for "rapture," "centaur" for "sender," "pressure" for "pleasure," and "scorpio" for "scrofula." She enjoyed frustrating him, and she made the most of his discomfiture. "Praise me!" she would say as he handed her a fountain pen and the documents, which she always waved away. "Praise me!" she would command again. He invariably reacted the same way. It had become a kind of ritual. "I repeat that I have not read a novel all the way through since 'The Crimson Sweater,' by Ralph Henry Barbour," he would say. His expostulations and his entreaties amused her for a while, but then she would poke at him with her cane and drive him off, crying, "He comes without armor who comes without art!"

Hadley, who ushered the attorney in and out every Wednesday afternoon, had one cold, impassive eye and one that he could cause to twinkle. It gave you the chill sense of being, at one and the same time, in the presence of advocate and

adversary. His duties in the final months were sparse, consisting mainly of serving Madeira to Chanda Bell and me, or to Chanda Bell and Vayne and me, in the Gray Room, after four o'clock, when she had had her egg and had dressed and was ready to receive. One always stood in her presence, for it was Chanda Bell's conceit to believe that only the uncomfortable are capable of pure attention.

Chanda Bell was fifty-seven when I first bent over her hand, and her mind seemed so keen and agile it was difficult to believe that she could confuse her guests, even her intimates, with one another. But she did. Charles Vayne was sometimes

Lord Rudgate, an Englishman of dim background and cryptic reference, and sometimes Strephon ("a Jung mad I cussed in the Sprig"). I was alternately Dennis, a deceased painter, who had specialized in gun dogs for the calendars of coal companies, and one McKinnon or McKenyon, an advertising executive, who had attempted to deflower Miss Bell in a speeding motorboat during the panic of 1907. This was highly exasperating to such scholarly critics as Hudson van Horne and Dantes Woodrow, and they never came back after their separate agonized hours in the underwater gloom of the echoing Gray Room.

It is not congenial to me, at this time, to expose in detail how I became lost—if lost I became—in the "brilliant wilderness" of Chanda Bell's prose, or to reënact the process of equation, synthesis, and integration by means of which I was able to reveal the subtle affirmation compounded of the double negative of her unmeaning and her unmethod. This was ably—if mistakenly, still ably—set forth in my "A Note on Chanda Bell."* Upon its publication, she had sent for me, and in the fine years of intellectual intimacy that followed, my faith in her genius was more often reinforced than not. It wasn't until the last few months, when, by design or aberration, she began to discuss herself, between teatime and twilight, as if she were discussing someone else, that the blackest of a critic's ravens, uncertainty of his soundness, came to dwell in my consciousness. It is a terrible thing not to be sure whether one has sought or been sought, not to be able to tell the hunter from the quarry, the sanctuary from the trap.

Chanda Bell had, in fact, commanded me to her salon, but had I not asked for it, had I not commanded the command, by the tribute of my unique and penetrating analysis of her work? She had cause to be grateful, and her summoning me to her side was, in my early opinion, the most natural of acts. Careless and churlish critics, in malice or mischief, had dismissed her bright and tangled intention with such expressions as "bloom and drool," "the amorphous richness of a thrown pie," "as dull as Daiquiris with the commodore of a yacht club," and "as far to the Right as a soupspoon." This last was

* *The Neutral Review*, October, 1943.

the sheerest nonsense. One might as reasonably have said that she was as far to the Left as a fish fork. The closest she ever came to mentioning politics was one day when, in a rare moment of merriment, she referred to Karl Marx as "Groucho." I myself had heard the faint and special obbligato of elfin horns in her work and the laughter in the dusty house, and I alone had seen the swift and single flashing of a naked nymph by moonlight.

It is hard to mark the hour and day when the thunderhead of suspicion first stains the clear horizon of an old admiration, but I came to be drenched, in the horrid mental weather of last autumn, by the downpour of a million doubts and dreads of Chanda Bell. I began to fear that she had perpetrated, in her half-dozen dense, tortured novels, one of the major literary hoaxes of our time, and to suspect that she had drawn me into the glittering web of a monstrous deceit, in order to destroy, by proxy and in effigy, the entire critical profession. We would sit in the Gray Room from four till dark—she had permitted me to sit, at last, with the compassionate concession of a queen—and she would pierce my thin armor of hope and prayer with sharp and studied flicks of her sardonic, allusive intelligence. "You have the scaffold touch of a brain certain," she told me one afternoon. This was in the best tradition of her infernal dialectic. I could figure, in accordance with her secret code, that I had the scalpel touch of a brain surgeon, or I could take her to mean, in perverted literalness, that I was doomed to die—and was about to—an awful death for my wrong and sinful certainties.

"You have found the figure, Thurber," she told me one afternoon, "but have you found the carpet?" This was accompanied by her shrewd, tiny smile. I could not determine whether she meant there was something to find that I had not found, or nothing to find at all, beneath the gleaming surface of her style. The devil of it was that I could not be sure of anything. I spent that night going over "The Huanted Yatch" with a fine-tooth comb, searching for esoteric anagrams, feeling for what she had called "the carpet." I scrutinized, investigated, explored, took apart, and put back together again the entire fibre and fabric, uncertain of what shape and texture I was looking for. I read the thing backward, and I even tried to read it upside down and in the mirror of my bureau. I copied out one disturbing sentence and carried it about with me for close study: "Icing mellow moony on a postgate doves snow and love surrender." Its once perspicuous feel-meaning deserted me, and its cool loveliness became the chatter of a gibbon in my distraught consciousness. I could no longer tell whether it was beauty or balderdash. If it was balderdash, the book degenerated into the vivid cackling of a macaw, and my critique stood as a monument to a fatuous gullibility.

Toward the end, Chanda Bell began to talk about herself in the third person, as if she were not there in the house but on her way to visit us. "I've asked her to tea," she would tell me, "but it will not astonish me if she fails to appear. Nobody has ever been able to pin her down." And she would study the effect of this upon me with her hooded gaze. She had lapsed into simple, declarative sentences, and this was a comfort, but I was deeply perturbed by the feeling that her outlandish fantasy and her revelations were new and planned inventions of her cruelty.

"Chanda Bell," she said one evening, "had an allowance of two hundred dollars a week while she was still in pigtails. Her father, the millionaire industrialist, doted on the awkward, big-eyed little girl. He would bring her curtsying into the library for his cronies to admire. 'By God, she'll be the first woman president of Standard Oil!' he exclaimed one night. He had a stroke when he discovered that she proposed to become a writer. 'By God!' he roared. 'I would sooner see you operate an unsuccessful house of ill repute!' At fourteen, a dreadful thing occurred. The small son of one of her father's gardeners sold two poems to the *Atlantic Monthly*, entitled 'Ruffian Dusk' and 'The Strangler of Light.' Chanda offered him fifty dollars a week to write poems that she should sign and publish. The little boy coldly rejected the proposition, and his father, a stern Presbyterian, informed Chanda's father of the deal and how it had fallen through. 'By God!' the old man roared. 'At least she's not guilty of integrity, and that's more than I can say for any Bell in four generations except my grandfather and myself.' "

Miss Bell let her reminiscence trail off here, and she watched me from her divan with her penetrating eyes. "Ah," I said hopefully, "but she learned that day the high and holy importance of integrity, I trust." Chanda Bell gave me her sign of dismissal, a languid lift of her left hand. "You are the critic," she said. "I am but the chronicler. Leave me now. You perceive she is not coming." I rose and bowed. "Perhaps," I blurted out, "there is no Chanda Bell." But she had closed her eyes and turned away.

The next day, they took her to the hospital. "I have a panther near my hearth," she said, the first time they let me call on her. I went to see her twice again, the last time with Charles Vayne, who carried, with polished hopelessness, two bulging briefcases, which the nurse would not permit him to open. Chanda Bell was wandering in a far land, but she contrived a faint smile for each of her visitors. "Dear Rudgate," she whispered to Vayne, "what will become of meaning, thank God, when you are dead?" He tried in silence to make her grip a fountain pen, but she shook her head and turned to me. "Pretension has no plinth, Dennis," she said. "Ah, what a dusty answer . . ." Her voice and her heart failed, and the most remarkable woman I have ever known was dead.

That night, I called at her house, in the East Sixties. Hadley let me in. I had suspected him for a long time of being joined in dark conspiracy with Chanda Bell to make an end of me. I wondered, as I glared at the cold eye and then at the warm one, whether he might not be a frustrated writer, a bankrupt publisher, or an editor who had suffered a nervous breakdown. I jumped over the amenities of sorrow. "Her dying request," I said, "was that I should examine her papers."

The eyebrow over his twinkling eye lifted. "This evening, sir?" he asked.

"Take me to her desk and open it," I demanded.

There was a full second's pause, then "Certainly, sir," he said, and led the way into the Gray Room. "If I knew what you seek . . ." he began.

I turned on him. "I think you do!" I snapped. "I am looking for proof of whether I am an egregious ass or a uniquely perceptive individual. The line is sometimes thinly drawn be-

tween a tranquil old age in this city and exile, say, in Nassau."
He seemed genuinely bewildered.

There was nothing in the desk except a large manila envelope, which bore my name on the cover. I tore it open with shaking hands. Inside was a single sheet of white typewriter paper on which there were three carefully drawn squares, one inside another. "What does it mean?" I asked. "What is it?"

"If you will permit me, sir," said Hadley, and he took the paper and studied it. "That, sir," he said, finally, "is what I should describe as a drawing of a plinth."

I seized him by the shoulder. "You *are* in on this!" I cried. "What does it mean? What's behind it? Who are you? What have you two devils been up to all these years? Why should you want to destroy *me*?"

He took a backward step and gaped. He was honestly frightened, or else he was a superb actor. There was no twinkle in his eye. "I do not understand, sir," he stammered, or seemed to stammer.

I let go of his shoulder. "My critical reputation is at stake," I said. "Has she ever written an explanation of her writing— perhaps to be sent to some journal or periodical after her death?"

Hadley appeared to frown. "That, sir, I could not say," he brought out.

I turned away from him and then whirled back. "What is the carpet?" I shouted.

He put several feet of the shiny floor between us. "I do not know what you mean," he said nervously.

"Would there be papers anywhere else?" I demanded.

He looked about the room. "Nowhere," he said hollowly.

I walked over and looked out a window for a long time.

Suddenly, Hadley began to speak. "She had promised to put me in one of her books," he said in a tone of sadness, or what came to my ears as a tone of sadness. Then his voice brightened. "I was to have been the uncharacter of the non-butler," he said.

I came back from the window and glared at him.

"Her phrase, sir," he added hastily.

I lighted a cigarette, inhaled the smoke, and blew it out slowly. "Didn't you appear in any of her novels?" I asked.

"Oh, but no, sir," he corrected me proudly. "I did not appear in *all* of them!"

It was as if Chanda Bell were in the room, her bright, dark eyes taking us both in with a look of veiled amusement. "It must have made you very happy indeed," I snarled. "Not to appear in any of her books was wonderful enough, but not to appear in *all* of them—the final accolade, Hadley, the final accolade." He acknowledged it with a grave bow. "What has become of her manuscripts and her letters?" I demanded.

Hadley put on a sad expression. "She burned them, sir," he said. "It was her last act in this house."

I looked for the last time at the Gray Room—the gray desk, the gray chair, the gray Hadley.

"Perhaps a glass of Madeira, Mr. Thurber?" asked the butler. I declined ungraciously and said that I must leave. At the door, with the welcome street so near and desirable, he coughed discreetly. "Do you wish to take this with you, sir?" It was the drawing of the plinth. I took it without a word. "If I may say so, sir," Hadley went on, "you were the closest of all of them."

I glared at him, but there was no twinkle. "How close?" I growled.

"Oh, very close, sir," he said. "Very close indeed." This time, I thought I detected the ghost of the twinkle, but I could not be sure. I could not be sure of anything.

It has been eight months since I found the plinth in Chanda Bell's desk. Nothing has happened, but I expect an editor to ring me up any day. "We've got a remarkable letter or manuscript here, apparently written by Chanda Bell," he will say. "Sent to us by her lawyer, in accordance with a request in her will. It isn't signed, but he says she wrote it, all right. Seems she never signed anything. Sort of laughter from beyond the grave, you might say. The old girl exposes her stuff as the merest junk. Proves her point, too. She takes a hell of a crack at your 'Note on Chanda Bell.' Thought you might want to read the thing and reply to it—we'll print you and her in the same issue. She calls the piece 'The Carpet,' for some reason. I'll shoot it along."

No such call has come as yet, but I keep a bag packed, ready at a moment's notice to fly to Zanzibar, or Mozambique, or East Liverpool, Ohio. Meanwhile, I have hit on a new approach to the works of Chanda Bell. I am trying to read them sideways.

Teacher's Pet

KELBY had not wanted to go to the Stevensons' for cocktails. It wasn't that he was tired out again, as his wife, Elizabeth, was always complaining. To prove this, he had, after making up his mind to go, insisted on walking, instead of driving, to the Stevensons' house, three blocks down and across the village green. He had wanted to have a quiet dinner at home, unpreceded by alcohol, and to retire to the library afterward and read du Noüy. Elizabeth would have at least three Martinis—he noticed, looking at her across the terrace at the side of the Stevensons' house, that she was already on her second—and that meant she might want to "go on" after dinner, or perhaps tear up dinner at home and drive to the Belleville Inn for more drinks and dinner there. She might even call up the Blakes from there and really get going.

"No, thanks," said Kelby as his host approached with the cocktail shaker; then, "Oh, all right, go ahead." And he held out his glass for his own second drink.

"Do you good," said Bob Stevenson, pouring. "Pep you up. You look a little gray—anything the matter?"

"No," said Kelby with the required smile. "No, not at all. I'm fine."

As a matter of fact, he was not fine. He had had, the day before, something very like a religious experience, of a darkly ominous nature. It had been brought on by his reading a magazine article dealing with the fears and neurotic disturbances of the human male in middle age. Kelby was three months past fifty, and the article had upset him, particularly in its reference to the sometimes disastrous shock caused by the aging man's recognition of the fact of death, the inevitability of his perhaps not too distant termination. Women, the article intimated, were better adjusted to the certainty of extinction and rarely gave it a conscious thought, but a man in his fifties or later—often earlier—might be stricken all of a sudden by the realization of impending death, with serious nervous or even mental sequelae.

Kelby had wondered, putting the magazine down, if the

dread experience had come to him in his forties, say, and he had forgotten it. He chose to think that it had and that he had weathered it like the contemplative scholar he was. Upon arriving at this comforting decision, he had struck a match to light his pipe, and for no reason at all, since it was a sound match and no breeze was stirring in the library, it had gone out, as swift as a wink, as swift as death. Kelby had recognized the Moment. It seized him by the throat, and he found it difficult to breathe. His heart seemed to skip, and objects in the room began to recede. His pipe fell to the floor, and he held on to himself with a great effort, gripping the arms of his chair. There was sweat on his forehead and his wrists when he came out of his seizure. In a minute, he was his rational self again. It had been nothing more than a senseless panic induced by autosuggestion. He had actually managed a smile and a careless gesture of dismissal.

The incident would not be dismissed so easily, it turned out. It set in train, as all Kelby's moments of weakness did, discomforting thoughts that took him back as far as his youth. It carried him relentlessly, against his will, to the awful day before the First World War when Zeke Leonard had faced him down, with a crowd of eager kids looking on and expecting a fight. Kelby marvelled that at fifty he still could not get that day out of his consciousness for very long.

The trouble had begun when Leonard, "a typical shot-putter," as Kelby, many years later, had described him to Elizabeth, started teasing him after school (they were in the eighth grade) by calling him "Willber, dear!" in a shrill falsetto, and repeating it at steady intervals all the way to the corner of Franklin Avenue and Pine Street. It was bad enough to be named Willber, with two "l"s, and to have his teacher call him by that silly name every day in class, but it had been unbearable when Miss Lemmert had called him "Willber, dear" one afternoon in the hearing of Zeke and several other kids as school was letting out. She had wanted Willber dear to post a letter for her, or to do some other small errand, a request that branded him at once a teacher's pet of the worst order. Willber Kelby was the smartest boy at Buchanan School, and from the third grade on his teachers had made no bones about it. Zeke Leonard, who had the brains of a pole vaulter, had hated Willber from the time they were seven for his intelligence, his name, his frail body, and his inability, according to Zeke, to do anything except study.

Kelby had turned on him that day, thirty-seven years before, but the grinning Zeke had pushed him, slapped him, bumped him, and kicked him around, holding one arm behind his back and calling attention to this handicap. Kelby had flailed his shorter arms a few times with ludicrous ineffectiveness, and then he had merely tried to cover his face against Zeke's pummelling. Finally, he had started to cry. The other boys had laughed and hooted and whistled. "Look—*both* hands behind me!" Zeke had sneered suddenly, and Willber Kelby had taken to flight, still crying.

"Break it up." The hearty voice of Bob Stevenson banged into Kelby's memories. "You having a conference with yourself? Here you go, Will."

"Thanks," said Kelby, holding his glass out for another Martini.

"Of course, I simply never get to know you, Mr. Kelby," babbled a woman, dropping into a chair next to his. "I've known Lizzie for simply ages, but you always seem to be *inside* yourself, as if you didn't want anyone to trespass on your thoughts. But here I am, a bold woman, determined to find out what you are thinking about, whether you want me to or not. Now, Mr. Kelby, what *are* you thinking about?"

Kelby fought off a frown and recrossed his legs. He was about to say something to the effect that he had been absorbed in the witty conversation going on about him, and then, perhaps because the gin had touched him, he came out flatly with the truth. "I was thinking about the time a boy named Zeke Leonard beat me up," he said. "I was a teacher's pet, and he beat me up."

"What in the world for?" exclaimed the woman. "What had you done?"

"A teacher's pet doesn't have to do anything," Kelby said. "It is the mere fact of his existence that makes the stupid and the strong want to beat him up. There is a type of man that wants to destroy the weaker, the more sensitive, the more intelligent." He must have let his gaze drift to his host, who was stirring up more Martinis.

"You mean the Bob Stevenson type?" the woman whispered into his ear in intimate understanding. Then, shifting back into high, "I know just what you mean. We have the *most* trouble with Elbert that way. He's so terribly sensitive. The older boys are always torturing him." She lowered her voice to a whisper again. "Young Bob Stevenson is the worst. He simply loves to badger Elbert. I do wish Elbert would stand up to him some day. It irritates my husband terribly that he won't take his own part. Do they get *over* it?"

Kelby's attention had wandered. "Once a fullback, always a fullback," he said.

"No, I mean the—well—teacher's pets," she explained. "You see, Elbert is really terribly smart—he's the brightest boy in his school. I wish *you* could talk to him, Mr. Kelby— it would do him a world of good. We are going to spend the winter here in Woodville, and he'll go into Junior High. It's terribly hard changing to a new school."

Kelby had been thinking while she ran on. Having finished his third drink, he was on the edge of his irritable phase, and the woman's babbling had not improved his mood. "I know Elbert," he said thinly. "He's like all the rest. They grow old, they die, and if they're lucky, they get buried. They do not change. The best that can be said for them is that they outlive the stupid and the strong. It isn't much, but it's something. They can snicker when they read the obituaries of the powerfully built. It is their only physical triumph."

"But they are not cowards," said the woman defensively, clipping the last word sharply. "At least, I know Elbert is not a coward."

Kelby had begun to twirl his glass by its stem. "There are a lot of comforting euphemisms," he said. "Hypersensitive, nonaggressive, peace-loving, introverted—take your choice."

The woman was beginning not to like the turn of the discussion. She had started to get up from her chair when from out of the house, letting the widely flung screen door bang behind him, came Robert Stevenson, Jr. He strode toward his mother, apparently oblivious of the guests. "Hey, Mom!" he said. "Geez, how's about some dinner—it's late."

Two of the guests arose at this broad hint, but Sally Stevenson waved them back to their chairs. "Sit down, sit down," she said. "It's early. We're not eating till seven-thirty."

"Geez, Mom!" said Bob.

"Speak to the guests, Robert," she commanded. "You know everybody." He let a scowlish grin trail from chair to chair.

"Got a belly like a moose," said his father proudly, hovering above Kelby with the shaker. "Can't think of anything but the nose bag. Healthy, though, God knows. What did they bring you up on, Will—marshmallows?"

"Yes," said Kelby. "Toasted, mostly." Stevenson burst into loud laughter. Kelby, who had covered his empty glass with his hand, suddenly held it out.

"Good boy!" chortled Stevenson, filling it.

"Easy does it, Will!" called Elizabeth from across the terrace. The apparently amiable laugh that accompanied her warning fooled everybody except the other women and Kelby.

He raised his glass with a defiant look at his wife. "Here's to Junior," he said, "the greatest future fullback in the world!"

"Make it tackle," said the boy's father. "Bob wants to be a tackle."

"We never call him Junior," put in Bob's mother.

"You know that, Will," said Elizabeth.

"Tackle, then," said Kelby, and drank half his cocktail.

"Say, I almost forgot," began Bob Stevenson, Sr., and he proceeded to tell the terrace at large a noisy story about the predicament of a friend of his.

Kelby, not listening, studied young Bob, who had dropped heavily but still gracefully onto the lawn and was moodily chewing a blade of grass and watching his father. The boy was thirteen, the same age Zeke Leonard had been in that faraway year of Kelby's humiliation. He was not unlike Leonard—big in the shoulders, long in the muscled arms, slender at the waist, restless, easy of movement and posture, and he had the same facile scowl and the sulky lower lip. Kelby hated his guts. He imagined that he was thirteen again, and he pictured himself squaring up to this big, ignorant boy. He spilled some of his drink as he indulged in the pleasurable fantasy of smacking Bob on the point of the jaw and sending him reeling backward to the ground. Kelby shook himself out of it with an effort. He finished his drink and stood up.

"How's about one for the village green?" asked Stevenson, who was an eager and watchful host.

"No, thanks," said Kelby. "Got some work to do tonight." He walked over to the only couple at the party that he liked and shook hands. He snapped a curt salute to the others and bowed to his hostess. Elizabeth could see that he was verging on his nasty state. She said goodbye to everyone hastily and joined him.

"Watch out for the marshmallows!" Stevenson called after him as they started around to the front of the house.

Elizabeth waited until they were out of earshot. "What did he mean—watch out for the marshmallows?" she asked suspiciously.

Kelby shrugged. "Once a fullback, always a fullback," he said.

"But what did he *mean*?" she persisted.

Kelby turned on her. "He loves marshmallows!" he shouted. "He dotes on them, he's crazy about them. They are responsible for his wonderful physique and his mushy brain. Didn't you know that?"

Elizabeth took a dozen steps in silence; then, "I won't talk to you when you're like this," she said in the artificially calm tone he knew so well. She kept her promised silence until they had crossed the green. "I never saw Bob Stevenson eat a single marshmallow in my whole life," she announced.

Kelby wasn't listening. He was back in school again, on an afternoon before the First World War. As he got to the driveway of their house, he caught Zeke Leonard a staggering blow directly between the eyes.

Elizabeth noted that his right fist was doubled and she saw the hard glint in his eyes. "What *is* the matter with you?" she demanded.

"Nothing's the matter with me," said Kelby. "I feel fine. You want to call up the Blakes and go over to Belleville?"

"Certainly not," said Elizabeth. "We've got a lovely roast of lamb, and we're going to stay right here. Besides, you'd be sure to get into one of your senseless arguments with Sam, and nobody would have any fun."

"We'll have another drink, then, before dinner," said Kelby. He could see her lips forming a firm protest. "I said we'd have another drink!" he almost shouted. She decided not to argue with him.

It was on Sunday, two days later, that Kelby, out for a walk, came upon young Bob Stevenson following Elbert truculently down Elm Street, increasing his cadence as his victim walked faster and faster. Elbert was almost at a dog-trot when he passed Kelby, who noticed that the boy's face was pale, and saw the hint of panic in his eyes.

"Hey, Ella!" Bob kept calling after the smaller boy.

Kelby was going to stop Bob and give him a sharp talking-to, and then something decided him to let the boy continue his pursuit. Bob passed Kelby without acknowledging that he saw him, calling "Hey, Ella!" in a mocking tone that had picked up an octave. Kelby turned around and followed the boys, but at a slower pace than theirs. Bob overhauled his quarry at the corner of Maple Street, and Kelby saw him reach out and whirl the smaller boy around. By the time Kelby came up to them, Bob, his back to the man, had flipped Elbert's cap off with a swift, insolent gesture. "You want to make anything out of it?" Bob was challenging. Elbert, panting, reached for his cap. "Leave it lay," said Bob, ruffling the boy's hair with his left hand. The future tackle stepped to where the cap lay and place-kicked it into the street. Then he strolled indolently toward the other boy, like a cop closing in on a traffic violator. He put out his hand slowly and took hold of Elbert's nose.

Kelby took two quick steps, grabbed Bob by the shoulder, and flung him around.

"Cut it out!" Bob said.

"Go on home!" snapped Kelby. "Go on!"

Bob scowled, and his lower lip stuck out. For three seconds, he tried to stare Kelby down; then he shrugged, made a noise with his lips, and started to saunter away.

"Wait a minute!" said Kelby harshly. Bob turned in surprise. "Pick up his cap and give it to him," said Kelby.

Bob glared. "Let him pick up his own cap," he said. "It ain't mine."

"Pick it up," yelled Kelby, "or, by God, I'll hold you over it by your ankles and make you pick it up with your teeth!"

Bob's eyebrows went up. He looked at Kelby's face and then away from it. He walked slowly to the cap in the street, spat neatly past it, and swept it up with his right hand. He tossed it at Elbert, who missed it. "So long, Ella," said Bob. "Keep your nose clean." He moved off down the street, whistling.

Through this scene, Elbert had stood where he was when the cap was knocked off his head. He was sniffling and whimpering. "Shut up!" shouted Kelby. "Shut up!" But the boy kept on. Kelby looked at his quivering lower lip and at the convulsion of his stomach. Elbert was fighting to gain control of himself, but he lost the battle and began to weep unrestrainedly. Kelby was suddenly upon him. He grabbed him tightly by the shoulders and shook him until his head bobbed back and forth. He let go of the boy's left shoulder and slapped him on the cheek. "You little crybaby!" sobbed Kelby. "You goddam little coward!"

Mr. Reynolds, who rounded the corner at that moment, had considerable difficulty pulling the grown man off the little boy. "I've seen some bullies in my time," Mr. Reynolds told the elder Stevenson later, "but I never saw anything to match that." Robert Stevenson, Sr., slowly struck a match and slowly lighted a cigarette. He put on his expression of profound wisdom, his lips tightening, his head slightly to one side. "Young Bob tells me Kelby threatened *him*, too," he said. He took in an enormous lungful of smoke and let it out gradually, studying its pattern on the air. "You never know about a man, Reynolds," he said. "You just never know."

FROM

THURBER'S DOGS

An Introduction

L EAFING through Plutarch's *Lives*, on a winter's day, I came upon the story of Xanthippus and his dog. It seems that the old Greek, fleeing Athens one time by ship, left his dog behind—or thought he left him behind. To his amazement and delight, the dog, in the finest whither-thou-goest tradition known to the animal kingdom, plunged into the sea and swam after the galley all the way to Salamis, a feat of which even a seal might well be proud. When the dog died, Xanthippus built a conspicuous tomb for it, high on a windy cliff, that men, infirm of purpose, weak of heart, might be reminded of the miracles which can be wrought by courage, loyalty, and resolution.

Man first gained superiority over the other animals not because of his mind, but because of his fingers. He could pick up rocks and throw them, and he could wield a club. Later he developed the spear and the bow and arrow. It is my theory that the other animals, realizing they were as good as cooked if they came within range of Man's weapons, decided to make friends with him. He probably tried to make a pet and companion out of each species in turn. (It never occurred to him, in those days, to play or go hunting with Woman, a peculiarity which has persisted down to the present time.)

It did not take Man long—probably not more than a hundred centuries—to discover that all the animals except the dog were impossible around the house.* One has but to spend a few days with an aardvark or a llama, command a water buffalo to sit up and beg, or try to housebreak a moose, to perceive how wisely Man set about his process of elimination and selection. When the first man brought the first dog to his cave (no doubt over and above his wife's protests), there began an association by which Man has enormously profited. It is conceivable that the primordial male held the female, as mate or mother, in no aspect of esteem whatsoever, and that the introduction of the dog into the family circle first infected him

---

*There is no deliberate intention here to offend admirers of the cat, although I don't really much care whether I do or not.

799

with that benign disease known as love. Certain it is that the American male of today, in that remarkable period between infancy and adolescence, goes through a phase, arguably atavistic, during which he views mother, sister, and the little girl next door with cold indifference, if not, indeed, outspoken disdain, the while he lavishes wholehearted affection on Rex or Rover. In his grief over the loss of a dog, a little boy stands for the first time on tiptoe, peering into the rueful morrow of manhood. After this most inconsolable of sorrows, there is nothing life can do to him that he will not be able somehow to bear.

If Man has benefited immeasurably by his association with the dog, what, you may ask, has the dog got out of it? His scroll has, of course, been heavily charged with punishments: he has known the muzzle, the leash, and the tether; he has suffered the indignities of the show bench, the tin can on the tail, the ribbon in the hair; his love life with the other sex of his species has been regulated by the frigid hand of authority, his digestion ruined by the macaroons and marshmallows of doting women. The list of his woes could be continued indefinitely. But he has also had his fun, for he has been privileged to live with and study at close range the only creature with reason, the most unreasonable of creatures.

The dog has got more fun out of Man than Man has got out of the dog, for the clearly demonstrable reason that Man is the more laughable of the two animals. The dog has long been bemused by the singular activities and the curious practices of men, cocking his head inquiringly to one side, intently watching and listening to the strangest goings-on in the world. He has seen men sing together and fight one another in the same evening. He has watched them go to bed when it is time to get up, and get up when it is time to go to bed. He has observed them destroying the soil in vast areas, and nurturing it in small patches. He has stood by while men built strong and solid houses for rest and quiet, and then filled them with lights and bells and machinery. His sensitive nose, which can detect what's cooking in the next township, has caught at one and the same time the bewildering smells of the hospital and the munitions factory. He has seen men raise up great cities to heaven and then blow them to hell.

The effect upon the dog of his life with Man is discernible in his eyes, which frequently are capable of a greater range of expression than Man's. The eyes of the sensitive French poodle, for example, can shine with such an unalloyed glee and darken with so profound a gravity as to disconcert the masters of the earth, who have lost the key to so many of the simpler magics. Man has practiced for such a long time to mask his feelings and to regiment his emotions that some basic quality of naturalness has gone out of both his gaiety and his solemnity.

The dog is aware of this, I think. You can see it in his eyes sometimes when he lies and looks at you with a long, rueful gaze. He knows that the bare foot of Man has been too long away from the living earth, that he has been too busy with the construction of engines, which are, of all the things on earth, the farthest removed from the shape and intention of nature. I once owned a wise old poodle who used to try to acquaint me with the real facts of living. It was too late, though. I would hastily turn on the radio or run out and take a ride in the car.

The dog has seldom been successful in pulling Man up to its level of sagacity, but Man has frequently dragged the dog down to his. He has instructed it in sloth, pride, and envy; he has made it, in some instances, neurotic; he has even taught it to drink. There once lived in Columbus, Ohio, on Franklin Avenue, a dog named Barge. He was an average kind of dog, medium in size and weight, ordinary in markings. His master and mistress and their two children made up a respectable middle-class family. Some of the young men in the neighborhood, however, pool-shooting, motorcycle-riding bravos, lured Barge into a saloon one day and set before him a saucer of beer. He lapped it up and liked it. From there it was but an easy step to whisky.

Barge was terribly funny, the boys thought, when he got stiff. He would bump into things, hiccup, grin foolishly, and even raise his muzzle on high in what passed for "Sweet Adeline." Barge's coat became shabby, his gait uncertain, and his eyes misty. He took to staying out in the town all night, raising hell. His duties as watchdog in the home of his owners were completely neglected. One night, when Barge was off

on one of his protracted bats, burglars broke in and made off
with his mistress' best silver and cut glass.

Barge, staggering home around noon of the next day,
sniffed disaster when he was still a block away. His owners
were waiting for him grimly on the front porch. They had not
straightened up after the burglars. The sideboard drawers were

He goes with his owner into bars.

pulled out, the floor littered with napkins and napkin rings.
Barge's ears, chops, and tail fell as he was led sternly into the
house to behold the result of his wicked way of life. He took
one long, sad look around, and the cloudiness cleared from
his head. He realized that he was not only a ne'er-do-well but
a wrongo. One must guard the house at night, warn the family
of fire, pull drowning infants out of the lake. These were the

sacred trusts, the inviolable laws. Man had dragged Barge very far down, but there was still a spark of doghood left in him. He ran quickly and quietly upstairs, jumped out of an open window, and killed himself. This is a true and solemn legend of Franklin Avenue.

FURTHER FABLES
FOR OUR TIME

The Bluebird and His Brother

It was said of two bluebirds that they were unlike as two brothers could be, that one was a pearl in a pod and the other a pea. Pearl was happy-go-lucky, and Pea was gloomy-go-sorry.

"I am in love with love and life," sang the glad bird.

"I am afraid of sex and flight," sang the sad bird.

Pearl flaunted his gay colors like a bonnie blue flag, and his song was as bold as the Rebel yell. He went South every winter alone, and came North every spring with a different female. His gay philosophy freed his psyche of the stains of fear and the stresses of guilt, and he attained a serenity of spirit that few male birds and even fewer male human beings ever reach. He did not worry because some of his children were also his nieces, the daughters of one of his sisters. He sat loose, sang

pretty, and slept tight, in a hundred honey locusts and cherry trees and lilac bushes. And every winter he went South alone, and every spring he came North with a different female. He did not worry because some of his grandchildren were also his grandnephews, the grandsons of one of his sisters.

At sunset in summertime, the gay bluebird flew higher than the lark or the wild goose, and he was pleased to note that, like himself, heaven wore blue, with a tinge of red.

The gloomy bluebird went South alone in the winter and came North alone in the spring, and never flew higher than you could throw a sofa. While still in his prime he developed agoraphobia and went to live underground, to the surprise and dismay of families of frogs and foxes and moles and gophers and crickets and toads, and of the bewildered dog who dug him up one day while burying a bone, and then hastily buried him again, without ceremony or sorrow.

MORAL: *It is more dangerous to straight-arm life than to embrace it.*

The Lover and His Lass

AN ARROGANT gray parrot and his arrogant mate listened, one African afternoon, in disdain and derision, to the lovemaking of a lover and his lass, who happened to be hippopotamuses.

"He calls her snooky-ookums," said Mrs. Gray. "Can you believe that?"

"No," said Gray. "I don't see how any male in his right mind could entertain affection for a female that has no more charm than a capsized bathtub."

"Capsized bathtub, indeed!" exclaimed Mrs. Gray. "Both of them have the appeal of a coastwise fruit steamer with a cargo of waterlogged basketballs."

But it was spring, and the lover and his lass were young, and they were oblivious of the scornful comments of their sharp-tongued neighbors, and they continued to bump each other around in the water, happily pushing and pulling, backing and filling, and snorting and snaffling. The tender things they said to each other during the monolithic give-and-take of their courtship sounded as lyric to them as flowers in bud or green things opening. To the Grays, however, the bumbling romp of the lover and his lass was hard to comprehend and even harder to tolerate, and for a time they thought of calling the A.B.I., or African Bureau of Investigation, on the ground that monolithic lovemaking by enormous creatures who should have become decent fossils long ago was probably a threat to the security of the jungle. But they decided instead to phone their friends and neighbors and gossip about the shameless pair, and describe them in mocking and monstrous metaphors involving skidding buses on icy streets and overturned moving vans.

Late that evening, the hippopotamus and the hippopotama were surprised and shocked to hear the Grays exchanging terms of endearment. "Listen to those squawks," wuffled the male hippopotamus.

"What in the world can they see in each other?" gurbled the female hippopotamus.

"I would as soon live with a pair of unoiled garden shears," said her inamoratus.

They called up their friends and neighbors and discussed the incredible fact that a male gray parrot and a female gray

parrot could possibly have any sex appeal. It was long after midnight before the hippopotamuses stopped criticizing the Grays and fell asleep, and the Grays stopped maligning the hippopotamuses and retired to their beds.

MORAL: *Laugh and the world laughs with you, love and you love alone.*

The Bachelor Penguin
and the Virtuous Mate

ONE SPRING a bachelor penguin's fancy lightly turned, as it did in every season, to thoughts of illicit love. It was this gay seducer's custom to make passes at the more desirable females after their mates had gone down to the sea to fish. He had found out that all the females in the community made a ritual of rearranging the sitting-room furniture, putting it back where it had been the day before, and they were only too glad to have a strong male help them move the heavier pieces. Their mates had grown less and less interested in housework and more and more addicted to fishing, as time went on. The bachelor penguin proved handy at putting on or taking off screen doors, removing keys wedged in locks meant for other keys, and rescuing the females from other quandaries of their own making. After a few visits, the feathered Don Juan induced the ladies to play Hide-in-the-Dark with him, and Guess Who This Is?, and Webfooty-Webfooty.

As the seasons rolled on, the handsome and well-groomed Casanova became a little jaded by his routine successes with the opposite sex. Then one morning, after the other male penguins had gone to the seashore to fish as usual, Don J. Penguin spied the prettiest female he had ever seen, trying, all by herself, to move a sitting-room sofa back to the spot where it had been the day before. Don gallantly offered to help the matron in distress and she gladly accepted, with a shy look and a faint blush. The next morning the bachelor, who knew how to play his cards, came back and helped the house-penguin put on the screen door, and the following day he fixed the broken catch of her necklace, and the day after that he tightened the glass top of her percolator. Each time that he suggested playing Hide-in-the-Dark or Guess Who This Is?, the object of his desire thought of something else for him to fix, or loosen, or tighten, or take off, or put on. After several weeks of this, the amorist began to suspect that he was being taken, and his intended victim corroborated his fears.

"Unless you keep on helping me take things off, and put things on, and pry things loose, and make things tighter," she told the dismayed collector of broken hearts, "I will tell my mate about your improper advances and your dishonorable

intentions." Don Penguin knew that the clever penguin's mate was the strongest male in the community, and also had the shortest temper and the least patience. There wasn't going to be any Hide-in-the-Dark or Guess Who This Is? or Webfooty-Webfooty. And so he spent the rest of his days working for the virtuous and guileful lady of his desire, moving sofas, taking things off and putting things on, loosening this and tightening that, and performing whatever other tasks his fair captor demanded of him. His bow tie became untied, his dinner jacket lost its buttons, his trousers lost their crease, and his eyes lost their dream. He babbled of clocks, and of keys caught in locks, and everybody closed her door when he came waddling down the street except the penguin who had taken him in with a beauty as unattainable as the stars, and a shy look, and a faint blush as phony as a parrot's laugh. One day her mate, returning early from the sea, caught a glimpse of Don leaving the house, and said, "What did old Droop Feather want?"

"Oh, he washes the windows and waxes the floors and

sweeps the chimney," the female replied. "I believe he had an unhappy love affair."

MORAL: *One man's mate may sometimes be another man's prison.*

The Peacelike Mongoose

IN COBRA country a mongoose was born one day who didn't want to fight cobras or anything else. The word spread from mongoose to mongoose that there was a mongoose who didn't want to fight cobras. If he didn't want to fight anything else, it was his own business, but it was the duty of every mongoose to kill cobras or be killed by cobras.

"Why?" asked the peacelike mongoose, and the word went around that the strange new mongoose was not only pro-cobra and anti-mongoose but intellectually curious and against the ideals and traditions of mongoosism.

"He is crazy," cried the young mongoose's father.

"He is sick," said his mother.

"He is a coward," shouted his brothers.

"He is a mongoosexual," whispered his sisters.

Strangers who had never laid eyes on the peacelike mongoose remembered that they had seen him crawling on his

stomach, or trying on cobra hoods, or plotting the violent overthrow of Mongoosia.

"I am trying to use reason and intelligence," said the strange new mongoose.

"Reason is six-sevenths of treason," said one of his neighbors.

"Intelligence is what the enemy uses," said another.

Finally, the rumor spread that the mongoose had venom in

his sting, like a cobra, and he was tried, convicted by a show of paws, and condemned to banishment.

MORAL: *Ashes to ashes, and clay to clay, if the enemy doesn't get you your own folks may.*

The Trial of the Old Watchdog

An old experienced collie, who had been a faithful country watchdog for many years, was arrested one summer's day and accused of the first-degree murder of a lamb. Actually, the lamb had been slain by a notorious red fox who had planted the still-warm body of his victim in the collie's kennel.

The trial was held in a kangaroo court presided over by Judge Wallaby. The jury consisted of foxes, and all the spectators were foxes. A fox named Reynard was prosecuting attorney. "Morning, Judge," he said.

"God bless you, boy, and good luck," replied Judge Wallaby jovially.

A poodle named Beau, an old friend and neighbor of the collie, represented the accused watchdog. "Good morning, Judge," said the poodle.

"Now I don't want you to be too clever," the Judge warned him. "Cleverness should be confined to the weaker side. That's only fair."

A blind woodchuck was the first creature to take the stand, and she testified that she saw the collie kill the lamb.

"The witness is blind!" protested the poodle.

"No personalities, please," said the Judge severely. "Perhaps the witness saw the murder in a dream or a vision. This would give her testimony the authority of revelation."

"I wish to call a character witness," said the poodle.

"We have no character witnesses," said Reynard smoothly, "but we have some charming character assassins."

One of these, a fox named Burrows, was called to the stand. "I didn't actually see this lamb killer kill this lamb," said Burrows, "but I almost did."

"That's close enough," said Judge Wallaby.

"Objection," barked the poodle.

"Objection overruled," said the Judge. "It's getting late. Has the jury reached a verdict?"

The forefox of the jury stood up. "We find the defendant guilty," he said, "but we think it would be better to acquit him, nonetheless. If we hang the defendant, his punishment will be over. But if we acquit him of such dark crimes as murder, concealing the body, and associating with poodles and defense attorneys, nobody will ever trust him again, and he will be suspect all the days of his life. Hanging is too good for him, and much too quick."

"Guilt by exoneration!" Reynard cried. "What a lovely way to end his usefulness!"

And so the case was dismissed and court was adjourned, and everybody went home to tell about it.

MORAL: *Thou shalt not blindfold justice by pulling the wool over her eyes.*

ALARMS AND DIVERSIONS

The First Time I Saw Paris

W HAT I SAW first of all was one outflung hand of France as cold and limp as a dead man's. This was the seacoast town of Saint-Nazaire, a long while ago. I know now that French towns don't die, that France has the durability of history itself, but I was only twenty-three then, and seasick, and I had never been so far from Ohio before. It was the dank, morose dawn of the 13th of November, 1918, and I had this first dismal glimpse of *France la Doulce* from the deck of the U.S. Transport *Orizaba*, which had come from the wintry sea like a ship out of Coleridge, a painted ship in an unreal harbor. The moist, harsh light of breaking day gave the faces of the silent staring gobs on deck a weird look, but the unreality was shattered soon enough by the raucous voice of a boatswain bawling orders. I had first heard this voice, strong enough to outshout a storm, snarling commands at "abandon ship" drill: "Now, light all lanterns!" and "Now, lower all lifeboats!" I had been assigned to a life raft that was rusted to the deck and couldn't be budged. "Now, what's the matter with Life Raft Number Six?" the boatswain had roared. A sailor next to me said, "She's stuck to the deck, sir." The boatswain had to have the last word and he had it. "Now, leave her lay there!" he loudly decreed.

The *Orizaba* had taken a dozen days zigzagging across the North Atlantic, to elude the last submarines of the war, one of which we had sighted two days before, and Corcoran and I felt strange and uncertain on what seemed anything but solid land for a time. We were code clerks in the State Department, on our way to the Paris Embassy. Saint-Nazaire was, of course, neither dead nor dying, but I can still feel in my bones the gloom and tiredness of the old port after its four years of war. The first living things we saw were desolate men, a detachment of German prisoners being marched along a street, in mechanical step, without expression in their eyes, like men coming from no past and moving toward no future. Corcoran and I walked around the town to keep warm until the bistros opened. Then we had the first cognac of our lives, quite a lot of it, and the day brightened, and there was a sense of beginning as well as of ending, in the chilling weather. A young pink-cheeked French army officer got off his bicycle in front of a house and knocked on the door. It was opened by a young woman whose garb and greeting, even to our inexperienced eyes and ears, marked her as one of those females once described by a professor of the Harvard Law School as "the professionally indiscreet." Corcoran stared and then glanced at his wristwatch. "Good God!" he said. "It isn't even nine o'clock yet."

The train trip down to Paris was a night to remember. We shared a sleeping compartment with a thin, gloved, talkative Frenchman who said he was writing the history of the world and who covered his subject spasmodically through the night in English as snarled as a fisherman's net, waking us once to explain that Hannibal's elephants were not real, but merely fearful figments of Roman hallucination. I lay awake a long time thinking of the only Paris I knew, the tranquil, almost somnolent city of Henry James's turn-of-the-century novels, in which there was no hint of war, past or approaching, except that of the sexes.

Paris, when we finally got there, seemed to our depressed spirits like the veritable capital city of Beginning. Her heart was warm and gay, all right, but there was hysteria in its beat, and the kind of compulsive elation psychiatrists strive to cure. Girls snatched overseas caps and tunic buttons from American soldiers, paying for them in hugs and kisses, and even warmer coin. A frightened Negro doughboy from Alabama said, "If this happened to me back home, they'd hang me." The Folies Bergères and the Casino de Paris, we found a few nights later, were headquarters of the New Elation, filled with generous ladies of joy, some offering their charms free to drinking, laughing and brawling Americans in what was left of their uniforms. At the Folies a quickly composed song called *"Finie la Guerre"* drew a dozen encores. Only the American MP's were grim, as they moved among the crowds looking for men who were AWOL, telling roistering captains and majors to dress up their uniforms. Doughboy French, that wonderful hybrid, bloomed everywhere. *"Restez ici* a minute," one private said to his French girl. *"Je* returny *après cet* guy partirs."

Cet guy was, of course, a big-jawed military policeman set on putting a stop to non-regulation hilarity.

"I do not understand the American," a Casino girl told me. "They fight at night with each other, they break mirrors, they become bloody, they say goddamn everybody, and the next day what do you think? They are in the Parc Monceau on all fours giving little French children a ride on their backs. They are marvelous. I love them."

The Americans have never been so loved in France, or anywhere else abroad, as they were in those weeks of merriment and wild abandon. When, late in 1919, most of our soldiers had sailed back home, *La Vie Parisienne* had a full-page color drawing of an American officer over whose full-length figure dozens of lovely miniature French girls were rapturously climbing, and the caption ruefully observed: "The hearts of our young ladies have gone home with the Americans."

My trunk had stayed on the *Orizaba*. Corcoran and I had been the only two civilians on board, and transports were not used to unloading non-military baggage. All I had was the clothes I wore—my hat had been claimed as a souvenir—and I set about the considerable task of buying a wardrobe, paying what amounted to five dollars for B.V.D.'s at the Galeries Lafayette. A suit I bought at a shop deceptively called "Jack, American Tailor" is packed away in the modest files of secret memory. It might have been made by the American Can Company. I tried on hats for an hour in a shop on the Avenue de l'Opéra, upon whose civilian stock the dust of four years of war had settled. There were narrow-brimmed hats, each with a feather stuck on one side, that made me look like Larry Semon, movie comic of the silent days, and some that would have delighted that great connoisseur of funny hats, Mr. Ed Wynn. They were all placed on my head with an excited *"Voilà!"* by the eager salesman, and they were all too small, as well as grotesque. In one of the famous black, broad-brimmed hats, long and lovingly associated with the painters and poets of Bohemian Paris, I looked like a baleful figure attending the funeral of Art. I nearly broke the salesman's heart when I turned down a ten-gallon white Stetson he had dug up out of the cellar. So I went through that cold, dank Paris winter without a hat.

I had bought a cane, which in Columbus would have identified me as a lounge lizard of dubious morals, and I acquired enough boulevard French to say, *"Où est la Place de la Concorde?"* and to reply to *"Voulez-vous une petite caresse?"* My *tout ensemble* was strange, but not strange enough to deceive doughboys and gobs wandering along the Champs Elysées, homesick and disconsolate after the elation died down. I helped them decipher the small red-and-black French-English dictionaries they carried and told them that, contrary to their invariable conviction, they would not be stuck in "this godforsaken city" forever. Once I translated, for a puzzled demoiselle, a mysterious note she had got through the mails from a doughboy who had returned to her one day before *cet* guy had partired. It began, "I am in a place I cannot leave." I managed to explain to her that her boy had been jailed for being absent without leave. I gathered that he had been, when on the loose, a great lover, fighter and piggy-back rider, like the others. "I wish to cry on your shirt," his girl friend told me, and she cried on my shirt. That astonished shirt, stained with Lacrimae Puellae 1919, must have cost a lot, but all I remember is that the amazing French shirttail reached to my knees.

When I got to France, the franc was worth almost a quarter, but pretty soon you could get fourteen francs for your dollar, and since prices didn't rise as rapidly as the franc fell, the $2,000 annual salary of a code clerk began to mean something. One amateur speculator among us, certain that the franc would come back with all the resilience of Paris, bought up francs and was wiped out when *la chute* continued. In my nearly forty years off and on in France I have seen this coin of a thousand values vary from 5.30 to 350. "It will be as worthless as dandelions," a dour concierge predicted in 1919, but she was wrong.

"Ah, *ces américains*," sighed a Folies girl one evening. "*Quels hommes!* They are such good bad boys. They wish to spend the night, even the weekend." She went on to explain how this complicated the economic structure of one in her profession. She was used, in the case of other foreigners, to a nightly transference of paid affections as neatly maneuvered as the changing of partners in a square dance. "These Americans are men born to marry," my informant went on. Many of them—thousands, I believe—did marry French girls and took them home to an astonished Brooklyn, a disapproving Middle West, and occasionally more amiable regions. I read somewhere in 1928 that about 75 per cent of these wartime marriages had ended in the return of the brides to France. One of those who stayed wrote me a letter a quarter of a century ago in which she said, dolorously, "There is not the life in Detroit. It is not Paris. Can you send me some books in French?" She had married a great big good bad American Army lieutenant. I sent her, among other books in French, the poems of Mallarmé and the book Clemenceau wrote after the war. I often wonder what finally became of another girl who married a sailor and went to live in Iowa, and what they thought of her English out there. She had learned it all from the plays of Shakespeare and it was quaint and wonderful to hear, but definitely not for Iowa. "How goes the night?" she asked me once, straight out of *Macbeth*, to which I was proudly able to reply, "The moon is down. I have not heard the clock." This Gallic Elizabethan had given up working for a few francs a week in a garment factory for a more lucrative and less monotonous career. Once I met her by appointment, and in pursuit of my sociological studies, on the terrace of the Café de la Paix, where, over vermouth cassis, she explained that she was going to meet, in half an hour, an American captain whom she had comforted one night long ago when he didn't have a sou. It seems he had promised to meet her at the café and pay his debt of gratitude, and he had written her from somewhere and fixed an hour. "He will be here," she said confidently, and she was right. A quiet, almost shy good bad boy, he slipped her a sealed envelope while I studied the passing throng in which, true prophecy has it, you will see everybody you know if you sit at your table long enough. I still remember that what he ordered was chocolate ice cream.

The City of Light, during most of 1919, was costumed like a wide-screen Technicolor operetta, the uniforms of a score of nations forming a kind of restless, out-of-step finale. The first Bastille Day celebration after the war was a carnival that dazzled the eye and lifted the heart. Chairs at windows of buildings along the route of march cost as much as fifty dollars, and stepladders on the crowded sidewalks could be rented for fifteen dollars. At night, in a thousand "tin bars," as our men called bistros, and in more elaborate *boîtes de nuit*, the Americans often changed the prewar pattern of Paris night life by fighting among themselves, or singly, in pairs, or in groups, the Anzacs, the waiters, the management, the *gendarmerie*, or whoever was looking for action. Chairs and bottles were thrown, and mirrors cracked from side to side. There was a conviction among Americans, more often false than true, that they were always overcharged, and this was the chief provocation for trouble, but high spirits, the irritating factor of unfamiliarity, triple sec, and a profound American inability to pick up foreign languages easily, often led to roughhouse. A civilian I knew who hailed from New Jersey, and constantly and profanely wished he were back there, asked me one morning how to say in French, "I demand the release of these Americans." It turned out that no Americans he knew were in durance anywhere. My unilingual companion simply planned to go out on the town that night with some compatriots and wanted to be prepared, in case his detachment was overwhelmed by the authorities in some bar. Like me, he worked at the Embassy, then on the Rue de Chaillot, and he had a code-room pass which he proposed to wave while shouting his command. I told him the French were always aroused, never intimidated, by civilians shouting orders, especially if they flaunted mysterious and doubtful official credentials. He would be taken, I told him, for that most despised of creatures, the *mouchard*, or police spy. Not the next morning, but a few days later, he showed up with bruised knuckles and a swollen jaw. "You were right," he admitted meekly.

Paris had been down on her knees, but now she got back on her feet, surely and resolutely, in the noble tradition of the world's most spirited city. Montmartre, when I first walked its deserted silent streets, had seemed down and out for good, but by New Year's Eve, 1918, it had begun to function, and before long the Moulin Rouge and the Chat Noir were gaily crowded again. Excellent food, the great pride of Paris, was naturally slow in reaching the tables of the famous restaurants, but I took an American Red Cross girl to Voisin's not many weeks after I arrived, and it seemed to have gone through the war as if nothing worse than a storm had passed. This was the quietly elegant restaurant celebrated for its calm, almost austere, survival of the Siege of Paris in the war with Prussia, when, undaunted by dwindling supplies, it served up the tender cuts of some of the more edible animals of the zoo. I remember being shown one of the remarkable and touching menus of those war years. I have forgotten just when it closed its doors forever, but in 1938, while accompanying my wife on a shopping trip, I was suddenly overcome by a curious and haunting sense of the past in a woman's glove store. Recognition flowed back like a film developing, and I realized that I stood within a few feet of where the American girl and I had sat for lunch one day. It was like meeting an old beloved friend who has undergone a sorrowful change and no longer knows who you are.

Paris during the months of the Peace Conference would have delighted Hadrian, Playboy of the Roman Empire, who enjoyed colorful spectacles brought together from the corners of the world. When President Wilson drove down the Champs Elysées, more people watched and cheered, more flags were waved, more eyes were bright, than I have ever seen in one place at one time. The way from there had to be down, because there was no higher place to reach, and the international highway of acclaim never runs straight and smooth very far. There had been, even on the day of armistice, voices that did not shout *"Finie la guerre!"* but solemnly warned, *"Maintenant ça commence."* But these prophets of predicament and peril were lost sight of in the carnival. I didn't hear them myself; I was too busy, between coding and decoding telegraphic messages, watching Premier Paderewski arriving at his hotel, catching glimpses of Herbert Hoover sitting erect in the back seat of his big Cadillac, identifying the impressive head of Lloyd George at one of the restaurants in the Bois de Boulogne. At the Casino de Paris, the famous straw hat and lower lip of Maurice Chevalier, not long before turned thirty, attracted crowds as his rising star dimmed a little the light of the great Mistinguette. He did a wonderful burlesque of an American gob, by turns melancholy and gay, excited and bewildered, taking the edge off Mistinguette's singing of "For Me and My Gal," a song the French loved. The Americans, of course, were singing "Smiles" and "Hindustan," and then a song of which someone had sent me a recording from America, "Dardanella." I remember taking the Red Cross girl to dinner at Noël Peters, where a trio of piano, violin and cello played many pieces, only one of them American. After brandy I had requested an American song, and the pianist finally dug up the sheet music of "Goodbye My Bluebell."

Everybody went out to Versailles, where the famous fountains had been turned on for the first time in years. All kinds of devices were used to get into the Hall of Mirrors. Never had so many fake passes been so elaborately contrived, but few of them worked. And through it all the Battle of Paris went on. Souvenir hunting by Americans reached a high point. They took things out of niches and tried to pry things loose from plinths, to add to the relics of war brought back from the front, including ornamental vases made by French soldiers out of the casings of French 75's. I got one of these at Fort Vaux outside Verdun, which had been stormed and taken and retaken so many times. Verdun had been the farthest north reached by me and another Embassy clerk in the week before Christmas, 1918. We had gone by train as far as the town of Vierzy, where my companion searched vainly for the grave of a friend from Illinois who had been a marine. Another marine from the Embassy guard, talking and dreaming of his ranch in Montana, had gone with us as far as Vierzy, mainly to find an open space in which he could practice firing a Luger he had picked up somewhere, but he would have no part of our plan to walk through the battlefields, day after day, as far as Soissons and Verdun. Up there we paid our way into Fort Vaux and the underground city of Verdun with American cigarettes. I often consume again, in fantasy, the light omelet, *pain de famille*, and good white wine served to us by a young French farmer and his wife who were bravely rebuilding their home in one of those landscapes of destruction so poignantly painted by the late English artist Paul Nash. It took long argument to persuade the couple to take money for the meal.

In our trek through the battlefields, with the smell of death still in the air, the ruined and shattered country scarred with ammunition dumps and crashed planes, we came upon the small temporary cemeteries arranged by the Graves Registration Service, each with a small American flag, such as the children of Paris waved at President Wilson, nailed to a post and faded by the rain and wintry weather. In one of these cemeteries my companion, a Tennessee youth, only a little taller than five feet, began singing "The Star-Spangled Banner" with his hat over his heart, and went on singing it in a sudden downpour of rain, for the anthem, once started, must be finished. He was loaded down with junk on our way back, most of which he had to abandon. He mourned his failure to wrench an ornamental iron gate from the entrance to a shattered château. The only thing I brought back, besides the vase, was the identification papers of an Algerian soldier named A. Mokdad, which were lying on the ground, punctured by two machine-gun bullets. Detachments of French labor battalions were trying to clear up the wreckage here and there, a task that seemed hopeless. But the French soldiers were tough, determined men. By the light of a Very shell one night in Soissons we had seen a company of *poilus* marching through the mud, singing "Madelon." In the muzzles of some of their carbines flowers from God knows where had been stuck. The soldiers looked enormous and indomitable, and it is good to know that one or two French painters of the time did justice to their stature, painting them to look like the rocks they were. Contrary to the prewar American notion of Frenchmen as small and dapper, there were scores of d'Artagnans in the armies of France for every Aramis—and he was tough enough himself.

Back in Paris, I made a brief survey of the souvenirs collected by Americans I knew. One man had brought from somewhere a machine gun, which he kept in his hotel room and left there when he went home. Legend had it that the upraised sword of the equestrian statue of George Washington in the Place d'Iéna had been replaced nine times, and one overenthusiastic vandal had been arrested while attempting to take one of the gilt cherubs from the superstructure of the bridge of Alexandre III across the Seine. A sailor I know collected, with the aid of chisel and screwdriver, ornate locks from old doors and gates, and his trophies must have weighed a good hundred pounds. A doughboy who fancied bronze and marble busts in museums was less successful. It was rumored, in the days of the Great Hunt, that not more than five servicemen were admitted to Napoleon's tomb at one time. Everybody heard, and retold, the wonderful myth of the bold and enterprising soldier in the Louvre who had got away with the arms of the Venus de Milo and the head of the Winged Victory.

I have nothing tangible to remind me of those tangled days, the Verdun vase and the papers of A. Mokdad having long since disappeared. The vase, wherever it is, must still bear the deathless hammered-out name "Verdun." From a separate trip to Rheims I brought back nothing but chill memories that still turn up now and then in nightmares. I see the vacant staring space from which the rose window of the cathedral had been carefully removed in time, and the gaping hole in one wall of the edifice, made by a shell hit. This great city of the Champagne country was all but deserted when I was there, and a walk through its streets was a walk on the moon. The disappearance of one wall had revealed a bedroom that looked like a dismal abandoned stage set. The works of a printing shop, its machines and type, were scattered across a street. The façade of a theater had been ripped off, revealing a crumbling stage, while empty seats and boxes, unharmed except by weather, gave the beholder the feeling that cast and audience had fled in horror during the showing of some kind of extravaganza in hell. And in Paris, so near in space, seemingly so far away in time, morbid visitors, looking for the effects of war, asked where they could find the church upon which a shell from Big Bertha had made its terrible direct hit.

All of us went to the grand opera many times, my own first visit being to hear "Aïda" and to see the *haut monde* of Paris once again in evening clothes, glittering up and down the marble staircases between acts. Someone pointed out René Fonck in the crowd, and I still remember the ribbon of the great airman's croix de guerre, as long as a ruler to accommodate all the palms he had won. There is a timelessness about grand opera in Paris, and except for the uniforms, there was no hint that the greatest war in history had come so recently to an end. I paid a dollar that night for a pack of American cigarettes, but this was not my most memorable financial transaction. A week or two after our arrival Corcoran and I had paid a dollar apiece for fried eggs, and almost as much for marmalade.

I sometimes ate with the doughboys, who never got used to French food, and groused about American Army grub. In Verdun one day we ate Army beans and the rest of the rations, using borrowed mess kits. "Look at them guys eat that stuff," one private said. "I'll be damned if they don't like it." We also liked the wheat cakes with genuine maple sirup served at an Army kitchen set up in the basement of the Crillon, the de luxe hotel in the heart of Paris which had been taken over by the Americans.

I saw no doughboys or gobs at the opera, but they crowded into the cinemas when they opened, to watch the American films of three actors popular with the French—W. S. Hart (*"le roi du ranch"*), Harold Lloyd, known as *"Lui,"* and Douglas Fairbanks *père*, lovingly called "Doogla" by the French.

When I finally sailed back home, sixteen months had elapsed since the Armistice, and the Brave New World was taking on its disillusioning shape. Theodore Roosevelt had died in 1919, which marked in its way the end of an era, and Woodrow Wilson had come down from his dizzy pinnacle of fame and hope, and was on his way to his own dismayed and frustrated end. Before long a celebrated room was to be filled with smoke out of which a political magician named Harry M. Daugherty would produce the shadowy figure of Warren Gamaliel Harding and the misleading motto of "Return to Normalcy" in a period of flagpole sitting, nonstop dancing, Channel swimming, ocean flying, husband murder, novels of disenchantment, and approaching financial chaos. I reached New York still without a hat. It was March and blustery in New York, and one of the first things I did was to buy one. It fitted my head, and seemed to my repatriated eye extremely becoming. It wasn't until later that day that I looked inside the hat to see the mark of the maker. I quote from a piece I wrote in 1923 for the Columbus, Ohio, Sunday *Dispatch*: "Something inside the crown caught my eye. I looked more closely. *'Fabriqué par Moissant et Amour, 25 Avenue de l'Opéra, Paris,'* it said."

Paris, City of Light and of occasional Darkness, sometimes

in the winter rain seeming wrought of monolithic stones, and then, in the days of its wondrous and special pearly light, appearing to float in mid-air like a mirage city in the Empire of Imagination, fragile and magical, has had many a premature requiem sung for the repose of its soul by nervous writers or gloomy historians who believe it is dying or dead and can never rise again. Paris, nonetheless, goes right on rising out of war, ultimatum, occupation, domestic upheaval, cabinet crises, international tension, and dark prophecy, as it has been in the habit of doing since its residents first saw the menacing glitter of Roman shields many centuries ago. Recently in the New York Sunday *Times* John Davenport sang sorrowfully of the Paris of today as a dying city, a city of ghosts, but his funeral arrangements were laughed off by, among others, a South Carolina reader who protested, "It is not Paris but an Anglo-American myth that is dying."

The Americans and English have never become an integral part of the anatomy of the city, which is forever French. Its visitors come and go, hopeful or despondent, comfortable or uneasy, looking in the wrong places for the pulse of the city, feeling in the wrong places for the throb of its heart. I have been in and out of Paris half a dozen times from 1920 to 1955, and I have had my moments of depression and worry about the great city, but I have never felt that I was sitting up at night with a fatally sick friend. I have seen her moods shift from confidence to despond, for Paris is a lady of temperament and volatility, but I have never felt she was mortally languishing, like a stricken heroine of grand opera.

I enjoy arguing with Parisian friends about the true gender of their fair city, pointing out that "feminine," in my lexicon, means neither frail nor frivolous, neither capricious nor coquettish, but female, and summing up with this sound paraphrase of Kipling: "The female of the cities is far tougher than the male." In my observation, the female of any species is not, in Simone de Beauvoir's pallid phrase, the Second Sex, but the First Sex, of which the Second is luckily born. Frenchmen jump too easily to the inference that "lady," when applied to Paris, means *poule de luxe*, or that what we feminists have in mind is the gay figure evoked when Monsieur Chevalier sings *"Paris, elle est une blonde."* What we really mean is Woman in the sense and stature, the sign and symbol, in which she is represented everywhere you look in Paris, from the celebrated statue of the fighting French woman called *"Quand Même,"* in the Tuileries, to the monumental figure on one side of the Arch of Triumph. Or take the statues in the Place de la Concorde representing eight great provincial cities of France, all of which are depicted as women. Perhaps the finest, that of Strasbourg, was shrouded in black when I first beheld it, but I was happily on hand when the lady was joyously stripped of her mourning after Strasbourg had been restored to France.

Street rioting has broken out in the streets of Paris from time to time, for Paris does not repress her anger any more than she suppresses her desires, and windows are smashed and buildings are burned, and now and then someone is killed. Once in a while the United States has been the object of Parisian wrath—thirty years ago I witnessed a *rixe* or two, but never a real *bagarre*—because of our failure to write off the French war debt. There were those at the time who feared that demonstrators might overturn the statue in the Place des Etats-Unis of Washington and Lafayette shaking hands. It has been marked with chalk, but it will never be overthrown. Not far from these sculptured hands across the sea stands an equally solid monument to the 118 Americans who lost their lives in the service of France during the First World War, sixty-one of them in the Lafayette Escadrille. The granite tribute contains the indestructible names of Raoul Lufbery, Norman Prince, Kiffin Rockwell, Victor Chapman and Alan Seeger.

This is the American quarter of Paris that I knew so well in the months after the Armistice. In front of what was once the chancellery of our Embassy at 5 Rue de Chaillot, a statue of Rochambeau salutes the mounted image of George Washington in the Place d'Iéna not far away. It was indeed *bien américain* the time of my first visit, for Woodrow Wilson lived at No. 11 Place des Etats-Unis, and a short walk from there was the Avenue du Président Wilson and a *pension* filled with Americans from the Embassy. The streets were loud with American voices and bright with our uniforms, and marines sometimes played baseball in the Rue de Chaillot. A bar advertised "American cocktails" and Yanks sang our war songs, including the one with the line "I'll bring you a Turk and the

THE YEARS WITH ROSS

A Dime a Dozen

HAROLD ROSS died December 6, 1951, exactly one month after his fifty-ninth birthday. In November of the following year the *New Yorker* entertained the editors of *Punch* and some of its outstanding artists and writers. I was in Bermuda and missed the party, but weeks later met Rowland Emett for lunch at the Algonquin. "I'm sorry you didn't get to meet Ross," I began as we sat down. "Oh, but I did," he said. "He was all over the place. Nobody talked about anybody else."

Ross is still all over the place for many of us, vitally stalking the corridors of our lives, disturbed and disturbing, fretting, stimulating, more evident in death than the living presence of ordinary men. A photograph of him, full face, almost alive with a sense of contained restlessness, hangs on a wall outside his old office. I am sure he had just said to the photographer, "I haven't got time for this." That's what he said, impatiently, to anyone—doctor, lawyer, tax man—who interrupted, even momentarily, the stream of his dedicated energy. Unless a meeting, conference, or consultation touched somehow upon the working of his magazine, he began mentally pacing.

I first met Harold Ross in February, 1927, when his weekly was just two years old. He was thirty-four and I was thirty-two. The *New Yorker* had printed a few small pieces of mine, and a brief note from Ross had asked me to stop in and see him some day when my job as a reporter for the New York *Evening Post* chanced to take me uptown. Since I was getting only forty dollars a week and wanted to work for the *New Yorker*, I showed up at his office the next day. Our meeting was to become for me the first of a thousand vibrant memories of this exhilarating and exasperating man.

You caught only glimpses of Ross, even if you spent a long evening with him. He was always in mid-flight, or on the edge of his chair, alighting or about to take off. He won't sit still in anybody's mind long enough for a full-length portrait. After six years of thinking about it, I realized that to do justice to Harold Ross I must write about him the way he talked and lived—leaping from peak to peak. What follows here is a monologue montage of that first day and of half a dozen swift and similar sessions. He was standing behind his desk, scowling at a manuscript lying on it, as if it were about to lash out at him. I had caught glimpses of him at the theater and at the Algonquin and, like everybody else, was familiar with the mobile face that constantly changed expression, the carrying voice, the eloquent large-fingered hands that were never in repose, but kept darting this way and that to emphasize his points or running through the thatch of hair that stood straight up until Ina Claire said she would like to take her shoes off and walk through it. That got into the gossip columns and Ross promptly had his barber flatten down the pompadour.

He wanted, first of all, to know how old I was, and when I told him it set him off on a lecture. "Men don't mature in this country, Thurber," he said. "They're children. I was editor of the *Stars and Stripes* when I was twenty-five. Most men in their twenties don't know their way around yet. I think it's the goddam system of women schoolteachers." He went to the window behind his desk and stared disconsolately down into the street, jingling coins in one of his pants pockets. I learned later that he made a point of keeping four or five dollars' worth of change in this pocket because he had once got stuck in a taxi, to his vast irritation, with nothing smaller than a ten-dollar bill. The driver couldn't change it and had to park and go into the store for coins and bills, and Ross didn't have time for that.

I told him that I wanted to write, and he snarled, "Writers are a dime a dozen, Thurber. What I want is an editor. I can't find editors. Nobody grows up. Do you know English?" I said I thought I knew English, and this started him off on a subject with which I was to become intensely familiar. "Everybody thinks he knows English," he said, "but nobody does. I think it's because of the goddam women schoolteachers." He turned away from the window and glared at me as if I were on the witness stand and he were the prosecuting attorney. "I want to make a business office out of this place, like any other business office," he said. "I'm surrounded by women and children. We have no manpower or ingenuity. I never know where anybody is, and I can't find out. Nobody tells me anything. They sit out there at their desks, getting me deeper and deeper into God knows what. Nobody has any self-discipline, nobody gets anything done. Nobody knows how to delegate anything. What I need is a man who can sit at a central desk and make this place operate like a business office, keep track of things, find out where people are. I am, by God, going to keep sex out of this office—sex is an incident. You've got to hold the artists' hands. Artists never go anywhere, they don't know anybody, they're antisocial.''

Ross was never conscious of his dramatic gestures, or of his natural gift of theatrical speech. At times he seemed to be on stage, and you half expected the curtain to fall on such an agonized tagline as "God, how I pity me!" Anthony Ross played him in Wolcott Gibbs's comedy *Season in the Sun*, and an old friend of his, Lee Tracy, was Ross in a short-lived play called *Metropole*, written by a former secretary of the editor. Ross sneaked in to see the Gibbs play one matinee, but he never saw the other one. I doubt if he recognized himself in the Anthony Ross part. I sometimes think he would have disowned a movie of himself, sound track and all.

He once found out that I had done an impersonation of him for a group of his friends at Dorothy Parker's apartment, and he called me into his office. "I hear you were imitating me last night, Thurber," he snarled. "I don't know what the hell there is to imitate—go ahead and show me." All this time his face was undergoing its familiar changes of expression and his fingers were flying. His flexible voice ran from a low register of growl to an upper register of what I can only call Western quacking. It was an instrument that could give special quality to such Rossisms as "Done and done!" and "You have me there!" and "Get it on paper!" and such a memorable tagline as his farewell to John McNulty on that writer's departure for Hollywood: "Well, God bless you, McNulty, goddam it.''

Ross was, at first view, oddly disappointing. No one, I think, would have picked him out of a line-up as the editor of the *New Yorker*. Even in a dinner jacket he looked loosely informal, like a carelessly carried umbrella. He was meticulous to the point of obsession about the appearance of his magazine, but he gave no thought to himself. He was usually dressed in a dark suit, with a plain dark tie, as if for protective coloration. In the spring of 1927 he came to work in a black hat so unbecoming that his secretary, Elsie Dick, went out and bought him another one. "What became of my hat?" he demanded later. "I threw it away," said Miss Dick. "It was awful." He wore the new one without argument. Miss Dick, then in her early twenties, was a calm, quiet girl, never ruffled by Ross's moods. She was one of the few persons to whom he ever gave a photograph of himself. On it he wrote, "For Miss Dick, to whom I owe practically everything." She could spell, never sang, whistled, or hummed, knew how to fend off unwanted visitors, and had an intuitive sense of when the coast was clear so that he could go down in the elevator alone and not have to talk to anybody, and these things were practically everything.

In those early years the magazine occupied a floor in the same building as the *Saturday Review of Literature* on West 45th Street. Christopher Morley often rode in the elevator, a tweedy man, smelling of pipe tobacco and books, unmistakably a literary figure. I don't know that Ross ever met him. "I know too many people," he used to say. The editor of the *New Yorker*, wearing no mark of his trade, strove to be inconspicuous and liked to get to his office in the morning, if possible, without being recognized and greeted.

From the beginning Ross cherished his dream of a Central Desk at which an infallible omniscience would sit, a dedicated genius, out of Technology by Mysticism, effortlessly controlling and coördinating editorial personnel, contributors, office boys, cranks and other visitors, manuscripts, proofs, cartoons, captions, covers, fiction, poetry, and facts, and bringing forth each Thursday a magazine at once funny, journalistically sound, and flawless. This dehumanized figure, disguised as a man, was a goal only in the sense that the mechanical rabbit of a whippet track is a quarry. Ross's mind was always filled with dreams of precision and efficiency beyond attainment, but exciting to contemplate.

This conception of a Central Desk and its superhuman engineer was the largest of half a dozen intense preoccupations. You could see it smoldering in his eyes if you encountered him walking to work, oblivious of passers-by, his tongue edging reflectively out of the corner of his mouth, his round-shouldered torso seeming, as Lois Long once put it, to be pushing something invisible ahead of him. He had no Empire Urge, unlike Henry Luce and a dozen other founders of proliferating enterprises. He was a one-magazine, one-project man. (His financial interest in Dave Chasen's Hollywood restaurant was no more central to his ambition than his onetime investment in a paint-spraying machine—I don't know whatever became of that.) He dreamed of perfection, not of power or personal fortune. He was a visionary and a practicalist, imperfect at both, a dreamer and a hard worker, a genius and a plodder, obstinate and reasonable, cosmopolitan and provincial, wide-eyed and world-weary. There is only one word that fits him perfectly, and the word is Ross.

When I agreed to work for the *New Yorker* as a desk man, it was with deep misgivings. I felt that Ross didn't know, and wasn't much interested in finding out, anything about me. He had persuaded himself, without evidence, that I might be just the wonder man he was looking for, a mistake he had made before and was to make again in the case of other newspapermen, including James M. Cain, who was just about as miscast for the job as I was. Ross's wishful thinking was, it seems to me now, tinged with hallucination. In expecting to find, in everybody that turned up, the Ideal Executive, he came to remind me of the Charlie Chaplin of *The Gold Rush*, who, snowbound and starving with another man in a cabin teetering on the edge of a cliff, suddenly beholds his companion turning into an enormous tender spring chicken, wonderfully edible, supplied by Providence. "Done and done, Thurber," said Ross. "I'll give you seventy dollars a week. If you write anything, goddam it, your salary will take care of it." Later that afternoon he phoned my apartment and said, "I've decided to make that ninety dollars a week, Thurber." When my first check came through it was for one hundred dollars. "I couldn't take advantage of a newspaperman," Ross explained.

By the spring of 1928 Ross's young *New Yorker* was safely past financial and other shoals that had menaced its launching, skies were clearing, the glass was rising, and everybody felt secure except the skipper of the ship. From the first day I met him till the last time I saw him, Ross was like a sleepless, apprehensive sea captain pacing the bridge, expecting any minute to run aground, collide with something nameless in a sudden fog, or find his vessel abandoned and adrift, like the *Mary Celeste*. When, at the age of thirty-two, Ross had got his magazine afloat with the aid of Raoul Fleischmann and a handful of associates, the proudest thing he had behind him was his editorship of the *Stars and Stripes* in Paris from 1917 to 1919.

As the poet is born, Ross was born a newspaperman. "He could not only get it, he could write it," said his friend Herbert Asbury. Ross got it and wrote it for seven different newspapers before he was twenty-five years old, beginning as a reporter for the Salt Lake City *Tribune* when he was only fourteen. One of his assignments there was to interview the madam of a house of prostitution. Always self-conscious and usually uncomfortable in the presence of all but his closest women friends, the young reporter began by saying to the bad woman (he divided the other sex into good and bad), "How many fallen women do you have?"

Later he worked for the Marysville (California) *Appeal*, Sacramento *Union*, Panama *Star and Herald*, New Orleans *Item*, Atlanta *Journal*, and San Francisco *Call*.

The wanderer—some of his early associates called him "Hobo"—reached New York in 1919 and worked for several magazines, including *Judge* and the *American Legion Weekly*, his mind increasingly occupied with plans for a new kind of weekly to be called the *New Yorker*. It was born at last, in travail and trauma, but he always felt uneasy as the R of the F-R Publishing Company, for he had none of the instincts and equipment of the businessman except the capacity for overwork and overworry. In his new position of high responsibility he soon developed the notion, as Marc Connelly has put it, that the world was designed to wear him down. A dozen years ago I found myself almost unconsciously making a Harold Ross out of one King Clode, a rugged pessimist in a fairy tale I was writing. At one point the palace astronomer rushed into the royal presence saying, "A huge pink comet, Sire, just barely missed the earth a little while ago. It made an awful hissing sound, like hot irons stuck in water." "They aim these things at me!" said Clode. "Everything is aimed at me." In this fantasy Clode pursues a fabulously swift white deer which, when brought to bay, turns into a woman, a parable that parallels Ross's headlong quest for the wonder man who invariably turned into a human being with feet of clay, as useless to Ross as any enchanted princess.

Among the agencies in mischievous or malicious conspiracy to wear Ross down were his own business department ("They're not only what's the matter with *me*, they're what's the matter with the country"), the state and federal tax systems, women and children (all the females and males that worked for him), temperament and fallibility in writers and artists, marriages and illnesses—to both of which his staff seemed especially susceptible—printers, engravers, distributors, and the like, who seemed to aim their strikes and ill-timed holidays directly at him, and human nature in general.

Harold Wallace Ross, born in Aspen, Colorado, in 1892, in a year and decade whose cradles were filled with infants destined to darken his days and plague his nights, was in the midst of a project involving the tearing down of walls the week I started to work. When he outlined his schemes of reconstruction, it was often hard to tell where rationale left off and mystique began. (How he would hate those smart-aleck words.) He seemed to believe that certain basic problems of personnel might just possibly be solved by some fortuitous rearrangement of the offices. Time has mercifully foreshortened the months of my ordeal as executive editor, and only the highlights of what he called "practical matters" still remain. There must have been a dozen Through the Looking Glass conferences with him about those damned walls. As an efficiency expert or construction engineer, I was a little boy with an alarm clock and a hammer, and my utter incapacity in such a role would have been apparent in two hours to an unobsessed man. I took to drinking Martinis at lunch to fortify myself for the tortured afternoons of discussion.

"Why don't we put the walls on wheels?" I demanded one day. "We might get somewhere with adjustable walls."

Ross's eyes lighted gloomily, in an expression of combined

hope and dismay which no other face I have known could duplicate. "The hell with it," he said. "You could hear everybody talking. You could see everybody's feet."

He and I worked seven days a week, often late into the night, for at least two months, without a day off. I began to lose weight, editing factual copy for sports departments and those dealing with new apartments, women's fashions, and men's wear.

"Gretta Palmer keeps using words like introvert and extrovert," Ross complained one day. "I'm not interested in the housing problems of neurotics. Everybody's neurotic. Life is hard, but I haven't got time for people's personal troubles. You've got to watch Woollcott and Long and Parker—they keep trying to get double meanings into their stuff to embarrass me. Question everything. We damn near printed a newsbreak about a girl falling off the roof. That's feminine hygiene, somebody told me just in time. You probably never heard the expression in Ohio."

"In Ohio," I told him, "we say the mirror cracked from side to side."

"I don't want to hear about it," he said.

He nursed an editorial phobia about what he called the functional: "bathroom and bedroom stuff." Years later he deleted from a Janet Flanner "London Letter" a forthright explanation of the long nonliquid diet imposed upon the royal family and important dignitaries during the coronation of George VI. He was amused by the drawing of a water plug squirting a stream at a small astonished dog, with the caption "News," but he wouldn't print it. "So-and-so can't write a story without a man in it carrying a woman to a bed," he wailed. And again, "I'll never print another O'Hara story I don't understand. I want to know what his people are doing." He was depressed for weeks after the appearance of a full-page Arno depicting a man and a girl on a road in the moonlight, the man carrying the back seat of an automobile. "Why didn't somebody tell me what it meant?" he asked. Ross had insight, perception, and a unique kind of intuition, but they were matched by a dozen blind spots and strange areas of ignorance, surprising in a virile and observant reporter who had knocked about the world and lived two years in France. There were so many different Rosses, conflicting and contradictory, that the task of drawing him in words sometimes appears impossible, for the composite of all the Rosses should produce a single unmistakable entity: the most remarkable man I have ever known and the greatest editor. "If you get him down on paper," Wolcott Gibbs once warned me, "nobody will believe it."

I made deliberate mistakes and let things slide as the summer wore on, hoping to be demoted to rewriting "Talk of the Town," with time of my own in which to write "casuals." That was Ross's word for fiction and humorous pieces of all kinds. Like "Profile" and "Reporter at Large" and "Notes and Comment," the word "casual" indicated Ross's determination to give the magazine an offhand, chatty, informal quality. Nothing was to be labored or studied, arty, literary, or intellectual. Formal short stories and other "formula stuff" were under the ban. Writers were to be played down; the accent was on content, not personalities. "All writers are writer-conscious," he said a thousand times.

One day he came to me with a letter from a men's furnishing store which complained that it wasn't getting fair treatment in the "As to Men" department. "What are you going to do about that?" he growled. I swept it off my desk onto the floor. "The hell with it," I said. Ross didn't pick it up, just stared at it dolefully. "That's direct action, anyway," he said. "Maybe that's the way to handle grousing. We can't please everybody." Thus he rationalized everything I did, steadfastly refusing to perceive that he was dealing with a writer who intended to write or to be thrown out. "Thurber has honesty," he told Andy White, "admits his mistakes, never passes the buck. Only editor with common sense I've ever had."

I finally told Ross, late in the summer, that I was losing weight, my grip, and possibly my mind, and had to have a rest. He had not realized I had never taken a day off, even Saturday or Sunday. "All right, Thurber," he said, "but I think you're wearing yourself down writing pieces. Take a couple of weeks, anyway. Levick can hold things down while you're gone. I *guess*."

It was, suitably enough, a dog that brought Ross and me

together out of the artificiality and stuffiness of our strained and mistaken relationship. I went to Columbus on vacation and took a Scottie with me, and she disappeared out there. It took me two days to find her, with the help of newspaper ads and the police department. When I got back to the *New Yorker*, two days late, Ross called me into his office about seven o'clock, having avoided me all day. He was in one of his worst God-how-I-pity-me moods, a state of mind often made up of monumentally magnified trivialities. I was later to see this mood develop out of his exasperation with the way Niven Busch walked, or the way Ralph Ingersoll talked, or his feeling that "White is being silent about something and I don't know what it is." It could start because there weren't enough laughs in "Talk of the Town," or because he couldn't

reach Arno on the phone, or because he was suddenly afflicted by the fear that nobody around the place could "find out the facts." (Once a nerve-racked editor yelled at him, "Why don't you get Westinghouse to build you a fact-finding machine?")

This day, however, the Ossa on the Pelion of his molehill miseries was the lost and found Jeannie. Thunder was on his forehead and lightning in his voice. "I understand you've overstayed your vacation to look for a dog," he growled. "Seems to me that was the act of a sis." (His vocabulary held some quaint and unexpected words and phrases out of the past. "They were spooning," he told me irritably about some couple years later, and, "I think she's stuck on him.") The word *sis*, which I had last heard about 1908, the era of *skidoo*, was the straw that shattered my patience. Even at sixty-four my temper is precarious, but at thirty-two it had a hair trigger.

The scene that followed was brief, loud, and incoherent. I told him what to do with his goddam magazine, that I was through, and that he couldn't call me a sis while sitting down, since it was a fighting word. I offered to fight him then and there, told him he had the heart of a cast-iron lawn editor, and suggested that he call in one of his friends to help him. Ross hated scenes, physical violence or the threat of it, temper and the unruly.

"Who would you suggest I call in?" he demanded, the thunder clearing from his brow.

"Alexander Woollcott!" I yelled, and he began laughing.

His was a wonderful, room-filling laugh when it came, and this was my first experience of it. It cooled the air like summer rain. An hour later we were having dinner together at Tony's after a couple of drinks, and that night was the beginning of our knowledge of each other underneath the office make-up, and of a lasting and deepening friendship. "I'm sorry, Thurber," he said. "I'm married to this magazine. It's all I think about. I knew a dog I liked once, a shepherd dog, when I was a boy. I don't like dogs as such, though, and I'll, by God, never run a department about dogs—or about baseball, or about lawyers." His eyes grew sad; then he gritted his teeth, always a sign that he was about to express some deep antipathy, or grievance, or regret. "I'm running a column about women's fashions," he moaned, "and I never thought I'd come to that." I told him the "On and Off the Avenue" department was sound, a word he always liked to hear, but used sparingly. It cheered him up.

It wasn't long after that fateful night that Ross banged into my office one afternoon. He paced around for a full minute without saying anything, jingling the coins in his pocket. "You've been writing," he said finally. "I don't know how in hell you found time to write. I admit I didn't want you to. I could hit a dozen writers from here with this ash tray. They're undependable, no system, no self-discipline. Dorothy Parker says you're a writer, and so does Baird Leonard." His voice rose to its level of high decision. "All right then, if you're a writer, write! Maybe you've got something to say." He gave one of his famous prolonged sighs, an agonized protesting acceptance of a fact he had been fighting.

From then on I was a completely different man from the one he had futilely struggled to make me. No longer did he tell White that I had common sense. I was a writer now, not a hand-holder of artists, but a man who needed guidance. Years later he wrote my wife a letter to which he appended this postscript: "Your husband's opinion on a practical matter of this sort would have no value." We never again discussed tearing down walls, the Central Desk, the problems of advertisers, or anything else in the realm of the practical. If a manuscript was lost, "Thurber lost it." Once he accused me of losing a typescript that later turned up in an old briefcase of his own. This little fact made no difference. "If it hadn't been there," he said, "Thurber would have lost it." As I became more and more "productive," another of his fondest words, he became more and more convinced of my helplessness. "Thurber hasn't the vaguest idea what goes on around here," he would say.

I became one of the trio about whom he fretted and fussed continually—the others were Andy White and Wolcott Gibbs. His admiration of good executive editors, except in the case of William Shawn, never carried with it the deep affection he had for productive writers. His warmth was genuine, but always carefully covered over by gruffness or snarl or a semblance of deep disapproval. Once, and only once, he took White and Gibbs and me to lunch at the Algonquin, with all the fret and fuss of a mother hen trying to get her chicks across a main thoroughfare. Later, back at the office, I heard him saying to someone on the phone, "I just came from lunch with three writers who couldn't have got back to the office alone."

Our illnesses, or moods, or periods of unproductivity were a constant source of worry to him. He visited me several times when I was in a hospital undergoing a series of eye operations in 1940 and 1941. On one of these visits, just before he left, he came over to the bed and snarled, "Goddam it, Thurber, I worry about you and England." England was at that time going through the German blitz. As my blindness increased, so did his concern. One noon he stopped at a table in the

Algonquin lobby, where I was having a single cocktail with some friends before lunch. That afternoon he told White or Gibbs, "Thurber's over at the Algonquin lacing 'em in. He's the only *drinking* blind man I know."

He wouldn't go to the theater the night *The Male Animal* opened in January, 1940, but he wouldn't go to bed, either, until he had read the reviews, which fortunately were favorable. Then he began telephoning around town until, at a quarter of two in the morning, he reached me at Bleeck's. I went to the phone. The editor of the *New Yorker* began every phone conversation by announcing "Ross," a monosyllable into which he was able to pack the sound and sign of all his worries and anxieties. His loud voice seemed to fill the receiver to overflowing. "Well, God bless you, Thurber," he said warmly, and then came the old familiar snarl: "Now, goddam it, maybe you can get something written for the magazine," and he hung up, but I can still hear him, over the years, loud and snarling, fond and comforting.

The First Years

I HAD never heard of the *New Yorker* when I sailed from
New York on the *Leviathan* in May, 1925, for a year in
France. My unawareness of Harold Ross's "little magazine"
(as Sam Goldwyn has always called it, in spite of its increasing
wealth and matronly girth) was not surprising. Only a dozen
meager issues had then reached the stands, all of them nervous
and peaked, and most of them pretty bad. ("There's that goddam 'pretty' again," Ross would say. The easy overuse of
"pretty" and "little" exacerbated his uneasy mind. Once, to
bedevil him, I used them both in a single sentence of a Talk
piece: "The building is pretty ugly and a little big for its surroundings." After stumbling upon these deliberate oxymora,
Ross poked his head into my office, made a pretty ugly sound
with his tongue and lips, and withdrew. We had been discussing the goddam pretty-little problem earlier that same
day.)

The *New Yorker* was the outstanding flop of 1925, a year of
memorable successes in literature, music, and entertainment,
and the only flop that kept on going. Its continued existence
may accurately be called life after death. The *Leviathan* was
still at sea on that eastward voyage of thirty-four years ago
when the weekly was officially declared dead at an executive
luncheon in New York, presided over by its chief backer,
Raoul Fleischmann. Then miracle, in the form of chance encounter, resurrected the deceased. Several hours after the cor-
oner's verdict, Ross ran into Fleischmann at the wedding of
Franklin Pierce Adams, and, in that atmosphere of hope, beginning, and champagne, they decided to have another go at
it. It was hard for the F and the R of the F-R Publishing
Company to believe that their cherished infant could die in
such a season of viability.

In 1925, the greatest of war plays, *What Price Glory?*, was
still running at the Plymouth, and two young men named
Rodgers and Hart wrote the music and lyrics for the unforgettable *Garrick Gaieties*, whose big song hit, "Manhattan,"
still gaily rides the national airwaves. It was the year of *The*

Great Gatsby and of *Arrowsmith* and *An American Tragedy.* In 1925, the new Madison Square Garden was opened, and presented its popular monstrosities to an eager public: the six-day bike race, the marathon dance, an indoor flagpole sitter, and strange men and women who took part in rocking-chair and gum-chewing contests, indefatigably entertaining the insatiable addicts of endlessness. *The Poor Nut*, starring its co-author Elliott Nugent, was a hit at the Henry Miller. Elliott came down to the ship to see me off. He was then making, we figured the other day, approximately a hundred times as much money as the twelve dollars a week I was going to get on the Paris edition of the Chicago *Tribune.*

Meanwhile, the *New Yorker* kept going downhill. From an original runoff of fifteen thousand copies in February, its circulation fell to a pernicious-anemia low of twenty-seven hundred copies in August. One evening, during that summer of Harold Ross's greatest discontent, the harried editor ran into Dorothy Parker somewhere. "I thought you were coming into the office to write a piece last week," he said. "What happened?" Mrs. Parker turned upon him the eloquent magic of her dark and lovely eyes. "Somebody was using the pencil," she explained sorrowfully. It gave a fair enough picture of the goings on in West 45th Street, where a small inexperienced staff strained to bring out a magazine every Thursday.

This is a memoir of my years with Ross, and so I shall take up, as tenderly and as briefly as may be, the troubles that beset the founder of the *New Yorker* before I became a party to his predicament and a witness of his woe. Ross could never have seriously believed his constantly reiterated "Writers are a dime a dozen." A great many writers were in Hollywood during his early struggles, others were in Paris—among them two future *New Yorker* authors, Robert Coates and Joel Sayre (Sid Perelman joined them in 1926)—and most of those he knew personally in New York were a million dollars a dozen and more amused by the *New Yorker*'s flounderings than by its contents.

There is little doubt that Ross's famous and busy writer friends of the Algonquin Round Table and its fringes took his fond enterprise lightly, as a kind of joke on him and Fleischmann. A few of them helped now and then, with left hand,

and tongue in cheek. "The part-time help of wits is no better than the full-time help of half-wits," a great wit named Herman Mankiewicz is reported to have said at the time. When I reminded Ross of this line years later, all he said was, "God knows I had both kinds."

He couldn't pay anybody much money, in an era when magazine word rates were extremely high. (Nunnally Johnson got ten times as much for his humorous stories in the *Saturday Evening Post* as Ross could have paid him.) When Elwyn Brooks White came to work for the *New Yorker*, part-time, in 1926, he got thirty dollars a week, with an additional five dollars for each of his first-page comments, which were soon to become one of the *New Yorker*'s best-known contributions to American letters.

The record of contributions by the men and women Ross must have expected to help him, out of the goodness of their hearts, during the first year is disheartening to look back upon. In 1925, Dorothy Parker turned in only one piece and two poems, and her celebrated book reviews, signed "Constant Reader," did not begin until October, 1927.

Robert Benchley waited ten months to lend a hand, and his first casual was printed in December, 1925. He didn't take over the *New Yorker*'s theater criticism until 1929, the same year that Ross's close friend Alexander Woollcott started his page called "Shouts and Murmurs." Ross's good friend Ring Lardner sent in one piece in 1925 and was not heard from again for two years. Marc Connelly and Arthur Kober got around to writing for Ross in 1926, and George Kaufman's name was first signed to a *New Yorker* casual as late as 1935.

It wasn't until 1930 that the names of Perelman and Ogden Nash showed up in the magazine's pages; Sally Benson's first story had been printed the year before. Clarence Day's reminiscences of a New York life were published in 1933. "If I had never printed anything but Clarence Day's stuff, it would have been enough," Ross once told Frank Sullivan, who, incidentally, wrote only three pieces for Ross in 1925; it would be ten years before his Cliché Expert first took the witness stand.

The *New Yorker* was a year old before Gluyas Williams began drawing for it. Peter Arno, who had sold Ross a spot in June, 1925, was first represented by a captioned drawing in

September of that year of ordeal. Helen Hokinson's first captioned drawing brightened the *New Yorker* in November,
1925. It showed a saleslady at a perfume counter holding up a
small phial to a woman customer and saying, "It's *N'Aimez
Que Moi*, madam—don't love nobody but me." The woman
customer, glory be, was the original garden club dowager
whose hilarious ilk became before long one of the ornaments
of *New Yorker* humor. This first Hokinson was, it seems to
some of us now, the funniest thing that Ross's tremulous
magazine printed in the year of our Lord 1925. The little magazine that died and came to life in the same day had the invaluable help and guidance of Rea Irvin from the start. He
was responsible for its format, its special type that bears his
name, and the famous figure that adorned its first issue and

every succeeding anniversary number, that of the nineteenth-
century dandy inspecting a butterfly through his haughty
monocle.

Nothing is so dated as an old prospectus, unless it be a
faded love letter to a lady who many years later divorced its
author, so I shall spare you the *New Yorker*'s prospectus,
drawn up in the chill winter of 1924, except for a couple of
sentences that are pertinent here: "There will be a personal
mention column—a jotting down in the small-town newspaper style of the comings, goings and doings in the village of
New York. This will contain some josh and some news value."

The word "josh," smelling remarkably of Ross's old-fashioned vocabulary, and the phrase "the small-town newspaper style" were unhappily lifted out of context and magnified into motto by Ross and his helpers. They got the young magazine off on the wrong foot, wearing the wrong shoe. Its early issues went in for a frivolous and curiously small-town kind of joke, an almost subcollegiate flippancy, and a self-conscious, intra-mural urbanality, all of which show up bleakly now in an old *New Yorker* folder labeled "Office Gazette," kept in a secret vault in the present offices and accessible only to those of us who are going on a hundred.

The contents of the Office Gazette consist of fragile and yellowing notes, suggestions, letters, and interoffice memos, stained with sweat and blood, mainly Ross's. Herein we en-counter a great deal of tittering about the Optimist Joke, a two-line joke that was accidentally printed like this:

> "A man who thinks he can make it in par."
> "What is an optimist, Pop?"

This sentimental souvenir of the old days was reprinted in every anniversary issue of the *New Yorker* for twenty-five years before it was abandoned. Even right side up it shows what was the matter—a kind of youthful lack of loving care. One poem was accidentally printed in two different issues in 1925; a building located by the *New Yorker* at Sixth Avenue and 55th Street was actually at Sixth Avenue and 54th Street; the name of George Eliot was spelled with two *l*'s, and Carolyn Wells was called Caroline, two mistakes that were pointed out by that old precisionist, F.P.A., whose hawk eye was ever alert for inaccuracies. When a verse of Philip G. Wylie's, signed with his initials, was reprinted in the New York Sunday *World*, it was credited to Pelham Grenville Wodehouse, and the Ga-zette had much rueful fun with this.

Among the notes in the old folder is one beginning "At a mass meeting of the two contributors to this magazine" and another reads "The magazine for people who cannot read." The intramural joshing turns up everywhere in the crumbling documents. Someone suggested a drawing showing "Harold Ross calling at the Martha Washington Hotel on his aunt from Dubuque." There is a lot of high school levity about the idea of using the face of Ben Turpin in burlesque reproductions of famous paintings, or to replace the countenance of Jimmy Walker, Calvin Coolidge, and others, in a series of cartoons. The Gazette reveals that *New Yorker* readers were instructed, in one issue, how to pronounce Rea Irvin's first name and Helen Hokinson's last name.

One 1927 item is worth reprinting in full, since it deals with two *New Yorker* immortals who soon rose above all the joshing:

> Lois Long, who writes under the name "Lipstick," was married to Peter Arno, creator of the Whoops sisters, last Friday. The bride wore some things the department stores had given her from time to time, and Mr. Arno wore whatever remained after his having given all his dirty clothes to a man who posed as a laundry driver last week. The romance had its beginning in The New Yorker office, and was greatly advanced by a summer spent abroad, the contrast between the two places being noticeable. Immediately after the wedding the couple left for 25 West 45th Street, where they will spend their honeymoon trying to earn enough money to pay for Mr. Arno's little automobile.

My own favorite item in the ancient collection is a suggestion from a reader, which goes like this:

March 20, 1927

THE NEW YORKER

> I have an idea for a cartoon. The cartoon is entitled, "Pouring over his Books." This is a pun. Have a student sit by a desk with a stack of books before him and reading out of one book. In the meantime have him pour some gin in a glass and is ready to drink it. All about him on the floor have bottles thrown about.
>
> The humor in this cartoon is in the words "pour" and "poir" one means to drink and the other means to study careful.

In the margin of this wondrous note, Ross had written "Too subtle."

Ross's sweating and straining to keep his faltering magazine above the level of Dubuque and in the sophisticated tonality of cosmopolitan New York both puzzled and annoyed some readers. One of them, objecting to a facetious piece about the Barnard Cloisters, wrote testily, "Flippancy in an elephant might be amusing, but flippancy in a flea doesn't even amuse its canine host." Ross's agitated reply to this began, "We are young." And young they were. Every effort to sound metropolitan in viewpoint and background brought the breath of Aspen, Colorado, to the journal's perspiring pages.

Ross was apparently intensely devoted to a continuing department called "Are You a New Yorker?", a series of questions such as "Where is the morgue?" and "On what days is admission charged to the Bronx Zoo?" Clipped to this particular questionnaire was a tart note from a male subscriber which read, simply, "Who gives a damn?"

But it was in this turgid area of odds and ends and beginnings that I found a refreshing letter to Ross from Elmer Davis, dated May 19, 1926. After a decade on the New York *Times*, Mr. Davis had resigned in 1924 to free lance and to write books. He sold the *New Yorker*, in its first three years, some twenty-five pieces, and in this letter he enclosed a contribution for "Are You a New Yorker?" In it there were ten questions, of which the ninth went like this: "Who was Josh DeVore? Bridgie Webber? James A. O'Gorman? Pat Kyne? Hugh McAtamney? Anna Aumuller? Lieutenant Percy Richards?" Mr. Davis's tenth question made my heart leap up. It said, simply, "Where Are They Now?" That was to be the standing title, ten years later, of a series of twenty-five pieces I wrote for the magazine under the name Jared L. Manley. For a whole decade Ross had fretted and fussed about this project, excited by the idea but dissatisfied with the title, as he was usually dissatisfied with everything, sometimes for weeks, sometimes for years. In the end, of course, he came back, as he often did, to the original suggestion, but I doubt that Elmer Davis was remembered as the originator of the idea for "Where Are They Now?" or that Ross's debt to him was ever acknowledged. The editor was always conscientious about giving credit where credit was due, but his head continually buzzed with a thousand different ideas, and in the flutter the Davis letter must have been forgotten.

The carelessness and confusion of the first two years, echoed and reflected in the Office Gazette, are undoubtedly responsible for Ross's later intense dedication to precision, order, and system. He studied the New York Telephone Company's system of verifying names and numbers in its directories, and used to say that, despite the company's careful checking, it had never got out a phone book with fewer than three mistakes. He found out about the *Saturday Evening Post*'s checking department, which he said consisted of seven women who checked in turn every fact, name, and date. He must have set up a dozen different systems, during my years with him, for keeping track of manuscripts and verifying facts. If the slightest thing went wrong, he would bawl, "The system's fallen down!"

He lived always in the wistful hope of getting out a magazine each week without a single mistake. His checking department became famous, in the trade, for a precision that sometimes leaned over backward. A checker once said to me, "If you mention the Empire State Building in a Talk piece, Ross isn't satisfied it's still there until we call up and verify it." When Robert Coates, in a book review, said that Faulkner sometimes seemed to write about the woodland of Weir instead of the American South, checkers ransacked postal guides, maps, and other sources looking for the Weir that existed only in the imagination of Edgar Allan Poe. When, in a piece I sent in from the French Riviera in 1938, I mentioned the Hotel Ruhl, the checkers found out that it was actually the Hotel Ruhl et des Anglais, and changed it to that in my copy. I wrote Ross a sharp note saying, "Where shall we meet for five o'clock tea—at the Waldorf-Astoria or the Ritz-Carlton?"

But overchecking was better than underchecking, in his opinion, even if it did sometimes lead to the gaucherie of inflexibility. Ross's checkers once informed Mencken that he couldn't have eaten dinner at a certain European restaurant he had mentioned in one of his *New Yorker* articles, because there wasn't any restaurant at the address he had given. Mencken brought home a menu with him to prove that he was right, but he was pleased rather than annoyed. "Ross has the most astute goons of any editor in the country," he said.

While Ross was sweating blood and baying the moon

during that awful summer of 1925, I was in a farmhouse in Normandy trying to write a novel. It didn't work out because I got tired of the characters at the end of five thousand words, and bade them and novel-writing farewell forever. In September I got my job as a rewrite man on the Paris *Tribune*.

"I got thirty men ahead of you who want jobs," the city editor said when I went to see him. "What are you, by the way, a poet, or a painter, or a novelist?"

I told him I was a newspaperman with five years' experience, and knew how to get it and write it and put a headline on it, and he hired me on the spot. That first month I wrote about the crash of the dirigible *Shenandoah* in Ohio, and in October the editor handed me six words of cable from America and said, "Write a column about that." The six words were "Christy Mathewson died today at Saranac," and I wrote a column about it.

It wasn't until the following month, November, 1925, that I first heard of the existence of a magazine called the *New Yorker*. I was sitting on the *terrasse* of the Café Dôme, reading our rival paper, the Paris *Herald* (which had wanted no part of my services), when I came upon a first-page story about a flutter in the dovecotes of Park Avenue. The story said that Ellin Mackay, daughter of the millionaire head of Postal Telegraph, and later Mrs. Irving Berlin (he dedicated two songs to her that year, *Always* and *Remember*) had written an "exposé" of Park Avenue society for a weekly magazine called the *New Yorker*. Miss Mackay's short article, called "Why We Go to Cabarets" and subtitled "A Post-Debutante Explains," seems as quaint and dated now as its title, but it got the *New Yorker* on the front pages of New York newspapers and gave it its first big shot in the arm circulationwise, as they say in American business circles. Miss Mackay slapped with her fan the wrists of all the sad young men in the Park Avenue staglines, whose dullness drove American society girls with stars in their eyes to cabarets, where they danced to jazz music on the same floor with "drummers" and other interesting barbarians from the hinterland.

After thirty-four years, the dusty pages of Miss Mackay's once vital prose seem less a souvenir of the Jazz Age than a dying echo of the days of silent movies and the era of Rudolph

Valentino. That great matinee idol, incidentally, was to collapse outside a New York cabaret in 1926 with an agony in his stomach that turned out to be a fatal perforating ulcer. When he fell, his opera hat rolled into the street, and was rescued by one of those who rushed to his aid, none other than Harold Ross, the young editor of the *New Yorker*. Several months before Valentino's collapse in New York, I had interviewed him at the Hotel Ruhl (et des Anglais) in Nice, where I had gone from Paris in the winter of 1925 to be assistant editor of the *Tribune*'s Riviera edition. I remember that Valentino proudly showed me the hundred pairs of shoes he always took with him on his travels, or it may even have been two hundred. Ross kept his opera hat, intending to return it to him when he left the hospital, which he never did alive. The hat was accidentally thrown out when Ross and his first wife moved from their house on West 47th Street in 1928. "I thought it was an old hat of Aleck's," Jane Grant, Ross's first wife, told me. Alexander Woollcott had shared the coöperative house in the West Forties.

The loss of Rudolph Valentino's opera hat might well stand as a kind of symbol of the ending of the *New Yorker*'s infancy and the beginning of its maturity. In 1928 Oliver Wolcott Gibbs joined the staff of the magazine, and in one issue of that year a short first piece, called "Alumnae Bulletin," appeared away back on page 101. It was written by a young man named John O'Hara, who was then twenty-three years old and whose short stories were to help set up a lasting literary barrier between the town of Dubuque and the city of New York.

I got back to New York in early June, 1926, with ten dollars, borrowed enough to hold on until July in a rented room on West 13th Street, and began sending short pieces to the *New Yorker*, eating in doughnut shops, occasionally pilfering canapés at cocktail parties (anchovies, in case you don't know, are not good for breakfast). My pieces came back so fast I began to believe the *New Yorker* must have a rejection machine. It did have one, too. His name was John Chapin Mosher, a witty writer, a charming man, and one of the most entertaining companions I have ever met, but an editor whose prejudices were a mile high and who had only a few enthusiasms. It was in the always slightly lunatic tradition of the *New Yorker* that he had been made first reader of the manuscripts of unknown writers. In the years that followed, we became friends, but I never had lunch with him that he didn't say, over his coffee, "I must get back to the office and reject."

In 1943 he rejected a story by Astrid Peters (then known as Astrid Meighan), called "Shoe the Horse and Shoe the Mare," which its author later read aloud to me one day. I sent it to Ross with a note saying it should have been bought, and he bought it. It was one of the stories included in *The Best American Short Stories 1944*. Mosher's only comment on it had been a characteristic "A tedious bit about an adolescent female." I sometimes wonder what Mosher would say, if he were alive now, about the *New Yorker*'s flux of stories by women writers dealing with the infancy, childhood, and young womanhood of females. "We are in a velvet rut," Ross once said many years ago, and this was amended not long ago by a sardonic male writer to read, "We are now in a tulle and taffeta rut."

I first called at the *New Yorker* office late in June, 1926, to find out what had happened to the only piece of mine that had not been returned like a serve in tennis. It was about a man named Alfred Goullet, the greatest of all six-day bike riders, with whom I had shared a stateroom on a liner returning from France in 1920. (I had been a code clerk in the American Embassy for two years.) Mosher came out into the reception room, looking like a professor of English literature who has not approved of the writing of anybody since Sir Thomas Browne. He returned my manuscript saying that it had got under something, and apologizing for the tardy rejection. "You see," he said, "I regard Madison Square Garden as one of the blots on our culture."

I didn't ask to meet Ross that day, but I did inquire if Mr. White was in. On the *Leviathan* going to France, I had met a married sister of White's with the lilting name of Lillian Illian. She had often talked about her talented brother, whose name I remembered as Elton Brooks White. His real first name, of course, is Elwyn, but he had been lucky enough to go to Cornell, where every male student named White is nicknamed Andy, after Andrew White, the university's first president. White wasn't in that day, and so nearly eight months went by before I met him and Ross. I must have seen him, however, without recognizing him, for he also lived on West 13th Street then, sharing an apartment with three other Cornell graduates. One of them, Gustave Stubbs Lobrano, later became an editor of the *New Yorker*.

By July first my money had run out again, but I didn't take the reporting job on the *Evening Post* that had been offered me by its city editor, whom I had met in Paris while he was on vacation. I had an idea for a parody of current best sellers, to be called "Why We Behave Like Microbe Hunters," and to finish it I threw myself upon the hospitality of Clare Victor Dwiggins, called Dwig, a well-known comic-strip artist, who was spending the summer at Green Lake, New York, with his family. (I had met him in Nice.) The wonderful Dwigginses took me in, and I finished the twenty-five thousand words of the book by the end of August. In September I peddled it about New York. It was rejected suavely by Harper's, and without a word by Farrar and Rinehart, unless you can count the "Here" of the secretary who handed me the manuscript when I called at the office. Herschel Brickell, rest his soul, almost persuaded Henry Holt to take the parody, but was overruled by the sales department: "We can't publish a first book of humor by an unknown writer." I sent the six chapters of the book piecemeal to the *New Yorker* and got them all back. Then I went to work on the *Evening Post*, but still kept trying to sell something to Ross's magazine.

In December I had about given up, and was thinking of going back to Columbus, when I sent one of my many rejections to F.P.A. on the *World*. It was the story of Hero and Leander done in newspaper headlines, and Mr. Adams printed it. It filled up one whole column of "The Conning Tower." I think it was ten years later that I told the conductor of "The Conning Tower" that I had written the thing. He had no way of knowing because I had signed it, for reasons too obscure to remember, Jamie Machree.

I now lived in a basement apartment on Horatio Street, near the Ninth Avenue El, with my first wife, who has somehow got lost in the shuffle of these reminiscences. She was convinced I spent too much time on my *New Yorker* efforts, and so one night I grimly set the alarm clock to ring in forty-five minutes and began writing a piece about a little man going round and round and round in a revolving door, attracting crowds and the police, setting a world's record for this endurance event, winning fame and fortune. This burlesque of Channel swimming and the like ran to fewer than a thousand words, and was instantly bought by the *New Yorker*. For the first time out of twenty tries I got a check instead of a rejection slip.

With the money we bought a Scottie, the same Jeannie that was later to be lost in Columbus and to cause the dog fight between Ross and me. The proof that no permanent scars resulted from that brief snarling and fateful encounter lies in an old incident I like to remember. In 1929 my wife began raising Scotties and poodles in Silvermine, and one day Ross asked me if he could buy one of her Scottie pups. "I don't want it myself, for God's sake," he explained hastily, "but Helen Hokinson said the other day that she would like to have a Scottie, and I thought I'd give her one for Christmas." Ross did countless thoughtful and generous things for the men and women he loved, often going far out of his way and spending a great deal of time hunting for gifts, arranging introductions, smoothing paths, and lightening personal burdens.

One of Jeannie's male offspring, three months old, was selected by my wife and, with a wide red ribbon around its neck and a card attached, was delivered by messenger to Miss Hokinson on Christmas Day. She loved the dog but said she couldn't possibly keep it in town, where she was then living, and returned it sadly to my wife. It had cost Ross seventy-five dollars, and my wife made out a check for this amount. He flatly refused to take it and promptly sent it back. Thus the strange story of Ross and Jeannie and me came, in its curious and somehow satisfying way, full circle.

It was easy for me to sell things to the *New Yorker* after the first one was taken, although, in rereading some of the earliest ones, I marvel that Ross put his approving R on "Villanelle of Horatio Street, Manhattan" and a short parody called "More Authors Cover the Snyder Trial." In this last I tried to imitate the style of James Joyce and that of Gertrude Stein, and Ross could never have read a single line of either author. The Stein part went like this:

> This is a trial. This is quite a trial. I am on trial. They are on trial. Who is on trial?
>
> I can tell you how it is. I can tell you have told you will tell you how it is.
>
> There is a man. There is a woman. There is not a man. There would have been a man. There was a man. There were two men. There is one man. There is a woman where is a woman is a man.
>
> He says he did. He says he did not. She says she did. She says she did not. She says he did. He says she did. She says they did. He says they did. He says they did not. She says they did not. I'll say they did.

In gritting his teeth, swallowing hard, and buying that, Ross must have depended upon the counsel of his literary editor, Mrs. Katharine Angell, graduate of Bryn Mawr, wife of a lawyer, and the author of articles and reviews for the *New Republic*, the *Atlantic*, *Harper's*, and other magazines before she was hired in 1925 as assistant to Fillmore Hyde, the magazine's first literary editor. Mrs. Angell, who hired Andy White in 1926 and was later married to him, was one of the pillars upon which Ross could lean in his hours of uncertainty about his own limitations. "She knows the Bible, and literature, and foreign languages," he told me the day I first met him, "and she has taste."

That day in February, 1927, when I first saw Ross plain and talked to him, I had been brought to his office by White. Andy had called me on the phone one day to say that his sister had mentioned meeting me on the *Leviathan* and that he was, like myself, a friend of Russell Lord, a man who had gone to both Ohio State and Cornell, later wrote *The Wallaces of Iowa*, and somewhere in between, like practically everybody else, took his turn as managing editor of the *New Yorker*. I didn't meet White until five minutes before he took me in to see Ross, but Ross always believed that White and I had been friends for years.

When he got an idea fixed in his head, it usually stayed

fixed, and time and truth could not dislodge it. He had decided thirty years ago that Wolcott Gibbs was Alice Duer Miller's nephew, and the fact that Gibbs was actually her cousin never registered in Ross's mind, although he was told this fact a dozen times. Gus Lobrano had worked for *Town and Country* before coming to the *New Yorker*, but Ross got the notion that he had been on *Harper's Bazaar*, and nothing Lobrano said through the years could correct this misconception. Ten years before Lobrano died in 1956, Ross said to him about something, "I suppose you learned that on *Harper's Bazaar*." Gus sighed resignedly and said, "Yes, and it wasn't easy."

Harold Ross had an exasperating way of pinning quick tags and labels on people he met, getting them cozily pigeonholed, and sometimes completely wrong. Ben Hecht, for example, was a police reporter at heart, Elmer Davis a corn-belt intellectual, Alan Dunn "the only recluse about town I know." When Morris Markey, the *New Yorker's* first reporter-at-large, was assigned to write a piece about what goes on behind the gates at Grand Central, he had to postpone his visit because of the illness of the station master, but for ten years Ross would say, when someone suggested an assignment for Morris, "He couldn't get into Grand Central."

After Ross found out, the hard way, that I was not an administrative editor, he had to think up a tag for me to make my task of writing the "Talk of the Town" department as hard as possible for both of us.

"Thurber's worked too long on newspapers," he told somebody. "He can't write Talk the way I want it. He'll always write journalese." I don't think Ross had ever read anything I had written outside the *New Yorker*. It wasn't much at the time, but I did have a scrapbook of unjournalese pieces I had sold to *Harper's* "Lion's Mouth," the *D.A.C. News*, *Sunset Magazine*, and the Sunday *World* and *Herald Tribune*. What stuck in Ross's head was that I had covered City Hall for the Columbus *Dispatch*, been central Ohio correspondent for the *Christian Science Monitor*, worked for the Chicago *Tribune* in France and the *Evening Post* in New York, and once contributed weekly jottings on Ohio politics to the Wheeling *Intelligencer*. So it was that in the new Ross-Thurber relationship of editor and rewrite man there were several months of another kind of ordeal, full of thrust and parry, doubt and despair, sound and fury. It wasn't until the issue of December 24, 1927, after three months of slavery, that a Talk piece of mine appeared which Ross had praised and not rewritten. It was a "personality" piece called "A Friend of Jimmy's," about William Seeman, intimate of Mayor Walker, brother-in-law of Rube Goldberg, canner of White Rose salmon, and crony of Harold Ross. It is no more worth bothering with than that old prospectus, and sticks in my mind only as the second turning point in my relationship with Ross.

Every Tuesday Afternoon

THE EARLIEST *New Yorker* ritual that any oldster can remember was the weekly Tuesday afternoon art meeting.
Philip Gordon Wylie was the second person in the history of
Harold Ross's magazine to "hold the artists' hands," as the
editor always described the task of dealing with artists and
their drawings. Before Wylie, there had been a young woman,
but, like most women, she made Ross nervous and he asked
Wylie to fire her, while he (Ross) was at lunch. Two hours
later Ross phoned Wylie to ask if the deed had been done,
and he was told the lady had left with two weeks' salary, and
then Ross came back to the office. He never had, to put a
blunt point on it, the guts to fire anybody himself, with one
exception. In the early thirties, Scudder Middleton, then the
official handholder, was emboldened one night at the Players
Club to say to Ross, "How am I doing at the office?" and
Ross, emboldened by Scotch, snapped, "You're fired!" Then,
to cover his own embarrassment, he blustered that he was
going to get Peter Arno on the phone and fire him, too. It
was way after midnight, and Ross's call aroused Arno from
sleep. He promptly bawled Ross out and ordered him never
to wake him up again.

In the very beginning, the art meeting was attended by
Ross, Wylie, and Rea Irvin. The invaluable Irvin, artist, ex-
actor, wit, and sophisticate about town and country, did more
to develop the style and excellence of *New Yorker* drawings
and covers than anyone else, and was the main and shining
reason that the magazine's comic art in the first two years was
far superior to its humorous prose. At the art meetings, Wylie
would hold up the drawings and covers, and Irvin would explain to Ross what was good about them, or wrong, or old,
or promising. Rea had done the first cover—the unforgettable
dandy with the monocle, known intramurally as Eustace Til-
ley, a name invented by Corey Ford—and for months it remained the composition most like the sort of thing Ross was
after, the sort of thing Rea Irvin spent several hours every
Tuesday teaching the "corny-gag editor-hobo" (Wylie's de-

scription) to understand. Ross learned fast, didn't always see eye to eye with Irvin, often stubbornly had his own way, but was never truly comfortable if his art editor was not at the meetings.

Phil Wylie remembers that Al Frueh did the second cover, and a pretty, shy girl named Barbara Shermund the third one. He recalls, too, the advent of Reginald Marsh, Johan Bull, and Covarrubias, and above all, Curtis Arnoux Peters, a young man not long out of Yale and playing the piano in a jazz orchestra in the West Fifties, who came into the office one day wearing sneakers and carrying a sheaf of drawings signed Peter Arno. Ross was later to write him a note that read, "You're the greatest artist in the world." Under Irvin's supervision and encouragement, other now famous cartoonists began appearing with their work, changed some of it at his quiet suggestion, took his ideas about their future stuff.

One of the last parties Ross ever gave was a cocktail affair at the Barberry Room in honor of Rebecca West, whom he always considered one of the two finest journalists of her sex. The other was Janet (Genêt) Flanner, the *New Yorker*'s Paris correspondent almost from the start. I remember only one artist at the West party, the late Helen Hokinson, for whom Ross had great admiration and affection. "Artists don't know anybody and they never go anywhere," he was still grumbling. "They stay home at night, drinking soft drinks in cold sitting rooms, and watching home movies." This Ross exaggeration was, and is, certainly applicable to many *New Yorker* cartoonists, but there were several others who went everywhere and knew everybody. The editor himself was socially close to Arno, Al Frueh, John Held, Jr., Rea Irvin, Gluyas Williams, Rube Goldberg, Wallace Morgan, and Ralph Barton, whose suicide in 1931 was a grievous blow to the editor ("When I called on Barton it was like talking to a man with a gun in his hand").

One of my 1927 chores, on top of everything else, was that of holding the artists' hands, but I didn't like it and was not good at it, and soon told Ross the hell with it. I think my first assignment in this touchy area came when Ross asked me to phone Al Frueh and tell him his caricature of Gene Tunney was not a good likeness. Frueh and I had never met, and when I gave him Ross's message he said, "You can go to hell," and hung up on me. Later I got to know and, like the rest of us, to love Al Frueh, who once came upon me in my garage in Connecticut, sitting ten feet in front of my Ford and trying to draw it head on. "You can't do that, Thurber," said Frueh, out of his vast knowledge and experience as a draftsman. "You'd better draw it from the side." I took his advice.

For several months in 1927 I was one of the editors that attended the art meetings, and every now and then after that year I used to drop in as an unofficial observer. In 1929 a sense of order was brought to the meetings by the advent of Miss Daise E. Terry, who comforted Ross by keeping track of covers and drawings (at one time with the assistance of a youngster named Truman Capote). Miss Terry ("She's vigilant about art," said Ross) also took down his comments and criticisms, mainly unfavorable, in shorthand. The art meetings began after lunch and often lasted until nearly six o'clock. One week, during the thirties, finished drawings, rough sketches, and typed suggestions reached a total of some twenty-five thousand. "We got a bank of drawings big enough to last two years," Ross once said, "but there aren't enough casuals to last three weeks."

In the center of a long table in the art meeting room a drawing board was set up to display the week's contributions from scores of artists, both sacred cows and unknowns. It was never easy, and still isn't, for a new artist to break into the *New Yorker.* Some of those whose names have become well known tried for months, or even longer, sending in dozens of rough sketches week after week. If an unknown's caption, or sketch, seemed promising, it was often bought and turned over to an established staff cartoonist. Arno usually got the cream of the crop; the wonderful Mary Petty has never worked from any idea except her own; James Reid Parker did most of Helen Hokinson's captions; and other artists either had their own gagmen or subsisted on original inspiration, fortified by captions and ideas sent in by outsiders or developed by the staff. In the early years, Andy White and I sent to the meeting scores of captions and ideas, some of them for full-page drawings, others for double-page panels for Gluyas Williams and Rea Irvin. If a caption didn't suit Ross—and he was as finicky about some of them as a woman trying on Easter bonnets—

it was given to White to "tinker." Gibbs and I did tinkering, too, but White was chief tinkerer to the art meeting.

No phone calls were ever put through to the meeting room on Tuesday afternoon, and only three or four of us could enter unannounced and watch without upsetting Ross. A dozen years ago I began writing a play about Ross and the *New Yorker*, a comedy whose three acts took place in the art room. When I showed the first draft of Act I to a famous man of the Broadway theater he said, "I have a sense of isolation about that meeting room, as if the characters were marooned there and there was nobody else in the building. There must have been people in the other offices on the floor, but I don't feel them."

There were plenty of people outside that quarantined room, surging about the offices and up and down the corridors. If there was an unusual racket of some kind, Ross would say to Miss Terry, "Go out and stop that, and don't tell me what it was." Once it was a workman with a pneumatic drill, who had begun tearing up the floor of the reception room. The area he was ripping up had been marked off by chalk lines. I think Ross wanted a staircase put through to the floor below. The work was not supposed to start until after office hours, but the man with the drill had begun too soon, not realizing that the magazine's working day was from ten to six. According to Ralph Ingersoll, I increased the racket by banging metal wastebaskets up and down the halls, as a form of protest. Miss Terry managed to quiet the drill and me, and to clear the corridors of bystanders.

Ross at one time had his own office soundproofed and thought of extending the system to the art meeting room, but someone at Riggs Sanitarium, where he had spent a couple of weeks resting up from the wrangle and jangle of life, advised him against it. Ross told White and me when he came back, " 'You can exclude noise by soundproofing your mind,' this man said. You don't hear racket if you know how to concentrate. Soundproofing walls is catering to weakness." One summer day, to demonstrate how this theory worked, he called me into his office. "They're putting up a building on the corner," he said, "and there must be twenty automatic drills going right now." He dismissed this tiny irritation with a jaunty wave of his hand and began discussing some office problem that annoyed him. Suddenly he whirled and bawled at the racket outside, "Stop that!"

The art meeting always began with the display of finished covers in color, one at a time. They were bought and scheduled six months in advance, so that in June we were studying Christmas covers. Ross sat on the edge of a chair several feet away from the table, leaning forward, the fingers of his left hand spread upon his chest, his right hand holding a white knitting needle which he used for a pointer. Miss Terry remembers the day he brought it in, having picked it up nobody knows where. She later bought a dozen more of them, so everybody could have one. Ross liked to have a lot of everything he needed, for nothing irritated him so much as not to be able to put his hand instantly on what he wanted. There was always a full carton of Camels, for instance, in the drawer of the long table, and it was kept replenished by his secretary, like the carton in the drawer of his office table. For a while he had used a pencil as a pointer, but he was afraid of marking up the drawings. Then he tried a ruler, but the goddam thing wasn't right, and fate directed him to the knitting needles that solved this little problem.

He became, I think, by far the most painstaking, meticulous, hairsplitting detail-criticizer the world of editing has known. "Take this down," he would say to Miss Terry, and he would dictate a note of complaint to the creator of the drawing or cover under consideration. The memory of some of his "sharpshooting"—I don't know who applied the word, but it was perfect—will last as long as the magazine, and perhaps even longer. I cannot vouch for the truth of his query about a drawing of two elephants gazing at one of their offspring with the caption, "It's about time to tell Junior the facts of life," but, valid or apocryphal, it has passed into legend. "Which elephant is talking?" he is supposed to have asked. I was on hand, though, when he pointed his needle at a butler in a Thanksgiving cover depicting a Park Avenue family at table, and snarled, "That isn't a butler, it's a banker." Suddenly, the figure was, to all of us, a banker in disguise, and Ross dictated a note asking the artist to "make a real butler out of this fellow." He once complained of a blue sky,

"There never was a sky like that." It is not true, as rumor has it, that he said, "It's delft, or Alice, or some goddam shade." The only blues Ross could have known are light, sky, and navy.

On another day, he doubted that the windows of the United Nations Building were anything like those shown in a drawing, and he ordered that a photographer be sent to take pictures of the windows. My favorite of all his complaints, in a career of thousands of them, was reported to me by Peter De Vries, who for years attended the art meetings and still helps go through the "rough basket," skimming off the best of hundreds or thousands of sketches. The cover on the board showed a Model T driving along a dusty country road, and Ross turned his sharpshooting eye on it for a full two minutes. "Take this down, Miss Terry," he said. "Better dust."

Idea drawings, as they were called to distinguish them from captionless spots, were raked by Ross's sharpshooting fire from the wording of the captions to the postures and expressions of the figures and the shape and arrangement of furniture or trees, or whatever else was in them. Sometimes it seemed to me and the rest of us that Ross was bent on wringing the humor out of a drawing by his petulant objections to details. This attitude reminds me of Gibbs's celebrated single-sentence criticism of Max Eastman's book, *The Enjoyment of Laughter*, whose advance proofs Ross had asked him to read. Gibbs wrote in a memo to Ross: "It seems to me Eastman has got American humor down and broken its arm."

Ross rarely laughed outright at anything. His face would light up, or his torso would undergo a spasm of amusement, but he was not at the art meeting for pleasure. Selecting drawings was serious business, a part of the week's drudgery, and the back of his mind ever held the premonition that nothing was going to be funny. Just as he searched writers' copy for such expressions as Dorothy Parker's office-celebrated "like shot through a goose," he scanned drawings for phallic symbols and such, and once found one, he thought, in a hat I had drawn on a man in one of my covers. He was imagining things, but I had to change it anyway.

The most prudish neighbor woman in H. L. Mencken's Bible belt could not have taken exception to any *New Yorker* drawing I can remember, including Arno's husbands and wives in bed and the series he did of a man and a woman on, or near, a porch swing in what was intended to be a compromising clinch, the while they talked such passionless words as "Have you read any good books lately?" Arno's first conception of this entanglement was warm without being torrid, it seemed to me, but it gave Ross the galloping jumps, and under his coaching and coaxing Arno finally drew a couple approximately as sexually involved as a husband and his sister-in-law at a christening.

One realistic detail of the kind that upset Ross was overlooked by him and the others, out of understandable ignorance. It was a Garrett Price that was published in the issue of December 20, 1930, and it showed a young woman on an operating table saying to a young surgeon entering the room, "Why, Henry Whipple, I thought you were still in medical college!" The scrub nurse in the drawing is holding a tray upon which lies what is known to the surgical profession as a double-spoon curette, an instrument used in, as Ross might put it, you know what. Wylie later wrote Ross kidding him about this, but if old Afraid-of-the-Functional exploded, I didn't hear about it. For one thing, the scene was what he called "clinical," which took some of the curse off the realistic and functional. However, he did direct Scudder Middleton to ask Price, "Were you trying to put something over on us?" Price is not that kind of man or artist, and just the other day he told me that his father was a doctor and he had drawn the curette from memory of instruments in his father's office. "I didn't know what it was for," he said on the phone (like many other famous *New Yorker* artists, Garrett Price is one I've never met).

Every drawing was a task for Ross, and a few were real problems. It took courage for a humorous magazine to publish the grim Reginald Marsh that showed a woman holding up her little child so that, over the heads of an assembled crowd, it could witness a lynching. Among the submissions that were too much for Ross was a full page of two Arab fighters leaving a field upon which bodies are scattered, one of the Arabs saying, "Some of my best friends are Jews," and there was another, whose central figures were two divinity students, their eyes bright with recognition, walking toward each other in Grand Central Station with outstretched hands, above the caption "Well, Judas Priest!" I substitute the name for that of the deity because I share Ross's deep conviction that major blasphemies have no place in comedy. Ross hated to lose this drawing, though, and he sent it to White for tinkering. Andy tinkered it into a line that he told Ross comfortingly would not offend the church. It was "Well, I'll be a son-of-a-bitch!" Ross chuckled about that all day and then sent White a memo reading, "No, but I'm afraid it would offend American mothers."

I never saw the editor of the *New Yorker* get more enjoyment out of anything than he derived from a Gluyas Williams full page showing a board meeting room in which all the chairs at the long table are empty while the chairman and the members of the board are crouched in a football huddle in one corner of the office. That one lingered lovingly in his memory along with the famous Williams drawing of the day a cake of Ivory soap sank at Procter & Gamble's, and the picture captioned "Oops, sorry," in which one trapeze artist misses the outstretched hands of another, high in the air—the work of George V. Shanks. There were hundreds of others, too, but I haven't got all year.

A magazine that has published nearly twenty thousand drawings was bound to run into repetitions and formulas years ago, and they formed another nightmare for Ross. There were too goddam many men and women on rafts and on desert islands, and too many talking animals, and too many guys in a jail cell—on and on the calendar of formula ran. I once made a series of drawings especially for Ross about the trials and tortures of the art meeting. One showed the scowling Ross himself shoving a drawing at a timid office employee and snarling, "Is that funny?" He was a great man for what he called the outside opinion, and sometimes sent a questionnaire to five or six of us on which we were to say yes or no about a drawing, or a casual, or a poem. Two of the other art meeting drawings I did for Ross ("You tease him too much," my mother once told me sternly. "You shouldn't tease him so much.") showed, respectively, an old woman asking for a cup of cold water at a storage dam, and the same old woman asking a fireman for a match at a great conflagration. The editor had the drawings framed and hung on the walls of his office to remind him of the threat of formula. That was Harold Ross. He could not only take a joke at his own expense, he could perpetuate it. Not long before he died, I discovered, in going through my scrapbook of drawings in the office library, that I had drawn one with the caption "The magic has gone out of my marriage—has the magic gone out of your marriage?" and another with "Well, who made the magic go out of our marriage—me or you?" I sent tear sheets of the two drawings to Ross, and he sent me a note that read, "Well, who's responsible for the magic going out of your marriage twice—you or me?"

It would not have surprised Ross if the sanity had gone out of any artist at the very moment he was saying good morning to the editor. Ross regarded writers as temperamental mechanisms, capable of strange behavior, and artists were just as bad, or even worse. Complexes, fixations, psychological blocks, and other aberrations of the creative mind had him always on the alert. "They have *sinking* spells," he would say. "They can't ride on trains, or drive after dark, or live above the first floor of a building, or eat clams, or stay alone all night. They think automobiles are coming up on the sidewalk to get them, that gangsters are on their trail, that their apartments are being cased, and God knows what else." This dissertation, with variations, always gave Ross his saddest look and his darkest sigh. After one of these enumerations of his woes, he and I had lunch at the Algonquin. It was in the years when I could see, and I suddenly stared blankly at the bill of fare as if I had never seen one before, got slowly to my feet, and began trembling. I tried to turn pale, too, but I doubt if I managed that. Ross's alarm bell rang. "Are you all *right*?" he demanded nervously. I kept on staring at the bill of fare. "What the hell is this thing?" I croaked.

"It's the goddam menu," Ross said, and then he got it. "Don't do that to me, Thurber," he pleaded. "Too many people I know are *really* ready for the bughouse." That was his invariable word for rest home, sanitarium, and such.

For Ross's developed taste and sense of humor in selecting cover art and idea drawings I have a firm and lasting respect.

Sitting and staring at a hundred pictures, one after the other, week after week, can become a tedious process that dulls perception, but Ross's eager, unflagging desire to get the best and the funniest kept a sharp edge on his appreciation. Picking drawings at a lengthy meeting is somehow comparable to producing a play. You're not going to know for sure whether something is good until the readers or the audience see it in print or on the stage.

One afternoon in the winter of 1928, when I was sharing an office with White, Andy interrupted my typing to ask my opinion of a caption he had just worked out for a drawing. He was a little solemn about it, and clearly uncertain that he had hit on the right idea. I looked at the drawing and the caption and said, "Yeh, it seems okay to me," but neither of us cracked a smile. This drawing, by Carl Rose, appeared in the issue of December 8, 1928, and it carried one of the most famous and laughed-at captions in the history of the magazine, the one in which the mother says, "It's broccoli, dear," and the little child replies, "I say it's spinach, and I say the hell with it." The youngster's expression of distaste was to become a part of the American language. A song was written about it called "I Say It's Spinach," it has been mentioned in hundreds of editorials and newspaper columns, and it was worked into the title of a book by Elizabeth Hawes, which I illustrated, called *Fashion Is Spinach*. (In *An American Dictionary of Slang* the definition of the word "spinach" as "nonsense or bunk" is attributed to J. P. McEvoy, who used it in his book, *Hollywood Girl*, in 1929.)

The experience of that winter afternoon so long ago, when Andy tossed the famous caption up for grabs and both of us darn near let it fall, served to moderate my disappointment whenever a caption drawing of mine was later turned down, or bought without comment, as a matter of routine. I suppose the best known of my own scrawls is the one of the seal on the headboard of a bed in which a wife is snarling at her husband, "All right, have it your way—you heard a seal bark." I hadn't thought enough of it to show it to anybody before submitting it, and I was as surprised as I was delighted when its appearance in the magazine in January, 1932, brought me a truly ecstatic telegram from Bob Benchley, than whom there was nobody whose praise a cartoonist or humorist would rather have had. I gave him the original of the drawing, and named my first book of pictures *The Seal in the Bedroom* because of what he had said.

The incredulous eye of Harold Wallace Ross fell for the first time upon a drawing of mine in the spring of that troubled year 1929. For years I had been scrawling drawings on pieces of yellow copy paper and throwing them on the floor or leaving them on my desk. I began drawing at seven, mostly what seemed to be dogs, and carried the practice into the years of so-called maturity, getting a lot of good, clean, childish fun out of filling up all the pages of memo pads on the office desks of busy friends of mine, seeking to drive them crazy. Ingersoll recalls that he was a frequent victim of the ubiquitous dogs when he tried to find a blank page to write down an address or a phone number, but he maintained his reason like a veteran of the artillery of infantilism. After all, he had gone through worse than dogs with Ross.

It was White who got the mad impetuous idea that my scrawls should be published and, what is more, paid for with money. I didn't think he could make it. It is true that, a dozen years earlier, I had filled up a lot of space with dogs and an improbable species of human being in the Ohio State *Sun-Dial*, but I was its editor-in-chief then (one of my predecessors was Gardner Rea, a *New Yorker* artist since its first issue), and nothing could be done to stop me. Some of the *Sun-Dial* drawings were about the same as those I had done when I was seven and the ones I did for the *New Yorker*, but others were elaborate arrangements of solid black and crosshatching. When White caught me trying this same style again one day, he spoke a sound word of warning that has gained a small deserved fame: "Don't do that. If you ever got good you'd be mediocre."

One spring day in 1929 I had done, in approximately thirteen seconds, a pencil sketch on yellow copy paper of a seal on a rock staring at two tiny distant specks and saying, "Hm, explorers." White inked it in, a task for which rough tremor disqualified me, and sent it to the art meeting. Anything that had the strong backing of Andy White was likely to impress Ross, who had bought and printed the year before my first serious casual, a thing called "Menaces in May," only after getting White's favorable opinion on it. I don't know what Ross said upon first gazing at a Thurber drawing, but he probably dismissed it lightly as a gag, a single buzzing fly that one could swat and then there wouldn't be any more. Rea Irvin drew a picture of a seal's head on the same paper with my seal and wrote under it, "This is the way a seal's whiskers go." Promptly the following Tuesday White sent the drawing back to the meeting with a note attached that read, "This is the way a Thurber seal's whiskers go." It came back again, this

time without a word. As the weeks went on, White kept inking in and sending on other drawings of mine, and they were all rejected. All that Ross ever said during this preliminary skirmishing was a gruff "How the hell did you get the idea you could *draw?*"

Soon Andy and I began writing *Is Sex Necessary?*, for which he insisted that I do the illustrations. We finished the book in the late summer and sent it to Harper's, who had published White's book of verses, *The Lady Is Cold*. Then one day we called on the publishers with a big sheaf of my drawings.

White laid them out on the floor, and three bewildered Harpermen stared at them in dismay, probably murmuring to themselves, "God, how we pity us." One of them finally found his voice. "I gather these are a rough idea of the kind of illustrations you want some artist to do?" he said. White was firm. "These are the drawings that go into the book," he said. There was a lot of jabber then about sales ceilings, the temper of the time, reader resistance, and the like, but the drawings went into the book, and the book was a success, and Ross kept hearing about it and about the drawings. He was mightily disturbed. Something created in his own office, something he had had first shot at, had been printed by a publisher, a species of freak with whom Ross never ceased to do battle. He came into my office, looking bleak. "Where's that goddam seal drawing, Thurber?" he demanded. "The one White sent to the art meeting a few months ago." I told him that he had rejected it and I had thrown it away. "Well, don't throw things away just because I reject them!" he yelled. "Do it over again." I didn't do it over again for two years, although he kept at me.

The first drawings of mine to appear in the *New Yorker* were of animals, illustrating a 1930 series called "Our Own Pet Department." In one of these, incidentally, a drawing of a horse's head with antlers strapped to it, the horse's teeth had been put in by a girl friend of mine. Everybody took liberties with my drawings. In one of them, showing a man and his wife and another woman at a table, a charming editrix blacked in the other woman's shoes with India ink to make it clear to readers that the designing minx was playing footy-footy with the husband. The startled husband, strained and bolt upright in his chair, had drawn from his wife the line, "What's come over *you* suddenly?" Benchley, always a kind of jealous guardian of my art, such as it was, was annoyed by this monstrosity of explicitness, and said so to Ross. My goddam drawings were beginning to close in on Ross. Now he had something new to fret and fuss about, something he had never dreamed God would let happen to him.

It wasn't until January, 1931, that I sent another idea drawing to the *New Yorker*'s art meeting. I had begun drawing straight away in India ink, without pencil foundation. Ross bought the drawing and asked for more. This was easy, since I could do a hundred in one week end, but I usually submitted only two or three at a time. (In 1939 I did all the drawings for *The Last Flower* between dinner and bedtime one evening, but spared Ross this flux of pictures, because I didn't want to be responsible for his having a seizure of some kind.) He still kept pestering me about the seal drawing, and one evening in December, 1931, I tried to recapture it on the typewriter paper I always used. The seal was all right, atypical whiskers and all, but the rock looked more like the head of a bed, so I turned it into a bed, and put the man and his wife in it, with the caption Benchley so generously wired me about. With its purchase and printing in the magazine, I became an established *New Yorker* artist, still to Ross's mixed bewilderment and discomfiture.

He never asked me if the couples I put in beds were married, but some of the drawings aroused his best Sunday alarm or perplexity. There was the one known around the office as "The Lady on the Bookcase," a nude female figure on all fours, about whom a man is saying to a visitor, "That's my first wife up there," and adding, "and this is the *present* Mrs. Harris." I have often told about what happened when *that* hit Ross squarely between his fretful editorial eyes. He telephoned me in the country to say, "Is the woman on the bookcase alive, or stuffed, or just dead?" I told him I would give the matter my gravest consideration and call him back, and I did. "She has to be alive," I told him. "My doctor says a dead woman couldn't support herself on all fours, and my taxidermist says you can't stuff a woman." He thought about it for a few seconds and then roared into the phone, "Then, goddam it, what's she doing naked in the house of her former husband and his second wife?" I told him he had me there, and that I wasn't responsible for the behavior of the people I drew. Just the other day I turned up a note of amplification that I had sent to him. In it I explained that I had tried to draw a wife waiting for her husband at the top of a flight of stairs, but had got the perspective all wrong and suddenly found I had a woman on a bookcase. This led naturally, I said, to the unnatural domestic situation I had drawn. "Thurber's crazy," Ross told someone later, but it wasn't the first time he had so diagnosed my condition.

There was another drawing that set off a memorable display of fireworks between the editor and me. It showed three hound dogs in the window of a petshop, one of them, sitting between the other two, having unusually sad eyes and gentle expression. A would-be woman purchaser is talking to the proprietor of the store, who is saying, "I'm very sorry, madam, but the one in the middle is stuffed, poor fellow."

"I don't think they have stuffed dogs in pet shops," Ross said. "Not in the show window, anyway."

"*This* shop has one in the show window," I said stubbornly.

"You have me there," Ross growled. Then I got into deeper difficulty. "It's a variant of that old story about the three men on the subway train late at night," I said. "They were sitting across from a fourth man, who is left alone on the train with the three others after still a fifth passenger hands him a note and gets off at the next stop. The note says, 'The man in the middle is dead.'" I never saw Ross look unhappier about anything. He said so much then, in such a splutter, that it doesn't come back to me coherently now. "I'll send that drawing in to every art meeting until it's bought and printed," I told him. I think it was bought on its third resubmission. Some of my drawings were held up much longer than that, and one night I got into Ross's office with a passkey, faked his R on three drawings I especially liked, and sent them through the works the next day. Nothing was ever said about that, but for weeks I expected all hell to break loose.

Ross's tormented forehead was always in creases of worry about some art problem. When, early on, he had decided to put captions in italics—bang! there was the problem of what to do about emphasizing words and phrases that needed it. Clearly they would have to be set up in roman, thus reversing an ancient convention, and Ross was not fond of being the first by whom the new idea is tried. Several times I tried to sell him the idea of romanizing only part of an emphasized word, on the ground that Americans, particularly females, often do that; a case in point is the caption I sent in (my last one, I think) for which Whitney Darrow did the drawing, an ardent girl saying to her gloomily intellectual young man, "When you say you hate your own species, do you mean *every-body?*" Actually, it seemed to my ear, our young ladies stress only the "ev" in that word, but this was the kind of hybrid that would have driven Ross into a new ulcer.

Since the great warrior was a worshiper of the gods of Clarity and Explicitness, that devotion sometimes led him into overelaboration of captions. I remember an early Arno of a husband and wife arguing *en boudoir*, the wife saying, "And after I've given you the best years of my life," and the husband snapping back, "Yes, and who made them the best years?" The point would be sharper if only the husband's speech were used, and Ross soon gave up dialogue for monologue in most captions. He could torture single lines, though, as in the case of a Hokinson dowager complaining to her pampered Pomeranian, *couchant* on a soft cushion in his cage at a dog show, "I'm the one that should be lying down." The caption had come in that way, but Ross changed it to "I'm the one that should be lying down somewhere," so readers wouldn't get the idea the dog's owner wanted to climb in and lie down on its cushion. I made my own mistakes in the same area, too, once drawing a tipsy gentleman, fallen prone at the feet of a seated lady and saying, "This is not the real me you're seeing, Miss Spencer." It should, of course, have been simply, "This is not the *real* me."

The editor was also often on the edge of panic about suspected *double entendre*, and after thirty-one years I recall his concern about an Arno drawing of one of his elderly gentlemen of the old school dancing with a warmly clinging young lady and saying "Good God, woman, think of the social structure!" Ross was really afraid that "social structure" could be interpreted to mean a certain distressing sexual phenomenon of human anatomy. He brought this worry to me, pointing out that "social diseases" means sexual diseases, but I succeeded in quieting his fears, and the caption ran unchanged. He was wary of fatality in drawings, sharing Paul Nash's conviction that "not even Americans can make death funny," and when Carl Rose, in 1932, submitted a picture of a fencer cutting off his opponent's head and crying *"Touché!"* Ross thought it was too bloody and gruesome, and asked Rose to let me have a swing at it, because "Thurber's people have no blood. You can put their heads back on and they're as good as new." It worked out that way. Nobody was horrified.

In the early thirties all the *New Yorker* cartoonists had to put up for months with the havoc and bother of a new Ross apprehension. He became convinced that somebody was giving away our captions to rival magazines before they could be used. The trouble began when two similar drawings with identical captions appeared in the *New Yorker* and the old *Life*. A snowbound traveler in the Alps is taking the brandy cask from a Saint Bernard and saying, "What, no White Rock?" The line had been invented by Donald Ogden Stewart, who told it to somebody, who told it to somebody else, and thus both magazines heard about it before long. After that alarm had sounded through the offices like a somber bell in Macbeth's castle, the originals of drawings the *New Yorker* bought came back to the artists with heavy strips of butcher's paper pasted over the captions. This ruined some of the drawings, since the paper often stuck to the caption like a collie's tongue to a frosty hitching post. A drawing of mine with the caption "What have you done with Dr. Millmoss?" got the super-secret treatment, and was obliquely described in the office records as "Woman with strange animal." The strange animal was a hippopotamus, but the *New Yorker* wasn't going to let any spy find out about that. This panic, like many another office panic, died down and was forgotten.

If I wrote of Ross's constant concern and kindliness about my eyes, it would embarrass him in heaven, as it would embarrass him on earth if he were still here. He was not a demonstrative man, or he thought he wasn't, but anyone who knew him well could see through the profane bluster and gruffness that covered great solicitude for the men and women he loved when they were in peril, or in any kind of trouble. He began by taking my drawings as a joke, went through a phase in which he dismissed them as "a passing fancy, a fad of the English," and ended up doing his darnedest, as my disability increased, to keep the drawings going by every kind of ingenious hook and crook. After I got so I could no longer see to draw, even with black grease crayon on large sheets of yellow paper, Ross began a campaign, recorded in a series of letters he wrote me, to reprint old drawings of mine with new captions. First he suggested reversing the old cuts, a simple mechanical maneuver; then, with the aid of others in the office who knew about such things, he experimented with taking figures or furniture out of one drawing and putting them in another, arriving at a dozen permutations of men, women, and dogs, chairs, bridge lamps, and framed pictures, upon which he must have spent hours of thought with his confederates in this conspiracy of consolation.

I did think up a few new captions for old drawings, but whatever device of recomposition was used, some readers got on to it. The first publication to point out what was going on was the *News Chronicle* in London. The interest of the English, or some of them, in my drawings both pleased and puzzled Harold Ross. He was puzzled by Paul Nash's enthusiasm for my scrawls, although he was delighted by Nash's having singled me out at a luncheon in the Century Club in 1931 from the very forefront of American painters, all present and lined up for introduction to the visiting British painter and critic. He loved my story of how Nash insisted that I be put on his right (on his left was a bottle of whiskey we had snatched from a sideboard), and by the distinguished visitor's asking a formidably bearded connoisseur of art, seated across from him, "What do you think of Milt Gross?"

When Nash was art critic for the *New Statesman and Nation* in London, he once wrote a piece about American comic art in which he mentioned that I apparently began drawing without anything particular in mind, in the manner of the early drawings of the great Matisse. This remarkable and somewhat labored comparison was distorted by word of mouth until some careless columnist printed the news that Henri Matisse was an admirer of my scrawls. So it came about that in 1937, when two bold young gallery men in London put on a one-man show of my drawings, one of them telephoned Monsieur Matisse, over my dead body, to try to arrange a meeting. The poor chap came back from the phone a little pale, and stammering, "Matisse's secretary says that Matisse never heard of Mr. Thurber *or* the *New Yorker*." That same year a short-lived magazine called *Night and Day*, too imitative of the *New Yorker* for its own good, was published in London, and it bought and printed a series of my drawings called "The Patient," which the *New Yorker* had rejected. I saw to it that Ross was immediately notified of the sale, and I sent him a copy of the magazine. That's when he really began telling people, "Thurber's drawings are a fad of the English, a passing fancy." He thought that some of my drawings were funny, all right, but what really got him, I could tell from his tone and look when he first mentioned it to me, was the praise they got from Ralph Barton and Wallace Morgan when Ross asked these friends of his about them. There was one *New Yorker* cartoonist, perhaps one of many that felt the same way, who yelled at Ross one day during the thirties, "Why do you reject drawings of mine, and print stuff by that fifth-rate artist Thurber?"

"Third-rate," said Ross, coming promptly and bravely to the defense of my stature as an artist and his own reputation as an editor.

In the last seven years of his life Ross wrote me dozens of letters and notes about my drawings. In one he said he had found out that the *New Yorker* had published three hundred and seven of my captioned drawings, of which one hundred and seventy-five had been printed in one or another of my books. He wanted to know if I would permit new captions by outsiders on those rearranged originals of mine. "There is a caption here on a sketch by an idea man," he wrote me, "that it is thought might do for a re-used drawing of yours, as follows: (Two women talking) 'Every time she tells a lie about *me*, I'm going to tell the truth about *her*.' Now that I've got it on paper, it may not sound so hot, but it might do. The women in your drawings used to say some pretty batty things." He wanted to pay me the full rate I had got for originals, but I said no on a project in which I would have no real creative part.

The whole idea was abandoned after I told Ross that I didn't grieve about not being able to draw any longer. "If I couldn't write, I couldn't breathe," I wrote him, "but giving up drawing is only a little worse than giving up tossing cards in a hat. I once flipped in forty-one out of the whole deck, at twelve feet." I may have been straining a point to cheer up

Ross, but cheering up Ross was a good deed, like lighting a lamp.

He was fond of two series I had drawn, "Famous Poems Illustrated" and "A New Natural History," and here are some of the things he wrote me about them. "Why in God's name did you stop doing the illustrated poems? There are forty million other verses in the English language, many of them unquestionably suitable for Thurber illustration." "I hereby suggest the Blue Funk as an animal or bird in the Natural History series. Also, I suggest the Blue Streak and the Trickle, and mention the fact that you might get a few more animals out of the bones of the human skeleton." "There might be a name for something in the Natural History series in 'Lazy Susan,' a flower or a butterfly, or something. Would 'antimacassar' be possible? I guess not."

Some of his written comments on the Natural History series show the old sharpshooter at work. "The checking of the names in your Natural History series revealed that one name is a real name: there is an actual fish called the pout. You have a bird called a shriek. In real life there is a bird called a shriker and also one called a shrike. I should think the approximation here does not matter. There is a bee called a lapidary, but you have drawn an animal. You have a clock tick. There is, of course, a tick. No matter, I say. There is a bird called a ragamuffin. You have drawn a ragamuffin plant. No real conflict." I wrote Ross that, for temperamental reasons, and such, I could draw only creatures suggested to me by my own thoughts about words, and said, "I've come to the end of this series, unless you want a man being generous to a fault—that is, handing a small rodent a nut. And I know you won't want a female grouch nursing a grudge. As for the illustrated poems, they began when I sent St. Clair McKelway, from Frederick, Maryland, the Barbara Frietchie drawings, and they ended when I tried Poe's Raven, and it turned into a common cornfield crow."

In 1955 my London publishers brought out a small paperback of some forty selected drawings of mine, with a short preface. It was called *A Thurber Garland* and cost five shillings, or about seventy cents. That year only thirty-seven copies of it were sold, and I can hear Ross now, as I so often hear him, pacing the chalcedony halls and complaining. Perverse, unpredictable, H. W. Ross is grumbling to some uninterested angel, "What the hell's the matter with the English? Thurber's drawings are not a fad, or a passing fancy, they are here to stay. Don't they know that?"

The paragraph above is the way this installment ended when it was printed in the *Atlantic Monthly*. After it appeared, I got a reproachful letter from my English publishers, Hamish Hamilton, Ltd., telling me that *A Thurber Garland* had sold more than five thousand copies during its first year. I don't know how I made such an appalling mistake, but it wouldn't have surprised Ross. It wouldn't have surprised the late Gus Kuehner, either. He was my city editor on the Columbus *Evening Dispatch* when I covered City Hall for that newspaper in the early 1920's, and he once put up a kidding notice on the bulletin board announcing that I would no longer be allowed to deal with sums running into more than five figures—it now turns out it should have been four, or maybe three. As I recall it, I'd written a story in which I magnified the municipal debt by some six million dollars.

Ross and Kuehner, incidentally, had a great deal in common. They had both started in as part office boy and part reporter when they were in their teens; they both got along well with cops; their frowns and snarls and moods were similar, and they talked the same language. One day in 1928 the phone rang in my office at the *New Yorker* and a voice as loud as Ross's tried to disguise itself, with about as much success as Ross would have had. "Are they serving tea and lady fingers at the *New Yorker* now?" said a strong falsetto that I recognized instantly. Kuehner could never get it out of his head that the *New Yorker* was a fancy pants place, with thick carpets on the office floors, and editors who smoked cigarettes in long holders. He said he had been in town for a convention of newspapermen, but was on his way back to Columbus. I told him to come over so I could introduce him to Ross. "I want you to meet him," I said. "He's a guy like you. In some ways he *is* you." Kuehner was unimpressed. "I'm taking a train in about ten minutes," he said. "Don't let your tea get cold. Kiss Ross for me." And that was the last time I ever heard his voice. He died one Christmas Day in Columbus, at the age of forty-nine. If heaven were a place in which guys could get together and talk, Ross and Kuehner would have a fine time exchanging newspaper and editorial experiences and taking Thurber apart, the guy who didn't know the difference between thirty-seven and five thousand.

The Talk of the Town

O NE of the already well-established rituals aboard the *New Yorker* when I joined its jittery crew in the wayward weather of 1927 was what skipper Harold Ross, alternately dauntless ("Don't give up the ship!") and despairing (" 'We are lost!' the captain shouted.") called the weekly Talk meeting. I survived hundreds of them—physically, at any rate. Named for "The Talk of the Town," the front-of-the-book department that was Ross's favorite and gloomiest preoccupation in the early years, the Wednesday morning meetings rambled on for anywhere from one to three hours, depending upon the mood of the master.

When Ross's secretary informed him that the rest of us—Katharine Angell, Andy White, Ralph Ingersoll, and I—were gathered around the table in the meeting room, Ross would saunter in, sometimes with the expression of a man who has heard an encouraging word but oftener with the worried brow of a bloodhound that is not only off the scent but is afraid it's losing its sense of smell. ("You're lousing up your metaphors," I can hear Ross grumbling. "Now you got a goddam bloodhound commanding a ship.") He would plop his briefcase on the table, sit down, sigh darkly, and open the meeting with some pronouncement, either a small fact about a big man: "William Randolph Hearst still has all his teeth," or a derogatory comment about an institution: "Medical science doesn't even know how to cure dandruff," or a running broad jump to some despondent conclusion: "Maude Adams lives in town now, but I haven't got anybody that can find out what she does and where she goes and who she sees."

Then the regular order of business began with a safari through the darkest regions ("Now, by god, I'm Stanley!") of the X issue, the one that would reach the stands the following day. It never satisfied Ross, and it rarely put him in a good humor. There weren't enough laughs in Talk, or any interesting facts; two drawings in the issue were too much alike; and "White and Thurber both mentioned novocain in their casuals. We're getting neurotic."

There was always, tossed in somewhere, a brief lecture about something: the lack of journalistic sense in the female of our species, everybody's ignorance of the rules of grammar and syntax, the wasting talent of a certain artist who was making a career of sex, or the incompetence of some doctor who was treating a friend of Ross's. He affected a disdain for doctors and other professional men, and once when I introduced him to a great eye surgeon, he shook hands with him and said, "I have little respect for professional men." He actually had great respect for this particular doctor, and for several others, but his rude generalization was prompted by the little boy in him, or the partly educated adult envious of specialized training and skeptical of technical knowledge, or some orneriness of mood aggravated by the peptic ulcers that bothered him during the last thirty years of his life. Alexander Woollcott explained the ungracious phase of the fabulous editor in ten words: "Ross has the utmost contempt for anything he doesn't understand."

Ross had a kind of mental file of prejudices and antipathies, some momentary, others permanent, and most of them of unrevealed origin. At one Talk meeting he scrawled on a memo pad "Hate Southerners," handed it to Ingersoll, and growled, "Keep bringing that up every week." It was brought up every week until Nancy Hoyt wrote a sharp satirical piece about a fictional Southern girl. Ross liked and admired many Southerners, among them Laurence Stallings and Nunnally ("Where I come from the Tobacco Road people are the country club set") Johnson. In 1926 Johnson had told Ross he would like to review motion pictures for the magazine. "For God's sake, why?" Ross demanded. "Movies are for old ladies and fairies. Write me some pieces." Ross had early conceived a violent dislike of movies, and hoped his cinema critic would have at them with a cudgel. His feeling was moderated somewhat after he saw *Public Enemy* and *Viva Villa*. On several visits to Hollywood he became a friend of James Cagney and Frank Capra, among others, and, a dozen of his letters prove, tried for years to interest Hollywood producers in my "The Secret Life of Walter Mitty," whose film possibilities he was the first to detect.

Ross almost never got through a Talk meeting without contriving to make Ingersoll say something to irritate him. When Ingersoll suggested a dope piece about the enormous ball that surmounts the Paramount building, Ross glared at him and snarled, "I wouldn't print a piece about that ball if Lord Louis Mountbatten were living in it." On another Wednesday, when Ingersoll told him, "I have the stuff you wanted on Thaw," Ross's eyes brightened darkly. Ingersoll always pronounced *Thaw* as if it were *Thor*, and Ross knew this, but he said, "I don't want a piece about Thor, or Mercury, or any of the other Greek gods." Ingersoll was the main target of his gripes, and I was next. "There isn't a single laugh in the Talk of the Town," he snapped one day, and I snapped back, "You say that every week," and he snarled, "Well, there are even fewer this time." Ross was not Ross until he had churned the hour, any hour, into a froth of complaint and challenge, and this was part of the inexhaustible, propulsive force of the magazine. I took up the challenge about Maude Adams, and a few days later laid on his desk her private phone number and enough data on her goings and doings for two separate pieces in "Talk of the Town." Ross stared at the stuff as if it had been dug up by a little child, and all he said was, "Well, I'll be damned!" It was a long time before he accepted me as a dependable reporter, but I was used to this because I had had the same experience of trial by ordeal with three different city editors of newspapers.

Russell Maloney, who took over from me in 1935 the task of writing most of Talk, once wrote in the *Saturday Review* that Harold Ross regarded perfection as his personal property, like his hat or his watch. This observation could be carried further without straining its soundness. In the first few years of his magazine Ross sometimes had as many as three men, in separate offices, writing pieces for Talk, each one unaware of the competition of the others. Most of them "went out like matches in the wind of Ross's scorn," as Ralph Ingersoll once put it. When the editor of the *New Yorker* became convinced that writers did not possess the perfection that was rightfully coming to him, out they went. Even when he decided that a writer probably did have his perfection, he liked to believe the fellow would never come across with it. He always hoped he would find perfection lying on his desk when he came to work, but he was pretty sure there would be no such luck.

Fifteen years ago I brought him a sheaf of some miscellaneous writings by Peter De Vries, whom I had met in Chicago, where he was then editor of *Poetry*, and told Ross I had found a perfect *New Yorker* writer. He stared at the material glumly, and said, "I'll read it, but it won't be funny and it won't be well written." Two hours later he called me into his office. Hope had risen like a full moon and shone in his face. "How can I get DeVree on the phone?" he demanded, his enthusiasm touched with excitement. Not many days after that Ross and I had lunch at the Algonquin with Peter DeVree—the name had become wedged in Ross's mind as French, not Dutch, and he was sure the sibilant should go unsounded, as in *debris*, and he never got it straightened out. I had warned Pete, since I was a veteran of such first meetings, that Ross's opening question might go off in any direction, like an unguided missile. "Hi, DeVree," said Ross as they shook hands. "Could you do the Race Track department?" This was the kind of irrelevancy I had in mind, and Pete was prepared for it. "No," he said, "but I can imitate a wounded gorilla." He had once imitated a wounded gorilla on a radio program in Chicago. Ross glared at me, realizing I had briefed De Vries, and then his slow lasting grin spread over his face. "Well, don't imitate it around the office," he growled amiably. "The place is a zoo the way it is." Thirty years ago Ross would probably have opened up on De Vries with "Maybe you could run the magazine" or "Could you write the Talk department?"

Ross couldn't have described perfection, because his limited vocabulary got tangled up in his fluency ("I don't want you to think I'm not incoherent," he once rattled off to somebody in "21"), but he recognized it when he saw it. He handled White's invaluable contributions as if they were fine crystal, and once stuck this note in Andy's typewriter: "I am encouraged to go on." Surely no other editor has ever been lost and saved so often in the course of a working week. When his heart leaped up, it leaped a long way, because it started from so far down, and its commutings over the years from the depths to the heights made Ross a specialist in appreciation.

In spite of preliminary ordeal, of which there was always plenty, it became a pleasure to write for a man whose praise was so warm and genuine when it came. Dozens of us cherish old memos from him, and letters, and the memory of phone calls, and it is surprising how quickly they come to mind. I often remember a single sentence he scribbled and sent to me about one of the drawings I had done, illustrating Leigh Hunt's "The Glove and the Lions." It read, "It's the god-damdest lion fight ever put on paper." But this is about "Talk of the Town," of whose significant figures White was perhaps the most important, because of his superb handling of the first, or editorial, page of that department.

Elwyn Brooks White, who had been God's gift to the Cornell *Sun* and to that university's English professors, gentlemen used to perfection in books but not in classroom themes, was getting thirty dollars a week writing automobile advertising in New York when Ross's magazine began. He sold Ross his first piece two months later, and then half a dozen light verses and some more "oddities," as he calls them. He did not meet Ross until after he was hired by Katharine Angell in the fall of 1926. I might as well admit, right here, that I have done a lot of brooding about the mystery that some literary scholars have wrought out of, to quote one of them, the central paradox of Harold Ross's nature; that is, his magic gift of surrounding himself with some of the best talent in America, despite his own literary and artistic limitations. Without detracting from his greatness as an editor, it must be pointed out that the very nature of his magazine, formless and haphazard though it was to begin with, did most of the attracting. Writers and artists of the kind Ross was looking for decided that here was a market for their wares, and to say that the head of such an enterprise, personally unknown to most of those who came to work for him, was the attracting force is to say that the candle, and not the flame, attracts the moths. I think the moths deserve most of the credit for discovering the flame.

White "brought the steel and music to the magazine," according to Marc Connelly, famous among his colleagues for such offhand lyrical flights. Others, White among them, have not been quite so definite about what it was that the *New Yorker's* "number one wheel horse" (Ingersoll's phrase) brought to the magazine from Cornell by way of the advertising business. In 1926 White began working part time for the *New Yorker* at thirty dollars a week. "I hung on to my advertising connection because I had no confidence in my ability in the world of letters," White has written me. "Nothing that has happened in the last thirty years has shaken my lack of confidence—which is why I still hang on to newsbreaks." Nobody else in the world of letters shares White's lack of confidence in White.

Andy quickly cured one of Ross's early persistent headaches, caused by the problem of newsbreaks, those garbled and often hilarious items from American journals and magazines which conveniently fill out, or "justify," *New Yorker* columns. For more than thirty years White has written the taglines for these slips of the linotype machine, and some thirty thousand of them have brightened the *New Yorker*'s pages. Nobody else, and many have tried, ever caught the difficult knack of writing the tags, or inventing the various newsbreak categories such as "Raised Eyebrows Department," "Neatest Trick of the Week," and a score of others. My one contribution to the categories was "How's That Again? Department," but I was baffled by the task of writing taglines.

Once when White was on vacation I tried my hand at it, and it turned out to have five thumbs. I invented a phony newsbreak, to see if I could get it past Ross. The item, which I credited to a mythical newspaper, went like this: "Oswego, New York, birthplace of William Tecumseh Sherman, has no monument or other memorial to the great Civil War general." Under this I had written, "Oswego marching through Georgia?" Sherman, of course, was born in Ohio, and this fact flickered into flame in the back of Ross's mind when the issue containing the fake break came out. Then he checked the newspaper and found out I had made it up. He banged into my office crying, "Goddam it, Thurber, don't kid around with the newsbreaks."

It would be like hunting for a broken needle in a hayfield to try to find a given newsbreak published long ago, and I doubt that even Miss Ebba Jonsson, the *New Yorker*'s incomparable librarian, could locate my own favorite newsbreak in the roughly seventeen hundred issues of the weekly that have been published so far. Fortunately it was printed in 1931 in a little book of *New Yorker* newsbreaks, called *Ho Hum*, with a foreword by White and drawings by Soglow. It goes like this:

The Departure of Clara Adams
[From the Burbank (Cal.) Post]

Among the first to enter was Mrs. Clara Adams of Tannersville, Pa., lone woman passenger. Slowly her nose was turned around to face in a southwesterly direction, and away from the hangar doors. Then, like some strange beast, she crawled along the grass.

Ross had been in the habit of peddling the newsbreaks around the office, letting everybody try his hand at writing lines of comment to round them out. White turned in his first batch one day in the fall of 1926, and then went out to his parents' home in Mount Vernon, New York, where he came down with chicken pox. Ross instantly knew he had found the one and only man who could handle newsbreaks perfectly, and he got White on the phone in Mount Vernon. "I had never heard such a loud voice over any telephone," White wrote me, "and I had never been encouraged before by an employer, so it was a memorable occasion. Then Ross asked me to come right back into the office and I had to tell him I had chicken pox. 'You have *what*?' bellowed Ross." It was one of those innumerable petty irritations that bedeviled him in his early life as an editor. He just couldn't believe that he had at last found someone who was willing to endure the boredom and triviality and fine print of newsbreaks—and then this man had contracted a child's disease. It was the kind of experience that used to make him bang his hand on the table and scream, "That's my life!"

The handling of newsbreaks, White and Ross soon found, had its special perplexities, of the kind that made the editor nervous: a couple, instead of a coupé, found in a ditch; a hippy in place of a happy bride; a ship's captain who collapsed on the bride, instead of the bridge, during a storm at sea; and a certain percentage of items skillfully counterfeited. There were also a few fanatics who made a hobby, or even a lifework, out of reading newspapers and sending in breaks, and most of them were touchy and temperamental. One of these career men wrote, "Do not put paper clips on my rejections. They leave marks." This complaint happened to Andy on a gloomy day. He poured Glyco-Thymoline on the breaks, instead of putting clips on them, and a few days later showed me a letter from the newsbreaker, thanking him for his care. "That's *my* life," said White.

White's "Notes and Comment," the first page of "Talk of the Town," through the years has left its firm and graceful imprint on American letters, and every now and then has exerted its influence upon local, or even wider, affairs. It was responsible for the moving of the information booth in the Pennsylvania Station out into the center of the main floor; for the changing of the lights, from colored to white, in the tower of the Empire State Building; and for directing attention to the captive audiences in Grand Central Station, where passengers had been forced to listen to broadcast commercials. This practice was officially abandoned after hearings by the Public Service Commission. The editor made few public appearances in his lifetime, but this was one of his finest hours, and he enjoyed every minute of it. It was White, though, who had inaugurated the campaign to free the captives of commercialism.

"Notes and Comment," called simply "Comment," did more than anything else to set the tone and cadence of the *New Yorker* and to shape its turns of thought, and White's skill in bringing this page to the kind of perfection Ross had dreamed of intensified Ross's determination to make Talk the outstanding department of the magazine. It was a great help when God sent him an efficient and tireless young reporter named Charles H. Cooke, the magazine's first "Our Mr. Stanley," who was often up at dawn and abroad at midnight, digging up data.

The prospectus had declared, "The *New Yorker* will be what is commonly called sophisticated, in that it will assume a reasonable degree of enlightenment on the part of its readers." Ross found it hard to keep in mind this assumption of enlightenment, and sometimes seemed to be editing Talk for a little boy or an old lady whose faculties were dimming. When I used *axe-haft*, Ross followed it, in parentheses, with "the haft is the handle of the axe." His profound uneasiness in the presence of anything smacking of scholarship or specialized knowledge is perpetuated in dozens of small changes he made in my copy. In the following excerpt from a Talk piece, which I wrote after a visit to the Metropolitan Museum, I have italicized his insertions: "For those who exclaim over armour, *a thing pretty rare with us*, the three new suits the museum has just come by will prove enthralling. One of them, a richly ornamented Spanish war harness, has more pieces of réchange, *or you might say accessories*, than any other battle suit in the world. . . . Among other prizes of the New Accession Room is the lid of an amphora, *but we never did find out what an amphora is*." In another Talk item about the demands upon his hosts of the difficult and imperious Count Keyserling, I wrote that he had to have, around midnight, after his lecture, "champagne or claret," and Ross had to explain to his sophisticated readers that claret was "French red wine," so they would not confuse it with its prize-ring meaning of "blood."

Harold Wallace Ross, who secretly enjoyed being thought of as raconteur and man about town, was scared to death of being mistaken for a connoisseur, or an aesthete, or a scholar, and his heavy ingenuous Colorado hand was often laid violently upon anything that struck him as "intellectual." Thus his avid mental curiosity balked at whatever seemed to him redolent of learning. I find I once wrote of him in a letter to White, "What are you going to do about a man who would rather listen to Jim Farley discuss Coca-Cola than to Robert Frost describing rings of lantern light?"

Ross had the enthusiasm of a youngster at a circus for a thousand different things, but none of them was in the realm of the recondite or the academic. One day, a year before he died, I brought him together at the Algonquin with an old friend of mine who had never met him but had always been eager to find out what he was like. Ross launched immediately into a breathless discussion of his enthusiasm of the moment, the history of Bull Durham tobacco. My friend sat entranced for a quarter of an hour and, after Ross had departed, exclaimed, "He's a Gee Whiz guy!" Ross was fascinated by facts and statistics about the big and costly, but he didn't like his

facts bare and stark; he wanted them accompanied by comedy
—you unwrapped the laugh and there was the fact, or maybe
vice versa.

The Gee Whiz Guy was forever enchanted by the size and
saga of the fabulous city's great buildings. He had long
wanted a profile on Jacob Volk, a building wrecker out of
Herculean mythology, who tore down two hundred and fifty
big structures in Manhattan during his lifetime and never
passed the Woolworth Building but what he dreamed of the
joys of razing it. I had wanted the piece for Talk, where it
seemed to me it belonged, but Ross assigned Robert Coates
to do the profile. (Ross also took Shipwreck Kelley, the flagpole sitter, away from me and profiled him. These enlarge-
ments into profiles of snapshots that belonged in Talk marked
the beginning of Ross's interest in long pieces instead of sharp
vignettes.) I got Jake Volk for Talk, in spite of Ross, because
the famous wrecker died while the Coates profile was in the
works, and we never ran profiles about dead men. I broke the
sad news to the editor. "Dammit," mourned Ross, "why
couldn't he have waited a week?" Ross believed that God and
nature owed the *New Yorker* a reasonable amount of consideration in the matter of life and death. We laid Jake Volk to
rest in "Talk of the Town," which dealt with the dead as well
as the quick.

He had died two months before another wrecker began
taking down the old Waldorf, on whose site the Empire State
Building was erected. The original Waldorf was a toughly constructed building, and the wrecker who took it apart was paid
nine hundred thousand dollars for the job—old Jake had paid
for the privilege of tearing structures down, and made his
profit by selling intact sections, but the debris of the Waldorf
was all taken out to sea and dumped. I wrote about the last
day of the famous hotel, and eighteen months later climbed
the still unfinished tower of the Empire State.

Jake shook his head at mention of Stanford White. "When
he built 'em they stayed built," he would say sadly. One that
stayed built has been made over into apartments for fifteen or
twenty families. It's the great Italian Renaissance mansion in
East 73rd Street where Joseph Pulitzer spent his last years and
died without ever having been in forty-five of its sixty rooms.

My bones still feel the cold of the mansion's deserted sprawl of rooms and halls littered with trash and covered with dust when I shivered in them one wintry day in 1934. The legends of Pulitzer and Stanford White are growing dim, but the famous mansion is as staunch as ever. I trust that the ghost of Jacob Volk, seeming to munch one of the caviar sandwiches he so loved, does not mournfully stalk the corridors of the old mansion just off Fifth Avenue.

In Columbus, or in France, or for the *Evening Post*, I had interviewed many celebrities: Eddie Rickenbacker, who had little to say; General Pershing, who had nothing to say; Harry Sinclair, who mumbled tonelessly; Thomas A. Edison, who kept repeating, "The radio will always distort the soprano voice." Interviews for "Talk of the Town" were easier, because most of the characters of that period were colorful and voluble: Jimmy Walker, always eager to say something; Al Smith, a born speaker; Huey Long, who paced the four rooms of his hotel suite delivering a political speech for an hour to an audience that consisted of me; Jack Johnson, who talked about himself in the third person—"Jack Johnson don't approve of the immorality of the Broadway theater." If the principal celebrities of the time were to be seeded, like tennis players, on the basis of number of mentions each got in Talk, the listing of the first seven would go like this: Jimmy Walker 63, Al Smith 60, Calvin Coolidge 43, Lindbergh 33, J. P. Morgan 29, Gene Tunney 25, Otto Kahn 21. Ross once tacked an order on the bulletin board which read: "Otto Kahn has been mentioned six times in Talk recently. There will be no more mentions of him for six months." Ross was sternly opposed to anecdotes about the Algonquin group, and when an excellent one required the use of the name Alexander Woollcott, he cursed awhile and said, "I'll tell you what we'll do—we'll misspell it," and we left out one of the "l's." He worried about overmention of others, too: Admiral Byrd, Rudy Vallee, Grover Whalen, and Fiorello La Guardia.

Harold Ross, ever hot for certainties in this our life, was also, being a true newspapermen, avid of exclusive stories for Talk. It wasn't easy, though, to get them, because of the danger of their being leaked out between press time and publication day. Once we broke to the world the news of the vast

Rockefeller Center project, only to find that the world knew all about it. Alva Johnston had written it up in a Sunday newspaper article before we hit the stands. We did manage what I called in my lead "A little miracle of secrecy" in reporting the first meeting of Gene Tunney and Charles A. Lindbergh, which took place at the studio of the artist Charles Baskerville in 1928. Ross and Tunney had become friends during the *Stars and Stripes* days in France. Ross got a great kick out of making me believe for a time, after the Tunney-Lindbergh story, that I had been hoaxed and that no such meeting had taken place—he himself had been out of town when I wrote the piece. But Gene Tunney has recently verified the old meeting in a letter to me, which he ended with, "Hal Ross was a great American," and Mr. Baskerville, riffling through the years, recently found a photograph of himself and Tunney and Lindbergh taken that day at his studio.

Every press agent in town dreamed of getting into Talk by throwing his fast ball past Ross (one day a story reached my desk about a cockroach race at the Nut Club in Greenwich Village), but Ross was struck out only once, by, of all people, Texas Guinan. She telephoned him one day to say, in a fine imitation of breathless excitement, that Ella Wendel, last of the three wealthy Wendel sisters, who lived in the gaslit past in a mysterious Fifth Avenue mansion, had visited her night club, accompanied by two elderly gentlemen out of the carriage days of old Gotham. "She talked to me about it for half an hour," Ross told me. I stared at the wise old newspaperman in disbelief. "She talks to everybody for half an hour on the phone," I told him. "She talked to me for half an hour one day when I was on the *Post*." Ross then went on to say that a few days after Miss Ella's visit Tex had received from her an elegant specially made handbag worth forty-five hundred dollars, to replace one given her by Larry Fay, which she had lost. "You can't believe that!" I yelled. "It's obviously a phony. Ask any woman you know, ask any little girl." But Ross ordered me to write the story—I told him he would have to make it an order—and it was printed, and Miss Wendel's attorneys called on Ross and demanded a retraction of the story. H. W. Ross gave up hard. He sent out three different reporters to call on every handbag maker in the East, and they

all came back with the word that he had been royally hum-
bugged.

One of the clearest pictures in my mental memory book of
the old days is that of Ross pounding away on his typewriter,
trying, by speed and finger power, to get facility and felicity
into his writing of Talk. "It should be like dinner-table conversation," he used to repeat, but although he could be an
entertaining dinner-table conversationalist, he was unable to
hammer it into written prose. This was because he became an
unreal Ross when he tried writing for the magazine, a strained
and artificial personality, completely different from the undis-
guised and articulate one that still breathes in almost every
line of the thousands of personal letters he wrote. He simply
was not a *New Yorker* writer, never got better at it, and in the
thirties gave it up, although he persisted in sticking into my
copy now and then such pet expressions of his as "and such"
and "otherwise." His "and such" spots old "Talk of the
Town" pieces like flyspecks. It was his idea of achieving ease.
In one story, "The studio walls are hung with oils and watercolors, with here and there a gouache and silverpoint" became
"The studio walls are hung with oils and watercolors, and
such." His sense of rhythm, often orally effective, failed him
on the typed page.

Sometimes I secretly rewrote his clumsier rewrites of my
Talk pieces and faked his R, which every piece of copy had to
bear when it went to the printers. He was capable of awkward
sentences that would have made him bellow if he had found
them in someone else's copy; such a prize monstrosity, for
instance, as "A man in a brown suit named Jones came into
the room." Once he hastily changed "colloid" to "collide,"
and I sent him a note of reproof and told him to look up the
word in the dictionary. He did and wrote back, "It's a hell of
a complicated world." Our clashes over Talk, frequent and
lengthy in the beginning, gradually quieted down with his
increasing interest in other departments of the magazine. But
the late twenties were full of scraps between us. When, as
something of an expert on the haunts of O. Henry in his
beloved Bagdad-on-the-Subway, I wrote that he had last lived
at the Hotel Caledonia, 28 West 26th Street, Ross yelled that

I was wrong. F.P.A. had told him that it was the Hotel Chelsea, and to Ross the great Frank Adams was infallible. He sent a reporter to City Hall to check the vital statistics on Porter, William Sidney, and then slouched into my room to say grudgingly, "Okay on the Caledonia, Thurber," not so much pleased that I had been right as sorry that Adams had been wrong. If I was a man who lost things, and he was sure I was, he couldn't understand how the hell I could get facts straight.

The harassed editor, always beset by anxieties, worried about the rigor mortis of formula in "Talk of the Town" style, the repetition of "a gentleman of our acquaintance," "a man we know," "a Park Avenue lady," and such. Anecdotes, of which we have printed thousands, many of them flat, some of them memorable, were like mosquitoes that pestered him continually. "Nobody in this whole goddam city seems to say anything funny except taxi drivers, children, and colored maids." "We get too damn many about telephones and Macy's." And he would stick up a notice on the bulletin board beseeching everybody to turn in some fresh anecdotes. Once he paced for days, off and on, wondering what to do about a story my brother had sent in from Columbus, Ohio, dealing with Calvin Coolidge. It seemed that Mr. Coolidge had lost a nightgown in a Pullman sleeper and had written the company asking that it be returned or that he be reimbursed for his loss. This one never did reach print, because Ross could not figure out how to "hang it," that is, how to account for our knowing about a fact that had originated in the Near Far West.

With rue my heart is laden for one anecdote printed in Talk. It reported an incident that occurred during a convention of monumentalists, or tombstone cutters, in White Plains. A local member of the craft had shown off his own handiwork during a tour of a cemetery with a visiting headstonist. As they left the cemetery, a whistling boy walked past them. "Son of that big granite job I showed you back there," said the White Plains man. Ross loved it and ruined it with his rewrite. He not only dragged Rotary into it, for no good reason, but tinkered clumsily with the pay-off line, so that it came out: "Son of that big granite and iron job I showed you back there." Ross had turned a deaf ear to the speech and, for all I know, may also have found out that there is always some ironwork in a granite monument.

When another superior anecdote was sent in—it is still known around the office to old-timers as the "grison anecdote"—I rewrote it and commanded Ross not to touch a single word. He read it, brought it into my office, said it was swell, looked as sad as if he had just lost a friend, and said, "Can't I please put a comma after 'My God'?" That comma, the record shows, is there. Here is the grison anecdote:

> The Harold Wilcoxes, of Nutley, New Jersey, have a grison, which they keep in a cage on their porch. A grison is a very odd-looking South American weasel-like carnivore. The other day a house-to-house salesman for a certain brand of dainty soap rang the bell (without noticing the grison) and Mrs. Wilcox answered. He launched right into his well-rehearsed praises of the soap, in the course of which he finally did see the grison. He blanched, but kept right on: "It preserves the fine texture of the most delicate skin and lends a lasting and radiant rosiness to the complexion my God, what *is* that thing?"

One day in 1931 Ross came into my office to say, after a lot of silent pacing, "Are we *important*?" The voice was not that of the man who had kept repeating a year before, "We're getting *grim*." I didn't encourage his implied ambition for higher things and longer pieces, but said, "We're just a fifteen-cent magazine." He left the room without saying anything, but half an hour later stuck his head in my door again. "I don't think so," he said, and went away.

The Talk meetings grew wearisome in the end and ran down like an old clock and stopped. "Thurber and White are sulky or surly or silent," Ross once told somebody, "and we're not getting anywhere."

Once, at meeting's end Ross said to me, "Have you got anything else to bring up, Thurber?" and I said I had, and I brought it up, and it turned out the others had just been discussing it. "Thurber is the greatest unlistener I know," Ross later complained. Then there was the day, very near the end, when I wrote doggerel during a meeting and shoved it across to White. Ross had figured I was making notes on something he had said, but the thing got into the magazine, I can't remember why, and there it is in the files, entitled "Bachelor Burton." It runs like this:

> Allen Lewis Brooksy Burton
> Went to buy himself a curtain,
> Called on Greenburg, Moe, and Mintz,
> Bought a hundred yards of chintz
> Stamped with owls and all star-spangled,
> Tried to hang it, fell, and strangled.

My eight years of wandering the city for Talk ended in 1935, and my last visit piece was about a melancholy stroll along 14th Street a few days before Christmas that year. It ends like this: "We missed this year the vendors of those old-fashioned German Christmas cards with the tinsel snow and the rich colors. There used to be several of them around, and a sad man who played 'O Little Town of Bethlehem' on a flute. Nobody seemed to know what had become of them." Most of the personalities of the Crazy Years between Lindbergh's flight and Hitler's heyday are dead and gone, and I had forgotten most of the tinsel snow and the colorful trivialities I gathered for "Talk of the Town" so long ago until I looked them up in the files the other day. There was a lot of stuff to hold the interest of the Gee Whiz Guy: Ely Culbertson pondering for forty-three minutes before playing a certain card in his celebrated bridge match with Sidney Lenz; the signature of Count Felix von Luckner, fourteen inches long and two inches high, in an enormous guest book; and an item about the thirty-six-ton meteorite that Admiral Peary brought back from Greenland and presented to the Museum of Natural History. "Geezus!" said Ross. "I hope they were expecting it."

There was always something to catch and hold his eager interest in the foibles, frailties, and wonders of human nature. When a certain toothpaste's "Beware of Pink Toothbrush" campaign was on, it pleased but did not surprise him when we found out that a drugstore on Broadway had received more than forty requests for pink toothbrushes in one week. He was also tremendously amused when the Schrafft restaurants stopped selling Lucky Strikes because of the far-flung slogan, "Reach for a Lucky instead of a sweet," only to discover, at the end of the year, that the sale of all kinds of sweets had gone up, not down, as the result of the cigarette advertising.

There were, also, many things that made him scowl and fret. One week I nodded, and rewrote an anecdote that someone had stolen from Homer's *Odyssey*, one about the weary seafarer who starts walking inland with an oar over his shoulder and says he is going to keep going until he comes to a land where nobody knows what the thing is for, and there he will settle down. "Now Thurber's falling for anecdotes a thousand years old," Ross complained, after some classical scholar had written in about it. But I also caught several old ones that Ross had sent me to rewrite, among them the one about the little colored girl called Femily who, her parents told a visitor, had been named by the family doctor. The name which the doctor had put on the birth certificate was, as you may know, Female. Everybody knows now the story of the woman at the zoo who asked the caretaker, "Is that a male or a female hippopotamus?" to which the man replied, "Madam, I don't see how that could interest anybody except another hippopotamus." It was Harold Ross who brought that anecdote into my office, and it was the *New Yorker* that printed it first. Everybody in town stopped him and told him stories, and he became an expert in telling the old from the new. And how, in those years, he loved a fact—a great big glittering exclusive fact! When the King of Siam was operated on for cataract in 1933, Ross wanted to know if I could find out how much he had paid the great surgeon who performed the operation. He said it was rumored around town that the amount was as high as a hundred thousand dollars. It wasn't until about seven years later that I brought him this particular fact, and laid it on his desk. The chamberlain of the king had inquired of the surgeon's secretary what was the largest fee a commoner had ever paid him and was told the answer was ten thousand dollars. Thereupon the chamberlain wrote out a check for twenty thousand dollars and gave it to the secretary. The fact fascinated Ross, but the story was cold and seven years old, and he wouldn't use it.

Ross gradually lost his high interest in "Talk of the Town," but the best of it, carefully selected, would be a valuable record of the Wonderful Town in the bizarre second quarter of this century. In 1950 I wanted to write for Talk two or three pieces about Houdini, but Ross wrote me that he didn't want to "piddle Houdini away on Talk of the Town." This was the epitaph for the old journalistic department as I had known it. Four years earlier he had written me a letter that clearly reveals the dying of an old passion of his. It begins "Dear Jim." (Ross rarely called men by their first names in talking to them in the office, but he often used first names in letters, and at social gatherings at his apartment, and otherwhere. Like me, both White and Gibbs were always a little surprised by the intimate salutation, and once Gibbs was disturbed. He had been in the hospital for several weeks, and Ross had visited him there. "I was about to have a third of my right lung taken out," Gibbs wrote me, "and, as I know now, without a very good chance of surviving the operation. He came to see me the afternoon before they were going to work on me, and he called me Wolcott, pronouncing it almost right, and I swear to God it was the first time it really occurred to me that I might be going to die. I called him Harold back, but it was quite an effort in my condition.") Here is the Ross letter, dated November 12, 1946:

The fault with Talk is mainly ideas. When you were doing the rewrite, we were getting better ideas. Shawn (peerless as an idea man) was on the job, and if I do say it myself, I was sparking some too. I was younger then. I've been very uneasy about the idea end of Talk for some time, now that the war is over and things aren't so obvious. I look over the ideas every week and am discouraged. If you should know of a man who can spark ideas, there's a job open for him, God knows.

It isn't true that there are many reporters. At the moment, we are weak there too, unless two or three absolutely new men should develop a flair, like Charles Cooke's (he also was peerless). We've had a couple of very good girls, but one got married and left town, and the other has gone on to working on longer pieces. We use reporters on long pieces more than we used to, but no more on Talk, I think, except for people trying out. We're trying to find young talent of all kinds and it's hard. And as to the writing, no one writer is making it a principal interest now, and I think that makes a difference. All the boys are doing Talk along with other things. Give me you, Shawn, and Cooke and I'll get out a Talk department. . . . It's up to God to send some young talent around this place, and He's been neglecting the job. That's the trouble.

When Ross wrote that, Bill Shawn, now editor of the *New Yorker*, was top man on the totem pole and remained there the rest of Ross's life, thus setting a world's endurance record. It was characteristic of H. W. Ross to forget that the two idea men in my day were Ralph Ingersoll and Bernard A. Bergman, who were never excelled, that Russel Crouse and Bob Coates had been two of the earliest and ablest Talk writers, and that the remarkable Haydie Eames Yates had been one of the first and liveliest reporters. Once, thirty years ago, I incorporated a line of her notes intact in one of my rewrites and sent it on to Ross. It was about a certain colorful celebrity and reported simply: "His love life seems as mixed up as a dog's breakfast." Ross blue-penciled it, of course, but the phrase remained a part of office lingo. As the years rode by, the love life of more and more *New Yorker* people became as mixed up as a dog's breakfast—but that's another story for another time.

Russel ("Buck") Crouse had been doing most of the Talk rewrite when I joined the staff. He would attend the Talk meetings, and then take a folder of stuff home with him to do in his spare time. As conductor of a column on the *Evening Post* called "Left at the Post" he had a job he didn't want to give up for the full-time anonymity of Talk, which in those days was signed *"The New Yorkers."* When Ross piled most of the Talk rewrite on me, in addition to my other work, he decided to save money by letting Crouse go and, as often happened, he did this while Crouse was on vacation. It wasn't until Buck came back and called at the office for his weekly folder of data that he found out that he wasn't going to do Talk any more. "I phoned Ross and asked him why he hadn't let me know I was out," Crouse says, "and Ross said, 'I was too embarrassed.' "

Buck Crouse had started two *New Yorker* departments, "That Was New York" and "They Were New Yorkers," and he had astounded Ross one day by telling him there were too many profiles about big successful Americans, and there ought to be one about a failure. Ross glared at him and said, "You're crazy," but Crouse turned in a profile of a typical Bowery derelict, and Ross read it and liked it and printed it. That was H. W. Ross—the editor who said you were crazy one day and then agreed with you the next.

Charles H. Cooke's career on the *New Yorker* was unique, which means it was like everybody else's, only different. The time of each of us there was peculiar in its own way, to come as close to definition as may be. Cooke was hired by Ingersoll at thirty-five dollars a week, worked twelve years, day and night, and never got more than sixty dollars. He turned in some twelve hundred Talk stories. No other reporter ever equaled his energy, or came close to his output. To Ross, whom he has called "the irascible, lovable genius," he was, more than most other men, a prize and a puzzle, a person to praise one day and lash out at the next. "I'm surrounded by piano players," Ross once said to me. "Why we haven't got a piano in this joint I'll never know." He meant not only Cooke, who wrote a book on piano playing, but Peter Arno, a real professional; Shawn, who once played a piano in a place in Montmartre; John McNulty, who had been a pianist in a silent movie theater; and Andy White, a parlor performer on the keys.

Cooke has sent me a long, fascinating summary of his Talk experiences, and the places he visited and the men he interviewed would make a book in itself, a book he has now and then started to write, but given up for the dozens of other activities he has crammed into his life, as novelist, short story writer, lieutenant-colonel in the Air Corps, and researcher in Washington. After the war, he wanted to get back on the *New Yorker*, but Ross told him, "I long ago decided not to keep any reporter for more than five years." What he meant by that I'll never know. Cooke had been a peerless reporter for him for twelve years. I'll never know, either, why he told Cooke, in 1946, he was going to give him the job of Talk editor, and then didn't do it. This happened at one of the many times when Ross admonished God for not sending him just such a man as Charles Cooke. Maybe Cooke will solve it all when he gets around to his own history of the *New Yorker*, and I hope he does.

I can't leave out a wondrous three-cornered exchange of notes involving Cooke and Ross and McKelway. Charles had turned in a piece about a performing dog, and it contained this sentence, "He stared at us and smiled affably." Ross read that and sent this note to McKelway, then managing editor (one of the fifteen Cooke worked for in his time): "Tell Cooke to for God's sake stop attributing human behavior to dogs. The dog may have stared but Cooke knows damn well he didn't smile." McKelway sent the memo to Cooke, and appended this: "Ross wants you to for God's sake stop attributing human behavior to dogs. O.K.?" Cooke sent it back to McKelway with this added: "O, for God's sake K." Later that same day Cooke got this message from McKelway: "Ross says your dog piece is swell. He put it through as is and left in the smile. Bow for God's sake wow."

Miracle Men

HELL, I hire anybody," Harold Ross told Ralph Ingersoll in the summer of 1925 when Ingersoll called on the editor of the *New Yorker*, asked for a job, and got one. It wasn't as simple as it sounds, though. Ingersoll had appeared in the editor's office dressed in a Palm Beach suit he had bought for the occasion, and Ross had talked to him for only a few minutes, gesticulating widely, when his big right hand struck an inkwell. Suddenly Ingersoll's new suit was dripping with ink and Ross was covered with embarrassment. Ingersoll had almost reached the office door on what he was sure was his way out of Ross's life when the editor shouted, "You're hired!" And then, a few moments later, sighed, "Hell, I hire anybody."

From then on Ross hired anybody, and everybody, in his frantic and ceaseless search for the Fountain of Perfection. A few of us came to realize that he didn't really want to find it, whether he knew it or not; that the quest itself was what kept him going. If he had found the Redeemer who, in Cabell's words, would make everything as "neat as a trivet or an apple-pie," he would have grasped his own starry scheme of things entire, smashed it all to bits, and then remolded it nearer to his heart's desire, or his mind's illusion, or whatever it was. A team of Freuds would have a hard time putting a finger on the Imp of the Perverse in Ross's psyche. I think he was looking for two separate kinds of Miracle Men: (1) the administrative genius who would sit at a Central Desk, push buttons, and produce Instant Perfection of organization, and (2) a literary wizard who would wave a magic wand over writers and artists and conjure up Instant Perfection in prose, drawings, and all other contents of the magazine.

H. W. Ross, being neither artist nor poet, was not equipped to bring "grace and measure" out of the chaos of man on earth, for his heart's ease or his peace of mind, but there was in him something of the powerful urge that has animated the human male from Sir Percival to Pasteur, from Marco Polo to Admiral Peary. He never knew exactly what he was after, since

he didn't have much self-knowledge and was afraid of intro-
spection, but I think he hoped it would be as shining as the
Holy Grail, or as important as the Northwest Passage, or as
rewarding as the pot of gold. He was afraid, though, that a
Gorgon would pop up at any time to frustrate him, or a Quest-
yng Beast, or a Gordian knot, and he realized that he damn
well better have a Perseus on hand to help him, or a Pala-
medes, or an Alexander the Great. These romantic compari-
sons would, I am sure, move psychiatrists to ridicule; they
would find in Sir Harold not a romantic, but a mixed-up modern man driven by the well-known compulsion to build with
one hand and tear down with the other. Well, that urge was
in him, too, along with fixation, defense mechanism, inferiority complex, and all the rest.

Many of us who went with him on his Quest, part of or all
the way, often became bored or infuriated, and wanted to
quit, and there were scores who did quit and found an easier
way to live and make a living. A few of us could not quit. We
had put on the armor and strapped on the sword and we were
stuck with them. Once, when E. B. White had taken all he
could, or thought he had, he said he was quitting and went
home. Ross paced his office all afternoon and then got White
on the phone at his apartment. "You *can't* quit," he roared.
"This isn't a magazine—it's a Movement!" Andy did not
leave the Movement.

The limits and limitations of Sir Harold's quest were defined by the very nature of his magazine, and no matter how
high, and ever higher, he set his goal, it was ludicrously low
compared with the objectives of the great pioneers and path-
finders whose listing above would nevertheless give Ross, I
think, more comfort than discomfiture. He had humor, but
he was never able to see clearly the essential comedy of a shining quest confined and constricted by mundane office walls
and all the mean mechanics of magazine production. Once in
a while he would say that he didn't really give a damn, and
that the only thing he had ever liked doing was getting out
the *Stars and Stripes* in Paris. "Every magazine has its cycle,"
he would say, "and this one has its cycle, too. It's a precarious
enterprise, at best, and I wouldn't encourage anybody to in-
vest in it." But if you concurred in his depressive views and

pretended to share his mood, he would snap out of it like a switch blade.

In the last months of his life, when he was trying to lean back and take it easy at his home near Stamford, on doctor's orders, one of those who called on him was Hobart Weekes, since 1928 a big cog in the *New Yorker* machine, a Princeton and Oxford man whose knowledge of and familiarity with make-up, proofreading, fact checking, English, and English literature frequently amazed his boss. Once Ross was about to scribble "Who he?" in the margin of a proof opposite the name William Blake, but one of those hunches or intuitions that stayed his hand made him send for Weekes. "Who's William Blake?" he demanded, and Weekes told him. "How the hell did you know that?" Ross said. He was also astonished by Weekes's knowledge of the differences, ecclesiastical and otherwise, between a virgin and a verger. (A virgin, instead of a verger, had crept into a Talk story about some church ceremony, but was hustled out by the learned Princeton-Oxford man before she could get into the magazine and mortify its editor.)

The day Weekes called on him at Stamford, Ross was lying on his bed, restless and disconsolate, smoking cigarettes against orders. "They don't need me at the office any more," said the man who had sometimes protested he didn't want to be there. Weekes straightened him out on that, implementing and underlying the *New Yorker*'s need for its founder. That night, I am sure, H. W. Ross slept better.

Nothing throws a stronger light on Ross's eternal questing, his incurable discontent, and his psychological, if not indeed almost pathological, cycle of admiration and disillusionment than the case history of Ralph McAllister Ingersoll from 1925 until he quit in 1930 to become a Luce editor, later the founder of *PM*, a controversial front-page figure during the war, a lieutenant-colonel in the U.S. Army, and the author of half a dozen books. In 1942 he was the subject of a two-part profile in the *New Yorker* written by Wolcott Gibbs. When Ingersoll was on the magazine, Ross would have bet a cool million to one that no such profile would ever be published. (Thirty years ago, when Ingersoll kept suggesting a profile of Walter Winchell, Ross said, "Dismiss it from your mind. There'll never be a profile of Winchell in this magazine." St. Clair McKelway's *New Yorker* profile of Walter Winchell in 1940 ran to six parts.)

Ingersoll, not yet twenty-five when he was hired by Ross, was a graduate of Yale's Sheffield, and he had been a reporter and a mining engineer, but all this meant little to his employer. What meant a lot was that Ingersoll was a grand-nephew of Ward McAllister and knew his way around Park Avenue and Long Island. "He knows what clubs Percy R. Pyne belongs to, and everybody else," Ross once told me. "He has entree in the right places. He knows who owns private Pullman cars, and he can have tea with all the little old women that still have coachmen or footmen or drive electric runabouts. It's damned important for a magazine called the *New Yorker* to have such a man around." Ross had sent him, for opinion, Ellin Mackay's "Why We Go to Cabarets," and it was Ingersoll's terse, emphatic "It's a must" that persuaded Ross to print it.

When I reached the *New Yorker* in March, 1927, Ross's enchantment with Ingersoll was undergoing its inevitable decline. Ross cast his own spells and broke them himself, and nobody has ever known just how or why. The great irony of Ross's quest, to me, was the simple truth that Ingersoll, who turned up when the magazine was a few months old, was the best of all the Central Desk men, the very administrative expert Ross spent his life looking for. I think he knew this unconsciously, would not admit it even to himself, and spent a lot of time after he had let Ingersoll go trying to justify and rationalize his bad judgment.

"He thinks he's a writer," he said to me when I told him he had lost his most valuable assistant. "He wrote a book called *In and Under Mexico*. I haven't read it, and don't want to, but it can't be good. The top drawer of his desk was always full of medicine. If I'd given him a thousand dollars a week to sit alone in a room and do nothing, in five days he'd have had six men helping him." Thus spake Harold Ross, the same man who kept saying, "We haven't got any manpower, we haven't got anybody who knows how to delegate anything." He had one final word the day I bawled him out for losing Ingersoll. "He brought Hush-a-phones into the office. I think he talked to brokers all the time, and people like Cornelius Vanderbilt. He knew too many people." Thus spake the man who had once boasted that Ingersoll knew everybody and that the *New Yorker* needed just such a man.

One of the hundred little things that plagued Ross was the postal regulation that requires all periodicals to print, at certain intervals, the names of their editors and principal stockholders. To satisfy this requirement, Ingersoll was listed as managing editor, all alone for several years, and then as co-managing editor with Katharine White. "Ross never stopped taunting me about it," Ingersoll says. "He would tell me that it didn't mean a thing, and that he was thinking of listing his butler as managing editor—'the way French newspapers name janitors or elevator men as their editors, so they can be the patsies in libel suits and such.'"

Ross kept bringing in other men, me among them, partly for the purpose of sticking pins in Ingersoll's pride. He told me, when I was "in charge," to give Ingersoll orders. "Don't let him write anything," he once said. "He did the captions on covering art this week. That's your fault. Change them." By "covering art" he meant a double-page spread of drawings that used to illustrate horse racing, open air concerts, and other goings on. Ingersoll had done the captions for a yacht race spread, drawn by Johan Bull: "The Start," "Midway," and "The Finish." Being sane at the time, or fairly so, I let them stand. "Did you change those captions?" Ross asked me later. "All you have to do is read them," I said. "They have my touch, it's unmistakable." He was satisfied.

Ralph Ingersoll and I became friends and nothing, even his passing into legend, has changed that. He spends his week ends now at his home in Castleton, Virginia, and is editor-publisher of the Middletown, New York, *Times-Herald* and the Pawtucket, Rhode Island, *Times*. Without his help and direction, always efficient and untiring, I could never have got "Talk of the Town" off the ground. He took care of a thousand managerial details that I was supposed to handle, couldn't have, and didn't want to, and Ross never knew about it. When Ingersoll began publishing *PM* in 1940, I wrote a brief column for it, called "If You Ask Me," twice a week until I went into a nervous tail spin following my fifth eye operation. Ross read a few of these columns and objected because, he said, "You're throwing away ideas on *PM* that would make good casuals." But I was out from under the strict and exacting editing for which the *New Yorker* was and still is famous, and I needed this relaxation and the hundred dollars a column Ingersoll paid me.

One column I wrote in 1941 dealt with an old *New Yorker* Talk item some contributor had sent to the magazine twelve years before, in 1929. My wife had turned it up in going through some old stuff of mine in the early summer of 1941 when we went to Martha's Vineyard. In my column I referred to the lost and found contribution, which had never got into print, as "an ancient fragment of urgency." It was a letter from a woman reader, and on it was clipped a pink memo reading "Must go this week" and signed with the initials of Arthur Samuels, one of the Miracle Men of 1929. When my wife found the thing, the item was not only a dozen years old, but Arthur Samuels had been dead for three years. Ross read that *PM* column, all right, but all he said to me was, "God knows how we got out a Talk department when you were writing it." Ingersoll could have told him how we managed it, and Bernard A. Bergman could have told him, too, and Raymond Holden, and Ogden Nash. All of them belonged to the Big Parade of Miracle Men that came and went across the years.

The pink memo slip for urgency is said to have been put into effect by Holden, and later to have been abandoned because one of the editors in charge of urgency was color-blind. Ross took as capricious, and laughed about it only grudgingly, my suggestion that we use shape instead of color to denote urgency. "Let's make the urgent memos round, like an alarm clock, and use rectangular or coffin-shaped ones for less immediate matters," I said. Some way or other, in the notable confusion of all *New Yorker* systems, first things usually came first and others trailed along. Ross, at bottom, had about as much grasp of system as I had, which was perilously close to zero, but the difference was that he worried about it constantly and it was the least of all my concerns. We needed a guiding hand, there is no doubt about that, but often a competent secretary or a well-trained office boy could have brought about the order and pattern that Ross was confident could be achieved only through the agency of a genius sent to him by God.

After Ingersoll left in 1930, Ross realized, but never said so, that he had left behind an empty space it would take at least two men to fill. In the next few years Ross brought in at least eight hopefuls. As Ingersoll put it, in *Fortune* in 1935, "Ross has hired them out of advertising agencies, from behind city desks, from the Social Register, from the Players Club. He brings them back from lunch, he cables for them." One day, in 1930, Ross brought Ogden Nash into my office and said, "I'm thinking of letting Nash here take a swing at running the Talk department." Ogden himself, in a letter to me, has told, better and more succinctly than I could, what happened to him, and I quote his letter:

My experience with Ross was brief but unfortunate. He started buying my stuff early in 1930; later that year we met for the first time—not in the office—but in a speakeasy.

I don't need to tell you that in many ways he was a strangely innocent man and he assumed that my presence in a speakeasy meant that I was a man about town. He was, I believe, still in mourning over the departure of Ingersoll, who had apparently been the ultimate in men about town, and was looking for a suave and worldly editor. He hired me practically on the spot. It took him less than three months to discover that it takes more than a collection of speakeasy cards to make a man about town. Besides this, he didn't need an editor anyhow, as anything he didn't do himself was capably handled by Raymond Holden and Mrs. White. The end of the third month, therefore, found me in the employ of what was then Farrar and Rinehart.

Shortly after I moved to Baltimore, where I remained for some twenty years; I was living there at the time of his death. I saw him occasionally when I visited the office.

He was an almost impossible man to work for—rude, ungracious and perpetually dissatisfied with what he read; and I admire him more than anyone I have met in professional life. Only perfection was good enough for him, and on the rare occasions he encountered it, he viewed it with astonished suspicion.

I suppose that in the twenty-odd years of our relationship I had half a dozen grudging kind words from him. Once, toward the end, he sat down and wrote me a letter of congratulation on a certain piece that was almost fulsome; those rare kind words meant more to me than any compliments from reviewers, and I wish I could afford a tombstone large enough to hold the letter.

Office legend has it that the first of the Miracle Men (they were also known in the early years as Jesuses and Geniuses) was Joseph Moncure March, but he soon got out from under and from on top. Someone has told me that, after a particularly rough session with Ross, March sat for hours in the make-up room one night, staring out the window, but he wasn't the only one of us to do that; sometimes we sat for hours after work, alone except for a bottle of Scotch or rye, planning just how to tell Ross where to get off. There were a few men who had the good sense not to listen when Ross said, "Maybe you can run the magazine," a famous epitaph for at least two dozen miscast Geniuses.

Fillmore Hyde, the *New Yorker's* first literary editor, was one of these wise men. He got out early, for greener and more tranquil pastures. Hyde was a sensitive, difficult, and able editor, who took no nonsense from Ross or anybody else. On my first day at the *New Yorker* he snapped at me, "Boy, take this telegram." I snapped something back at him and walked away, annoyed because he had spotted me for an office boy and not the new Redeemer. The last episode involving Fillmore Hyde at the *New Yorker* resulted from a letter to him that Bergman had dictated to a secretary. Bergman sent the letter back to her with instructions to do it over because she had misspelled Hyde's name, but he had made the mistake of writing in pencil in the margin, "For God's sake get this man's name right. Hyde is a touchy blankety blank." The secretary retyped the letter, incorporating the penciled sentence in it, and, the tale tells, Bergman signed it without rereading it and sent it off. I don't know what happened after that.

Others, besides Hyde, who turned down the Big Job included Hobey Weekes, Wolcott Gibbs, and Clifton Fadiman. Ross piled so much work on Weekes just after the war years, Big Job or not, that this invaluable editor came down with a serious illness requiring a major operation and a long siege in the hospital. Ross never seemed to know when a man had reached the limit of his endurance. If you kept taking it, he kept piling it on. His strange ambivalence—admiration and disenchantment, faith and distrust—went through a series of undulations in regard to Weekes. Once, mad about something trivial, he picked up his desk phone and threw it during a conference with Hobey.

At an earlier time, Weekes felt that he was being "put in the icebox," that some of his editorial duties were quietly being taken away from him, not to lessen the pressure of his work, but out of some Ross dissatisfaction with it. A new Genius, named Don Wharton, had appeared on the scene, and Ross had said of him, "Wharton can handle anything." Weekes sensed that the ancient formula of hiring and firing was about to be repeated again, but he didn't know what he had done to offend Ross. Hobey had started out as a checker and sometime Talk reporter, and had come up the hard way to chief of the copy desk, later taking on added heavy chores in the make-up and proofreading departments. He finally went to Ross and said, "There seems to be a move on foot to get rid of me. If I'm not wanted here, I'll leave in ten minutes." Ross didn't say anything, just sat staring at him. A good three minutes went by, during which Ross didn't move a muscle or speak a word. When Weekes couldn't stand it any longer he just got up and left the room. He wasn't fired.

When I was, at least in Ross's stubborn mind, top man, we were dealing heavily with some slight problem in his office one day (circa June, 1927), when his secretary tiptoed in and laid on the desk an enormous typescript, bound in imitation leather and seeming to me now, in retrospect, at least as thick as a desk dictionary. It was labeled "Mistakes Made by J. Thurber as Managing Editor." Ross stood up and stared at it, his tongue coming out of the corner of his mouth, his eyes

getting darker and darker. Then he said to his secretary, "Get
that thing out of here. Get rid of it. I don't want to know
what you did with it." Since the monumental compendium
of my mistakes, many of them deliberate, seemed to me a sure
safe conduct out of the job I hated, I said, "Aren't you going
to read it? Don't you want to find out what's in it?" What he
wanted to do, it came out after a lot of silent pacing, was to
fire the man he held responsible for this assumption of authority, this gross insubordination, this rude interruption of
his routine. I told him he would have to fire the man himself, that he was one of the best on the magazine. After a
long pause and much coin jingling, he said, "I'm mistaken
for him by some people, right here in the goddam hallways.
It's embarrassing. People probably think he's me, too." I
laughed him out of that finally, but not out of his firing
mood.

"I want you to fire So-and-so," he said, changing the object, but not the subject, of his wrath. So-and-so was a young
woman, long since in heaven with the angels, who wrote one
of the back-of-the-book departments. "She makes me nervous," Ross said. "Last night, at Tony's, she was damn near
sitting in the lap of the man she was with." It happened that
I had been at Tony's the night before, too, and had seen the
couple, sitting and drinking and talking like any other couple
in Tony's, and I told Ross that. Then he came out with one
of his accusations that were pure, patented Ross. "They were
talking in awful goddam low tones," he said. It wasn't often
that I laughed in the inner sanctum in those first months, but
that was too much for me. Then I said, "Don't you know
your Shakespeare: Her voice was ever gentle and awful goddam low, an excellent thing in woman?" Ross turned away so
that I couldn't see his grin, but his torso had one of those
brief spasmodic upheavals that so often served as a sign of his
amusement in the art meeting when he looked at a drawing
he thought was really funny. When he turned around he was
scowling. "Goddam it, Thurber, don't quote things at me,"
he said. The firing mood was gone.

It was at a restaurant called Martin and Mino's, that Ross
rarely went to, but some of the rest of us haunted during
Prohibition, that he said to Gibbs, "Maybe you can run the

magazine." Gibbs quickly and sharply returned this serve, which had been both unexpected and expected, leaving Ross flatfooted. It was one of Ross's silliest attempts to get his administrative rocket into the wild blue yonder. He should have known by then that Wolcott was much too important a writer and copy editor to be launched gaudily into a meaningless orbit in the great managerial Nowhere. Years later, when somebody wrote in an article in *Harper's* that Gibbs didn't like anything, Ross said to me, "Maybe he doesn't like anything, but he can do everything."

This high praise was little short of plain fact. White and I and Gibbs had joined the *New Yorker* staff in that order between the fall of 1926 and the end of 1927. Before Wolcott arrived, to take on a dozen different jobs and do each one superbly, Alexander King had done an interview with Alexander Woollcott in a now dead magazine called *Americana*. I remember only one sentence, in which Woollcott was quoted as having said, "The *New Yorker* is got out by a shiftless reporter with the help of two country bumpkins." The bumpkins were White and I, and the reporter was, of course, Harold Ross, but "shiftless" was an unintentional misquotation. What Woollcott had actually said was "ship news reporter," a job Ross had once had in San Francisco. " 'Shiftless' is perhaps the only derogatory adjective that does not fit Harold Ross," Woollcott later said.

The two country bumpkins have been written about quite a lot here and there, but Wolcott Gibbs has never got the attention he deserves. He was easily, not just conceivably—to use one of his favorite words—the best copy editor the *New Yorker* has ever had. For years he had to deal with the seventy per cent of *New Yorker* fiction that has to be edited, often heavily, before it reaches print. Gibbs, an accomplished parodist, was always able to fix up a casual without distorting or even marring its author's style. He was inimitable, as such word experts are, but when he quit as copy editor in the fiction department to become the magazine's dramatic critic and to write some of its best casuals and profiles, he wrote and sent to Ross—this must have been twenty years ago—what he called "Theory and Practice of Editing *New Yorker* Articles," based on his experiences, often melancholy, with the output of scores of writers, male and female. The final straw, in his editorial career, was a casual that began: "Mr. West had never been very good with machinery." Here was the little man, a genre sometimes called, around the office, the Thurber husband, popping up for the thousandth time, and it was too much for the Gibbsian nerves. The Gibbs essay on editing, which has not been published before, follows:

THEORY AND PRACTICE OF EDITING
NEW YORKER ARTICLES

The average contributor to this magazine is semi-literate; that is, he is ornate to no purpose, full of senseless and elegant variations, and can be relied on to use three sentences where a word would do. It is impossible to lay down any exact and complete formula for bringing order out of this underbrush, but there are a few general rules.

1. Writers always use too damn many adverbs. On one page recently I found eleven modifying the verb "said." "He said morosely, violently, eloquently, so on." Editorial theory should probably be that a writer who can't make his context indicate the way his character is talking ought to be in another line of work. Anyway, it is impossible for a character to go through all these emotional states one after the other. Lon Chaney might be able to do it, but he is dead.

2. Word "said" is O.K. Efforts to avoid repetition by inserting "grunted," "snorted," etc., are waste motion and offend the pure in heart.

3. Our writers are full of clichés, just as old barns are full of bats. There is obviously no rule about this, except that anything that you suspect of being a cliché undoubtedly is one and had better be removed.

4. Funny names belong to the past or to whatever is left of *Judge* magazine. Any character called Mrs. Middlebottom or Joe Zilch should be summarily changed to something else. This goes for animals, towns, the names of imaginary books and many other things.

5. Our employer, Mr. Ross, has a prejudice against having too many sentences beginning with "and" or "but." He claims that they are conjunctions and should not be used purely for literary effect. Or at least only very judiciously.

6. See our Mr. Weekes on the use of such words as "little," "vague," "confused," "faintly," "all mixed up," etc. etc. The point is that the average *New Yorker* writer, unfortunately influenced by Mr. Thurber, has come to believe that the ideal *New Yorker* piece is about a vague, little man helplessly confused by a menacing and complicated civilization. Whenever this note is not the whole point of the piece (and it far too often is) it should be regarded with suspicion.

7. The repetition of exposition in quotes went out with the Stanley Steamer:

Marion gave me a pain in the neck.

"You give me a pain in the neck, Marion," I said.

This turns up more often than you'd expect.

8. Another of Mr. Ross's theories is that a reader picking up a magazine called the *New Yorker* automatically supposes that any story in it takes place in New York. If it doesn't, if it's about Columbus, Ohio, the lead should say so. "When George Adams was sixteen, he began to worry about the girls" should read "When George Adams was sixteen, he began to worry about the girls he saw every day on the streets of Columbus" or something of the kind. More graceful preferably.

9. Also, since our contributions are signed at the end, the author's sex should be established at once if there is any reasonable doubt. It is distressing to read a piece all the way through under the impression that the "I" in it is a man and then find a woman's signature at the end. Also, of course, the other way round.

10. To quote Mr. Ross again, "Nobody gives a damn about a writer or his problems except another writer." Pieces about authors, reporters, poets, etc. are to be discouraged in principle. Whenever possible the protagonist should be arbitrarily transplanted to another line of business. When the reference is incidental and unnecessary, it should come out.

11. This magazine is on the whole liberal about expletives. The only test I know of is whether or not they are really essential to the author's effect. "Son of a bitch," "bastard," and many others can be used whenever it is the editor's judgment that that is the only possible remark under the circumstances. When they are gratuitous, when the writer is just trying to sound tough to no especial purpose, they come out.

12. In the transcription of dialect, don't let the boys and girls misspell words just for a fake Bowery effect. There is no point, for instance, in "trubble," or "sed."

13. Mr. Weekes said the other night, in a moment of desperation, that he didn't believe he could stand any more triple adjectives. "A tall, florid and overbearing man called Jaeckel." Sometimes they're necessary, but when every noun has three adjectives connected with it, Mr. Weekes suffers and quite rightly.

14. I suffer myself very seriously from writers who divide quotes for some kind of ladies' club rhythm.

"I am going," he said, "downtown" is a horror, and unless a quote is pretty long I think it ought to stay on one side of the verb. Anyway, it ought to be divided logically, where there would be pause or something in the sentence.

15. Mr. Weekes has got a long list of banned words, beginning with "gadget." Ask him. It's not actually a ban, there being circumstances when they're necessary, but good words to avoid.

16. I would be delighted to go over the list of writers, explaining the peculiarities of each as they have appeared to me in more than ten years of exasperation on both sides.

17. Editing on manuscript should be done with a black pencil, decisively.

18. I almost forgot indirection, which probably maddens Mr. Ross more than anything else in the world. He objects, that is, to important objects or places or people being dragged into things in a secretive and underhanded manner. If, for instance, a profile has never told where a man lives, Ross protests against a sentence saying, "His Vermont house is full of valuable paintings." Should say "He has a house in Vermont and it is full, etc." Rather weird point, but it will come up from time to time.

19. Drunkenness and adultery present problems. As far as I can tell, writers must not be allowed to imply that they admire either of these things, or have enjoyed them personally, although they are legitimate enough when pointing a moral or adorning a sufficiently grim story. They are nothing to be lighthearted about. "The *New Yorker* can not endorse adultery." Harold Ross vs. Sally Benson. Don't bother about this

one. In the end it is a matter between Mr. Ross and his God. Homosexuality, on the other hand, is definitely out as humor, and dubious in any case.

20. The more "As a matter of facts," "howevers," "for instances," etc. etc. you can cut out, the nearer you are to the Kingdom of Heaven.

21. It has always seemed irritating to me when a story is written in the first person, but the narrator hasn't got the same name as the author. For instance, a story beginning: " 'George,' " my father said to me one morning"; and signed at the end Horace McIntyre always baffles me. However, as far as I know this point has never been ruled upon officially, and should just be queried.

22. Editors are really the people who should put initial letters and white spaces in copy to indicate breaks in thought or action. Because of overwork or inertia or something, this has been done largely by the proofroom, which has a tendency to put them in for purposes of makeup rather than sense. It should revert to the editors.

23. For some reason our writers (especially Mr. Leonard Q. Ross) have a tendency to distrust even moderately long quotes and break them up arbitrarily and on the whole idiotically with editorial interpolations. "Mr. Kaplan felt that he and the cosmos were coterminus" or some such will frequently appear in the middle of a conversation for no other reason than that the author is afraid the reader's mind is wandering. Sometimes this is necessary, most often it isn't.

24. Writers also have an affection for the tricky or vaguely cosmic last line. "Suddenly Mr. Holtzmann felt tired" has appeared on far too many pieces in the last ten years. It is always a good idea to consider whether the last sentence of a piece is legitimate and necessary, or whether it is just an author showing off.

25. On the whole, we are hostile to puns.

26. How many of these changes can be made in copy depends, of course, to a large extent on the writer being edited. By going over the list, I can give a general idea of how much nonsense each artist will stand for.

27. Among many other things, the *New Yorker* is often accused of a patronizing attitude. Our authors are especially

fond of referring to all foreigners as "little" and writing about them, as Mr. Maxwell says, as if they were mantel ornaments. It is very important to keep the amused and Godlike tone out of pieces.

28. It has been one of Mr. Ross's long struggles to raise the tone of our contributors' surroundings, at least on paper. References to the gay Bohemian life in Greenwich Village and other low surroundings should be cut whenever possible. Nor should writers be permitted to boast about having their telephones cut off, or not being able to pay their bills, or getting their meals at the delicatessen, or any of the things which strike many writers as quaint and lovable.

29. Some of our writers are inclined to be a little arrogant about their knowledge of the French language. Probably best to put them back into English if there is a common English equivalent.

30. So far as possible make the pieces grammatical—but if you don't the copy room will, which is a comfort. Fowler's *English Usage* is our reference book. But don't be precious about it.

31. Try to preserve an author's style if he is an author and has a style. Try to make dialogue sound like talk, not writing.

WOLCOTT GIBBS

Harold Ross said to me, one dark day during the 1930's, "If you and Gibbs and White ever leave this place, I'll go, too." Years later, when he didn't have long to live, he told me one day that he had stayed late at the office the night before and flipped through some back copies of the magazine, on a lonely journey through the regrets and triumphs of the past. "There wasn't anything the three of you couldn't do," he snarled. The snarled sentence was a brief preface to, "You could have got the magazine out without any other help if your private lives weren't so damn tangled up." He had made a list of the things he said the three of us had done in our time. It was written in pencil and I lost it long ago, but I remember most of what he wrote down, and it may be that I have added a few he forgot: covers, Goings On, Notes and Comment, The Talk of the Town, idea drawings, spots, captions, casuals, verse, newsbreaks, The Theatre, The Cinema,

Books, Profiles, A Reporter at Large, Onward and Upward with the Arts, Where Are They Now?, Our Footloose Correspondents, fact and fiction editing, proofreading, some make-up, and The Tennis Courts.

I covered tennis for several years (and so did Gibbs), and something I wrote in January, 1937, upset Ross when Franklin P. Adams told him I had gone out on a limb and didn't know what I was talking about. (The limb was a place that scared Ross. He used to say he was going to write an autobiography called *My Life on a Limb*.) I had predicted that Donald Budge would win the singles titles at both Wimbledon and Forest Hills in 1937 and beat Baron von Cramm once or twice. I offered to bet Ross and Frank I was right, but there were no takers. In my dotage, I often sit cackling in the chimney corner when I think of my old prophecy, for Budge won at both Wimbledon and Forest Hills in 1937 and, in July that year, beat von Cramm in the Davis Cup singles. Ross didn't play or know anything about sports, unless you count croquet, and he read such departments only for mistakes in grammar, and such. Once he broke Frank Adams's heart, when Adams was doing the tennis column, by striking out the phrase "the Red Budge of Courage." He hated puns, but I once got a beauty past him: "I'm tired of seeing our tennis hopes brought back home on our Wood Shields." Ross had never heard of Sidney Wood or Frank Shields, then our two outstanding Davis Cup players, and I'm sure he didn't know about slain warriors being brought back home upon their shields. I often wonder how he bore up under the strain of me. And vice versa.

Somebody has asked me, "Do you think the *New Yorker* was successful because of, or in spite of, Harold Ross?" The answer is: The *New Yorker* was created out of the friction produced by Ross Positive and Ross Negative. He tried, and failed, to make an executive editor out of me, and wanted to do the same thing to Gibbs. This was Ross Negative at its worst. He had the good sense, from the first, to let White alone. This was Ross Positive at its most perceptive. He got from this one trio, in the end, the "productivity" he was after from the very first. How much productivity he lost, through the years, because of the mixture in him of the perspicacious, the perverse, and the preposterous, nobody could ever measure. The files of the magazine, during his years as editor, are the only dependable record of Harold Wallace Ross Positive and Negative. My own conclusions are, at best, only one man's footnotes, personal and debatable.

"Sex Is an Incident"

ONE lovely day in October, 1933, Harold Ross, the unimperturbable editor of the *New Yorker*, went running to Katharine White, his office confidante in times of emotional crises, with a new and wild alarm: "Now Thurber's playing with dolls!" What had scared him could have been figured out quickly and calmly by a lesser man, a man untrained in the difficult art of how to approach everything the hard way. My daughter's second birthday was coming up, and I had bought her a big, beautifully dressed French doll. One of the girls at the office had taken it out of its box to show to the others, and had then set it up on my desk with its arms extended toward the door. Ross, banging into the office, deeply worried by the state of the world, or a comma, or something, had come face to face with what he regarded as new evidence that I was getting curiouser and curiouser, and likely to stop writing for his magazine any minute.

Mrs. White had a much easier time allaying his fears about me that day than she had had four years before when Ross lurched into her office one morning wailing, "Now Thurber's going with actresses!" My private life, like that of everybody else on the magazine, was a constant concern and puzzle to Ross. Married in 1922, separated in 1929, later reunited, and then divorced, and married again to a second wife, I was too much for Ross to keep track of, and my status at any moment disturbed him. The night before he plopped his new worry into Katharine's lap, he had seen me at Tony's with an actress, but only one actress, and had sat down at our table. My companion, who didn't like to drink, had a glass of lemonade on the table in front of her, but Ross, gesticulating recklessly, knocked it over. Then he ordered the lady another lemonade and knocked that over, too. This is not exaggeration, but simply the cold, damp facts.

Sex, in or near the office, in any guise or context, frightened Ross. Sex was, to him, an ominous and omnibus word that could mean anything from the first meeting of a man and a woman, through marriage and the rearing of children, to extra-marital relations, divorce, and alimony. When he swore, as he often did, that he was going to "keep sex, by God, out of this office," and then added, "Sex is an incident," he meant hand-holding, goo-goo eyes, fornication, adultery, the consummation of marriage, and legal sexual intercourse. Whether or not Ross knew it, there was a wistful and comic military-head-quarters quality in his oft-repeated directive about sex. He brusquely ordered it confined to quarters, or assigned it to KP duty to keep its mind off itself, or simply declared all the offices and personnel of the *New Yorker* magazine off-bounds for the biological urge. Sex, normal and abnormal, legal and illicit, paid little attention to Ross and his imperious commands. It hid from him, and went on about its affairs as it had been doing for thousands of years.

There were many office marriages during Ross's lifetime, among them the unions of Peter Arno and Lois Long, Andy White and Katharine Angell, Bernard Bergman and Frances Dellar, who had been Lois Long's assistant. Lois, whom Ross had been lucky enough to steal from *Vanity Fair* at the very start of the *New Yorker*, had once been an actress. She knew just how to embarrass the girl-shy editor, and loved to do it. The first time I ever saw her, the day after I went to work on the magazine, she came into his office with the devil in her eye. Ross said hastily, "Don't kiss me, Long. This is Thurber. He's going to make some sense out of this place." Lois Long, alias Lipstick, alias L. L., who could tell more about a man in two minutes than Ross sometimes found out in two years, plainly doubted it. Arno was not the only New Yorker who fell in love with Lois Long. A middle-aged gentleman, who was in his twenties at the time, has written me that after Lois became Mrs. Arno, he was heartbroken and for several days and nights did little except play a record of "Who?" over and over on his Victrola. This lovelorn fellow, by the way, was the man who first suggested that Arno should turn the Whoops Sisters into a series. (It ran with great success until Ross decided the uninhibited sisters were becoming too drunken and bawdy for his family magazine.)

There had been a large reception room, with easy chairs, a couch or two, and screens, in the old offices in West 45th Street, but Ross had once had a shattering experience there, and he ruled out a reception room when he moved to the present quarters of the magazine. Men and women now meet in a widening of the hall, sparsely furnished, just as you step off the elevator on the nineteenth floor. It's as open as a gold-fish bowl.

Ross's shattering experience, his first dismaying brush with sex in the office, occurred during the first summer of the magazine's existence. A young woman, one year out of Vassar, called on Ross with a letter of introduction from an old friend of his. He read the letter in his office and then ventured out into the reception room to interview the fair applicant for a job. She might have gotten it if she hadn't said, in conclusion, "Of course, I realize what would be expected of a girl in a place like this—I mean in addition to her regular work." Ross blenched, I have no doubt, mumbled something, turned tail, and fled from the room. Then he called a meeting of all the male members of the staff, of whom there must have been at least seven or eight at the time, and blamed them for what had just been said to him. "You're giving this magazine a bad name around town," he roared. "People are getting the wrong idea about it and about me." Nobody knew what he was talking about, but they were all used to that.

One of the chill traditions of the *New Yorker*, and I think it grew out of Ross's determination to dehumanize or at least de-emotionalize the place, was soon sensed by all of us when we went to work there. Almost nobody was ever introduced to anybody else, and there was never a general assembly of the staff to talk things over, for propinquity must have seemed to Ross a danger outweighing any benefits of staff coopera-tion. St. Clair McKelway had been working on the magazine for three months before we met. Lillian Ross had been there a couple of years before I met her on the stairs with someone who introduced us. Nobody has caught this cool state of un-familiarity among co-workers better than Edmund Wilson, who became the magazine's literary critic in 1944. This is from a letter he wrote me recently:

It was only after Russell Maloney's death that I real-ized that the person I had been thinking was Maloney must actually be somebody else. Since I was seeing him

still in the corridors, I knew that it could not be Maloney. I thought that Geraghty was Lobrano for years.
That girl with the built-in tape-recorder who did those
articles on Hemingway and the Stephen Crane movie—
about whom I had a certain curiosity—I have never been
able to identify or get anyone to introduce me to.

I must have been working in the office for years before
Ruth Flint identified me correctly, and I should undoubtedly never have known her if she had not been a
friend of my wife's. At about the time I started in, a new
messenger to the printer's appeared. He was old-fash-
ioned-looking and shabby genteel, carried a briefcase,
wore a black derby and an old dark overcoat; his face
was pallid and faded, and he walked with averted eyes;
his features were rather refined. He looked, as Ruth said,
like someone who might have absconded from an English bank and come to the United States. She thought
that this man was me. When she told me this, I became
rather curious about him and found, on inquiry, that she
was so far right that he was actually a disbarred Virginia
lawyer. At one time I played with the idea of hiring him
to impersonate me and deliver the lectures and after-
dinner speeches for which I am sometimes asked.

Wilson was used to the office luncheons of the *New Republic* staff, and to even more intimate fraternization on the
old *Vanity Fair*, where, on certain rainy days, charades were
actually played by men and women of the staff. The game was
instituted by the editor, Frank Crowninshield. Games at the
New Yorker, or the merest suggestion of games, would have
given Ross the jumps or an even worse seizure. Furthermore,
the *New Yorker* people were not gregarious. White was a sol-
itary luncher, for example, and I had been on the *New Yorker*
a year before I had lunch with him. Most of us played our
own versions of Post Office and Pillow here and there about
town, but there was nothing doing in this area at the *New
Yorker*. Oh, I could tell you a few stories, but I won't. There
was another cause for the ungregariousness of the people. The
first of a series of three or four *New Yorker* parties was held
in the offices, in the American tradition, but there was so

much spooning and goo-goo eyes, and drinking and worse, that Ross issued an edict saying that all office parties would be held elsewhere after that.

H. W. Ross was married three times to women, and once, and for keeps, to the *New Yorker* magazine. He differed from most men in that his office, not his home, was his castle. His inviolable, and formidable, selfness had no permanent fusion point with any woman. The only entity he ever fused with was the *New Yorker*. It was the deadly and victorious rival of each of his three wives. Neither I nor any other man ever heard Ross tell a dirty story, but when he became what he called "clinical" he could take your breath away with his forthrightness about the sexual nature, exploits, and disabilities of friends and acquaintances, true or just guessed at. I heard him only once in my life talk about a conquest of his own, and that time he was what Mencken used to call "spifflicated."

Ross, as I have said, divided women into good and bad, but there was a subdivision of the bad, which, while not exactly good, was somehow privileged. These were the women of great talent, especially in the theater, whose deviations from convention and morality in their private lives were, by the very nature and demands of talent, excusable—"I *guess*," he might well have added.

One night in the 1920's Ross persuaded a country bumpkin to go with him to Texas Guinan's night club—he never took me there, perhaps because he was afraid I would lose my innocence and the winsome, childlike quality of my prose. Between marriages, and not yet permanently "off the sauce," as O'Hara puts it, he was in a merry mood, and all of a sudden, to his companion's dismay, jumped up from his chair and crossed to a table where two couples were drinking and talking and watching the show, whatever it was. The charm of one of the ladies had caught Ross's fancy and he made a gallant, though misguided, effort to bend over and kiss the back of her hand. The kiss ended up on the nape of her neck. Chairs were pushed back and the two men at the table stood up. They did not enter into the spirit of Ross's merriment. An experienced bouncer appeared. The experienced Miss Guinan disappeared. The bouncer, stiff and firm, helped Ross and his friend into their overcoats and gave them their hats. Fifteen seconds after the editor's kiss, he and his companion were out on the sidewalk. Ross was bewildered and hurt. "I thought it was gay," he said dejectedly.

A few years after that, during a hiatus in both Ross's married life and mine, we made the rounds of a few night spots in the company of Burgess Meredith and Franchot Tone. Some time after midnight, in one of the gathering places of café society, I told Ross I would demonstrate how gentlemen manage a proper approach to the Strange Lady at the Next Table. She happened to be one of the more famous post-debutantes of her day, and Tone and I, arm in arm, went over to her table, bowed, and presented ourselves. We were not thrown out of the place, but we did get a cold and wordless rejection, becoming in a lady of quality. Her breeding and her hauteur were untouched by both my dark sinister Latin charm and Tone's boyish demeanor and frank open countenance. The next day I found Ross stalking the corridors of the *New Yorker*, his shoulders sagging, his mood depressed. To my "What's the matter now?" he replied, "Goddam it, I have a certain reputation to keep up in this town, and I spend one whole night helping you and Franchot Tone chase *girls* around night clubs." Once again the Great Multiplier of Menace had turned one girl into girls and was worrying about the bad effect of all women on all men.

About this same era he came upon me one evening in the Oak Room of the Algonquin having drinks with three or four other persons, including Lilyan Tashman, whom I had never met before and never saw again, and Humphrey Bogart, a drinking companion of mine since well before he played Duke Mantee in *The Petrified Forest* and went on to Hollywood and fame. Ross wouldn't sit down with us, and I detected all the signs of his discomfiture. The next day he said to me, "What the hell are you going around with *Tashman* for? She's way out of your league, Thurber." I explained that I was not going around with Miss Tashman, and that my woman companion the evening before was a housewife and homebody and the mother of four children. "A likely story," said Ross, and then, "Well, the hell with it. Now in this casual of yours here, you use a colon where anybody else would use a dash. I'm not saying you can't do it. I'm just bringing it up." After an argument, he agreed to let the colon stand, for he was, as I have said and now say again, at once the most obdurate and reasonable of editors.

The first time I met Ross's mother, she suddenly said, "Harold was always bashful with the girls, even as a little boy." Harold was embarrassed and shushed her instantly with "Don't tell Thurber things like that. He blabs everything. Besides, it isn't true." It was true, though. Harold Ross employed the technique I once called the "Get-Right-at-It Move" in a series of drawings I did for the *New Yorker*, "The Masculine Approach." He printed all of the drawings except that one, which showed an impassioned male wrestling with a girl on a sofa, the gleam of Pan in his eye. The troubled gamin from Aspen, Colorado, had no subtleties of approach

to the female, no routine of sweet nothings, no romantic build-up. Before marriage, and between marriages, he was, various lovely and desirable ladies have told many of us, inclined to make a sudden and unexpected dive at them, which usually ended in chaos and the laughter of the love object. He seemed to believe that "sweep her off her feet" was to be taken literally, in the physical sense. Once, to a laughing lady he had brought down with a veritable Catfish Smith football tackle, he moaned, "What did I do wrong?" This Lochinvar, American Western style, was not alone in his shock tactics; they were practiced on ambushed damsels by a poet I know, a young publisher I used to know, and an English novelist I once met who has written of "tumbling lassies in the bracken," which puts him one up on Ross, for bracken is rougher than carpet.

It doesn't take a psychiatrist to realize that the sudden pounce, similar to what was known in the old six-day bicycle races as a "jam," is the natural reverse of the coin of masculine shyness, especially in the virile Western type, unlettered in the literature of love. There is desperation and high impatience in it, as well as desire, a restless determination to get it all over with in a smoke screen of blustery action. Ross was ever afraid that sex would forget it was an incident and become an episode, and then an interlude, and, before long, the whole story, God help us all, of a man's life.

The psychic trauma of Ross's experience with the Vassar girl in 1925 stayed with him to the end. He jittered at the sight of an unfamiliar female face in any of the offices, and told Katharine White, as the *New Yorker* increased in size and more and more women typists and secretaries were employed, that he had to find a woman of strong character and firm hand to ride shotgun on the goddam girls on the editorial floor. He found what he was looking for in Daise Terry, in 1929, and she is still there, her hand as firm as ever, though she has ten times as many girls to control as there were thirty years ago. The editor carried a lot of his "problems of a personal nature" to her. When my daughter was born, spang in the middle of the afternoon of Wednesday, October 7, 1931, Ross turned to Miss Terry with a nervous monologue that must have gone like this: "I hear Thurber has just had a daughter. I hope somebody's looking after him. Send Mrs. Thurber some flowers and say on the card they're from the *New Yorker*. I thought babies were born early in the morning or late at night. I'm surrounded by women and children. I have to look after everybody's personal life. Sometimes I wonder how the hell I ever get out a magazine. I hear the baby only weighs seven pounds—is that *enough*? I know damn well *I* weighed nine pounds. It has something to do with diet now, and is probably a fad of the doctors." Then he must have stared about him morosely and harped on a theme he never left unharped on long. "This place isn't a business office, it's a sitting room, and it's becoming a, by God, nursery."

Ross didn't like it at all when he found out, bumbling into

what we called the Goings On room, that the girls there brewed both tea and coffee every afternoon, and he was appalled when he bumped into a Coca-Cola machine that had been installed while he was away. "If we have a *candy* counter, I don't want to know where it is," he bawled. "I heard somebody's daughter running up and down the hall yesterday, as if this were a goddam playpen. I understand she fell and hurt herself. I hope they found the arnica—oh, we *must* have a medicine chest somewhere in this *house!*"

At about that time a series of my drawings called "The War Between Men and Women" was running in the *New Yorker*, and I got a telegram one day from Dr. Logan Clendenning in St. Louis that read, "Help. I'm surrounded by women." I showed it to Ross, and he was off on his well-worn lecture again. "Doctors don't know what it is to be surrounded by women. They can turn women patients over to nurses, or psychiatrists, or something. What we need here is a registered nurse and a trained psychiatrist. It's the only office in the world where paste and scissors are kept in desk drawers. The women do that. And if they don't show up for work, you can't ask why. I wish the hell I was back on the *Stars and Stripes*—it's the only place I ever really enjoyed working."

It takes two or more women to surround the average man, but Harold Ross could look as beleaguered as Custer in the presence of only one. He let an editor go in the early years because the man brought his wife into Ross's office to meet him. Ross looked up and there she stood, seeming to be closing in on him from all sides. Very few women, even among those employed there, could enter the inner sanctum of old Surrounded. Of the privileged females, my second wife, Helen, was one. We walked into his office one day unannounced, and he didn't start or turn pale. He had known her for quite a while by then, liked her personally, relaxed in her company, and admired her because she had been a magazine editor and once got out two monthlies all by herself, from cover to cover. More than once he grumbled, "I got *fifty* men and women I don't even know walking around here with pieces of paper in their hands, getting in each other's way, and Helen Thurber used to get out *five* magazines a month all by herself." It was on that day in his office that Ross, discussing some guilty pair, said, "I'm sure he's s-l-e-e-p-i-n-g with her." He was the only man I've ever known who spelled out euphemisms in front of adults.

Ross had not liked the idea of my getting married again when he first heard about it, and he asked Bob Benchley to "talk to Thurber. See if you can't do something about it." Benchley did talk to me one evening, over cocktails, in his suite at the Royalton. He was repeating, I knew at once, Ross's concern: that if I became happily married, something bad would happen to my drawings and stories. Benchley was married only once and told me he didn't believe in second marriages. A man had his wife, whatever their relationship might be, and that was that. The rest was his own business. A woman friend of Bob's once gave him a drawing of mine for Christmas. It showed a man hiding in a tree while a woman on the ground is calling for him, and the donor of this Christmas gift said, "The man is poor Bob, and the woman is all those women who keep after him all the time." Later Bob met Helen, liked her, and said to me in an aside, "Why don't you marry the girl? What are you waiting for—Ross's permission?"

All that Ross ever said to me about Helen, before he met her, was, "Is she quiet?" Afterwards, I suppose, he was sorry, in his fashion, that he had told Benchley to see what he could do about changing my mind. It must have gratified him no end when the people in my drawings suffered no noticeable beatification except in one spot I did deliberately to scare him, which showed a man and a woman and a dog drifting dreamily among the stars; and he was further reassured when a piece called "A Couple of Hamburgers" indicated no lessening of tensions in my prose war between men and women.

We were often at Ross's apartment, especially during his second marriage—to the former Frances Clark, mother of his only child—the marriage in which he was still young enough and well enough to seem comfortable at home, if I can use such big words as comfortable and home about him. Slowly he turned every apartment into an annex of his office and a gathering place for his men friends. "I got too many personal possessions," he would say. There were only a few he wouldn't have got rid of, out of a sense of escape, and among these was a collection of Gideon Bibles sent to him, from time to time and from most American cities, by his great friend Joe Cook when he was on tour. Ross kept his possessions, including his house near Stamford, but toward the end he lived in a suite at the Algonquin, looked after by a male nurse. He kept rejecting his third wife's efforts to take care of him, partly because he wanted to be let alone when he was sick. Being looked after, or cared for, at such times only fretted him. He didn't want any woman around. When, toward the end, we called on him in his Algonquin rooms, he complained about being "fussed over" and said, "I usually get rid of women callers by saying I have to lie down. One woman didn't go, even then. Two hours later when I got up, she was still sitting out here." After his death, it is said, an envelope containing a considerable amount of cash was found in a safety deposit vault marked "Getaway money." It meant, I think, get-away-from-the-world-of-women money.

He didn't want to get away from work, and kept at it until his final visit to the hospital in Boston where he died. One of his last projects, and one of his keenest interests, was the five-part profile on Duveen by S. N. Behrman. He had one of the galley proofs in his suite on our last visit there. He had put it aside momentarily to eat what he called supper. Its nature shocked Helen a little, as it would have any woman. He was eating sardines right out of the can. "It's practically the only thing I can taste," he said. I still keep thinking, against my will, of that brief visit, and of the tired, cloyed, but dogged efforts of Ross to fight against the disease that was killing him, and I like to turn from it to brighter thoughts of him.

I remember his panic the evening he got home from work and was told that he was going to be a father. He leaped to the phone, called a woman friend who gave him the name of an obstetrician, and then called the doctor, who came running. After a brief examination, the doctor came out of the bedroom, as annoyed as Ross was distraught. "It is possible that your wife is pregnant," he said, "but it's too early to tell for certain. As it happens, this is not an emergency, as your call indicated. I could actually have taken time to eat my dinner."

"Judas, I didn't know," Ross told me the next day. "I thought you had to act fast."

Ross's daughter, Patricia, was one of the great things in his life, and the only female who could handle him with ease. When she was only seven he brought her to the Algonquin at lunchtime to show her off to his friends. She had a good time and didn't want to leave. "I have to get back to the office," he told her as she lingered in the lobby talking to people. "Just wait," she told him, and he sat back in a big chair, with a deep sigh of restive resignation, and waited. Like any other father of a first daughter, he was sure that a girl in her infancy was a fragile object. "Can she *breathe*, lying on her stomach like that?" he asked her nurse when the baby was not yet one year old, and again, "Is it all right for them to sleep with their hands above their head? I think my mother said it's bad for them, but I forget why." I remember the day he tiptoed into Patricia's room to show her to my mother. She quieted his fears about the baby's fragility. "They usually outlive their husbands," she told him, "and they always outlive their fathers, so I wouldn't worry about her."

The Gee Whiz Guy became utterly enthralled by the miraculous phenomena of conception, gestation, and parturition, and was always lecturing to one or more of us on the subject. This was his "being clinical," that attitude of mind toward the functional which was privileged—in conversation, that is, not in type. When he had been a father for less than a year he went to a party one night at the home of Charles MacArthur and Helen Hayes in Nyack. "I had gone out into the kitchen to shake up some fresh drinks," MacArthur told me, "and when I came back I stood there in the doorway listening to Ross. He was haranguing our guests, most of them fathers and mothers, and some of them grandparents, about the goddam miraculous cycle of menstruation. 'Nature is wonderful,' Ross was saying. 'The damn thing stops at the right time and then resumes without any interference or help.'" The MacArthur guests were, I gathered, mostly men and women of the world of literature and the theater, and far from being shocked or bored, they listened in fascination to this lecture by the editor of the *New Yorker*. Charlie ended his description of the scene this way, "Ross has the charm of gaucherie."

At about that same time, the spell of the miracle of birth

still being upon him, he came over to me during a party at the apartment of Elliott and Norma Nugent. "I understand there's an obstetrician here, a friend of yours and Nugent's," he said. "Can we get him in a corner for a minute? I want to ask him a clinical question." The obstetrician, one of America's most distinguished, had been a fraternity brother of Elliott's and mine at Ohio State. I got him and Ross together in a corner. The clinical question he asked him was a hypothetical one, it turned out, and it had been troubling Ross's waking hours. He wanted to know how many women could be impregnated, theoretically, all things being equal and all women being nubile and willing, by a single seminal ejaculation. The doctor told him 300,000,000. I had never seen Ross look more profoundly thoughtful. "Geezus, nature is prodgidal," he said, "nature is prodgidal."

One morning, circa then, I found Ross, worried and stoop-shouldered, pacing a corridor, jingling those pocket coins. He came right out with his current anxiety. "Goddam it, I can't think of any *man* that has a daughter. I think of men as having boys, and women as having girls."

"I have a daughter," I said, "and I wanted a daughter."

"That's not natural, is it?" he demanded. "I never heard of a man that didn't want a son. Can you name any, well, you know, goddam it—terribly masculine men with daughters?" After protesting that I could outmasculine him the best night he ever saw, I said that Morris Markey, a masculine Virginian, had a daughter, and so did Joel Sayre, once described by Stanley Walker as "the wandering behemoth . . . a great man." Ross brightened, but the sun and moon of reassurance shone in his face when I came up with "Jack Dempsey has two children, both girls." His day was saved from the wreckage of despair, but he still had one final depressed word. "Goddam it, I hate the idea of going around with female hormones in me."

Ross kept going to Boston during his last few years, first to see a specialist about his ulcers, and then to endure the torment of the bronchoscope and other ordeals after tests had shown that he had a minimal cancer. On one of these visits the man who knew almost every actress of his time called on one of his favorites backstage at a theater in which she was

UNCOLLECTED PIECES

An American Romance

THE LITTLE MAN in an overcoat that fitted him badly at the shoulders had had a distressing scene with his wife. He had left home with a look of serious determination and had now been going around and around in the central revolving door of a prominent department store's main entrance for fifteen minutes.

The knot of annoyed shoppers had been augmented to a sizable crowd by the time a floorwalker arrived and rapped sharply on the glass panels as they flashed by. "Here," he called. "Here, stop this."

But the little man kept going around and around.

"Use the other doors," called an assistant department superintendent who came up. "There are plenty of other doors."

He was unheeded and the crowd continued to gather about the relentlessly whirling door.

The store carpenter was sent for and he tried vainly to slip a wedge under the door and arrest its progress. A policeman attempted to hurl himself into the door and was badly bruised.

"It's not a case for the police," said one onlooker. "For shame. This man is a patient, not a criminal. It's a case for a psychoanalyst."

A psychoanalyst was called.

"How old are you?" he demanded.

The little man did not answer. Nor did he answer when the specialist asked him where his boyhood had been spent, and if he had ever been in a cyclone and if he had ever had a severe shock while out walking.

Soon the newspapers heard about it and the crowd was pushed aside to make room for the photographers. The little man had now been going around for two hours.

At this point a richly dressed gentleman in a greatcoat shouldered through the crowd and spoke loudly.

"I'll give him $45,000 if he can go for another two hours," he said. "I'm a big chewing gum magnate from the West."

Bets of ten to one were immediately placed that the little man couldn't do it. He was such a little man.

At five minutes of eight, just before the additional two hours ended, firemen were helping hold back the crowd. Flares were lighted. As the store clock sounded eight, the little man fell out of the doors, exhausted. Willing hands supported him to a nearby hotel where the management had thrown open the Presidential suite. By midnight the little man had received more than $100,000 worth of offers from the vaudeville and moving picture companies.

"I did it for the wife and children," he said.

The New Yorker, March 5, 1927

A Visit from Saint Nicholas

In the Ernest Hemingway Manner

It was the night before Christmas. The house was very quiet. No creatures were stirring in the house. There weren't even any mice stirring. The stockings had been hung carefully by the chimney. The children hoped that Saint Nicholas would come and fill them.

The children were in their beds. Their beds were in the room next to ours. Mamma and I were in our beds. Mamma wore a kerchief. I had my cap on. I could hear the children moving. We didn't move. We wanted the children to think we were asleep.

"Father," the children said.

There was no answer. He's there, all right, they thought.

"Father," they said, and banged on their beds.

"What do you want?" I asked.

"We have visions of sugarplums," the children said.

"Go to sleep," said mamma.

"We can't sleep," said the children. They stopped talking, but I could hear them moving. They made sounds.

"Can you sleep?" asked the children.

"No," I said.

"You ought to sleep."

"I know. I ought to sleep."

"Can we have some sugarplums?"

"You can't have any sugarplums," said mamma.

"We just asked you."

There was a long silence. I could hear the children moving again.

"Is Saint Nicholas asleep?" asked the children.

"No," mamma said. "Be quiet."

"What the hell would he be asleep tonight for?" I asked.

"He might be," the children said.

"He isn't," I said.

"Let's try to sleep," said mamma.

The house became quiet once more. I could hear the rustling noises the children made when they moved in their beds.

Out on the lawn a clatter arose. I got out of bed and went to the window. I opened the shutters; then I threw up the sash. The moon shone on the snow. The moon gave the lustre of mid-day to objects in the snow. There was a miniature sleigh in the snow, and eight tiny reindeer. A little man was driving them. He was lively and quick. He whistled and shouted at the reindeer and called them by their names. Their names were Dasher, Dancer, Prancer, Vixen, Comet, Cupid, Donder, and Blitzen.

He told them to dash away to the top of the porch, and then he told them to dash away to the top of the wall. They did. The sleigh was full of toys.

"Who is it?" mamma asked.

"Some guy," I said. "A little guy."

I pulled my head in out of the window and listened. I heard the reindeer on the roof. I could hear their hoofs pawing and prancing on the roof. "Shut the window," said mamma. I stood still and listened.

"What do you hear?"

"Reindeer," I said. I shut the window and walked about. It was cold. Mamma sat up in the bed and looked at me.

"How would they get on the roof?" mamma asked.

"They fly."

"Get into bed. You'll catch cold."

Mamma lay down in bed. I didn't get into bed. I kept walking around.

"What do you mean, they fly?" asked mamma.

"Just fly is all."

Mamma turned away toward the wall. She didn't say anything.

I went out into the room where the chimney was. The little man came down the chimney and stepped into the room. He was dressed all in fur. His clothes were covered with ashes and soot from the chimney. On his back was a pack like a peddler's pack. There were toys in it. His cheeks and nose were red and he had dimples. His eyes twinkled. His mouth was little, like a bow, and his beard was very white. Between his teeth was a stumpy pipe. The smoke from the pipe encircled his head in a wreath. He laughed and his belly shook. It shook like a bowl of red jelly. I laughed. He winked his eye, then he gave a twist to his head. He didn't say anything.

He turned to the chimney and filled the stockings and turned away from the chimney. Laying his finger aside his nose, he gave a nod. Then he went up the chimney. I went to the chimney and looked up. I saw him get into his sleigh. He whistled at his team and the team flew away. The team flew as lightly as thistledown. The driver called out, "Merry Christmas and good night." I went back to bed.

"What was it?" asked mamma. "Saint Nicholas?" She smiled.

"Yeah," I said.

She sighed and turned in the bed.

"I saw him," I said.

"Sure."

"I did see him."

"Sure you saw him." She turned farther toward the wall.

"Father," said the children.

"There you go," mamma said. "You and your flying reindeer."

"Go to sleep," I said.

"Can we see Saint Nicholas when he comes?" the children asked.

"You got to be asleep," I said. "You got to be asleep when he comes. You can't see him unless you're unconscious."

"Father knows," mamma said.

"I pulled the covers over my mouth. It was warm under the covers. As I went to sleep I wondered if mamma was right.

The New Yorker, December 24, 1927

Tom the Young Kidnapper,
or, Pay Up and Live

A kind of Horatio Alger story based on the successful $30,000 kidnapping in Kansas City of Miss Mary McElroy, who had a lovely time, whose abductors gave her roses and wept when she left, and whose father said he did not want the young men to go to the penitentiary

I WOULD admire to walk with youse to a small, dark cellar and manacle you to a damp wall."

The speaker was a young American, of perhaps twenty-five years, with a frank, open countenance. Betty Spencer, daughter of old Joab Spencer, the irate banker and the richest man in town, flushed prettily. Her would-be abductor flushed, too, and stood twisting his hat in his hands. He was neatly, if flashily, dressed.

"I am sorry," she said, in a voice which was sweet and low, an excellent thing in woman, "I am sorry, but I am on my way to church, for my faith is as that of a little child."

"But I must have sixty or a hundred thousand dollars from your irate father tonight—or tomorrow night at the latest," said Tom McGirt, for it was he. "It is not so much for me as for the 'gang.'"

"Do you belong to a gang?" cried Betty, flushing prettily, a look of admiration in her eyes. In his adoring embarrassment, the young kidnapper tore his hat into five pieces and ate them.

"My, but you must have a strong stomach!" cried the young lady.

"That was nothing," said Tom, modestly. "Anybody would of done the same thing. You know what I wisht? I wisht it had been me stopping a horse which was running away with you at the risk of my life instead of eating a hat." He looked so forlorn and unhappy because no horse was running away with her that she pitied him.

"Does your gang really need the money?" she cried. "For if it really does, I should be proud to have you kidnap me and subject me to a most humiliating but broadening experience."

"The gang don't work, see?" said the young man, haltingly, for he hated to make this confession. "They're too young and strong to work—I mean there is so much to see and do and drink, and if they was working in a factory, say, or an old stuffy office all day, why—" She began to cry, tears welling up into her eyes.

"I shall come with you," she said, "for I believe that young men should be given hundreds of thousands of dollars that they may enjoy life. I wear a five-and-a-half glove, so I hope your manacles fit me, else I could easily escape from those which were too large.

"If we ain't got ones your size," he said, earnestly, drawing himself up to his full height, "I'll go through smoke and flame to git some for you. Because I—well, you see, I—"

"Yes?" she encouraged him, gently.

"Aw, I won't tell youse now," he said. "Some day when I have made myself worthy, I'll tell youse."

"I have faith in you," she said, softly. "I know you will pull this job off. You can do it, and you *will* do it."

"Thanks, Betty," he said. "I appreciate your interest in me. You shall be proud some day of Tom the Young Kidnapper, or Pay Up and Live." He spoke the subtitle proudly.

"I'll go with you," she said. "No matter where."

"It ain't much of a basement," he said, reddening, and twisting an automatic between his fingers. "It's dark and the walls are damp, but me old mother ain't there, and that's something. She's no good," he added.

"I know," she said, softly. They walked on slowly down the street to a nasty part of town where an automobile drew up alongside the curb, and they got in. Four young men with frank, open countenances were inside, their faces freshly scrubbed, their dark hair moistened and slicked down. Tom introduced them all, and they put away their automatics, and took off their hats, and grinned and were very polite. "I am quite happy," Betty told them.

The cellar in which the young gang manacled Betty to a wall was, as Tom had promised, dark and damp, but the chains which fitted around her wrists were very nice and new and quite snug, so she was quite content. Two of the boys played tiddlywinks with her, while the others went out to mail a letter which she had written at the gang's dictation. It read: "Dear Father—Put a hundred thousand berries in an old tin box and drop it out of your car when you see a red light on the old Post Road tonight, or your daughter will never come home. If you tell the police we will bite her ears off." "That's nice," said Betty, reading it over, "for it will afford Father an opportunity, now that I am in mortal danger, to realize how much he loves me and of how little worth money is, and it will show him also that the young men of this town are out to win!"

Betty was kept in the cellar all night, but in the morning Tom brought her chocolate and marmalade on an ivory-colored breakfast tray, and also a copy of Keats' poems, and a fluffy little kitty with a pink ribbon around its neck. One of the other boys brought her a table badminton set, and a third, named Thad the Slasher, or Knife Them and Run, brought her a swell Welsh pony named Rowdy. "Oh," said Betty, "I am so happy I could cry," and she jangled her manacles. Several of the boys did cry, she looked so uncomfortable and so happy, and then Betty cried, and then they all laughed, and put a record on the Victrola.

That night, Betty was still chained to the wall because her old father had not "come through." "He's holding out for only forty grand," explained Tom, reluctantly, for he did not wish her to know that her father was stingy. "I don't guess your father realizes that we really will make away with you if he don't kick in. He thinks mebbe it's a bluff, but we mean business!" His eyes flashed darkly, and Betty's eyes snapped brightly.

"I know you do!" she cried. "Why, it's been worth forty thousand just the experience I've had. I *do* hope he gives you the hundred, for I should like to go back alive and tell everybody how sweet you have been and how lovely it is to be kidnapped!"

On the second morning, Betty was sitting on the damp cellar floor playing Guess Where I Am with Tom and Ned and Dick and Sluggy, when Thad came in, toying with his frank, open clasp knife, his genial countenance clouded by a frown.

"What is wrong, Thad," asked Betty, "for I perceive that

something is wrong?" Thad stood silent, kicking the moist dirt of the floor with the toe of his shoe. He rubbed a sleeve against his eye.

"The old man come across with all the dough," he said. "We—we gotta let you go now." He began to cry openly. Tom paled. One of the boys took Betty's chains off. Betty gathered up her presents, the kitty, and the table badminton set, and the poems. "Rowdy is saddled an' waitin' outside," said Thad, brokenly, handing tens and twenties, one at a time, to his pals.

"Goodbyeee," said Betty. She turned to Tom. "Goodbyeee, Tom," she said.

"Goo—" said Tom, and stopped, all choked up.

When Betty arrived at her house, it was full of policemen and relatives. She dropped her presents and ran up to her father, kindly old Judge Spencer, for he had become a kindly old judge while she was in the cellar, and was no longer the irate old banker and no longer, indeed, the town's richest man, for he only had about seven hundred dollars left.

"My child!" he cried. "I wish to reward those young men for teaching us all a lesson. I have become a poorer but a less irate man, and even Chief of Police Jenkins here has profited by this abduction, for he has been unable to apprehend the culprits and it has taken some of the cockiness out of him, I'll be bound."

"That is true, Joab," said the Chief of Police, wiping away a tear. "Those young fellows have shown us all the error of our ways."

"Have they skipped out, Betty?" asked her father.

"Yes, Father," said Betty, and a tear welled up into her eye.

"Ha, ha!" said old Judge Spencer. "I'll wager there was one young man whom you liked better than the rest, eh, my chick? Well, I should like to give him a position and invite him to Sunday dinner. His rescuing you from the flames of that burning shack for only a hundred thous—"

"I didn't do *that*, sir," said a modest voice, and they all turned and looked at the speaker, Tom the Kidnapper, for it was he. "I simply left her loose from the cellar after we got the dough."

"It's the same thing," said her father, in mock sternness. "Young man, we have all been watching you these past two days—that is to say, we have been wondering where you were. You have outwitted us all and been charming to my daughter. You deserve your fondest wish. What will you have?"

"I'll have Scotch-and-soda, sir," said Tom. "And your daughter's hand."

"Ha, ha!" said the kindly old Judge. "There's enterprise for you, Jenkins!" He nudged Jenkins in the ribs and the Chief nudged back, and laughed. So they all had a Scotch-and-soda and then the Judge married his blushing daughter, right then and there, to Tom the Young Kidnapper, or If You Yell We'll Cut Your Throat.

The New Yorker, June 10, 1933

How to Relax While Broadcasting

THE EVENING I went up to the studios for my first radio broadcast I got off by mistake at the sixteenth floor instead of the seventeenth. I decided not to wait for the elevator but just run up the stairs to the seventeenth floor, because elevators in broadcasting buildings are always crowded with small Italian musicians carrying 'cellos; furthermore, when the "Up" sign above the elevators in these buildings lights, the operator of the car that stops for you usually says "Down," and before you can think, you find yourself on the first floor again without any way of getting back up, because you surrendered your pass to the man at the desk in the lobby the first time you went up.

I walked to a door on the sixteenth floor marked "Stairs" and stepped out into a cold, dark staircase shaft and walked up one flight. I found that the door on that floor wouldn't open. It was after seven o'clock in the evening and the door had been officially locked. I hurried back down to the sixteenth floor and discovered that the door there had locked behind me, too. I began to beat on it and kick it. From far off a faint voice came to me finally, saying, "Cut that out!" The only thing to do was walk down fifteen flights to the main floor, which I did, but the door out into the lobby was also locked and nobody answered my screams and poundings. Screaming and pounding is "not radio," as the broadcasting people say.

I went down into the basement, which was dark and gloomy, and hunted for the elevator shaft. I found it, but there was no bell to push, so I sat on an old chair until the car came down. The operator was surprised to see me and asked me for my pass. I told him I didn't have a pass. He thought a while and then asked if Mr. Hayman knew I was down there. I said I didn't think so. He was pretty much alarmed by that, but he took me up to the seventeenth floor after warning me never to come down to the basement again without a pass.

There was nobody on the seventeenth floor who understood my case, although the people I talked to were patient and courteous. They said the seventeenth floor was entirely given over to the business department and had no studios or microphones. What I probably wanted was the twenty-seventh floor. Up there I found some people I had met before, but they were pretty busy and seemed to think it was the wrong night. I sat down in a chair, and presently a man came up to me and asked me if I was Mr. Totherer. I said I wasn't sure and he said to follow him. I was shown into an office where there were some officials I knew and some friends of mine. One of the officials was denying a story somebody had been telling about a man who fell dead in front of the microphone. It seems he had merely had a stroke.

In a little while I was led, in a solemn march, to a small and lonely studio, heavily draped and silent. I took out a cigarette, but saw a sign saying "No Smoking," so I put the cigarette away again. Some men in the glassed-in control-room began to look at me. I could see their lips move, but I couldn't hear anything. A man tiptoed into the room where I was and shook hands with me and tiptoed out again. He never came back. I walked over to a regular microphone such as I had talked over once or twice before and had got used to, but someone led me away from that and said I was to talk over a table microphone, because it would help me to relax. This turned out to be a table about the size of a card table with a microphone set innocently in its centre, face up, more or less like an ashtray. Its studied simplicity caused me to tighten up slightly and I mentioned this to a man. "Be at your ease," he said.

I stood over the table, grasped its edges firmly, and leaned down toward the microphone. Someone grasped me. "No, no," he said. "You just sit down at the table as if you were sitting in a chair at any table, and talk." I sat down, trying to remember how I sit in a chair at a table, especially a card table at which nobody else is sitting. "Relax," said someone, with a note of command. I slumped back in the chair and placed on the table the papers I was going to use and began fussing with them. "Shhh!" somebody hissed. "Don't rustle them! This is a very highly sensitized mike which picks up every slightest sound. It would sound like a waterfall if you rustled them." I began to drum my fingers on the table top, but a courteous official put his hand on mine and stopped that. "Tapping would sound like cavalry crossing a bridge to your listeners," he explained. "Just take it easy." I leaned back in my chair and adjusted my tie, doubtless giving the effect of someone trying to take a leather belt away from a bulldog.

In a moment an announcer came in and said we were all ready to go. "Okay," I said, standing up. "Let's get out." He smiled with calm assurance and said no, he meant that we were about to start the program. Everybody but him tiptoed out of the room. I sat down at the table again. I could see them all watching me from the control-room. Somebody in there raised his hand sharply and let it drop sharply. I expected to hear the faint hiss of lethal gas escaping into the chamber, but instead the announcer started to talk. I creaked nervously in the chair at this, and the listeners heard, along with his calm announcement, the sound of a buckboard falling over a cliff. Finally he pointed a finger at me. I sat bolt upright and began to talk to the ashtray. . . .

When it was all over everybody tiptoed whisperingly into the room and congratulated me on being only five seconds too slow—not bad for a beginner. The record is one five-hundredth of a second. I got up and started out of the room, but a man followed me and took me by the arm. "Where are you going?" he asked. "Let's all go out and get a drink," I said. "But you haven't got time," he said. "All this has just been the rehearsal." I must have tightened up horribly at that, for he said soothingly, "Take it easy. You got plenty of time to relax in." He looked at his wristwatch. "You got four minutes."

The New Yorker, May 5, 1934

E. B. W.

ONCE, a few years ago, a gentleman came to the offices of *The New Yorker* and asked for E. B. White. He was shown into the reception room and Mr. White was told that someone was waiting for him there. White's customary practice in those days, if he couldn't place a caller's name, was to slip moodily out of the building by way of the fire escape and hide in the coolness of Schrafft's until the visitor went away. He is not afraid of process servers, blackmailers, borrowers, or cranks; he is afraid of the smiling stranger who tramples the inviolable flowers of your privacy bearing a letter of introduction from an old Phi Gam brother now in the real estate game in Duluth. White knows that the man in the Reception Room may not be so easy to get rid of as a process server—or even a blackmailer; he may grab great handfuls of your fairest hours, he may even appropriate a sizable chunk of your life, for no better reason than that he was anchor man on your brother's high school relay team, or married the sister of your old girl, or met an aunt of yours on a West Indies cruise. Most of us, out of a politeness made up of faint curiosity and profound resignation, go out to meet the smiling stranger with a gesture of surrender and a fixed grin, but White has always taken to the fire escape. He has avoided the Man in the Reception Room as he has avoided the interviewer, the photographer, the microphone, the rostrum, the literary tea, and the Stork Club. His life is his own. He is the only writer of prominence I know of who could walk through the Algonquin lobby or between the tables at Jack and Charlie's and be recognized only by his friends.

But to get back to the particular caller whom we left waiting in the reception room. On that occasion, out of some obscure compulsion, White decided to go out and confront the man and see what he wanted. "I'm White," he told the stranger he found sitting alone in the room. The man rose, stared for a long moment at the audacious fellow in front of him, and then said, with grim certainty, "You are not E. B. White." White admits that his hair leaped up, but it is my fond contention that his heart did, too. I like to think that he was a little disappointed when he realized, as he was bound to, that the man was wrong. I like to insist that he resumed his burden of identity with a small sigh. (Where the remarkable interview got to from the tense point to which I have brought it here I shall leave it to my memoirs to tell.)

In the early days of *The New Yorker* the object of this searching examination signed his first few stories and poems with his full name: Elwyn (as God is my judge) Brooks White. I cannot imagine what spark of abandon, what youthful spirit of devil-may-care prompted a poet who loves to live half-hidden from the eye to come out thus boldly into the open. He didn't keep it up long; he couldn't stand that fierce glare of polysyllabic self-acknowledgment. For some years now he has signed his casuals and his verses merely with his initials, E. B. W. To his friends he is Andy. It was a lucky break that saved him from Elly or Wynnie or whatever else one might make out of Elwyn in the diminutive. He went to Cornell, and it seems that every White who goes there is nicknamed Andy for the simple if rather faraway reason that the first president of the University was named Andrew White.

It used to be a wonder and a worry to White's boss, Mr. Harold Ross, the mystic and wonderful editor of *The New Yorker*, that his favorite and most invaluable assistant avoided people, lived along the untrodden ways, hid by mossy stones, and behaved generally in what Ross was pleased to call an antisocial manner. For a restlessly gregarious man who consorted with ten thousand people from Groucho Marx to Lord Dalhousie it was difficult to comprehend the spirit of Walden Pond. As long ago as the late 1920's there were hundreds of people who implored Ross to introduce them to the man who wrote, on the already famous first page of *The New Yorker*, those silver and crystal sentences which had a ring like the ring of nobody else's sentences in the world. White declined to be taken to literary parties, or to any other kind of parties, but one day Ross lured him to the house of a certain literary lady who, White was persuaded to believe, would be found alone. When the door of her house was opened to them, Ross pushed White into a hallway loud with the chatter of voices proceeding from a crowded living room, the unmistakably assertive voices of writers and artists. Ross made the serious mistake of entering the living room first. When he looked around for White, that shy young man had quietly disappeared. He had proceeded deviously through the house, to the disciplined dismay of the servants, out the back door, and over trees and fences, or whatever else may have been in his way, to the freedom he so greatly cherishes, leaving the curtsy, the compliment, and the booksy chat to writers who go in for that sort of thing.

"Isn't there," Ross demanded of him one time, "*any*body you would like to meet?" White gave this difficult question his grave consideration and said, at long last, "Yes. Willie Stevens and Helen Hayes." It is a proof of the reckless zeal and the devoted energy of Harold Ross that he instantly set about trying to get hold of Willie Stevens for the purpose of inviting him to a dinner in New York at which White and Miss Hayes were to be the only other guests. I am desolated to report that this little coming together could not be accomplished: Willie apparently knew too many people the way it was and declined the invitation with that gentle old-world courtesy of which he was so consummate a master. Ross did manage finally to bring White face to face with Helen Hayes. Our hero, I am informed, was discontented and tongue-tied during their brief, jumpy conversation and was glad when it was all over. I suppose Miss Hayes was, too.

E. B. W. was born in Mount Vernon, N.Y. He had an ordinary, normal childhood, monkeying with an old Oliver typewriter, shooting with an air gun at the weather vane on his father's barn. At Cornell he charmed and astonished his English professors with a prose style so far above Cayuga's ordinary run of literary talent as to be considered something of a miracle. The *Cornell Sun* under White's editorship must have been the best-written college newspaper in the country. After Cornell he drove a model T Ford across the country with a friend named Howard Cushman. When they ran out of money, they played for their supper—and their gasoline—on a fascinating musical instrument that White had made out of some pieces of wire and an old shoe or something. In Seattle the young explorer got a job as reporter on the *Times*, the kind of newspaper that did not allow you to use the verb "to mangle." Accurately reporting, one day, the anguished cry of a poor husband who had found the body of his wife in the municipal morgue, White wrote "My God, it's her!" and when the city editor changed this to "My God, it is she!" our wanderer moved sadly on to where they had a better understanding of people and a proper feeling for the finer usages of the English tongue. He became mess boy on a ship bound for Alaska, commanded by an old whaling captain, and manned by a crew who knew that a man says it's her when he finds her dead.

Shortly after *The New Yorker* was founded, its editors began to get occasionally manuscripts from an unknown young man named E. B. White who was a production assistant in an advertising agency. Harold Ross and Katharine Angell, his literary editor, were not slow to perceive that here were the perfect eye and ear, the authentic voice and accent for their struggling magazine. It took months, however, to trap the elusive writer into a conference and weeks to persuade him to come to work in the office; he finally agreed to give them his Thursdays. It is not too much to say that Andy White was the most valuable person on the magazine. His delicate tinkering with the works of *The New Yorker* caused it to move with a new ease and grace. His tag lines for those little newsbreaks which the magazine uses at the bottom of columns were soon being read joyfully aloud around town. His contributions to the Talk of the Town, particularly his Notes and Comment on the first page, struck the shining note that Ross had dreamed of striking. He has written a great many of the most memorable picture captions, including the famous one that has passed (usually misquoted) into song and legend, editorial and, I daresay, sermon: "I say it's spinach and I say the hell with it." He had a hand in everything: he even painted a cover and wrote a few advertisements. One day he decided that some pencil drawings I had absently made and thrown on the floor should be published in *The New Yorker*, so he picked them up, inked in the lines, and, to the surprise of us all, including Ross, got them published in *The New Yorker.*

Andy White understands begonias and children, canaries and goldfish, dachshunds and Scottish terriers, men and motives. His ear not only notes the louder cosmic rhythms but catches the faintest ticking sounds. He plays a fair ping-pong, a good piano, and a terrible poker (once, holding four natural jacks, he dropped out of the betting under the delusion that there were eight jacks in the deck and all he had was half of them). He has steadfastly refused to learn to play bridge or to take out life insurance. Once he offered an airplane pilot a thousand dollars to take him through a stormy dawn from Roosevelt Field to Chicago because a mysterious phone call had made him believe a friend was in great distress. The pilot had to make a forced landing in Pittsburgh, so that all White had to pay to see for himself that all was quiet along Lake Michigan was eight hundred dollars and his railroad fare from Pittsburgh. When a band of desperadoes stole his Buick sedan out of a quiet Turtle Bay garage and used it in the robbery of an upstate bank, White was suspected by the New York police of being the "brain guy" who devised the operations of a large and dangerous mob. For days detectives shrewdly infested his office, peering under tables, asking questions, staring in suspicious bewilderment at the preposterous array of scrawls, dentist's dates, symbols, phone numbers, photographs, and maps that littered his walls. Eventually they went shrewdly away, but every time I hear the sirens scream, I think they are coming for White. The former suspect is a good man with ax, rifle, and canoe (for several years he was part owner of a boys' camp in darkest Canada), and he sails a thirty-foot boat expertly. Two of his favorite books are *Van Zanten's Happy Days* and Alain-Fournier's *The Wanderer*. In the country he is afflicted with hay fever and in the city with a dizziness that resembles ordinary dizziness only as the mist resembles the rain. He expects every day of his life that something will kill him: a bit of mold, a small bug, a piece of huckleberry pie.

Some years ago White bought a farm in Maine and he now lives there the year around with his wife, who was Katharine Angell. He spends most of his time delousing turkeys, gathering bantam eggs, building mice-proof closets, and ripping out old fireplaces and putting in new ones. There is in him not a little of the spirit of Thoreau, who believed "that the world crowds round the individual, leaving him no vista, and shuts out the beauty of the earth; and that the wholesome wants of man are few." Now and then, between sunup and milking time, Andy White manages to do a casual or a poem for *The New Yorker*, or write a book. Many of the things he writes seem to me as lovely as a tree—say a maple after the first frost, or the cherry hung with snow. What he will go on to do I have no idea. If he simply continues to do what he has always done, it will be all right with me.

The Saturday Review, October 15, 1938

from *I Believe*

E VERY MAN is occasionally visited by the suspicion that the planet on which he is riding is not really going anywhere; that the Force which controls its measured eccentricities hasn't got anything special in mind. If he broods upon this somber theme long enough he gets the doleful idea that the laughing children on a merry-go-round or the thin, fine hands of a lady's watch are revolving more purposefully than he is. These black doubts creep up on a man just before thunderstorms, or at six in the morning when the steam begins to knock solemnly in the pipes, or during his confused wanderings in the forest beyond Euphoria after a long night of drinking.

"Where are we going, if anywhere, and why?" It will do no good to call up the *Times* or consult the Britannica. The Answer does not lie in the charts of astronomers or in the equations of mathematicians; it was not indicated by Galileo's swinging lamp or the voices of Joan of Arc; it evaded Socrates and Archimedes and the great men of the Renaissance and it has evaded everybody else from Francis Bacon to John Kieran. The fearful mystery that lies behind all this endless rotation has led Man into curious indulgences and singular practices, among them love, poetry, intoxicants, religion, and philosophy. Philosophy offers the rather cold consolation that perhaps we and our planet do not actually exist; religion presents the contradictory and scarcely more comforting thought that we exist but that we cannot hope to get anywhere until we cease to exist. Alcohol, in attempting to resolve the contradiction, produces vivid patterns of Truth which vanish like snow in the morning sun and cannot be recalled; the revelations of poetry are as wonderful as a comet in the skies, and as mysterious. Love, which was once believed to contain the Answer, we now know to be nothing more than an inherited behavior pattern.

Before we can pronounce any judgment on Man's destiny, we must have a peek at the dilemma into which he has gotten himself. We must examine his nature before we can measure his hope of Heaven. For some curious reason Man has always assumed that his is the highest form of life in the universe. There is, of course, nothing at all with which to sustain this view. Man is simply the highest form of life on his own planet. His superiority rests on a thin and chancy basis: he had the trick of articulate speech and out of this, slowly and laboriously, he developed the capacity of abstract reasoning. Abstract reasoning, in itself, has not benefited Man so much as instinct has benefited the lower animals. On the contrary, it has moved in the opposite direction. Instinct has been defined as "a tendency to actions which lead to the attainment of some goal natural to the species." In giving up instinct and going in for reasoning, Man has aspired higher than the attainment of natural goals; he has developed ideas and notions; he has monkeyed with concepts. The life to which he was naturally adapted he has put behind him; in moving into the alien and complicated sphere of Thought and Imagination he has become the least well-adjusted of all the creatures of the earth, and hence the most bewildered. It may be that the finer mysteries of life and death can be comprehended only through pure instinct; the cat, for example, appears to Know (I don't say that he does, but he appears to). Man, on the other hand, is surely farther away from the Answer than any other animal this side of the ladybug. His mistaken selection of reasoning as an instrument of perception has put him into a fine quandary.

The survival of almost any species of social animal, no matter how low, has been shown to be dependent on Group Co-operation, which is itself a product of instinct. Man's co-operative processes are jumpy, incomplete, and temporary because they are the product of reasoning and are thus divorced from the sanity which informs all natural laws. The lower animals co-operate in the interest of the preservation of their species. Man no longer has the natural, earthy sense which would interest him in the preservation of his species. The co-operation of the lower social animals is constructive, that of man destructive. "Group struggles to the death between animals of the same species, such as occur in human warfare, can hardly be found among nonhuman animals," says W. C. Allee in his enormously interesting *The Social Life of Animals.*

The animals that depend upon instinct have an inherent knowledge of the laws of economics and of how to apply them; Man with his powers of reason has reduced economics to the level of a farce which is at once funnier and more tragic than *Tobacco Road.* One has but to observe a community of beavers at work in a stream to understand the loss in sagacity, balance, co-operation, competence, and purpose which Man has suffered since he rose up on his hind legs. His grip on the earth and its realities began to lessen in that hour; he could walk, but he had lost the opposability of his hallux, and his feet were no longer prehensile. Two of his parts increased enormously in size: his gluteus maximus and his cerebrum. He began to chatter and he developed Reason, Thought, and Imagination, qualities which would get the smartest group of rabbits or orioles in the world into inextricable trouble overnight. Man, the aloof animal, has deteriorated in everything except mentality and in that he has done no more than barely hold his own for the past two thousand years. He no longer understands the ways of the lower animals and they no longer understand the ways of Man. Here again it is Man that has suffered the loss.

Next to reasoning, the greatest handicap to the optimum development of Man lies in the fact that his planet is just barely habitable. Its minimum temperatures are too low and its maximum temperatures are too high. Its day is not long enough and its night is too long. The disposition of its water and its earth is distinctly unfortunate (the existence of the Mediterranean Sea in the place where we find it is perhaps the unhappiest accident in the whole firmament). These factors encourage depression, fear, war, and lack of vitality. They describe a planet which is by no means perfectly devised for the nurturing, or for the perpetuation, of a higher intelligence. The effect of all this on Man is everywhere apparent. On his misfit globe he has outlasted the mammoth and the pterodactyl, but he has never got the upper hand of bacteria and the insects. "This is not even the age of Man, however great his superiority in size and intelligence," writes Mr. Allee, "it is literally the age of insects." It is surely not going too far, in view of everything, to venture the opinion that Man is not so high as he thinks he is. It is surely permissible to hazard the guess that somewhere beyond Betelgeuse there may be a race of men whose intelligence makes ours seem like the works of an old-fashioned music box. The Earth, it seems to me, may well be the Siberia, or the Perth Amboy, of the inhabited planets of the Universe.

Now that we have got Man down on his back, so to speak, let us look at the tongue of his intellect and feel the pulse of his soul. There is a great deal to be said for his intellect, in spite of the fact that it is unquestionably coated. It has produced Genius and out of Genius has come Art, the one achievement of Man which has made the long trip up from all fours seem well-advised. Most of the faint intimations of immortality of which we are occasionally aware would seem to arise out of Art, or the materials of Art. This brings us to God and Heaven, the last stop which this exploration into the known and the unknown will make.

Everybody is supposed to have some opinion as to whether there is life after death. Intelligent persons are expected to formulate "an integrated and consistent attitude toward life or reality"; this is known as "a philosophy" (definition 2c in *Webster's New International Dictionary*). Unfortunately, I have never been able to maintain a consistent attitude toward life or reality, or toward anything else. This may be entirely due to nervousness. At any rate, my attitudes change with the years, sometimes with the hours. Just now I am going through one of those periods when I believe that the black panther and the cedar waxwing have a higher hope of Heaven than Man has.

The Dignity of Man and the Divine Destiny of Man are two things which it is at the moment impossible for me to accept with wholehearted enthusiasm. Human Dignity has gleamed only now and then and here and there, in lonely splendor, throughout the ages, a hope of the better men, never an achievement of the majority. That which is only sporadically realized can scarcely be called characteristic. It is impossible to think of it as innate; it could never be defined as normal. Nothing is more depressing than the realization that nobility, courage, mercy, and almost all the other virtues which go to make up the ideal of Human Dignity, are, at their clearest and realest, the outgrowth of Man's inhumanity to Man, the fruit of his unending interspecific struggle. The pattern is easily traceable, from Christ to Cavell.

In spite of everything, it is perhaps too easy to figure Man as merely an animal of the earth whose cerebrum developed extraordinarily, like the peacock's tail or the giraffe's neck, and to let it go at that. There is always Browning's "plaguy hundredth chance" that the mysterious inner eye which seems to see God, actually does see God; and that God sees it, too. There is always Browning's "grand Perhaps." If it is hard to Believe, it is just as hard, as our poet's Bishop Blougram points out to the cynical Mr. Gigadibs, to "guard our unbelief." You remember: "Just when we are safest, there's a sunset-touch, a fancy from a flower-bell," and all that sort of thing—and we believe again. And then there's a man with a little mustache, and a man with an umbrella, and all *that* sort of thing, and we are safe once more in our conviction that there can be no God watching over this sorrowful and sinister scene, these menacing and meaningless animals.

We come back, in the end, to all that we can safely feel we know: a monkey man in the Eolithic times, wandering through the jungle, came upon a jewel and stuck it into his head. Since that day his descendants have given off light, sometimes a magic and blinding light. The question whether the jewel was carelessly flung off from a whirling star or carefully planned and placed by a supernatural hand has engaged the interest of mankind for a million years. The question will go on and on: is this light a proof of God or is it no more remarkable than the plumage of a bird of paradise?

"Come, come, it's best believing, if we can," says the jovial Sylvester Blougram, over his wine. "Why not," he asks, " 'the Way, the Truth, the Life'?" Why not, indeed? It is all right with me, I say over my own wine. But what is all this fear of, and opposition to, Oblivion? What is the matter with the soft Darkness, the Dreamless Sleep? "Well, folks," the cheery guard may say, as the train rushes silently into a warm, dark tunnel and stops, "here we are at good old Oblivion! Everybody out!" Come, come, what is the matter with that? I ask— over my scotch and soda.

I Believe, I Believe: The Personal Philosophies of Certain Eminent Men and Women of Our Time, 1939

I Break Everything I Touch

I AM interested in forming a little club of miserable men. No man can belong to it who can fix anything or make anything go. No man can belong to it who is handy around the house—or the garage, or anywhere else.

I was born with an aversion to tools. When I was in the eighth grade I had to go to manual training class every Thursday and I was still planing away at a bread-board when the other boys were putting the finishing touches on kitchen cabinets, davenports, and pianos. The bread-board was as far as I ever got and when I finally had it done the instructor, a temperamental and highly strung man named Buckley, who really loved carpentry and cabinet-making, picked it up and looked at it and said, "Thurber, I weep for you." I wept for me, too. I was covered with cuts and bruises from gouges, planes, bits-and-braces, saws, and hatchets. None of the other boys had a mark on them.

The only thing I can really do is change the ribbon on a typewriter, but it took me 22 years to learn that and every now and then I have to call in a friend or neighbor to help unravel me. When I was younger, I once changed a fuse in the fuse box, but I am too old and too smart to try that again. They tell me that electricity has been harnessed, and I say yes and so was King Kong. I don't even like to monkey with the thermostat that regulates the oil furnace. Every time I put the thing down to 55 before going up to bed, I expect to be blown out through the roof.

I come by my ineptitude with contraptions of any kind quite naturally. My grandmother on my mother's side was afraid of doorbells; she always took the receiver off the telephone hook during a thunder storm; she believed that if you unscrewed an electric light bulb, electricity would drip invisibly all over the house and if you then struck a match, you would be blown to hell. My mother was confident that the Victrola we bought in 1913 would explode if you wound it too tight, and she was forever warning me not to drive the family

Reo without gasoline, because she had heard it was bad for it if you did.

About the only thing I really know about an automobile is that you can't run it without gasoline. The Lord knows that enough of my men friends have explained the principles of the gas engine to me, but I am always just where I was when they started—and so is the gas engine. For all I know the distributor regulates the pressure on the manifold. I can run a car and I can stop one; I can also turn right and left and back up; but I don't know exactly what is happening. The thing has never become any more clear to me than the third law of thermodynamics—or the first one as far as that goes.

I have, of course, been in any number of embarrassing situations with automobiles, from my grandfather's old Lozier to my 1935 Ford. In England (I drove 15,000 miles in Europe and lived to tell it) my battery went dead near one of the cathedral towns, and I phoned a garage. A young mechanic in a truck appeared after a while and said he would pull me and I could get my engine started that way. I had been pulled and pushed in the old Reo days and I knew that you could start the engine that way. I knew that you pushed the clutch in (or is it out?) and then let it out (or in) suddenly. So the garage man attached a rope to the back of his truck and to the front of my car and away we went—over the hills and through the dales of England.

Every quarter mile or so he would stop and come back to see what was the matter. He lifted the hood, he got under the car, but there was nothing doing.

At the end of five or six miles he got out and said, "What gear you got her in?" He had me there. I didn't have her in any gear. I had her in neutral. He just stared at me, not in anger or resentment, not with an injured look, but as Cortez must have stared when he stumbled on the Pacific. I know now that you can't make her turn over if you've got her in neutral, but I don't know why. You can make her turn over with the starter when you've got her in neutral. The hell with it.

My worst embarrassment came one day in Connecticut when my engine began to heat up until the red fluid in the gauge was almost up to the top. I stopped at a garage and pointed this out to a mechanic. I got out of the car and stood looking in at the dashboard, thus seeing it from an unfamiliar angle.

Suddenly I saw what I thought was the matter. A needle on one of the dials pointed to 152. "For God's sake!" I said to the mechanic, "that shouldn't be registering so high, should it?" (I always swear around mechanics to make them think I have an easy, profane knowledge of motors.) The garage man gave me a long, puzzled look—the old Cortez look. "That's your radio dial, brother," he said.

Sure it was. I just hadn't recognized it. Half the time I look at the oil-pressure gauge instead of the speedometer and I think I am doing only 17 miles an hour.

One of the presents I got for Christmas was a handsome new-fangled soda syphon complete with a set of directions. I put the thing away until just the other day, and then I got the directions out and looked at them, the way ladies look at the snakes in a zoo.

The first three directions were simple enough but the fourth began to make me suspicious. It reads like this: "Place a Super-Charger in the charge holder with small end pointing out (see Figure C). Then screw back cap of charge holder. Do not use force." They don't know that the first thing I use is force—I use it on linked-nail puzzles and olive bottles and everything else. An engineer or a mechanic or my brother-in-law or the next door neighbor would go about a thing like this simply and gently, but what I do is get panic-stricken, the way you would if somebody grabbed you in a dark room, and the first thing you know I have the contraption on the floor with my knee on its chest. Pretty soon something makes a sharp snapping noise and the device has to be taken to the attic to join all the other contrivances whose bones I have broken in a series of unequal struggles. Psychologists would explain this by saying that I don't really want the things around so I break them while pretending to be trying to make them work. Psychologists are often right.

But to get back to the syphon. Rule Six says: "To puncture Super-Charger and to charge the syphon push down charging button (marked A in Figure D) with heel of hand (see Figure E); or give button a tap with palm of hand. Some people find it easier to push charging button against edge of kitchen sink or table." I haven't got up enough courage yet to experiment with this syphon, for while I am sure it would work fine for nine men out of ten, I have a feeling it would fight to a draw with me. Next year the makers might even have to add a line or two to Rule Six: "Mr. Thurber of Woodbury, Connecticut, finds it easier to grasp the syphon with both hands and whang it against the kitchen stove. See Group F: the cut and bleeding figure is Thurber."

When I was 12 years old, an uncle gave me a little box Brownie, the simplest camera in the world. A folder of directions came with it, and I warily approached the section where it explained how to put in a film. "First," it said, "spring out the spool pins." I knew right there the thing had me. I knew that far from being able to spring out the spool pins, I wouldn't even be able to find them. I gave the camera to the first little boy I met on the street, a youngster of eight, who I was sure could spring out the spool pins with his eyes blindfolded and mittens on his hands.

This is not the world for me, this highly mechanized world. I can only hope that in Heaven there is nothing more complicated than a harp and that they will have winged mechanics to fix mine when I get it down and break its back.

The Man, 1941

CHRONOLOGY

NOTE ON THE TEXTS

NOTES

Chronology

1894   Born James Grover Thurber on December 8, 1894, in Columbus, Ohio, second son of Mary Agnes ("Mame") Fisher and Charles Thurber. (Maternal grandfather William M. Fisher founded what became a prosperous wholesale produce business in 1870; he was noted in Columbus for his eccentric and sometimes pugnacious behavior. Mother, born 1866, also became known locally for her extravagant storytelling, elaborate practical jokes, and deep interest in astrology, numerology, and various systems of self-help. Father was born in Indianapolis, Indiana, in 1867; he came to Columbus in 1878 to stay with his aunt Margery Albright. Parents met in elementary school, then corresponded after father returned to Indianapolis to support his ailing mother; after a three-year engagement, they married in July 1892. Their first child, William, was born in October 1893.) Father works as clerk for Ohio secretary of state.

1895   Father begins working as clerk for Ohio governor Asa S. Bushnell in December.

1896   Brother Robert born in December.

1900   Thurber begins attending Ohio Avenue Elementary School in September.

1902   Family moves to Washington, D.C., in April after former Ohio congressman David K. Watson hires father as stenographer; they later rent summer house in Falls Church, Virginia. In August, Thurber is accidentally shot in his left eye with a toy arrow by William while playing. Mother takes Thurber to general practitioner who dresses the injured eye; several days later eye is removed by specialist Dr. Swann Burnett, but uninjured right eye is gradually damaged by "sympathetic infection." (In later years Thurber becomes convinced that early removal of the injured eye would have averted damage to the other eye.) Thurber stays at home during the next school year.

1903   Family returns to Columbus in June, where father works as freelance stenographer (his jobs are sporadic and short-term, and he is frequently unemployed). Thurber starts third grade at Sullivant School, which he will attend for the next four years; schoolmates include future humorist Donald Ogden Stewart.

1905   Father becomes seriously ill, and is unable to work; family moves into home of Thurber's maternal grandparents for several months. (Thurber, who is often the object of his grandfather's fierce temper, frequently stays with great-aunt Margery Albright over the next five years.)

1907–9   Transfers to Douglas School for seventh and eighth grades. Enters Columbus East High School in the fall of 1909.

1913–14   Publishes first story, western adventure "The Third Bullet," in high school magazine in May 1913. Enrolls at Ohio State University in September 1913. Vision problems prevent his participating in athletics; he suffers ostracism, and no fraternity pledges him. Attendance at classes, military drill, and physical education is erratic. Registers as sophomore for 1914–15 school year, but drops out for the entire year.

1915–17   Registers again as a sophomore for 1915–16, then drops out when denied admission in the second semester because of failure to attend gym classes and military drill; is reinstated on appeal in the fall of 1916. Forms close friendship with fellow student and professional actor Elliott Nugent (son of well-known playwright and actor J. C. Nugent); with Nugent's help is accepted into Phi Kappa Psi fraternity, and becomes active in student newspaper *The Lantern*, humor magazine *The Sun-Dial*, and drama club The Strollers. Deeply influenced by literature classes taught by Joseph Taylor, who introduces Thurber to work of Henry James.

1918   Becomes editor of *The Sun-Dial*. Eager to help war effort, drops out of Ohio State in the spring and travels to Washington to train for three months as State Department code and cipher clerk. Arrives in Paris shortly after end of World War I in November.

1919   Works at American Embassy and lives in a pension. Looks up places mentioned in Henry James's novels and visits Normandy. Loses his virginity in the fall, under circumstances that he never clarifies; writes to a friend that he has "had a very bad time of it with nerves in Paris."

1920   Returns to Columbus in February. Rents typewriter and tries to write; spends much of his time courting childhood schoolmate Eva Prout. Hired in August as cub reporter for *Columbus Dispatch*. Active in The Scarlet Mask, campus theatrical group that stages yearly musicals; collaborates as writer and performer on musical *Oh My, Omar!*

1921   Forms friendship with newspaperman John McNulty, a New Yorker then working for the *Ohio State Journal*. Meets Althea Adams (b. 1901), an Ohio State undergraduate involved in Strollers drama club. Travels to New York in October to review plays for the *Dispatch*; attends wedding of Elliott Nugent, who is currently appearing on Broadway. Writes script of Scarlet Mask production *Many Moons*.

1922   Marries Althea Adams in May; they honeymoon in Washington, D.C., and New York. Collaborates on writing of Scarlet Mask production *A Twin Fix*.

1923   Contributes Sunday humor column "Credos and Curios" to the *Dispatch*. Travels in April to New York and Connecticut, going to the theater and visiting with Nugent. Collaborates on Scarlet Mask production *The Cat and the Riddle*.

1924   With Althea's encouragement, quits the *Dispatch* and spends the summer working on script for a musical and writing essays and stories in a cabin in the Adirondacks; only one piece is accepted for publication. Returns to Columbus, where the *Dispatch*, following standing policy, refuses to rehire him. Works as press agent for various local entertainment businesses. Writes and directs Scarlet Mask production *Tell Me Not*.

1925   Sails with Althea to France in May; tries unsuccessfully to write a novel at a farmhouse in Normandy before settling in Paris. Works at night copy desk of Paris edition of *Chicago Tribune*; forms friendship with fellow reporters William L. Shirer and Elliot Paul. Meets F. Scott and Zelda Fitzgerald. Thurber and Althea spend winter in Nice working on Riviera edition of *Tribune*. Freelances for other publications including the New York *World*, Kansas City *Star*, and *Harper's*.

1926   Marriage is troubled; Thurber returns to New York alone in June and settles in Greenwich Village. Submits a batch of articles to *The New Yorker*; all are rejected. After Althea returns from France, she and Thurber spend the summer in Gloversville, New York, then settle in an apartment on Horatio Street in Greenwich Village. He considers returning to Columbus until his brief humor item is printed in Franklin P. Adams' syndicated column "The Conning Tower." Hired as reporter by *New York Evening Post*.

1927   Sells his first short piece to *The New Yorker*, "An American Romance." Meets *New Yorker* staff writer E. B. White, who becomes close friend and mentor, and is introduced by White to magazine's founding editor, Harold W. Ross, who hires him immediately to handle administration. (Magazine's regular contributors include Alexander Woollcott, Robert Benchley, and Dorothy Parker; staff includes Katharine Angell, who later marries White, and Ralph Ingersoll, and will later be joined by Wolcott Gibbs, Brendan Gill, Gus Lobrano, Robert Coates, and William Maxwell, among others.) Demonstrates no aptitude at administration and after several months begins working as copy editor and rewrite man, while continuing to contribute "casuals" to the magazine. Shares an office with White for the next three years, and with him writes much of the "Talk of the Town" section of the magazine for the next eight years. During summer meets Ann Honeycutt, with whom he forms intense friendship.

1928   Writes first in series of stories about the Monroes, couple whose married life is modeled on the marriage of Thurber and Althea.

1929   Separates from Althea; he lives at the Algonquin Hotel in Manhattan while she stays at rented house in Silvermine, Connecticut, where he sometimes visits her. Collaborates with E. B. White on *Is Sex Necessary?*, parody of contemporary sex manuals, with Thurber contributing four chapters, preface, and glossary; at White's insistence, the book is illustrated with Thurber's drawings. The book is published in November by Harper & Bros.

1930   Meets magazine editor Helen Muriel Wismer at New Year's Day party at Ann Honeycutt's apartment. In the fall Althea and Thurber share an apartment in New York City.

1931   *The Owl in the Attic*, collection of pieces originally published in *The New Yorker*, published by Harper in February. Buys farm in Sandy Hook, Connecticut, in August. Daughter Rosemary is born on October 7.

1932   Publishes first of 307 captioned cartoons in *The New Yorker* in January. Visits Bermuda, where he forms enduring friendship with young English couple Ronnie and Jane Williams. *The Seal in the Bedroom and Other Predicaments*, a collection of cartoons and other drawings, published by Harper in November.

1933   Lives at the Algonquin, occasionally visiting Althea and Rosemary in Sandy Hook. *My Life and Hard Times* published by Harper in November.

1934   Althea files for legal separation in March. Thurber substitutes for Alexander Woollcott on his radio show for several weeks in April. One-man show of Thurber's drawings opens at Valentine Gallery in New York City in December.

1935   Suffering effects of anxiety and heavy drinking, rests at a sanitarium in Ellenville, New York, in March. Divorced from Althea in May. Marries Helen Wismer June 25; they honeymoon on Martha's Vineyard and afterwards move into an apartment on Fifth Avenue. Invites Thomas Wolfe up for drinks but is insulted by Wolfe's lack of regard for his writing (later notes of Wolfe: "For an hour he was very amusing and then he became a drunken writer and exactly as disagreeable as all drunken writers"). *The Middle-Aged Man on the Flying Trapeze* published by Harper in November. Visits Columbus with Helen at Thanksgiving. Gives up staff position at *The New Yorker* to work on freelance basis.

1936   Spends spring vacation with Helen in Bermuda, where they spend an evening with Sinclair Lewis, who recites passages by Thurber from memory. (Thurber later describes Lewis as "the only drunken writer I ever met who said nothing about his own work and praised that of another writer present.") Rents house in Litchfield, Connecticut, for summer. On a trip to Columbus in November, enjoys evening exchanging stories and singing songs with Carl Sandburg.

1937   Cataract begins to cloud vision in his remaining eye, but he postpones necessary surgery. Sails with Helen to France in May; in Paris they encounter Ernest Hemingway, Dorothy Parker, and others; in London visits an exhibition of his drawings. *Let Your Mind Alone! and Other More or Less Inspirational Pieces* published in September by Harper.

1938   Returns to France; during four-month stay at villa at Cap d'Antibes, meets Winston Churchill (delighted by Churchill's description of him as "that insane American and depraved artist"). Travels in England, Scotland, and France; returns to U.S. in September, settling in rented house in Woodbury, Connecticut. Writes to Elliott Nugent about idea for play set at Ohio State.

1939   Works with Elliott Nugent on play *The Male Animal.* "The Secret Life of Walter Mitty" published in *The New Yorker* in March. Father dies in Columbus in April. Travels to Los Angeles in June to continue collaboration with Elliott Nugent; meets Charlie Chaplin and others in film community during three-month stay. *The Male Animal* staged in San Diego, Santa Barbara, and Los Angeles in October. Antiwar parable *The Last Flower*, created in one evening at the Algonquin, published by Harper at Christmas.

1940   After considerable rewriting, *The Male Animal* opens on Broadway in January to good reviews. Thurber visits Bermuda in the spring; begins contributing pieces to *The Bermudian*, edited by friend Ronnie Williams. Undergoes cataract surgery in June, but vision continues to deteriorate. Begins contributing humor column "If You Ask Me" to *PM*, left-wing tabloid edited by his friend Ralph Ingersoll (column runs from September 1940 until July 1941). *Fables for Our Time and Famous Poems Illustrated* published in September by Harper. Thurber undergoes major operation for glaucoma and iritis in October, but it fails to halt deterioration of his vision; undergoes another operation in December.

1941   Virtually blind, is released from hospital under care of nurses and goes to live at Grosvenor Hotel with Helen. Undergoes two more eye operations in March and April. Suffers a breakdown followed by a long period of deep depression (refers later to "a five-year nervous crack-up"). Rents house for summer on Martha's Vineyard; meets poet Mark Van Doren, who becomes a close friend. "The Whip-Poor-Will" appears in August, first story published in *New Yorker* in fourteen months. Rents apartment in Manhattan in the fall.

1942   Attends premiere of film version of *The Male Animal* in Columbus in March. Alternates between apartment in Manhattan and house in Cornwall, Connecticut. Leaves Harper & Bros. for Harcourt Brace, which publishes *My World—And Welcome To It* in October.

1943   Moves into East 57th Street apartment with Helen in January. Despite failing vision, continues drawing with the aid of the Zeiss loop, a magnifying device used in defense plants. Publishes children's book *Many Moons* (September) and cartoon collection *Men, Women and Dogs* (November), both with Harcourt Brace; *Many Moons* wins American Library Association award for best children's book. Pleased by serious critical appreciation of his work in December number of *Poetry*, written by Peter De Vries, who becomes a close friend.

1944   Suffers in the fall from pneumonia, followed by a ruptured appendix and peritonitis, for which he undergoes emergency surgery. Spends time at the Homestead resort in Hot Springs, Virginia, where he returns frequently in subsequent years. *The Great Quillow* published in October by Harcourt Brace.

1945   *The Thurber Carnival*, a retrospective anthology covering Thurber's entire career, is published in February by

Harper, and becomes a bestseller. Buys 14-room colonial house on 60-acre property in West Cornwall. *The White Deer* published in September by Harcourt Brace. Works on film adaptation of "The Secret Life of Walter Mitty" (none of his work is used). Turns down membership in National Institute of Arts and Letters because E. B. White has not been asked to join.

1946   Visits Columbus in January for mother's 80th birthday celebration. Works at a slower pace as he continues to suffer from depression.

1947   Vacations in Bermuda, February–April. Movie version of *The Secret Life of Walter Mitty*, starring Danny Kaye, is released in August. Publishes final original drawing in *The New Yorker* on November 1. Writes letter to the New York *Herald Tribune* in November protesting an editorial calling for American government workers to take loyalty oaths.

1948   Visits Columbus in May. "Soapland," a five-part series on radio soap operas, is published in *The New Yorker*, May to July. *The Beast in Me and Other Animals* published in September by Harcourt Brace.

1949   Visits Nassau (March) and Bermuda (April). Begins contributing feature "Letter from the States" to *The Bermudian*.

1950   During March stay in Bermuda writes *The 13 Clocks*, which is published in November by Simon & Schuster with illustrations by West Cornwall friend Marc Simont. Visits Columbus in June on his way to receive honorary doctorate from Kenyon College. Meets T. S. Eliot in December. "Photograph Album," series of articles about Thurber's family and early life, begins appearing in *The New Yorker*.

1951   Thurber draws self-portrait (his last drawing for publication) for cover story in *Time* (July 9); T. S. Eliot, in an interview for *Time*, comments on Thurber's work: "There is a criticism of life at the bottom of it. It is serious and even somber . . . His writings and also his illustrations are capable of surviving the immediate environment and time out of which they spring." Offered honorary degree by Ohio State University, but refuses in protest of university policy of barring politically controversial guest speakers. Harold Ross dies of lung cancer on December 6. (Thurber writes in a letter: "He was the principal figure in my career and I don't know what I would have amounted to without his magazine, in which 90 percent of my stuff has appeared . . . Ross was a part of my daily life for almost exactly a quarter of a century.")

1952   *The Thurber Album*, book version of "Photograph Album" series, is published in April by Simon & Schuster. Suffers from worsening thyroid condition.

1953   *Thurber Country* published in October by Simon & Schuster. Television adaptation of *The 13 Clocks* is broadcast in December. Returns to Columbus to spend Christmas with his family.

1954   Behaves erratically, exhibiting outbursts of violent anger under influence of thyroid condition and heavy drinking. Vacations in Bermuda and on Martha's Vineyard.

1955   Spends summer and fall in Europe. *Thurber's Dogs*, consisting mostly of previously published pieces, appears in October from Simon & Schuster. Spends a month in Columbus after his mother suffers a stroke and sinks into a coma; mother dies in December.

1956   Relations with staff of *The New Yorker*, now under editorship of William Shawn, become increasingly difficult, and Thurber makes public statements about his problems with the magazine. *Further Fables for Our Time* published in October by Simon & Schuster; awarded $5,000 prize from American Library Association for promoting "the cause of liberty, justice and fair play."

1957   Quarrels with *New Yorker* fiction editor William Maxwell over editing of children's story *The Wonderful O*; withdraws manuscript and writes to Katharine White, "I need a long holiday from the magazine and its high pressures." *The Wonderful O* published in May by Simon & Schuster. *Alarms and Diversions* published in November by Harpers. "The Years with Ross," series of articles on Harold

Ross and the early years of *The New Yorker*, begins appearing in the *Atlantic* in November.

1958 Travels to Europe with Helen for five-month stay; honored by staff of *Punch* at luncheon in July; meets Adlai Stevenson in Paris. Disagreements over articles on Ross lead to final breach with E. B. and Katharine White.

1959 *The Years with Ross* is published in expanded form by Atlantic, Little, Brown, and becomes a bestseller; many veteran *New Yorker* contributors find fault with book's accuracy.

1960 *A Thurber Carnival*, revue adapted from Thurber's works by Haila Stoddard, opens in Columbus; show moves to Broadway in February, but closes due to actors' strike despite excellent reviews. After a run in Central City, Colorado, it reopens on Broadway in September, with Thurber playing himself in one sketch; he appears on stage for 88 performances before the show closes in November. Behavior continues to be erratic and sometimes violent, possibly because of series of undiagnosed minor strokes. John "Jap" Gude (Thurber's agent for many years) and writer Peter De Vries remain close friends, while others avoid him.

1961 Receives a Tony award for *A Thurber Carnival*. Travels with Helen to England in January, in unsuccessful effort to promote an English production of *A Thurber Carnival*; sleeps little and explodes often in fits of rage. *Lanterns and Lances* published in May by Harper. Returns to U.S. in May. Collapses after leaving party for Noel Coward on October 3; is rushed to Doctors Hospital in New York City where doctors remove a brain tumor. Lapses into semiconsciousness and dies November 2. Ashes buried at Green Lawn Cemetery in Columbus on November 8.

Note on the Texts

This volume contains the complete texts of four works by James Thurber, *The Seal in the Bedroom* (1932), *My Life and Hard Times* (1933), *The Last Flower* (1939), and *The 13 Clocks* (1950); two chapters by Thurber from *Is Sex Necessary?* (1929), his collaboration with E. B. White; six chapters from his memoir *The Years with Ross* (1959); a selection of short pieces and drawings taken from 13 collections published during Thurber's lifetime; and seven pieces never collected in book form by Thurber. The contents are arranged in the chronological order of their initial book publication, with the exception of the seven uncollected pieces, which are placed in a separate section at the end of this volume.

Thurber arrived at the final versions of even the shortest of his pieces through a process of extensive revision. In an interview published in 1940 in *The New York Times Book Review*, he said of his writing: "I rarely have a very clear idea of where I'm going when I start. Just people and a situation. Then I fool around—writing and rewriting until the stuff jells." Speaking to *The Paris Review* in 1955, he remarked: "Well, my wife took a look at the first version of something I was doing not long ago and said: 'Goddam it, Thurber, that's high-school stuff.' I have to tell her to wait until the seventh draft, it'll work out all right." His cartoons, by contrast, were dashed off as spontaneously as possible; Thurber told *The Los Angeles Sunday Times Magazine* in 1939: "I'm not an artist. I'm a painstaking writer who doodles for relaxation." Thurber occasionally made small revisions, and sometimes altered the captions of cartoons, when preparing work that had appeared in *The New Yorker* and other periodicals for book publication. (When compiling material already published in book form for subsequent collections, Thurber sometimes made further revisions, updating or retitling previously collected pieces. After he lost his eyesight, *The New Yorker* experimented briefly with using new captions with previously published cartoons.)

The texts printed in this volume are taken from their first book publication, except for the texts of five of the uncollected pieces, which are taken from their original periodical publication. Pieces taken from collections by Thurber are presented in this volume in the same order as they appeared in the volumes in which they were first collected.

The following annotated list gives the source of the texts and drawings printed in this volume and the dates of their original periodical publication (all page numbers refer to this volume):

"The Nature of the American Male: A Study of Pedestalism" and "The Lilies-and-Bluebird Delusion" appeared as the first and fifth chapters in *Is Sex Necessary?: Or, Why You Feel the Way You Do* by James Thurber and E. B. White, published in New York by Harper & Brothers on November 7, 1929. The texts printed here are from the Harper edition.

"Mr. Monroe Holds the Fort" and "The Pet Department" are taken from *The Owl in the Attic and Other Perplexities*, published in New York by Harper & Brothers on February 5, 1931. "Mr. Monroe Holds the Fort" appeared in *The New Yorker* on November 30, 1929. Fourteen of the pieces in "The Pet Department" appeared in *The New Yorker*, under the heading "Our Pet Department," as follows: p. 38, February 22, 1930; p. 39, April 5, 1930; p. 40, June 7, 1930; p. 41, May 3, 1930; p. 42, March 1, 1930; p. 43, March 15, 1930; p. 44, February 22, 1930; p. 45, March 15, 1930; p. 46, May 17, 1930; p. 47, May 17, 1930; p. 49, March 1, 1930; p. 51, April 5, 1930; p. 53, June 7, 1930; p. 54, May 3, 1930. The remaining drawings in "The Pet Department" appeared for the first time in *The Owl in the Attic*. The texts printed here are from the Harper edition.

The Seal in the Bedroom and Other Predicaments was published in New York by Harper & Brothers on November 23, 1932. The following drawings appeared in *The New Yorker*: p. 59, January 30, 1932; p. 60 (top), December 5, 1931; p. 61 (bottom), June 20, 1931; p. 62, February 14, 1931, February 28, 1931; p. 63, August 29, 1931, October 3, 1931; p. 64, November 7, 1931, August 13, 1932; p. 65, October 10, 1931, August 22, 1931; p. 66 (top), May 7, 1932; p. 67, July 11, 1931, June 11, 1932; p. 68, May 16, 1931, February 27, 1932; p. 70 (top), July 25, 1931; p. 72, September 12, 1931, May 28, 1932; p. 73 (top), September 26, 1931; p. 74, July 2, 1932, July 4, 1931; p. 75, April 16, 1932, March 19, 1932; p. 76, March 12, 1932, April 2, 1932; p. 77, January 23, 1932, August 20, 1932; p. 78, January 2, 1932, May 14, 1932; p. 79 (bottom), November 21, 1931; p. 80, April 9, 1932, July 30, 1932; p. 81 (top), November 14, 1931; p. 82, April 30, 1932; pp. 83–84, February 6, 1932; p. 104 (top), October 15, 1932; p. 107 (top), June 25, 1932; p. 113 (bottom), May 28, 1932; p. 114 (bottom), July 23, 1932; p. 115 (bottom), April 9, 1932; p. 118, April 23, 1932; p. 119, July 16, 1932, June 4, 1932; p. 120, June 4, 1932, July 16, 1932; p. 121, July 16, 1932, June 4, 1932; p. 126 (top), December 19, 1931 (the remaining drawings appeared for the first time in *The Seal in the Bedroom*). The text printed here is taken from the Harper edition.

My Life and Hard Times was published in New York by Harper & Brothers on November 10, 1933. Eight of the chapters had previously appeared in *The New Yorker*: "The Night the Bed Fell," July 8, 1933;

"The Car We Had to Push," July 15, 1933; "The Day the Dam Broke," July 29, 1933; "The Night the Ghost Got In," August 12, 1933; "More Alarms at Night," August 26, 1933; "A Sequence of Servants," September 9, 1933; "University Days" (as "College Days"), September 23, 1933; "Draft Board Nights," September 30, 1933. The text printed here is that of the Harper edition.

Nineteen pieces in this volume are taken from *The Middle-Aged Man on the Flying Trapeze*, published in New York by Harper & Brothers on November 15, 1935. All appeared in *The New Yorker*: "The Departure of Emma Inch," August 10, 1935; "There's an Owl in My Room," November 17, 1934; "The Topaz Cufflinks Mystery," July 23, 1932; "A Preface to Dogs," January 2, 1932; "The Private Life of Mr. Bidwell," January 28, 1933; "Mr. Preble Gets Rid of His Wife," March 4, 1933; "A Portrait of Aunt Ida," November 10, 1934; "The Luck of Jad Peters," December 8, 1934; "I Went to Sullivant," June 22, 1935; "If Grant Had Been Drinking at Appomattox," December 6, 1930; "How to See a Bad Play," September 14, 1935; "The Funniest Man You Ever Saw," August 15, 1931; "The Black Magic of Barney Haller," August 27, 1932; "Something to Say," July 30, 1932; "Snapshot of a Dog," March 9, 1935; "The Evening's at Seven," October 22, 1932; "The Greatest Man in the World," February 21, 1931; "One Is a Wanderer," March 2, 1935; "A Box to Hide In," January 24, 1931. The texts printed in this volume are taken from the Harper edition.

Eighteen pieces in this volume are taken from *Let Your Mind Alone! And Other More or Less Inspirational Pieces*, published in New York by Harper & Brothers on September 8, 1937. Seventeen of them appeared in *The New Yorker*: "Pythagoras and the Ladder," November 28, 1936; "Destructive Forces in Life," December 5, 1936; "The Case for the Daydreamer," December 19, 1936; "How to Adjust Yourself to Your Work," January 9, 1937; "Anodynes for Anxieties," January 30, 1937; "The Conscious vs. The Unconscious," February 20, 1937; "Sex ex Machina," March 13, 1937; "Sample Intelligence Test," April 3, 1937; "Miscellaneous Mentation," May 1, 1937; "The Breaking Up of the Winships," January 11, 1936; "Nine Needles," January 25, 1936; "A Couple of Hamburgers," November 16, 1935; "Aisle Seats in the Mind," December 21, 1935; "Mrs. Phelps," December 12, 1936; "Wild Bird Hickock and His Friends," May 29, 1937; "Doc Marlowe," November 2, 1935; "The Admiral on the Wheel," February 1, 1936. "A Dozen Disciplines" appeared for the first time in *Let Your Mind Alone!*. The texts printed in this volume are taken from the Harper edition.

The Last Flower: A Parable in Pictures was published in New York by Harper & Brothers on November 17, 1939. None of the text and drawings in the book had previously appeared in periodical form. The text printed here is taken from the Harper edition.

Thirty-two pieces in this volume are taken from *Fables for Our Time and Famous Poems Illustrated*, published in New York by Harper & Brothers on September 18, 1940. All of them appeared in *The New Yorker*: "The Mouse Who Went to the Country," "The Little Girl and the Wolf," "The Two Turkeys," "The Tiger Who Understood People," January 21, 1939; "The Fairly Intelligent Fly," "The Lion Who Wanted to Zoom," "The Very Proper Gander," "The Hen and the Heavens," February 4, 1939; "The Moth and the Star," "The Shrike and the Chipmunks," "The Hunter and the Elephant," "The Scotty Who Knew Too Much," February 18, 1939; "The Bear Who Let It Alone," "The Owl Who Was God," "The Sheep in Wolf's Clothing," April 29, 1939; "The Stork Who Married a Dumb Wife," "The Crow and the Oriole," "The Elephant Who Challenged the World," July 29, 1939; "The Courtship of Arthur and Al," "The Hen Who Wouldn't Fly," "The Glass in the Field," "The Rabbits Who Caused All the Trouble," August 26, 1939; "The Bird and the Foxes," "The Tortoise and the Hare," "The Unicorn in the Garden," October 21, 1939; "The Seal Who Became Famous," "The Green Isle in the Sea," "The Patient Bloodhound," February 17, 1940; "Excelsior," March 11, 1939; "Lochinvar," April 8, 1939; "Curfew Must Not Ring To-night," June 17, 1939; "Barbara Frietchie," September 16, 1939. The texts printed in this volume are taken from the Harper edition.

Ten pieces in this volume are taken from *My World—And Welcome To It*, published in New York by Harcourt, Brace and Company on October 29, 1942. All of them appeared in periodicals: "The Whip-Poor-Will," *The New Yorker*, August 9, 1941; "The Macbeth Murder Mystery," *The New Yorker*, October 2, 1937; "The Man Who Hated Moonbaum," *The New Yorker*, March 16, 1940; "The Secret Life of Walter Mitty," *The New Yorker*, March 18, 1939; "Interview with a Lemming" (as "If You Ask Me"), *PM*, March 3, 1941; "You Could Look It Up," *Saturday Evening Post*, April 5, 1941; "The Gentleman in 916" (as "If You Ask Me"), *PM*, January 27, 1941; "The Letters of James Thurber," *The New Yorker*, October 8, 1938; "Here Lies Miss Groby," *The New Yorker*, March 21, 1942; "A Ride with Olympy," *The New Yorker*, April 30, 1938. The texts printed in this volume are taken from the Harcourt edition.

The drawings in this volume taken from *Men, Women and Dogs: A Book of Drawings* are printed from the edition published in New York by Harcourt, Brace and Company on November 10, 1943. All of the drawings appeared in *The New Yorker*. The drawings in the section titled "Selected Cartoons" appeared as follows: p. 587, March 27, 1937, July 6, 1935; p. 588, December 15, 1934, May 27, 1933; p. 589, December 3, 1932, June 2, 1934; p. 590, August 19, 1939, November 9, 1940; p. 591, May 21, 1938; p. 592, February 6, 1943; p. 593, September 12, 1936, July 14, 1934; p. 594, December 17, 1932, March 4, 1933; p. 595, March 27, 1943, June 9, 1934; p. 596, April 1, 1939, September 21, 1940; p. 597, December 17, 1938, March 14, 1936; p. 598, December 30, 1933, February 6, 1937; p. 599, April 22, 1939, February 2, 1935; p. 600, June 10, 1939, May 5, 1934; p. 601, August 31, 1935, December 31, 1932; p. 602, June 24, 1933, November 10, 1934; p. 603, February 13, 1937, April 13, 1940; p. 604, June 5, 1937, October 29, 1932; p. 605, March 23, 1935; p. 606, February 21, 1942, October 21, 1933; p. 607, August 18, 1934, October 27, 1934; p. 608, May 4, 1935, March 16, 1935; p. 609, January 7, 1933, December 9, 1933; p. 610, April 6, 1935, July 22, 1939; p. 611, November 19, 1938, March 7, 1936; p. 612, December 24, 1932. The drawings in "The Masculine Approach" appeared as follows: p. 613, November 13, 1937; p. 614, November 13, 1937, November 20, 1937; p. 615, November 20, 1937, December 4, 1937; p. 616, December 4, 1937; p. 617, December 25, 1937; p. 618, December 25, 1937, March 19, 1938; p. 619, March 19, 1938; p. 620, February 12, 1938; p. 621, February 12, 1938, January 15, 1938; p. 622, January 15, 1938. The drawings in "The War Between Men and Women" appeared as follows: p. 623, January 20, 1934; p. 624, January 27, 1934, February 3, 1934; p. 625, February 10, 1934; p. 626, February 17, 1934; p. 627, February 24, 1934, March 3, 1934; p. 628, March 10, 1934, March 17, 1934; p. 629, March 24, 1934, March 31, 1934; p. 630, April 7, 1934, April 14, 1934; p. 631, April 21, 1934, April 28, 1934.

Two pieces in this volume are taken from *The Thurber Carnival*, published in New York by Harper & Brothers on February 1, 1945. Both of them appeared in *The New Yorker*: "The Catbird Seat," November 14, 1942, and "The Cane in the Corridor," January 2, 1943. The texts printed in this volume are taken from the Harper edition.

The pieces in this volume taken from *The Beast in Me and Other Animals: A New Collection of Pieces and Drawings About Human Beings and Less Alarming Creatures* are printed from the edition published in New York by Harcourt, Brace and Company, on September 17, 1948. All of them appeared in periodicals. "The Princess and the Tin Box" was published in *The New Yorker*, September 29, 1945, as "Fairy Tales for Our Time: The Princess and the Tin Box." "The Lady on the Bookcase" was published in *The New York Times Magazine*, January 28, 1945, as "Thurber As Seen By Thurber." "A Call on Mrs. Forrester" appeared in *The New Yorker*, June 19, 1948. The drawings in "A New Natural History" appeared in *The New Yorker* under the heading "Our New Natural History" as follows: p. 672, April 14, 1945; p. 673, March 10, 1945, March 2, 1946; p. 674, May 11, 1946, March 31, 1945, May 11, 1946; p. 675, November 3, 1945; p. 676, June 2, 1945, January 19, 1946; p. 677, December 8, 1945, July 7, 1945; p. 678, December 8, 1945, (bottom left) March 31, 1945, (bottom right) July 7, 1945; p. 679, June 2, 1945, March 17, 1945; p. 680, July 7, 1945, April 14, 1945; p. 681, August 11, 1945, October 6, 1945; p. 682, April 13, 1946; p. 683, March 31, 1945, May 5, 1945, October 6, 1945; p. 684, March 10, 1945, January 19, 1946; p. 685, March 17, 1945, May 11, 1946; p. 686, March 10, 1945, April 14, 1945; p. 687, March 2, 1946, (bottom left) June 2, 1945, (bottom right) May 5, 1945; p. 688, March 2, 1946, (bottom left) October 6, 1945, (bottom right) May 5, 1945; p. 689, March 17, 1945, December 8, 1945.

The 13 Clocks was published in New York by Simon and Schuster on November 15, 1950. The story had not previously appeared. This volume prints the text of the first edition (the illustrations by Marc Simont published in the 1950 edition are not included here).

Two pieces in this volume are taken from *The Thurber Album: A New Collection of Pieces About People*, published in New York by Simon and Schuster on April 29, 1952. Both appeared in *The New Yorker*: "Daguerreotype of a Lady," April 28, 1951, as "Photograph Album: Daguerreotype of a Lady," and "Lavender with a Difference," July 28, 1951, as "Photograph Album: Lavender with a Difference." The texts printed here are taken from the Simon and Schuster edition.

Four pieces in this volume are taken from *Thurber Country: A New Collection of Pieces About Males and Females, Mainly of Our Own Species*, published in New York by Simon and Schuster on October 26, 1953. All of them appeared in *The New Yorker*: "File and Forget," January 8, 1949; "Do You Want to Make Something Out of It?," September 29, 1951; "A Final Note on Chanda Bell," October 15, 1949; "Teacher's Pet," August 20, 1949. The texts printed here are taken from the Simon and Schuster edition.

"An Introduction" first appeared in *Thurber's Dogs: A Collection of the Master's Dogs, Written and Drawn, Real and Imaginary, Living and Long Ago*, published in New York by Simon and Schuster on October 17, 1955. The text printed here is taken from the Simon and Schuster edition.

Five pieces in this volume are taken from *Further Fables for Our Time*, published in New York by Simon and Schuster on October 31, 1956. Four of them appeared in *The New Yorker*: "The Bluebird and His Brother," May 19, 1956; "The Lover and His Lass," May 26, 1956; "The Bachelor Penguin and the Virtuous Mate," June 23, 1956; "The Peacelike Mongoose," June 23, 1956. "The Trial of the Old

Watchdog" appeared for the first time in *Further Fables for Our Time.* The texts printed here are taken from the Simon and Schuster edition.

The text of "The First Time I Saw Paris" printed here is taken from *Alarms and Diversions,* published in New York by Harper & Brothers on November 12, 1957. The piece had previously appeared in *Holiday,* April 1957.

"A Dime a Dozen," "The First Years," "Every Tuesday Afternoon," "The Talk of the Town," "Miracle Men," and " 'Sex Is an Incident' " appeared as the first, second, third, fifth, sixth, and ninth chapters in *The Years with Ross,* published in Boston by Little, Brown and Company on May 28, 1959. Portions of the book were serialized in *The Atlantic Monthly,* November 1957–August 1958, then revised for book publication. The texts printed here are taken from the Little, Brown edition.

The seven uncollected pieces included originally appeared as follows: "An American Romance," *The New Yorker,* March 5, 1927; "A Visit from St. Nicholas [In the Ernest Hemingway Manner]," *The New Yorker,* December 24, 1927; "Tom the Young Kidnapper, or Pay Up and Live," *The New Yorker,* June 10, 1933; "How to Relax While Broadcasting," *The New Yorker,* May 5, 1934; "E.B.W.," *Saturday Review,* October 15, 1938; Credo from *I Believe, I Believe: The Personal Philosophies of Certain Eminent Men and Women of Our Time* (New York: Simon and Schuster, 1939), edited by Clifton Fadiman (also published as "Thinking Ourselves into Trouble" in *Forum and Century,* June 1939); "I Break Everything I Touch," *The Man: An Anthology of the Best Articles of the Year for Men* (New York: Farrell Publishing Corporation, 1940), edited by Leigh Quackenbush.

This volume presents the texts of the original printings chosen for inclusion here, but it does not attempt to reproduce features of their typographic design, such as display capitalization of chapter openings. The texts are printed without change, except for the correction of typographical errors. Spelling, punctuation, and capitalization are often expressive features, and they are not altered, even when inconsistent or irregular. The following is a list of typographical errors corrected, cited by page and line number: 25.17, brightening,; 27.10, "Bon,"; 27.10, '*Alors,* 63.1, Gran pa; 193.35, Why; 195.7, Littlefield,; 214.2, know; 229.17, McNally's; 229.19, McNally's; 279.2, photogragh; 319.17, country).; 320.27, woman,; 334.24, men; 334.40, underating; 516.11, "Curfew; 548.25, street; 828.17, .75's; 831.38–39, "*Fabriqué . . . Paris,*"; 831.39, said.; 848.15, become; 880.20, "The; 888.19, (You're; 954.40, waterfalls; 967.2, Here.

Acknowledgments

Notes

In the notes below, the reference numbers denote page and line of this volume (the line count includes headings and captions). No note is made for material included in standard desk-reference books such as Webster's *Collegiate, Biographical,* and *Geographical* dictionaries. For references to other studies, and further biographical background than is contained in the Chronology, see Harrison Kinney, *James Thurber: His Life and Times* (New York: Henry Holt, 1995); Neil A. Grauer, *Remember Laughter: A Life of James Thurber* (Lincoln and London: University of Nebraska Press, 1994); Burton Bernstein, *Thurber: A Biography* (New York: Dodd, Mead & Co., 1975); Charles S. Holmes, *The Clocks of Columbus: The Literary Career of James Thurber* (New York: Atheneum, 1972); Edwin T. Bowden, *James Thurber: A Bibliography* (Columbus: Ohio State University Press, 1968); *Selected Letters of James Thurber*, edited by Helen Thurber and Edward Weeks (Boston and Toronto: Little, Brown and Co., 1981); and *Conversations with James Thurber*, edited by Thomas Fensch (Jackson and London: University Press of Mississippi, 1989).

3.2   *Pedestalism*]   Defined by Thurber in the Glossary appended to *Is Sex Necessary?* as: "PEDESTALISM: The American male's reverence for the female or, better yet, her insistence on being revered, which amounts to the same thing."

4.18   pother (see Glossary)]   Defined by Thurber as: "POTHER: Uncalled-for interest in something—almost always sex."

5.1   *Übertragung*]   German: transfer or carrying over. In the Glossary of *Is Sex Necessary?* Thurber defined it as: "ÜBERTRAGUNG: Period of transition during which the male strives to transmute his ardor for women into the semblance of ardor for games."

7.20   charades,*]   Defined by Thurber in the Glossary as: "CHARADES: (1) Parlor game devised by women to fend off men (1900–1909); (2) acting up in a skittish manner about the facts of life, instead of getting right down to them; twitching, nervous twitching."

10.1–3   Bob Fitzsimmons . . . Julia Marlowe]   Bob Fitzsimmons, New Zealand boxer (1862–1917) who held three world titles, 1891–1905; G.A.R., Grand Army of the Republic; Julia Marlowe, English actress (1866–1950) noted for her Shakespearean roles.

20.4   the Thaw case]   Harry K. Thaw fatally shot architect Stanford White at the roof garden of Madison Square Garden in June 1906; he was acquitted on grounds of insanity after a sensational trial. Thaw suspected White of having had an affair with his wife, Evelyn Nesbit.

138.38   Stuart Chase's]   Economist and writer (1888–1985), whose books included *The Tragedy of Waste* (1925) and *Men and Machines* (1929).

139.29   F. Hopkinson Smith]   Popular novelist (1838–1915) whose books included *Colonel Carter of Cartersville* (1891) and *The Fortunes of Oliver Horn* (1902).

149.15   Mantell]   Robert Mantell (1854–1928), Scottish-born American actor who played romantic leads in such plays as *The Corsican Brothers* and *The Lady of Lyons*, and in later years toured the United States in Shakespearean roles.

151.8–9   "Come Josephine . . . Machine"]   Song (1910) by Alfred Bryan and Fred Fisher.

160.8   *Marie Celeste*]   The American ship *Mary Celeste*, sailing from New York to Genoa with a cargo of alcohol, was found adrift midway between the Azores and the Portuguese coast on December 5, 1872, with no crew members on board. Various explanations, some extremely fanciful, have been proposed for the ship's abandonment.

169.22–23   Nat Wills]   Wills (1873–1917) was known for his stage performances as "The Happy Tramp."

176.20   "Rasputin and the Empress,"]   Film (1932) directed by Richard Boleslawski, starring John, Ethel, and Lionel Barrymore.

187.35   "Flights of angels . . . rest"]   *Hamlet*, V.ii.360.

187.38–39   "Cave Canem."]   Latin: Beware the dog.

205.2   "Horses, Horses, Horses" . . . "Valencia."]   "Horses" (1926), song by Byron Gay and Richard A. Whiting, based on Tchaikovsky's "Troika"; "Valencia" (1926), French song with music by Jose Padilla.

205.21   Tondelaya . . . "White Cargo,"]   Tondeleyo, an African woman who seduces the English manager of a West African rubber plantation, is the leading character of Leon Gordon's play *White Cargo* (1923).

215.3–4   famous passage . . . grass, alas]   Cf. Gertrude Stein, *Four Saints in Three Acts*: "Pigeons on the grass alas. Pigeons on the grass alas. Short longer grass short longer longer shorter yellow grass. Pigeons large pigeons on the shorter longer yellow grass alas pigeons on the grass."

237.28–29   Judge Crater . . . Starr Faithfull case]   Joseph Force Crater (b. 1899), a New York Supreme Court justice, disappeared without a trace in June 1930. The Rev. Edward Hall and Mrs. Eleanor Mills were murdered on September 14, 1922, in New Brunswick, New Jersey; Hall's wife and three other defendants were tried for the murders but were acquitted. The body of Faithfull, a 25-year-old woman, washed up on a Long Island beach in June 1931;

the investigation into her apparent suicide led to scandalous revelations about her personal life, including sexual abuse at an early age by a prominent Boston politician.

238.5–8   Willie Stevens . . . Wendel house]   Stevens was among the defendants charged and ultimately acquitted in the Hall-Mills murders (see note 237.28–20); Thurber's *New Yorker* profile of him, "A Sort of Genius," was included in *My World—And Welcome to It.* "Jafsie" was the nickname of John F. Condon, a Bronx resident who in 1932 served as intermediary between the family of Charles Lindbergh and Bruno Hauptmann, kidnapper of Lindbergh's infant son. John G. Wendel and his six sisters inherited a large fortune, but lived in squalor in the same New York town house for fifty years; the last sister died in 1931.

254.7–8   an army surrenders on its stomach]   Cf. remark attributed to Napoleon: "An army marches on its stomach."

260.4–5   "Merton of the Movies,"]   Satirical comedy of Hollywood (1922), by George S. Kaufman and Marc Connelly, based on a novel by Harry Leon Wilson.

322.25   Victor McLaglen]   Actor (1886–1959) featured in many Hollywood films, including *What Price Glory* (1926), *The Lost Patrol* (1934), and *The Informer* (1935).

326.25   "Oh, to be . . . April's there,"]   Robert Browning, "Home Thoughts from Abroad."

326.33–34   "The Ring and the Book."]   Book-length narrative poem (1868–69) by Robert Browning.

332.10   Oxford Group]   Religious and anti-communist movement promulgating absolute standards of morality and "the dictatorship of God," organized in the 1920s in Oxford, England, by American evangelist Frank Buchman (1878–1961); subsequently known under the name Moral Rearmament.

339.25–26   Marx brothers . . . justly famous scene]   In *Animal Crackers* (1930).

344.20   "Mourning Becomes Electra"]   Dramatic trilogy (1931) by Eugene O'Neill, based on the *Oresteia* of Aeschylus.

350.13–15   Ernest Boyd . . . Dave Chasen]   Boyd (1887–1946), Irish author who became well-known as a speaker and editor in New York; Chasen (1899–1973), vaudeville partner of comedian Joe Cook and later a prominent Los Angeles restaurateur, was a close friend of *New Yorker* editor Harold Ross.

352.34–35   McDougallians]   Followers of psychologist William McDougall (1871–1938), who rejected behaviorism in favor of what he called "hormic" psychology, and later conducted experiments in parapsychology at Duke University. His books included *Introduction to Social Psychology* (1908) and *Outline of Abnormal Psychology* (1926).

355.36   Max Adeler] Pseudonym of Charles Heber Clark (1847–1915); his collections of humorous stories and sketches included *Out of the Hurly Burly* (1874), *Elbow Room* (1876), and *Random Shots* (1879).

366.21–24   The Assyrian . . . deep Galilee.] Lord Byron, "The Destruction of Sennacherib" in *Hebrew Melodies* (1815).

371.20   "Camille."] Film (1937), starring Greta Garbo and Robert Taylor and directed by George Cukor, adapted from the novel by Alexandre Dumas the younger.

386.17   Mr. Lasky] Jesse L. Lasky (1880–1958), pioneering film producer who was among the founders of Paramount.

386.37   "Jumbo."] Elaborately staged musical (1935) produced by Billy Rose, with songs by Richard Rodgers and Lorenz Hart.

395.14–15   "The Plainsman,"] Film (1936) directed by Cecil B. De Mille, starring Gary Cooper and Jean Arthur.

395.37   Nick Carter] Hero of dime detective fiction who made his first appearance in the *New York Weekly* in 1886, and whose adventures were recounted by a long series of writers, most notably Frederic Van Rensselaer Dey (1861–1922), who wrote over a thousand Nick Carter stories.

396.1   John L. Stoddard] Stoddard (1850–1931) became well known for his travel lectures accompanied by stereopticon slides; they were collected in fifteen volumes, 1897–1901.

407.5   Poictesme] Imaginary medieval country featured in a series of romances by James Branch Cabell (1879–1958), among them *Jurgen* (1919), *Figures of Earth* (1921), and *The Silver Stallion* (1926).

408.1   Moxie] Popular soft drink, first marketed in 1884 as a "nerve food" with curative powers.

498.1   *Excelsior*] Longfellow's poem was published in *Ballads and Other Poems* (1841).

504.1   *Lochinvar*] Sir Walter Scott's poem was published in *Marmion* (1808).

510.1   *Curfew Must Not Ring To-night*] Thorpe's (1850–1939) poem first appeared in book form in *Ringing Ballads* (1887).

517.1   *Barbara Frietchie*] Whittier's poem was published in *In War Time and Other Poems* (1868).

536.19–20   Hercule Poirot] Belgian detective who is the protagonist of dozens of novels and short stories by Agatha Christie (1890–1976), including

The Murder of Roger Ackroyd (1926), *Murder on the Orient Express* (1934), and *The A.B.C. Murders* (1936).

536.22–23   Mr. Pinkerton . . . Inspector Bull]   The amateur detective Evan Pinkerton and his friend, Scotland Yard inspector J. Humphrey Bull, are featured in a series of novels written by Mrs. Zenith Jones (1898–1983) under the pseudonym David Frome, including *Scotland Yard Can Wait* (1933) and *Mr. Pinkerton Goes to Scotland Yard* (1934).

544.9   'Gallegher,']   *Gallegher and Other Stories* (1891).

571.14   Unglaub]   Bob Unglaub (1881–1916) played, between 1904 and 1912, for the New York Highlanders, the Boston Pilgrims, and the Washington Senators.

572.15–16   "Snow-Bound"]   Narrative poem (1866) by John Greenleaf Whittier.

574.27–28   Cornishmen . . . Trelawny]   Cf. Robert Stephen Hawker, "The Song of the Western Men" (1825): "And shall Trelawny die? / Here's twenty thousand Cornish men / Will know the reason why."

574.29–31   Housman's lad . . . hung with snow.]   Cf. A. E. Housman, *A Shropshire Lad* (1896), 2: "And since to look at things in bloom / Fifty springs are little room, / About the woodlands I will go / To see the cherry hung with snow."

575.9   Palamides]   Knight who figures in Arthurian legend; sometimes identified as being unbaptized or a Saracen.

577.37–578.1   *enfant du premier lit*]   French: child by the first wife.

578.2   *cordonnier*]   French: shoemaker.

578.6–7   "*Il est mort . . . de chagrin.*"]   French: He died of grief.

580.5   *Embrayage*]   French: clutch.

580.15   *Frein*]   French: brake.

581.25–26   "*A gauche . . . toujours à gauche!*"]   French: Left, left, keep left!

582.8   "*Lentement!*"]   French: Slowly!

582.10   "*Ça va mieux, maintenant,*"]   French: It's better now.

583.7–8   "*Où est votre mari?*"]   French: Where is your husband?

583.14–15   *mauvais quart d'heure*]   French: A bad fifteen minutes.

583.30   *tintamarre . . . hurlement*]   French: hubbub . . . howling.

583.38–40   *Galerie . . . hors texte).*]   *Gallery of Masterpieces and Summary of Art History in the Nineteenth Century, in France and Abroad (1000 engravings, 58 plates).*

590.1   *"I come . . . hern!"*]   Alfred, Lord Tennyson, "The Brook" (1855).

636.15   Red Barber]   Walter Lanier "Red" Barber (1908–92), baseball commentator on radio and television.

646.34   'Sanctuary']   Novel (1931) by William Faulkner.

666.4–16   Sweet Water . . . Frank Ellinger]   Location and central characters of Willa Cather's novel *A Lost Lady* (1923).

668.18   crokinole]   Croquignole, a method of waving the hair with the use of curlers.

669.24   Madame de Vionnet]   Character in Henry James's *The Ambassadors* (1903).

671.22   "Louise,"]   Opera (1900) by Gustave Charpentier.

731.37–39   "Is it not . . . pennyroyal?"]   Cf. Emerson, "Country Life" (1858), first collected in the 1904 edition of *Natural History of Intellect and Other Papers*.

741.27   Verdi's Violetta]   Courtesan heroine of *La Traviata*.

753.27   Julia Marlowe]   See note 10.1–3.

756.13–18   'It Happened . . . Wednesday."]   *It Happened One Night* (1934), directed by Frank Capra and starring Clark Gable and Claudette Colbert; *One Sunday Afternoon* (1933), directed by Stephen Roberts and starring Gary Cooper and Fay Wray; *I Loved You Wednesday* (1933), directed by Henry King and William Cameron Menzies and starring Warner Baxter and Elissa Landi.

756.39–757.3   Evangeline Adams . . . Dianetics]   Evangeline Adams (1868–1932), astrologer and author of *The Bowl of Heaven* (1926) and *Astrology for Everyone* (1932); Professor Emile Coué (1857–1926), exponent of a self-help system based on auto-hypnosis; Dianetics, theory propounded in a 1950 book by science-fiction writer L. Ron Hubbard (1911–86) and subsequently developed into the doctrines of the Church of Scientology.

758.5   John Aloysius McNulty]   John Augustine McNulty (1895–1956), *New Yorker* writer who was a close friend of Thurber.

780.1–2   'The Crimson . . . Ralph Henry Barbour,"]   Barbour's sports novel was published in 1906.

782.29–30   "You have found . . . the carpet?"]   Cf. Henry James's short story "The Figure in the Carpet."

788.9   du Noüy]   French writer Pierre Lecomte du Noüy (1883–1947), author of *Human Destiny* (1947).

823.29–30   Larry Semon]   Movie actor and director (1889–1928) who starred in many films including *Babes and Boobs* (1918), *The Stage Hand* (1920), and *The Sportsman* (1921).

824.20   Lacrimae Puellae] Latin: Girl's Tears.

827.37   Mistinguette] Mistinguett, stage name of Jeanne Marie Bourgeois (1875–1956), French music hall star whose repertoire included "Mon Homme" and "Je cherche un millionaire."

830.29   Big Bertha] Popular Allied name for German gun used to shell Paris at a range of over 70 miles between March 23 and August 12, 1918; 256 people were killed during the bombardment.

833.26–27   Raoul Lufbery . . . Alan Seeger.] Raoul Lufbery (1885–1918), fighter pilot in the Lafayette Escadrille, killed in action; Norman Prince (1887–1916), fighter pilot who helped organize the Lafayette Escadrille, killed in landing accident while flying with the squadron; Kiffin Rockwell (1892–1916), fighter pilot in the Lafayette Escadrille, killed in action; Victor Chapman (1890–1916), first Lafayette Escadrille pilot killed in action; Alan Seeger (1888–1916), poet, author of "I Have a Rendezvous with Death," killed in the battle of the Somme while serving with the Foreign Legion.

837.6–7   Rowland Emett] English cartoonist and inventor (b. 1906), whose drawings often appeared in *Punch*.

838.11   Ina Claire] Actress (1892–1985) who appeared on Broadway in the *Ziegfeld Follies* of 1915 and 1916 and *The Gold Diggers* (1919), and starred in such films as *The Awful Truth* (1929) and *The Royal Family of Broadway* (1931).

838.18   *Stars and Stripes*] Ross edited the army newspaper *Stars and Stripes* while stationed in France during World War I.

839.15   Wolcott Gibbs's comedy *Season in the Sun*] Gibbs's play opened on Broadway in 1950 and enjoyed a successful run.

839.17   *Metropole*] William Walden's play, in which the central character Frederick M. Hill is modeled on Harold Ross, opened on Broadway in 1949.

841.3   Lois Long] *New Yorker* columnist who covered night clubs ("Table for Two") and fashion ("On and Off the Avenue").

841.22   James M. Cain] Cain (1892–1977) worked as managing editor of *The New Yorker* for nine months in 1931.

842.5   *Mary Celeste*] See note 160.8.

842.11–12   Herbert Asbury] Journalist and author (b. 1891) of many books including *The Gangs of New York* (1928) and *The Barbary Coast* (1933).

842.26   *Judge*] Humor magazine which began publication in 1881 and remained popular into the early decades of the twentieth century; its contributors in the 1920s included Ring Lardner, S. J. Perelman, and John Held, Jr.

842.37   a fairy tale] *The White Deer* (1945).

846.11   Niven Busch . . . Ralph Ingersoll]   Busch (1903–91), an early contributor to *The New Yorker*, later had a long career as a novelist and screenwriter; Ingersoll (1900–83) left *The New Yorker* in 1930; he founded the
left-wing tabloid *PM* in 1940 and was the author of a number of books about
his war experiences, including *Action on All Fronts* (1942) and *The Battle Is
the Payoff* (1943).

846.20   lost and found Jeannie]   See "Look Homeward, Jeannie" in *The
Beast in Me and Other Animals* (1948).

850.33   *What Price Glory?*]   The drama by Maxwell Anderson and Laurence Stallings, set in World War I, opened on Broadway in 1924.

851.7–8   *The Poor Nut* . . . Elliott Nugent]   Nugent's play, written in collaboration with his father J. C. Nugent, opened on Broadway in 1925.

851.32   Robert Coates . . . Joel Sayre]   Coates (1897–1973) was art critic
of *The New Yorker* from 1937 to 1967 and author of a number of books,
including *The Eater of Darkness* (1929), *The Outlaw Years* (1930), and *Yesterday's Burdens* (1933); Sayre (1901–79), *New Yorker* writer, Hollywood screenwriter, and childhood friend of Thurber in Columbus, Ohio.

851.38   Algonquin Round Table]   The circle of writers and wits who gathered informally at the Algonquin Hotel in New York from the 1920s to the
1940s included Dorothy Parker, Robert Benchley, George S. Kaufman, Alexander Woollcott, Marc Connelly, and others.

852.2–3   Herman Mankiewicz]   Screenwriter and movie producer (1897–
1953), best known for the screenplay of *Citizen Kane* (1941).

852.7   Nunnally Johnson]   Journalist, fiction writer, screenwriter, and film
director (1897–1977).

852.27   Arthur Kober]   Kober (1900–75) was best known for his long-
running comedy *Having Wonderful Time* (1937).

852.31   Sally Benson]   Short story writer (1900–72) whose books include
People Are Fascinating (1936) and *Meet Me in St. Louis* (1942).

853.12   Rea Irvin]   Cartoonist (1881–1972) and original art editor of *The
New Yorker*.

854.39   Ben Turpin]   Slapstick comedian (1874–1940) who starred in many
of Mack Sennett's films.

858.12   crash . . . *Shenandoah*]   The U.S. navy dirigible *Shenandoah* was
wrecked over Ohio in a thunderstorm in 1925, resulting in the deaths of 14
crew members.

861.32   "The Conning Tower."]   Influential syndicated humor column
edited by Franklin Pierce Adams; Thurber contributed an item to it in 1926.

862.38   the Snyder Trial."]   Ruth Snyder and her lover Henry Todd Gray were executed after a sensational trial for the 1927 murder of Snyder's husband, Albert.

883.25   Milt Gross]   Cartoonist (1895–1953), whose illustrated books included *Nize Baby* (1926), *Hiawatta with no Odder Poems* (1926), and *Famous Fimales from Heestory* (1928).

885.32   St. Clair McKelway]   Long-time *New Yorker* writer (1907–80) who was the magazine's managing editor during the 1930s.

889.34   *Public Enemy . . . Viva Villa*]   *The Public Enemy* (1931), directed by William Wellman and starring James Cagney and Jean Harlow; *Viva Villa* (1934), directed by Jack Conway and starring Wallace Beery and Fay Wray.

898.35   Grover Whelan]   New York City police commissioner, known for his role in organizing public ceremonies, including homecoming parades after World War I.

899.23   Wendel sisters]   See note 238.5–8.

903.28   Count Felix von Luckner]   German naval officer (1881–1966) who as commander of a small surface raider in World War I sank approximately 20 Allied ships; he lectured extensively in the U.S. after the war.

909.25   Imp of the Perverse]   "The Imp of the Perverse," short story by Edgar Allan Poe, first published in 1845.

912.9–10   Percy R. Pyne]   Percy Rivington Pyne II (1882–1950), prominent New York banker and philanthropist.

913.38   *PM*]   Left-wing daily newspaper edited by Ralph Ingersoll (see note 846.11).

916.15   Joseph Moncure March]   Journalist (1899–1977) best known for his narrative poems *The Wild Party* and *The Set-Up*.

923.20–21   Leonard Q. Ross]   Pseudonym used by Leo Rosten (b. 1908) when he published in *The New Yorker* the stories later collected (under his own name) as *The Education of H*Y*M*A*N K*A*P*L*A*N* (1937).

930.3–4   That girl . . . Stephen Crane movie]   Lillian Ross, whose book *Picture* (originally published in *The New Yorker*) was an account of the making of John Huston's 1951 film of Crane's *The Red Badge of Courage*.

932.27   Lilyan Tashman]   Screen actress (1899–1934) noted for sophisticated roles; her films included *A Broadway Butterfly* (1925), *Manhattan Cocktail* (1928), and *The Marriage Playground* (1929).

932.29–30   Duke Mantee . . . *The Petrified Forest*]   Humphrey Bogart played the role of the gangster Duke Mantee in Robert E. Sherwood's *The Petrified Forest* on Broadway in 1935, and repeated it the following year in the film version directed by Archie Mayo.

937.2–3   Joe Cook]   Stage comedian (1890–1959) who starred in such productions as *Rain or Shine* (1928) and *Fine and Dandy* (1930).

937.21   profile on Duveen by S. N. Behrman]   Behrman's profile of the celebrated art dealer was published in book form as *Duveen* (1952).

958.12–13   Willie Stevens]   See note 238.5–8.

960.26–27   *Van Zanten's Happy Days . . . The Wanderer*]   *Van Zanten's Happy Days: A Love Story from Pelli Island* (1908), novel by the Danish writer Laurids Valdemar Bruun (1864–1935), published in English in 1922; *The Wanderer*, English translation of Alain-Fournier's novel *Le Grand Meaulnes* (1913).

966.17   Bishop Blougram . . . Mr. Gigadibs]   Characters in Robert Browning's poem "Bishop Blougram's Apology" (1855).

CATALOGING INFORMATION

Thurber, James, 1894–1961.
    [Selections. 1996]
    Writings and drawings / James Thurber.
       p.   cm. — (The Library of America ; 90)

    1. Humorous stories, American. 2. American wit and
humor, Pictorial. I. Title. II. Series.
PS3539.H94A6   1996
818'.5209—dc20   96-5853
ISBN 1–883011–22–1 (alk. paper)   CIP

THE LIBRARY OF AMERICA SERIES

This book is set in 10 point Linotron Galliard,
a face designed for photocomposition by Matthew Carter
and based on the sixteenth-century face Granjon. The paper is
acid-free Ecusta Nyalite and meets the requirements for permanence
of the American National Standards Institute. The binding
material is Brillianta, a woven rayon cloth made by
Van Heek-Scholco Textielfabrieken, Holland.
The composition is by The Clarinda
Company. Printing and binding by
R.R.Donnelley & Sons Company.
Designed by Bruce Campbell.